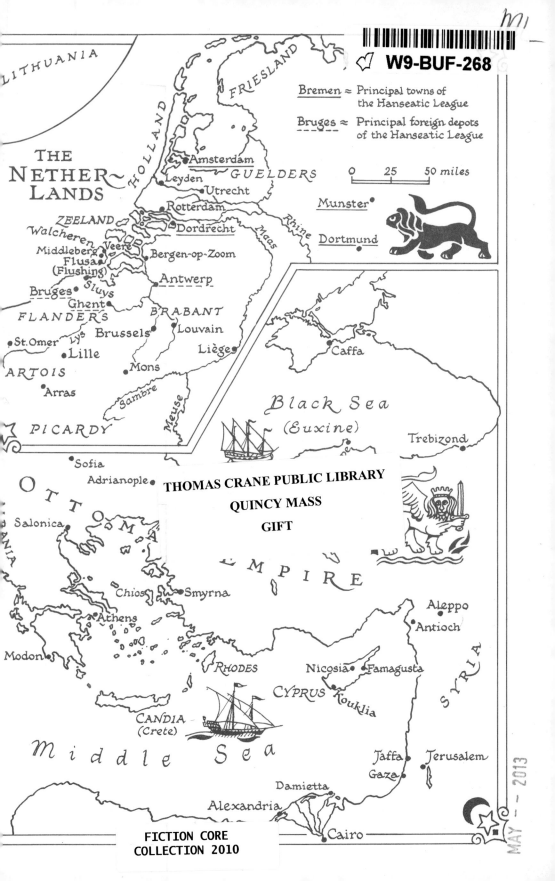

LITHUANIA

FRIESLAND

HOLLAND

THE
NETHER~
LANDS

Bremen ≈ Principal towns of
the Hanseatic League

Bruges ≈ Principal foreign depots
of the Hanseatic League

Amsterdam

Leyden   GUELDERS

Utrecht

Rotterdam

ZEELAND

Dordrecht

Rhine

Maas

0   25   50 miles

Munster

Dortmund

Walcheren

Middleberg Veere

Flusa
(Flushing)

Bergen-op-Zoom

Bruges

Sluys

Antwerp

Ghent

BRABANT

FLANDERS

St.Omer Lys Brussels Louvain

Lille

Liège

Mons

ARTOIS

Arras

Sambre

Meuse

PICARDY

Caffa

Black Sea
(Euxine)

Trebizond

Sofia

Adrianople

OTTOMAN

Salonica

EMPIRE

Chios   Smyrna

Athens

Modon

Aleppo

Antioch

RHODES

Nicosia Famagusta

CYPRUS Touklia

SYRIA

CANDIA
(Crete)

Middle   Sea

Jaffa Jerusalem

Gaza

Damietta

Alexandria

Cairo

To Lie
with Lions

The House of Niccolò

To Lie with Lions

Dorothy Dunnett

ALFRED A. KNOPF   NEW YORK   1996

THIS IS A BORZOI BOOK
PUBLISHED BY ALFRED A. KNOPF, INC.

http://www.randomhouse.com/

Originally published in Great Britain in slightly different form by
Michael Joseph Ltd., London, in 1995.

Library of Congress Cataloging-in-Publication Data
Dunnett, Dorothy.
To lie with lions / Dorothy Dunnett.
p. cm. — (The house of Niccolò; 6th)
ISBN 0-394-58629-8 (hard)
1. Vander Poele, Nicholas (Fictitious character)—Fiction.
2. Fifteenth century—Fiction. 3. Bankers—Europe—Fiction.
I. Title. II. Series: Dunnett, Dorothy. House of Niccolò; 6th.
PR6054.U56T6 1996
823´.914—dc20 95-50422
CIP

Manufactured in the United States of America
FIRST AMERICAN EDITION

For Halliday Alastair Dunnett

Characters

February 1471 – November 1473
(Those marked * are recorded in history)

Rulers
*England: King Edward IV, House of York, vying with
  *Henry VI, House of Lancaster
*Scotland: King James III
*France: King Louis XI
*Burgundy: Charles, Duke of Burgundy, Count of Flanders
*Pope: Paul II, Sixtus IV
*Venice: Doge Nicolò Tron
*Cyprus: King James de Lusignan (Zacco)
*Ottoman Empire (Istanbul): Sultan Mehmet II
*Mameluke Empire (Cairo): Sultan Qayt Bey
*Muscovy: Grand Duke Ivan III, Autocrat of All Russia
*Scandinavia: King Christian I
*Poland: King Casimir IV

House of Niccolò
  Nicholas de Fleury, governor of the Banco di Niccolò
  Gelis van Borselen, dame de Fleury, his wife
  Jordan (Jodi), their son
  Clémence de Coulanges, senior nurse
  Pasque, nursemaid
  Bita, temporary nursemaid
  Alonse, servant to Nicholas
VENICE COUNTING-HOUSE:
  Gregorio (Goro) of Asti, lawyer and manager
  Margot, his wife
  Tasse, former servant to Jaak de Fleury, Geneva
  Julius of Bologna, notary and manager
  Cristoffels (Cefo), under-manager
BRUGES COUNTING-HOUSE:
  Diniz Vasquez, manager, nephew of Simon de St Pol
  Mathilde (Tilde) de Charetty, his wife
  Marian, their daughter
  Catherine de Charetty, Tilde's younger sister

SCOTTISH BUREAU & ESTATES:
  Govaerts of Brussels, manager, Canongate bureau
  Oliver Semple, factor
  Wilhelm of Hall, goldsmith
  Tom Yare, lawyer from Berwick
*John Bonkle, natural son of the Provost of Trinity College
PERIPATETIC:
  Father Moriz of Augsburg, chaplain and metallurgist
  John le Grant, engineer, sailing-master
  Michael Crackbene, shipmaster
  Astorre (Syrus de Astariis), mercenary commander
  Thomas, deputy to Astorre
  Tobias Beventini of Grado, physician to Count of Urbino
OTHER NAMED AGENTS:
  Lazzarino, agent in Rome
  Jooris, agent in Antwerp
  Eric Mowat, agent in Copenhagen
  Achille, agent in Alexandria
COMPLEMENT OF THE *SVIPA*:
*Lutkyn Mere, Danish pirate
  Yuri, from Muscovy
  Dmitri, his son
  (with Nicholas de Fleury, Mick Crackbene, John le Grant and Father
    Moriz)
PAST ASSOCIATES:
  Ochoa de Marchena, former master of the *Ghost/Doria*
  Filipe, former boy on the *San Niccolò*

Duchy of Burgundy
BURGUNDIAN HOUSEHOLD:
*Charles, Duke of Burgundy and Brabant, Count of Flanders, Holland,
    Zeeland etc.
*Margaret of York, his wife and sister of King Edward IV
*Isabella of Portugal, Dowager Duchess of Burgundy
*Marie, daughter of Duke Charles by previous wife
*Bastard Anthony, natural brother of Duke Charles
*William Hugonet, lord of Saillant, Chancellor of the Duchy
*Philippe de Commynes, Master of Ducal Household, later chamberlain to
    King of France
*Loyet, the Duke's goldsmith
*Peter von Hagenbach, Duke's High Bailiff in Alsace
BRUGES AND GHENT:
*Anselm Adorne, merchant, magistrate, of the Hôtel Jerusalem
*Margriet van der Banck, his wife
*Jan Adorne, lawyer, their oldest son
*Katelijne (Kathi) Sersanders, Adorne's niece
*Anselm Sersanders, her brother, Adorne's nephew
*Dr Andreas of Vesalia, physician in Bruges and Scotland

*Louis de Bruges, seigneur de Gruuthuse, merchant nobleman
*Marguerite van Borselen, his wife
*Tommaso Portinari, Medici manager in Bruges
*Maria, his wife
*Angelo di Jacopo Tani, former Medici manager at Bruges
*Alexander Bonkle, merchant in Bruges and Scotland
*Justus of Ghent (Joos van Wassenhoven), painter in Urbino
*Hugo van der Goes, artist, sponsored by Joos
*Hans (Henne) Memling, German artist working in Bruges
*Jehan Metteneye, host to Scots merchants in Bruges
*Lambert van de Walle, merchant kinsman of Adorne
*Colard Mansion, scribe and illustrator
*Pieter Reyphin, merchant kinsman of van de Walle
*João Vasquez, secretary to Duchess Isabelle of Portugal
*Henry Cant, Scots merchant
*William Caxton, former Governor of the English merchants; adviser to
    Duchess of Burgundy
VEERE AND MIDDLEBURG:
*Henry van Borselen of Veere, Count of Grandpré, 'uncle' of Gelis van
    Borselen
*Wolfaert van Borselen, his son
*Charlotte de Bourbon, Wolfaert's second wife
*Lodewijk van Borselen, their son
*Anna van Borselen, their daughter
*Paul van Borselen, bastard son of Wolfaert
*Stephen Angus, Scottish agent at Middleburg
DIJON/FLEURY:
  Enguerrand de Damparis, friend of Marian de Charetty's sister
  Yvonnet, his wife

The Vatachino Company
  Martin, broker, merchant and agent
*David de Salmeton, the same, in Cyprus
COMPLEMENT OF THE *UNICORN*:
  Svartecop of Revel, master
  Mogens Björnsen, pilot
  Reinholdt, Cologne merchant
  (with Martin, and Anselm and Katelijne Sersanders)

Anjou and the Loire
ANGERS:
*René, Duke of Anjou, Count of Provence and titular King of Naples and
    Sicily
*Jeanne de Laval, his wife
*Margaret, his daughter, wife of King Henry VI of England
*Edward of Wales, her son
*Nicholas of Calabria, Duke of Lorraine and grandson of King René

*René, grandson of King René and Duke of Lorraine after Nicholas, his
  cousin
*Fleur de Pensée, herald
*Ardent Désir (Pierre de Hurion), herald
*Jehan du Perrier ('Le Prieur'), chamberlain
*Master Guillaume, keeper of lions
*Bertrand, master of works
*Cresselle, Bertrand's Moorish wife
*Pierre de Nostradamus, physician to René's late son John
*Pierre Robin, physician and architect
*John Perrot, Abbot of Angers, King René's confessor
VALLEY OF CISSE:
  Bernard de Moncourt, seigneur de Chouzy
  Claude d'Échaut, dame de Chouzy, his wife

France and Franco–Scots
*King Louis XI
*Francis II, Duke of Brittany, his nephew
*Charles, Duke of Guienne (Aquitaine), the King's brother
  Jordan de St Pol, vicomte de Ribérac, merchant-magnate of Scotland and
    France
  Simon de St Pol the Younger of Kilmirren, his son
  Henry de St Pol, son of Simon's late wife Katelina
*Andro Wodman, former Archer of the King's Scottish Guard
*Louis de Luxembourg, Count of St Pol, Constable of France
*William, Lord Monypenny, lord of Concressault, envoy to Scotland
*Gaston du Lyon, equerry, seneschal of Toulouse
*Guillaume Fichet, rector of Sorbonne and printer, Paris
*Jacques d'Orson, master gunner
*Odet d'Aydie, Gascon lord of Lescun, chief counsellor to Duke of Brittany
*Colombo, French privateer

Scotland
ROYAL HOUSEHOLD AND NOBLES:
*James Stewart (Third of the Name), King of Scotland
*Margaret, daughter of Christian I of Denmark, his Queen
*Georgie Bell (Little Bell), King's chamber valet
*Mary Stewart, Countess of Arran, the King's elder sister
*Thomas Boyd, Earl of Arran, her husband
*James and Margaret, their children
*Robert, Lord Boyd, father of Thomas
*Alexander Stewart, Duke of Albany, the King's brother
*Sir James Liddell of Halkerston, Albany's steward
*John Stewart, Earl of Mar, the King's younger brother
*Margaret Stewart, the King's younger sister
*Colin Campbell, 1st Earl of Argyll, Master of the Royal Household
*Archibald Whitelaw, Royal Secretary
*Andrew Stewart, Lord Avandale, Chancellor

*John Laing, Treasurer
*Patrick Graham, Bishop of St Andrews
*William Tulloch, Bishop of Orkney, Keeper of the Privy Seal
*William Scheves, cleric, royal apothecary
*James Hommyll, royal tailor
*David Guthrie of Kincaldrum, Clerk-Register
*Master Conrad, physician
*Archibald Crawford, Abbot of Holyrood
*Robert Blackadder, Abbot of Melrose, brother of John Blackadder, Rome
*David Arnot, cleric, kinsman of Henry, Abbot of Cambuskenneth
*William Sinclair, Earl of Caithness
*Sir William Knollys, Preceptor in Scotland of the Order of the Knights Hospitaller of St John of Jerusalem
*David Lindsay, 5th Earl of Crawford
*James Hamilton of Cadzow, 1st Lord Hamilton of Kinneil
*Sir Robert Semple of Elliotstoun, sheriff of Renfrew
*William Semple his son, 'second cousin to Oliver Semple'
MERCHANTS AND OTHERS:
*William of Berecrofts (Old Will), Canongate merchant
*Archibald Berecrofts the Younger (Archie), his son
*Robin, son of Archie
 Isobella (Bel) of Cuthilgurdy, neighbour to the St Pols of Kilmirren
*Elizabeth, Prioress, Cistercian Priory, Haddington
*Elizabeth (Betha) Sinclair, daughter of the Earl of Caithness, widow of Patrick Dunbar, Haddington Priory
*Catherine Sinclair, daughter of the Earl of Caithness by another wife, wife of the Duke of Albany
*Euphemia (Phemie) Dunbar, Betha's cousin, daughter of George Dunbar, Earl of March, Haddington Priory
*Dame Alisia Maitland, nun of same priory
 Ada, servant at Coldingham Priory
*William Roger (Whistle Willie), Court musician
*Thomas Cochrane, master mason
*Edward Bonkle, Provost of Trinity College, Edinburgh
*John Lamb, Leith merchant
*Thomas (Thom) Swift, Edinburgh merchant
*Andy Crawford, merchant
 Richard, his son
*John Muir, merchant-burgess of Canongate
*John Lauder, burgess of Canongate
*Sir Alexander Napier of Merchiston, merchant, vice-admiral
 Constantine (Conn) Malloch, Borders landowner and merchant
 Benedict (Ben) Bailzie, landowner and merchant

The Duchy of the Tyrol
*Sigismond, Duke of Austria & Styria and Count of the Tyrol
*Eleanor Stewart, his wife, aunt to the King of Scotland

Urbino
*Federigo da Montefeltro, Count of Urbino and mercenary leader
*Battista Sforza, his second wife

Rome (including envoys)
*Pope Paul II, Sixtus IV
*Henry Arnot, Abbot of Cambuskenneth, and procurator of James III at the
     Curia
*John Blackadder, brother of Abbot of Melrose, Scotland
*Bessarion (John) of Trebizond, Cardinal Legate, Archbishop of Nicaea,
     Patriarch of Constantinople
*Jacques Scéva, his Greek-Cypriot major domo
*Nicolò Perotti, his secretary, Archbishop of Manfredonia
*Antonio Bonumbre, Genoese Bishop of Accia, Corsica, and papal envoy to
     Muscovy
*Zoe Palaeologina, grand-daughter of Manuel II, past Emperor of Constanti-
     nople, and protégée of Bessarion
*Andrew and *Manuel, Zoe's brothers
*Father Ludovico de Severi da Bologna, Patriarch of Antioch
*Hadji Mehmet, legate of Uzum Hasan, Turcoman Prince, Persia
*Nicholai Giorgio de' Acciajuoli, Greek-Florentine kinsman by marriage of
     Pierfrancesco de' Medici
 Nerio of Trebizond, exile, Burgundian Court and Rome
*Michael Alighieri, of Florence and Trebizond, counsellor and chamberlain
     to Duke Charles
*Benedetto Dei, seamaster and Florentine merchant trading in Africa
*Marco Barbo, Cardinal of San Marco and nephew of Pope Paul
*Oliviero Caraffa, Cardinal of Naples, Admiral of papal fleet
*Lorenzo de' Medici of the Republic of Florence, envoy
*Donato Acciajuoli, Florentine orator
*Domenico Martelli, Florentine envoy
*James Goldwell, Bishop of Norwich, English delegate
*Philibert Hugonet, Bishop of Mâcon, later Cardinal (brother of Chancellor
     Hugonet of Burgundy)
*Prospero Schiaffino de Camulio de' Medici, Genoese and Milanese agent

Cyprus
*King James de Lusignan (Zacco)
*Charlotte (Charla), Eugène and Janus, his natural children
*Marietta of Patras, his mother (Cropnose)
*Jorgin, his servant
*Sir Rizzo di Marino, Sicilian chamberlain to the King
*Sor de Naves, Sicilian Constable of Cyprus
*Louis Perez Fabrice, Catalan Archbishop of Nicosia
*Peter Davila, constable of men-at-arms, Cyprus
*Catherine Corner, Zacco's Queen
*Marco Corner of Venice, sugar-grower in Cyprus, her father
*Fiorenza of Naxos, his wife, sister of Violante & Valenza

*Andrea Corner, his brother, Auditor of Cyprus
*Violante of Naxos, wife of *Caterino Zeno, Venetian envoy to
    Uzum Hasan, Persia
*Marco Bembo, cousin of Queen Catherine
*Nicolas Pasqualigo, Venetian Bailie
*Josaphat Barbaro, Venetian envoy and trader of Tana
*Muzio Constanzo, Admiral of Cyprus
*Gabriel Gentile, royal physician
*Toma Phicard, King's chancellor and notary

Rhodes
*Carlotta de Lusignan, half-sister and rival of Zacco
*Giambattisti Orsini, Grand Master of the Knights of St John
*Tobias Lomellini, Treasurer of the Knights of St John

Faroes
Torolf Mohr, sea pilot

Hanseatic League: Poland
COMPLEMENT OF THE *PRUSS MAIDEN*:
*Paúel Benecke, Danzig privateer
Stanislas, lodesman

*Filippo Buonaccorsi (Callimachus), Italian humanist in exile

England
Jonathan (Jo) Babbe, master of the *Charity* of Hull

Ultima Thule
Tryggvi-Sigurdsson, fisherman, guide from Markarfljót
Glímu-Sveinn, fisherman, farmer, wrestler
Hristin, his wife
Herra Oddur, Bishop's bailiff, Skálholt
Sigfús Helgason, guide from Skálholt

The Germanies
*Frederick III of the House of Habsburg, German Emperor and King of
    the Romans
*Archduke Maximilian, his son
*Jacques, Comte of Montfort, an Imperial chamberlain
*John of Baden, Archbishop of Trèves
*Charles, Margrave of Baden, his brother
*Albert-Achille, Margrave of Brandebourg
*Frederick, Count Palatine of the Rhine (Fritz le Mauvais)
*Adolf de Nassau, Archbishop of Mayence and Grand Chancellor of the
    Empire
*Calixtus Ottomanus (Bayazid Osman), half-brother of Sultan Mehmet II,
    protégé of Emperor
Gräfin Anna von Hanseyck, Cologne, widow of Graf Wenzel von Hanseyck
Bonne, her daughter

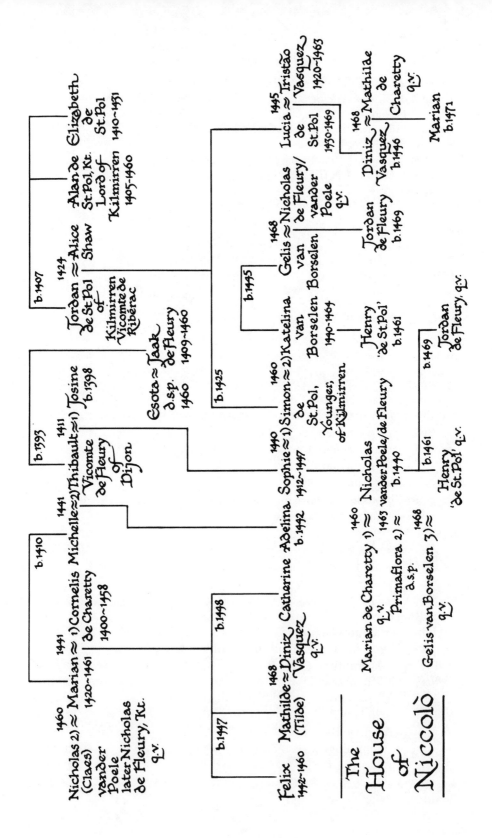

The House of Niccolò

INTRODUCTION

T HE ELEGANT WORKING out of designs historical and romantic, political and commercial, psychological and moral,
over a multivolume novel is a Dorothy Dunnett specialty.
In her first work in this genre, the six-volume "Lymond
Chronicles," suspense was created and relieved in each volume, and
over the whole set of volumes; the final, beautifully inevitable,
romantic secret was disclosed on the very last page of the last volume.
"The House of Niccolò" does the same.

The reader of *The Unicorn Hunt,* then, may wish to move directly
to the narrative for a first experience of that pattern, with a reader's
faith in an experienced author's caretaking; the novel itself briefly
supplies the information you need to know from past novels, telling
its own tale while completing and inaugurating others. What follows,
as a sketch of the geopolitical and dramatic terrain unfolding in the
volumes which precede *The Unicorn Hunt,* may be useful to read
now, or at any point along the narrative, or after reading, as an indi-
cation of which stories of interest to this volume may be found most
fully elaborated in which previous volume.

VOLUME I: *Niccolò Rising*

"From Venice to Cathay, from Seville to the Gold Coast of Africa,
men anchored their ships and opened their ledgers and weighed one
thing against another as if nothing would ever change." The first
sentence of the first volume indicates the scope of this series, and the
cultural and psychological dynamic of the story and its hero, whose
private motto is "Change, change and adapt." It is the motto, too, of
fifteenth-century Bruges, center of commerce and conduit of new
ideas and technologies between the Islamic East and the Christian
West, between the Latin South and the Celtic-Saxon North, haven

of political refugees from the English Wars of the Roses, a site of
muted conflict between trading giants Venice and Genoa and states
in the making and on the take all around. Mrs. Dunnett has set her
story in the fifteenth century, between Gutenberg and Columbus,
between Donatello and Martin Luther, between the rise of mercantile culture and the fall of chivalry, as that age of receptivity to—
addiction to—change called "the Renaissance" gathers its powers.

Her hero is a deceptively silly-looking, disastrously tactless
eighteen-year-old dyeworks artisan named "Claes," a caterpillar who
emerges by the end of the novel as the merchant-mathematician
Nicholas vander Poele. Prodigiously gifted at numbers, and the
material and social "engineering" skills that go with it, Nicholas
has until now resisted the responsibility of his powers, his identity
fractured by the enmity of both his mother's husband's family,
the Scottish St Pols, who refuse to own him legitimate, and his
maternal family, the Burgundian de Fleurys, who failed his mother
and abused him and reduced him to serfdom as a child. He found
refuge at age ten with his grandfather's in-laws, especially the Bruges
widow Marian de Charetty, whose dyeing and broking business
becomes the tool of Nicholas' desperate self-fashioning apart from
the malice of his blood relatives.

Soon even public Bruges and the states beyond come to see the
engineer under the artisan. The Charetty business expands to
include a courier and intelligence service between Italian and
Northern states, its bodyguard sharpened into a skilled mercenary
force, its pawnbroking consolidated toward banking and commodities trading. And as the chameleon artificer of all this, Nicholas
incurs the ambiguous interest of the Bruges patrician Anselm
Adorne and the Greco-Florentine prince Nicholai Giorgio de' Acciajuoli, both of whom steer him toward a role in the rivalry between
Venice, in whose interest Acciajuoli labors, and Genoa, original
home of the Adorne family. This trading rivalry will erupt in different novels around different, always highly symbolic commodities:
silk, sugar, glass, gold, and human beings. In this first novel the con-
tested product is alum, the mineral that binds dyes to cloth, blood
to the body, conspirators to a conspiracy—in this case, to keep secret
the news of a newly found deposit of the mineral in the Papal States
while Venice and her allies monopolize the current supply.

Acciajuoli and Adorne are father-mentor figures Nicholas can
respect, resist, or join on roughly equal intellectual terms—whereas
the powerful elder males of his blood, his mother's uncle, Jaak de
Fleury, and his father's father, Jordan de Ribérac, steadily rip open
wounds first inflicted in childhood. In direct conflict he is emotion-

ally helpless before them. What he possesses superbly, however, are the indirect defenses of an "engineer." The Charetty business partners and others who hitch their wagons to his star—Astorre the mercenary leader, Julius the notary, Gregorio the lawyer, Tobias Beventini the physician, the Guinea slave Lopez—watch as a complex series of commodity and currency maneuvers by the apparently innocent Nicholas brings about the financial and political ruin of de Fleury and de Ribérac; and they nearly desert him for the conscienceless avenger he appears to be, especially after de Fleury dies in a fight with, though not directly at the hands of, his nephew.

The faith and love of Marian de Charetty make them rethink their view of this complicated personality. Marian, whose son was killed beside Nicholas in the Italian wars, and whose sister married into his family, is moved towards the end of the novel to suggest that Nicholas take her in marriage. It is to be platonic: her way of giving him standing, of displaying her trust in him and his management of the business, and of solacing him in his anguish. Once married, however, she longs despite herself for physical love, and Nicholas, who owes her everything, finds happiness also in making the marriage complete.

That marriage, however, sows the seeds of tragedy. The royally connected Katelina van Borselen, "characterful," intelligent, and hungry for experiences usually denied a genteel lady, has refused the vicious or vacuous suitors considered eligible, and seeks sexual initiation at the hands of the merry young artisan so popular with the kitchen wenches of Bruges. Against his better judgment, Nicholas is led to comply, for, however brusque her demands, she has just saved his life in one of the several episodes in which the St Pols try to destroy him. Two nights of genuine intimacy undermined by mismatched desires and miscommunicated intentions culminate in Katelina's solitary pregnancy. Unaware of this, Nicholas enters his marriage with Marian, and Katelina, alone, fatalistically marries the man in pursuit of her, the handsome, shrewd, and fatally self-centered Simon de St Pol, the man Nicholas claims is his father. Sickened at what she believes is Nicholas' ultimate revenge on his family—to illegitimately father its heir—Katelina becomes Nicholas' most determined enemy.

VOLUME II: *The Spring of the Ram*

Simon de St Pol, the overshadowed son of Jordan de Ribérac, husband of the bitter Katelina, father of the secretly illegitimate Henry, has clearly had his spirit poisoned long since by the powerful and malignant de Ribérac, and is as much pitied as loathed by Nicholas vander Poele, who sees in Simon something of his own deracinated brilliance. Looking to find a sphere of activity where Simon and Nicholas can no longer injure each other, Marian de Charetty, now the wife of Nicholas, persuades her husband to take up an exciting and dangerous project: to trade in Trebizond, last outpost of the ancient empire of Byzantium.

It is less than a decade since Sultan Mehmet took Constantinople, and the several forces of Islam—Mehmet's Ottomans, Uzum Hassan's Turcomans, Kushcadam's Egyptian Mamelukes—ring the Christian outpost while delegates from the Greek Orthodox East, led by the very earthy and autocratic Franciscan friar Ludovico de Severi da Bologna, scour the Latin West for money and troops to mount still another crusade. With Medici backing and Church approval, Nicholas sets out for Trebizond to trade as Florentine consul, bringing his skilled mercenaries as a show of support from the West—a show that will soon turn real as the Sultan moves against the city more quickly than anyone had anticipated.

Nicholas' rival, and in some ways alter ego, is the gifted, charming, and amoral Pagano Doria, trading for Genoa, gaming with Venice's Nicholas in a series of brilliant pranks and tricks which include, terribly, the seduction of the thirteen-year-old Catherine de Charetty, one of Nicholas' two rebellious stepdaughters. Pagano, who is secretly financed by Nicholas' enemy Simon de St Pol, has invited the adolescent Catherine to challenge her stepfather, and no pleas or arguments from Nicholas, her mother's officers, or the new figures joining the Company—the priest Godscalc and the engineer John le Grant—can sway her.

In Trebizond, Nicholas deploys his trading skills while he assesses Byzantine culture, once spiritually and politically supreme, now calcified in routine, crumbling in self-indulgence. Nicholas must resist the Emperor David's languidly amorous overtures while he takes the lead in preparing the city for, and then withstanding, the siege of the Sultan. The city, however, is betrayed by its Emperor and his scheming Chancellor, and Pagano Doria suffers his own fall, killed by a black page whom he carelessly loved and then sold to the Sultan. Nicholas has willed neither fall, yet has set in motion some of the psychopolitical "engineering" which has triggered these disasters, and he carries, with Father Godscalc's reflective help and the more robust assistance of Tobie and le Grant, part of the moral burden of them.

The burden weighs even during the triumphant trip back to Venice with a rescued if still recalcitrant Catherine and a fortune in silk, gold, alum, and Eastern manuscripts, the "golden fleece" which this Jason looks to lay at the feet of his beloved wife. A final skirmish with Simon, angry at the failure of his agent Doria, ends the novel abruptly, with news which destroys all the remaining dream of homecoming: Marian de Charetty, traveling through Burgundy in her husband's absence, has died.

VOLUME III: *Race of Scorpions*

Rich and courted, yet emotionally drained and subconsciously enraged, Nicholas seeks a new shape for his life after visiting his wife's grave, establishing his still-resentful stepdaughters in business for themselves, and allowing his associates to form the Trading Company and Bank of Niccolò in Venice. Determined to avoid the long arm of Venetian policy, attracted to the military life not precisely for its sanction of killing but for the "sensation of living through danger" it offers, Nicholas returns from Bruges to the war over Naples in which he had, years before, lost Marian's son Felix and contracted a marsh fever which revisits him in moments of stress. When he is kidnapped in mid-battle, he at first supposes it to be by order of his personal enemies, Simon and Katelina; but in fact it is Venice which wants him and his mercantile and military skills in another theater of war, Cyprus.

The brilliant and charismatic but erratic James de Lusignan and his Egyptian Mameluke allies have taken two-thirds of the sugar-rich island of Cyprus from his legitimate Lusignan sister, the clever and energetic Carlotta, and her allies, the Christian Knights of St. John and the Genoese, who hold the great commercial port of Famagusta. Sensing that, of the two Lusignan "scorpions," James holds the winning edge, Nicholas agrees to enter his service. He intends to design the game this time, not be its pawn, but he doesn't reckon with the enmity of Katelina, who comes to Rhodes to warn Carlotta against him, or the sudden presence of Simon's Portuguese brother-in-law Tristão Vasquez and Vasquez's naïve sixteen-year-old son Diniz, all three of whom do become pawns.

Nicholas is now the lover of Carlotta's courtesan, the beautiful Primaflora, whose games he also thinks he can control, and he recognizes a crisis of countermanipulations brewing between Katelina and Primaflora. Only at the end of the novel, after Katelina's love/hate for Nicholas has been manipulated to bring Tristão to his death and Diniz to captivity under James, after Nicholas and Katelina rediscover intimacy and establish the truth of their relationship, after a brilliant and deadly campaign waged by Nicholas for James has brought him to ultimate tragedy—the siege of Fama-gusta which he planned and executed has resulted, without his knowledge, in the death of Katelina and the near-death of Diniz, trapped in the starving city—only at the end does Nicholas fully admit even to himself that much of this has been planned or sanc-tioned by Primaflora, intent on securing her own future.

In the end, too, the determinedly rational Nicholas gives vent to his rage. Punishment for the pain of the complex desires and denials in his private and public history cannot be visited upon the complex and only half-guilty figures of his family or his trading and political rivals and clients. But in this novel, for the first time, he finds a person he can gladly kill, the unspeakably cruel Mame-luke Emir Tzanibey al-Ablak, whom he fatally mutilates in single combat while James, unknown to him, has the Emir's four-hundred-man army massacred in a preemptive strike carrying all the glory and damnation of Renaissance kingship.

Like Pagano Doria, like Nicholas himself, Primaflora is a "mod-ern" type, a talented and alienated "self-made" person. Unlike the other two, Nicholas has the memory of family in which to ground a wary, half-reluctant, but genuine adult existence in the community. At the same time, however, he avoids close relationships: he has established the Bank of Niccolò as a company, not a family. But, resisting and insisting, the members of the company forge bonds of varying intimacy with Nicholas, especially the priest Godscalc and the physician Tobie, who alone at this point know the secret of Katelina's baby and carry the dying woman's written affirmation of Nicholas' paternity.

Nicholas' only true intimate, however, is a man of a different race entirely, the African who came to Bruges as a slave and was befriended by the servant Claes, who first communicated the secret of the alum deposit, who traveled with him to Trebizond to run the trading household, and to Cyprus to organize and under Nicholas reinvent the sugar industry there. His African name is as yet unknown, his Portuguese name is Lopez, his company name Loppe. Now a major figure in the company, and the family, he listens at the end of the novel as both Nicholas and his new rival, the broker of the mysterious Vatachino company, look to the Gold Coast of Africa as the next place of questing and testing.

VOLUME IV: *Scales of Gold*

For those who know the truth, the deaths of Katelina, Tristão, and Tzanibey, the brutal forging of a new monarchy for Cyprus, even

Nicholas' alienation from and reconciliation with young Diniz, have stemmed from honorable, even noble motives. But gossip in Europe, fed by de Ribérac and St Pol, puts a more sinister stamp on these events. Under financial attack by the Genoese firm of Vatachino, the Bank of Niccolò undertakes a commercial expedition to Africa, which young Diniz Vasquez joins partly as an act of faith in Nicholas, while Gelis van Borselen, Katelina's bitter and beautiful sister, joins to prove him the profit-mongering amoralist she believes him to be. They are accompanied by Diniz' mother's companion Bel of Cuthilgurdy, a valiant and razor-tongued Scottish matron who comes to guide the young man and woman and ends up dispensing wisdom and healing to all; by Father Godscalc, who desires to prove his own faith by taking the Cross through East Africa to the fabled Ethiopia of Prester John; and by Lopez, whose designs are the most complex of all. Through Madeira to the Gambia and into the interior they journey, facing and eventually outfacing the competition of the Vatachino and Simon de St Pol.

Like everyone but the Africans, both companies have underestimated even the size, let alone the cultural and religious complexity, of Africa: no travelers in this age can reach Ethiopia from the East, and the profits from the voyages of discovery and commerce recently begun by Prince Henry the Navigator are as yet mainly knowledge, and self-knowledge. There is gold in the Gambia, and there is a trade in black human beings which is, as Lopez is concerned to demonstrate, just beginning to take the shape that will constitute one of the supreme flaws of the civilization of the West. There is also, up the Joliba floodplain, the metropolis of Timbuktu, commercial and psychological "terminus," and Islamic cultural center, in which Diniz finds his manhood and Lopez regains his original identity as the jurist and scholar Umar; where Gelis consummates with Nicholas the supreme relationship of her life, hardly able as yet to distinguish whether its essence is love or hatred.

On this journey, Godscalc the Christian priest and Umar the Islamic scholar both function as soul friends to Nicholas, prodding him through extremities of activity and meditation that finally draw the sting, as it appears, from the old wounds of family. Certainly there is no doubt of the affection of Diniz for Nicholas, and surely there can be none about the passion of Katelina's sister Gelis, his lover. As the ships of the Bank of Niccolò return to Lisbon, to Venice and Bruges, success in commerce, friendship, and passion mitigates even the novel's first glimpse of Katelina's and Nicholas' four-year-old son Henry, molded by his putative father, Simon, in his own insecure, narcissistic, and violent image.

On the way to his marriage bed, the climax and reward of years of struggle, Nicholas is stunned by two blows which will undermine all the spiritual balance he has achieved in his African journey. He learns that Umar—his teacher, his other self—is dead in primitive battle, together with most of the gentle scholars of Timbuktu and their children. And on the heels of that news his bride Gelis, fierce, unreadable, looses the punishment she has prepared for him all these months: she tells him how she has deliberately conceived a child with Nicholas' enemy Simon, to duplicate in reverse—out of what hatred he cannot conceive—the tragedy of Katelina. As the novel closes, we know that he is planning to accept the child as his own, and that he is going to Scotland.

How Nicholas will be affected by the double betrayal—the involuntary death, the act of willful cruelty—is not yet clear. There is a shield half in place, but Umar, the man of faith who helped him create it, is gone. Nicholas' own spiritual experience, deeply guarded, has had to do with the intersection of mathematics and beauty, with the mind-cleansing horizons of sea and sky and desert, and with the display in friend and foe alike of the compelling qualities of valor and joy and empathy: the spiritual maturity with which he accepts the blows of fate here may be real, but he has taken his revenge in devious ways before. More mysteriously still, the maturity is accompanied by a curious susceptibility he cannot yet understand, a gift or a disability which teases his mind with unknown events, unvisited places, thoughts that are not his. As much as his markets, his politics, or his half-hidden domestic desires, these thoughts seem to draw him North.

VOLUME V: *The Unicorn Hunt*

Thinner, preoccupied, dressed in a suave and expensive black pitched between melodrama and satire, between grief and devilry, our protagonist enters his family's homeland bearing his mother's name. Now Nicholas de Fleury, he comes to Scotland with two projects in hand: to recover the child his pregnant wife says is Simon's, and to build in that energetic and unpredictable northern backwater a new edifice of cultural, political, and economic power. Nicholas brings artists and craftsmen to Scotland as well as money and entrepreneurial skill, making himself indispensable to yet another royal James. But are his productions there—the splendid wedding feasts and frolics for James III and Danish Margaret, the escape of the king's sister with the traitor Thomas Boyd, the skillful exploitation of natural resources—the glory they seem? Or are they the hand-set maggot mound, buzzing with destruction, of Gregorio's inexplicable first vision of Nicholas' handsome estate of Beltrees? Is Nicholas the

vulnerable and magical beast whose image he wins in knightly combat—or the ruthless hunter of the Unicorn?

The priest Father Godscalc, for one, fears Nicholas' purposes in
Scotland. Loving Nicholas and Gelis, knowing the secret of Katelina
van Borselen's child, guessing the cruel punishment which her sister
has planned for Nicholas, the dying Godscalc brings Nicholas back
to Bruges and extracts a promise that he will stay out of Scotland for
two years, and so remove himself from the morally perilous proximity of Simon, the father-figure whom he seeks to punish, and Henry,
the secret son who hates him more with every effort he makes to help
him. Nicholas agrees, and turns to other business, mining silver and
alum in the Tyrol, settling the eastern arm of his banking business in
Alexandria, tracking a large missing shipment of gold from the
African adventure from Cairo to Sinai to Cyprus. These enterprises
occupy only half his mind, however, for the carefully spent time in
Scotland has confirmed what he suspects, that the still-impotent
Simon could not in fact be the father of the child whom Gelis has in
secret borne and hidden, and who, dead or alive, is the real object of
his quest. In a stunning dawn climax on the burning rocks of Mount
Sinai, Nicholas and Gelis, equivocal pilgrims, challenge each other
with the truth of the birth and of their love and enmity, and the conflict heightens.

The duel between husband and wife finds them evenly matched in
business acumen and foresightful intrigue, tragically equal in their
capacity to detect the places of the other's deepest hurt and vulnera-
bility. But Nicholas is the more experienced of the two, and wields in
addition, or is wielded by, a deep and dangerous power. One part of
that power makes him a "diviner," who vibrates to the presence of
water or precious metals under the earth, his body receiving also, by
way of personal talismans, the signals through space of a desperately
sought living object, his newborn son. The other part of the power
whirls him periodically into the currents of time, his mind aflame
with the sights and sounds of another life whose focus is in his name,
the name he has abandoned—the vander Poele/St Pol surname
whose Scottish form, Semple, is startlingly familiar to readers of the
Lymond Chronicles, Dorothy Dunnett's first historical series.

The professionals Nicholas has assembled around him have always
tried to control their leader's mental and psychic powers; now a new
group of acute and prescient friends strives to fathom and to guard
him, from his enemies and from his own cleverness. Chief among
these new friends is the fourteen-year-old niece of Anselm Adorne,
the needle-witted and compassionate Katelijne Sersanders, who
finds some way to share all his pilgrimages as she pushes adventur-
ously past the barriers of her age and gender. The musician Willie
Roger, the metallurgical priest Father Moriz, and the enigmatic

physician and mystic Dr. Andreas of Vesalia add their fascinated and critical advice as Nicholas pursues his gold and his son through the intricate course, beckoning and thwarting, prepared by Gelis van Borselen. In the endgame, as Venetian *carnivale* reaches its height, this devoted father, moving the one necessary step ahead of the mother's game, finds, takes, and disappears with the child-pawn whose face, seen at last, is the image of his own.

Yet there is a Lenten edge to this thundering Martidi Grasso success. Why has Nicholas turned his back on the politics of the crusade in the East to pursue projects in Burgundy and Scotland? Who directs the activities of the Vatachino mercantile company, whose agents have brought Nicholas close to death more than once? Have we still more ambiguous things to learn about the knightly pilgrim and ruthless competitor Anselm Adorne? What secrets, even in her defeat, is the complexly embittered Gelis still withholding? Above all, what atonements can avert the fatalities we see gathering around the fathers and sons, bound in a knot of briars, of the house of St Pol?

Judith Wilt
Boston, 1995

Part I

Summer, 1471

Prologue:

THE CHUTE OF LUCIFER

Chapter 1

AMONG THE RICHER class of dealers and traders, the kidnapping of the heir to a bank signifies trouble. Some investors snatch back their ducats at once, assuming that half an ear and a ransom note are about to arrive at the counting-house. Those with propositions to make do not make them. Invitations drop off. The market oscillates; the Bourse proceeds to lose bottom.

Finding itself assailed by such rumours in Venice, the Banco di Niccolò took immediate measures to quash them. Fortunately, its management was adroit. Business clients were calmed by Gregorio, the company lawyer. The well born were embraced by the handsome notary Julius, and left heartened. The heir to the Banco di Niccolò, they all learned, was aged two. And the kidnapper was the Bank's founder himself, the child's legitimate father.

The client was occasionally puzzled. 'Ser Niccolò, you say, *stole away his own son?*'

'Following a disagreement with the lady his wife. An irrational impulse. Ser Niccolò will tire of the boy in a week.'

'Tell me if he does,' said one client at least. 'He can have my son instead. I would pay to have the turd stolen. And meanwhile, the Bank goes on as usual?'

'As usual,' the notary Julius always agreed, tilting his classical head and occasionally smoothing the silk on his uppermost knee. 'That is, Master Gregorio will be in Venice, as always. I may have to go to Cologne.'

That was between February and March.

The news spread.

The Duchess Eleanor of the Tyrol heard the tale from a band of noble pilgrims from Venice on their way home to Bruges in the Low Countries. Their leader Anselm Adorne broached the subject. 'You

will have heard. Nicholas de Fleury has disappeared. A dispute over a
child. I am sure his company will keep you informed of it.'

'Nae doubt,' said the Duchess, who was Scottish. They had been
hunting from her castle of Brixen. She finished feeding her dogs and,
wiping her hands, picked up her embroidery. Despite her lack of
youth and her girth, she was as adept in the field as she was at
fending off probes about mineral rights. She said, 'And how's the
wife taking it then? Glad to get rid of them baith?'

'Glad!' exclaimed Adorne's son drolly. Adorne's niece Kathi
screwed up her face.

'Katelijne?' encouraged the Duchess.

'Gelis is very sad,' said the girl.

'Sad. Deary dear,' said the Duchess. 'Mind you, that's a handful,
that fellow Nicholas. And you're a mite peaky yourself, my wee lass.
Come to me later, and I'll find ye a potion. And how did ye manage
on Cyprus? Is yon feckless lad Zacco properly married yet?'

That was in the middle of March.

The King of Cyprus, who was not properly married yet, heard the
news in the third week of March, in the hills where he was hunting
with leopards. Two days later, his party somewhat depleted, he rode
back to Nicosia and called to the table the envoys of Venice, of
Rhodes, and of all those other peoples who were immediately threatened by Turkey.

'It appears,' said Zacco of Cyprus, 'that despite all he promised,
the padrone of the Banco di Niccolò is not to fight at our side. De
Fleury has fled. He has abandoned us, and his God. I cast him off. I
wait to hear what you offer instead.'

The man from Cairo sighed; the Venetians shuffled; and the
Treasurer of the Knights of St John muttered under his breath. The
consul for Venice said, 'There is, my lord, the joy of your coming
consummation with our daughter your Queen.'

In Rome, the news was handled by the Bank of Niccolò's agent
Lazzarino, who sought to present his patron's dramatic exit as an
episode in a family tiff. Such acceptance as this received was then
abruptly overturned by the Patriarch of Antioch, come in March with
an envoy from Persia to press a Crusade on the Pope.

'Nicholas de Fleury?' roared the Patriarch, a hirsute Franciscan
blessed with resonant organs. 'The self-serving Ser Nicholas de
Fleury, who put the fleshpots of the West before the fight for his
Church in the East? Well may he vanish. And when he materialises
once more, wherever in Christendom that may be, he will find my

crucifix at his jaw and my fist at his snout to change his mind for him.'

'He has taken a child?' said the Persian thoughtfully.

'Because the mother annoyed him. He himself is no more than a scab on the good name of huckstering. But of such persons the Lord can make use – with your help and mine,' said the Patriarch.

The news came in April to Scotland, where Nicholas de Fleury had several homes. The high-born ladies of Haddington Priory were especially shocked. 'A baby so young! He snatched the child from its mother and vanished! What will the poor lady Gelis do now?'

A letter from Bruges had acquainted them with the news. 'Sir Anselm declares,' said Phemie Dunbar, to whom it was sent, 'that the lady Gelis was quite wild in her despair, combing Venice for news of the boy. Sir Anselm grieved for them all, and so did young Katelijne, but they could do nothing about it. We are to give the news to Sersanders his nephew.'

'So what will the lady Gelis do now?' said Betha Sinclair her cousin.

'In her place,' said the lady Phemie, 'I should wait.'

'Obviously. M. de Fleury will tire of the child,' the Prioress said.

'No,' said Betha. 'But I'll make you a wager. When he's ready, he'll make sure his lady wife knows it. And if she wants the boy, she'll have to come to him, not the other way round.'

'How terrible!' said the youngest nun, her face rosy.

Most importantly of all, the news came that same month to Picardy, where the armies of France faced the armies of the dukedom of Burgundy across the banks of the Somme. Trivial though it might seem, the report caused each ruler to act.

The Duke of Burgundy sent for his captain of mercenaries. 'I am disappointed, Astorre. Your company is serving me well. But I am told that your patron has vanished – fled, some are saying, to the detriment of his Bank. Is this true?'

Captain Astorre had fought under better men than the Duke, including the Duke's own late father. He employed his comfortable voice. 'My lord Duke, you well know that Master Nicholas turned his back on the gold of the East in order to help you settle this quarrel with France. No doubt he or his officers will come to tell you themselves, but I can assure you of this: the Bank stands in good name, and I and my men have all the arms and silver we need to keep our bond to the Duchy of Burgundy.'

As it happened, the Duke knew this was true. It didn't lessen his annoyance with the vanished Nicholas de Fleury.

In the castle of Ham, over the river, the King of France sent for his fiscal adviser. 'You were in Venice. Indeed, my dear vicomte de Ribérac, you have been absent these two months when we needed you. Now we hear this troublesome banker is to support Duke Charles instead of ourselves. Or has he some other patron in mind? We are told he has vanished.'

One could seldom tell, within such a volume of flesh, whether Jordan de Ribérac was disturbed. His voice remained mellow. 'Monseigneur is well informed. M. de Fleury has left his lady wife, and wishes apparently to deny her access to their son. The situation will resolve itself. The Bank is secure.'

'We spoke of this before,' said King Louis. 'You were unable to bring me the child.'

'I have not given up hope,' said Jordan de Ribérac. 'A banker's son reared at the Court of France might prove a jewel of some price. We speak of maintaining Lyons, reversing the Tyrol, seducing Savoy, keeping Scotland in thrall. My lord knows what de Fleury has done to our harm.'

'He may be reconciled to his wife,' said the King. 'He may have many more sons. Where is the lady?'

'Searching for him, of course,' said the vicomte. 'But I am told that latterly she has abstained from her quest, no doubt recognising that her husband cannot remain absent for ever. She is on her way to Cologne, I am told, with the company notary Julius.'

'A comely man?' said the King.

'A man who has found a fortune and a place in society through the success of the Bank. But not, I understand, an athlete of the bedchamber.'

'Perhaps his tastes will now change. Tell me again about the redoubtable M. de Fleury. He is a kinsman of yours?'

The vicomte did not sigh, but the cost of his restraint could be glimpsed. 'He is a bastard of my son Simon's dead wife. My son Simon, who keeps my castle in Scotland.'

'I remember,' said Louis. 'Then if he comes here, I expect you to bring him to see me. I speak of M. de Fleury, not your son.'

'I have sent my son to Madeira,' said the vicomte; and this time he exhaled like a jet from a pudding.

Of the three people who all this time knew where Nicholas de Fleury might be found, two had been trained to distrust him, and one was too young to hold an opinion.

Several weeks before the baby (now kidnapped) was born, Clémence de Coulanges had come to serve Gelis the mother, and had stayed to tend mother and baby. Convent-reared, convent-trained, Mistress Clémence was a lady as well as a nurse, even though her parents (report said) had neglected to wed before dying. Her elderly amanuensis Pasque was neither a nurse nor a lady, but, grumbling, fetched and carried and washed, and chivvied the wet-nurse when the time came to hire her.

Pasque was in the last resort respectful of Mistress Clémence, who held herself upright as a hat-stand of wood, and had been born, you would say, middle-aged. Pasque was even more in awe of her employer, the lady Gelis van Borselen, who carried her babe with the spunk of a countrywoman, even though the child was her first, and a desperate burden. It did not seem right to Pasque that the Lady's husband should stay so long overseas, and never ask for her.

It seemed downright cruel that the Lady gave birth to her fine son alone, struggling in agony hour after hour, while her husband neither sent nor tried to come till weeks after. And by then even Mistress Clémence knew that something was wrong, although the Lady never offered a confidence. It was Madame Margot, the Lady's companion, who told them that the lady Gelis was afraid that her husband would take against his new son, and so the boy must be hidden.

And concealed he had been, sometimes in this house or that, but always with Mistress Clémence and old Pasque to look after him, and his mother too, when it was safe. And it even seemed that the Lady's fears must be right, because the husband did actually come, and bring a troop of armed men to the convent, and try to torture the servants, Heaven preserve us! But the child had been taken away, and was safe, of course, with his nurses.

Then the Lady had followed her husband to the Holy Land, so they were told, to soften his heart towards her and the child. From that she had come back full of hope for the future, only to be betrayed by her so-called friend Margot. So the father, Nicholas de Fleury the torturer, had been able to kidnap the baby at last, and have his nurses brought to the ship where the child was, and demand that they serve him.

Nicholas de Fleury. Pasque would never forget the day she first set eyes on him; neither would Mistress Clémence, for all she planted herself on the floor of the cabin, chin up and hands clasped at her apron, as if about to complain to a tradesman. Being small, Pasque stood behind.

He was a very big man, M. de Fleury. She had seen smiths of that build, although none buttoned up to the chin in his pourpoint like this one, seated at a tidy chart-desk like a clerk, with pen and paper before him. He didn't rise. His voice, smartly outlining his proposals, alarmed her by the excellence of its Burgundian French: they had been told he was Flemish. His hair was brown like the child's, but there seemed, at first, no other resemblance that hit you. His eyes, although of the same grey, were big and fixed and bright as a drunk Marseilles monkey's. Pasque had edged closer to Clémence.

He said, 'I recognise you have long served my wife. I am not asking you to be disloyal to the lady, but to extend the devotion you have shown since his birth to my son. For that, I am prepared, as I have said, to improve your fees and maintain your conditions of service. If you wish anything more, you must tell me.'

'Thank you,' had said Mistress Clémence, in the bold way that Pasque would have called cheeky. 'A little clarification, perhaps? We are still, so far as I know, in the dame de Fleury's employment. When the child returns to her care, she may well accuse us of breaking a contract.'

'The child will not return to her care,' said M. de Fleury. Pasque shuffled.

'I see,' said Mistress Clémence. 'Then, monseigneur, I have to ask you what prospect we have for the future, with a broken contract behind us? What are your plans for the boy?'

'To rear him myself, with your help,' said M. de Fleury. He paused. He added, 'It is even possible that the lady my wife may join us one day. Should that occur, I am sure she would feel nothing but gratitude for your continuing care of her son.'

Mistress Clémence said nothing. Sometimes her silences maddened Pasque. M. de Fleury waited and then produced a curious smile. Two dents appeared in his cheeks. Pasque stared at them.

He said, 'I am buying your commitment to Jordan de Fleury, not to me, Mistress Clémence. Be his friend, and when the day comes to part, I shall see that you both lack for nothing. I shall write it into your contract, if you wish.'

Be his friend. Pasque grinned to herself, even as Mistress Clémence narrowed her gaze. Mistress Clémence said, 'I am a nurse. I train a child in my own way. The dame de Fleury has been pleased to support both me and my methods. I should expect the same freedom at least.'

'You would have it,' he said. The two dimples had gone.

Then Mistress Clémence glanced round for Pasque's nod, and said in her firm voice, 'In that case, monseigneur, we agree.' And just as she spoke, they both heard a high voice outside: a child's voice; the voice of a child calling their names.

Upon that, M. de Fleury had opened the door, and there stood Jordan de Fleury, thumb in mouth, his upturned eyes swimming about like two fish-floats until he saw his own *Clemme* and *Paque*. The thumb trailed down at once over the sopping wet chin, and there were the two shining front teeth and the dimples, growing deeper and deeper just like the father's. And now there was no doubt about it. Here was a man and his son, and whatever was to come, Pasque and Mistress Clémence were contracted to serve them.

Although she had exacted the best terms she could, the decision, for Clémence de Coulanges, had been unavoidable. She owed it to the child she had reared for two years, and who still required her protection.

Against what, she was not as yet certain. Her view of the Lady differed slightly from Pasque's. Every nurse knew what reliance to place on the claims of quarrelling parents. Consistently the mother had hidden the child – perhaps from fear; perhaps because of threats from the father. Or perhaps from nothing but shame, because the boy had been conceived far too soon.

Naturally, as the child grew, its precise age was no longer apparent. Yet it had remained out of sight, however far off its father might be. And this frightened lady had abandoned her son for four months, for six months at a time.

Mistress Clémence did not believe in according blame lightly. She could judge the depths of anguish to which M. de Fleury had now subjected his lady. She saw that there was some sort of battle engaged between husband and wife. It was for her, with Pasque's help, to ensure that the child came to no harm from it all.

She did not realise, at the start, that M. de Fleury intended to keep them at sea for five weeks. Fortunately, she was impervious to the motion of vessels, nor could she complain of her quarters or treatment. A meeting was called, at which she explained the child's routine and requirements, while a quartermaster made notes, like a commissary preparing for war. Everything she asked for she got. She enquired at which hours the child should be brought to his father, and was told that the boy should be kept out of sight unless summoned.

'I knew it!' said Pasque, when informed. 'The man is set on chastising his lady, and the baby is nothing!'

'Then we should be thankful,' Mistress Clémence replied. 'At least M. de Fleury has not abstracted the child in order to disfigure or harm it.'

M. de Fleury himself, she had seen, bore a scar: a thin white line many years old, which scored his face from eye to mouth on one side. She studied him whenever she could, for much of a man's nature by thirty could be judged from his body and face. It struck her, in those early days, that the well-dressed M. de Fleury looked jaded, bleak as a mercenary returned starving from war – although, of course, he had not come from war.

His upbringing was not easy to guess. To carry such muscle and bone he had not been stinted in childhood; but then masters made sure of strong servants: the broad hands knew how to handle a sword, but might be equally at home in a workshop. Somewhere he had been taught to hold himself properly; or perhaps it was a trait born of pride. A straight back was worth more than a smile; she believed and taught that herself.

This man did not smile. She registered the bulk of brown hair, professionally cut to dip under his cap, and the broad jaw and strong neck within it. The face was Burgundian; that curious mixture of races in which, here, the broad mask of the Low Countries predominated, although the austerely drawn nose hinted at some strain of Latin or Celtic. The whole was dominated by the pellucid and widely set eyes which in a boy's face might spell merry innocence, but here produced the immense leaden gaze which had so alarmed Pasque. His skin was pale, unless you counted the faint jaundiced tint left by last year's Egyptian sun. She thought, if he made a threat, he would fulfil it. She could detect no wish to be liked, or to like.

The ship that carried them all was a small merchant vessel with no passengers but for themselves and the servants of M. de Fleury. Such a ship was almost independent of shore, carrying livestock and water and plentiful food with her cargo. There was a cow, milked every morning.

M. de Fleury had been true to his edict, and had made no effort to see them. For the first day, in any case, she had kept the child quiet. Although it was February still, the waters of the Gulf of Venice were kind, and the boy slept to their motion. None the less, she assembled the ropes she had asked for, and by the time the child made his first journey on deck, she had arranged a composition of lashings among which he moved, a little uncertain, his brown hair flicked by the wind, his eyes round. That day she saw M. de Fleury in the distance, talking to one of the seamen. He moved off shortly without looking round, but she saw the child stand and gaze.

The next day, she heard the page lifting the pail, and carried the child in his wake to witness the milking. The page, an unexceptional youth, expected the boy to be frightened or thrilled, as if dairies were unknown in nunneries. Yet, having small brothers, he talked to the boy, and gave him a drink. Coming up, they saw M. de Fleury again in the distance, kneeling over something on the deck. She felt the child halt, but a moment later, M. de Fleury had gone. It annoyed her.

She made no effort therefore, the following day, to stop the child when, seeing the familiar figure again, the boy suddenly tugged his hand free and went forward. Did the man think the child had no wits? This was the person who had brought him from Venice, who had stayed with him until she, Clémence, had reached him. Only perhaps a matter of hours, but a child, a friendly child, would remember all that. And now he was being ignored. She watched him cross the deck in his harness, his cheeks red, his brows straight; and this time M. de Fleury looked up, and paused. Then he said, 'Look at these,' and sat back on his heels.

She could not see to what he referred: she thought the objects were raisins. The child sat and M. de Fleury bent forward. The two heads, hessian brown, leaned together. She could hear the child's high, erratic voice and the other leisurely, masculine one, but could not distinguish the words. Then the man started to rise and the child, getting itself to its feet, faced towards Clémence and said, 'Que Jodi mange?'

'Jodi?' said the man.

She winced. 'I am training him out of it. He finds his name hard to say. The nuns called him Bouton de Fleury.'

'I prefer either to Jordan,' said M. de Fleury. 'Jodi wants to eat carob seeds. There is a carob seed.'

'Carobs are nasty,' said Mistress Clémence, looking him in the eyes.

'Carob seeds are very nasty,' he agreed. He had let the child take one. Jodi opened his mouth.

M. de Fleury said, 'Put it in, have a taste, spit it out. Now here are some raisins . . .'

The child threw the seed down and stretched out his hand.

'. . . but we must ask Mistress Clémence if it is a good time to eat them. Is it allowed?'

'I think it is,' she said, using her agreeable voice, and the child backed confidently into her arm, pleased, his cheeks full of fruit. M. de Fleury dusted his fingers, nodded, and began to walk off.

The child half took his weight from her arm and then stopped. The man continued to walk. Just as she thought he had gone he turned and lifted a hand, and she saw the child's face break into its own private, generous smile, a dimple deep as a pool in each cheek. Then Mistress Clémence took him below and gave him to Pasque, for she wanted time to consider whether the reason for the long meandering journey had now been explained.

The days and weeks that followed proved her correct. Never in her experience had courtship of lovers been conducted with the finesse of this wordless dialogue between a man and his son. It progressed as it had begun, forming a relationship which included small treats, small adventures, small gifts; but was not built upon them. After a very few days a trust formed; the preternatural tension began to relax.

On the fourth day, M. de Fleury did not come at the usual time. The child strayed, inattentive, from one side of the deck to the other, and hardly replied to the seamen who called to him. When the man did appear, the boy slipped his hand free and went forward. Mistress Clémence halted and watched as M. de Fleury slackened his pace and strolled over.

His appearance had changed. There was a faint warmth in his skin, and fewer hollows, and his shirt was unjewelled and creased. He looked like the student sons she remembered, who used to sleep deeply and late, and then invade her busy nursery, demanding breakfast. He stayed with the child longer than usual, and once laughed aloud.

Mistress Clémence said nothing, but from the next day took her deck-walk much later, to accommodate whatever deferred convalescence was taking place. More: as their patron came to himself, so the disembodied ship, the meandering voyage seemed to find positive focus. The sea turned blue and sparkled with light. Approaching an island, the spaces of canvas and timber would fill with the aroma of flowers. Fish would splash in the waves and nesting birds pause in the rigging, where the nameless pennant flew among stars. Jodi said, 'Where is maman?'

He had asked Mistress Clémence before, and she had replied plainly as she usually did, although making no promises. And the child seldom fussed since, in the past, his lady mother had always come back, and he was used to friendly faces about him.

But this time, the child asked M. de Fleury, who happened to be in the cabin improving his horse. Latterly it had become apparent that wooden articles bought in the marketplace lacked a certain character which M. de Fleury could supply. A knife, a brush, a paint pot and, it seemed, endless patience had already produced articles which decorated not only the child's room but the ship, and chirped, rang or clattered to order. As its patron had revived, so the ship itself had begun to stir with new life.

But now, the question was put, and not, this time, to Mistress Clémence. The child began to finger its toy; a stranger would think that its interest had wandered. Mistress Clémence said nothing. M. de Fleury wiped his brush, laid it carefully down and turned his full gaze on the child. They were both on the floor. He said, 'Ta maman te manque?'

You miss your mother? Mistress Clémence gave a dry cough. The child wanted an answer, not an abstract expression of loss. Then she saw the man had suddenly got to his feet and was holding out first one hand, then two. The child scrambled up, and let himself be lifted and swept to the poop windows.

The man swung him round. 'You see that land over there, far away? Madame ta mère is over there. She cannot come, she is busy. But there are horses for riding over there, and fine boats, and hound-puppies, and cows to be milked. And one day you and I and Mistress Clémence and Pasque will sail to that shore, and find some boats, and some horses, and will ride to where maman will meet us.'

'Soon?' said the child. He looked up and round.

'Soon,' said M. de Fleury. His voice was easy but his gaze, turned to Mistress Clémence, was dense and unyielding as pewter, as it had been when first they met.

That time, the play with the horse was resumed and the child, she saw, was content. Only, several days later, he said again to the man, 'And so, where is maman?'

And the man, looking at him, picked him up and seated him again in the crook of his arm and walked again to the windows. 'Why, you see that land over there, far away? Madame ta mère is over there. She cannot come, she is busy, M. le bouton.'

'Horses,' said the child.

'But there are horses for riding over there . . .'

'Boats.'

'And fine boats . . .'

'Puppies.'

'And hound-puppies, and cows to be milked.'

'Soon?'

'Of course, soon.'

The next time, man and boy chanted the recital together, and Mistress Clémence got up and left. To Pasque she said, 'My head ached.'

Although a peasant, Pasque also came from Coulanges. She said, 'He hates his lady wife. Do you believe he is truly planning to meet her?'

And Mistress Clémence replied, after a while: 'He is taking a great deal of trouble to attach the boy to himself. His purpose I do not know. He tells me we are sailing now for Marseilles.'

'To land?' said Pasque. When she was pleased, she displayed her
very few teeth. When she was extremely pleased, she would dance.

'Eventually. He is in no hurry. Then we have to prepare the child for a
journey through France. Provence; Burgundy. To Dijon in Burgundy.'

'Dijon?' said Pasque. 'The vicomtes de Fleury come from near
Dijon. Ser Nicholas wishes to show off his son to his mother?'

'Hardly,' said Mistress Clémence. The family château at Dijon was
a ruin. M. de Fleury's disgraced mother was dead; the grandfather
locked away in his dotage. M. de Fleury was without brothers and
sisters. The child would find no aunts or uncles to greet him at
Dijon, no cousins to play with.

'Then why Dijon?' said Pasque.

'I have not been told,' said Mistress Clémence. She had herself
considered the question. The child's mother might have been sent
for, or have demanded a meeting. It might be nothing to do with the
child, but merely denote M. de Fleury's return to the world of affairs.
The head of a bank could not vanish for ever. And a child of two
years had no place in a bank.

'M. de Fleury has an army,' Pasque remarked. 'They say it is a
good way to train up a boy, to put him among men in an army.'

Quite simply, Nicholas de Fleury had bought himself time. For five
weeks the vessel of which he was owner floated in the Middle Sea,
and gold made it invisible. Even when he finally set foot on shore at
Marseilles, quietness followed him still. He was well served, and
although René its ruler was absent, the comté of Provence embraced
the child and himself with the spring.

The child bloomed. To the uninitiated, Nicholas de Fleury reflected the blooming: a sunlit wall of unknown composition. The
journey continued northward through France. For as long as it
lasted, Nicholas conducted his life with perfect and costly simplicity,
as he had done for three months. Then, reaching Dijon at last, he sat
down one day in his room and, taking out his pen and his seals, sent
out the commands that would set into motion the plan he had already
long formed: the plan interrupted that night in Venice, as he stood
with the child in his arms and studied the weeping, desperate face of
his wife.

In none of the letters did he say where he was, only that he was
travelling in France, and would shortly make his whereabouts public.
He was leaving Dijon in any case: the secrecy was for the protection
of Jordan, who would stay there in retreat until sent for. They would
not be parted for long, and Nicholas made light of his leaving. The
child was well served, well protected. Mistress Clémence would

manage the rest. Now, turning his back on the boy, he rode north to where the road joined the Loire, and from there found a boat – a fine-enough boat – to sail him to the castle of René at Angers.

It was the third week in May, and the air over the leafy river was moist, the clouds low, the lions of thunder grumbling faintly abroad in the ether. Unknown to him, a kingdom had fallen, and his plan was already in motion.

Chapter 2

B Y THE FOURTH day of June, the house of the Banco di Niccolò in Bruges knew that Nicholas was in France, and by the eighth the news reached Cologne and his child's mother, Gelis van Borselen.

The company notary Julius, who was also in Cologne, was candidly thankful. Not himself a family man, he had taken little interest in the (somewhat overdue) marriage of Nicholas to this strong-minded young woman. He had shared Nicholas's evident lack of interest in the resulting progeny. He had found himself quite astonished when Nicholas, performing a total volte-face, actually quartered Venice one night and snatched the child from the arms of its mother.

Julius had found it amusing until he saw the sober faces of all the others who witnessed the kidnapping. Gregorio and his partner Margot; Anselm Adorne and his son and his niece Katelijne; Simon, the chevalier son of Jordan de Ribérac, stared after the vanishing boat as if someone had died.

After Nicholas disappeared, Julius was concerned, as Gregorio was, to restore public confidence. Cursing his wayward padrone during those chaotic first days of planning, Julius was relieved to find less sympathy than he had expected for Gelis, visibly raging through Venice, pouring out threats, gold and a fierce demoniac energy in the effort to track down her son. No one in authority helped. In this quarrel, Venice chose to stay neutral.

Others, too, had held back. Kathi, the niece of Adorne, the Burgundian Envoy, had sided with Nicholas, not the child's mother. So had Margot, once moved by her fears for the baby to leave even her beloved Gregorio. When, bereft and alone, Gelis van Borselen had stood weeping by the waterside that terrible night, it had been Gregorio who had walked forward in pity and led her back to her home. But he had done nothing since to help her find the child or her husband. And no one knew where Nicholas and the baby had gone.

At first Julius was too busy to care; but he was by nature inquisitive, and finding Gelis hurrying through a public place, would stop and speak to her. At first, learning that he had nothing to tell her, she would treat him with stony reserve. But that changed. Julius enjoyed the pleasant aspects of life and was not a man to cast blame on others. Nor was he shy. When, one day, he asked her why Nicholas had done such a thing, his brashness unexpectedly brought him an answer. Gelis, at first silent, spoke slowly. 'I kept the child from him. I was afraid.'

Julius knew that much, from Margot. He said, 'Afraid Nicholas would harm it? Surely not?'

'I had a reason,' she said. From a plump child in Bruges, she had grown into a lissome, fair woman of twenty-six with the looks to make a lusty man happy. Although uninterested in her himself, Julius was conscious, at these meetings, that they made a fine pair.

He said, 'And now?'

She had looked at him. 'Will he harm Jordan? He might. Even if he does not, how can he heal the shock of that night, stealing him from all that he knows? And he will teach him to hate me.'

Julius said, 'Margot tells me his nurses have gone.'

'Even his nurses,' she said. Her voice was bitter. After a moment she said, 'But if they are with him, of course it will help.'

Then, as she fell silent, Julius said, 'What are you going to do?' He supposed she realised that if Nicholas didn't want to be found, she wouldn't find him. And meantime she was friendless in Venice, and in Bruges would find no warmer reception, he suspected. He doubted if she had any close relatives living, apart from her cousin Wolfaert at Veere. On the other hand, she had money. Nicholas had endowed her as his wife with a fortune. He must be regretting it now.

She said, 'What are your plans?'

It was not the sort of question a man like Julius would answer out of hand. Ten years older than Nicholas, he had once helped to run the small dyeworks in which Nicholas had begun as an apprentice. Since then, he had risen with Nicholas, and watched Nicholas surpass him without any real rancour. To Julius, the best years of his life had been spent serving the Bank with Gregorio in Venice or Bruges.

He had no ties. At present, there was urgent business demanding his presence in the Imperial city of Cologne, six weeks' journey from Venice. He proposed travelling there through the Tyrol, where he was to leave two of his colleagues. It struck him that the presence of Gelis van Borselen in Cologne might not be unsuitable. The story of the dispute over the child would be known, but would not, as in Bruges, be fiercely debated. She could act as his hostess, chaperoned by the wife of their agent. And Cologne was only four days from Bruges. Sooner or later Nicholas would emerge, or resume contact. Julius could not see Nicholas living in limbo, without numbers, without puzzles, without schemes: a hermit rearing a baby.

He said, 'I have some business in Cologne. Perhaps, if you are going to Bruges, you might like to stop there on the way?'

She accepted his offer. If there was no outburst of passionate gratitude, he sensed she was deeply relieved. His fellows at the Bank were less so, although Father Moriz, who was also bound for the Tyrol, described his scheme as humane. John le Grant, their other expert on mines, swore in German when told and banged the door, leaving.

To Margot, Julius said, 'I think you will have to tell me what Gelis did that was so terrible.' He tried to sound less enjoyably interested than he felt.

Margot did not answer at first. Then she said, 'She kept the child from him.'

'I know that,' Julius said. He looked to Gregorio for more.

Gregorio studied his hands. When Margot took one of them quietly in hers, he glanced at her. Then he turned his gaze on Julius and spoke slowly. 'Gelis tried to persuade Nicholas that this child was not his, but the son of Simon of St Pol. It is not so, of course. They have been competing with one another, Gelis and Nicholas. They have been looking for new ways to hurt each other.'

'She and Simon were lovers?' Julius said.

'I didn't say that,' said Gregorio stiffly. 'Only that she claimed the child might be his. It is not so, of course. The child and Nicholas are alike as two peas. By hiding the child, she prevented him from realising as much. It was a cruel deception, carried out cruelly, and Gelis has received her deserts. I am sorry for her, but not deeply sorry.'

Julius left Venice entranced by this insight into the marital relations of Nicholas, and remained privately entranced all the way north with Father Moriz and John, although impeccably courteous to the lady de Fleury. At Bozen, he enjoyed practising his charm on the Duchess Eleanor, who was short, stout and Scots. She knew most of their news: Anselm Adorne and his party, it seemed, had passed that way five days before. Then, leaving Moriz and John to their mining, he and Gelis made for the Rhine and Cologne.

Residence in the prince-bishopric proceeded much as he had expected. Although exhausted at first by the journey, Gelis soon became self-sufficient: making acquaintances; fulfilling the Bank's social obligations in style with her fine jewels and rich gowns and royal manners. Indeed, Julius had no cause for complaint.

Nevertheless, after six weeks of serious trading, he began to feel hampered, and even uneasy. Gelis was still there, and no word had come from her husband. She said nothing about it, but his agent's wife thought she was pining. Ever since the loss of the child, the girl had had the look of a starving dog kept in a pit.

No one, therefore, was happier than Julius when the courier from Diniz in Bruges burst into his office with news. Nicholas and the child were in France. Within five days they were to learn his exact whereabouts.

'You will go to Bruges?' Julius said, in the girl's chamber. She was sitting. She had dropped into a seat as soon as he started to speak.

'Don't you recognise a summons when you hear it?' she said.

The words were scathing, but her eyes were deep as two ice-pools in snow, and her hands were cramped in her lap. He said, 'He won't hurt you.' It was hardly worth the pretence. She was married to Nicholas. She knew what he did. She deserved to suffer, according to Margot.

She left the following day. Julius realised that in some practical ways he would miss her. But for her, the Hanse correspondence would have fallen behind, and she had a natural aptitude for ciphers. It was only away from his desk that he had begun to feel the want of his freedom.

His doublet-maker was due. He set down his beaker of wine and took up and emptied a packet of buttons. He studied them, smiling, and smoothing the silk on his uppermost knee.

The town of Angers was in mourning. The sadness which had dimmed the warm sun of Provence hung like a pall over Anjou and the capital where René, King of Sicily, Duke of Anjou, Count of Provence, mourned the fighting son lately dead in Barcelona, and now the death of Blanche, the little matron, the love-child he had looked to, with his wife, to comfort him in old age.

Nicholas, careful of such things, had advertised his coming in terms of subdued condolence, but would have been surprised to learn that he would be unwelcome at René's Provençal castle at Tarascon, or could not be entertained by the bereaved monarch at Angers. A merchant banker with Burgundian connections was not likely to be ignored at this juncture in Anjou's affairs. The greeting he received at Marseilles from René's godson and namesake confirmed this.

He was expected, therefore, at Angers, even though the royal boat which met his at the junction of the Loire and the Maine was pinned with black taffeta, and Fleur de Pensée, the herald who welcomed him, had discarded his beautiful livery of white and dove-grey and black for one of mourning. So too had Ardent Désir, the second herald who awaited him with a small cavalcade on the quay. High on its rock a hundred feet over their heads loomed the seventeen striped dark towers of the castle in which, ceremoniously, Nicholas de Fleury, banker of Venice and Bruges, was about to be received.

He felt no qualms. He was trained to formality; knew to appear in some dark colour that was not the black of the sorrowing family; knew that everything about him would be documented, including his own feud with Jordan de Ribérac, finance officer to the King of France, René's nephew and overlord in this duchy. The vicomte de Ribérac's grandson, Henry, had been in training here as a page. He would be ten now.

The heralds preceded him. Behind the romantic names were two experienced courtiers and trusted friends of the King. Ardent Désir, whose name was Pierre de Hurion, was a writer and poet. So was the King's maréschal des logis, Jehan du Perrier, commonly known as Le Prieur, who soon joined them. Nicholas de Fleury was shown to his chamber, in which there was no food but a lavish provision of wine, which his companions were happy to share with him. Then he was sent for.

Poet, painter, musician, maker of buildings and gardens, prince of learning and of pleasure, René King of Sicily had withdrawn in bereavement into a shadow seated in a great chair, his hand at his cheek. About him stood his courtiers, among whom were no pages whom Nicholas recognised. Beside René was Jeanne, the second of the two queens whom he had coaxed, like his peach trees, into long ripening at his side. Ysabelle, mother of all his legitimate children, had brought him Lorraine, the duchy his dead son had held, and thirty-three years of successful partnership. After Ysabelle had come Jeanne, twenty-one when he had married her seventeen years ago. For her, young and loving to him and to all his children, he had sought to lead a simpler life away from the grand palaces such as Saumur and Angers where now perforce he sat in splendour below the painted ceiling and the heavy tapestries, among the tables laden with treasures.

He was in Angers because his heir was dead, and all he had planned had to be replanned. He was in Angers because France and Burgundy were face to face to his north, and he did not wish to lose Anjou to either. He was in Angers because his daughter Margaret was the Queen of Henry of England, and striving, her son at her side, to maintain her husband's throne claimed by another. He would not begin, however, by referring to any of that.

'M. de Fleury,' said the King. 'You have come to condole with me on the loss of my son. You fought against him at Naples and Troia.'

'Nine years ago. My company did. As monseigneur knows, there is no ill will in such cases. He was a gallant opponent. There are no words to salve such a loss.'

'No.' The King stirred. Below the black brim of his hat, something winked: his eyeglasses, left hung at one ear. He said, 'You were travelling, I was told, with a child.'

'With my son. I left him at Dijon. He is a little young, or he would have wished to thank you himself for the generosity of your captain at Tarascon. He produced all a child could wish save for the monster La Tarasque himself.'

'I trust he fares well at Dijon,' said the King dryly. He indicated a stool, and Nicholas sat. The wine had been strong. He supposed he knew why. 'He is with his mother your wife?' the King added.

'Not at present. But his nurse is of frightening competence, although not a Tiphaine, a Caieta.'

'You know my theories, I see. The master may make the warrior, but the nurse makes the man.'

He broke off abruptly. There was a little silence, during which the Queen his wife turned her head. Nicholas said, 'I am sorry. You are waiting for news.'

'From England, yes,' said the King. 'It would suit the Duke of Burgundy, of course, if Edward of York wins back the throne, and my grandson dies in the field, whatever the quality of his nursing. That is why you are here?'

His face was grim. This was not to be an exchange of formalities. The King, oppressed, was obeying his moods. Nicholas kept his voice calm. 'The Duke of Burgundy is my master, as the King of France considers he is your overlord and the Duke's. An observer would say that if Lancaster prevails, Burgundy will be at the mercy of France. If York wins, the King of France, fearful of Burgundy, may turn next to master your Anjou.'

'And Burgundy would save me?' said the King. 'Your observer has a confidence that perhaps others lack.'

'I think,' said Nicholas de Fleury, 'that the King of France would find it hard to fight against England and Burgundy both.'

He said no more, for he had been out of touch with his spies, and had no intention of guessing how far the secret talks between René and Burgundy might have gone. That they were taking place he had no doubts. He himself was concerned, here and now, merely with demonstrating which side he had chosen, and why.

René said, 'You have land in Scotland, M. de Fleury.'

He was shrewd. The remark should not have been unexpected. René knew Jordan de Ribérac; had entertained his son and his wife

and his wife's offspring. The Loire was awash with retired Scottish
Archers.

Nicholas answered elliptically. 'Scotland has always been a friend
to the lady Margaret your daughter and France. But if York retakes
the throne, Scotland will have to court York, just as Burgundy must.'

'You think Edward of York will prevail.'

'I am married to Gelis van Borselen of Veere,' Nicholas said. 'And
the opponents of York have been unwise enough to promise Zeeland
and Veere to their supporters. It is why the fleets of Veere and the
Hanse support York.'

René did not speak. His Queen smiled. She said, 'We should like to
meet your lady wife. You said she was elsewhere?'

Nicholas said, 'She is in Cologne with some friends, but I expect
her to join me this summer.'

'Then we shall receive her,' said René. He rose, his palm on the
arm of his chair. 'Unless affairs forbid. The play for Corpus Christi
has suffered already. Perhaps you have noticed the suspended tortures
of St Vincent? But of course you would. You are an expert in the
engines of illusion. Go and look at ours before supper. Madame will
conduct you through the gardens.'

Outside, he was offered more wine, and did not refuse, although he
drank slowly. Then the Queen led the way through alleys and arches
while her ladies scurried behind and Le Prieur and Ardent Désir
brought up the rear. She said, 'It needs irrigation. We have difficulty
with leading in water. You are an expert in water?'

'I employ those who are,' Nicholas said. 'They are in the Tyrol at
present. Perhaps they could help you.' Afterwards, he realised that he
had been thinking more slowly than he should.

'We have heard of them,' said the Queen. 'But you yourself are
curiously gifted, are you not? I am told that you can divine the
presence of anything: water, silver. They say you divined the whereabouts of your own son.'

They had walked so quickly that there was no one within earshot.
By now he was fully on his guard. He said, 'The Church does not
approve. What I achieved was by accident. I have stopped now.'

'Can you predict the future?' she said. They passed a pavilion. Her
veils swirled in reflection across the glass of the windows; her cloak
rustled over the grass. He said, 'No, madame. In any case, you have
your own astrologers.'

'But they cannot tell us,' she said. It was a cry. When he didn't
answer, she continued. 'You named your child Jordan, they say, after
the seigneur Jordan de Ribérac?'

'My wife named him,' he said. The wind was cold on his skin.

'A fine name,' said the Queen. 'Breton, surely? Simon, Jordan, Gaultier de St Pol. Your wife preferred it to the van Borselen names? What of Wolfaert, or Francis, or Henry?'

'She has a nephew called Henry already,' Nicholas said. 'As you know, madame. By your kindness, he attends your school of children here sometimes, I am told.'

'You might have found him here, had you been a week or two earlier,' said the Queen. 'His grandfather took him away to reunite him with his father, who was going to his Portuguese property. A beautiful boy. Father Perrott will miss him. And now here are the lions. Or perhaps you are tired?'

To visit the gardens was to visit the menagerie. He had known he would be thrust again among animals; the ubiquitous animals; the intrusive, inescapable bestiary which sometimes seemed more real than his life. He could see ostriches in the distance. He disclaimed being tired, was introduced to Master Guillaume, and heard of the gross consumption and ferocious temper of lions – six hundred sheep, the butcher kept handy to feed them! – and of poor Martin who died, despite the ministrations of the barber, the surgeon and the King's physician Pierre Robin himself.

Of course, René's ring bore a lion as one of its supporters. The Queen, smiling, made a joke about St Pol de Léon and his son's Breton name. The Lion of St Mark was the symbol of Venice; the lion flew on the flags of Cyprus, of Scotland, of England, of Burgundy; it appeared on the royal arms of Denmark, and on the badge of Eleanor of the Tyrol. The Queen was offering him a cured lion skin (that of Martin, he belatedly realised), and he was refusing.

He saw the monkeys, the dromedaries, the peacocks. He visited the aviary gallery and met Master Bertrand, who wished to show him a cage full of parrots. Some of them mimicked the human voice in langue d'oc, which was different from Greek. In Amboise, they said, all the parrots shouted *Péronne*; being sequestered by Louis for having been taught to insult him. Poor France.

He was introduced to the wife of Master Bertrand who was black and slender and Moorish. Her name was Cresselle and she spoke Mandingua. He said one word in automatic response and when she looked at him in shock, turned blindly away.

No one had heard. He found himself at the edge of the moat which, instead of water, held a grunting, stinking group of wild boars. This time, Nicholas turned so abruptly that he had to sway to avoid a man who had just walked quietly down from the drawbridge. From his features he was a Jew, a race which King René tolerated more than most rulers, but his scarlet robe and cap carried no emblem.

'M. Pierre,' said the Queen, who was nearer than Nicholas had realised. 'I hoped you would be here. This is Ser Nicholas de Fleury of Venice and Bruges, the guest of monseigneur.'

'I am sorry,' Nicholas said. 'The boars startled me.'

The man smiled. 'You mistake. I am not their keeper, but merely a doctor of medicine. Although I do not feel as violently about them as you do. You have always disliked them?'

'M. de Fleury has had enough of animals,' said the Queen. 'And I must go back. You will allow M. de Hurion and Le Prieur to show you where the play is to be staged? Truly, it would interest you.'

'Perhaps I too might accompany M. de Fleury,' said the Jew baptised Pierre. 'The tortures of St Vincent are certainly not to be missed. You may find it hard to choose what you wish to see first: Paradise or the gridiron?'

'How reassuring,' said Nicholas, 'unlike St Vincent, to be given a choice. The gridiron, of course.'

The Queen gave a faint smile and turned to leave. He bowed and saw that she had stopped, as if by impulse, to add something in private. 'Forgive us if we seem preoccupied. You have seen the King in his sorrow. The prince his grandson is only seventeen. And whatever may happen in England, the King of France has a power which my lord has no means to resist. We cannot even protect our friends.'

'Your friends understand that,' Nicholas said. He kept his breathing quite even.

'Do they?' she said. 'Do they understand that if York regains the throne of England, if my lord can be accused of sympathising with Brittany, or entertaining thoughts of turning to Burgundy, Anjou will be taken from him?'

'Whether monseigneur your husband is guilty of them or not,' Nicholas said, 'he will be accused of either or both of these things, should King Louis decide to evict him. Or I should not be here, endangering both you and myself.'

They looked at one another. 'What you say is true,' said the Queen. 'And indeed, Provence is beautiful. The grape is better here, and the Loire is sand, and not salt. But Provence is beautiful.' She turned to leave. There had been tears in her eyes.

'You have seen the gridiron, M. de Fleury,' said the herald Ardent Désir with bitterness. 'Come now and see God and His angels.'

The play was to take place in the Cattle Market. The immense elevated frame of the royal stand was already there, its new-shorn wood protected by sheets of tarred canvas. As they arrived, a youth in leather apron and leggings hurried forward calling 'M. Le Prieur!' The flapped cap on his head enclosed a fresh face of painful anxiety.

'Eve,' indicated M. Le Prieur. 'Also Isachor, Architriclin and Tubal the Paralytic. The son of a smith. His father has just given us five thousand nails.'

'How . . .?' Nicholas said. He had noticed a man with two hutches of rabbits. The alcohol stirred in his veins. Despite himself, happiness, recently rediscovered, suddenly appeared like a ghost.

'With a fig-leaf,' said Le Prieur briefly. 'Both Adam and Eve are born with a fig-leaf. Excuse me.' He stepped aside.

'M. Le Prieur is Adam,' said Ardent Désir mellifluously. 'If, that is, we are to present *The Creation*, as planned. Since the death in Spain of the prince, roi monseigneur has asked us to consider instead the *Mystère* of St Vincent of Saragossa, the Catalonian martyr. It has caused certain problems. Come. Come to the workshop.'

'Problems?' Nicholas said. They began to cross over the square. The Jew followed.

'Six months of preparation,' said Ardent Désir. 'Bestow a little thought on what must be arranged for these plays? For the *Multiplication des Pains*, six dozen loaves from some baker, to be replaced at starvation prices when eaten. For the *Décollation of St Jehan Baptiste*, a second head, with the best type of blood. *Sodom and Gomorrah* one could run for a month, except that more wish to take part than to watch. As for the Judas's death! *Yci creve Judas par le ventre et les trippes saillent dehors*: it sounds simple. But the Superintendent must fashion the tripes, order the soul, commission the device for their ejection.'

'And produce the rabbits for *The Creation*,' Nicholas suggested helpfully.

'You see the trouble?' said Ardent Désir with exasperation. 'No play demands so much as *The Creation*! You say it is easy: a snake, a cloud, a maisonette for Adam and Eve. But the doves, the coneys, the fish, what of these? Compared with which, St Vincent is simple – a mere engine of torture, and some blood.'

'Heaven and Hell,' said the Jew. They had come to a large shuttered warehouse.

'One can hardly escape Heaven and Hell,' said Ardent Désir, 'in any play. It is my contention that the Creation should be abandoned. Let us have the noble St Vincent, whose instruments, if well greased, will suffer no harm however long the play is deferred.' He began to declaim. '*O l'aide Dieu, createur tout puissant; par le congé de vous, tresnoble roy; noble prince, nature cognoissant . . .*'

'You have a rôle in St Vincent?' asked Nicholas.

'I,' said M. de Hurion, 'am the Prologue,' and, flinging open the doors, walked into the workshop.

Nicholas hesitated. 'As you perceived,' said the Jew at his ear. 'The flaming city of Ai reflecting the infernal city of Dis. Each gentleman has a stake in one play, and each is reluctant to concede. But indeed, M. de Hurion is eloquent as the Prologue, just as M. Le Prieur is a magnificent Adam. Have you a minute?'

He held one in his hand: a thick wad of paper slipped from the sleeve of his robe.

'The script?' said Nicholas.

'A summary of it. The blanks represent the comedy interludes, in the hands of Les Chinchins.'

'It seems a very long play,' Nicholas said. The floor of the ware-house was littered with half-made artefacts, some silent, some receiv-ing the attention of groups of people employing saws, brushes or knives. Men argued with one another; greeted M. Pierre; smiled at Nicholas from a platform dominated by a great wheel. In a corner a towering object suddenly opened its jaws, revealing a flood of scarlet light and two dwarves.

'Le Crapault d'Enfer,' said M. Pierre. 'It *is* a long play. Fifteen thousand verses, sixty actors and three days to perform it. Text in French, directions in cooking-Latin, comedy inadvertently in bas-auvergnat, but we needn't go into that. I am told that you practise the art of divining.'

'You are mistaken. What is the wheel?'

'According to requirements, the Wheel of the Damned, or that which represents nine choirs of angels in nine circles of fire. Come down. It is not at all safe.'

There were platforms at the end of each spoke, some with dummies on them. Having climbed halfway up, Nicholas inserted himself beside a pliant angel with tall feather wings. He made no attempt to come down.

He had seen a lot of Mystery Plays. He had acted in some. Ardent Désir had reappeared and the other officer, Le Prieur, walked in and stood by the door, somewhat flushed. The doctor Pierre, standing still, had no expression on his upturned face at all. But then, he was sober.

So damn them all. 'Thunder for God, if you please,' Nicholas said. Without particular haste the thunder basket was brought and the handle turned. The stones rumbled. The copper sheet rippled and sighed. In the voice of God, Nicholas addressed himself, with sonor-ity, to the doctor.

> '*Ha! Meschant homme, qu'as tu fait*
> *Fors ordure et sterilité!*'

He paused, to permit a chorus of sardonic approval. The actor Le Prieur moved forward, looking astonished. The angel said, 'You have stood on my toe!'

'Don't interrupt. I thought you were a dummy,' Nicholas said. He saw, looking closer, that the angel sharing his platform was a boy in a mask. Half of the angels were children.

'He is a dummy!' someone roared from the floor. 'Vacquenet the butcher's son! Stamp on his other toe, God!'

'Merde!' said the angel. 'Get off!'

There was a vacant platform above him. Nicholas swung himself up, the wheel rocking. A voice addressed him from below. 'M. de Fleury! Our friends are here to rehearse some of the music. Perhaps . . .'

'Perhaps what?' said Nicholas. Somewhere, a little drum had started to beat. The angels ruffled their feathers and coughed. A flute added itself to the drum.

'Perhaps,' said M. Pierre the doctor, stooping gently, 'we should test the wheel and the music together.' Then he straightened and looked up at Nicholas as the wheel began to revolve. The angels shrieked, engraving a fillet of sound as they wheeled.

Nicholas said, 'So what music?'

The piece was in three parts for the Trinity: the minute, when he thumbed over the pages, remarked, *Icy parle Dieu à III voix.* The wheel creaked, moving slowly; each time it shook, the angels cried. Nicholas said, 'Well, let's get going. I'll count three, then come in.' He reached up and laying hands on a very young heavenly body, plucked him down and sat him on his knee. He said, 'Come. Take off your mask, and we shall do it together.' He wondered whose son this was.

Cheeringly, this angel was friendly. Uncertain at first, its voice gradually strengthened, and another voice joined it. The music was simple. Nicholas sang peacefully along with it, picking it up, following the three strands as they appeared until the entire choir was in voice, interrupting itself at intervals as the wheel jolted or jammed, less to cry than to giggle. Then he called for a drum and two sticks and, when they were tossed up, launched into a staccato outburst of sound, to which with effortless clarity he added the words of a tavern song everyone knew.

The choir tittered and sang; the workers below roared along with them, and swayed. A man on the Ascension pulley swung himself

rhythmically up and down bawling, and two devils mounted the
wheel, which rocked and began to move faster. Nicholas set down his
drum, singing still. 'And that's enough,' he said placidly to the
cherubim on his knee. 'When we arrive close to the ground, you will
jump. And you, monsieur, and you.'

The wheel turned. His hands round its waist, Nicholas released his
angel, a butterfly, into the waiting hands below. A second jumped,
and a third. Last of all he stepped down himself, a devil under each
arm, his drum hung round his neck and the sticks in his belt. Le
Prieur and Ardent Désir were waiting for him, brandishing scripts,
uttering blandishments.

'Abraham! Noah! Monsieur, the blessed St Vincent himself!'

The angels were tugging his arms. He laughed. 'You flatter me.
Anjou can provide all the talent you need. And in any case, alas, I
must go.'

M. Pierre had not spoken.

'You are a guest of monseigneur,' said Le Prieur. 'He will invite
you, as I do, to stay.'

'I have obligations,' said Nicholas. 'And at present, monseigneur
awaits. Please forgive me.' He had to raise his voice against the
shouting and singing.

'Come with me,' said M. Pierre.

Nicholas was sorry to leave. He liked people, and music and
laughter. He would like to have investigated the circles of fire, and
braced the wheel really well. He was hungry, not for royal food but
for bread and cheese and radishes and cheerful company. Thinking of it,
he followed M. Pierre carefully along a passage and through a doorway
into a room which became perfectly quiet when the door closed.
Nicholas returned from his thoughts with some suddenness.

He had moved out of the warehouse to another house which clearly
adjoined it. He stood in a chamber whose furnishings – trestles, brazier,
instruments – were familiar to him from other rooms, including that
of his own company doctor and another, in Cyprus. Except that
Tobie had never employed a table covered in black, with a copper
bowl of liquid set in its centre, the rim engraved with strange letters.

The only seats in the room stood before it. Nicholas looked at the
man who had brought him and spoke, slurring a little. 'I have
nothing to say to you.'

'You are not surprised,' said the Jew baptised M. Pierre. 'The
Queen, I suppose, asked if you predicted the future. And you said
you did not.'

'It is the truth,' Nicholas said.

'Perhaps. Sometimes we perceive one truth, and a bystander sees another. But if I ask you directly, now we are alone, whether using a rod or a pendulum, you can trace a human being, you would not deny it?'

'No,' said Nicholas at length. All the laughter had gone, but not all of the wine. A wave of anxiety turned him cold.

'No. This is not some idle test. I do not ask you to prove it. I wanted to meet you. Our mutual friend Dr Andreas of Vesalia sometimes visits the Loire. I wished to offer you a present.'

'*Fa me indovino, et iou te davo dinare?*' Nicholas said.

'I ask for no money. The gift is your own, and I propose only to free it. I know what rumours have said of your son and your lady. I know that if you have left them, you must be very sure where they are. Is your pendulum with you?'

'No,' said Nicholas.

There was a silence which he made no effort to break. Then the other man said, 'So be it. I could not harm him, you must know that. As his father, your power is unbreakable. If I had something of his, I could answer your question.'

Nicholas walked to the stool and subsided. 'Which is?'

'It need not be spoken,' said M. Pierre. He sat opposite. His gaze remained level. 'A pendulum is only a weight on a cord. You ask it questions and it replies yes, or no. This is a little different. Your answer is more complete. It is spelled.'

Nicholas sat, his unseeing eyes on the bowl. In his purse was a thread, and bound to one end was a carob seed: the pendulum whose presence he had denied. His son was in Dijon. The pendulum told him that every day, as any expert could guess: his finger was inflamed with the rub of the thread. The man said, 'Please accept. I should balance one thing with another.'

Nicholas looked at him then. The eyes, darker grey than his own, remained level, and the lips within the brown beard, although authoritarian in set, were not without sensibility. Against his better judgement, Nicholas drew the fragile thing from his purse and handed it over.

It dangled over the bowl. The warmth of the sinking sun roused the oil in the fabric that covered the window, and hazed the copper with light. The little play-token hung, motionless, its cord in the Jew's strong, clean hand. Then it stirred.

It was very quiet. If the revels continued in the next building, they didn't penetrate here. The only sound was the chime of the seed as it shivered, and swung, and, spacing each swing and each movement, touched the rim of the vessel five times.

The doctor holding the cord had not been told what its owner was

asking. Nicholas, bedevilled by the mists of the future, hardly knew
himself what most he needed to know, so ominous and diffuse he felt
the shades around him to be. He simply opened the doors of his
mind, so that there was nothing between him and the man who held
his son's treasure. And the carob set to its work, and spelled out a
name.

The seed stilled. The Jew looked at him. He must have worn a
puzzled expression because M. Pierre drew back and said, 'You are
disappointed. Would you like me to do it again?' His gaze remained
calm, although this time Nicholas was conscious of some sounds of
activity distantly in the passage and the trampling of horses outside,
enough to break the concentration. But when, as he nodded, the
pendulum began its travail again, the result was the same.

A name. Not a place-name, the name of a person. The name
ROBIN.

It was a relief. Nicholas stood. He collected the pendulum from the
long palm of the other and, holding it for a moment, made it his own
again before putting it away. Architects, glass-makers, doctors, the
family Robin were known throughout Anjou and Provence. He
thought of the lion Martin and smiled. It was a crooked smile,
because the trampling was coming nearer. Not the feet of angels, but
of six men at least, outside the window and door. He had been kept
there very artfully. But then he had known what might happen. *We
cannot even protect our friends.*

The door opened.

'I am sorry,' said the man opposite.

'You had no choice, I am sure. It would have happened in any
case,' Nicholas said. The men who came in were armed. Their leader
was a man he had seen before, at long intervals in strange places, in
Bruges, in Louvain, in Scotland. He remembered his name, Andro
Wodman. Until not so long ago, a member of the King of France's
Scottish Guard; now accompanied by soldiers, every one of whom
wore the royal badge of France on his tunic.

Wodman walked in and glanced at the table. 'We had finished,'
said the physician. 'Do your duty. I shall tell the Duke of Anjou what
has happened.'

Wodman turned. 'M. de Fleury, my master begs you to forgive the
hasty invitation, but I have to ask you to come with me at once.'

'It is, indeed, remarkably short notice,' Nicholas said. 'My boxes,
for example, are up at the castle.'

'They are here,' Wodman said. 'My lord apologises, as I have said,
for the inconvenience. There is, however, no possibility that he could
be refused.'

'Then I shall not try,' Nicholas said. He turned. 'So I must say goodbye, M. Pierre Robin.' It amused him, a little, that the man had troubled to do no more to fill time than tap out his own name. And yet despite himself, watching the pendulum, Nicholas had been touched by a sadness he had not felt before.

His remark drew a sharp look, as he expected. Then the doctor gave a mild sigh. 'Ah! My name is not Pierre Robin, M. de Fleury. You have confused me with King René's physician.

'We share the name Pierre, it is true; but I am not the Robin whose life, whose fate touched you today. My name is Pierre de Nostradamus.'

Chapter 3

THE RED AND white chequered fortress of Ham, powerful as a walled city, had for two hundred years commanded the village, the church and the River Somme whose moat surrounded it. Because of its strategic importance it had changed hands many times. At the moment it was defended by the Constable of France, and occupied by Louis XI, King of France and nephew and overlord of René of Anjou, who had no army with which to protect either Anjou or his guests.

Nicholas de Fleury was not brought to Ham in bonds, nor deprived of his senses, but he was under guard, and had been for the week of the journey from Angers. On the way, they stayed only at the King's lodges. The Burgundian was allowed his own horses and his own servants, who were considerably better acquainted with fighting than they looked. Of his escort, only Wodman stayed at his side from the first, but answered no questions.

Nicholas waited. On the first night, eating alone with him in the chamber they shared, Nicholas set down his cup and said, 'And now.'

Under previous monarchs, the Archers of the Royal Guard of France were handpicked for their looks, as well as for their skill and their courage. In array on the field, they resembled an army of Attic comeliness, with their plumes of red, white and green and their sleeveless three-coloured jackets covered with golden embroidery. Andro Wodman by contrast was an ugly man; short-necked and short-legged and burly under the plated jack which he removed with his helmet and cap. His hair was dark and thick as a bear's, and the stubble darkened his jowls below a nose squashed in some argument. He seemed to have no objection to scrutiny but spoke through his meat. 'Ask away. You'll get some answers. Not many.'

'You were an Archer of the King's Scottish Guard?'

'That's no secret. Eight years under Pat Flockhart. Jordan Semple had gone by that time – him that's now Jordan de St Pol, vicomte de

Ribérac. We all thought we'd nothing to do but rise to be a commander like him, and suck up to the King and get land and titles and a post at the Court, but we didna have the genius the vicomte was born with, it would seem. I got out of it seven years ago, none the richer, although I do serve King Louis here and there, when he has need of me. And I give a hand to the good vicomte de Ribérac, whiles in France, whiles in Scotland. Your friend and mine. Him that gave you the scar on your face.'

It was interesting that he knew that. It was easy too to forget that Jordan de Ribérac had once been a soldier in France; a celebrated leader of armies; the confidant of kings. The fat, indolent man who had tried to buy his son Jodi from him.

'And which of them has sent for me to Ham?' Nicholas said. 'The King, or M. de Ribérac?'

'Oh, the King,' said the Archer. 'He seems to think you could be useful. And whether or not, he could always exchange you for your son.' He grinned. 'I ought to congratulate you. We thought we could lift him at Dijon, but I've never seen a lad better guarded.'

'Thank you,' said Nicholas. 'And M. de Ribérac? Shall I see him as well?'

'Ye could hardly overlook him,' said the Archer. 'Forbye, did ye kill his daughter in Scotland?'

'I can't remember,' Nicholas said. 'I thought you were there at the time.'

'Master Simon certainly thought that you did. M. de Ribérac's son. He's been sent away with his boy Henry – packed off for safety to his places in Portugal. You're not afraid?' said Andro Wodman, wiping his platter. 'The King is a hard man, and ye ken the vicomte. He kills what he catches.'

'So do I,' Nicholas said. He stretched back in the settle and studied the Archer. 'You admire him.'

'I admire a clever man,' Wodman said. 'And a cunning man. And a man who pays me what I'm worth. If you are not afraid of him, then you ought to be. Let me tell you: you'll never leave Ham until Louis is sure of a hostage. They'll make you send for the child.'

'What makes you think that I won't?' Nicholas said. It amused him, the way it stopped Wodman talking.

Little more was said, either then or during the rest of the journey. This was a disciple of Jordan's: Nicholas had no wish to court him. Only, occasionally, he caught the man's face turned to his, full of puzzlement.

At Ham, he was handed over to the Constable's men and taken at once to a chamber in one of the towers where he was locked in. His

servants were removed, despite his one, chilly protest. In fact he had
been prepared for it. No one explained or apologised. Strangers
brought him a meal. His window, too high to need locks, showed him
a courtyard noisy with the aftermath of a hunting-expedition; it was
known that even in war, Louis moved nowhere without his dogs, his
huntsmen, his birds. And this was not war. It was a long, mutually
agreed lull during which peace talks between the King of France and
the Duke of Burgundy could continue for as long as both sides
awaited the outcome of the struggle in England.

Across the Narrow Sea to the north, it might already be decided
whether Lancaster was to keep the throne, or York was to recover it.
Over there was Margaret of Anjou, daughter of René; first cousin of
Louis; wife of the Lancastrian King Henry VI. The triumph of
Lancaster would be the triumph also of Louis of France, and the end
of Burgundy's hopes of pushing over the Somme into France. The
armies of Lancastrian England would soon prevent that.

If Lancaster won. If, having landed in England, Edward of York
was unable to maintain his initial successes, and was imprisoned or
killed. As René waited in Anjou, so Louis waited here, in his castle in
Picardy. It was not surprising that, at a juncture so momentous, the
King's minor designs should have been set temporarily aside. Nicholas was resigned to a long wait for his audience. He knew, in any case,
who would examine him first.

Jordan de Ribérac came to his door as evening fell. Nicholas heard
the ponderous tread, accompanied by the footsteps and clank of
armed soldiers. He rose as the key was put in the lock. For a moment,
despite all his wealth in Venice, his power in Bruges, his growing
influence in the Levant, Nicholas de Fleury faced again the fears of
his boyhood: the emotions of more than ten years of confrontation
and struggle against this gross man who had always despised him,
had always proclaimed him to be none of his blood, but the bastard
child of his son's wife. For if he was not, Nicholas the Burgundian,
the farouche apprentice of Bruges, would have to be known to the
world as his grandson.

The vicomte never altered. His attire – the vast hat, the swathed
scarf, the doublet and coat over the mighty shoulders – was of the
same style as in the fifties. Whereas René of Anjou, slender, active,
only two years the younger, led every fashion in dress and in art when
not, as now, living in apprehension and mourning.

There was no trace of distress in the vicomte's clean-shaven pink
face with its ripple of chins. His brow was smooth except for the
curling arch over each eyebrow; his brief mouth still owed its character to unbroken strong teeth. His eyes studied, dissected, recorded

from bantering purses. 'You don't object? His Sacred Majesty is uncommonly busy. You and I understand each other so well that one brief conversation may well save King Louis an hour of the sand-glass.'

'He could have saved even more by not bringing me,' Nicholas remarked. He had chosen to remain where he was, perched on the ledge of the window embrasure. At a sign from the vicomte, the soldiers withdrew smartly outside the door, and the vicomte lowered himself into a seat and smoothed out his sleeves.

'But, Nicholas, you wanted to come. And you had taken care that your little treasure, your boy was well guarded. In Dijon, they say. How sentimental. Did you visit the deserted estate that you managed to ruin? Did you take him to the tomb of your first wife? Did you reverently show him the coffin of your poor over-liberal mother? Does he now understand some simple expressions, such as chienne?'

'His name is Jordan. I expect he does,' Nicholas said.

The fat man leaned back. 'I remember now. You have learned to talk. There is this small store of insults, painfully accumulated through long years of dumb cowering. Perhaps, however, we should try to pass straight to business. What have you to tell me about Duke René's intentions?'

Nicholas thought. 'That he has tried to cancel *The Creation* in favour of the *Mystery of St Vincent*,' he said. 'It has caused a great upset.'

The fat man sighed. 'Nicholas. Your present purpose is to manipulate the courts of France and of Burgundy to what you think is your best advantage. Otherwise you would not have come. Anjou's plans are your bargaining counter. So bargain.'

'What do you want to know?' Nicholas said.

'His plans for his grandson in Lorraine. His plans if his daughter wins England. His plans if she doesn't. And his plans for the throne of Aragon, now his son John is dead.'

'And in return?'

'What do you want?' said the fat man. 'Pick from the stall. Money? A little manor house somewhere? Or a contract for something more permanent? A pension, leading to a little title, a big title even? Louis rules France. The lands of the Duke of Burgundy are certainly rich, but they may not stay with him long if he insists on provoking his overlords. You know, and I know, that Duke Charles is a conceited, impetuous dullard whose ambitions will probably wreck him. He is not spending his favours on you, but on that noble pilgrim, that merchant aristocrat Anselm Adorne of Bruges, who is already our rival in business. You should be working for France against the Vatachino and Burgundy.'

'You would like me to bankrupt the Vatachino,' Nicholas said. It was something he had frequently attempted himself, as had others. The company Vatachino, brokers, dealers, traders with an unproved connection with Genoa, were not popular in the merchant community. Better men than the vicomte longed to have them exterminated.

'It would suit me,' agreed the fat man. 'It would suit you as well. Every company with a fleet suffers from them, and I have had enough vessels plundered this year without that. Bring your army over the Somme, and together we can crush the Vatachino.'

'My army!' said Nicholas. He tried to sound surprised. Outside, the courtyard, which had cleared, became suddenly busy again. A groom ran to the stables and was followed by several others. A man emerged from the castle dressed for travelling, servants hurrying after. Below the cloak was a sparkle of gold and a glimpse of fringed crimson. Nicholas said, 'My army, as well as Duke René's plans?'

'We spoke of a scale of reward. And of the joint destruction of the Vatachino interests.'

'But,' said Nicholas, 'I want to destroy your interests much more than I do those of the Vatachino.'

'Have I ruled that out?' said the vicomte. 'You may join France and still try to defeat me in business, as you might stay with Burgundy and match yourself against Anselm Adorne. The difference is that Adorne has Duke Charles to protect him, whereas the Vatachino have no friends in France. Give your support to King Louis, and I shall help you destroy Anselm Adorne and the Vatachino. After that, you may attempt anything against me that you wish.'

'Now you interest me,' Nicholas said. 'But still I feel I should like to know what support the King has in mind beyond the plans of Duke René and my army.'

'Must we spell it out? You will receive in the measure in which you give. Withdraw from the Tyrol. Duke Sigismond will break any promises that don't suit him. Hamper the Burgundian schemes for Lorraine, whatever you promised Duke René. Instruct your splendid emissary in Cologne to leave. He will do it. He has found a beautiful gräfin whom he is hoping to tempt to his bed. Reconsider your loans to Duke Charles. Your managers in Venice and Bruges will make no demur – Master Gregorio is in the first delirium of wedded bliss, and my grandson Diniz has contrived to become a father at last, although unfortunately not of a son. Are you enjoying my bulletin upon your neglected affairs?'

'So far as it goes. You don't mention Scotland.'

'I thought you were frightened of Scotland,' the vicomte said. 'But of course, if you thought of returning, His Sacred Majesty would be greatly moved to feel that you went as his servant, since Anselm Adorne is undoubtedly returning as the envoy of Burgundy. You know he is sheltering the Scottish King's exiled sister in Bruges?'

'Still?' Nicholas said.

'She is awaiting the birth of a second child. Her plans must also depend on the outcome of the struggle in England. Her husband meantime serves with the Duke. It would really not be suitable, Nicholas, for you to serve the Duke of Burgundy also,' said the fat man. 'There is so much against it, and so many benefits to be had from joining France. For example, when Fleury is French, not Burgundian, the vicomté could be restored and given to you. The present holder is senile, they say?'

'I am tempted,' said Nicholas. 'But you said, didn't you, that whatever I promised, they would never let me leave here without some security?'

The vicomte paused. He said, 'It would require, of course, to be considerable, but not beyond your means. Ships, or gold perhaps. A bond for your good faith.'

'Or the child,' Nicholas said. 'I shall do as you suggested, and send for the child. It would be cheaper.'

There was a silence. For a space, he could not tell how far he had been believed; any more than he could weigh precisely the reality behind the fat man's mocking, unhurried offers. Then Jordan de Ribérac said, 'How remarkable. When I offered to buy the brat from you once, I remember being given a very short answer.'

'I think I felt vulnerable,' Nicholas said. 'At the time, he was my only legitimate heir, and my wife had just formed a conjunction with your son. But now that Gelis is joining me, I hope to be blessed with a whole warren of others. Enough to stock a Creation. I can afford to risk this one, if pressed.'

'Your wife is joining you?' The fat man's face showed simple surprise, but one hand was a fist.

'I have sent for her. She is unlikely to refuse,' said Nicholas, smiling.

'Even if the child is out of your hands?'

'All the more reason. Is that all?' Nicholas said. He pulled himself from his seat at the window. Three more couriers had left, but the courtyard was still busy.

The fat man didn't stand. He said, 'All the more reason? Because she expects you to get it back? I hear some rubbish about your pretending to meddle with necromancy. You claim to divine.'

'That's M. de Nostradamus,' Nicholas said. 'A knowledge of charming, prophecy and other abused sciences. They have a menagerie, too.

Apes and japes and marmosets tailed. You wanted to know about
Angers.'

The other man stood. One forgot, because of his bulk, how nimble
he was. Unprepared, Nicholas found his wrist gripped and his fingers
splayed in the fat man's painful grasp. Then his hand was thrown
away. 'Afraid of the past, afraid of the present, afraid of the future,'
Jordan de Ribérac said. 'Afraid the churchmen will burn you, as they
probably will, if it suits them. My advice would be to attempt the real
world without talismans. But you are probably inadequate to it. What
have we settled? Nothing. How typical.'

Nicholas walked to the door. 'We have settled, I hope, the question
of whether or not I deal with messengers. Tell the King that if he
places a proposition before me himself, I shall give him an answer
myself. Good day, my grandfather.'

The broad face contemplated his with contempt. Then the fat man
rapped on the door and, when it opened, walked off without looking
back.

Next day, an escort of the King's Archers came to conduct Nicholas
de Fleury, Burgundian, to the presence of His Most Christian Majesty
of France.

Eleven years had passed since his other brief audience with Louis,
then not yet King. The wiry frame was the same, kept so by incessant
activity at work and at sport, and often at both together. But the skin
on either side of the long nose was sallow and lined, and the bright
eyes deeper under the elderly hat. He wore only the badge of St
Michael, although the courtiers grouped behind him were expensively
robed. The table at which the King sat was deep in papers.

The King said, 'Ah, M. Nicol de Fleury. *Ser* Nicholas, I am told; a
worthy honour from my nephew of Scotland, if not so remarkable as
the barony he seems to have given M. Anselm Adorne. Are you
troubled by haemorrhoids?'

'Who is not?' Nicholas said. He rose from the formal obeisances
and obeyed the finger which pointed to a station in front of the desk.
'You obtain your unguent from Tours, from your apothecary, monseigneur?' There was a box on the desk.

'To a recipe from the Professor Giammatteo Ferrari in Pavia.
The uncle of Dr Tobias, your company doctor. Dr Tobias has left
you, I am told. Your Bank is dissolving?' said the King. After the
first glance, he had returned to his papers. He signed two, and
handed them over his shoulder; one of his officers took them and
left.

'The reverse, monseigneur,' Nicholas said. 'It is too healthy to require medication. We can barely store the pledges which are offered us daily. We even have to refuse those we once dealt with most often.'

'Ah,' said the King. His hand did not falter, but as he completed his name, he laid down his pen and looked up. 'M. de Ribérac told you my wishes. I hope he conveyed them correctly.'

'As I understand them,' Nicholas said, 'they range, monseigneur, from the provision of privy information to the open transfer of my army and services from Burgundy to yourself. Including my financial services.'

'That is what I told the vicomte to say,' said the King. 'There is, of course, scope for many permutations between. But the greatest honours are reserved for the man who makes the boldest move. The Constable of France and the Receiver-General of Normandy spring to mind.'

'And monseigneur's financial adviser from Scotland,' Nicholas said. 'That is the position, I must confess, that I would covet most. In fact, the only position.'

The King smiled. Even his eyes smiled. 'Come. Land, wealth, a vicomté, compared with the cares of a kingdom's income and outlays? Leave M. de Ribérac to his burdens.'

'Monseigneur, of course. But in that case – it pains me – I cannot serve you.'

Behind the King, a man suddenly bent over and whispered. The King made an irritable gesture while pinching his lips. His eyes still rested on Nicholas. He said, 'I am aware, of course, that there is bad blood between you and the vicomte. Do you really consider that you can replace him, or do you seek rather to shame and embarrass him? Is that what you ask?'

'You ask me for information about Burgundy and Brittany and Lorraine. You ask me to cease making loans to Duke Charles, and to withdraw my army from his service. You ask me to counteract Burgundian influence in the Tyrol, and hinder Duke Charles from final possession of Guelders. You ask me to work for you in Scotland against the Burgundian influence of the Baron Anselm Adorne.'

'Leave me,' Louis said. He spoke not to him, but to the men around him who stirred and left the room quietly, in order. They had not looked surprised.

The door closed. Louis said, 'Do I understand that you would do all of this, in return for the degredation of M. Jordan de Ribérac?'

'No, monseigneur,' Nicholas said. 'You understand that I shall perform half of what you ask. I shall not withdraw my army, because in the present truce there is no need of that army. I shall not overtly transfer to your service because I could not supply you with information if I did. I shall not refuse loans to Duke Charles of Burgundy, but I shall delay what loans I promise, and I shall reduce them. The rest I shall do, fully and unconditionally as you suggest, at a rate of payment that takes account of the fact that no public honours can be bestowed. And I shall not do it at all without an undertaking that Jordan de Ribérac will meet the fate of Jacques de Coeur, when I choose to supply proof of his errors.'

'Is he cheating me?' said the King.

Nicholas smiled. He said, 'Let us say that he is the last person monseigneur should have sent to persuade me to join you. If I joined you openly, I should be dead.'

'So,' said Louis. He rose and strolled to the bed. His knees, above the knotted calves, were bent slightly inwards. He turned. 'So you think you are worth more to me than he is?'

'I think,' Nicholas said, 'that monseigneur needs us both today. But tomorrow, when you have enjoyed the fruits of all I can bring you, you may find that M. de Ribérac is not the only numerate man in your kingdom.'

The King was silent. Then he said, 'M. de Ribérac's advice was to make no agreement that would not involve a considerable forfeit if broken. He suggested I demand from you a lodgement of gold.'

'Or my son?' Nicholas said.

'We have small use for what may be simply replaced by an active man attentive to his marriage. No. But suppose,' Louis said, 'suppose that our discussion had gone otherwise. Suppose that we demanded you openly serve us, and refused to let you depart without such a bond?'

Nicholas pursed his lips. 'Monseigneur, the situation could never arise. As I explained, to join you openly would destroy half my worth. The world must think I have refused what you are offering. That is why my other servants have gone straight to Hesdin, to inform Duke Charles of their anxieties over my whereabouts. Of course, as soon as I appear, the truce talks will continue without impediment.'

There was a long silence. At last: 'But how charming,' said the King. 'You expect a pension; you promise to serve me. But what guarantee do I have that you will do anything for me at all?'

'As much as you have,' Nicholas said, 'from any other of your myriad pensioners. With this difference, perhaps. You will see results very soon. I am going to Scotland. I shall do all in my power to see that Scotland sends you all that you dream of. An army, led by her King.'

'You will?' said the King slowly. He came close, until he stood face to face, looking up. He said, 'Yes, my friend. My ambitious, clever young friend. You do that, and France will be generous. Do that, and indeed, you will receive what you ask.'

Freed, Nicholas rode out next day with his servants. A mile from the castle, he was halted by a small group of horsemen. Among them, vast in the saddle, was Jordan de Ribérac. 'A word,' he said.

The forces were evenly divided. They made no attempt to attack or to mix, but waited facing each other while Nicholas and the vicomte moved apart. De Ribérac halted and spoke. 'You are a fortunate youth. I hear you refused the King, and yet he released you.'

Nicholas smiled. 'Did he tell you why? I had sent ahead to warn Burgundy.'

The fat man gazed at him thoughtfully. 'You had no intention, when you came, of joining France. Or of sending your son. You can rout the Vatachino, you think, on your own.'

'I should have been a fool to join France,' Nicholas said. 'Considering what was happening in the courtyard as you and I spoke. I never, saw a more depressed set of couriers. Are all the members of the royal House of Lancaster dead, or merely in fetters?'

'Was it so obvious?' de Ribérac said. 'I suppose, to a second-class sort of diviner, it was. Yes, the news had just come from England. Edward of York has regained the throne. Henry of Lancaster is dead; his queen Margaret of Anjou in prison.'

'And the boy?' Nicholas said.

'Edward of Wales died on the battlefield. A fierce, silly child, mad for war.'

'The news will have reached Angers,' remarked Nicholas. 'They will probably cancel St Vincent.'

'You are going to the Duke of Burgundy now, at Hesdin?' the fat man asked.

Nicholas looked surprised. 'Who in his senses would miss such an occasion? Fireworks, bonfires, rejoicing: York on the throne, and his ducal good-brother en fête? It'll be like Negroponte. Of course I am going to the Duke. I have my wife Gelis to meet.'

He rode off, and did not know how long Jordan de Ribérac brooded alone in the saddle, looking after him.

Chapter 4

ON THE THIRTEENTH day of June, ten days after her husband left Ham, the lady Gelis van Borselen completed her journey from Cologne to Bruges, which she had left sixteen months before in the train of Anselm Adorne's so-called pilgrimage.

From that extraordinary journey, Adorne had returned in April to his own grand house in Bruges, together with his son and his niece. Gelis had not seen him since he left Venice, and she avoided him now, not least because his home was sheltering the little royal lady she had once served, Mary of Scotland. Gelis did not want to meet the lady Mary at present, and have to answer her puzzled enquiries.

She had had to decide, before leaving Cologne, where best to settle in Bruges, to wait out the interim until her husband chose to communicate. She made the choice on her own. For three months, Julius had helped her balance her life with his careless goodwill and ample energy and total lack of involvement, but she refused to yield to his insatiable curiosity. Fortunately his interests at present were deeply engaged somewhere else.

On her own, therefore, she had determined to make no present demands on the courtesy of Adorne or invite the anxious questions of her former mistress by calling at the Hôtel Jerusalem, or risk the condemnation of her cousins by descending upon the Wolfaert van Borselens at Veere. She could have leased again the house she had shared with Margot and the child, together with Clémence de Coulanges and old Pasque, who had been so quick to desert her for Nicholas – or so she assumed. If they were not with Nicholas, no one had heard of them. If they were not with Nicholas, the child was lost as perhaps Nicholas wanted him lost, with everything taken away that was dear.

It was four months since she had seen her son, and he had only been two. She tried not to think of it, for even though she believed she had wrung her throat dry, fresh rivers still came. And because the house would have cried for the child, she did not want to go there.

Which left the married home she had never occupied: the great Charetty–Niccolò house in Spangnaerts Street. This, besides the apartments of Nicholas and his staff, held the bureau of the Bank and the offices of the Charetty company, and was also the home of Tilde de Charetty, the step-daughter of Nicholas, and Catherine her sister, and Diniz Vasquez her husband who managed it all. The message which had reached Gelis in Cologne had been sent from there: it was to this house that Nicholas was communicating. Whatever it demanded from her in terms of brazen defiance, that was where she must go, for this channel was the only channel, she had long recognised, that would lead her, perhaps, to her son.

She had written therefore to Diniz, proposing herself. Nicholas would expect it, and for his sake they wouldn't refuse her. She would not be welcome. Since the events of last year, all that masculine coterie at the Bank had become aware of her war against Nicholas, and after the kidnapping of the child, they had felt no call to continue to shield her. It was common knowledge by now that she had lain with Simon, Jordan de Ribérac's son, in an effort to bastardise the legitimate child she was carrying.

The response of her husband, whom nobody blamed, had been to trace the child and take it away from her. Simon, who had thought the baby his own, had found himself a laughing-stock and a dupe, and had been dispatched quickly to his Portuguese property before he could harm her or himself. His spoiled brat Henry had been sent with him. Despite their absence, however, Bruges would not be a friendly place for Gelis van Borselen any more than Venice had been, where indifference and distaste had surrounded her. Adorne had shown her courtesy, and Gregorio pity, that was all.

It would not stop her from entering Bruges. Nicholas had come close to breaking her this time. She could think of nothing, attempt nothing against him until she knew the child to be safe. Meanwhile she still had her pride, and her courage. And later, they would find out, all of them, what she could do.

Nicholas forced her to wait for a month, during which he sent her two messages. The first told her that he was in Hesdin. The child was elsewhere. If she moved without orders, she would not see him. The second summoned her, at last, to the Burgundian camp.

By that time, even Tilde de Charetty had begun to lose her aversion for Gelis van Borselen, two years older than herself, once the plump, wilful child who had been so enchanted by Nicholas the apprentice. As she, Tilde, once had been, before she met and married her beloved Diniz.

At first, learning that Gelis proposed to come and stay, Tilde had refused point-blank to have her. Her sister Catherine shared her view. In vain, Diniz had argued that the house belonged to the Bank, and that Gelis had at least as much right to live there as they had. In fact his arguments lacked some conviction. They all knew, now, what Gelis had done. It was Adorne's niece Katelijne who, dropping in at the height of the dispute, changed their opinion.

Since returning from pilgrimage with her uncle, Katelijne Sersanders had occasionally called on Diniz and Tilde de Charetty. The attraction, naturally, was Tilde's baby – a daughter called Marian after Tilde's mother. Adorne's wife sent it presents. Paying her first visit in May, Katelijne, seventeen, single and active, ate the cakes her aunt sent, talked to Tilde, talked to the baby, folded napkins, mended a fringe, finished some sewing, offered to make a straw basket and dispensed news.

Some of it, but not very much, concerned her recent pilgrimage, during which she had briefly run across Tilde's stepfather Nicholas de Fleury, who had taught her how to weave baskets. Having disposed, without detail, of the pilgrimage, Katelijne entertained Tilde with an account of the present war being waged in the Adorne household, currently lodging a branch of the Scottish royal family together with fifty attendants. They had been there for over a year.

'Officially,' said Katelijne, unpacking three papers of powders, 'the Duke of Burgundy doesn't know they are there, because the Princess's husband has been condemned as a traitor in Scotland, and Burgundy shouldn't be sheltering him or his children.'

'When is the second one due?' Tilde enquired. She brought a bowl, and watched Katelijne start mixing.

'In the late summer, they think. They ought to leave now, while the Princess can travel, but they won't know where to go until the English succession is settled. The Earl of Arran can't go back to Scotland, and the Princess his Countess won't leave him.'

'A fine-looking man,' suggested Tilde, with all the complacency of one married to another such.

'It wouldn't matter if he looked like a boot. She worships him. It makes Jan puke,' Kathi said. Jan was Adorne's son, her cousin, who had returned from his pilgrimage with the offer of a good job in Rome, and was not at all pleased to be stuck in Bruges with a household of foreigners.

'And you?' Tilde had said. 'Do you want to stay with the Countess, or go back to help with her sister in Scotland?'

Kathi's eyes, as sometimes happened, had lost focus. She concentrated again. 'I liked Scotland,' she said. 'I shouldn't mind going back. There's your mixture.'

'What is it?'

'Flea paste,' the girl said. 'I wondered if I remembered how to make it.'

'Dr Tobias,' said Tilde. 'Of course, he was with you as well. Do you know he has gone? Back to his hated uncle the physician in Pavia. No one knows why.'

'He keeps doing that,' Kathi said. 'He's waiting for his uncle to die, so that he can get hold of his books and his printing press. I don't think it's an omen. Master John and Father Moriz left as well, but just to see to the mines in the Tyrol.'

'I wish we knew where Nicholas was,' Tilde said fretfully. But she was certain by then that neither Kathi nor the Adorne family knew.

The next time Kathi came, Tilde did know where Nicholas was, because he had sent to tell them. He had also sent to have his wife directed from Cologne to Bruges to await orders. 'She wants to stay here, but I'm not having her,' Tilde had said flatly. As a solid, narrow-faced matron of twenty-three she was acquiring something of her mother's authority. At first, Tilde and her sister had bitterly resented Nicholas when he had married their mother. Now they resented his present wife, who had cheated him in ways no woman should.

Tilde de Charetty seldom talked about Nicholas, and never to Catherine, who had learned to deal with life at second hand through a shifting circle of suitors. Tilde supposed that every girl child in Bruges at some time had dreamed of receiving the merry, loving, undemanding attentions of Claes, the Charetty apprentice. A sweetheart for the season, not a lord to preside at your table, however gentle his manners.

But then, building upon the Charetty business, a lord was what he had become. To Tilde, he had always behaved as a member of the household as much as a stepfather. It was his planning which had brought her Diniz Vasquez her husband. Tilde thanked God for that daily, even if Nicholas often occupied the rest of her thoughts; Nicholas whose ability had always been there under the generous, inconsequential demeanour. Hidden there.

But for Gelis to marry and cheat him had been unforgivable. Tilde inadvertently wakened the baby, slamming down the basket which Katelijne had brought, and had to march up and down with the child over her shoulder declaiming, while Kathi unpacked the pannier. There were two oranges in it, which Kathi set out and peeled. She said, 'I keep wondering why the lady Gelis did what she did.'

Tilde put down the baby, which was annoyed but no longer alarmed. 'I thought you'd know. Didn't you help get the boy away from her in Venice? She hates Nicholas.'

'Everyone helped. It was time, for the boy's sake. But if she hated M. de Fleury, why keep the child?'

Tilde held a section of orange and thought briefly. 'She wanted a baby, she didn't want Nicholas. Or she hoped the baby was Simon's.' She ate the orange.

'She knew it couldn't be. Margot told me.'

'So what do you think?' Tilde asked. She knew from report that Adorne's niece had been popular on the pilgrimage in the way a mascot was popular: small, spry and ever willing to help, with her hazel eyes and brown hair and air of perpetual eagerness. Only Jan Adorne had found her tiresome, but Jan Adorne was a plodding student who had over-celebrated at Venice and disliked everyone who knew about it.

Katelijne considered. She ejected some pips. 'I think that some ladies like freedom, and resent it if a child comes too soon.'

'So she didn't want the child? She certainly left it a lot.'

Katelijne shook her head. 'I think she fell in love with it, when she couldn't have M. de Fleury.'

Tilde laughed. 'Well, it's a theory. So what does Nicholas think of his wife? He chose her.'

'I don't know,' the girl said. 'But in Alexandria, he was told she was dead, and it was as if –' She stopped. She was frowning.

'As if?' prompted Tilde.

Kathi turned. 'He loved your mother. What did he do when she died?'

Tilde felt herself flush, and then recollected it was Kathi she was talking to, who censured nobody, and helped whom she could. Tilde said, 'He tried to come home to us, but we wouldn't have him. We were stupid. He went off on his own for a long time, until the Venetians caught him and took him to Cyprus. With Primaflora.' She spoke without thinking. In Cyprus and Rhodes, the lady Primaflora, now dead, had briefly been married to Nicholas. She had been a beauty. She had been a professional courtesan.

'That was when and how he met Primaflora?' Kathi had stopped eating, her eyes unfocused again.

It occurred to Tilde, for the first time, that indeed, that was how the affair with Primaflora had begun. She said tentatively, 'And so ... It must have been terrible. Was it terrible? What did he do when he thought Gelis had died and left him as well?' She drew a shocked breath. 'Was he *glad*?'

The speckled gaze, refocused, was minatory. 'Couldn't stop laughing,' said Kathi. 'What are you talking about? I don't really think he'd go through all that with her in Africa and then marry her, without feeling something when he heard she was dead. The point is, what? She wasn't your mother, so of course it was different.'

Tilde said nothing. The girl said after a bit, 'He seemed to be lost. He cares about something, but Dr Tobias isn't sure either what it is. It may just be that his plan had been spoiled. His future may have depended on this intricate duel with Gelis, and he had nothing to put in its place.'

'Not the child?' Tilde said. 'After all the efforts to find it?' She was not eating now. In passing encounters, in exotic places, this little girl had seen more of Nicholas as he was now than anyone else. Tilde thought the girl's view over-simple, but it had a clarity about it which she trusted. Adorne possessed it as well: this gentle, unsentimental appraisal which did not stop him from correcting and chastising those whom he perceived to err.

'He would have thought of that eventually, I expect,' Kathi said. 'As it is, Margot believes that the nurses have been with the boy all along, so the child hasn't suffered. And if M. de Fleury is planning to have his wife join the baby again, it sounds as if he means a reconciliation. But he may not make it easy, and Gelis will have to find somewhere private to wait where she can be sure of getting his message. It will be very hard for her, because she's been stupid. As you say, people are.'

Tilde was silent. 'And after they are together?' she said. 'Where will Nicholas go?'

'It depends what he wants,' Kathi said. 'Not a hot country for the sake of the child – and he has walked away from his business there anyway. To Bruges or Venice or Florence if he wants to humiliate Gelis. If he wants to appear, briefly or permanently, like a family, then to somewhere more distant, like Scotland. He can do what he likes there. And he had planned to go back.'

Tilde found she had shivered. She said, 'But he couldn't. Simon and his father live there. Simon won't stay in Madeira and Lagos for ever. And he must hate Gelis now.' Forgetting her sticky hands, she picked up the baby and laid its face to her cheek. It began to mouth, its eyes closed, and she dabbed kisses on it.

Kathi said, 'I should trust M. de Fleury to hold his own against M. de St Pol and the vicomte. They won't harm your baby, Tilde, she's a girl. And really, Gelis has been terribly punished, and is going to have a hard time. She will need all her strength if the reconciliation is going to work.'

'I don't want it to work,' said Tilde abruptly.

'I know. But maybe he does,' Kathi said. 'Give her a room. I shan't come. Let her stay.'

Later, talking to Diniz, Tilde was not sorry she had agreed, although Catherine was harder to convince. Then Gelis came, a white formal stranger who became from that moment a white formal recluse, making brief, silent forays to houses which received her with neutrality: that of Tommaso Portinari of the Medici Bank; of the Baltic merchants; and, very briefly, that of her cousin in town.

Occasionally, seeking common ground, Diniz would take her into the counting-house and let her listen and watch. She recognised the messages coming in from Cologne but made no offer to handle them. Although not physically ailing, she seemed as tired as if she had travelled a long way for many years. Anger with their unwanted guest turned to a pity that was not expressed either, for it was not invited. The brutal silence lasted a month; and then the messenger came with the summons which caused Tilde to fall silent, and look at her husband. But Gelis, hearing, simply rose and said, 'It is time, then,' and went steadily to complete her arrangements. When she came to leave, there seemed nothing to say that had meaning. They were Nicholas's family, and she was not. She was whiter than when she had come, with circles under her eyes, but was quite composed, thanking them.

Just before leaving, she had asked Diniz and Tilde to her room and had brought out and handed over two parcels. One contained a child's golden pendant of Italian workmanship. The larger enfolded a silver-gilt object: a warming-apple.

'The pendant is for Marian your daughter,' Gelis said. 'The apple was always meant for your family. If your daughter one day has to leave you, give her the pendant, and keep the apple for Nicholas. He will find her for you.'

'He gave you the apple,' Tilde said. She remembered the precious object brought by Claes with such care from Milan, and never presented to anyone. He must have been very young. Claes, not yet Nicholas. She remembered Gelis, loud and baleful and triumphant, showing it off. Her sister Katelina had been angry.

'It was always meant for your family,' Gelis repeated, with her sister's anger.

In Dijon, M. le bouton de Fleury began to make his desires known in Burgundian French, instead of the Blésois, the Blois tongue of his nurses. His voice, swooping from high to low, could be heard in every part of the fortified farmhouse his father had taken for him, so well defended that even the bullies of the vicomte de Ribérac had been unable to bribe or beat their way through.

Since he had arrived there in May, his father had visited him twice – possibly a mark of affection, and certainly one of efficiency, since it meant twice setting aside his affairs to make the long, hard ride to and from the north. Whatever his motives, Clémence de Coulanges welcomed the reinforcement to her rule, and the benefit to the child. His mother lost, the boy needed the reassurance of his father's interest, and the father, unlike most, did not bribe or cosset or ignore, but treated the toddling boy of two and a half years as friend, companion and page. Mistress Clémence, who did not believe in spoiled children, was by turn impressed and suspicious.

The rest of the time she spent sparring with Pasque who perceived in M. de Fleury's absence the perfect opportunity for a quick foray abroad to display their darling Jodi in Coulanges. Mistress Clémence did not lack the gift of command, or she would never have controlled princely nurseries. She was more relieved, however, than she would have admitted when the running battle was arrested. Instead of their attempting to go to Coulanges, Coulanges came to Dijon in the form of a chance visit from her own Chouzy cousins.

Entertainment at the farm was forbidden, but M. de Fleury had already taken them, when first they arrived, to the hospitable home of friends of his first wife. Enguerrand and Yvonnet de Damparis had several times invited the child back, impeccably guarded, and had won Mistress Clémence's approval by filling the house with other children for Jodi's inspection. Childless themselves, the couple – it transpired – were friends not so much of M. de Fleury as of Marian his first wife and her sister. Both were buried here: the sister who had married an old man and made Dijon her home, and Marian de Charetty who, taken ill, had paused there on a journey and died.

The child had been taken to both tombs. In general, Mistress Clémence understood the importance of teaching children the lessons of mortality, but thought that a crypt below ground was no place for a boy quite so young, even though M. de Fleury made nothing lingering or solemn of it, but simply talked to the child as they walked with their lamp, hand in hand. It seemed that his own mother Sophie was buried there, which made the lapse more comprehensible – indeed quite understandable, had M. de Fleury been an old man. Mistress Clémence had made no attempt to take the child there a second time, and the boy had asked no questions about it.

It was not a nurse's place, either, to question; but, on joining the family, Mistress Clémence had made it her business to learn all the popular gossip about her charge's father. M. de Fleury's mother,

buried here, had been Sophie, daughter of Thibault, vicomte de
Fleury. Report said that the vicomte, still living, had long since been
taken away to be cared for, and his only daughter by a second, late
marriage had been placed in some convent. The family home, now in
ruins, had sheltered Sophie de Fleury for seven years from the birth
of Nicholas to her death, still in disgrace. Simon de St Pol had never
accepted M. de Fleury as his son, as Jordan de St Pol had rejected
him as his grandson. The true father had never been named.

It was an old scandal. There seemed no bitterness, at least on the
de Fleury side, although there was with the Scots-French St Pols.
People said that old Thibault de Fleury had done his best for his
grandson while in health, and the girl, Adelina, was probably better
off as a nun: the title carried no money, and the estate was tied up in
debt from some family concern that had failed.

Mistress Clémence had thought, from the excessive time M. de
Fleury spent examining his grandfather's property, that he had a
mind to restore it. Nothing, however, seemed to come of it, and she
sensed that the family friends around Dijon were not displeased that
this should be so. They were polite to M. de Fleury, as well as fond
with the child. Yvonnet de Damparis especially asked after the servant
who had nursed Marian de Charetty in her last illness. The name
Tasse was unknown to Mistress Clémence. It appeared that the
woman was in pensioned retirement, arranged for her by Master
Gregorio, the lawyer who had attended her mistress's burial.

Mistress Clémence listened, surprised. Knowing better than most
the value of old, trusted servants, she deduced that Tasse was unused
to small children, or too old for M. de Fleury to bring back to serve
his new son. Then she remembered that it was the lady Gelis who
had chosen Pasque and Mistress Clémence herself for young Jordan,
and that a servant loyal to her husband would not then have suited
her plans.

It reminded Mistress Clémence that a difficult phase of her contract
was now approaching. She and Pasque had successfully accomplished
the transfer from the mother's employment, and had no complaints
about their new patron. But everyone knew there was nothing worse
for young children than two quarrelling parents, the prospect they all
must presently face. Very soon, M. de Fleury had said, Mistress
Clémence would be asked to bring Jordan to Hesdin, where he
expected his wife to join him forthwith. His plans after that would
depend on events.

And that was certainly true. Whatever the rights of the case, the
mother had been forcibly deprived of her child for four months and
might arrive with some sort of mandate to seize the child and cancel

the marriage. Or she might do worse than that. Mistress Clémence had seen other clever, solitary girls who repressed all emotion until it exploded in blows, or steel, or self-destruction. She herself intended to support neither side nor allow Pasque to do so, but she would certainly shield the child from distress. She had not been responsible for the upbringing of M. de Fleury or his lady, but come what may, she would make a respectable citizen of this petit mafflu, their little Bouton de Fleury. When the summons came, in mid-June, the child and his nurses were ready.

The command dispatched by Nicholas de Fleury to his representatives in the Tyrol arrived a week later, and received a more guarded welcome. John le Grant had no wish to witness the terminal encounter between Nicholas and this dangerous girl he had married. His colleague Father Moriz, whose acquaintance with Nicholas was shorter, reminded John of their obligations to the Bank. Nicholas had been absent since February, and consultation on alum and silver, on guncasting and mining was imperative. He did not mention what his own personal remit to do with Nicholas was. As usual, their common deep professional interest carried the day. They carried out their instructions, took their leave of the Duke and the Duchess and set off in the heat of late June for the Somme, bearing a material gift for the child and several intangible ones for the Banco di Niccolò.

In the same heat, in the north, Nicholas de Fleury, *machiniste*, *fatiste*, Master of Secrets, set the last of his chiselled wheels spinning and crossed into Burgundian Artois where lay his mercenary troops under Astorre and his present titular employer, Charles, Duke of Burgundy.

He felt satisfied. Happiness was something different; generally fleeting and born from the unexpected, like the wheel of angels in Angers. Contentment came from intellectual satisfaction. There was something in between, which he had recently felt, but then he had been ill, or at least not himself.

The audience before him was the last, and perhaps the most important, but he was not at all apprehensive. Everything he had done, ending with this, had been precisely planned. It was appropriate, if unnecessary, that this, the second wing of his triptych, should have brought him to the acme of artifice, the Duke of Burgundy's palace of Hesdin in Artois. Unnecessary because there was no danger, here, that he would be received as a man imported to mend the ingenuities. The Duke and he had done business already. It was known that the Bank, to oblige Burgundy, had withdrawn from a

lucrative proposition in the East. More particularly it would be
known that, at this moment, the sieur de Fleury came to him warm
from the embraces of Louis of France, who had equally failed to
seduce him.

It was true, so far as it went. Nicholas had ridden from Ham
directly to Hesdin, crossing the Somme, then crossing the Authie
without attempting to halt at the Burgundian camp and appear to
consult with his captain. Instead, a few miles short of Hesdin,
Astorre himself had slipped unseen into M. de Fleury's small cavalcade and briefly ridden along with him, under a ceiling of night
clouds shot through with crackling fireworks and flushed with the red
light of bonfires.

'They're happy. York on the throne. The French'll be sick. How
was it at Ham?' Astorre said. He was riding where his good eye, not
his sewn one, could observe his employer. His beard had turned
black.

'Just as we hoped. The army stays for the season in Burgundy.
High pay, reasonable weather and no fighting. A lot of comforts in
camp?' Nicholas said.

'Anything you want. It's like a town. You'll be sorry your lady
wife's coming so soon. Or maybe you've grown out of all that.'

'Do I look dead?' said Nicholas.

Astorre grinned. 'And the boy? You'll turn him into a banker?'

'If he's good enough,' Nicholas said. 'If he isn't, I may just have to
pay some poor troop of soldiers to keep him out of my way. He's got
hands.'

'I've made him a sword,' Astorre said. Above the dyed beard, a
touch of pink coloured his cheek-bone. He said, 'Body of God, I
don't know who taught you. No fighting because of some truce? The
Duke wants the Somme valley cleared, and he's hoping for a great
English army to help him.'

'Will they?' said Nicholas.

'Boyd says yes, but who knows. He's with us in camp, waiting to
kiss you. Tom Boyd, Earl of Arran. The lad you helped get out of
Scotland with his wife the King's sister. They've landed on Adorne.'

'I know. I arranged it. So now York is back on the throne, are the
Boyds going to settle in England?'

'Earl Tom's not so sure, but his father wouldn't risk anywhere else.
I'm told Adorne isn't so keen.'

'Why not? He must be desperate to get rid of them all. Unless, of
course, he thinks the English will plot with the family, and Scotland
will blame him. So what else? Tell me more. What about Guelders?
Paris? Anjou? Brittany . . .?'

Astorre talked, and he listened. Outside Hesdin they parted, and Nicholas rode on thoughtfully to his meeting. In Ham, he had been greeted by Jordan de Ribérac. Here, he would be delivered first to the Chancellor and his lawyers and clerks. Nicholas knew Guillaume de Hugonet from several meetings in Brussels. He could guess his present agenda, and knew how he wanted to adjust it to his own. After that, Hugonet would report to the Duke, and Nicholas would have his audience. Hugonet was pedantic and humourless, but he was the third member of his family to serve Burgundy, and had been with Charles since he was young, as had his brother. He generally knew what the Duke would accept, and how to present it.

It happened much as he expected. Nicholas had been in Hesdin before. It was one of the three houses in Flanders large enough to contain both the Duke and the Duchess. Margaret of York was at present away, supervising the victory feast acclaiming her brother. Nicholas was therefore spared the need to mention his wife and his son, although Hugonet, greeting him, asked out of courtesy. The Duke had forgotten Gelis had ever served as a lady of honour.

There were two sets of talks, and might have been more had other business not been so pressing. The English success of King Edward had led, as at Ham, to urgent consultations behind guarded doors. The meetings moved politely through the areas of desire and contention; the quicker because he had brought no lawyers or clerks of his own, which was new and surprised them at first. It was noted that the mercenary troop of Captain Astorre had eighteen months of its contract to run, and was prepared to complete it. An advance payment was discussed for the cannon presently being made in the Tyrol, and for the gunners who would accompany it. It was noted that, from the following summer, the Bank's own master gunner would be available for hire, at a price.

They proceeded to loans. He proposed changes; they were opposed; there were some expected concessions. He was reasonably satisfied.

They mentioned Scotland. He agreed that he had interests there, and might expand them without interfering with the influence of Anselm Adorne, now Baron Cortachy. He might persuade the Scottish King to withdraw his pretensions to the duchy of Guelders, as he had encouraged Sigismond of the Tyrol to take Duke Charles's part with the Emperor. Frederick, Emperor of the Germanies, was overlord of Charles's eastern possessions and no longer so young; soon he would have to turn his mind to his own successor. Nicholas mentioned nothing of that. It was enough to refer to the Bank's metallurgic successes in the Tyrol, and Duke Sigismond's consequent gratitude. Sigismond was the Emperor's cousin.

They mentioned his own valued status as banker and adviser to Burgundy. He assured them he was ready personally to undertake any service, so long as it could be confined to the summer. He preferred to devote the winter to the Duke's business abroad. In Scotland, for example.

After the two meetings were over, he was called to the Duke.

For this audience, Nicholas appeared in dull grey (less ostentatious than black), having spent more time than he wanted trying to flatten his hair. The Duke, austere amid the blinding glare of his wealth, did not favour curled hair or frivolity.

The matters he had discussed with Hugonet were reviewed and, in the main, received ducal approval. The Duke said, 'And Anjou? I understand you spoke with my lord René?'

'Yes, monseigneur. He seems, although a vassal of France, afraid and ready to look to his friends. I had an impression, I do not know from where, that he was wistful for the goodwill of Burgundy.'

'Yes?' said Duke Charles. 'Did he say so?'

'He said,' Nicholas answered, 'that if his daughter failed, he would have little ambition beyond foiling France in its wish to usurp him.'

'Do you say?' said the Duke. 'And France? You saw our uncle the King, we believe. But you nobly resisted his offers?'

'I wish I could say so,' Nicholas said. 'But only children follow their impulses. My fees fall heavily enough on your coffers, I know. It seemed only right that, as in other lands, the enemy should contribute towards them. I offered to spy, for an annual pension. And I offered to incite James of Scotland to bring an army to help him.'

The Duke sat very still. 'M. de Fleury, why are you telling me this? I should make you answer for it if you did. And monseigneur my uncle will stop your pension, certainly, if you don't.'

'But I shall!' Nicholas said. 'That is, I shall urge the King to the best of my powers. Fortunately, there is no chance at all that his country will vote him the money to do it. And I shall make sure he has no surfeit of money, and recommend that the Baron Cortachy does so as well.'

He waited. There was a small chance he would not be believed. The punishment in that event would very likely be perpetual prison or worse. The gamble gave the moment an edge. Then the Duke said, 'Hugonet?' and the Chancellor bent forward and spoke.

'And, M. de Fleury, your undertaking to persuade the King of Scotland to withdraw his claim to Guelders? Is the basis for that equally derisory?'

'Forgive me,' Nicholas said. 'But so far as I know, the King had no intention of sending an army to Guelders. He merely staked a claim, in the hope that some concessions would follow. I should hope to mitigate his expectations, without harming monseigneur's reputation for generosity. He will play off France against Burgundy.'

'As you are doing,' the Duke said.

'I am a Burgundian,' Nicholas answered. 'There are no friends of mine at the French Court.' They knew his history. They knew about Jordan de Ribérac. The hostility of Jordan de Ribérac was the strongest card in his favour. He was sorry the fat man couldn't appreciate it. He said, 'If I break my trust, it will be evident. It is not in my own interest to do so. I hope to see my Bank rise with the fortunes of Burgundy, the one aiding the other. I hope to see my Bank become an Imperial Bank, financing the war which will throw the Turk out of Christendom.'

He had not said that before. He still had not said – no one had – if and when Charles of Burgundy becomes the next King of the Romans. If and when he is anointed in Rome as the Holy Roman Emperor following Frederick. But of course, it had been in his mind ever since Venice.

'Is that your intention?' said the Duke.

'As it was your illustrious father's,' said Nicholas. 'I have been in the land of the Golden Fleece. I would return with an Emperor.'

The Duke stared at him, his expression unchanging. 'We shall hold you to those words,' was all he said.

It was all he needed to say. The danger was over. He had given his tacit agreement; the details would be worked out elsewhere. He had a vast contract; security; leave to take money from France; leave to appear an agent for both; leave to pursue the Duke's business in Scotland (and his) at the same time as Anselm Adorne, Baron Cortachy, the Duke's accredited envoy, who was currently housing Thomas Boyd, Earl of Arran and his wife.

Humbly and in good order, Nicholas presently left the Duke's presence, and entered that of the Duke's lawyers, where the necessary papers were drawn up and signed. Humbly and in good order still, he rode with his servants from Hesdin. Behind him was turmoil: the household was preparing to move; soon the palace would be empty of all but its controller, and the long lines of wagons would be taking themselves somewhere else.

They went without him. He was going to the Burgundian camp, the acres of ground upon which were marshalled the pavilions and worksheds and barracks of the Duke's standing army, where the timber house stood that held his officers, and the other, set apart, built by Captain Astorre for himself and for any visiting official of the Bank. By now he would have got rid of the girls, and he and the rest would be waiting for him to tell them what had happened, and to give him their news.

Thinking of it, Nicholas rode with a high heart, and talked now and then with his escort, who answered him cautiously until he thought to buy them some wine. He felt as he had felt before, filled with a pleasant excitement. He had a month with Astorre, in the company of men whom he knew, with the couriers of his Bank bringing back to his touch the great golden web of his business. A month at the end of which – yes, there lay the prospect of much that was unpredictable, as well as events he could control. In a month, John and Father Moriz would arrive from the Tyrol, bringing their news. In two weeks, his summons would reach Mistress Clémence in Dijon and, safe in the custody of his men, she and the old woman and the child would set out to come north and join him. The child Jordan de Fleury.

And as the child came to Artois, so would Gelis his wife, hoping to see it; as once in despair he had called to see the baby he believed had been born, and had been denied. In July they would be here, all of them. All of those he had forced to come to him.

Thinking about it, he realised that he had fallen into silence again, disappointing his men. He roused. There was a month. There was a month still before the prologue gave way to the play. He thought of Angers. *Cruciffiez!* they had cried. And René's grandson had died.

He rode, thinking that a month lasted for ever, and without calling to mind that one day he would wake to find the prologue was over, and the play had begun.

Chapter 5

SUMMER MADE A charming début in Artois that year. The hazy curtains of spring drew back to present greening fields where there had been trampled mud, and peaceful smoke rising from thatches where once stackyards had blazed. The palace of Hesdin lay empty but for its token caretakers. In Picardy, Ham kept its garrison but the French King had dashed back to the Loire, pulling on this rope and that; resetting his mines and his darts. Wisps of tinsel remained from the great victory over the Narrow Sea: a banquet here, an aubade there for some royal envoy; but the public stage remained empty, the actors in the wings awaiting the script still being written. The Burgundian army, its commanders gone, exercised and rehearsed under its captains, indulged in rough sport, drank and quarrelled, thieved and womanised, as men do awaiting a war.

Riding up, saddle-sore from their long journey from Innsbruck, the priest Moriz and the red-headed engineer John le Grant heard the wind-snatched roar from the exercise park an hour before they reached the stockade, and had to wait longer than they wanted before Thomas, Astorre's deputy, shoved his way out to meet them and bring their short train inside. It took half an hour after that to fight their way to their lodging, and almost as long before Thomas tracked down Astorre, red-faced in the shouting throng of soldiers and civilians at the edge of the sports field. He hardly spared them a glance.

'Aye, ye got here. Jesus Christ, will ye look at that!'

'By God's leave, what?' said Father Moriz, who was as weary as John but could see that John's response was about to match the hair under his hat.

'You're the priest? Glad to meet you. We're winning,' said Astorre.

'Good,' said John le Grant. 'You don't mind if we turn and go back, then? We could sell the guns somewhere else.'

Deaf to irony, Astorre smartly brought round his beard at the mention of guns. 'Ye brought them. Good lad. Is the cannon coming?' And as a shout throttled the air: 'Damn it, I missed it.'

'It's Nicholas!' said John, his enraged eye falling at last on the field. 'What's he doing there?'

'I told you,' said Astorre. 'We challenged the countryside to a series of contests. For the Feast of the Magdalen. We're winning.'

'It isn't the Feast of the Magdalen yet,' said Father Moriz. On the field, now he looked, the considerable debris pointed to an assortment of lethal engagements involving mass football, mass wooden-sword play, shooting at the mark, shooting at the popinjay, spear-throwing, bowling and horse-racing. A good deal of the litter was bloodstained, and there were five men lying at one side of the field and a dozen more reclining in various attitudes of unease. At a table nearby, a man in a cap and apron was cracking a joke as he threaded a needle. He was surrounded by flies.

'No, we're practising,' said Captain Astorre. 'A wagon of ale for the winners. I couldn't stop him. You try. Look at that.'

On the field, in a glittering display of high chivalry, twenty Burgundians, each borne on the neck of another, were attempting to beat down with staves twenty similar pairs of Artésiens. One of the upper Burgundians was Nicholas, black and blue above his torn hose and shrieking insults, and opposing him was a naked man built like a tithe barn and brown to the crabs of his toes. Beneath each was a broad, sweating carrier.

They were almost the last in the field: at that moment, one of the remaining pairs toppled and smacked to the ground and the tally was marked to deafening cheers. There were three couples left on each side.

It would have seemed harmless enough, if one of the contestants hadn't been the genius of the Banco di Niccolò with, resting in turn on his shoulders, the entire weight of the Bank's future in the West. The naked giant, lifting his pole, caught Nicholas a cutting blow on the shoulder before inducing his bearer to lurch sideways to help out another pair. The third couple, momentarily freed, began a staggering run towards Nicholas.

John said, 'Has he been doing a lot of this?'

'Not as much as he should,' Astorre said. His good eye, seen in profile, was baleful.

The priest said, 'It must come as a relief.' The Captain's eye flickered. The charging pair reached Nicholas, the pole swung and Nicholas ducked, while his mount, side-stepping neatly, tripped up the other carrier with his foot. With a scream, the pair fell apart in different directions while the pole bounced to the ground. Nicholas patted his mount on the head and spoke to it approvingly. Grinning, it turned, just in time. The tithe barn had not only rescued its oppressed comrade, it had dispatched both the Burgundian couples, leaving Nicholas and his bearer alone in the field. And poles at the tilt, both Artésien pairs were now lumbering towards him.

'Oh well,' said John le Grant. 'I can go back to the Tyrol. You can look after the Duke. Thomas can take on Alexandria. Astorre's cook can help Diniz in Bruges and the parrot can manage in Scotland. Who's worried?'

No one was listening, and his own words, towards the end, were coming out pale and flat as the ghost of a die-stamp. The two poles, from converging angles, were aimed at Nicholas: one to his head, one to his chest. There was no possibility of evading them. The noise, reaching fortissimo, stayed there. People threw things into the field. The patient on the table sat up, the needle stuck like a quill in his ear. The man under Nicholas dropped to his knees.

It took some effort. He had to balance, so that he neither pitched off his rider, nor allowed his feet to rest on the ground. Then he had to rise, taking his cavalier safely with him. The result, however, was well worth the labour. Father Moriz, warmed despite himself, watched the two opposing couples converge; watched the poles thrust into space, cross, and clash as the two human mounts staggered past their destination and collided. The tithe barn, knocked sideways, grasped his pole with one hand and snatched at his mount with the other, clinging on while his bearer recovered. The other rider, less lucky, soared through the air with his stave and landing, knocked himself out and cracked his carrier on the head with the pole. His carrier lay flat on the ground. Astorre was crying. John said, in an ecstasy of horror, 'Christ. He'll kill him.'

It was indeed clear that the tithe barn was angered. He kicked his mount on the ear, swung his pole, and then, two-handed, raised and lowered the bar like a weight-lifter. With an effort that brought him applause, the man supporting Nicholas put his weight on one foot, then two, and drew himself up while Nicholas, talking, shifted his balance like a Tzukanion-player. When they ended up at their full height again, it was seen that Nicholas was being steadied by one hand alone. In the other, his mount had snatched up the dropped stave.

The rules said nothing against it. It was a joke, in that it gave Nicholas mixed advantages: it weakened his seat while giving his mount a heavy weapon easily knocked from one hand. The beauty of it was the spice of variety; the challenge to the other's ingenuity, already affected by anger. The couples turned and faced one another, and began to advance. Nicholas was grinning, and so was his mount. The noise slackened. Then, with an audible grunt, the tithe barn's mount drew breath and charged. 'Moriz! Pray!' said le Grant.

'What do you think I've been doing?' said Father Moriz.

About what happened next there were as many versions as there were spectators, although the wagon of ale might have had something to do with the lack of consensus. The couples approached. Nicholas brandished his stave. His mount also brandished his stave, as well a man might with another large man on his shoulders. Then, just before the pairs met, he ceased to brandish it and instead braced it forward and up, as might a man playing a boar with his spear. And as a man would with a spear, he kept the point, as they closed, aimed at the one sensitive target where it would be most unwelcome, however softly it arrived, however promptly it fell.

The tithe barn didn't notice the threat, but his bearer did. The bearer, with a squeak, veered to the right just as his rider was preparing his blow. His rider yelled, clutched him and lowered his stave, upon which Nicholas knocked him off his perch. The tithe barn crashed to the ground followed by his mount, curled protectively against the sheer force of his imagination. Nicholas, shaken loose by the impact, was hanging round his mount's neck, helplessly laughing. His mount, frothing with laughter and sweat, dropped his stave and put up his hand, but too late to save Nicholas who tumbled down to the ground, somersaulted twice and, jumping up, seized his mount to fling up their joint arms and face round to all sides of the park, tattered and strutting.

The big man, limping, crossed to him and, after a moment, slapped him on the back and embraced him. The noise was annihilating. Above it all, the sound of trumpets announced the arrival of the cart with the prize. It was declared that, honours being so well divided, the ale would be shared among all the participants, and M. de Fleury had added a second wagon-load at his own expense. The noise was such that the ears of Father Moriz went dead.

'Well?' said John le Grant.

'That's a man!' said Astorre.

Father Moriz returned John le Grant's glare. 'It is the man we work with,' he said. 'We have not taken him in marriage, so far as I know.' Le Grant flushed. Astorre's attention had already gone back to the field, followed promptly by his person.

Father Moriz said, 'You can go and congratulate the victor, or come back to the lodging with me. I am hungry. And I prefer wine to ale.'

They walked back to the barracks together.

'That was deliberate,' John le Grant said.

'Of course it was,' said the priest. 'We last saw him with a child in his arms. He is telling us that he is not a father, but a soldier. Presently he will show us that he is not a soldier, but a banker. It is interesting to follow his mind. It is not our duty to admire it.'

Later, he was ashamed to have paraded his perspicuity, when it came to be exactly justified by events. It was the banker who had them brought from their rest two hours later; who sat them down, thanked them briefly for coming, and obtained from them, with admirable economy, an accounting for all that had happened in the Tyrol and since. They were then given a matching report of the Bank's progress elsewhere, and told to prepare to leave shortly for Scotland.

Through it all, Nicholas was wholly impersonal, as was his custom when conducting negotiations in public; as he had been, no doubt, in those vital interviews in Ham and in Hesdin. To remain detached here, alone in a private room with two men as close to him, in their separate ways, as John and Father Moriz himself, was either an aberration or a notification which required thinking about. He sat before them with the childish bruises and cuts showing above the immaculate chemise and doublet, and ignored what they had just seen as easily as he was ignoring their common past. Father Moriz thought, John is perhaps right, and I am perhaps wrong. He did not even know we were about to arrive. He was cultivating Artois and the army as he was cultivating Anjou, Burgundy, France. I suppose we should thank someone that he is not troubling to cultivate us.

They had reached the end of the curious interview and were about, he thought, to be dismissed when someone tapped on the door and Nicholas opened it. When he came back, his manner was the same, but there was a change of some sort in his face, which was already coloured with the open air. He said, 'I've disturbed your rest. Alonse will take you back to your rooms. Send if you want something to eat; you know Astorre's cooks are always superb. I'll have someone bring you at first light tomorrow to go over the detail.'

'And that's all?' said John. His annoyance at the dismissal was justified. It was only mid-afternoon. Instead of intervening, Father Moriz trod peacefully to the window. He was aware that the gaze of Nicholas followed him.

Nicholas said, 'If you're not tired, there are a hundred men out there, and you know at least half of them. Go and enjoy yourself. I have some things I must do.'

'The camp has visitors,' the priest said. The perpetual haphazard traffic between buildings, tents and sheds had coalesced at one point

into a huddle of horses and packmules with, here and there, the
ruddy glitter of steel. In the middle he thought he glimpsed the high
shape of a veil, and the folds of a gown on a side-saddle. As he
watched, grooms ran up to the leading horse and began to lead it to
another part of the encampment.

'A lady,' remarked Father Moriz. 'But not for you, Nicholas, it
would seem.' He heard footsteps coming to join him and knew it was
John, and that Nicholas had stayed where he was.

Nicholas said, 'I am enthralled. Alonse is waiting.'

Below, the procession had stopped. Father Moriz remained looking
down. Captain Astorre, fastening his points, came trotting into view.
Taking the reins from the groom, Astorre turned the horse round and
began to bring the leading members of the cavalcade towards the
door of the house in which they stood. John turned. He said, 'Is it
Gelis, Nicholas? Astorre is bringing her here.'

Moriz turned as well. Nicholas stood by the door, gazing outwards.
There was only one staircase. Whoever it was, there was no avoiding
meeting her now. Nicholas said, 'It is not Gelis.' There were footsteps
below, and then the clatter of Astorre's spurs on the stairs, followed
by other, softer feet. With a hiss of impatience, Nicholas drew back
until he stood with the furthermost wall at his back. His expression
was lost in the shadows. Moriz remained at the window, his fingers
holding back John. The clatter reached the top of the stairs, and the
threshold.

Captain Astorre, bent double, came into the room, his face red, his
eye glittering madly. He straightened. On his shoulders, miniature of
his stave-bearing father, was a grey-eyed child, crowing, his brown
hair tight-curled in the damp, his rotund cheeks merry with dimples.
John straightened. Father Moriz increased his grip, studying Nicholas.

'Well!' said Captain Astorre, looking round. 'What's all this about
a room of his own, when a lad wants the house of his father? Here are
his nurses to tell you as much. And where is your father, then, young
Master Jordan?'

The boy looked round the strange room, cast into dusk by the
strong light outside. Reassured by Astorre's jovial voice by his ear,
the child seemed quite at ease. He looked first at the window and
smiled at Moriz and John, although they too were strangers. Then
the smile, travelling on, reached the wall. 'M'sieur mon p'p . . . a . . .
a . . . a!' said Jordan de Fleury, in the moderate shriek of a child who
has found a promised toy, and is pleased as much with himself as
with the enjoyment ahead. 'R'garde! R'garde! R'garde!'

Nicholas stood free of the wall. 'Eh bien, c'est M. JeMoi,' he said.
'Comme tu est gros.' He spoke direct to the child, his voice calm.

'Nenni! 'Suis ici!' said the child. It was more than an announcement. His head tilted.

'Go to him, then!' said Astorre, raising his hands. But before he could lift him down, the child in turn had stretched his arms to his father. 'I am here! Where is maman?'

Beside Moriz, John le Grant breathed through his nose. Moriz continued to grip him. At the door he could see two women standing still, saying nothing. The nurses. Astorre hesitated, looking at Nicholas. And Nicholas, after the shortest pause, strode forward and sweeping the boy into the crook of his arm, looked him in the face.

'Toujours! Encore? That the gentlemen stand aside from the window?' And when the way was clear, the man with the child took their place, talking. His voice was low, but the child's was clear and confident, as if reciting some incantation. 'Horses! Boats! Cows to be milked!'

Then the child said, 'But she is still busy?'

Nicholas turned, facing the room, still with the child in his arms. 'No,' he said. 'She is coming. She is coming here.' His gaze fell on Moriz, who felt himself wince. The same gaze travelled over John, and Astorre, and the two women who stood in the doorway.

Nicholas said, 'Ta maman will be here in three days.' On the hand spread to hold the child so securely was a mark. Father Moriz knew what it was, and that it had not been there earlier in the day. Tracking Gelis, Nicholas had not realised that the child was so near. Or this encounter would have happened, as intended, in private.

Father Moriz said, 'Your son will be tired. Let the nurses take him,' and was surprised to find his help accepted.

Nicholas said, 'You hear that? To Mistress Clémence. I shall see you tomorrow. You will get fatter.'

'Always,' said the child. The woman Clémence, coming forward, lifted the child and set him on his feet, curtseying to the room before she went out, the elderly maid at her heels. He had had his nurses, then, through all his absence. Moriz knew about them from Mistress Margot, and thought, momentarily confused, that he must send to Venice to tell Mistress Margot and assuage some of her fears. And of course, those of the mother as well. Then he remembered what had just been said. The lady Gelis was coming herself. In three days she would be here. And what would happen then, he could not predict.

Astorre, wiser perhaps than anyone, had left. Moriz was afraid John would linger, in the belief that Nicholas wanted their company. On the contrary, the engineer had walked to the door and was waiting for him, too, to leave. Nicholas watched them sardonically. Moriz wondered what resources of imagination or skill or ingenuity, what quality of callousness had enabled him to carry off what had just happened, betraying nothing, jeopardising nothing. So far.

That night, he said aloud to John what he felt. 'There is nothing now to be done but to wait.'

To the rest of the camp, the three days that followed were little different in character from the busy, brawling good humour of the month that had passed. Certainly, Astorre took time, now and then, to drop into the temporary nursery of Master Jordan de Fleury and show him how to wield his new wooden sword. Mistress Clémence, who could unbend now and then, would send him away with one of her exceptional pies, and Astorre came to the view that she was rearing the boy well enough, although she didn't cackle like Pasque at his jokes. Astorre suspected that little Pasque, as a matter of history, was not unaccustomed to the attentions of rough soldiery.

Father Moriz, too, was reassured. He spent time with the child and both nurses, and sometimes found Nicholas there, looking entirely at home in a way that both touched and surprised him. For Nicholas, those sparing but regular calls were the only departure from a schedule crammed with meetings and paperwork. There were no more boisterous excursions into the exercise field. Only, as the bruises started to fade, the weal on his finger grew angrier.

John, as well as Father Moriz, knew what it meant. He was sufficiently aggravated, by the second day, to remark on it. 'So where is she, Nicholas? Where is Gelis?'

And Nicholas, looking at him with indifference, had pulled open a drawer and, spreading a map, had said, 'There. No, since last night possibly there. If you have five minutes, I can show you exactly, if that is what you really want to know.' The pendulum lay on the desk. It looked like an ordinary pebble.

'I want to know why you are doing it,' John had said. 'You know she is coming. She's got to come.'

'Of course. So she should have a welcome,' Nicholas said.

The foreboding which others experienced had already touched Mistress Clémence, an expert in the aberrant conduct of fathers. Studying M. de Fleury, she had watched, unsurprised, the dulling of the glow brought about by those long leisurely days at sea, and distrusted the extreme urbanity which seemed to have replaced it. Either M. de Fleury was unmoved by the approach of his wife, or was able to cover his feelings by a feat of acting which defied the imagination.

She held this view until the third day when, coming to visit the child, he took Mistress Clémence aside and informed her that his wife was expected tomorrow, and that he wished her to travel with him to meet her.

'But naturally. I shall prepare Master Jordan,' she had said.

'No,' he said. 'The boy is not to come. You will be there instead, to assure my wife of his wellbeing. I have arranged to meet her at the palace of Hesdin.'

'The lady is staying there?' she had asked. The palace was empty. Everyone knew the palace was empty.

'She will be taken there. I have the Duke's kind permission. I have in mind,' continued M. de Fleury, 'to show madame some of Hesdin's particular splendours. You will be pleased, I hope, to accompany us.'

She was disturbed. She would have thought him a little drunk, were it not that she had placed him as a temperate gentleman, except when it suited him. Even as she agreed, Mistress Clémence conveyed mute dissatisfaction. She disapproved of what happened at Hesdin. She agreed because her Christian conscience (and human curiosity) would not have allowed her to refuse. A good nurse is the link between child and parent: the person who interprets one to the other and is respected by both, if not loved. Although she had been loved, in her time.

The following morning she set off to Hesdin with a liveried escort from the company. With her rode Nicholas de Fleury, husband and father, ready now to end a long parting.

Chapter 6

MOVING INESCAPABLY in her turn towards him, Gelis van Borselen was conscious that, whatever she did, her foe her husband was watching her. She made no effort this time to evade him. She wore the ring which his pendulum knew, and travelled slowly, because he would not expect that, and it might disturb him a little.

She had thought, sitting alone, considering – hour by hour, week by week – what she knew of his mind, that the summons would come on the day that marked the third anniversary of their marriage. But he, no doubt guessing as much, had amused himself by avoiding it. The command, when it came, arrived at an hour of no special portent, and she left immediately, so that he should be in no doubt that she was willing.

It would have been a relief to be tracked by human beings, by spies such as ordinary businesses used. Instead, she was being monitored by a shadow, and felt reduced to a shadow herself. A shadow, an echo. Whereas no one could monitor Nicholas, who moved to his prey like a cat, traced from field to field, grove to grove by the streamers of terrified birdsong.

She had one servant with her, and an escort to protect her whole baggage, which she had been expected to bring. Despite her leisurely progress, she might, by hastening, have arrived at his camp before dusk, but instead chose to pass the night at an inn in St Omer. She spent money freely. It was her marriage endowment from Nicholas. There was plenty of it.

Movement by night from a town was forbidden, or possible only for officials or burgesses. Nicholas was neither, but gold or threats must have served, otherwise she would never have been roused by a terrified maid in the night, with a message that she was to dress and depart. Outside, her own escort had gone and strangers waited. The sergeant carried a note in the script that, in Arabic, in Italian, in

Flemish, she had seen on tablets in Africa, in Venice, in Spangnaerts Street: the quick, clear, tutored handwriting of her husband. She was to go with his soldiers to Hesdin, leaving her maid and her boxes behind. He did not mention the child.

Because of the child, she must go. She understood perfectly what was happening. As she had drawn him from Scotland and Bruges, dispatched him painfully on fool's errands, chasing the will-o'-the-wisp of the child, so he now held the same lever. Only he, the ultimate engineer, manipulator, Master of Secrets, would use it in his own way, and this time to punish her.

Wherever she was going, the child would not be there. Whatever, whoever awaited her at the end of this night, she did not think it would be Nicholas. It was strange then that, wrested from her bed, thrown on horseback, she found herself possessed by a vast and painful excitement, a surge of exhilaration that fell upon the chance, at last, to ride fast and hard to where, of all the world, she longed most to go.

The journey occupied four hours, and was made with fresh horses, changing twice to maintain the highest level of speed. No one spoke. Gelis van Borselen was a good horsewoman, and had set out well rested from Bruges at a pace whose agonising slowness she had cause now to be thankful for. She regretted only that, riding, it was not practical to arrive at her destination as finely gowned as she would have preferred. The boy of the Sinai desert, the travel-stained woman of Venice were due to be forgotten. Then she bit her lip, thinking how seldom appearance had ever had anything to do with him, or with her. The night fled by, and in the torchlight no one saw that sometimes she wept unawares as she rode.

They arrived with the first of the dawn. Already her shadow was moving before her when she saw a powder of lights far ahead and, suddenly, the high ruddy twinkle of glass. She had known, since they entered the parkland, that this was not the road to the Burgundian camp. She was being brought somewhere else to stand trial for what she had done. All the same, even when coursing the green wooded vale of the Canche, she still dismissed the ducal château as a likely destination. Hesdin was too unsubtle a choice for the subtle Nicholas of this brittle war.

And again, Nicholas had used her expectations to trick her. The great building blurred in the distance could be nothing other than Hesdin, enchanted theatre of marvels. The towers and turrets crowded the sky, and presently the walls could be seen, and the great sculptured mass of the gatehouse. The vaulted entrance was dark, but there were lights visible throughout the château, its walls flushing now with the dawn. Even unoccupied, a ducal stronghold would merit a garrison.

She saw the flash of armour from outside the entrance, and discerned double doors standing open, and men-at-arms in the tunnel behind them. She could not see who else waited among them. Then her sergeant brought her troop to a halt and, jumping down, helped her dismount. She found with anger that she was shaking, and was curt with him, to show she was not afraid. She saw she was to go onwards alone. She shook back her hood and walked forward.

Within the vault, no one moved. Her eyes strained, she thought she could distinguish civilian headgear mixed with the helms: the hat of the governor, perhaps; the veil of some lady proposed as her servant or chaperone. She was a van Borselen, related to princes. She would be treated with ceremony. She was sure, then, that Nicholas was not here, or if he were, that he waited for her indoors. Inside Hesdin, palace of mischief.

She was still thinking so when she realised that among the anonymous watchers was a man of greater height than the rest, richly and quietly dressed. His identity was lost in the gloom, but she knew him as if he had called. It was Nicholas.

He let her traverse almost the whole way to the gatehouse before he stirred, and strolled out with his shadow to meet her, alone in the roseate light. She stopped and waited.

Once, from a window in Florence, she had looked down on someone she thought was fashioned like this: brown-haired and solid and calm. She had forgotten, till now, how different Nicholas was. It was like forgetting birth, or the sea. The seething, chopped tides of the sea, with combers of violet and crimson emerging. The walls of the palace were red, and behind him the spires of the gatehouse were burning like torches. He lifted his head, deigning to give her at last his attention, and met her gaze with his own.

Time stopped. For almost five months she had meditated on what she would say to him, and how she would say it. She had planned it in anguish and bitterness. She had not forced herself further: to visualise how he would look, or what she would feel when she saw him. Perhaps he had not either, or perhaps the long silence from which, bemused, she began to emerge was deliberate. She realised that her escort was waiting behind her, and that the group by the gatehouse was murmuring.

Now the sky flamed; the air they breathed was dyed red; the palace windows glittered and burned. She choked, her throat clearing at last, and saw Nicholas smiling at last: the brilliant, deep-dimpled smile that filled her with horror. Before she could speak, he unloosed a hand and, smiling still, indicated the way through the yards to the palace.

'Walk over with me,' he said.

Clémence de Coulanges heard the words from the entrance, and caught the suffocating change on the young woman's face. It arose perhaps from debility. Once of exceptional looks, the girl had grown hollow, as many wives did in a crisis of marriage. The husbands were most often unmoved, unless to guilty bad temper.

To Mistress Clémence, M. de Fleury had shown nothing that morning of either impatience or temper. They had been at Hesdin for an hour. All the time his wife's cortège approached, dim against the dawn light, and even when the Lady dismounted, M. de Fleury had stood motionless; had indeed let her walk for some distance before he moved forward to greet her. Then, cruelly perhaps, he had said nothing. Mistress Clémence saw that the Lady herself was struck dumb, either from fear or from nervousness. The silence, as it stretched, became ominous, like the deadening of sound when a cannonade stops. Then M. de Fleury had uttered four simple words.

Mistress Clémence didn't know what inner meaning they bore, but saw that they had one. After a while, Gelis van Borselen visibly called on her will-power and spoke. 'My lord? I shall go, of course, wherever you wish. So long as I still have a son.'

Clémence de Coulanges clicked her tongue and walked forward. She observed that M. de Fleury was smiling. Then, as if he knew she was near him, he turned, and drew her out where the Lady could see her.

The lady Gelis sprang forward. Her fingers, clutching Clémence by the wrists, were painfully fierce. Then she loosened her grip and stepped back. 'Mistress Clémence. You are well?' She was a lady of style, Gelis van Borselen, dame de Fleury.

Clémence said, 'Madame, I am well and so is your son. Pasque and I have cared for him. He is safe in the Burgundian camp.' Halfway through, she slackened the rate of her speech, realising that M. de Fleury would not stop her; that this was why she was here.

You could see the Lady thinking so, too, the Nordic blue eyes studying M. de Fleury. He returned her gaze, smiling still. The Lady said, 'When did you leave camp?'

She spoke to Clémence, who replied as a good servant should. 'Early this morning, madame. The child was sleeping, well guarded, with Pasque.'

It was the truth; that was all you could say for it. 'Guarded by whom?' said Gelis van Borselen. It was a remark, not a question. A remark touched with weary contempt.

'By my men,' said M. de Fleury at once. 'Do you doubt therefore that he is safe? Pleasures, as someone said, are best when deferred.' He paused. 'Shall we go in? The sun is up, and food awaits us, and entertainment of one kind or another. In case the conversation should fail.'

He had turned. He looked unsurprised to find Mistress Clémence blocking his way. Mistress Clémence addressed him with firmness. 'Your lady wife, M. de Fleury, is tired. Once she has rested, we shall be glad of the refreshment you offer.'

'And the entertainment,' M. de Fleury said agreeably.

'This is a palace of springes,' said Clémence de Coulanges. 'If your wife does not know, she should be warned of it.'

'I felt sure,' said M. de Fleury, 'that you would deem it your duty to tell her. But she knows. Everyone knows, but not everyone has first-hand experience of them. You have no objection to touring the château, have you, madame?'

He was smiling again. The lady Gelis said, 'If it would really amuse you. Either you have changed, Nicholas, or you believe that I have. As we walk round, would you like me to scream? Pray? Weep? Call for my mother? I shall do what I can.'

'I thought you didn't like your mother,' he said.

'Then I shall call for my sister,' she said. 'You know how close we both were. Shall we go?'

The refreshment he had spoken of was there, laid out on fine cloths in a parlour. Despite what he had said, M. de Fleury did not join them. His lady wife sat, while Clémence set wine before her, and food which only Clémence ate. The lady said, 'Does he treat you well, Mistress Clémence? And Pasque?' Her eyes said, Is this a trap? Can I trust you?

'It is not a settled life,' said Mistress Clémence. 'But he treats us well, and it is suitable enough for the child. You know that we have chosen to stay for the sake of the child.' She saw the mother relax, as she ought. She, Clémence, had spoken the truth.

'I pray to God you will continue to stay,' said Gelis van Borselen. 'Mistress Clémence, what else will he allow you to tell me? Whatever happens, you must not offend him.'

'I shall say what I please,' Clémence said sharply, clearing her mouth. 'Master Jordan is in no distress; eats well; grows; M. de Fleury has done all that he should, and has told the child you are coming. In my opinion, you should insist on going straight to the camp. There is no call for you to go through this nonsense.'

'Well, madame?' said M. de Fleury. She had not heard him return.

The lady Gelis looked up. She said, 'You have the esteem of your nurse. She believes that I may refuse to do this with impunity. I prefer to pay my price, and be free.'

'Free?' he said.

She looked at him. She said, 'I understand. It is a relative term. I place myself in your hands.'

'Entre cuir et chair as of old: I know how secrets attract you. Then what are we waiting for?' said Nicholas de Fleury expansively.

This is a palace of springes. Springes, and springs. The Counts of Artois, two hundred years since, had made this fortress a playground for mockery; a place where high-born lieges paid for their suppers by suffering, overcoming, enjoying – if their natures were hearty – a series of practical jokes, devised to mortify and to hurt, to shock and to shame. Forty years ago, Duke Philip of the black wit and sardonic mind had had the devices repaired and improved. His son, the single-minded, the dour Charles, did not use them. But they were still there.

As Nicholas said, everyone knew about Hesdin, including herself. Apprehension, then, was part of her punishment, followed by mortification, ridicule and discomfort. She had no redress. In losing the child, she had placed herself in his physical power, not only today, but for as long as he wanted. But whatever happened, she would see that he received no satisfaction; saw no trace of anger or fear. It struck her as curious, frightening even, that he had expected this circus to cow her. Unless, of course, he had heard what had happened when he left her childless in Venice. She had broken down then. She had shown fear and anger and every aspect of agony then.

But that was over four months ago. She had recovered. And – blessing and pain at one time – the child was not here, distressed witness of her humiliation. Unless, suddenly, Nicholas would overstep even that boundary and produce him. Apprehension of that, too, was her lot, she assumed. Apprehension mixed with terrible hope. Nicholas generally employed only the finest of weapons, and dealt in largely invisible wounds.

By twisting words, for example. A secret is kept *between skin and flesh*: a cliché for some; an intimate term, as it happened, for her. No one noticed. No one would comprehend the other phrase he had used at their meeting: *Walk over with me.*

Die with me, the words meant. Or had meant when last he spoke them, holding her on a dawn such as this. Die with me if we cannot live without hurting each other. She had refused, in a cry of derision. And he had repeated the words in derision just now.

She believed she was not going to die in the palace of Hesdin. So long as the child lived, or interested him, the long duel would afford

Nicholas pleasure. He had brought her here to suffer indignity. He would mortify her, as the Dukes made buffoons of their courtiers. And then he might or might not allow her the child.

They had begun to walk through the château, Nicholas a little removed from her side. By some alchemy, contrived by distance, contrived perhaps by nothing more potent than soap and water, he had sterilised the sense of the familiar which had seized her when they met. Mentally, physically, she had no sense of him any longer. He had not touched even her hand. She walked before him through every doorway, and Mistress Clémence, as due to her sex, followed next. Built over the centuries as palace, fortress, pleasure-house, the place was a concoction of wings, each containing chambers and salons, parlours and staircases and galleries, sleeping rooms and rooms for retiring, rooms for courtiers and servants and guard. She would not know, until it happened, where the first trap would be sprung.

She said, 'Might we pass the time in conversation? Or is it forbidden to talk?' Her voice echoed. In all their journey so far, they had seen no one else. This was to be a private performance, it seemed, for her husband alone. Yet Clémence was here.

He was smiling faintly again. 'I could prevent you? What do you want to know?'

'Nothing that you would want to tell me. I wondered whether some of my womanly gossip might be new to you. Does the Bank inform you of romances, of weddings, of infants born or expected?'

'Of such stuff,' said Nicholas, 'is good banking made.' He opened another vast door and stood aside. 'But it is news, indeed, if you have developed an interest in feminine tattle. I am arranging for a decree of divorce.'

Her heart stopped, and so did she. Then, thudding, it brought back her blood and her voice. She said, 'Now you have surprised me.'

He wore his puzzled, amiable face. 'Have I insulted you? I thought you wanted one.'

She gazed at him. Mistress Clémence, grimly attending, had taken three ostentatious steps from the door. Disregarding her, Gelis lifted her brows. 'Then we are both mistaken,' she said. 'I thought you wanted the child.'

'That would be the condition,' he said. 'So you don't want a divorce? Stay there a moment.'

'Not on that condition,' she said. 'Not on any terms that give you sole rights to my son.' She was looking down. Below her feet was a grating. She made no effort to leave it. She observed, 'Is the mechanism usually so slow? It will be dark in twelve hours.'

'No, you can move. Your skirts were supposed to fly up to your shoulders. Some of the pumps, like the Koy's, have got rusty, and there is not quite the same inducement to mend them. So go on. You were saying?'

She gazed at him, then began to walk through the door. Clémence followed. Gelis said, 'You didn't mean what you said? You were simply putting off time?'

'No, I meant it. I keep the child. If you want a divorce, you can't have him.'

'Who says so?' said Gelis.

'Money,' he said. 'Julius loves lending money to Cardinals. Do go on. Do you want a divorce?'

'I thought you said you were obtaining one,' Gelis said. She walked obediently forward. Half her mind was focused on what he had said and why he was saying it. The rest was surveying the room for devices. Some might work and some might not: a typical de Fleury refinement. But she would prefer, on the whole, to have warning.

'I could cancel it,' Nicholas said. 'It would be very much more economical. I could go to Heaven instead.'

No gratings, no jets but a distorting mirror, shifting and leering at the edge of her sight. She turned, not without cost, and surveyed herself in it, but nothing happened. She ran a finger down the holes in the frame and drew it off orange with rust. Nicholas shimmered behind her. He said, 'Some of them work. May I interest you in the next room? How is Julius, Stupor Mundi? Romances, weddings, infants born or expected?'

The next room had a grille in the threshold. She paused there, but again nothing happened. Gelis said, 'I don't wish to spoil your enjoyment, but perhaps Mistress Clémence was right. Rather than a long, fruitless walk, why not sling a bucket of soot at me now, and let me ride on to the camp? I promise not to rinse off till I get there.'

'Would you?' Nicholas said. 'Of course, I'd rather you stayed, but if you want to go off to camp, I shan't stop you.'

She turned quickly and saw the two dimples: the code she knew better than anyone. She said, 'You are lying.'

'No,' he said. 'You can go. Naturally, the boy isn't there. He was moved as soon as we left. You won't find him.'

'I will,' said Mistress Clémence unexpectedly.

He glanced at her. 'Yes. You will. But not my wife, unless she completes the certified course. No Hesdin, no Jordan.'

He had hidden the child. It was what she would have done – had done often enough. Confirmation of it still made her feel sick. She said, 'I thought I had sent you to Heaven. Is this my reward?'

The dimples smoothed. He was studying her. 'You are asking me to withdraw the divorce?'

'Until the state of your soul is secure.'

'Then we stay married,' said Nicholas. His voice echoed. He added, 'How simply these things are arranged. So will you kindly walk forward? It will be dark in twelve hours.'

'I am sorry,' Gelis said. 'I was waiting for the noose round my neck. In here, would you say?' Behind her, the nurse gave a click of impatience. She had forgotten her.

The room she had entered seemed to hold nothing but an old lectern with a book of some kind laid open upon it. The stem of the lectern was thick, and there was a mark on the ceiling above. Nicholas spoke. His voice, without the echo, was good-humoured enough: 'The book is a volume of ballads. Go and turn over the pages. So what about Julius? You didn't tell me.'

'You know more than I do by now,' Gelis said.

'I know, certainly, about the Gräfin von Hanseyck and her daughter, the rich, the beautiful and the widowed. Then tell me about something else. Who has married, apart from Margot and Gregorio? Or is that all? Even masculine gossips know of that.'

'And do they know of the second Marian?' Gelis said. She walked to the lectern and looked. To turn the pages, it was necessary to stand under the mark on the ceiling. She did so, maintaining a weary forbearance, and set her hand to the book. Nothing happened.

'Of course. Marian de Charetty's grandchild. Mine too, since I married Marian de Charetty. You have married a grandfather. The song in the book is what the soldiers made up when Warwick died and the Yorkist King won. Do you sing? Like a lark?'

She sighed. 'Not as you do. *Bien vienne.* How could I forget? How could I forget your songs in the brothels of Cairo? I was flattered,' said Gelis, 'to hear you mourn me so eloquently.'

'I was singing to you,' he said. Mistress Clémence, behind, was standing in silence.

Gelis smiled. 'Another failed jest. So what was supposed to disconcert me here, do you think?' She indicated the lectern, and surprisingly he strolled up to look at it. He was chanting under his breath: she realised it was the soldiers' song from the book.

> *'Or a-t-il bien son temps perdu*
> *Et son argent qui plus lui touche*
> *Car Warwic est mort et vaincu;*
> *Ha! Que Loys est fine mouche!*

'You should sing. What failed here? Soot from overhead, it is evident. And jets of water, of course, from the book. I must lodge a complaint. The schedule allowed for a fall of flour in the doorway, and a second cascade as you fled to the mirror. The catoptric flour of parrots and poesy. If nothing works, then I shall certainly send for some buckets. The second verse is worse:

'*Entre vous, Franchoix*
Jettez pleures et larmes:
Warwic vostre choix
Est vaincu par armes.'

He crossed to the window, singing in a concentrated way. As she followed, he stopped. 'And so, find something to tell me. Whose is the child not yet born?'

There was a face outside the window: a grotesque mask which hovered, mouthing and grinning. Below it was a box, and below that nothing but air. The box was too small for a man. She said, 'What does it do?'

'It answers questions,' he said. 'More quickly than you do.'

She peered at the mask. 'The coming child? It is Anselm Adorne's, born of his welcome home to his family in Bruges. His lady will be delivered in January.'

He did not answer. Looking up, she saw he was watching the mask. Gelis said, 'What are you doing?'

'Asking a question,' he said. He opened the window and ducked. Eyes rolling, the mask emitted a brief spurt of water, and a portion of Mistress Clémence's sleeve became soaked. She sprang back. Nicholas, straightening, addressed the face gravely. 'Master, tell me the truth. Will the family Boyd go to England?'

There was a pause. 'Bien sûr,' said the box under the mask. Its voice, a little flustered, was adult. A dwarf.

'It doesn't know,' Gelis said, out of breath. Nicholas stood frowning quite close beside her. His doublet was scentless and new, but there was a warmth in the sun from the window. He turned away and walked out of reach again.

'Of course it doesn't know,' he said. 'But I do, and so do the Boyds: they're not stupid. They've made off with the hermit.'

'The Boyds have? What hermit?' she said. He marched to the door and she followed him, talking. 'Why not ask the dwarf?' she was saying. 'He must be horribly cramped.' Mistress Clémence was looking at her. Gelis stopped talking abruptly.

He didn't seem to have noticed. He said, 'There should be a room with a hermit. Now there's only the Medea.'

'The Medea?' she said.

'Called after Jason's enchantress. Duke Philip named the room after her. Otherwise known as Violante. There are eight conduits under that doorway, and three outlets for flour. Go and stand there.'

None of them worked. She realised that she didn't care if they did, and that in itself that was dangerous. Her fear and anger were fading; her resolve was melting; her sense of conflict was already half lost, fool that she was. Fool that she was, how could she forget whom she was fighting? There was a pain in her throat: she had to ignore it. She had to prevent herself from entering the game. His game.

Today had been planned as a trial, a punishment, a means of underlining and studying her helplessness. He had also wanted to know what value she placed on the boy. He had probably found out all these things quite quickly and now, you would say, had tired of his role and was playing; was releasing, seductive as a drug, that uninhibited genius for mischief which could bind people to him for life. And you had to resist the enchantment, for it was never spontaneous.

She collected herself, and saw him watching her. Then he laughed: an acceptance of failure. He was standing outside a pair of great doors, waiting for her to go in. The last room, the room of Medea. And this time, she knew, as if she had been told, that everything would work.

Just before she walked through, she spoke to Clémence: 'Be careful.' She wondered what the nurse thought of them both. She thought suddenly that, if they both died, she and Nicholas, Jordan would have no one else. Then she thought of nothing but of what was before her.

Here was no sign of neglect. This chamber was as big as a hall, its high ceiling painted blue with gold stars. Angels stood about with silver-gilt wings, their limbs and appendages turgid with pent water. Gelis said, 'The lady Violante's husband is going to Persia. Were you not one of her lovers?'

'Julius would remember,' said Nicholas. 'Didn't you mention romances? Not that the lady Violante was quite what he fancied. So what did you think of the Gräfin Anna von Hanseyck and her daughter? Is Julius serious?'

'It was the talk of Cologne,' Gelis said. 'Beautiful, wealthy and widowed. You should divorce me and cuckold Julius. Give me my son and take the Gräfin's charming daughter. She is eight.' She stood in mid-chamber, Clémence beside her. The floor was cut into recesses and channels, and Nicholas was closing the shutters. A lantern flickered. Somewhere, she could hear the sound of a drum, like a heartbeat.

'Too young for me,' Nicholas said. 'I should tell Julius to ship her to Simon. We know that Simon can't get her with child, and someone ought to give him a virgin instead of all these used matrons he tries out.' He turned. 'Did you think I should let you walk free?' His voice was sweet.

'Of course not,' she said. The air sighed. The drum deepened its sound. Beside her, Mistress Clémence took a quiet step and placed a hand under her arm. The hand was steady.

The last shutter closed. The lantern glimmered, the only light in the room. There was another sigh, and another, and the ground began to slide under her feet. She sprang aside, taking Clémence with her, and, scrambling, made for the wall. The floor in the centre had changed. The uneven paving had sunk, forming a broad rectangular pit which barred her way to the end of the chamber. Across it lay a finely wrought bridge, upon which Nicholas stood, his eyes wide.

He said, 'The door behind you is locked.' Somewhere, someone started to chant. Mistress Clémence, pressing her arm, had brought them both to stand with their backs to the wall along which the paving still ran, high and firm. Immediately ahead lay the edge of the chasm. Other voices joined in the singing: the sound was serious, liturgical, soft, the sound of a blessing or maybe a curse. Something materialised from the gloom of the pit and rose, whirring. It was joined by another. Its flight, inconsequential as that of a dragonfly, stirred her hair and fluttered the nurse's stiffened voile, so that she put a hand to her throat. The voices were those of women. Dim in the light, the golden stars glittered and the panelled walls faded, replaced by shadowy boughs, glimmering fruit, floating garlands. Mistress Clémence said, 'Toys.'

She spoke to Nicholas. 'Toys,' he agreed. He stood, substantial among the weaving denizens of the room, dark but for the lantern-glint that stood in his eyes, and the flame from his ring. The jewel burned. The black rectangle below him had begun to breathe smoke, and a flicker of red burnished the bridge and dimly illumined his face from below, distinguishing the high Latin nose within the plain Burgundian mask. Mistress Clémence moved.

'It is not fire,' Gelis said. Now you could see the dragons above, and the angels. It was the angels who were singing. It was Latin. It was not a blessing. She said, 'You should, I think, let Mistress Clémence leave. She has caused you no annoyance that I know of.'

'Presently,' Nicholas said. The singing reached a climax and broke off. The drum beat. The pit glowed. Unexpectedly, far above, a bird started to sing. Its voice was frightened and loud. Nicholas said, 'Mistress Clémence? You know why we are here?'

The bird sang. Mistress Clémence's voice, when it came, was

surprisingly steady. 'My training is with children, not adults, M. de
Fleury. They chastise one another with blows.'

'And you think that better? Perhaps you are right. But I reserve
some rights as a husband, or else my son, when he grows, would
despise me. When I am abused, I make some complaint. It seems a
mild one, to me. As you see, my wife is not easily frightened.'

'It is not my place to comment,' said the nurse. 'I only hope, as he
grows, that your son will forgive you the part allotted him in this
experience.'

'You would tell him?' said Nicholas.

'Others will, soon enough. It is as well to remember,' said Mistress
Clémence. 'The bond between mother and child cannot be broken. A
son will defend even a mother he hates.'

'Thank you,' said Gelis. 'I am here, do you remember?'

The nurse turned. 'Your son loves you, madame.'

'Who can doubt it?' Nicholas said. 'But in time, he will learn, as
you say, what has happened. So will others, and sooner. You have
heard my lady wife express her wish to continue our marriage. I am
overwhelmed – for my own sake, for that of the child. But I would
begin our new married life in public accord. Being young, she fell
into error. I have exacted my own form of punishment. I have
forgiven her.'

'Thank you,' said Gelis. About her, the air swam with flickering
shadows, red with a breathing malevolence. The bird screamed. Her
flesh, fighting to preserve itself, tore open her mind to the channels of
instinct while she sought, breathing fast, to control it.

The announcement he had just made was a travesty. The promise
he had not made was the one she wanted to hear. She said, 'And
Jordan? *Jordan?*'

The name was the trigger. She was in the lair of a Professor of
Secrets, and the levers under his hand were his playthings. As she
spoke her son's name, the bird's song reached the highest point of its
terrified screech and darkness fell. A fissure of light, sizzling high in
the air, showed the pit at her feet, showed the bridge, showed
Nicholas standing immobile still, looking down at her. The dragons
and angels had gone and the walls had turned black. The ground
under her shook. A roar swept through the room: a rolling crash that
hammered into her eardrums; withdrew and thundered again. The
lightning seared through the air and the fingers of Clémence dug into
her arm.

'Toys, my lady,' said Clémence. 'The louder the noise, the smaller
the harm. There'll be rain.' As she spoke, the hiss started.

It fell from above. At first, it drummed into the bed of the floor;

then the rush of sound altered as the water fell on itself, surging, rising, filling the pit. The spray coated her face, her hair, all she wore. She pressed back on the wall. 'I am sorry, my lady,' said Clémence.

There were jets on the wall. As he had touched off the storm, so the silent controller of Hell brought to life, one by one, all the other devices. Water poured under her skirts, over her shoulders, streamed down her hair and her face, stopping her breath. Thunder crashed as she choked, and lightning flickered and swam through the air, showing her the bridge of the secrets again and again and again. The last time, it was empty.

She was halfway across when someone seized her, dragging her back. For a moment she fought, then saw it was Clémence, and obeyed. As she moved, the bridge broke where she had been, and loosed its planks in the water below. The nurse said, 'Now. Now you can jump.'

It was possible. It was just possible, running, to launch oneself over that gap and reach the rest of the bridge: the stump that led to the far side of the room and the exit. There was no sign of Nicholas anywhere.

Her skirts were leaden with water. Gelis lifted them in both hands, threw back her soaked hair and, measuring, precipitated herself onwards and upwards and jumped. She landed staggering, clawing the rail. Then she turned, hands outstretched, and caught Clémence. They touched hands for a moment. Next, turning, Gelis slithered down from the bridge and led the way across the short stretch of polished wood to the door.

She didn't know, then, what warned her. A small sound of some kind, a creak that hardly made itself heard against the relentless crash of the mechanical thunder and the hissing roar of the fall in the pool. She felt a movement. She saw Clémence plunging towards her. Gelis stopped and flung out her arm. She thrust the nurse to one side, following with her shoulder and the whole of her body; occupying the place where the woman had been. Clémence stumbled and knelt by the wall.

Beneath Gelis, a rectangle of floor thudded open. Below was nothing but space. She grasped air. Her arm seared against wood. She touched a bracket, and lost it. Her sleeve caught, then her skirt, and ripped free. Clémence flung out a hand, but it was beyond Gelis's reach, and already her momentum was too great to check. So she fell.

It was a long way. She called his name, once.

Chapter 7

GELIS WOKE TO a sickening pain in her arm, and the sound of somebody screaming. A man.

She was in the sunlit guest-parlour in Hesdin. Her eyes, moving from her bound shoulder and arm and an unfamiliar robe, came to rest on the concerned, impatient face of the nurse. Mistress Clémence sitting wrapped in a cloak, and a gown beneath it which reached to her calves.

The rain. The rain, the deep pool, and the bridge; and the Master smiling upon it. Then she looked round.

Two strangers, both in armour, both looking angry. A man in court dress, his face pale. And Nicholas, standing half-turned as if stopped in mid-sentence, who made a furious, dismissive gesture and turned fully to her.

The men left. Nicholas stood looking down at her. 'I am sorry,' he said. 'The mattresses should have been there.'

His eyes were distended, as they had been on the bridge. He sounded childish, or mad. It occurred to her for the first time to wonder if he was mad. She said, 'I am rather sorry as well.' Outside, the screaming had started again.

'You could have been killed, either of you,' Nicholas said. He spoke as if answering some question. Then he dropped his eyes to her arm. 'Mistress Clémence tended it for you. It should never have happened.'

Shivering, she tried to make him talk sense. She said, 'But you meant me to fall.'

'I explained that,' he said.

'So it has all turned out as you wanted. You have been abused. You have abused in return. I am forgiven. May I go now?' Gelis said. 'Or was there anything else?'

It was risky, but she wasn't going to whine, or he would think he had won. Everything ached, and she couldn't stop trembling. While she talked, she tried to assess the full extent of her hurts. She had fallen a long way, and there had been no mattresses. She wondered if she could run if he said she could go. Or if he didn't.

'No. That is, we are all leaving,' he said. 'There is a covered cart you can have. Mistress Clémence thinks it will be best for your arm. You think you can travel?'

'Of course,' Gelis said.

She felt sick. She was not sure if she could stand. With such coin she had purchased her freedom and, maybe, permission to rejoin her son. She thought, anger piercing the faintness, that, purged, she might at least be allowed to mention his name. She said, 'And Jordan. Is it far to the camp?'

The nurse moved. Nicholas said with unusual irritation, 'I told you. The boy is not at the camp.'

She stopped. 'But you are bringing him there?'

'He has left camp for good,' Nicholas said. He sounded impatient. 'You are not going to the camp. You are going with me to Scotland. That is why you left your maid and your bags at St Omer. You agreed. Or do you want a divorce?'

'You lied. You said nothing of this. What is happening?' she said. Turning painfully, she looked for Mistress Clémence.

The nurse, her hands folded, returned a calm gaze. Mistress Clémence said, 'I had not been told either, my lady. All I know is that I stay with Pasque and the child.'

'Then I stay,' Gelis said. She could hear the hopelessness in her own voice. *You won't find him*, he had said. She stared at him, her eyes dry, and then flinched.

He had done her no harm; simply dropped on the floor the glass beaker which had stood on the table. It broke not in fragments, but in half. He said, 'Will it ever mend, or are you now an idiot for life? Have you followed nothing of what I have told you?'

She stared at him, shivering. Behind her, Mistress Clémence rose and placed a hand firmly on the shoulder that was unhurt. It felt reassuring and calm. Nicholas said, 'I shall see you below,' and went out.

The cavalcade was four times larger than she expected: a troop of glittering men-at-arms in the black and white unicorn livery of the Banco di Niccolò. There were some well-dressed riders among them, one a priest in black robes, one a man with an extravagant jewel in his hat. A chain of laden mules sagged behind that, and three disconnected baggage-carts to one side of a huddle of draught oxen chained to a gun-carriage. A team of four horses stamped and jingled before a long padded cart whose hooped cover was incongruously pinned with cheap streamers.

The man with the jewel in his hat was John le Grant, whom she had last seen at Innsbruck, and who had shown her courtesy but little else. The priest was Father Moriz the German, who had also been in the Tyrol. She had received a homily from him on her departure, but he had not been unsympathetic; he might help. Especially now, when she saw that he seemd to be disputing with Nicholas. Then Nicholas himself turned, and came over.

She had recovered enough to need only a groom at her elbow. Mistress Clémence stood at her side. Nicholas, ignoring them both, jerked his head at the groom, saying 'There!'

He had indicated the wagon. Gelis said, 'You owe me a little. May we speak?'

He looked at her. 'Later, of course. Can you climb, or may we lift you into the wagon?'

'I can climb,' Gelis said. The groom, none the less, took her arm.

Dust eddied and rose. Men scurried over the cobbles; a horse staled; a mélange of eye-watering odours hung in the air, accompanied by a cacophony of human and animal voices. The hall of Medea, al fresco. The hooded cart, as she drew near, rocked as if crammed with vigorous passengers. Vigorous, talkative passengers, of which one at least was a woman.

The camp followers. Captain Astorre, come to escort his patron to the coast, had brought his women, and she, Gelis, was expected to travel with them. She would rather ride, broken arm and bruises or no. Gelis halted again. Up in the cart, a flurry of activity culminated in a view of a woman backing out from under the canopy, scolding. It was not a camp follower. It was a woman no camp would have invited to follow. It was Pasque.

Astonishing her groom, Gelis thrust him from her and began to limp to the cart. She was halfway there when Pasque saw her, and dropped her jaw with its yellow-pegged teeth. She had almost arrived at the wheels when the person Pasque had been admonishing scrambled out from the hood and stood, viewing the scene with delight. The childish brow, stuck with brown hair, was unchanged, but in nearly five months the soft lips had firmed; the nose and chin had wickedly redefined themselves.

Here; here; here, Jordan her son. Jordan her son, not in camp, not in hiding but here. She stood gasping, her heart leaping and failing within her. Jordan her son, last seen in Venice, with twenty weeks' worth of living that she would never know lying between them. Jordan, son of his father.

Then the grey gaze swept round and opened, and the lips parted, and the dimples, black as devils, flew into the round cheeks. 'Maman!' cried Jordan de Fleury, his voice rising in delight. 'Maman! R'garde!'

'I see you,' said Gelis, and set foot on the step, and received the rush of his body in her arms, hardly marking the pain.

Nicholas de Fleury turned away, and then stopped, because Mistress Clémence's iron hand was clamped round his wrist. He had apologised to her. He had been, in fact, royally generous. She said, 'If you went forward now, it would be better.'

His eyes reflected the light, bright as mirrors. He said, 'I have to lead this party to Calais, Mistress Clémence.'

Mistress Clémence dropped her hand. 'You need not stay with him long. You are . . .' She hesitated, then went on: 'You are a new possession to the child. He will continuously ask. It can cause jealousy.'

M. de Fleury went forward without further comment. She followed. The child saw her first, and looked pleased if not overwhelmed: with Pasque at his side it was axiomatic that the other half of his household would follow. Then he saw his father and cried out again. In front of his mother, the cry was a trifle theatrical: Clémence sighed. Then M. de Fleury spoke to his son, and to his wife, and after a reasonable time, took his leave and turned back. He did not go near Clémence again.

It had been necessary. Anyone would agree who knew something of children. These three were going to Scotland together. They had to establish some sort of surface relationship, or the situation would be worse than before. And he himself had, after all, taken some trouble to lay the foundations.

'. . . And so he hates his wife,' said Pasque indulgently that night, sharing a bed at St Omer with her superior, their shifts decorously side by side on a coffer. 'To subject her to that! She might have been killed! Well might he have the man whipped for forgetting the mattresses. And she! What wife will she make to him now, compelled out of her country, frightened out of her wits! I tell you, you and I will have our work cut out to bring up that child.'

Mistress Clémence lay as if asleep. In many ways, old Pasque was right. Stubborn, bitter and devious, the family they were now to accompany to Scotland offered small prospect of happiness or normality to themselves or to those who lived with them.

Nevertheless . . .

Nevertheless, why, subjecting his wife to this trial, had the sieur de Fleury also put at risk the child's nurse, upon whom depended the boy's whole security?

Mistress Clémence de Coulanges would not say to Pasque what she thought the real test had been. She would not say to Pasque that she had seen a man whipped almost to flaying because he might have killed Mistress Clémence, as much as his wife. She would not say that the lady Gelis had, in the end, been allowed to hold her son in her arms because, in the face of hurt and possible death, she had put her son first. She had pushed Clémence aside from that trap so that Clémence would live, no matter what happened. And because of that, she was here with her child.

Hatred? Perhaps. She had seldom seen husband and wife behave as relentlessly as these two had, in that unchivalrous cavern of artifice. The mother had not given way, and the so-called mishap had followed at once.

Yet in falling – to her death, she would think – the girl had cried only one name, and that in anguish, not anger. And the man so entreated had moved faster than thought: had been first to sink to her side; first to touch her brow and her hair; first to gather her up, until others came to carry her out. Then had come the annihilating explosion of anger.

The commerce and torments of marriage were not a servant's concern. Clémence lay as if sleeping, and thought of the child, and of where she was going. She smiled.

On the twenty-eighth day of July, 1471, on a ship leased for the purpose and handled by his own sailing-master Mick Crackbene, the padrone of the Banco di Niccolò sailed out of Calais on his long-deferred voyage to Scotland. With him he carried his wife and his son, Jordan de Fleury. The two years of absence he had promised his dying chaplain, Father Godscalc, were done.

Just two days before, on a warm Roman evening, the Holy Father (Pietro Barbo, Paul II), dined in his garden bareheaded and sadly expired of a stroke, directly after enjoying a dish of three melons. He was aged fifty-four. The news reached the Hôtel Jerusalem, Bruges three weeks later.

Anselm Adorne, Baron Cortachy, received it first from the hands of a courier, whom he sent off with gold. Afterwards, he sat alone at his table, his gaze on his fine painted windows. All their plans gone for nothing. All the credit he had acquired from this Pope for himself, and for his Genoese kin, and his Burgundian master. And a loss greater than that, the post his son Jan was to have found in the Curia.

All gone; and a new Pope to be elected, who might be of any nationality, any persuasion. Weeks would go by, perhaps months, while Jan would exacerbate with his ill temper the appalling, abnormal life in this house.

Mary of Scotland, Countess of Arran had been here with her husband, her husband's father and their household for sixteen months. Last year, their first child had arrived. Within a week, the second was due. Once the child was born and the Princess could travel, they could leave Flanders. Now that Edward of York was on the throne, they could ask for shelter in England. They could only go back to Scotland if Tom Boyd, the Earl her husband were to be pardoned.

Adorne had tried, through the Duke, to persuade King James to take back his sister and her family. The King was fond of his sister, and might be petulant over her misplaced loyalty, but would do her no harm. But the effort had failed: the courier (Alex Bonkle) had come back from Scotland wincing from a violent refusal. And so the royal pair were still here, and would very likely remain here for weeks.

Everything now was in disarray. As legate of the young King, Adorne had concocted with Jan this marvellous manuscript of their travels which was to be gifted to James when it was finished. With the Boyds off his hands, Adorne could have carried it to Scotland this month, reinforcing his special position. But the coming of the second Boyd child had made that impossible. And now there was Margriet.

Anselm Adorne rose. Knight of the lists, financier, diplomat, he was only just past middle years, and kept the considerable beauty of face and form that he had always had. He had married Margriet when she was fourteen and he nineteen; and in the twenty-eight years that followed had been loving and faithful in all that mattered. If, here and there in the world, he had lapsed, the interludes had been brief, and tempered with passions other than physical: with friendship and laughter; with a love of music, of poetry, whose absence he never complained of at home, for he had given Margriet too little cause to learn either, with her great house and her children. And now . . .

And now, when she should have been safe and coming to harbour, he had given her another child. He had not intended it: they had grown long accustomed to caution. But she was his dear wife, and on his return after great dangers and absence, he had met in her a dizzying welcome such as he did not remember since the early days of their marriage. That she meant to make of it more than that, he now knew. He had not thought; he had not realised what resolve she had made until April advanced into May and she came to him illumined with triumph. There was to be a last child.

He would cherish it. He had made her happy, as he was happy with the news. But she had never had such trouble when pregnant as she had faced in those first early weeks, and was still facing, although the child was four months on its way. Without Katelijne his niece, they would never have managed. But Katelijne had returned to her duties in Scotland and was not here to pacify Jan, comfort his wife, reassure the little Scots Countess, so near to her time.

The lady Mary was young: she was twenty. She was grateful to Nicholas de Fleury, who had helped her Tom escape his execution in Scotland with the King her brother's reluctant approval. The lady Mary's friend, young de Fleury, who had so cleverly planned that Adorne's house would bear the brunt of the exile.

Thomas Boyd, Earl of Arran, was hardly less devoted to Nicholas. The two men had recently met, Adorne heard, in the Burgundian camp. De Fleury had spent some time, it would appear, advising Arran to take his wife and settle in England. Adorne had not yet fathomed why.

As for de Fleury's reunion with his wife and his child, Adorne was glad, as he knew Kathi would be. During their long pilgrimage to the East, Adorne and his young niece had encountered Nicholas many times, sometimes as rival, sometimes as companion, sometimes, he feared, as an enemy. At the end of it, Katelijne, with misgivings, had helped remove the man's child from its mother. It had been a wretched affair, and Adorne was pained still to think of Jan's part in it. But it was over; the estrangement apparently finished, and child and parents together once more.

Good news, except that the prospect of young Nicholas in Burgundian employment was not one which gave Adorne any pleasure. He bore a wound in his thigh from the last time. And now, it seemed, the man was making for Scotland. Nicholas would have time to refresh all his friendships before Adorne staged his own impressive return, with his winning account of his travels. And meanwhile, the Holy Father was dead, and no one could tell what would happen.

Adorne stood still at the window, unseeing. He must go. He must take on the burden of transmitting the news to his friends. Bishop Patrick Graham was in Bruges, on his way to beg from a man who was dead. A Pope succumbs, and graveyards fill with lost hopes.

The very morbidity of the thought brought back his sense of proportion, and his will to act with his usual resolve. He would go at once to his wife, and to Jan. And presently he would write a letter to Katelijne Sersanders his niece, who was waiting in Scotland.

By a delightful disposition of fate, the death of the stricken Pontiff, Paul II, occurred just when the Bank's notary Julius had abandoned Cologne to do business in Venice. Clearly, with all Christendom roused and all Italy held in suspense, the Banco di Niccolò should be seen where it mattered. A message was sent to its agent in Rome to inform him that Gregorio and Julius were coming.

The journey to Rome in the thick heat of August occupied nine busy days on thronged roads and through excited towns hoarse with speculation and gossip. Despite Gregorio's inconvenient interest in ruins, the two men travelling together got on extremely well: Julius because he was about to attend a number of public events of unimaginable grandeur; and Gregorio because he was happy.

He was unselfishly pleased because Nicholas was communicating once more, and in the interval had kept his son safe. And he was selfishly possessed with the joy that had come with his marriage. Margot and he were to have their first child. They were to have a child in December.

Julius knew. It had been the first thing he had learned, arriving in Venice. He had arrived with a pang, because when Gregorio was absent, Venice was managed by Julius. When Diniz was made director in Bruges, Gregorio and Julius worked in Venice together, except when Nicholas decreed otherwise. It concerned Julius, now and then, to know where the priest Moriz was going to end up. Gossip now declared that Moriz had insisted on going to Scotland. And good luck to him, Julius thought. He remembered the banquets in Scotland. In any case, as he had recently realised, the senior managers of a Bank of this standing really required to be married. Nicholas of course had seen to that. So had Diniz and Gregorio. A man needed a hostess.

He and Gregorio arrived in Rome to find it full as a beehive and buzzing. As they had already been told twenty times, the new Pope was now chosen: a blameless della Rovere from the coast west of Genoa who was going to call himself Sixtus. Milan and Bologna were happy. Venice, which would have preferred its good friend Bessarion of Trebizond, was reserving its judgement. There were sixteen Cardinals and their trains in the city, and all but three of the Electors. The crowning would take place in three days; and Julius was glad he wasn't arranging it.

They stayed with Lazzarino their agent in a rather large house which had just been renamed the Casa Niccolò. It had a garden, a fountain, a chapel and a Franciscan priest awaiting them under a fig tree. He was eating. 'Ha!' said Father Ludovico da Bologna, Patriarch of Antioch. 'The funds improve when the patron disappears for four months. So where is that son of Babylon, Nicholas?'

The solid frame and black tangled hair were the same, and the stained gown of nondescript colour under his robe, but the Patriarch's tonsure was practically visible and he had recently shaved. The Curia clearly had him in hand.

Julius, who had a long memory, looked at him with disfavour. It was forty years since this unpleasant man, when merely an Observatine monk, had first heard the call to unite the Christian churches of the East and the West, and persuade them to raise money and arms against the Ottoman Turk. To that worthy end, Ludovico da Bologna had since travelled across half the known world, collecting his instructions and expenses from four Popes. Now he was here to urge another Crusade, and the death of the Pope had detained him.

Ten years ago, the Patriarch had embarrassed Julius in Florence by exposing his youthful errors when clerk to the Cardinal Bessarion. Time and again, Nicholas, too, had been forced to wrest the course of his life from those black-pelted fists, most recently early this year, when he had declined to commit his army and funds to the East. Hence, now, the man's evil enquiry.

Julius was happy to offer enlightenment. 'Nicholas? On the high seas for Scotland, if not actually there, with his wife and his son. I thought you knew. That was the plan he propounded in Venice.'

'I wasn't in Venice,' said Ludovico da Bologna. 'I saw him in Cyprus, walking quadrilles in the street like the sodomitical partridge and vowing to venture his stock in Heaven for a concerted attack on the Turk. Then he denied it. But thus in all countries is the artisan class. And to this he has now added, I gather, the diabolical practice of necromancy.' He presented his teeth to a chicken leg.

Julius, wincing, drew breath to retort, but Gregorio, in his calm lawyer's way, forestalled him. 'Nicholas is the custodian of a Bank which must have regard to great events affecting its coffers. Moreover, his commitment was made, as I remember, on certain conditions. You offered him a meeting with his son. This he achieved by himself.'

'Through the aforesaid skills, forbidden by Mother Church. The offspring will be damned, or the parents be driven to responses of abominable violence. I saw your Dr Tobias in Urbino.'

'You stayed in Urbino?' said Julius. The Count, a well-known leader of mercenaries, kept a lavish table.

'With my Persian delegate, yes. There was a Flemish painter at work on a masterpiece, and nothing would do but Hadji Mehmet should have his portrait included. It flatters him. Your Dr Tobias thinks, as I do, that Burgundy will cost the Bank more than it offers, and that Scotland should be left to Adorne. Is Adorne's niece in a nunnery yet?' A jelly was set on the table, with a spoon. Julius averted his eyes.

'Katelijne Sersanders?' said Gregorio. 'She lives in one, when in Scotland. That is, she serves the young Scottish Princess in a priory. But she is not, so far as I know, taking the veil.'

'I shall remind her,' said the Patriarch. 'Her barbs would rust, sunk in a husband.'

He swallowed. Julius was surprised. Then he recalled that the Patriarch and Katelijne Sersanders had both been in Egypt and Cyprus last year, and Adorne had spent time with the Pope. The last Pope. Julius said, his voice dulcet, 'Are you worried, Patriarch, about the new Pontiff? You'll have to use all your charm: I hear he doesn't like Observatine Franciscans. You must have hoped they would vote for Bessarion.'

'The Cardinal Bessarion is still with us,' the Patriarch said. 'And a house full of erudite Greeks, and those less so. Zoe, the Cardinal's ward, has also been painted. It is the salve of rich men: as a scalded head calls for lard, so they apply coats of paint to their vanity. The Duke of Muscovy has requested a portrait of Zoe.'

Julius sat up. 'He wants to make her his Duchess?'

'Perhaps. Moscow and Rome have discussed it. Then the business hung fire when Paul migrated to the Lord with his melons. Tell Nicholas. The King of Cyprus will be sad to lose Zoe.'

'Zacco would never have married her,' Gregorio said.

'He bid for her. Zacco will do anything, will he not, to avoid consummating his marriage with Catherine of Venice? Tell Nicholas. Zacco needs him. So how is the Banco di Niccolò?'

'Like all banks,' Julius said. 'Calling in its debts rather than lending money.' He knew the Patriarch. If he couldn't get Nicholas, he would be looking for gold. And they had lost enough gold already.

'And what debts do you have in Cologne?' said the priest. The pudding was finished, and the splashes had caked in the sun except where they still rimmed his lips, like salt round a goblet. 'Or is it pledges you have been collecting?'

Gregorio grinned. Julius said stiffly, 'Every merchant who sells to the Baltic has to have an eye on Cologne at the moment. Caxton's there, writing books for the Duchess Margaret.'

He waited for the Patriarch to grunt. Caxton was English. He might be writing books, or even learning to print them, but he was in Cologne, everyone knew, because the town distributed cloth, and England's exports had been blocked by the Baltic trading alliance called the Hanse. Cologne had broken away from the Hanse. In retribution, the Hanse had intensified its feud against England. Ships were being robbed, wrecked and sunk, to the extent that no one could even send an army anywhere safely. There might come a point – hence Caxton's presence and his own – when Cologne's privileges were costing too much.

He said something of all that to da Bologna. The Patriarch listened.

'So you are working for the Lord's peace. I commend you. Anna von Hanseyck, isn't she called?'

'The Gräfin Anna von Hanseyck,' said Julius haughtily, 'is a widowed lady of my acquaintance who lives in Cologne with her daughter, yes. She has been gracious enough to consult me about financial matters.'

'She's rich?' the Patriarch said.

'Not rich enough to finance a Crusade,' Julius said. 'And too much of a lady to merit having her name bandied about. May I offer you something to drink?'

'Water. Water will do,' said the Patriarch. 'So tell me: what else you were doing in Cologne?'

He had heard rumours, obviously. Julius told him something, not entirely made up, about the Bank's long-term plans. The Patriarch listened. He had paid for it with news of his own, and Julius didn't mind gossiping.

Later, when the Patriarch had gone, Gregorio lay back in his chair, his scoop-nose red with the sun, and said, 'You told him too much. Never mind. I don't want to know about Denmark, it's time I heard about Anna von Hanseyck. Tell me everything.'

Julius ran out of patience. He said, 'You know everything. Christ God, you've read the documents; we've talked about it often enough. She's the widow of Graf Wenzel von Hanseyck. When he died, she exchanged his land in the Rhine valley for gold, and I've helped her invest it. Half the Bank's new ship is hers, and she'll have a share in the profit.'

'If there is a profit,' said Gregorio mildly.

'There'll be a profit. My God, with Nicholas going to do what he's doing? Anyway, she's grateful. She needs help with her money and wants the Bank to advise her. I've said I'll introduce her to Nicholas next summer. You'll see her before that, if you're keen. She's coming to Rome with her daughter for Christmas.'

'Her daughter?' said Gregorio. Behind the question, Julius saw his wife Margot's prompting.

'Name of Bonne,' Julius said. 'Wenzel adopted her.'

'But she's the Countess's daughter?'

'I expect so,' said Julius. 'They have the same eyes and the same hair. I assume the child was the result of an earlier marriage, but of course she might be a daughter of sin. You must ask the Countess to tell you.'

Gregorio was grinning. 'Touchy, aren't you? I'm delighted. Really. We all thought you were going to die without ever coming across anyone worthy.'

'She is just a client,' Julius said. 'Mary Mother, if I went to bed with everyone I did a deal with, I'd die of exhaustion. You've got marriage fever, that's all. Go and find Tobie or John and drag them to the altar.'

'There aren't enough rich German widows to go round,' Gregorio said, and ducked as Julius threw a plate at him. But as a matter of fact, Julius wasn't angry at all, any more than he was disappointed that Nicholas was going to Scotland without him. Julius was quite content, ensconced in the splendours of Rome, and waiting for Christmas.

Chapter 8

LONG BEFORE HE left Calais, it was known in Scotland that Nicholas de Fleury was returning to take up his business, accompanied by two mining experts and a pedigree cannon from Innsbruck.

As seed quickens to rain, so from east coast to west, the Bank's dormant fleurets awoke to the touch of their master. Indolent on the high seas, Nicholas lived, as once before, from wave to wave, for the moment. With him in a locked chest were the letters which still had to be delivered, this time by himself. The documents for King James, from the Duke and the Chancellor of Burgundy. And the personal note for King James from His Most Christian Majesty Louis of France, to be handed over at a time of discretion, for it, like the other, requested the sender's dear kinsman of Scotland to receive the sieur de Fleury with favour, and to give credence to what he would ask. Thus Nicholas de Fleury, serving two masters.

For the two weeks of the voyage, Gelis van Borselen and her husband were together for the first continuous spell since their marriage. Together, that is, in the sense that they travelled aboard the same vessel.

After Hesdin, the journey to Calais had been made bearable by the logistics of travel. Nicholas had a convoy to lead, and his wife was injured and needed attention. Her maid had departed, refusing to sail off the top of the world with two nurses. Gelis travelled to the coast in the cart with the child, and slept with the child and Mistress Clémence and Pasque, who cared for Gelis too. Nicholas shared the quarters and table of his officers: Michael Crackbene, le Grant and Father Moriz.

All of these came to pay their respects, but the first two had little to say and did not return. Only the sturdy bow-legged pastor sometimes remained, passing the time with the child and his nurses whom he had already befriended in camp. She was aware that he was available if she wanted to talk. She had no wish to talk to a henchman of Nicholas. She had to build, and was still finding the bricks. She did not know, and would have been horrified to learn, that Mistress Clémence had asked Father Moriz to be her confessor.

The child had dropped readily into his old confiding relationship with her, which was exactly the same as the one he had with his nurses. Time spent with Mistress Clémence had confirmed what she could now deduce for herself: that in her absence Nicholas had been impeccable with the child, and consistently agreeable to the nurses. Mistress Clémence, true to her training, had offered no further comment on what had happened at Hesdin, and her manner to Gelis was precisely as it had been since the birth of the child.

In this at least, Nicholas had played fair: neither child nor nurses had been set against her. Only sometimes, in the knowledgeable eye and hoarse banter of Pasque (*c'est un bachique!*) did Gelis guess that something about Nicholas had appealed to the outrageous old dame and might, too, have touched the nurse of superior education, better able to conceal it. It was not unexpected. Gelis knew how Nicholas set about making friends.

She should have expected, therefore, that on board ship he would do what he did, which was to turn the same skills on herself. For the sake of the child, she shared as before the child's sleeping quarters. The intimacy of marriage was therefore plausibly lacking, but in every other way he remained in public her husband and friend. When, watching the coast recede, she had found him at her side, the screaming Jordan clutching his neck, she had been dazed by the affectionate ease of his manner. He spoke to her as she had heard him speak to Tilde or Margot, or – long, long ago – to the gentle black girl whom his friend Umar had married. And Gelis, staring back at him dumbly, had had to fight an impulse to tears, because Umar and Zuhra were dead, and because he was acting.

Her son was screaming with joy. She had forgotten that Jordan had recently made his home for many weeks on a ship. She had forgotten that his father had first come to him like this, between water and air, on swaying decks, among the cords which Clémence had put up so deftly in the first moments on board.

The truth was, of course, that Nicholas was not playing fair. To Jordan, his father was the first person, the only person who belonged to a ship: the magician who might be anywhere from helm to forecastle, from the depths of the hatches to high by the flag in the rigging. And she had forgotten that Nicholas was happy at sea. Sailing out from Lagos bound for Africa on his wonderful ship the *San Niccolò*, she had never seen him so happy, except when she had made him so herself.

Jordan was crowing, and Nicholas was looking at her with an easy replica of the open, generous smile that he had turned, too, on Tilde and Margot, on Katelina and Marian, on Umar and Zuhra and herself. His eyes were pin-sharp as a kite's and even held some amusement. She walked away.

Of the others on board, John le Grant saw what was happening but ignored it. He belonged to Scotland and was reasonably interested in coming back, and extremely interested in the opportunities lying ahead of him. He was not at all interested in the marital problems of Nicholas. That said, he twice received the rough edge of Mistress Clémence's tongue for showing the child tricks with tinder and alum.

Moriz, being a priest, was here for the opposite reason. He should be in Venice, not here: there were sensible reasons why Nicholas had expected him to stay behind, apart from the fact that he knew nothing of Scotland. Both he and Nicholas knew that he was here because of what had happened with Gelis. When Nicholas allowed him to come, it had been a sign of exasperation, not acquiescence. These days, Nicholas wouldn't lose sleep over a small German priest threatening hellfire.

The same view, Father Moriz had found, was held by the lady. She had kept him at a distance on the journey from Venice to Brixen, as she was polite on the journey to Calais and after. He was not a patient man. The first rough day at sea, when the child was to be seen drenched to the skin and whooping with glee in the grasp of Mistress Clémence or his father, Moriz marched below to the lady.

She had looked surprised but had admitted him. She had been writing, with difficulty. He helped her stopper her ink; she had already turned over her papers. She was undisturbed, he saw, by the motion. He wished he could say the same. Shortening matters, he sat down and said, 'I am here to tell you, madame, that I am not your husband's spaniel nor am I yours. I see you are in difficulty, and I am a man of experience. I propose therefore to offer myself as a mediator. What may I do for you?'

She secured the last of her pens and sat back, her free hand nursing the arm that was bound. 'Difficulty?' she said. 'You are very kind, but truly there exists no special difficulty. Or if there did, it has been resolved.' Her colouring was so fair that he couldn't determine the state of her health, or her feelings. Her eyes, of a very pale blue, were not as grave as her voice.

Moriz said, 'In my opinion, your husband has forced you to come, perhaps by threatening to deny you the boy. I am willing to speak to him, if you will tell me what to say.'

She looked at him. Something slid over the floorboards, hesitated, and slid back again. Above, there was a regular bumping. Gelis van Borselen said, 'I am not, myself, short of words. If it seemed that a third person might help, then I should gladly invite you. But Nicholas and I understand one another very well.'

'I am sure you do,' Moriz said. 'I think you are under pressure to stay.'

Gelis rose, steadying herself with one hand. She said, 'Please don't trouble. There is no pressure. I want to stay.'

'Because you want this wrangling to go on?'

The motion was slackening. He rose as well, keeping his balance, trying to read her calm face. She said, 'Ask him if he wants to stop.'

She was waiting for him to leave. He stood in thought. Then he said, 'I have to tell you that I think he is stronger than you are.'

She returned his look, swaying in silence. 'You think so?' said Gelis. She watched him shake his head and walk to the door. When he got there she said, 'Speak to Nicholas. He will tell you the same.'

Isolating Nicholas, as he must, was more difficult. The chance came on a day of light seas, and Moriz's journey was vertical, since Nicholas was perched high aloft in the mast-basket. He showed no surprise as the priest settled beside him. 'You've come to talk about Gelis,' he said. His voice, snatched by the wind, sounded mild.

'You haven't thought,' said Father Moriz, 'that she might take her own life if you go on? She was close to it in Venice.'

'No, she wasn't,' Nicholas said. 'And she won't, any more than I should. You don't know her.'

'And you do?' said Father Moriz. 'So tell me what she holds against you.'

'That my name is no longer Claes. That I marry too many people. That I have an illegitimate child. Godscalc surely told you,' he said.

'But this has gone on for three years between you,' said Moriz.

'We like it,' said Nicholas. 'That is why we never quite kill one another. But those who interfere might be less lucky.'

'No one could be less lucky than Gelis,' said the priest. 'What will happen next time? Do you reduce her to her bed, or her grave?'

'You speak,' said Nicholas, 'as if I meant to chain her for the rest of her life to the bed-foot. She is free to leave at any time.'

'But without the child.'

'Of course, without the child.'

'So she is chained. What life is that for her, or for the boy? Or for you, for that matter? She is a good mother,' said Moriz. 'Don't be stupid. Let her go, and the child. She won't prevent you, surely, from seeing him.' The ties of his cap flew whipping under his chin and the wind tugged at his sleeves. The mast swayed and Nicholas, shifting his grip, pulled a considering face.

'You think so?'

'Am I talking in the right language?' said Moriz. 'I am telling you: let me say to the woman that she can go, and take the boy with her.'

The light from the sails moved over their faces. 'Perhaps you are right. So yes. Why not?' said Nicholas.

Moriz gazed at him, full of suspicion. 'Then I may? And obtain her promise to let you see the boy when you wish?'

'Oh no,' said Nicholas, glancing at him with a smile. 'That would be too much, don't you think? If she goes, she goes. I shouldn't be interested in any child brought up wholly by Gelis.'

Ask him if he wants to stop. Father Moriz prayed under his breath. So that was it. Nicholas meant what he said. Gelis could take the child if she liked and depart. The offer was genuine, but Nicholas had made it in the absolute confidence that it would not be accepted.

Father Moriz said, 'I want you to listen to me. A child with one parent, or no parent, is better off than one reared in a household of hate. Are you telling me that you and your wife will live in accord from now on?'

'I am telling you,' Nicholas said, 'that we are both very good at dissembling. The child, at least, will not suffer.'

'But Gelis will.'

'Then she has only to leave,' Nicholas said. His voice had become curt.

'But she won't,' Father Moriz said slowly. 'Because she, too, is bent on this extraordinary duel. Can neither of you understand it is wicked? I shall tell her to go, with the boy. I shall compel her, if need be.'

'Do,' Nicholas said. 'Although I should point out that the challenge was hers, and not mine. She may even win. She has scored quite a few points, most of them visible, were I to undress. She won't go.'

Moriz restrained his voice with some trouble. 'So what are we to expect for the future? A reign of fear? A sequence of impossible trials?'

'An interlude of picardesque fougousité? I dare say,' Nicholas said, 'she will have some such in mind, but I shall try to match and even survive it. I'm sorry. You've done your best. The Patriarch would have been proud of you. It isn't your fault that the maiden turned into the dragon and sent the unicorn off with two horns. I shall try to confine the harm to ourselves.'

'Will you?' said Moriz.

'I don't aim at Père Dieu,' Nicholas said. His voice was easy. 'Only a small speaking part with a gridiron. You might even discover that Gelis schemes better than I do.'

'I know how you scheme,' Moriz said.

'I have a Bank to run,' Nicholas said; and looked at him, finally.

The clouds passed and repassed. The bows crashed, like a bucket slamming into a well. The shadow of seabirds slid over the sails and snatches of talk rose from the decks, and the rattle of rings, and the clank of pails, and the bleating of animals. And the shrill sound of a young, imperious voice.

Abruptly, Nicholas released him from scrutiny. Moriz turned his eyes away, more exercised than he wanted to show. Far off, a line of green, the English coast hung in the mist. Down below, the helm creaked in the grip of the big Scandinavian shipmaster whose name had been mentioned so casually at camp, and who for some reason always disturbed him. Moriz said, with sudden annoyance, 'Who is that person?'

Nicholas glanced down at the helmsman. 'Michael Crackbene? Not a churchgoing man. Prefers the sea to the land. Is currently the Bank's personal pirate, retained at a basic fee topped up by booty, plus a Yule timber of furs for his Ada. He's the reason you're here. It's true that he's friendly with Andreas, but to forgive us for what Crackbene does, we need more serious help than the Fortune Books.'

Father Moriz laid a hand on the rail and prepared to get up. He said, 'I don't mind your insulting my intelligence and my cloth. But there is a child down there, and innocent families where you are going. Unless you come to your senses, you are going to harm both.' He was so angry it obliterated all his dislike of heights. He had descended crook-legged to the deck before he realised that the shipmaster's narrow blue gaze had been examining him. He stumped off below.

The last person to express his opinion on the voyage was the same Michael Crackbene. He did it ten minutes later, when his duty was over, and Nicholas had slid to the deck to stand with him.

Crackbene said, 'The priest'll wreck it. You said he wasn't to come. He'll stop your divining.' His eyes were like Gelis's: chilly.

'I didn't know I was going to divine,' de Fleury said. 'He's just jealous. You're going to Valhalla and he's only going to Heaven like me.'

'Le Grant is over-free with his talk,' Crackbene said. 'The priest is learning too much.' Then he swore, for the leather cap he had been carrying had been lifted out of his hands and tossed to hang high on a yardarm.

'You're overweight,' de Fleury said. 'The priest is one of your truly great metallurgists. He is going to have to be told what to do

when we're ready. Meantime, we want him to think we need saving.'
He threw back his head. 'Two ducats I'll beat you.'

Crackbene got to the cap first, but only just. It didn't matter: it
kept the ship cheerful. Later, he and de Fleury got drunk.

Over the years, Michael Crackbene had sailed both for and against
vander Poele, now de Fleury. He liked working a ship at his side.
Liking didn't mean fondness: Crackbene's only attachment was to a
woman whom de Fleury didn't know he had married, and two
children de Fleury didn't know had been born.

It was one of the reasons why Crackbene was tolerant of this
infestation of wife and nurses and child. He had had experience of the
van Borselen woman in Africa, and knew she was of good, active
stock, capable of making a life of her own. As for children, he spoiled
his own but was uninterested in others, unless they were training for
sea. He had brought one such lad back with him from Africa, and had
got him a good post. He meant to tell de Fleury, some time, about
Filipe. He would be pleased.

You could say that de Fleury and he were the same, for all that he
was a seaman and de Fleury a banker, or supposed to be. They were
both attracted by the kind of crazy, high-paying jobs that no man of
sense would risk his skin for. Northern waters were Crackbene's
native habitat, but he had also sailed to the Euxine and Cyprus and
Africa, and had lost a few ships, and a few crews, and more than one
owner. De Fleury had near-killed him once, and so had the Turks
and the Gambia. But you would come back from the dead for this
game.

Even John le Grant hadn't been told the whole story at first. Some
of it had been discussed in February with the lawyers at Venice.
Some of it had been planned before even that. De Fleury had known
he was coming back to Scotland one day. He had left orders. And
then, surfacing in Dijon this summer, he had extended them.

The present voyage had been arranged at that time: Crackbene was
to charter King James's *Rose of Bremen* and pick up the padrone and
party from Calais in July. When, as it turned out, the *Rose* had been
reduced to chips in an battle with pirates, a smaller caravel had been
leased. The Bank, of course, had no ships of its own in the north: its
roundship and caravel were both in Venetian service, and its elderly
galley confined to calm waters.

Wading through the English bureacracy at Calais, Crackbene had
found de Fleury's party installed in a house of the Staple with the
priest and le Grant. The domestic tangle had evidently been regulated
at last: the child was there, indisputably a de Fleury, and so was the
wife, with her arm in a sling. Among the grooms and the archers, the

story had been the same one that he'd already picked up elsewhere: the girl had slept with St Pol, that stupid philanderer, and de Fleury had sent for her and taught her a lesson. It matched what Crackbene already guessed, including de Fleury's attempted fight to the death with her lover. It continuously surprised him that St Pol had survived it.

Greeting Crackbene at Calais, the padrone and the lady now looked and sounded reserved, as was understandable. In a month, the scandal would all be forgotten. The girl made a lot of the child. Crackbene deduced, without too much trouble, that the wellbeing of the child was why de Fleury had troubled to continue his marriage. Also, she was a handsome young woman, worth taming. Crackbene was satisfied, with his mind on his business, to dismiss the private problems of Nicholas de Fleury.

And the business, discussed in a private room with a view of the Ruisbank Tower, had been all that Crackbene had anticipated. Face to face, freed from the importunities of his women, de Fleury had unfolded at last the detail of the Bank's particular venture in Scotland and John le Grant, the only other participant, had listened in silence, his white-lashed eyes round as sea-anemones; his fading carrot hair twisted in spikes. From time to time he ejaculated.

'Danzig! Ye have a caravel building in Danzig!'

'Bristol! It was you that captured that wine-ship!'

'Jordan de Ribérac! How in the name did ye sell off his cargoes!' His accent, set adrift with excitement, travelled to Aberdeen from the Ruhr in three sentences.

Finally he sat back, alight but indignant. 'All you mentioned in Artois was putting a man of your own into Denmark, and getting a new specialist lawyer from Berwick.'

'We have both,' de Fleury said. 'The first thing you need, capturing ships, is a letter of marque, and the next thing is a bloody good lawyer. If you mean to meddle with fishing rights, you need the Archangel Gabriel. Who did you say we have, Mick?'

'Tom Yare the agent. He knows about ships, he knows about fish, he knows about customs. And our man in Copenhagen is Eric Mowat of Orkney. Recommended by Lord Sinclair: he's related.'

'I know him. They're all related,' said John le Grant. 'He'll speak the language and keep his mouth shut. I thought I was coming to build for the King. What are you capturing ships for?'

'Mick can't help it: they give themselves up,' said de Fleury. 'You'll still build for the King. There's a small yard already at Leith, and Mick will tell you where else. You'll need a foundry for your guns and your gear – Lamb can help you. But these are small ships:

fifty tons, and doggers and balingers. We don't want to be seen to
have large ones.'

'Because of the Baltic merchants?' le Grant said.

'And the Vatachino,' Crackbene said. 'Their man Martin has been
all over Scotland this month.'

There was a silence. The Vatachino, merchants, brokers and ship-
owners, were the Bank's nearest rivals. And of their three principal
factors, Martin had been in the Middle Sea recently with Anselm
Adorne.

De Fleury said, 'When is Adorne coming to Scotland? Does anyone
know?'

Crackbene said, 'Not for two months or perhaps even three, rumour
says. He wants to bring away the Earl and Countess of Arran at the
same time.'

'But Scotland has refused to pardon Tom Boyd?' de Fleury said.

'That is so,' Crackbene said. 'They said they'd hang him. You
didn't see him to talk to?'

'You speak of my soul-mate Tom Boyd?' de Fleury said. 'Of course
I saw him. He was fighting for Burgundy: Astorre was giving him
tips. I have strongly advised him to take his sweet wife and find
shelter in England. As far as I know, he's going to do it.'

'That's dangerous,' John le Grant said.

'I know. Do you think they'll make him the next King of Scotland?
It's not going to make Adorne very popular either. Do we still think
he's helping to lead the Vatachino?'

'I thought we were sure,' Crackbene said. 'He's been looking for a
ship.'

'Has he?' said de Fleury.

'Are you surprised?' said John le Grant. 'He took shares once
before in a voyage. You should remember that, if anyone does.'

'I remember,' said de Fleury. 'So what kind of ship? And what
master?'

'Nothing yet,' Crackbene said. 'Martin isn't a shipmaster and their
second man, David, is in Cyprus while Egidius, rumour says, is in
Rome. Adorne will have to hire. He's got time. The sailing season
doesn't open until the New Year. You can get your own little ships
built before then, and start on the drainage and mining. And the
alum has come. And Govaerts is fairly itching to get you into a
cellar.'

'What it is to be loved,' de Fleury said. 'You realise what we are
going to do?'

'I'm trying not to realise it,' said John le Grant. 'Gregorio *sanctioned
this?*'

De Fleury smiled. Crackbene said, 'The bits he knew about.'

Later, embarked on their ship, Nicholas had cause, like Crackbene, to remember that meeting. Much depended on Crackbene; but though he drank with him after the wager, it was not to excess. Not on board ship. Not with Gelis there, and the child. Although he had not spoken to Gelis since that first day, when she had looked so shocked to find him beside her, with the child in his arms. She, too, had thought it advisable to treat the new proximity with caution; to remain apart in space and in time, only their thoughts touching, circulating. He knew Moriz had seen her again. He knew he would have told her to leave.

Now, gazing alone out to sea, he was thinking of nothing worth mentioning when the shadow moved, catching his eye by its very familiarity, for it had crossed his path before under hotter suns than this; darkening dust, darkening stone, darkening the colour and spray of a fountain. Gelis had come from her chamber and stood lifting her face to the sun, the white wool cloud of her robe like a galabiyya. He turned and looked at her.

She looked better. Instead of braiding her hair, she had left it to toss beneath the wide band at her brow. It had grown, in a year, and the ends were bleached by the sun of the wilderness. She said, 'Jodi has learned to say, *Gel, gel, gel.* Are you his camel?'

It was the first time she had used the short name. It was the first time she had spoken familiarly. The decision was made.

Nicholas said, 'I am the saddle. A perfect seat, as you know, for any horseman. I think John is the camel. How are you?' His voice, obscured by the wind, sounded as normal as hers.

'Anxious to arrive,' Gelis said. 'Where shall we stay? You have a pretty *cassino*, you once told me, in Edinburgh.'

He had bought it for her, long ago. Long ago, before the day of their wedding. Now he said, 'I still have it. It is yours as soon as my tenants have moved. Until then, there are passable living quarters in the house of the Bank in the Canongate. You remember the Canongate? Like Spangnaerts Street sloped like a chute, with Holyrood Abbey in place of the mattresses. Is your arm painful?'

He didn't know why he said it, except that there was no one within earshot, and he found himself suddenly impatient of pretence.

She read him at once. 'You would rather I said what I thought? Yes, my arm is extremely painful. I assume that is what you wanted to hear. Nicholas?'

'Gelis?' he answered immediately. He saw her flush, and pale with mortification before she went on.

She said, 'About Hesdin. I wondered what would have happened to Jordan, if Mistress Clémence or I had been killed. Did you consider that?'

'Naturally,' he said. 'As much as you ever did. How was Cologne? Did you enjoy being free for four months?'

'I had no choice,' Gelis said. 'And before that, I had to divide my time between Jordan and his father. And you?' She paused and spoke as if against her own will. 'What do you think of him?'

The lapse was surprising. 'Who?' he said.

'Jordan!' She loosened her hands, a little too quickly.

'Do you need to ask?' Nicholas said. 'If I could kill him I would, but I might lose my freedom for rather more than four months. However. My chance will come.'

She was staring at him.

He said, 'You are talking about Jordan de Ribérac? No? These identical names are so confusing.'

She always had courage. She didn't leave. She said hardily, 'What do you think of him then? Or what would you like me to believe?' A long way off, a high voice was talking. She must have heard it as well.

He made a gesture. He said, 'I have found him useful, as you have. It is convenient that he shows his paternity – although not to you. How you must have hated him when he was placed in your arms! And I suppose he will grow up as any foster-child does, paying with embraces for favours. He has pretty ways.'

'Foster-child!'

'Clémence stands for his mother. The world is his mother and father,' Nicholas said. 'He will grow up trusting no one, loving no one. A very good thing.'

'Like you?'

'Like both of us,' Nicholas said.

Then she left, walking away without help, a little unbalanced by the sling. He watched her go.

She was staying. So was Jodi, his son.

This time he had what he wanted; and no one could stop him.

Down below in her cabin, painfully, shakily, stubbornly, Gelis was writing again.

Chapter 9

AS ARRANGED BY a master of illusion, the return of Nicholas de Fleury to Scotland lacked no ceremonial. Scotland welcomed its adopted knight, its brilliant banker Nicholas de Fleury and his superb wife and his thriving small son: a handsome and loving young family.

The grand entrance took place at Leith, as Nicholas wanted. His caravel rowed into harbour, its sails shipped, its sides washed and shining, its banners taut, its trumpets piping and blaring. Lighters fled to and fro at their keel; the pilot boat which had brought them saluted; and, far ahead, glossy in satin and silk, men stood arrayed on the riverside wharf: the magnates of Scotland, come to welcome their Knight of the Unicorn. And among the fringed flags that flapped and crackled above them was the Lion of Scotland. The royal house had sent one of its members.

Three years before, on the verge of her marriage to Nicholas, Gelis had slipped into Scotland to finish her tour as maid of honour to the King's sister Mary, the Countess of Arran. She had made some friends, but not many, for she knew what she was going to do. And now everyone knew. This arrival, arranged with such flamboyance, might turn out to be as uncomfortable for Nicholas de Fleury as it was for herself. No honest woman, about to be promised to a man she respected, would have taken Simon de St Pol as a lover.

The priest knew it, and le Grant: both looked sober. The senior nurse, too, looked sedate, although Pasque was hopping on her elderly feet with excitement. Crackbene, in expert control of the landfall, gave an impression of suppressed satisfaction. Oddly, Nicholas conveyed the same sense. In immaculate black and white, with the chain of the Unicorn across the width of his shoulders, he was scanning the river-bank as he had scanned the shore of the estuary. His gaze, far from apprehensive, was proprietorial.

Then they were over the bar, and in due course the ship's boat was

lowered to take them to the wharf. Gelis had taken her seat with the
child when Nicholas, smiling, bent and scooped up the boy, saying,
'Come, Courtibaut, there is a better view over here.' The child put its
arms round his neck.

'It is natural,' said Mistress Clémence at her side. 'Fathers are
proud. You have left your arm unbound?'

'It is much better,' Gelis said; and then wished she had answered
her differently, for the nurse had meant well. Gelis had abandoned
her sling because she was Gelis van Borselen, kin to the princes of
Scotland and Burgundy, and soliciting pity from no one.

The boat touched the jetty timbers and Nicholas held it steady, the
child on his shoulder, while the rope was secured. He let Crackbene
guide his wife up the steps. His page followed. The child smiled at
her as she passed and so did her husband: two liberal smiles, one of
them genuine; two pairs of grey eyes, one of them freely affectionate.

Nicholas said, 'What a pity you don't have a hennin.' She didn't
know what he meant. It was a private joke, the kind he made for
himself, and sometimes against himself, and sometimes very much
against her. She made no reply but, reaching the top of the steps,
waited for him, the page at her side.

The wharf had been recently paved. She saw a line of new sheds
and a crane. At the end, a gate had been opened and a great many
people seemed to be standing there. Behind them, she had an impression of riding horses and liveried servants. A man, separating from
the crowd, was making his way without haste towards them.

Nicholas, arriving noiselessly, set the child on its feet, retaining the
grasp of one of its hands and directing the other to Gelis. 'Smile,' he
said. 'Unless you really dislike him.'

She had thought it would be Govaerts his factor. Instead, she saw
the noble features and soldierly bearing of Jamie Liddell, a man she
knew well from Bruges. Sir James Liddell of Halkerston, steward to
the King's brother Alexander, Duke of Albany. Which meant . . .

She looked at Nicholas, but he was already exchanging greetings;
indicating her, indicating the child. Liddell, smiling, bowed to her
and went on talking to Nicholas. 'You are none the worse of the
journey? There is a perfect army ridden here to give you a welcome,
my lord Duke has not the temerity to deny them. Speak to them
quickly if you can. He owes me money.'

'Where . . .?' said Nicholas. As they looked, the crowd shifted,
revealing the sparkle of armour and behind it a group of horses
harnessed in velvet. The flag which hung over the group was the
royal standard.

Liddell said, 'He'll probably take you to the Wark. Your lady can go straight into town with the boy. But, of course, meet your friends on the way. You see how pleased we are to have you returned.' He smiled and walked past, she heard him greeting Crackbene, and being introduced to the priest and le Grant. She found Nicholas was already walking across to the welcome party by the gate, the child trotting with him. She recovered its hand, moving now with conscious grace, as she had been trained. As Nicholas, too, had been trained. She perceived, belatedly, the handsome picture they all three were presenting: the tall young man, the elegant girl, the beautiful child. She had, for a moment, the impulse to tear herself away, to scream at him, to ruin it. She tried to open her hand, but Jordan had gripped it too tightly. Then she came to herself.

On the surface, it was no trouble at all to exchange simple courtesies with well-dressed people of different stations, some strangers, some formal acquaintances, some known to her by reputation. They were all men. That was natural. The head of a bank, bearing the goodwill of Burgundy, would be met by his equivalent in authority: by city councillors and merchants; by high officials of the church which was his landlord; by the officers from a few lordly households. She saw some lawyers in a group and, surprisingly, Archibald Whitelaw, the King's Secretary, in person. She walked beside Nicholas, linked to him by his child, and was exposed to no hint of embarrassment. Behaving impeccably, she watched how Nicholas greeted each man, and memorised it.

She was taken unawares twice. Once, when her hand was touched, then taken by a young man of much her own age whom she saw to be Adorne's nephew Sersanders. Whatever formalities he was uttering, they could not wholly conceal his unease. He had heard the rumours, and did not know what to think. She spoke to him serenely, and moved on without haste.

The next time she was surprised by a clear-eyed man who, having welcomed her diffidently, immediately squatted and held something out to the child. Jordan released both hands and received it, then burst into rapturous squeals. As she leaned to see what it was, the man exchanged smiles with Nicholas, who suddenly laughed. Then Nicholas himself was engulfed by the last of those waiting, and Gelis drew the child to her side as she watched.

Do you sing? Like a lark? One of the men now greeting Nicholas was Will Roger, the royal musician. Whistle Willie, the girl Katelijne had called him. As Gelis recognised him, he released her husband and whirled, his eyes moving from her to the child.

He took her hand. 'Unless this is painful? I trust you are better? You are a brave woman, to throw in your lot with this idiot. And now you have permitted him to set foot in Scotland, an act of charity for which other countries will vote you a pension. And this is Lancelot du Lac, I presume? And what is that?'

He was crouching, like the other, in front of the child. The object in the child's hand was a whistle.

She cleared her throat. 'His name is Jodi,' she said.

The musician looked up. 'Is it? I thought it was Jordan. Jodi, blow.'

He blew. He knew how to blow. He had learned, on the little whistle Nicholas had thrown into the water in Venice. He made it cheep, his cheeks inflated, and stopped.

Nicholas said conversationally, 'This is a man called Whistle Willie. Will you let Whistle Willie blow for you? He will give it back. You will also get leprosy.'

The child looked up, at first puzzled; and then reassured by the ordinariness of his father's expression. The musician took up the whistle and, still kneeling, set it to his lips. Gelis stood, watching.

'One must be musical, which I am not, to appreciate it,' said a voice. 'But I am told the man is a master performer. May I make myself known? My name is Martin, of the Vatachino company. I came as a courtesy to your husband and to make the lords happy: they think it will benefit prices if they see two financiers vying for trade. I trust your arm does well now?'

She turned. The speaker smiled. Beneath the triangle of his hat was a short, coarse pelmet of hair, orange as carrots. His eyes, round and pale, were fixed on her. The notes of the whistle yelped and swooped and chortled: Jodi was crowing. She knew that Nicholas, who had not turned, had heard.

She said, 'It is well, thank you. And here is my husband.'

Nicholas rose. 'We know each other,' he said. 'I pushed him downstairs as well. I was hoping to see David, your colleague.'

'Overseas, to his regret,' Martin said. 'But all that he told me of the good looks of your wife is quite true. And now you are a family man, with responsibilities. You must tell me if we push you too hard. It would never do if you, too, had a fall.'

That was all. He dropped behind, smiling, and they moved on. There was no one left to see now but Jamie Liddell, waiting alone. Nicholas said, 'I am sorry. It took longer than I expected. The Duke will have left.'

'He waited,' said Liddell. 'Come across. You may wish he hadn't.'

Of course, she had been presented to Alexander of Albany before. She had been in the entourage of his sister, and remembered him when he was a child, living with her uncle in Bruges. She was familiar with the Stewart colouring: the pale freckled skin, the auburn hair; the lack of height; the uncertain temper that went with the pride. He greeted her with the correct words, but it was hard to tell what he recalled, and what he owed to Liddell's reminding. She curtseyed to the required depth, her back straight, her neck bent, and then rose. The child, released, looked up at his father who said, 'Mon bouton, this is a prince. You must bow.'

Mistress Clémence had taught him. Someone had required Mistress Clémence to teach him. The child dipped his head and lifted it, his shining gaze bestowed between the Duke and his father. The Duke smiled cursorily, his head turned already to Nicholas. 'You traitor, you've taken the turban. Or whose money did you prefer to ours? England? Burgundy? Anjou? Cyprus?' His eyes were very bright.

'Berne, my lord,' Nicholas said. 'I thought of joining the Switzers. They live on draughty mountain-tops too, and don't train their hawks properly, and drink too much ale, and never pay their debts on time. But they got tired of me.'

'Or you of them?' said the boy. Despite the damask, the jewels, and the marriage imposed on him by the state, he was only seventeen. He had spent half his childhood in Bruges, and was not interested in Gelis van Borselen or her son. He said, still to Nicholas, 'What have you brought?'

'All I promised,' said Nicholas. 'Let them unload it and fetch it to you. We'll need draught oxen.'

The lad's throat was faintly freckled and long, the jaw-blade as sharp as a spear. He said, 'We can stay here while it is freighted ashore. Lamb's house, or the Wark. Did you bring them? The engineers?'

'They are here,' Nicholas said. 'Le Grant and Moriz of Augsberg. Do you really want to wait? It's heavy stuff, and takes a long time to move.'

The Duke stared at him. 'We have said so,' he said. 'No doubt the lady de Fleury will wish to proceed into town. The luggage can follow.'

'If there are enough carts,' Nicholas said. 'When Duke Charles was aged one, so they say, his toys and dresses filled two travel-wagons. The household de Fleury does not stint itself either.'

'You do not surprise me,' said the Duke. He had begun to stroll back to the shore as he spoke. Nicholas turned and walked with him. Their voices floated back to where Gelis stood in silence. She heard Albany say, 'The water is warm.' He added, 'I can of course swim.'

'I should hope so,' said the voice of her husband. He spoke without prefixes or titles. 'Who taught you? If it was Whistle Willie, you'll drown. They ululate from mountain to mountain in the Tyrol. Ululate, with two l's. And they whistle in the Canaries. I'll show you. You'll hate it.'

'He made a drum for you,' said the boy. 'And who taught you, my good sir? Is this how you address your ducal master in Burgundy?'

'No, my lord,' Nicholas said. His voice, even from the middle distance, held mild surprise, and some flatness.

She heard the Prince laugh, and saw him reach up and grip the sleeve nearest his arm like a bridle. 'It's, "No, Sandy,"' Albany said; and walked on like a king with Bellepheron tamed at his shoulder. His retinue followed, including John le Grant and the priest; leaving her standing behind with the child.

Sir James Liddell had waited. He spoke to her, smiling. 'Forgive them. My lord Duke holds your husband in great fondness. I am sure they will follow tomorrow.'

She answered gracefully. Mistress Clémence was approaching, with Pasque, and the man who had given Jordan the whistle, whose name was Archie of Berecrofts. She could see now that there was a small cavalcade waiting on shore: horses and mules, and men in the Bank's livery. She could see even that Nicholas, detaining the Duke, had turned aside to speak to them for a moment. Then they went on. She looked down at a sound and saw that Jordan was silently weeping.

Mistress Clémence picked him up. 'Now wouldn't the Duke of Burgundy have been proud of Jordan de Fleury this day! I never saw a boy bow better. And where is that whistle?' She dried his cheeks with two dabs.

He put his thumb in his mouth.

'Pasque has it,' said Mistress Clémence. 'And there is Pasque with the horses. Come! Let us hurry to Pasque!'

Gelis followed. The arrival she had dreaded was over, and she had been received, with her husband. Received because Nicholas had coolly introduced them all three as a family: father, mother and child. Received because the contentious name of her child was already known, and patently tolerated by its father. Received because news of her accident had already been broadcast, inviting sympathy or satisfaction, and demonstrating impartially that whatever had passed was either atoned for or forgiven. None of it was for her sake. This small, portable Arcadia had been engineered solely for Jordan de Fleury. Bouton, he had called him.

Her arrival was over, and none of the traps she had expected had opened for her except one – and that had dealt a blow to her self-esteem, not her arm. The little delicate girl, Adorne's niece, had talked to her once about the doings of Nicholas in Scotland. Gelis

had discounted what Kathi had said because it smacked too much of
the legend of Claes, the mischievous, foolhardy apprentice of Bruges,
and Nicholas had been far from that, since his wedding. His months
in Scotland in reality had been ugly with incident: Simon's sister had
died; Simon himself had nearly lost his life to Nicholas, and so had
Adorne. Why else had Godscalc, dying, forbidden Nicholas to return
for two years?

So Gelis had come back to Scotland, confident that for Nicholas,
too, this would not be a cloudless return. She knew Scotland by now.
No country could afford to spurn the foreigner come to engage in
banking or fighting or trade to their mutual benefit, but such occasional visitors were treated with caution. It had been her experience.
It had been the experience, too, of Anselm Adorne, of Louis de
Gruuthuse, of those van Borselen lords who had come to negotiate, to
serve, to impress. Provided their conduct conformed, a courteous
forbearance would not be denied them.

But of course Nicholas had not conformed, as Kathi had once
attempted to warn her. Actor that he was, unpredictable as he was,
foreigner as he was, Nicholas had come to this same people, and left
love behind.

Sensibly, Katelijne Sersanders applied for no special leave to travel to
Leith to witness the riveting arrival of Nicholas de Fleury and Gelis
his lady. She did however pounce on her brother next day when,
fulfilling a promise, he brought the news to the priory of
Haddington.

There was no prospect, of course, that she would see him alone; or
not until he had run the gamut of the senior nuns and the more
powerful of the distinguished residents, among whom would certainly
be the King's sister her mistress. All of them already knew all the
best rumours about M. de Fleury and his family, and Kathi only
hoped that Anselm realised what was expected of him. At times she
felt that he was the person who was seventeen and she the middle-
aged woman ten years older. She noted he was wearing one of his
very best hats, a bad sign.

'So?' said Kathi. They weren't even inside the priory; his audience
had all flowed into the yard the moment he appeared at the gatehouse
and dismounted. She herself had come straight from the schoolroom.

'So?' repeated her brother in a voice that went with his hat. 'How
impressive, this hunger for news. What shall I tell you about first?
The vital English conference just summoned for Alnwick? The dis-
tressing dispute over Coldingham Priory? The monarch's generous
offer to mediate between France and Burgundy?' He reeked of

contempt. 'Or would it interest you more to know that God's
darling, King David sailed into Leith yesterday, or perhaps it was
only my lord Nicholas de Fleury and his wife and his son? One could
hardly tell, such was the splendour.'

'Was he wearing big jewels? Sandy says his son is a bastard. Sandy
was going to be there,' said the King's sister Margaret, hopping up
on one foot. 'I wanted to go. I can swim.'

Optimism ran in the Stewart family. Kathi gazed at her eleven-
year-old mistress, thereby avoiding her brother's eye. Anselm said,
'The Duke of Albany was there, my lady. He and M. de Fleury spent
the night at the Wark but didn't swim, so far as I know.'

'Perhaps the bastard can swim,' said the Princess Margaret.

'I think,' said Anselm Sersanders, 'that my lord your brother
found he had made a mistake. From his looks, the boy is certainly the
son of M. de Fleury. But I am sure he cannot swim. Should we pass
indoors, ladies?'

They began to walk. Kathi captured her mistress, allowing her
brother to receive the full attention of the two Sinclair cousins. 'So
where is the lady Gelis?' asked Betha, the one who didn't write
poetry. The other kept quiet.

'She and the child have gone to the Canongate house. The two
engineers stayed with M. de Fleury to see the cargo unloaded.'

'But you spoke to them?' Betha said. 'You managed to ask about
the Countess's baby? And of course the lady your aunt, although she
has much longer to wait.'

She stopped, with Phemie beside her, and Kathi stopped also. You
never knew, with Anselm. He would never have put such a question
to M. de Fleury, but he was fond of their aunt, as she was. And he
had made the enquiry of somebody, for he answered at once. 'The
Princess was well when they left, and the child expected by the end of
this month. My uncle hopes to come to Scotland soon after.'

'With the Princess and her husband?' It was the other nun, who
taught Margaret.

Anselm said, 'Their plans are not known.'

'And Aunt Margriet?' Kathi said.

'She could be in better health but is cheerful, it is said. A courier
from Bruges came to the ship just before they left. One of the child's
nurses told me.'

'He has nurses?' said the other Sinclair, called Phemie.

'Apparently. They have been with the child all along. What more
can I tell you?' said Anselm.

When she got him to her chamber at last, he was flushed and cross.
'Women!'

Certainly, the youngest nun had giggled too much. Kathi said, 'It isn't all prurience. If he stays, M. de Fleury is going to change things for this country, and also for Uncle Adorne when he comes. And it looks to me as if he is planning to stay.'

'Because he has patched up his marriage?' He sat down, causing some strips of vellum to hop on her desk. He said irritably, 'What are you doing now?'

She had been helping the bursar with last month's accounts and was almost ready to sew them. Lying beside them was the alphabet-board from the school room. She picked it up by the handle and gazed at it as in a mirror with the aim of picking out simple words. 'Because he wants it to look as if he's patched up his marriage. Maybe he has.'

'Well, you know what happened,' her brother said. 'She allowed Simon the ultimate privilege, and Nicholas paid her back in her own coin. Stole the child, hid it, and refused to produce it until Gelis promised to resume the marriage, adding in a bit of physical punishment to help her remember, so it seems. If that is patching up a marriage, then it is patched.'

She said, 'Do you believe that? Of M. de Fleury?'

'The Duke of Albany believes it,' he said. 'Or at least, it doesn't disturb him. But then, he's seventeen himself, with three sons already, one of them a bastard.'

Kathi sighed. 'You know Sandy likes M. de Fleury. It doesn't automatically mean the end of the Adornes.'

Her brother gazed at her. 'Why do you use the first name of a Duke, and the second name of an illegitimate artisan?' He got up and taking the board from her looked at it with astonishment.

She said, 'Because one of them has given me leave, and the other hasn't. Tilde calls him Cousin Nicholas and he detests it. You liked him well enough when you fell off your horse.'

'That was two years ago,' her brother said shortly. He laid down the board and started to walk up and down. After a moment he added, 'As a matter of fact, I hardly blame him. She should never have done what she did.'

'But you're wary of him again. You think, don't you, that Uncle Adorne is going to bring the Boyd family with him to Scotland, and that the King will have Thomas Boyd put to death, and deprive Uncle Adorne of his lands and title and send him home, if not worse; for by that time Nicholas de Fleury will be the King's Burgundian favourite?'

Her brother stopped walking. He said, 'If you can see that, why keep taking his side?'

There was no point in being exasperated because Anselm was fond of his uncle. Kathi said, 'It's a game. Think of it as a game. He'll try to best you. He'll play against anybody, even his own wife. So make your move first. Write to Uncle Adorne. Tell him not on any account to bring the Earl and Countess of Arran to Scotland. Tell him not to bring Jan. If I thought he would do it, I should tell him not to bother coming himself. Or not until this business of the Boyds has worked itself out.'

'Are you crazy?' said her brother. 'You've just pointed out that one man can hardly bring about the end of the Adornes. Anyway, the Vatachino are here. Martin, the red-headed agent. He'll take care of Nicholas.'

'Well, fine,' Kathi said. 'Let him take care of Nicholas first, and then Uncle Adorne can decide whether it's worth his while coming or not.'

'You said Nicholas,' said Anselm, diverted.

She permitted herself a howl of frustration which split into three unintentionally at the end. 'So help me God, but I did. I shall take my parrot and enter an enclosed order. The Patriarch of Antioch advised it.'

'He was talking to the parrot,' her brother said. After a moment he added, in a different voice, 'Kathi? Nicholas owes you a favour. Tell him to go home.'

'Tell him to go home,' repeated Katelijne. She gazed at him. 'Do you know what he brought in on that ship?'

'Of course he's trading,' said Anselm. 'Of course he won't want to land himself with a loss. But there are rich pickings in Burgundy, surely.' He paused. 'Do you know?'

Kathi picked up and unfolded a paper. It was not part of the bursar's accounts. She read aloud. 'Four culverin. Twenty handguns. One great cannon. Five baths with tables and canopies; a mechanical clock, and a bell.'

'Tables and canopies! What!' said her brother.

'Plus fifty boxes of Secrets, packed in straw along with Heaven and Hell, fourteen haloes, twelve suns, nine choirs of angels, pulleys for Judas, harness for the Ascension, two vats of thunder and the Red Sea in a bundle of sheepskins. Also a barrel of souls.'

She held out the paper. 'The bill of lading. And that's just the first page of it.'

He took it. 'How did you get it?'

'Poisoned bird seed,' said Kathi obscurely. She clarified. 'The caravel put into Berwick, and word got out to Coldingham. It's not the whole list.'

'It's enough,' said her brother, looking blank. 'A clock?'

'And a rather nice spinet, Ada says.'

'Ada?'

'She's here on a visit from Coldingham. She works for the nuns. So M. de Fleury isn't going home,' Kathi said. 'And I'm not going to spy for you or for him. If I were you, I'd stick by him and see what happens. Can you bang on a drum?'

He looked impatient. 'Anyone can bang on a drum.' Then, evidently reading her face he said, 'What good would that do? I don't want to be rolling drunk in the Castle with Willie Roger.'

'It was only an idea,' she said. She wished he understood what a glorious privilege it was to be masculine, and able to bang on a drum, and be invited to join in the lunatic making of music that took place in Will Roger's room in the Castle. And the talk, the gossip, the camaraderie that was the portion of everyone who was allowed to go there.

She thought of it again when her brother had finally gone and she sat alone, making tentative noises that split into three, and thinking of Gelis van Borselen seated somewhere like this, but with a broken arm contrived by her husband, and in the full cognisance of the small, clever scheme in which she had been compelled to take part. And perhaps learning as well about that tumultuous room in the Castle of Edinburgh, and aching also to be male, and free, and part of that joyous, private, vital assembly, the key to so much.

If Gelis had music. If, like Anselm, she had not, the handicap was truly unfair. Katelijne Sersanders stared into space, filled with compassion and exasperation combined, and then laughed at her own naïveté and jumped up. For of course, unlike the Sersanders family, Gelis had no need of music. She knew what she had.

Part II

Autumn, 1471

JOYOUS ENTRY AND FARCE

Chapter 10

IN LATER TIMES, men were to say that spring came in August that year, along with Nicholas de Fleury.

It sounded wistful. It was not really true. No land such as this, with its powerful neighbours, its loosely knit far-flung communities, its small towns battling towards civic development could afford to be seduced into lunacy: Scotland was not Rome or Milan. The truth was a mixture, as it usually is.

On the one hand, the chameleon M. de Fleury might initiate the younger members of the Court into the game of Florentine football: a public disaster. On the other, he might provide useful advice to those travelling to England that autumn, to treat on matters left in contention through the Lancastrian wars. Matters such as piracy, and the family Boyd, and Coldingham Priory on the Scots side of Berwick, historically a dependant of the cathedral priory of Durham until liberated (to the delight of King James) by the family Hume. The Humes, the monks, the King were all aware that the revenues of Coldingham Priory were rich. So was the Pope. For four years, nothing decisive had happened. Resolution needed a miracle.

It was M. de Fleury who pointed out that, this time, the delegates might expect some concessions. A reconciliation between France and Burgundy, brought together by Scotland, was the last thing that King Edward wanted. They did obtain some concessions at Alnwick, and the miracle occurred. When the belated news of Pope Paul's death closed the meeting, the returning Scots sped to consult the Burgundian, a man who had spent part of last winter in his own accommodating bureau in Rome. The value of his past loans and his present counsel almost paid for the cost of rebuilding the site of the football match.

Equally, the news of the election of Sixtus took precedence over the plans for the Mystery Play the King had demanded for Christmas. The King and his Council, which had been progressing rather well in the direction of independent ecclesiastical appointments, retired to replan the future, and Will Roger took Nicholas off to his room in the Castle to rehearse.

While Nicholas sang, Roger picked up his cittern and composed (in a different key) an extempore requiem for Pope Paul in the futile hope of pushing the singer off pitch. He talked as he played. 'Poor Bishop Patrick, he'll never trust melons again. He was relying on Paul to forgive him all his annates and those who annated against him. Look at the music, you fool. We're troping. You've missed out the tropes.'

'I saw your bloody tropes,' Nicholas said. 'And they stink; you couldn't sell them to Judas. Poor Bishop Patrick? What about poor Jan Adorne's promised post, gone for a melon? The Baron Cortachy will weep into his money bags. And before you try to cover it up, I know you got some of the Boyd land. I'm going to win it off you at cards. I'm tired of this. Where's the drum?'

They wrangled, and the room filled up as usual with people and wine fumes and music. Those present had found out, as Roger had, that Nicholas bore no grudges towards friends who had done rather well while he was away. He had come back the same casual, competent man he had been, and bringing his voice. His precious, beautiful voice.

Much later on, when he had drunk enough and laughed enough, Roger sat down beside the voice's owner and said, 'Nicol? You'll get the King to see he can't go ahead with this Passion thing? It takes ten months to set up something that big, and it can't be done on the cheap.'

'I brought a lot of stuff with me,' Nicholas shouted. He was rousing his new drum into a frenzy, the way he used to do with the old, and everyone else was yelling at him to stop.

He stopped. Roger moderated his answering shout in a hurry. 'Even so. It would be crazy.'

'Don't you want to do all the music?' Nicholas said. 'The Dufay of the North? I don't know about crazy. Getting the King to tamper with Coldingham Priory is crazy.'

'We need the revenues for the Chapel Royal,' Roger said, alerted suddenly. 'Bugger your Passion. I want James's money for a proper choir and a set of proper musicians.'

'Contradiction in terms,' Nicholas said. 'Say I get both, what's it worth? Say I get your Chapel Royal and my impossible Passion?'

Roger stared at him. 'My bloody tropes,' he said. 'I'd give you my bloody tropes for the chance of both. Or another drum. But you won't. It'd be ruinous.'

'It's a wager,' Nicholas said.

Later, when the Burgundian had gone off at dawn with the others, entwined and indistinctly chanting downhill, Roger realised, thinking it over, that Nicholas hadn't said what he'd pay if he lost.

After two months of it, Gelis had become used to Nicholas returning home late, sometimes drunk, sometimes sober, sometimes in between. It was not to say he was wholly absent. He used the Canongate mansion a great deal, as a base for his work and his meetings. She became accustomed to finding one or other of the resident officers installed at her table: the correct figure of Govaerts the manager, or John le Grant arguing percussively about his multifarious projects, or Father Moriz making known his requirements or the duties of Nicholas, which were usually the same thing. Occasionally a battered man in a black apron appeared and talked German in a hoarse voice with Father Moriz. He was a goldsmith from the Tyrol called Wilhelm.

The men who lived elsewhere, like Crackbene, seldom came to her part of the Casa to eat. There were many of them, she knew; and other projects which were taking shape on the business side of the edifice, where the bureau and counting-house were, and the clerks' sleeping rooms, and the office of the padrone her husband. It had a separate entrance.

She did not feel unwelcome. The house was well built and meticulously furnished to a high level of comfort; Govaerts, a steward by training, had established an excellent routine and collected a good, willing staff. Her own chambers, and those of the child and his nurses, were fresh and pleasant, and she learned early to value the amiable goodwill of the Berecrofts family, on whose tenement holding their house had been built. Archie in particular had struck up a friendship with Jordan since the first day of the whistle, and often crossed the wall from his house to her own to bring something or suggest something that might divert the child. In return, she let his own son Robin spend as much time as he wished in the nursery. The boy was fourteen and lonely, she judged. Jordan liked him and, more to the point, so did Mistress Clémence.

She saw Nicholas from time to time. His chamber, adjoining her own, contained a bed and a desk and a number of presses for books and nothing else of great interest, although all of it was of good quality. Entering the house the day after their arrival in Leith, he had come to knock on her door and ask after her comfort. He had already called to see Jordan; she had heard their voices together. Now, coming in, he must have read her expression. He said, 'I admit everything, but I didn't bring him a present. Will this suit you?'

She said, 'I see your room is next door.'

He sat down on her fine cushioned settle. He smelled of horse and looked unslept, but quite tranquil. 'That doesn't please you? I have a bed in my office, but I can't pursue my conjugal duties from there. That's all really that still interests the populace. Once they are reassured, I shall remove myself and my books to my quarters. You should see your face.'

'I imagine it expresses my feelings,' said Gelis.

'I suspect I knew them already,' said her husband. 'Your chastity will remain strictly inviolate. I shall come to see Jodi, and you and I shall make some ceremonial visits. Inquisitive ladies will send their chamberlains to you, and I expect you will bring yourself to visit them. You have horses and servants and money, your own and mine, and must use it all as you please and go where you wish – so long, of course, as you are discreet. Alonse will tell you what I am doing and when we have any mutual engagements. If you want anything, tell him, or Govaerts, or me.'

He rose without haste, preparing to leave. She said, 'As you have devised, so it shall be done.'

'I should hope so,' he said. The door closed. She felt like an overwound wheel, as after all their meetings alone. There had only been a handful since Hesdin and all had been equally brief, tailored to the span of their mutual tolerance. The span would lengthen, no doubt, as their nerves calmed, or their indifference strengthened. At present the ark of their marriage was secured by a line made of hyphens.

She lay in bed listening for many nights after that, learning how often he came home and when, and in what condition. She won, in time, the reticent acceptance of Govaerts, but failed with Alonse.

In October, when it was known that, despite everything, Anselm Adorne was coming to Scotland, Katelijne Sersanders paid her first visit to the Ca' Niccolò in the Canongate since its owner's return. She carried a cage with a parrot.

Being inquisitive but not having a chamberlain, she had already examined both the child and its mother from a distance. She approved of both, but thought that M. de Fleury's rearranged marriage would have a better chance of success if the person who purloined his son did not feature in its earlier stages.

Before coming at all, she had consulted four different people at Haddington. Her brother Anselm held that Gelis the wife was a bitch, but that she regarded Kathi as no more than an officious young meddler, which is what she had been. Her friend the equable Mistress

Phemie thought that it was time for a friendly, impersonal call so long as Kathi didn't make too much of the child. In this Kathi concurred. Will Roger, the royal musician, emerged from working on the high notes of the lady Margaret and the chest notes (deeply rewarding) of the servant nurse Ada to express doubts.

'I thought they were reconciled,' said Kathi, puzzled. She was learning to knit. 'Just because she isn't sharing his business . . .'

'More than his business,' Roger said. 'Who the hell taught you that?'

'Bishop Tulloch's housekeeper,' Kathi said, sticking her needle back into her waist and beginning to flicker her fingers again. 'What do you mean? I heard they were together.' The son of Archie of Berecrofts came to Haddington for his lessons.

'Well, tell me what you find out,' said Will Roger sarcastically. 'But pick a time when he's sober.'

She laid down her needles. 'Ah.'

'It may just mean he's happy,' said Roger. 'In fact, he *is* happy. Don't go and spoil it.'

The last person she consulted was her physician. Dr Andreas said, 'Of course you must go. But remember. You are bad for each other. No escapades.'

She had smiled. 'I'm not fourteen any more, Dr Andreas.'

And he had gazed at her with the intentness he sometimes applied to his charts before saying, 'Katelijne, there is a fourteen-year-old in the oldest of us; in men like M. de Fleury as well. Let it sleep.'

Walking up the turnpike stairs and from room to room of the Ca' Niccolò, Katelijne saw immediately that nothing had changed – something unremarkable when a man moved into a woman's home, but unusual when the other way round. The manservant called Alonse walked before her, courteously bearing the cage. The parrot under its cover was silent, although it had once belonged here, and occasionally still repeated a phrase of M. de Fleury's, as well as the wrangling voices of the family Boyd. When the manservant halted, it was not to introduce either her host or her hostess, but because he faced a white-coiffed, white-aproned woman who could only be the child's nurse.

The woman said, 'I am Clémence de Coulanges, demoiselle. I shall see to her, Alonse. Give me the parrot.'

'You know about it?' said Kathi, pleased. The woman, thin as a scaffold, had the same look as Phemie Dunbar: a tutelary look. It could be good, or it could be bad. If she had survived eight months with M. de Fleury, it was probably good. Kathi added, 'Perhaps you would give it to Jordan? I'm really here to see his mother and father.'

'M. de Fleury is away,' said Mistress Clémence. 'He thought you might bring the bird. Madame is here. I have to take you to her in the orchard.'

A door opened behind her. 'But since you are here,' the nurse continued calmly, 'I am sure that Master Jordan would like to be presented. Jordan, this is the demoiselle Katelijne Sersanders.'

'Demoiselle Kathi,' said Katelijne. The child came forward, instantly friendly. Since Venice, his resemblance to his father had grown. She knew he would not remember her. He smiled, nevertheless, with both dimples, although his eyes were already fixed on the cage.

'Bonjour, demoiselle Kathi,' he said. 'Qu'est-ce que c'est?'

'It belongs to your father,' said Kathi. 'I hope he will let you have it.'

'Perhaps,' said Mistress Clémence. 'We shall place it here, Jordan, and you and I will show the demoiselle Kathi how to reach madame your maman in the garden.'

'Thank you,' said Kathi, turning to follow. The child, parting from the cage with reluctance, ran ahead. She added, 'He looks well.'

'The climate suits him,' said the nurse. 'Children are resilient creatures, so long as they receive sensible treatment. He has made a great friend of the boy Robin.'

Kathi grinned. 'In that case,' she said, 'there is nothing you don't know about me. The parrot swears.'

'In Greek and Spanish, I am told,' said the nurse. 'As yet, Master Bouton is not conversant with these tongues.'

'Bouton?' said Katelijne.

'His father's name for him. Mademoiselle?'

The nurse had stopped walking. 'Yes?' said Kathi.

'Forgive me, but as the lady Margaret's attendant, you must visit the Castle at times?'

'The King is fond of his sister,' said Kathi slowly.

The woman lowered her gaze. 'And you, like M. de Fleury, speak the tongue of the Queen, and so must be especially welcome at Court.'

'I have met the Queen once or twice,' Kathi said. 'I expect M. de Fleury knows her much better.'

'He is at the Castle now,' said the nurse. 'The King likes to bring them together. The King has asked to see Master Jordan tomorrow. I am to take him to their chambers.'

'And the lady Gelis?' said Kathi.

'Only the child. As mademoiselle perhaps knows, the Queen . . . is young.'

She said nothing more. Kathi looked at her. She said, 'You will be with Jordan?'

The woman said, 'Perhaps not all the time.'

'I see,' Kathi said. 'When do you go?'

'In the evening,' said the nurse. 'After supper. It is late, for a child.'

'We are often there in the evening,' Kathi said. 'My mistress will snatch any excuse to attend a feast, or a dance. If we happened to be there, I might see you.'

'It would be an honour,' said Clémence de Coulanges. 'If there is any change, the lad Robin makes a good courier. You know it is his dream to be a page to M. de Fleury?'

'I should never have guessed it,' said Kathi wryly. She paused, to gather her courage. She said, 'Mistress Clémence. You were at Hesdin. What happened?'

The woman's eyes met hers directly. The woman said, 'You were in Alexandria, I believe, when M. de Fleury was told that his wife might be dead?'

It was put as a question. Perceived as an answer, the implication took away speech. 'Hesdin was an accident,' Kathi observed at length.

'Hesdin was an accident, deeply regretted. Here is Jodi and this is where we must leave you. Beyond the door is the courtyard, and the archway leads direct to the garden.'

'Thank you,' said Katelijne. The nurse inclined her head and retired, the child racing ahead. She had not expected her to smile; in that one discreetly contrived meeting, Clémence de Coulanges had conveyed and gathered all that either of them needed to know. Her mind thronged, Kathi walked down the stepped slope from the mansion.

She had met the adult Gelis van Borselen only twice: the last time on that fraught night in Venice. Since then, so far as was known, Gelis had kept silence about the whole episode. The initial fault, after all, had been hers. And Kathi's part in uniting M. de Fleury with his son had been less, on the whole, than that played by the lawyer Gregorio and Margot now his wife, or by the doctor, Tobias.

She was prepared then for civilised behaviour. She was unprepared for a young woman she hardly recognised as Gelis van Borselen seated under the trees, lightly gowned in the warm autumn air, her fair hair parted over her shoulders. Archie of Berecrofts was sitting beside her.

He scrambled to his feet. 'Kathi! I thought you were bringing the parrot.'

'I did. Robin and Jordan can teach it together. Unless you mind?'
She smiled down at the pretty woman below her.

Gelis van Borselen said, 'Not at all. The parrot seems to have
become an integral part of our lives. Come and sit. I am told Nicholas
expects to be here. We have been talking about this prodigious Play
he is evolving for Christmas. Will your uncle be here in time?
Perhaps he or your cousin will act in it.'

Kathi sat on the rug beside Archie. 'He should be here, but I
don't think he'd take part. Jan isn't coming. He has to get back to
Rome.'

'And the Earl and Countess of Arran?' said the other woman.

'No one knows. But you've heard that the second Boyd baby is
born, a daughter this time?'

'Just as weel,' said Archie cheerfully. He picked up a well-riddled
apple and tossed it. 'A wheen too many knaves round the Scots
throne already. Is Nicholas directing the Play? I thought he'd got
Tom Cochrane over from Beltrees.'

'He has,' Gelis said. 'And another man, his factor in Renfrewshire.
Oliver. Oliver Semple?'

'You haven't met him?' said Kathi. 'But you've been to your castle
at Beltrees? M. de Fleury has taken you?'

'Not yet,' Gelis said. Her eyes, of a very clear blue, held a look of
perpetual amusement. 'Should he? Is it worth seeing?'

'It ought to be,' said Archie. 'No, that would be clyping.'

'Go on,' said Kathi. 'Tell her.'

'It's a fine, ample tower,' said Archie, obeying good-naturedly.
'Theiked with skaillie, and lined with panelled joined work throughout. Nicholas saw to the building, but left Govaerts to manage the
gear. Cochrane put up a scheme, and a neighbour-woman offered to
help him. Bel. Bel of Cuthilgurdy. You know her?'

Bel had been in Africa with Gelis and M. de Fleury. Gelis said,
'Yes, I know her. And so?'

Archie said, 'So Bel and Cochrane got the notion they were outfitting Cafaggiolo. When Govaerts was sent all the bills, he thought the
Bank would have to sell up to pay them. I never heard what Nicholas
said when he found out. But you ought to see it. And the wee fellow
would like it just fine.'

'Go and see it,' Katelijne said. 'If M. de Fleury won't take you, we
shall. Or Master Cochrane. There's a lake, and meadows and hills.
It's a beautiful place.'

'Oh, I know the district,' said Gelis. Beneath her smiling gaze,
Kathi fell temporarily silent. Of course she did. It was close to the
home of Jordan de Ribérac and Simon his son. Kilmirren was at

present unoccupied, but it was not hard to imagine why Nicholas de Fleury had not encouraged his wife to return west.

But that was behind them, or should be. Kathi said, 'Go to Beltrees. Take Jordan. Get M. de Fleury to go.'

'And become a country laird?' Gelis said. 'It would suit the Vatachino, I suppose.'

'Business isn't everything,' Kathi said.

'Tell Nicholas that,' said Archie; and then flushed with embarrassment. 'But of course —'

'But of course, at heart Nicholas is a family man,' Gelis said.

Kathi took her leave presently. M. de Fleury had not succeeded in arriving, if he had ever intended it, and she was not invited to meet the child she had once helped to steal. She thought, looking back as she left, that perhaps Robin's intuition was right, and this softer Gelis, the Gelis of Bruges and their courting days, might truly mean that she and M. de Fleury had mended their marriage.

If not, it meant something else, that she would rather not think about.

Next time, leaving Haddington, Katelijne Sersanders needed no special advice, since the King's youngest sister, the fount of all royal information, was travelling with her. It had not been difficult to arrange an excuse to visit the Castle. Will Roger was adept at deception, and Margaret's only stipulation had been that if she were going to dance, she should not have to talk to her miserable namesake, the Queen. It was going to be Kathi's job to do that, in sign language.

It was a little unfair on the monarch. After two years of marriage, her grace the Queen's grasp of English was reasonably good: she had some phrases off pat. *This is a disgrace* was one of them. *This would never happen in Denmark* was another. Her frame of mind was not due to lack of material comforts, esteem or loving attention; rather to an excess of some of these things. The King needed heirs, and she was childless.

It was not Jamie's fault, as his courtiers would gravely explain, before bursting into suppressed laughter. Jamie had been known to rise from his table, wife in hand, in the middle of dinner; or skip off during a dance; or disappear in the course of a hunt, dragging Margaret. Margaret, wearing her steady smile, always went with him. She never conceived.

His sister, aged eleven, had several theories which she aired again on the journey to Edinburgh. 'She doesn't like what he does. Sandy knows what he does. They used to share the same girls.'

'Then he's probably very good at it,' Kathi said. Their servants, riding about them, could hear perfectly what they were saying.

'But I wager that they would never do it that way in Denmark. Anyway, he broke the church rule.'

'My lady . . .' began Katelijne warningly.

'It doesn't matter. Everyone does, everyone knows. You can't be married and keep off for ever. He started a year ago. He told Sandy.'

'She must have been frightened,' said Kathi.

'I don't know about frightened. She was angry: she gave him great scratches. But of course, she couldn't complain once the time came. Six months. She hasn't conceived in six months. She's fourteen, and childless.'

This wasn't about James and his disappointments. Kathi knew what it was about. She said, 'My lady, your turn will come.'

'When?' Margaret said. 'The King of France has a son, the Duke of Burgundy has a daughter, the King of England has babies, and all of them have to wait until James gets a baby on Margaret, because his baby's marriage has to come before mine. It isn't fair,' Margaret said. 'I want to be married.'

'You will be,' said Kathi. She had already told Phemie what Robin, in his young, calm way had told her. Thank God, this Margaret was too young as yet to conceive. Bleezie Meg, the farm laddies called her. She was a Stewart.

Slightly feverish with laughter, like the courtiers, Kathi visualised her forthcoming unscheduled encounter with Nicholas de Fleury placed side by side with a crisis of dire royal carnality, and wondered if he could handle it. She was happy to think that, on past form, he could. Then she remembered the child.

Although she had accompanied her mistress many times to the Castle since August, Katelijne had always avoided M. de Fleury as she had until now avoided his wife. As with his wife, she had not been above snatching a look at him. Unlike the lady Gelis today, he had always been formally dressed, in cap and doublet or pourpoint or jacket. Apart from that, she could only describe him in negative terms: that the exhaustion of Venice had gone, and the despair and the anguish, if they were there, were invisible. Will Roger had said he was happy. He had his son, and his wife. The whole shabby business might be over at last.

The King's lodgings were in David's Tower and the men were still there, it appeared. To Margaret's disgust, she was expected to join the ladies in the Queen's parlour, where someone was singing and someone else was playing a spinet. Kathi was thankful to see Willie Roger, an expression of martyrdom on his face. He began to cross over to join her, but she was forced to sit between Margaret and the

Queen. There were six or seven of her grace's own attendants already there, most of them pretty young matrons and most of them in varying stages of pregnancy, which was why they had been selected.

As a very active small person herself, Katelijne Sersanders always felt depressed beside Margaret of Denmark, who possessed a pale clear Nordic face with plucked brows, and a pretty pink mouth, and white polished hands, and opulent shoulders half concealed by the round modest neck of her gown. She was given to hennins, perhaps because high veiled cones were less easy to shed than more approachable headgear. They were always bound with massive bands of great jewels, and she always looked as if her head ached. If it did, there were no compensations. According to Meg, the apothecary and Dr Andreas supplied the King with her dates every month.

Meg was going to give trouble. Expecting a grand occasion, she was discovering that there were no guests, no great lords; no one, in fact, but the present company, soon to be joined by the King and his brothers and by M. de Fleury, with whom they had been attending to business. From the subdued levity around her, Kathi judged that the business had been going on for some time, and was liquid in character. She engaged in stilted conversation with the Queen while watching the door. Will Roger went back to the spinet and played as if filling in time.

The Queen, catching something of the surrounding atmosphere, suddenly began to explain the delay. 'All last night they talked business. These are great events. This will be a year the world will remember. You know my lord is to lead a Scottish army to France?'

She was as bad as the other Margaret. 'My lady?' said Kathi. 'Perhaps this is not something to speak of in public.'

'These women have none but base tongues,' the Queen said. 'Messer Nicol is to make my lord a war leader. Like Alexander, King Arthur, Charlemagne.'

'Ghengis Khan. Mehmet the Conqueror,' Kathi said.

'They are not Christian!' said the Queen.

'No, of course not. Your husband will be a great Christian warrior. M. de Fleury is arranging it?'

'M. de Fleury will lead his own army. My lord the King will seize back his loyal Brittany, the land of his fathers!'

'His aunt married the Duke,' Kathi said.

'He will take back Saintonge!'

'Where?' said Kathi.

'He will become Duke of Guelders, his mother's heritage!'

'I thought the Duke of Burgundy had been promised the dukedom of . . . it doesn't matter,' said Kathi. 'You mean he is going away? My lord your husband?'

'Soon!' said the Queen. 'Messer Nicol is arranging it. As soon as they can build us some ships, and the Three Estates can vote us some money.'

'When the apricots come,' Kathi said. She didn't translate it into Danish. She sat furiously sympathising with Gelis, tied to a man who did this. She was so angry that she missed the opening of the door when it came, and only when the music died did she turn her head and catch sight of the glimmer of white in the entrance. Then she saw that Mistress Clémence was being brought in, her hand steering a small boy in skirts.

The Queen jumped up. The Queen said, 'I will bless no more children! Take it away!' Her voice trembling, she had shouted in English. Below her, all the wired, nodding heads turned.

Kathi stood quickly too. She said, 'It is the son of M. de Fleury, madame. He has not come to be blessed. It is M. de Fleury's son, come to join him.' Across the neatly tiled floor, beyond the spinet where Roger had risen, the child stood looking up. He must have been wakened to come: his round face was drained of all colour and his eyes were enormous and black.

The nurse said, 'Madame, we shall wait somewhere else.'

The King had sent for the child. He would not be permitted to leave. Kathi moved, but already Whistle Willie was speaking. 'Or, your grace, he could sit here by his nurse until his father arrives. This is a boy who can play on a whistle. He could play the spinet, I am sure.'

A cooing sound made itself heard. The Queen's ladies were much attached to young children. The nurse waited, her hand on the boy's shoulder. The Queen hesitated, then sat. She said, 'He may stay.'

The Princess Margaret said, 'For all the good it will do, he might as well go back to his cradle. But you were right, Kathi, he's Nicol all over; he can't be another man's after all. Is he going to scream?'

'Maybe,' Kathi said, since it was the answer Meg wanted. She saw the grey-black eyes rest on her and on Roger, then wander; Jordan's expression, of dazed resistance, was fixed. Mistress Clémence knelt down beside him and spoke. The words, which Kathi couldn't quite hear, were in French. The nurse waited; the child nodded; then, guiding him forward, Mistress Clémence settled herself on the chest beside the musician, and set the child on her knee. He leaned his head into her shoulder and Whistle Willie, conductor of souls, had the wisdom to turn his back and ignore him.

The Queen discussed what Master Roger should play and agreed, when Meg suggested it, that it might be pleasant to dance. The little matrons rose, chattering, and took each other's hands, deciding what to do, and how to do it. After a while, the child unburied his head and looked up. Once, the Queen, passing by, touched his cheek and smiled at him. She was the same age as his Robin. He smiled back. Kathi thought of a very bad Greek word the parrot had taught her. Then she began to watch the door again as she danced.

Chapter 11

I T WAS THE scene which Nicholas de Fleury came upon presently
when, opening the door, he stood aside to let the King enter,
along with his brothers Sandy and John and their households.
He received an immediate impression of a great deal of movement
and laughter: it was not a very large room, and it was filled with a
number of young women, dancing. They stopped and, turning, sank
into curtseys; Nicholas scanned them.

The music, which had also stopped, had been provided by Whistle
Willie, of course, who sat looking straight at him. Not far from him,
Kathi – Katelijne Sersanders, whom he should have met yesterday, if
the King had allowed him to leave. Whom he had not met since
Venice, when she had decided to help to free Jordan. Next time, she
might just as easily offer her services to Jordan's mother: Katelijne
Sersanders had very flexible prejudices, or an enlarged sense of fair
play, depending on your viewpoint. Just now, she was glaring. He
supposed he knew the reason. It had nothing to do with a broken
appointment.

And there, of course, superior as ever, was Clémence of Coulanges,
seated on a stool and restraining his son by the arms until the ladies
rose from their salute. Then Jordan broke away and came speeding
towards him. The child's face was red, but not swollen. Nicholas
said, 'What a good son I have. You have kept mademoiselle company
until I came. Have you danced?'

'No,' said the child.

'Well, we shall dance now,' Nicholas said, bending to lift him.

Mistress Clémence said, 'He is perhaps heavier than you
think.'

He smiled, the child in his arms. He said, 'I see my young friend
Katelijne is of the same opinion. I shall be careful, mademoiselle.' He
knew it was apparent that none of them was quite sober. The King
had been persuaded to put on his pourpoint again, but his shirt was

visibly torn from the last bout of horseplay, and the young men of the chamber were worse.

It had come to swords in the end, and he had had to get Liddell to help him calm it down. The euphoria of war, or hopes of war. It might, at least, divert young James from his other obsession. He walked forward. The girls were coy, the men drunk. Using all his masks, all his voices, God help him, he could exhaust them and get Jordan home. And himself.

Truth to tell, it was tiredness he was fighting, rather than anything else. It had been a long thirty-six hours. The worst of it had been at the end, when he had had to explain that his wife was not coming.

Little Bell and Guthrie and Hommyll and even Liddell had been half amused; the King had not. 'We commanded your son, and the lady Gelis your wife.' The royal complexion, less freckled than Sandy's, still ebbed and flowed with his temper. He was nineteen, and had as yet no issue to prove his virility. He said, 'You know why.'

Nicholas said, 'Perhaps my lord has forgotten. My son will be here, but Gelis suffers still from her accident. The break was a bad one.'

'I see,' said the King. 'We thought that she might be sick of a child. Of another child.'

'Alas, no,' Nicholas said. 'Perhaps your own good fortune, when it comes, will restore ours.' He could hear John of Mar murmur, then giggle. He wished, fleetingly, that he had not intervened, years ago, to prevent the young bastard's eye being skewered.

'In three years?' James remarked. 'You have managed one birth in three years? Your case is worse than our own. We told you. Your wife should have come. And now we have this potion from your own doctor, it seems, or his family. It surprises us that you have not tried it, or recommended it to us before.'

'My own doctor?' Nicholas had repeated. He had none at the moment. Andreas looked after the Princesses at Haddington, and Scheves treated the King. Pierre de Nostradamus served King René alone, and King René had been driven to Provence.

The King said, 'Your army's doctor. Tobias. The nephew of the greatest physician of Pavia, who treats our uncle of France for his ills. You told me about him, and I have sent for this fertility potion. It has come, straight from France.'

'*Dr Tobias* has brought it?' Nicholas said. Tobie had left after Venice, vowing never to come near him again.

'No. I did,' said Andro Wodman, coming in. He bowed to the King and his brothers and turned. 'Dr Tobias wasn't involved. We asked for the recipe from his uncle. His grace asked me to make you a copy.'

He held something out, and Nicholas took it. Across the paper smiled the face he had last seen at Angers, at Ham: the broken nose; the thick, heavy hair; the short neck. Andro Wodman, former body-guard to Louis of France; former Archer with Jordan de Ribérac. One of them must have sent him. Louis at least would be impressed by today's news when he heard it. His secret envoy de Fleury had persuaded King James to lead an army in person to France. When the apricots come.

All the same, it was as well that Crackbene had gone, and the moneyers. Nicholas laughed aloud. He said, 'Thank you. I must think who to give it to. And how is the vicomte de Ribérac? I assume that you brought him.'

'I wish I had. No, I came with Monypenny, the other grand lord serving two masters. Like yourself.'

'No, I have three,' Nicholas said. 'Four, if you want to count Burgundy. You have come to join in the swordplay?'

'He has business elsewhere,' said the King. 'And we have to join her grace the Queen for some music.' His face was still clouded, and his vexation flared again in the Queen's room, even as he watched Nicholas with his son. He said, 'The lady van Borselen should have been here. We are displeased. Tell her.' Then he touched the boy and said, 'A fine son. He likes water?'

'I am afraid he cannot swim,' Nicholas said.

'No, no. Warm water. Come. We shall dance. Take a partner. My lady, here is Nicol.'

The boy clung. Kathi Sersanders said, 'He can dance with us both. He could even hold one of us up. Bouton, did you look at the cage?'

'You have met him? Since Venice?' Nicholas said. 'I haven't thanked you for what you did there. You will probably live to regret it.'

'I met him through Mistress Clémence,' said the girl. She was dressed with exceptional neatness, her hair-caul ribboned, her sleeves tight to the knuckle. The few jewels she was permitted were exception-ally fine. She was Adorne's niece. He could see the coloured specks in her eyes, she was so angry. She said, 'I believe I regret it already.'

He said, 'It was unavoidable. Jordan is going home soon.' He had picked, reluctantly, the only language he was sure no one else but themselves could understand.

'Before the warm water?' said the girl. Here, the Arabic sounded ridiculous. She had flushed. 'Before or after you lead an army to France?'

It was unexpected. Considering the implications, he said something impolite under his breath. Now he knew why she was angry. The child said, 'I speak to the parrot.'

The girl's face changed. Nicholas looked down at his son. 'You have heard the parrot say that? Well, only parrots and fathers say that, never Jodi. There is Kathi's hand; there is mine. Now we shall dance.' It closed the conversation with Kathi. He would have to reopen it some time, but certainly not now.

They parted soon enough and presently he was able to restore the boy, heavy-lidded and fractious, to Mistress Clémence. Will Roger said, 'I heard what you told her to do. It won't work.'

'Yes, it will,' Nicholas said. 'We're all sick of your playing. I want some real action.'

'Games?' said Roger. 'Kathi has some good ones. Nicol, be careful with Kathi.'

It surprised him. 'She must be better now,' Nicholas said. 'Anyway, she's sober, and I'm not.'

Once before, when they were all three years younger, he had got the children of the royal family into trouble on Leith sands. Now two of the three present were married, and James had experienced the weight of his position, and carried the authority to match it. It meant that sometimes, they felt the need to break out. It meant that when they did, there was no one to gainsay them.

The crown of the Castle rock, on which the royal lodgings were built, was not large, but many people lived in its towers, and crammed the lower offices that crowded round the hall, the chapel, the arsenal and the barracks, the archery ground and the stables. Ringed by its stout walls, the Castle of Edinburgh stood above the smoke and noise of the town, and its own smoke and noise affected only itself and the angels, which was fortunate.

The party spilled outside after the first few games, and the next barrel of wine had been broached. The men by then were all in their loose shirts and hose: the current wager had to do with a ball, bouncing between them. The Queen trotted among them, not quite screaming like Meg, but with her eyes bright and her face heated. Her brother's friends, you could imagine, played rough games sometimes like this in the snow, on the sands, in the forests. She had begun not to notice when James, between vicious attacks on the ball and his rivals, set his hand at her waist, or pulled her running close beside him.

Nicholas noticed, in between fending off the same vicious attacks, and worse ones from Sandy and John. So did Kathi, sprinting beside him. Neither commented. Nicholas said, 'I still want to thank you for Venice. I have something for you.' A brick sliced through his hair and he ducked. He had lost his cap and her hair, short like Gelis's, had escaped from its caul.

'That was John,' the girl said. 'He doesn't like you. Whatever I did, it was for Gelis and Jordan as well. I don't want anything.'

'Oh,' he said. The ball, flying over their heads, landed on the top of the citadel wall and for a moment seemed lost. Then James was streaking after it whooping, banging into people regardless, followed by his two younger brothers. They started up the nearest flight of wall-steps, three at a time. The ball, rebounding, had trickled safely down to a roof. Nicholas said, 'Then I should have said that the gift is from us all, but two of us don't realise it yet. However. I take the point. I'll give it to Willie, and you can play on it anyway. Why are they all running up there?' The Princess, Meg, was making a purposeful dash at the gun-ramp.

'Because they want to win the wager,' Kathi said. 'I gather we are having a game of Florentine football on the parapet, six a side instead of twenty-seven. I thought it was your idea.'

It had been, earlier in the evening. The curtain wall of Edinburgh Castle was four hundred feet long and twenty-four feet in height, with a sheer drop of another thirty-odd feet on the outside. The top was wide enough to take culverin, or three people running abreast, and the inner side was lined with interesting roof-tops. It made an irresistible playing field for two teams. Two teams, all of them men. He said so.

The girl said, 'If Meg is going, I have to go, don't I? I don't mind. Willie will come. We need three more to make up a side. Can't you go and get them? Or it'll spoil all the fun.'

He suddenly saw that it would. By the time he found Crackbene and brought him back, two other applicants had appeared. One was Robin of Berecrofts, who had apparently escorted Jodi and his nurse from the Canongate. The other was Martin of the Vatachino, stripped like the rest to his unbuttoned shirt. The pelt on his chest was as orange as sheep-dip.

Behind the broker, Kathi was conveying helpless apology. He could see her eyes gleaming. Martin said, 'I offered to give you a hand. I've not a bad head for heights. Otherwise you would have lost your wager, wouldn't you?'

He was grinning. Without losing face, there was no chance of refusing him. Nicholas said, 'Who have the other side got?' Straw fell on to his shoulders and hair: the ball was being retrieved. People were running up and exclaiming: household officers and servants of the Court, clerks and servants of the chapel, soldiers of the garrison. There were three hundred people quartered within the walls of Edinburgh Castle. He saw two trumpeters he knew, gesturing at Willie Roger.

A lot of torches had arrived, illuminating the uneven ground, and the houses that clustered against and under the wall, and the ramp and the two ranges of ladder-like steps fitted between them. Black against the sky, the tall rectangle of the royal palace called David's Tower rose at one end, all its windows now lit, while far at the other end rose the round tower known as the Constable's, guarding the staircase to the inner citadel. But the top of the wall running between was quite dark, except where its crenellations blocked out the stars, and the forms of young men running along it. He could just make out the King, along with Sandy and John, and Meg scrambling and screeching beside them. Three princes of the blood and one princess. Someone would stop them.

Kathi said, 'They've called up Jamie Liddell and someone called Wodman. Who's he?'

'A Scottish Archer,' Nicholas said. 'In the employment of Jordan de Ribérac. He left the Guard after he'd killed a man, says Astorre. I like your skirts up like that. It reminds me of Sinai. The Queen isn't playing?'

'The King wouldn't let her,' Kathi said. 'She's to stand down here and admire him.'

'Or catch him,' said Mick Crackbene mildly. It was wonderful, Nicholas thought, to be about to enjoy oneself surrounded by sour faces like Willie's and Mick's. At least Robin appeared excited and happy while Kathi stood translated in the usual way, with the intense concentration of a pup at a rathole. His rival merchant Martin was smiling. He was probably quite happy, too.

There was no reason not to be. If he climbed quickly, it would be too late to stop it. He climbed quickly.

The high officers of the kingdom were informed and brought out quite fast, but there were not so many of them in the Castle that evening. Of the two whom the King had leaned on from boyhood, only Will Sinclair of Caithness, once Orkney, was using his rooms in the citadel. And of the very few with some hold over de Fleury, none was there but Lord Hamilton, taking wine with the Abbot of Holyrood.

Their lordships knew better than to countermand the whim of a monarch. These aberrations occurred with young men. Long rides and strenuous jousting were supposed to allay them, in between wars. Otherwise one took what precautions one could, and fingered one's rosary.

It was terrifying, all the same. *All* the royal children were there. All, that is, but the Princess Mary, Countess of Arran, at present with her children in Burgundian Bruges. And the King had no heirs.

What could be, was done. Light was brought. The elder statesmen themselves paraded an air of mild exasperation. But covertly, all the same, men scurried with bales from the stables, and mattresses and sacks from the storerooms, and laid them where they might save an inebriated boy, tumbling from the parapet to the steps, or from the parapet to the roof-tops inside, and thence to the ground. Outside, the rock at the foot of the citadel remained unquilted and bare. Nothing could save a boy, or a girl, or a man who was dropped, or was pushed, or who overbalanced over the outer side of the parapet. It was the brave little Fleming, the Baron Cortachy's niece, who leaned over a roof and informed Sinclair which were the goal posts. His daughter Betha was fond of the girl but often said, all the same, that she was crazy.

Once the young people were all on top of the wall, they crowded into the middle and there was a short preamble fixing the rest of the rules: the first team to score two goals, one gathered, would win. They used straws to choose ends, and to see who would cast the ball for a start. The King won, and took the ball in his hands. His hair flickered like fire in the wind. He slammed the ball down at an angle and they all jumped at it and each other.

Kathi had seen the big game they held when M. de Fleury had taught them how to play, and all the damage was done. The rules adapted well enough to small teams. The two front runners on each side – the *corridori* – were the smallest and nimblest: Kathi and Robin, opposing Meg her mistress and Meg's brother Mar. Behind the front line on each side hovered the two *sconciatori*, the spoilers, whose job was to stop the other team's runners: Roger and Crackbene for the non-royals; Liddell and Wodman for James. And at the back of each team were the hitters, who were allowed to use hands: M. de Fleury and Martin on one side and the King and his brother Sandy on the other.

The hitters were the ones who usually scored. The King's team had to knock the ball through the midway belvedere on the wall-walk. M. de Fleury's side had to drive it through the door which led into the upper floors of David's Tower itself. Two hundred feet of parapet lay between the two doors, with a crenellated wall lining its outer side. Heaped against the inner side of the walkway like an avalanche were the thatched and stone roofs of service buildings and lodgings of varying elevations and pitches, some far below the parapet level, one or two projecting above. David's Tower at the south end was sixty feet high, rising above the wall and all other buildings, just as the Castle itself stood nearly three hundred feet above the deep valley around its three sides. The outer side of the curtain wall was quite sheer.

Kathi herself was drunk only as a starving man feels himself drunk: a euphoria born of the fresh cold air and the height and the danger; a sharpening of wits honed against other sharp wits and agile bodies. For a moment, she was a participator in the same sexless bonhomie denied her in Will Roger's room, whose crooked roof was one of the jumble below her.

Then Robin said, 'Kathi!' and she saw that he had the ball at his feet, and the others were trying to take it. She raced forward, stooping and twisting, and had actually hooked it when Liddell's shoulder pushed through and he put his foot under it. It rose over their heads and bounced once on the top of the ramp before John of Mar ran down and, catching it, punted it back to Sandy the hitter, who caught it, screaming, and began to charge forward, all five of his players around him.

It was intimidating, like a stampede. M. de Fleury said, 'You two, let them through. *Sconciatori*, stand firm. Martin, it's that ball or your head. I'll cover you.' Then the stampede had reached and passed her, and the players seemed to have coalesced in a buffeting mass where everyone appeared to be hitting, no matter what they were called. For a moment Martin did get the ball and she danced about, struck with awe, to see him achieve the one magnificent throw which would let her catch it, or Robin, and race with it to goal. But at that point the whole interlocked body lost its balance and tumbled kicking on to the slats, and when the ball made its appearance it was sluggish, passing from foot to foot and hand to hand like something tame. Then someone punted it hard, and soon enough the impacted mass was back again in the centre and deploying itself into its component parts, only to break loose again as the ball was slapped out of the walkway and bounced its way down a stone-slatted roof with a chimney.

This time, John of Mar was followed by his sister and Robin, and the three scrambled about in the darkness, spurred on by the shouts from above and below, their faces, hands, elbows caught here and there by the torchlight. Then Robin, his face incandescent, appeared balancing himself on a roof-ridge, the ball at his feet, and kicked it straight towards M. de Fleury, even as Meg hurled herself at his side. Then the ball was in play again on the wall-walk, bouncing between foot and hand, wall and ground as the lot of them ran, this time streaming forward towards David's Tower.

Kathi ran and hopped in the front, looking over her shoulder. Robin joined her, soot on his face, hardly breathless. If the ball went over again, she would jump down as well. She was lighter than Robin. She was seventeen, the same age as Sandy. Robin was fourteen

years old and Meg, pounding behind was eleven, and John beside her
was only thirteen. Even the King, crouched and waiting for them
ahead, was not yet twenty. They were all light and supple as acrobats:
six youngsters at home on these heights compared with six grown
men who were not. Kathi had been up on the roof-tops before: they
all had. Childhood was climbing.

Childhood was also temper, especially as they got near to their
goal. She could laugh at Meg, delirious with excitement, attempting
to wrap her arms round Will Roger's ankles so that he nearly toppled
headlong down the steps. She found it harder to forgive John of Mar
the jab in the stomach that made Robin double up, and the kick to
the back of Crackbene's knee that made the big shipmaster stagger,
exclaiming. She saw the set face of the Scandinavian, prevented by
protocol – as Mar well knew – from retaliating. Just as M. de Fleury
had to sustain the hard knocks he repeatedly received from his grace
the King and almost as often from Sandy his brother.

She was happy to see that M. de Fleury, although thirty, could
look after himself. If Martin cannoned into him more than once, he
failed to fall. On two separate occasions at least, as the play flowed
one way or the other, he swerved in such a way that an intended blow
fell upon stone, to painful effect. This did nothing, unfortunately, to
cool the ardour of the King's team, which took further umbrage
when M. de Fleury's elbow carelessly implanted itself in Mar's eye
the next time they met in a pack. Mar, staggering back palm to face,
groped for his knife-sheath and turned like a being demented. The
ball, appearing in front of his nose, abruptly took his attention. He
jumped aside and, trapping it, staggered off.

'Well done,' said someone to Kathi. It was one of the other team's
spoilers. Wodman, the Archer who had killed a man once.

'That's all right,' Kathi said. 'Your side could do with some help.'
She dodged round him while he was speaking, treading on his foot as
she went, in case he thought she really meant it.

Robin joined her, brightly purposeful. He said, 'I'll keep an eye on
the Earl if you'll watch Master Martin.'

The ball, hopping about, was moving towards the belvedere again
and she could see Martin in front of the door, braced to resist. M. de
Fleury was just in front, and Martin was watching him. So was John,
Earl of Mar. Kathi suddenly understood what the boy had assumed
she had noticed. She said, 'Listen, look after yourself. M. de Fleury
knows what he's doing.'

'Not always,' said Robin.

'Then he'll have to learn to keep sober,' said Kathi tartly. The ball
came out at her feet and she could hardly believe it: she and Robin

fled with it a full four yards before they were felled by the rush from behind. The ball, squeezed among all the bodies, squirted up in the air and began to descend again to the roof-tops below. This time, she was the quickest to follow it, sliding down slopes and crawling up inclines and jumping from one roof to another. Meg was chasing her, screaming and giggling, and, out of sheer good nature, Kathi let her have the ball.

Once returned, however and into the game, she found herself glancing from time to time to see what their red-headed hitter was doing, as she observed Robin's gaze was following Mar. She refused to consider whether Wodman, the servant of Jordan de Ribérac, might also harbour designs against M. de Fleury. There was a limit to what one could do. The simple truth was that the whole opposing team was out to murder M. de Fleury if it led to winning the game, as he could hardly have failed to notice. She felt rather the same way herself about them. She saw Whistle Willie laughing at her, and she laughed back as she ran.

It had not occurred to Nicholas up to that point that he was the object of anyone's concern. He was vaguely sensible that all four royals were capable of any extreme of misconduct, with John of Mar the worst offender by far. Against that, he seldom obeyed rules himself. It was true that he didn't much like having the representative of the Vatachino at his back, but he had found ways of dealing with it which Martin didn't much like either. The weak links in his own side were Adorne's niece and Robin; not because they were young, but because they were vulnerable. He also felt some confused responsibility for Roger who, however willing, was far from being a natural athlete.

On the other side, he welcomed the moderating influence of Liddell, but faced a continuing enigma in Wodman.

Nicholas, after all, was a secret pensioner of the French King, and should have Wodman's support, if he knew as much. On the other hand, accidents happened. Especially accidents to a man who had humiliated Jordan de Ribérac's son. He thought, hazily, that it was time to start taking charge of this game. He thought it was even time that someone began scoring goals.

Down below, a spreading sense of relief caused an increase in the noise, in the shouting and even the laughter, as the wagering became less discreet, and as more emerged to jump about and comment and watch. Lamplight from windows and doors picked out the coifs and aprons of women, as the torchlight made ruddy the faces and tunics of men, and sparkled on half-armour and helmets, and picked out the gold thread of livery badges and the chain across Will Sinclair's shoulders and the jewel in James Hamilton's hat. The Abbot's cloak tossed in the wind, as the smoke and flame from the torches streamed sideways and joined the peat smoke and the soot in the air. The King burned coal in his fires.

The King, it was clear, was hot enough with his present exertion not to think about fires, although the wind on the battlements was strong enough now to bustle the ball in the air, and deflect its angle of fall. It showed against the black, starry sky from time to time, a dull blister of light, and sometimes its rap could be heard amongst the pounding of feet and the chorus of twelve people shouting. The sounds descended in waves, sometimes faint and sometimes loud, with the young voice of the lassie screaming highest. Bleezie Meg. A survivor.

It had begun to seem likely now that all might be well. The outer wall of the parapet was four feet in height and the space between the crenellations was narrow. It would take a very drunk man to climb up and fall over that, and as time went on, the effects of the wine must be lessening. It silenced them still when the damned ball came thudding down yet again in the roof-tops, and two or three of them sprang whooping down to recover it. Twice it dropped to the ground and someone quickly threw or kicked it back to the parapet, usually for very small thanks from one side or the other that thought it had been disadvantaged. All the same, the spectators' fears had diminished, and they were almost able to enjoy the first concerted move of the game that seemed likely, at last, to bring a score.

It started, clearly, with de Fleury's side and was not, this time, haphazard. To James Hamilton, who had experience of the Burgundian's cunning, it was not perhaps entirely surprising. To Sinclair, intently studying the man from a smaller acquaintance, it was as informative as watching a battle. Each of the five in the team, it was clear, had his or her orders. Also, the fiction that restricted the use of the hands had been abandoned, as had already happened in the King's team. This time, no holds would be barred.

'The girls are young,' said Will Sinclair, Lord Caithness.

Hamilton smiled. 'There are young boys on shipboard,' he said. 'They play a part, too, in the battle, but not the same part as the men. Watch. This is a clever man.'

'Too clever?' said Sinclair.

'For some,' Hamilton said. 'Take the right precautions, and you have him at your heel. There he goes.' The noise about them increased. Like embers fanned by the wind, the upturned faces burned against the dark rock, their breath rising like smoke.

*

Afterwards, it was easy to see how maddening his strategy must have been. From below, it had the look of a dance: in front, the slight forms of the runners slid round the opposing bodies as in a pavane, sometimes touching hands, sometimes diverging to skip down to a chimney or descend a few steps to run along some shallow roof before regaining the ramparts. The spoilers behind did the same, and the hitters. The ball, too, moved like a tapestry shuttle, sometimes from hand to hand, sometimes from foot to foot, or high in the air, or neatly directed to rebound from wall or gable or gutter or window-stanchion. As they drew near David's Tower, the players even started to signal to one another, beginning with a chirrup from the musician Will Roger, answered by a seaman's whistle from the shipmaster Crackbene, and followed by a triplet from the girl Katelijne, high above the angry shouts of their opponents. The ball followed the sound. The ball flew into the shadow of David's Tower, and the noise suddenly redoubled and became rather more ugly. There was a sudden check, then a roar.

'*Colpito! Colpito! Colpito!*'

Dancing figures appeared on the skyline, surrounded by other figures, shouting and arguing. The mass moved slowly back to the centre, still shouting. James, Lord Hamilton, looked at his companion. He said, 'M. de Fleury appears to have won the first point. Now it becomes dangerous.'

Will Roger, whose nose was bleeding, said to the shipmaster, 'They won't let us do that again.' He felt quite friendly to Crackbene, who had twice got him out of serious trouble, and had picked up a few scars himself.

'So we do something different,' said Nicholas, appearing. 'Are you sober yet?'

'No,' said Roger. 'Neither are you.'

'No. But Martin is, and Crackbene, and the children.'

'Children?' said Kathi.

'Children. *Quanto juniores tanto perspicaciores.* I'm switching you and Robin to the back; Martin and myself to the front. Go and be wise.'

'Then it isn't Florentine football,' Kathi said.

'You noticed. Tactics as follows.' His proposals, heard in cold blood, were lurid.

'You really ought to let the King win,' said Roger at the end. He knew it was useless.

'No!' said Kathi. She saw Martin smiling, and scowled. Then they were off.

There was no dancing this time: it was war. For a few moments, the unexpected weight of the foreigners' team carried it forward, brushing aside the royal runners. Then they were up against Wodman and Liddell, James and Sandy, and someone's wits had been at work: Meg and John of Mar hopped and scrambled along the inner side of the wall, deflecting the ball, and preventing the use of the roof-tops for overtaking. Then the King and Sandy got the ball, and began to push back; soon after which the weapons appeared.

They were simple enough: a stob of wood; a length of piping torn off a wall; a bar from a grille. Robin was the first to be sent staggering by a crack on the shins; he couldn't see from what, or who did it. The next victim was Crackbene, clipped by a brick just before the ball was wrested from him. The attacker this time was Sandy Albany. Crackbene, shaking his head, took two strides and tore the thing from him. Then they both turned and ran, for the ball was in free play again. But both sides, by that time, were armed, if by nothing more than a belt strap. And the play, swaying back and forth from the middle, became inconclusive.

It was Mar, in the end, who went further than anyone else by deciding, it seemed, to remove Nicholas. It began with a mild pincer movement, aided by Wodman and aimed at tipping him down the nearest ramp. When Nicholas, although incoherent with laughter, contrived to turn himself inside out and escape, Mar pursued him instead of the ball, and produced the iron stanchion he had thrust into his waistband. As it whistled over his head, Nicholas ducked. Wodman, running up from behind, slackened pace. Then Mar lifted his other hand, with the stone in it.

Had he been entirely clear-headed, Nicholas might have seen it in time. As it was, it slammed into his temple, knocking him half senseless between the teeth of the machiolations at his back, where the parapet wall was at its lowest, with nothing but sixty feet of air to the rocks at its foot. He had enough consciousness left to half turn, grasping at the high stone on one side. But by then, Mar had the bar again in his hands and was single-mindedly kicking and thrashing him upwards and over. The boy's freckled face shone in the dull light like amber, and his eyes were bright as the stars. At the same moment, Wodman got to his other side, his knife in his hand.

Whatever he had been going to do, it was forestalled by the flight of the ball, which turned the game and brought the players jostling back, James at their head, and Sandy and Liddell behind him. The King himself had a stick in his hand, and had shown himself as brutal as anyone in the way he used it. For a moment, swaying a little, he surveyed the scene; then he spoke. It was an order, couched in obscene terms, to his brother. Mar looked up. Nicholas, more than half aware, wrenched himself almost free and was caught again by the stanchion, this time against his shoulder and neck, thrusting him back yet again to the half-empty space in the wall. The King stepped up to John of Mar. He slapped his brother, and wrested the bar from his hand. And John of Mar, his face scarlet, stretched and seized the dagger from Wodman's grasp and lifted it high.

It was Wodman who disarmed him, with one swift movement which recalled the Archer he had once been. Against that, a thirteen-year-old had no defences. The Prince screamed in pain and frustration and his brother slapped him again and turned to Nicholas who was slowly straightening. Martin, bending over him, moved aside.

'You deserved that,' said the King, frowning vaguely.

'My lord,' Nicholas said. He cleared his throat. There was blood on his brow, and the skin of his face and neck was red and blue down one side.

'It isn't Florentine football,' the King said. 'It doesn't count.'

'I am,' Nicholas said, 'Florentine in my nation, not in my customs. Dante. It doesn't count.'

'Yes it does,' said the King's sister. Her hair, lit from below, framed a face as bright as her brother's. She said, 'I've just scored.'

'What?' said the King. Everyone turned, including Mar. Nicholas sat down on the machiolation over which he had just escaped being thrown, and pressed his face into a kerchief.

'You all ran away,' Margaret said. 'Master Crackbene had the ball, and I kicked him till he dropped it. It's in the door. *La porta.* I've scored.'

'My mistake,' Nicholas said. 'We *have* been playing Florentine football.'

'And so?' Margaret said. She jumped up and down, hitting the King. There was a short silence. She stood still, breathing threateningly. 'Now there has to be a third game.'

'If I might make a suggestion,' Nicholas said.

Chapter 12

To the betting men far below the ramparts of Edinburgh Castle, it gradually became clear that there had been another score up on the battlements, allotting one point to each side. When the teams failed to re-form it became a source of some speculation. Sinclair said, 'They're tired of it, thank God.' Then he said, 'What in God's name are they doing?'

Archie Crawford, the Abbot, had joined them. He said, 'Word from aloft seems to indicate that they are choosing the victor by trial of single combat. His grace the King and M. de Fleury are to race one another to the top of David's Tower.'

'Stop it,' said Sinclair.

'And impugn my lord's courage?' said Hamilton. 'Watch. His grace has done it often before. The Burgundian hasn't.' He did not add what they both knew: that the young men were drunk.

'He mustn't. He doesn't know the footholds,' said Robin.

'He'll find them,' said Kathi.

'The way he is? After that iron bar? In the dark?'

'It'll be light soon enough,' Kathi said. When she was delirious with invention like this she looked, with her Adorne cheekbones and wide eyes, like the kitten of her little name, except that kittens were sensual creatures, and all the essence of Kathi was in her mind.

Robin said, 'I know it's fun, but it's real mischief. He shouldn't do it.'

'All right, I'll stop him,' said Kathi, and began to walk to the parapet.

Robin said, with exasperation, 'No, I'll go,' and pushed her aside. He knew he couldn't stop M. de Fleury any more than Kathi could, but he was better at climbing. He had climber's feet, arched and tough, with sharp supple ankles. His father and grandfather said he would do for a monkey if he kept his mouth shut. Monkeys were wiser than men. They knew if they spoke that someone would set them to work. He grinned, thinking of monkeys and feeling for his first handhold.

The King and M. de Fleury were in full public view by the other wall, awaiting the signal to race. Robin's plan was to find his way up the wall just ahead of them and stand by to help. Round his waist was his belt, and a short length of rope Kathi had found for him. If either of them just slipped and fell, he couldn't do anything. If they got stuck, then he could. He moved upwards, listening. The signal came: a flourish from one of the trumpeters. Then the roar told him the race had begun. He went on picking his way, his heart aching with love and with worry.

Nicholas saw him when he was a third of the way up, and ahead of the King. Deafened by the waves of applause from below, he was progressing up the face of the tower in a way that owed more to the spirit of adventure than to climbing technique. The dressed stone was fairly new, and the mortar was grudging of footholds. On the other hand the string-courses were firm, and so were the cages over the windows. Only the wind now and then tugged him between one trifling hold and the next, and his hands were growing chilled, like the rest of him. The smoke swirling up from below caught his throat, and the glare of the torch-fire flickered and writhed on the stone, or blinded him from a window as he paused to recover. He only paused once, because James, his face set in a rictus, came scrambling past him, and he had to leave his hold to regain his lead. He was a bigger man. It was not all that difficult.

He had felt James snatch at his ankle as he came level to pass, but he had expected it, and was well dug in on that side. Mar had not been allowed to dispatch a Burgundian banker, but the King's honour was now directly involved. He supposed that ruthlessness was a good sign in a king, as it was a prerequisite for anyone who planned to be a victor in life. He wondered if the King knew enough about human nature to realise the rashness of rousing anger in a dangerous sport. If the Burgundian banker had begun the race feeling lenient, he might have changed his mind now.

Certainly, James had no idea how to handle his own youngest brother, and seemed as impervious to the isolation of Albany as to the loneliness and revulsion of the Queen. Yet around James were family men, if he would take their advice. Nicholas had seen Sinclair below, and James Hamilton. Hamilton would not be displeased if the King suffered an accident. *Oh Doge, as a flower shall you fall.*

It was not so hard after all. Nicholas was moving up quite methodically when he saw something move at the edge of the tower, a yard away from his hold. A hand appeared, grasping the edge, and there followed the knee and face of Robin of Berecrofts. There was only one storey to climb. 'Kathi sent you,' Nicholas said. '*Jeu de Robin and Katherine.* Infants are guiltless when they have not been instructed by the sane.'

Robin's hair and shirt were both flying loose, but he looked surprisingly comfortable. He said, 'No. She's gone to let the dogs out. Stay where you are; let the King get to the top, and then come down as you like. No one will notice.'

'Well, I beg your pardon,' said Nicholas, climbing again. 'I should notice. I'm going to win. *'Zione!'*

Robin said, 'What about Jordan?'

'What?' said Nicholas, gazing upwards. The top of the tower was dark, beyond the reach of the torchlight. He began to edge round, to the face that was better lit. Too late he remembered why it was better lit. He began to laugh, then realised that James was within kicking distance again and started to clamber.

Robin shouted, 'If you fall, what happens to Jordan?'

'You look after him,' Nicholas said. 'You and the parrot.' His fingers slid, coated with white, and he began to laugh again. They had been lime-washing and harling this side before the weather broke down. He crawled further up and over the painted side, encouraging James to climb faster and follow. Half of the King's hair was now white, and his cheek, and his arms. The surface to which they both clung was covered, like Turkish sweetmeat, with soft red and white marks from their fingertips. It was slippery.

Nicholas said irritably, 'Robin, go back. Your grandfather will evict me.'

He wondered what the Queen would do if the King fell. She must be watching with horror. The Scots, the *sconciatori*, the spoilers, who were about to make her a widow and send her back to her furious father. *Questo gioco è uno sconcio.* Now, perhaps, she would perceive the advantages, if not the joys of insemination.

Jodi.

Warm water.

Never mind. There are solutions to everything.

Blasts of music could now be distinguished amid the continuous roar from below: Willie's friends had brought out their instruments. A yapping sound added itself to the compound, followed by an impassioned and sonorous baying. Nicholas leaned his sticky hair into the wall and took breath, deeply amused. Every muscle complained. His gaze, moving from the glare and noise and emotion below, rested on the darkness beneath the outer wall of the Castle, and the silent glimmering mass of the town plunging beyond, with the black pool of the Nor' Loch below it. And far beyond that, over dark country ridges and the faint lights of towers and townships, was the broad grey span of the estuary and the black hills of Fife brooding behind. The estuary where his ships would pass, very soon.

He had paused for a moment too long; he was cold, and his concentration was lapsing. He had just realised it when a vicious blow, utterly unexpected, took him on the shoulder and side, and shook him free. The King.

Nicholas started to fall. He saw James's face, red and white like the wall, the mouth beginning to open. The King shouted. Slithering, clawing, Nicholas saw that the King was sliding as well, that the violence of his blow had dislodged James's own grip on the glistening wall. A shriek rose from below. Nicholas's hands, raking down, found a crack: a moment's purchase long enough to see, black on white, a past foothold and two marks for his hands. He chanced releasing his grip and, stepping rather breathlessly down, brushed the marks and settled precariously into them. James, kicking, was directly above.

So was the boy. The child Robin, his hair white with lime-wash and blackened with sweat, was clinging to the wall by the King, and the King had gripped him by the wrist, immobilising him, while he sought a hold for his feet. The boy's face, bearing the other man's shifting weight, was fierce with determination and pain. He said something. It sounded like, 'Sir!'

Nicholas said, 'I'm all right. The King will be all right in a moment. He'll lose the wager if he gets any more help. Monseigneur? You'll lose the –'

He ducked, missing the King's kicking foot by an inch. The King's other foot was firmly set in a crack, and the kicking foot withdrew and found another crack almost immediately. The boy's wrist was released, and the hand that had gripped him stretched up. James was climbing again.

Nicholas watched him with some admiration. He probably deserved the throne. He shifted his own insecure grip, and prepared to climb again. The boy said, 'No.'

He was above, and in his way. Nicholas said, 'Don't be tiresome. If I have to climb round you, I'll fall.' James was reaching the top storey, and the roaring had started again. The boy said nothing. Swearing, Nicholas pulled himself up beside him, his eyes searching above for new holds. He said, 'I ought to kick you, too, as I go.' He had almost passed when he glanced back and saw that the boy's face, half hidden, was itself as white as the paint, and that he was holding by only one hand. The hand slackened.

Nicholas swore, crossly, in Greek. He took one step down and, holding one-handed himself, gripped the boy's nearer arm. The boy gave a half-stifled scream, and Nicholas shifted his grip to his belt. There was rope there. Nicholas said, 'If you faint like a cowardly turd, I will forbid you my house. Dig your feet in. Use your right hand.'

'I can't,' said the boy. Sweat was glistening on his temples.

'Yes you can,' said Nicholas, knotting the rope. 'Do you suppose that idiot girl . . . *Katelijne!*'

The voice that answered him came from above, accompanied by the squealing of pulleys. She had been waiting. She must have run up inside, as any intelligent person would, of course, do. Nicholas was so busy manoeuvring the boy to the edge of the tower face that he hardly heard the violence of the noise from below, or the final concerted shriek as the whitened figure of James, King of Scotland, clambered triumphantly on to his roof, accompanied by the hysterical barking of dogs.

Dangling against the unpainted wall, when Nicholas finally reached it, was the object that very few people would have noticed, he supposed, unless they were fatally inquisitive to begin with, like himself. Like Katelijne.

He said, 'She had some sense, after all. She's sent down the plasterers' hurdle. Come on. Your carriage awaits.'

They were halfway down when everything became illuminated: roofs and towers, men and women and dogs; when the Castle's great inky shadow spread its skirts over a countryside and a town suddenly bathed in red light, as if a false dawn had broken forth from the coping of David's Tower, or Hell had opened its gates. The basket fire on the roof had been lit by the winner, as sworn.

The great fire took hold, its flames leaping. Moments passed. Then, one by one, all round the spaces of night, dulled by distance to moth-colours, other fires appeared and hung burning, part of the great unseen constellation that waited, day and night, to be summoned to fire: Haddington and Dunbar; Eggerhope and Dalkeith and Hume, Fife to Stirling and the north; Tantallon to Berwick and the south. The balefires of Scotland, wakened to summon the lieges.

'Why did I think . . .' Roger said as, the cradle lowered, the boy was lifted out of the hurdle. 'What made me think that whatever you said, you weren't going to be first at the top of that tower?'

'I was cheated,' said Nicholas. 'It's all right: his arm got a crack in the fighting and the King's grip finally did for it. Anyway, what to me are the windy plaudits of the multitude? That is, next time you will do better at Florentine football, or else. Do I see Kathi? Kathi descended: *la quale è molto utile et humile et pretiosa et casta*; who is going, please, to get the bloody dogs out of the way before their tongues all turn white? Does lime-wash affect –'

He stopped, largely because the King was standing in front of him, slapping him on the shoulder. 'You villain! Try to throw your King to his death! But here is the hero who stopped you. Robin of Berecrofts, I'm told?'

The boy's eyes were open. He began to struggle up from where he was resting, but the King pushed him back masterfully, on the wrong shoulder. 'No, no. My own doctors will visit you. And then we shall receive you, and see what can be done. You are old enough to hold a position. Yes, Nicol?'

'He was courageous, my lord,' Nicholas said. He remembered what he had said to get the boy's head to clear. It had worked.

'Then he should join some household that would train him. Do you not agree?'

The dogs were still licking Nicholas, and he pushed them aside. The boy's gaze was fixed on his. Willie Roger said, 'I think we all know, my lord, which household would be best. Nicol should take him himself. He has an army. A Scottish squire would embellish it.'

Nicholas had begun, a while ago, to realise that some such thing was going to be inevitable, if he were to continue staying close to the Berecrofts. Mistress Clémence ought to be pleased. 'I should leave it to my lord King and to his family,' Nicholas said. 'But of course, I should have no objection.' The boy's pale face had crimsoned.

The King said, 'Then that is settled. And now for the business I brought you for, and you cannot say, my friend, that it is not necessary. What you need – what we all need – is warm water.'

Very occasionally, when he was drunk, Nicholas came home talking, Gelis had learned. On this day, so exquisitely devised in all its features, it was his voice she heard first, as she waited fully dressed in the silence of the Canongate house where, at last, her son was at home, and asleep.

She had known since yesterday that something subversive was happening: the message had come from the Castle direct. The King, it appeared, requested the presence of young Master de Fleury this evening. He might be brought by his nurse, but not by the lady his mother. The note did not bear the King's seal, but was brought by a man in royal livery from whom she learned that her husband had had a hand in composing it. The command was still, she was assured, that of the King.

She had been considering what to do when Archie of Berecrofts vaulted over as usual, and was casually helpful, as usual. 'There's a theory that barren bellies warm to other dames' nurslings. Queens and Kings are like other folk: they want bairns.' She had listened in silence, digesting that.

Then for reasons quite unconnected, Katelijne Sersanders had come: disingenuous, thoughtful, steering her way through all the shoals surrounding their past relationship in a way one couldn't help but find disarming. She had left apparently undisturbed by the absence of Nicholas, who failed to make his expected appearance, and whose bed remained empty all night.

He had been kept by the King, so they said. He did not appear in the morning, and had not returned by this evening, when Mistress Clémence went off to the Castle with Jordan, reluctant and sleepy in velvet. She was glad when Archie's boy offered to carry him, and she sent two men to escort them, with lanterns. The porter, gossiping, mentioned that the wee lady Margaret had gone up the hill with some ladies from Haddington. The Flemish lass had been with them. The one that brought Master Jordan's new parrot.

The hours dragged. Bit by bit, the house quietened; the lights began to go out. No one came. It was later than Jordan had ever been allowed out before. Gelis walked from window to window, floor to floor. After a while she found a crooked shadow at her elbow: Pasque, snorting and grumbling. She was company. Gelis didn't send her away. Twice she climbed to the top of the house and stood on the balcony that looked uphill towards the Netherbow Gate and the buildings of Edinburgh. The glow of the Castle, as usual, underlit the October clouds, and the wind turned her cold.

She was in her parlour when Pasque came running to take her out to the street, where folk were gathering to look at the glare to the west, steadily brightening. Govaerts, roused and running to join her, explained. 'It's the Castle balefire, my lady. It spreads the word that there's trouble. The news can run from coast to coast before a courier has foot in the stirrup, and all Scotland can be under arms in two hours.'

'What kind of trouble?' said Gelis. 'M. de Fleury is there, and our son.'

'Armed ships in the estuary,' Govaerts said. 'Or word from the south that an army is crossing the Border. Or a mistake.'

'You think it is a mistake,' Gelis said. He was composed enough now, but running towards her, Govaerts had been hissing under his breath. '*Zot! Zot! Zot!*'

'It would be strange if it wasn't,' Govaerts said. 'This office has better advance information than even the King.' He cleared his throat. 'They will put the fire out. That will cancel it.'

'If they are sober enough,' Gelis said. No one answered. After a few minutes, the light from the west became unsteady. After ten minutes it had gone. A sour, lingering smoke drifted downhill, and Gelis went in. Half an hour later, her son Jordan returned, asleep in the arms of his nurse. With him came her two servants and a filthy creature with her skirts round her knees, whom Gelis recognised, with misgiving, as Katelijne Sersanders. Then she saw the litter.

The girl said, 'It's all right. That is, Robin's had his arm broken: M. de Fleury again, but it all worked out for the best. Is his father about?' Her face was smeared with dirt and there were great circles under her eyes.

'What happened?' said Gelis. She sent someone for Archie and brought the small cavalcade into the house. Mistress Clémence, on a nod, took the sleeping child upstairs.

'Nothing,' said the Baron Cortachy's niece. 'That is, they took Jodi to Willie's house, and by the time it was all over, they'd forgotten about him, and M. de Fleury told us to bring him back quickly.' She stopped and then said, 'The King was annoyed you didn't go, but M. de Fleury explained. It turned into a sort of race, and I'm afraid we all got rather dirty. I've got to go back to Margaret.'

'Wait,' said Gelis. 'I was invited?'

The expression in the fevered eyes altered. 'Oh dear,' said Katelijne Sersanders. 'He didn't tell you.' She considered. 'There would be a reason.'

'There usually is,' Gelis said. 'No doubt he will tell me himself. Unless he is staying permanently at the Castle?'

The girl looked at her. 'I shouldn't think so,' she said. 'Aren't you moving into the High Street tomorrow? That is, we shall all go back to Haddington in the morning, and the house is yours after that.' She paused. 'He didn't tell you that either.'

Gelis said, 'No. It doesn't matter. I knew he had a house inside Edinburgh.'

'Leased to the Prioress. He asked her to move. She wasn't too pleased, but she has taken another. Look,' said Kathi. 'He may have decided to refurbish it. He could have planned to tell you everything yesterday, but the King didn't let him come home. He can be very single-minded. I should find it most annoying, in your place.' She suddenly smiled. 'I'd better go.'

Gelis looked after her. For three years, it seemed, the pretty house Nicholas had bought for his wife had been occupied by the Prioress of Haddington and her household. Now, suddenly, the Prioress had been asked to leave, and his wife was expected to live there. Once, the possibility had been mentioned, but he had said nothing since. She settled, for perhaps the last time, to listen for Nicholas coming home. But not, this night, in her own room.

The town was asleep when, finally, Nicholas de Fleury made his way down Castle Hill, down the High Street, through the Netherbow Gate (for a price) and towards the staircase that led up to his door.

Alonse, lighting his way, had not been especially helpful, although he gripped his employer's arm once when he tripped, and twice waited, with resignation or patience, when various impediments made progress difficult. Alonse was the nearest thing Nicholas had to an automaton: that was why he had him. As time went on, Nicholas discovered that he was walking with a limp and tried to correct it. It was only his neck and arm which had stiffened.

The lamp at the stairhead was still lit, and so was the other, through the pend and over the door that led direct to his offices. The moon had come up: in its brightness, the wick flames burned ochre. The watchman came out, and answered his questions satisfactorily enough, his eyes curious. Alonse waited neutrally, lantern in hand, to learn which door he would choose.

He didn't especially want Govaerts or the clerks to find him comatose in his room in the morning. He turned up the steps to the house and told the night staff and Alonse to go to bed. He waited until they had gone, and without taking a light, found his way to a sink and got rid of the rest of what he had drunk.

He hoped it was the rest. His clothes, still sodden from neck to feet despite the long walk, were now freezing as well, engendering spasms of shivering. The water at the Castle, as promised, had been warm, and it had been his own choice to jump into it fully dressed. It had provoked another blurred expression of irritation about his wife's absence; but the girl they had got for him to bathe with instead was silly and eager and presented no more problems than he had ever met as an apprentice, full of ale and joyous lustfulness in the secret corners of Bruges.

Remembering that made it easy. His booth had no curtain, but he removed from his mind the smells of food and wine, the squeals, the laughter, the splashing of others. Nevertheless, however he turned the girl in her excitement, he couldn't escape the spectacle of the King, swollen-faced in his watery lodge, his little Queen clutched soaked on his knee, her immobile face turned outwards to the scented steam and all that was happening within it. Her face was staring out still when the King lifted his red-pelted arm from the water, and whipped the hood curtain in front of them both.

All of them had felt hot enough then. But not now.

The new glass windows of the Ca' Niccolò were brilliant with moonlight. Aiming for his own quarters, Nicholas found he had stopped by the room where his son slept. The door was a little ajar. By stepping softly up to the threshold, he could just distinguish the cot with the child's head sunk dark on the pillow. It did not stir. He might have gone in, but heard a movement beyond, by the window, and realised that Mistress Clémence was there, and awake. He lifted a hand in apology, and drew the door closed as he left.

The door of his own room was shut, but he saw underneath the line of flickering gold from the fire he always kept there, warming the cushions, the bedlinen, the heavy soft bedrobe and towels. He thought of them, walking towards it. Then he saw the twelve inches of shadow, blocking the light.

He made to turn, but too late. The door opened, and Gelis stood there. 'Come in, please,' she said.

She didn't know how many women Nicholas had. She knew, of course, that in the months before Jordan was born, he had methodically bedded every mistress of Simon's, as a journeyman of the lower grade would, laboriously proving his theory that Simon was infertile. It had proved unnecessary after Jordan, his image, had been born, but he had presumably enjoyed it. In any case, she was quite sure that on this his return, he had found similar sources of pleasure. He had indicated that she was equally free, so long as she observed discretion.

She therefore remained dressed tonight, presenting no diaphanous silhouette to her husband, and adduced by the heaviness with which he stood surveying her that she had been right. But she had guessed that already by the effortful quality of his voice, speaking to the watchman outside, and the vagaries of his step. She said, 'A word. I am afraid I am going to insist.' She raised her voice at the end of the sentence.

It was enough. He moved, closing the door between themselves and the way to the little boy's room, and crossing to the platform of his bed, stepped up and disposed himself comfortably on the quilt, his bare head inclined on the pillow bere. Within the dark of the bedposts, she could not even distinguish his features. He said, 'Shake me if I drop off to sleep. Jab me if you like; there is my knife. What drunken truths are you hoping for?'

The fire crackled. He had built a chimney-piece, such as they had now in some rooms at Bruges, and the light rippled and leaped over the hearth and the handsome tiled floor. She chose a stool halfway between the fire and the bed and sat down. She said, 'On the ship, you told Father Moriz that I was free to take Jordan and go.'

'Of course,' he said. There was no hesitation.

'Provided I never come back, and provided you never see Jordan again.'

'So when are you going?' he said. He had tucked his right hand behind his head; otherwise he lay still, completely at ease.

'Tomorrow,' she said. 'Now you can let the Prioress stay.'

'Ah,' he said. There was a space. She even thought, dazed with anger, that he had fallen asleep. Then he added, 'One of my sins, I perceive. Are there more?'

She said, 'Not even that; although I should like to have had warning, and to know whether you have a chamber there, too. No. I heard about your interesting evening: the King and his family brought to risk their lives on the towers of the Castle; Robin's injury; the Adorne girl's exhaustion; the men of your company whom only luck saved. I heard all about that, and the drunken idiocy of the balefire. But all that is your responsibility, not mine. You and I, as I understand it, are playing a different game, and I have decided to end it.'

'Good,' he said.

'Good? After all those elaborate plans?'

'*Io son mercatante e non filosofo.* I might say the same thing of you. If you can't stand one day of reverses, then you have saved me from wasting my time. A game is only worth while between equals.'

She said, 'You took Jordan into danger without me. That removes our common ground. And am I not wasting my time on a game so little regarded by you that all its course can be spoiled by some pointless demonstration of drunken bravado?'

He took the hand from behind his head and let it flop straight from the shoulder, fingers open. 'My God,' he said.

She could see his eyes were closed. When he spoke again, it was with insulting patience. 'When,' he said, 'did you ever know me embark on a pointless demonstration of anything? Is Jordan injured in any way? No.

'Did I suffer any form of impairment that will prevent me from pursuing this game, as you call it, and winning it whenever I choose? No.

'So leave because you are losing. Leave because you are cowardly. Leave because you are jealous. But don't pretend you are leaving because *I* have abandoned the game. I promise you I have not.'

'Jealous!' she said. 'Of your bedmates!' Then she felt herself slowly flush.

He did not reply.

She said, 'He is my son. I have nothing to be jealous of. I won't have him used.'

'He wouldn't have been,' Nicholas said. 'He was to have stayed in the High Street with you and his nurses, and with young Berecrofts as playfellow. Robin is to come as my equerry and page.'

She said, 'You are moving as well?'

'It is time to separate house and office,' he said. 'And it suits me to be near Adorne's lodging. His ship has put into Leith.'

She sat up. 'It has! Whom has he brought?'

'His pregnant wife,' Nicholas said. 'But no son. They have left their doleful author behind, forced to try his luck with the new Pope in Rome.'

'And the Boyds?' said Gelis quickly. 'The Earl and Countess of Arran and their children? Did they leave them behind?'

'No,' said Nicholas.

'They're here! But Tom Boyd and his father will hang!'

'Didn't you work it out?' Nicholas said. 'They couldn't afford to leave them in Bruges, the Duke forbade it. They couldn't bring the men here, they'd be hanged. But if Adorne left the whole tribe in England, the Princess and her children would be a threat to the Scottish throne all their lives, and James would never forgive Adorne for letting it happen. So Adorne was left with only one thing to do.'

'Which was?' Gelis said. All the anger had gone, leaving the bright, clear calculation of the game: her schemes against his; the delight of exposition. His voice was shallowly drink-hoarse, but surprisingly unblurred.

He said, 'Which was to take Tom Boyd to London and leave him there, with the prior consent of King Edward, who may keep him as long as he wishes. Lord Boyd has been given a pension, and left in some sinecure of a post in the north.'

'And Mary? The King's sister?'

Nicholas began to change his position. 'She is on board Adorne's ship with her children. He persuaded her to come. No doubt Margriet helped. The Countess thinks she is here to plead for her husband's redemption.'

There was a silence. Gelis said, 'Is that what you advised her to do?'

'I didn't see her,' Nicholas said. 'I told her husband to keep her with him in London.'

Gelis stared at the shadowy bed. She said, 'Of course you would. And doting on Tom as she does, she would rush to agree to all that at once: to settle with Tom and her children in London. It was Adorne, then, who had to persuade her, for his own sake and the King's, to come to Scotland alone with the children. Adorne must have had to pretend she could plead for Tom's safe return and reinstatement. And when she gets here, and finds the King will do no such thing, nor let her go back – it is Adorne she will blame.'

'I should think so,' he said. 'Also, Adorne will have to give up the Boyd land, or some of it. She'll need something to live on while she hates him. But the King will be forever grateful, I'm sure. Adorne may even thank me some day.'

His voice was calm. A triumph of planning. A vindication of what he had said: for him, no demonstration was pointless. Save for Nicholas, the King's sister Mary would never have left to roam with her husband. But for Nicholas, Mary would have spent the last three years in comfort in Scotland, her marriage safely annulled, her controversial children unborn. Gelis said, 'Does the King know his sister is here?'

'By now, he will. Crackbene told me in private.'

'What will he do?'

'Did you not hear the horses go by? Send to Leith to bring her ashore. After that, to the Castle. After that, I don't know. He was full of good humour tonight,' Nicholas said. She could not interpret the change in his voice.

She said, 'But you didn't send to warn her away. That might have cost you your Order.' He reclined, without troubling to answer. As always, it offended her. She said, 'So what do you get out of Mary's return, apart from ruining her and her faith in Adorne?'

She knew that, in the shadows, he was smiling. 'You'll never know, will you?' he said. 'You're going away.'

The fire burned. He watched her, his weight indolently transferred to one hand. In a moment he would go, or would force her to leave. She said, 'I have never shared a house with a piece of clockwork. I am tempted to stay.'

He said, 'Indeed. I thought an excess of carnality was the issue. Perhaps not. Now I come to think of it, the King was on the same theme. He gave me a paper. Where did I put it?'

He began to search, and then stopped. 'That is, there is no point if you are going away.'

'No,' said Gelis. 'I shan't go away yet. Not before I have made all my points.'

There was another silence. 'Why not make them now?' Nicholas said.

There was a tap on the door. He turned his head. Gelis said, 'I should be delighted, but unfortunately, someone seems to wish to speak to you. I had better see who.'

It was Govaerts, huddled into a night-robe as if he had been sent for. He looked past her into the room. Behind him, she noticed, the door to Jordan's room stood a little ajar.

Govaerts said, 'I am sorry, madame. I wondered if . . .'

'I am coming,' Nicholas said. He had stepped from the bed. His face, glimpsed in the firelight, looked strange; a composition of dislike and amusement, or even just a freakish effect of the shadows. Then he was outside the door, talking quietly to Govaerts. He turned and spoke in the same subdued voice to her. 'I have to leave. I shall probably sleep in the office. So you are going to stay?'

She looked round the room, before she realised what he referred to. She said, 'In the house in the High Street. Oh, yes.' Something white on the bed caught her eye.

'The note I told you about,' Nicholas said. 'From the King. With his especial good wishes. Good night. You have made the right decision, I'm sure.'

He left with Govaerts. She thought he was smiling. She prepared to take herself to her room. She felt a fool, in her heavy skirts and long sleeves and rolled hair while all sane people were sleeping. She crossed to the bed to take up the paper.

The pillow was wet. All along the depression where he had lain, the linen was grey with cold moisture from which arose a faint, costly scent. The paper, when she lifted it, was dimpled with moisture as well. She carried it to the fire in order to read it.

She had expected a letter. It seemed, instead, to represent an exhortation, perhaps to a son going abroad:

Avoid dampness. Thy room should possess a north window, and a juniper fire. Choose to consume fowl of all kinds, and quench thy thirst with almond water, or a little sweet wine, poker-heated. Avoid milk, and refrain from partaking of cheese, or of paté, or vegetables. Sleep for seven or eight hours; less in winter. Be merry: eschew contention and anger, and pay special heed to the gut, which requires rest for seven hours after food. When the hour of consummation is come, teach thyself to linger in preparation, and to recognise when preparation is ended. In parting, assume infinite care; so that two hours shall pass in the most expedient and lofty position. When all is done, keep thy bed for three days.

There were two paragraphs more.

Reject the mixtures of charlatans. Instead, take some hare meat and sugar and tooth dust, and serve with one testicle, chopped, from a wolf. That on his right side will make thee a son, whilst thou must eat of his left for a daughter.

And:

Should all fail, change thy country; for some cities can cure barren women.

It *was* an exhortation, of a kind. It was advice. Advice on how to conceive her next child.

She threw the paper into the fire. Then she went and sank by the wet, scented sheets and clenched her hands, because they were shaking.

Chapter 13

WEEPING MOTHER WITH two screaming children, the King's elder sister arrived that same night on a Burgundian ship, and the waves of news rollicked about like the gouts from a bath-stall. The next morning, betimes (so they said), the Princess and her household were fetched to the Castle and put into her old rooms in David's Tower, although the walls reeked of smoke and there were white footprints all over the stairway.

A Council meeting was called, and after that, the King sent for the man who had sailed in with the bairns and his sister: Anselm Adorne, the Duke of Burgundy's counsellor. He also called for the other Burgundian, Nicol de Fleury, him that was to blame for the King's sore head this morning, and a deal else, the callant. But Nicol had gone out of town, so it seemed, no one knew where. That was a lad.

Anselm Adorne, for his part, stoically endured the disaster. He had no alternative. But for Nicholas and the Boyd family, the Baron Cortachy might have made this return glorious, with his first-hand reports of the lands he had visited and his gracious letters from princes. And but for the death of the Pope, his handsome son Jan would have been with him, to present on one knee the book of their travels so painfully written, now encased in velvet and jewels and dedicated to King James himself.

Instead, Jan was travelling to Rome, with no more promising companion than the bankrupt and belligerent Bishop of St Andrews, and no sure prospect yet of a post. Instead, his dear Margriet, with her poor raddled face and swollen body, had been forced to come with him to Court, because the Princess Mary would not travel without her. And instead, the splendid gift of this book would be forgotten; cast aside by the other gift he had inescapably brought, to everyone's misery.

He could not have left the King's sister in Bruges. He could not leave in England a family so dangerous to the Scottish throne that his

own future in Scotland would have been forfeit. He had only cajoled
the girl herself into coming by exaggerating the hope he knew did not
exist – that she, favourite of James, would persuade him face to face
to let her husband come back to Scotland.

The outcome had been as he feared. James, in the act of opening
his arms to a penitent sister, had learned that Mary, shining and
scented with milk, had no regrets; no wish to be released from her
marriage vows. Her sole mission was on behalf of the traitor her
husband, so that they might come back to Scotland in state, their
lands returned, Lord Arran's death sentence quashed. She not only
wished it. She seemed to expect it.

The open arms had not remained open. Instead of her brother's
embrace, the walls of David's Tower had closed around Mary Stewart
and her household and children. And the door to the enclosure was
locked.

Returned from his difficult audience, Adorne found Sersanders his
nephew awaiting him in the big house he usually leased in the High
Street. His niece Katelijne, it seemed, was in bed, having overtaxed
herself the previous evening. Katelijne Sersanders was delicate. Her
brother thought the family wrong to wish her to marry in Scotland,
but Sersanders did not know, as his uncle did, what ageing princes
could do to a country. Or young ones, for that matter.

Anselm Adorne listened therefore to his nephew, although he was
tired, and asking him to sit down, had poured him some wine. The
beaker was from home. So was all their linen and silver and glassware.
Margriet had insisted. He had gone just now to her room to reassure
her, but had found her asleep. He was thankful. She had been
weeping all day for the Princess.

Now he said, 'Why revile Nicholas? It was not his fault that the
Pope died, or if it was, I have not yet heard the details. As for the
rest, the King will recover his equanimity. In his heart, he knows that
we have brought home his sister, whom he had lost, and that her
children are better brought up under his eye. What we lose, we shall
recover in other ways. And I have great hopes. You have spoken to
Martin. You have not yet heard all I have to tell you.'

'De Fleury has a Bank behind him.' Sitting four-square, with his
father's energy and his mother's muscular neatness, his nephew and
godson looked very young.

Adorne said, 'Nicholas *is* the Bank. That is its greatest strength and
its greatest impediment. Nicholas bestowing his undivided attention
upon any project is a sight worthy of awe: it leads naturally to
success. It does not lead to stability; to consistent leadership; to the
broadest vision which will carry a company or a family safely into the

future. Nicholas is not concerned with the future – for his country, his town or himself.'

'But surely!' Sersanders said. 'He has plotted and planned all his life! What was he doing in the Tyrol, in Hesdin, in Ham? What has he been attempting to carve for himself here?'

'You would think so,' said Adorne. It had come to him recently, the truth about Nicholas, or what he thought was the truth. He said, 'And you are right, when you speak of his mind. But what the core of Nicholas lives by is not the present, nor what is to come. It is the past.'

To the exasperation of all except, perhaps, the King, the sieur de Fleury continued to be absent all through the first days of the lady Mary's arrival and imprisonment and, having by now virtually a doctorate in disappearance, remained lost.

John le Grant, at whose side he unexpectedly appeared, bruised and sneezing, did nothing to give away the whereabouts of his padrone; but was cheered by the concentrated violence of both his language and his labours – a phenomenon often associated with a man thankfully returned from his wedding bed, or from doting dutifully over a crib.

The business being gun-casting, there was plenty of hard work to do, and meticulous planning. When it shifted to the new boat-yard, it was scarcely less strenuous. By the time the sufferer was ready to go back, the cold had gone and the marks on his face were hardly noticeable. He had said nothing that was not to do with the work, but of that he had said a great deal to the point. John gathered that Crackbene had been left in attendance in Edinburgh, but would shortly set sail as was planned. It would be necessary soon to be seen to be divining, with which Father Moriz could concern himself or not, as he pleased.

Father Moriz was at present with the Cistercians in Culross, conducting an experiment with a pump. John thought that, with Nicholas in this mood, it would be as well if Moriz stayed there. He did not discuss either Nicholas's son or his wife, whom he assumed to be at the bottom of this displacement. He did enquire about the future of the lady Mary, who was known to have come back to Scotland.

Nicholas, his face smeared, had sat back and picked up a beaker. He was drinking water again. 'The King will keep her fast until he's persuaded her that she's Tom's only chance, and that if she leaves, he'll make sure that Tom dies. In any case, Edward will only wait so long to see if she's coming, and then he'll get rid of poor homeless Thomas.'

'You helped her leave Scotland,' John said. He was not in the business of protecting the sensibilities of Nicholas.

'She would have left anyway. The King knows that. And I got her a nice home with Adorne.'

'So now she stays indefinitely locked in the Castle?'

'Not necessarily,' Nicholas said. 'In fact, she's probably left there already. I've suggested she moves into the High Street with Gelis.'

'*What!*' said John.

Nicholas looked at him. 'You remember. Gelis used to be one of her ladies. The nurses will help, and the nuns. Adorne will have no more to do, and the children will love it. Margaret, Jordan and James.'

'Does she know?' John le Grant asked.

'Gelis? She will by now,' Nicholas answered.

It had been left to Govaerts to carry the message to the dame de Fleury in her new house in the High Street, which she had occupied for less than a week.

The prospect didn't entirely displease him. He felt some slight proprietorial interest in the King's sister, whom he had helped originally to escape, and had never formed a close relationship with the wife and child with whom the padrone had saddled himself. Now, when he called with his message, it was as if the Lady had fathomed its contents. Or perhaps it was lack of sleep and not shock which gave her skin its extreme pallor. She was a very fair girl, with a tart way about her.

She said, 'You have something to tell me.'

'I have two messages, my lady,' he said. 'One from his grace the King, and one from your husband, to be passed to you at the same time.'

She said, 'You have heard from M. de Fleury?' And then: 'No. He would arrange it beforehand. What is it?'

'A great honour, madame,' Govaerts said. 'The King proposes that his sister the Countess of Arran should leave the Castle and come to lodge with you here. She will bring her household and children. The message from M. de Fleury endorses this. He relies on you. No expense is to be spared.'

'You mean he suggested it,' the Lady said. She was gazing past him. There was a commotion, he realised, in the doorway. The Lady added, 'And when will the Princess arrive?'

Govaerts had no need to answer. 'Tomorrow,' said Katelijne Sersanders, whipping past him and planting herself on a seat, having snatched up the sewing which occupied it. 'You didn't know? He didn't tell you? And of course, he's got himself safely out of the way. You'll have to do it. I can help you.'

'Of course,' said the Lady. She was quick to recover, you could give her that. She said, 'She stayed with your uncle and aunt. I'm surprised –' She broke off.

'It's because of Aunt Margriet's health,' the girl said gently. 'Or she and my uncle would have been happy to have her. And of course, M. de Fleury wishes to please the King. And if M. de Fleury does well, it will build a secure future for you, and for Jordan. I am sure M. de Fleury had all that in mind.'

By sheer chance, she was putting all the arguments most calculated to be helpful. Govaerts decided to keep quiet. The lady Gelis said, 'I see. I am sorry about your aunt. But this is not a large house. They tell me your uncle crossed with a retinue of a hundred.'

'Some of them stayed in England with the Earl and his father,' said the girl. 'Some were my uncle's. The Countess will have no more than a dozen, and some of them can stay with us. We are only next door.'

'We?' said the lady Gelis.

'The Edinburgh house of the Priory,' said the girl. She had reddened a little, but her voice remained instructive and bright. 'When the Prioress couldn't find satisfactory premises, M. de Fleury bought the house next to this, and presented it to them. I think,' said Katelijne Sersanders, 'that you will find the nuns very helpful, and the King's own household as well.'

'I am sure,' said the Lady slowly. She gazed at the girl. She said, 'I am surprised by one thing. Does the King trust M. de Fleury not to enable the Princess to cross the Border and join her husband a second time?'

Govaerts moved, and saw the girl glance at him reassuringly. She said, 'He wouldn't dare: he has nothing to gain by it this time. And anyway, there will be a guard on the door, you can depend on it. Also, you might disguise her, but you couldn't easily smuggle out a small boy and a baby. Should I speak to Mistress Clémence about them?'

'Mistress Clémence may decide to leave,' the lady Gelis said. 'She and Pasque. And what then?'

'Betha Sinclair,' said the girl. 'And they have a wet-nurse and a maid of some kind. But Mistress Clémence won't leave. You know she won't. Jordan is safe.'

Shortly after that, Govaerts left. He saw the two women watch him go, but didn't hear what they said.

'He disapproves of me,' Gelis said.

'He'll come round. He's a little jealous. He's loyal to M. de Fleury, but doesn't understand him a bit,' Kathi said. 'It's Robin you'll have all the trouble with. You know he's going to be here as a page when he's better?'

'So I heard. Jordan will be delighted. Trouble?'

'He thinks he's M. de Fleury's grandfather,' Kathi said. 'M. de Fleury gets irritated. Robin's father is good with them both. And I thought the parrot might help. To relieve the emotion.'

'Nicholas experiencing emotion?' Gelis said.

There was a silence. Then the girl said, 'No. It was Robin I meant.'

By the time Nicholas came back, the lady Mary was installed in the house with the orchard in Edinburgh; and nurses, children, cooks, stewards, chamber servants, maids, attendants and the changing ranks of the Countess's bodyguard had all been variously established, dispersed, and given their orders by Gelis. The orchard had been partly dug up, and the household, to hear Will Roger, was being run on the lines of a military establishment. 'If you ever lose Astorre, your lady wife could take his place.'

'I really wanted to marry Astorre,' Nicholas said automatically. 'Gelis was just a substitute.'

He had come back to the house in the Canongate, and had already called to see Robin next door. The boy had been jumping about with a spear in the garden, his arm all strapped up, and had wanted to join him at once. Nicholas had told him he was going away, but would see him when he came back. He didn't want Robin with him when he was divining, or not on this trip. Archie, at least, had been relieved.

Now he had to reassure Willie, who had come into the counting-house ostensibly to speak to one of his altos, but actually to quarrel with Nicholas over the Mystery Play.

Nicholas said, 'Willie, you have every expert I possess, plus the entire resources of the Abbey of Holyroodhouse, plus all the stuff I brought over from France. You don't need me.' On his desk in the next room were five sacks of dispatches and Govaerts, glued to his seat.

Willie said, 'Henry Arnot's being sent off to Rome. Why don't you do something properly, just for once?'

'I do,' said Nicholas. 'I'm trying to run a Bank properly.'

'You're back on water,' said Willie Roger. 'You always have a bloody short temper when you're on water. Well, you're wrong. I've spoken to your Julius. I've spoken to your Gregorio. I've spoken to your Govaerts. I don't think you've ever done anything with

everything you've got, except perhaps music. And that's just impro-
vising. That's not striving for perfection.'

The clerks, their necks red, were writing assiduously. Nicholas
sighed. 'You think I've forgotten about the Chapel Royal money.'

'I know you have. Haven't you?' Roger said.

'Drums, you promised me,' Nicholas said.

'*If* you managed to extract the money for your Passion and my –
You haven't?' said Roger.

'Why do you think Henry Arnot is going to Rome?' Nicholas said.
Someone was hovering. Alonse.

'Why?' said Will Roger. His face, too, had turned pink.

'The King,' Nicholas said, 'has reached the conclusion that the
Priory of Coldingham ought to be suppressed, and its revenues
directed instead to the Chapel Royal of St Mary the Virgin at St
Andrews. I know Henry Arnot is going to Rome. Why the hell do
you think he is going to Rome?'

Will Roger kissed him. It was highly unpleasant but not unexpected, and the clerks, turning round, had raggedly embarked on a
round of applause. His grip must be slipping. Alonse, his face neutral
said, 'Messire?'

Nicholas pulled himself away and gave Roger a blow between the
shoulderblades that was a quarter bonhomie and three-quarters meant
to rattle his teeth. Then he turned to Alonse.

'Messire,' said Alonse. 'The lady of Cortachy has called. She asks
if she can speak to you privately. I have taken her to sit in your
chamber.'

Of course. Anselm Adorne's pregnant wife, come to beg; come to
quarrel. Everyone did.

At home, she made small jokes about her size, since the swelling this
time was everywhere, and she was hard put to disguise it: wearing her
robes extra long to hide the grotesque feet and legs, and enfolding
half her neck and her chest in the drapes of her white linen headgear.
Even her face felt inflated. Whereas Claes vander Poele – Nicholas,
now de Fleury – looked at first sight the same as the troubled,
determined lad of nineteen who had asked her help and Anselm's to
marry the widow Charetty his employer in the Jerusalemkirk.

He was not the same, of course. He was thirty, and made to seem
taller by some change in the shape of his muscles, and the way he
now stood. His eyes held the attention now the way Anselm's did, by
their authority, and not just because they were wide-set and grey. She
thought he had probably modelled himself on Anselm, and set her
lips, remembering the wound he had given her husband, and the tiff

she and Anselm had had over it. Anselm had always been soft with
the boy. But now, of course, the boy himself had had his first son,
and she had not been one to harbour a grudge.

She said, because she was thinking of it, 'I've been to see your
young Jordan. A babe to be proud of, and a lovely young mother.
You are lucky.'

'I know,' he said. He had remained in the doorway while she
spoke, but now he came quickly in and sat down beside her. He said,
'I would have come to you. What can I bring you? What do the
doctors say?' That was the other difference. The dimples had gone.

She smiled. 'Alonse was kind. He is bringing some milk. Dr
Andreas says I have to rest, that is all. Jan was no trouble, nor will
this one be.'

He said, 'Jan is safely on his way to Rome, so far as I know. He will
come to no harm from me. Is that what you wanted to know?'

He was direct. She supposed she looked tired, and he wanted to
shorten the encounter. She said, 'He was a silly boy. Yes, I did want
to know that, and about Sersanders and Kathi. Although Kathi has
taken your part more, I must say, than I think she should.'

Unexpectedly, the dimples appeared. He said, 'Kathi takes everyone's part, that of Gelis included. I think she has made her peace
there. And Sersanders and I have an understanding, I think. We
spent a great deal of our boyhood together. I haven't forgotten. Nor
what you did for me and for Marian and the girls.'

'Tilde's baby!' said Margriet, flushing again with happy remembrance. 'And Gregorio and Margot, whose child will come just before
mine! All to grow up together, companions to your Jordan! Are we
not blessed?' She broke off. 'You knew about Margot?'

His smile returned. 'Yes, of course. We are blessed, as you say. But
you are still anxious about something? Or my lord your husband has
a message?'

She sat up. She should have made things plain at once. 'No, no.
Anselm has no idea I am here. Anselm thinks he can do everything;
asks no help; takes no advice. All the time he was away . . .' She bit
her lip and stopped. She said, 'Everything that was correct, we all
did. Two births, two christenings, with the great from every land in
attendance. My home was not my home for eighteen months. My
own children stayed away; Jan was put out of temper . . . We did our
best.'

'No saint could have done more,' the young man said. 'No one
knew, I think, that the whole burden would fall upon you.' He
sounded reserved.

'I did,' Margriet said. 'I knew as soon as –' She broke off again.

'But Anselm was thinking only of us, and of Jan. The sacred relics he would bring back; the thanks he would receive from the Duke and King James; the goodwill of the Pope – that was for us, for his family.' She had a kerchief somewhere and started to hunt for it in her layers of clothing.

Claes said, 'The Princess will remember all that. She is only suffering because the King will not let her join her husband.'

'She wouldn't see me!' Margriet said. 'I called to see the babies, and your Gelis, and Mary would not come from her chamber! And when I told Anselm, he said he had known all along. He knew the King wouldn't let Tom return. He knew the King would imprison her. And yet he got her to come.'

There was a silence. She blew her nose. Claes said, 'Demoiselle? Wasn't that, too, for the family? It would have been bad for you and for your husband if you had left the Countess in England.'

He was a man. Even so. Margriet van der Banck looked up and rammed down her fist with the kerchief. She said, 'Have you seen that poor girl? She thinks of nothing, wants nothing but her Tom. And so do her poor fatherless children. What is Anselm's future or mine compared with that? This is not our country! We could go back to Bruges tomorrow!'

Alonse came in with the milk, looked at her, and left after laying it down. Claes said, 'You think I can help?'

Her mouth was dry. She picked up the beaker and gulped from it. She said, 'The Countess will see *you*. Gelis says she never stops asking for you. Tom said it was your advice to stay together, a family in England, and they would have done that if Anselm hadn't overruled them. You helped Mary get away once.'

'I see,' he said. He seemed to be thinking. He said, 'I can go and see her, of course. I shall do that. But simply because I helped her before, the house is guarded. It would be almost impossible to get her away. And even if that weren't so, I might find it harder than you or Ser Anselm to suffer the consequences. I have Gelis and the baby to think of.'

'Of course,' she said. Put like that, it was plain. Her throat was painful, and she cleared it. She said, 'It's just that I'd like Mary to know that we wouldn't hurt her, and did what we thought best. Anselm is so . . . He sometimes can't see beyond his own family. And the King is grateful enough, but sore that Mary has not come to stay of her own accord, and cooler than Anselm expected. If you could tell the King that we did all we could. Not,' said Margriet, in a sudden burst of recollection, 'that I could ever take to Thomas Boyd or his father.'

'That should earn you the King's pardon for almost anything,' said Claes with a faint smile. The lids had dropped over his eyes. He said, 'I'm not sure that the King would welcome interference, but I shall do what I can. I'll see the Princess, of course. I'll try to tell you what happens. But go home now. Alonse will take you. Say nothing to Ser Anselm. And above all, I beg you, make sure that no one else helps the Countess run back to her husband. Whoever does so will pay, and she herself might live to regret it. Tom Boyd is a disagreeable man. He wanted position and wealth through his wife. As soon as the Queen starts to bear, his last chance will have gone.'

She looked at him in horror. 'You think –'

'I don't know,' he said. 'But you may have done the right thing, even though the lady Mary might not think so at the moment.'

He helped her rise, and as she took her leave, she gave him a kiss. She felt him recoil. It upset her, thinking how she had intruded on him her thick heated body and wet face. She went home.

Chapter 14

A WELL-RUN CHILDREN'S establishment, to the mind of Mistress Clémence, had much in common with a well-run military barracks. It was the extreme competence of the Burgundian camp under Captain Astorre which increased the hopes she had already formed of M. de Fleury's capability as a parent. The talents of his wife, the lady Gelis van Borselen, had now also been demonstrated, to Mistress's Clémence's satisfaction, in the transformation of the house in the High Street

The lady Gelis was, of course, already conversant with the requirements of a royal household. The King's sister and her attendants were suitably quartered, with neatly erected extensions for their housing and service in the gardens and the Priory's mansion next door. The cooks were reconciled, and some of the lesser servants turned off in favour of better-qualified ones from the Canongate house.

The nurse of the two royal children went back to Bruges after a week; but the wet-nurse, a humble creature called Scone, appeared glad to remain. The royal children were aged eighteen months and three months and on the point of being irremediably spoiled: it was fortunate that they arrived when they did. Jordan, introduced to them carefully, had shown no sign of jealousy.

His father, with remarkable good sense, had left the household alone for two weeks, but had arranged to communicate with the child at regular intervals. Most parents sent presents. M. de Fleury sent questions: *What have you eaten today? What is the parrot saying? Have you new gloves for winter?* Mistress Clémence doubted whether the answers, returned through some servant, ever reached M. de Fleury himself; but composing them gave his son great satisfaction.

Indeed, the child had to be protected from over-much attention: members of the royal bodyguard sometimes found their way indoors, the foremost being the man Andro Wodman, who spoke her own kind of French and whom she tended to keep, perhaps, longer than she should. And then the boy Robin came often, and the girl Katelijne stopped by very occasionally when on her way with her mistress to see the Countess. But both these young people were level-headed, while the lady Gelis, managing it all, was clearly better suited than she had been, alone in her rooms in the Canongate. But for the silly, poor-spirited girl they were housing, Mary Stewart, Countess of Arran, the new life might have been close to ideal.

She hinted as much, once, to the young girl Sersanders on one of her visits. The girl, who had taken up knitting, had come in with a large woollen object which proved to be a hat destined for Jordan. As always, it was to be given to the lady Gelis and not direct to the child.

The girl had sat down, knees akimbo and balanced the hat on her head. 'She isn't interested in *anything*. Even the children. Would you miss Tom Boyd as much as that?'

The nurse had smiled. 'I don't know him.'

'I did,' said Kathi. 'I think he was just the first man she saw outside the nest. Like the chickens in Cairo. The King thinks if she can be made to make friends with the Queen, the Queen will feel the same about him. He wants them both to go with the children and stay in Kilmarnock. He gave the Queen the Boyd lands in the west.'

'I do not think,' said Mistress Clémence, 'that such a plan would have much chance of success.'

'No. Not, anyway, while Mary blames her brother for everything. Although you wouldn't be any worse off in Kilmarnock. Dean is a fine castle, and the children would like it. And M. de Fleury has his new keep nearby at Beltrees. The Countess likes him,' said the girl thoughtfully. 'I don't know where he's gone, but I shouldn't be surprised if he solves all the Countess's problems when he comes back.'

She left the hat and went off. An old head on young shoulders. A fast intellect running a body scarcely able to keep up with it, from what the Adorne physician, Dr Andreas, said. She had seen it in other children, poor things. It sometimes struck her to wonder whether, in M. de Fleury, she was not witnessing a survivor of the same combination. She had looked for it in the boy but found nothing but balanced good health and normality. Of course, she had had the upbringing of Jordan.

Nicholas returned to Edinburgh exactly when his wife calculated he would, and called on her almost immediately. Gelis heard the body-guard's challenge below, followed immediately by the familiar voice. She dismissed Mistress Clémence in the middle of what they had been arranging; the nurse curtseyed and bent, before leaving, to pick up and replace the object of their discussion, which had slipped to the floor. Then Nicholas was shown in. 'Arrested at my own door!'

Their eyes met. The message was always something quite different; something which threatened to stifle her plans, as at Hesdin. She forced her five senses to work for her, not against her, and sat down gracefully, folding her hands. 'Andro should have been on duty. Perhaps the others will now tell one another who you are. Or you could leave them a drawing. Your bruises have faded quite nicely.' She could see the marks still, which in the dusk of the bedchamber she had taken for shadows. Such vanity. She added, 'The coverlet was badly stained.'

'I was sure you would hear all about it,' he said. He leaned against the door, his head almost touching the beams of the ceiling, his thumbs in his belt. He had left his cloak below, and was not therefore leaving immediately.

'The Countess heard, from her sister,' Gelis said. 'The Countess thinks it was thoughtful of you to spare me the ultimate embarrassment of the bath-stalls. She is anxious that, despite all, we should have a marriage as happy as hers. What a brute you have been to that girl. And to the Adornes.'

'So you have already said. Save your sympathy. *Le feu épure l'or.* The good Baron Cortachy as usual will emerge glowing richly,' Nicholas said.

'And his wife Margriet?' Gelis said. 'In case you are interested, Betha Sinclair goes across every day to see if she can help. Phemie too.'

'Phemie?' Nicholas said. Phemie was Betha's cousin, and shared her rooms in the Priory. In the midst of her disgust, it pleased Gelis to have tripped Nicholas into that question.

'Margriet asked for her. They met in Bruges, at the christening of the Countess's first child. Bel of Cuthilgurdy as well.'

This time she received only the flick of a dimple. 'I know Bel isn't here. The shrine of sanity has presumably found better things to do than follow our family *carroccio*. She has left us to the angel of distributive justice.'

'I hope not,' Gelis said. 'Justice is not what I had in mind. Are you here for some reason, such as to apologise; or merely on your way to visit the Countess?'

'Apologise for what? You are enjoying this,' Nicholas said. 'I am here to see the Countess, and the little broquette, and yourself. Govaerts and your steward have solved most of the problems, I gather, but there may be others to settle. Also, I shall divide my time now between this house and the other. There are rooms set aside, I am told.'

'With a separate entrance,' she said.

'But within earshot,' he said. 'People have been known to conceive by the ear. The Virgin Mary. Two or three friends we both know. Did you read the paper I left you?'

'I burned it,' she said.

'Oh,' he said. He wore one of his clown's faces, full of disappointment. 'You should have kept it for when Simon comes home. Simon needs it.'

'Certainly,' Gelis said, 'you do not.'

'No,' he said. He pushed himself thoughtfully off the door. 'But one must keep up the average. The Marquis of Ferrara had sixty-six bastards, they say:

> *'De ce côté-ci du Pô*
> *Tous sont fils de Niccolò.*

'I aim,' Nicholas said, 'for both sides of the Alps.'

'Why not?' Gelis said. 'You may have made a better start than you know. I have no complaints, and no questions. Go and see the Countess and make her even happier.'

He went to see the Countess, since that was why he was here, but first he visited Jodi, who had been smartly switched into a fresh tunic, he deduced, to receive his unheralded parent. Both Jodi and Mistress Clémence, for different reasons, looked rather pink.

Mistress Clémence was a choice of Gelis's with which Nicholas had no fault to find – but then, he had always had a respect for his wife's managerial powers. Whether employed by Gelis, by himself, or now within their joint ménage, Clémence of Coulanges had successfully steered her correct way through the changing relationships, while keeping her main task firmly before her: the wellbeing and training of Jordan.

He took her advice, within limits. When it was brought home to him now that Jodi was one of three children, and that he must give some attention to the others, he accepted that it was necessary for Jodi as well as for the Countess's brood, and acted accordingly. He had grown up among child apprentices, serving-maids' children, the children of his own employer who became later his wife. He had carried Tilde about on his back, who now had her own child, named Marian. As he sat, obtaining strange sounds from the whistle, he thought, not for the first time, of Margot's coming child, so long deferred because of the taint in her family. He had been prepared to find the same thing in Jordan. He supposed Margot felt as he had. Sometimes, in the stream of such thoughts, he wondered why he was doing what he was doing; but not for very long. Soon, he got up and went to see the King's sister.

The first-born of a young king and queen, Mary was the weakest of the five surviving orphans, having neither the ambitious intensity of the King, nor the wilful vigour of Sandy, nor the stupid belligerence of John of Mar, which showed itself more forgivably in the vivid, spoiled wildness of Margaret. Mary, with her wired headdress, her stiffened gown, her pallid skin, had been born frightened. Thomas Boyd, Earl of Arran, had offered her refuge after the death of her strong Flemish mother, and after the spectres of all those deadly contracts which would have married her to men who spoke another language, in parts of the world she had never known. It had happened to all her aunts. It would happen to her.

And instead, Fate had married her to Tom, whom she knew; who was Scots and well born and virile. She knew that, because her maids of honour told her everything. She would have an experienced lover. A glorious lover. Girls – women – married women – were dying of envy.

And so it had turned out. And now they had taken him from her.

She did not quite say all this to M. de Fleury, but when he kissed her hand she held it tightly, and made him sit close by her chair, to show kindness to him as he had shown it to her all those years ago, receiving her secretly in his house, though with respect, and agreeing to help her escape with her Tom. Before the dear children were born, whom it seemed he had befriended. Her dear fatherless children whom M. de Fleury was now going to help. Because now he was here, surely he would reunite her with her Tom?

She had sent her maids from the room. Nicholas, his hand trapped by hers, let her talk. The years of marriage, of intimacy, of childbirth had dispelled the shyness of their early encounters. Gradually, as she spoke, he realised that – as Gelis had said – she knew from her siblings all that had happened at the Castle, and his share in it. And she knew of course why it had been done. She did not even feel contempt for the Queen: she was uninterested. But it gave Nicholas, in her eyes, a physical kinship. He understood desire, her desire for her husband.

He listened, and occasionally spoke. Chiefly, she wanted to be heard. When she finished she wept, and he drew away his hand and found her a kerchief. Then she said, 'Now you must help me.'

It wasn't difficult. His shoulder had been cried on often enough by girls who couldn't read the signs; who didn't know when to let some lover go. The only difference was that in this case, the lover himself had not made the first move as yet. He said, 'My lady. The King your brother is not threatening your life.'

'But he has sentenced my husband to death,' said the Countess.

Nicholas said, 'My lady, he has sentenced your husband to death, but he has not tried to force him to return to face his sentence. He has not used his friendship with Burgundy or his new friendship with England to compel the Earl to come back, because his concern all along has been for you. So long as the King's beloved sister is in Scotland, he will not hound her husband.'

'But he won't let Tom return,' the Countess said. 'He won't forgive him.'

'He won't forgive him just now,' Nicholas said. 'The King is fond of you, my lady. He is hurt that you came back for love of Tom Boyd, not for him. That is why he is angry. His anger may take some time to fade. But once it does, is there not a chance he may reconsider? Young James will grow, and the baby. The King will learn to love them. One day, God willing, he will have his own children and will no longer see the Earl as a threat to his throne.'

Her face showed simple astonishment. 'A threat to the throne! Tom wishes only to return to his lands, and live as he has always done!'

'I am sure that he does,' Nicholas said. 'But your brother is King, and has his country to think of. Just now, with the Earl sheltered in England, the ruler of Scotland must be prudent. England is friendly now, but what if she fell out with your brother, and decided to launch some token attack with your husband as leader? I cannot know,' Nicholas said, 'if your grace has some ambition to be Queen: I do not think so. But I have to tell you that it would be more likely that your husband would die, and that you, if you had joined him, could not be spared execution. You and your children.'

'Tom would never –' she began.

'I am sure not. But if you returned now to your husband, your brother would have to think of that chance. He would be angry once more: you could no longer rely on his love. England would be required to ask you to leave. Burgundy would not accept you again. France would return you immediately to Scotland. So would Denmark. Where are your children going to be reared? Where will you die? In what country will your tomb lie?'

She stared at him. She said, 'I wish I were dead.'

Nicholas touched her hand. He said, 'You are at home, in your own land, with your sister and brothers about you. Your children will speak their own tongue. Wait. Have patience. Let the King's anger die. Wait until his new alliances are made, his way clear. Then you may plead again for your husband's return. Is it so much to ask?'

He waited. After a long time, she spoke. 'And if he doesn't forgive?'

He said, 'By that time you will know what you want, and what your husband wants. But to join him may be to kill him. You may have to think of his future more than your own. You may have to free him.'

He waited again. She said, 'How could we part?' Then she said, 'If I were free, they would send me away. They would send me away like Isabella, and Margaret and Eleanor.'

He said, 'There are not so many lords fit for you here, it is true. Some are old, or much-married, although kind enough.'

'I would marry anyone,' she said. 'If I couldn't have Tom, I would marry anyone, so long as I could stay at home.'

There was no one to hear it. It didn't matter: it had been said. He felt some pity, and let her see it. He said, 'Will you understand and forgive, then, if I do not help you? While you are here, your husband has hope. And the King may relent.'

'You are very kind,' Mary said. 'I am afraid I am not very clever. Tom is clever.'

'He knows he can rely on you,' Nicholas said. 'You are his bulwark.'

He had said nothing of Anselm Adorne.

He left almost at once, sweeping up his cloak down below, and brushing aside Katelijne Sersanders unseeing, so that she stood looking after him. He was already striding downhill when his way was barred.

His eyes blind, his mind wheeling, he was in no mood for that. He had his sword half from its sheath when he was set upon. He fought and then abruptly relaxed. The man before him was Roger, and the rest were the men of his choir: nine of them.

'Christ!' said the musician. 'Have they fired you from Martha and cracked you? You nearly broke my damned tooth.'

'No one would have noticed,' Nicholas said. 'You play as if they're all broken. Gumflute music. Gumpipe music. Gumkrumm . . .'

There was another scuffle, slightly less vicious this time, during which he took a lot of blows and recovered his self-possession. At the end, panting, they all turned him about and marched him downhill, away from his own house and the nuns' and Adorne's. Willie Roger said, 'You're coming to the Trinity with us.'

'Why?' said Nicholas.

'A mature falsetto,' said Roger approvingly. 'I have this bathing-tub –'

He broke off in order to let the renewed struggle run its course which it duly did, ending near the top of Halkerston's Wynd with four men shackling Nicholas by the arms and another hitched in immobilising fashion on his back. Halkerston's Wynd led to the church of the Trinity. Will Roger said, '– or we could roll you down. Yes or no?'

'No,' said Nicholas, and staggered to a resigned standstill. When Roger disapproved of something or somebody, he was apt to do this. He hadn't liked the sport at the Castle: Nicholas knew that well enough. He added, 'But I haven't much time.'

'I have plenty,' said Roger.

It sounded grim. Since, however, the many spectators were grinning, so Nicholas smiled in return equally broadly. He said, out of the side of the smile, 'Clacquedent, they'll call you. I'll have your embouchure for orderly garters. Tuscan drawn-work. Punto tirato. Molar merletti. And I'll wear your tongue in my hat. In the Name of the One, why the Trinity?'

They had let him go, and they were all walking normally. Roger said, 'Because it has an organ.'

It was too late by then to make another protest. The mellow sun shone on the loch; the moorfowl croaked; the Castle brooded against the bright sky. He walked on, and tried not to show how angry he was.

It was a sumptuous church, the one founded eleven years ago here at the lochside by the King's mother Mary of Guelders for her own weal, and the weal of her people. It was even complete enough to be used; at least to the extent of an apse and three bays of its choir, owing to the zeal of its Provost, Edward Bonkle his neighbour. Bonkle was not there when they reached it; but the doors were flung wide by the Sacristan and the Master himself, twinkling; welcoming. They walked under the hood of the porch and entered the spaces within.

Silent; cool as a forest the pillars receded, seemingly empty, leading the eye to the east, where a single lamp hung above a group of gowned men round a lectern. As he distinguished them, they were briskly joined by two boys, and then by the priests who had admitted him. Roger's friends followed after. Murmuring, smiling, they composed themselves surrounding the stand: a loose half-circle of underlit faces, reflective and brilliant as carollers in the snow.

Someone stretched to the lectern and furled back a skin of what lay there. It hung, speckled and supple, holding the light for a moment like honey. The speckles on it were music. And seated to the side of the sacristy door, almost concealed by the pipes of the organ was his metallurgical priest, Father Moriz.

Nicholas turned.

'Oh no,' said Roger.

They looked at one another. Nicholas said, 'This has nothing to do with you.' No one listening would have understood what he meant. He knew what he meant, and he thought Roger did.

Roger said, 'Then it won't touch you. Nicol? Your Passion, and my Chapel. This is what my Chapel will be like, when I have the money for it. Today, they are singing for nothing. This performance is for you. You and him.'

He indicated the near side of the church. Nicholas stretched back his head, expecting to be shown Father Moriz; but the man quietly sitting in one of the stalls was Anselm Adorne. A man who studied his enemies.

Ludere, non ledere. He was no longer an apprentice. He nodded to Adorne, but didn't join him. There were stone benches lining the aisles, and he seated himself on one of those, and watched Roger walk to the circle of singers and take his place in the centre. The Master nodded. Moriz bent to the bellows. The organist lifted his hands. Nicholas reclined, embracing one knee, and studied the floor.

The tiles were glazed. They glimmered green and yellow and brown, double-netted like fish where the window-leads caught them. When the first rumbling sound shook from the organ you would have expected them to heave up in shock, to writhe and to glint, but they didn't. The coloured designs on the windows hugged the shafts of the piers like embroidery on an Angevin doublet, in and out of the pleats, teasing up to the floriate collar of the capitals, which promptly exploded in clamour. The stone pealed. The capitals became the surrogate mouths of the organ. He removed his eyes from the capitals and gazed at the tiles all through the noise of the organ, and the echoing silence, and the lifting of the first human voices.

Gaude, flore virginali honoreque speciali, the two trebles sang. He knew the text, but had never heard the music before. It was to be a motet, not a Mass. The Seven Joys of the Mother of God. It shouldn't take long. His neck ached with looking down. He looked up.

He approved of the roof. It was simpler than at Roslin, where Sinclair had barred the aisles with carved timbers. Sinclair, whose daughter was sitting by Anselm Adorne's wife Margriet, struggling to carry her child. No one blamed Adorne. An aristocrat with a dozen children might still demand more; and none would blame him. *Gaude sponsa cara Dei*, sang the altos, weaving, blending as all the five parts came into play.

There was a virtue in simplicity. Here, the beauty lay in the strictness of the lines and the delicacy of the colour, complementing each other, so that the proportion of the whole was deeply pleasing: an imposing ninety feet from the bright cup of the apse to the rood tower behind him. The back of his own house could be viewed from the tower; he had climbed up there once to verify how much an outsider might see. Now he had less need to trouble; it was generally known that the King's guest-gifts were made in Wilhelm's private furnace, and accounted for the strong chests and the charcoal sheds and the smoke. It had amused him to accommodate Gelis, all unknowing, in the nuns' house which had also, in its time, been a mint. But time enough, of course, for all that.

Gaude splendens vas virtutem . . . In pictures the Nativity was the Third Joy, and the Adoration of the Magi the Fourth. Nicholas had met John le Grant through a Magi procession in Florence, organised for Cosimo de' Medici. He had met Cosimo's small grandson, who had also had a whistle, and who had died. John le Grant was wary of children but had proved his worth on that mining expedition in the Tyrol, and would do so again very soon. Nicholas gave some thought to his plans.

Ut ad votum consequaris quicquid virgo postularis, the basses were singing, while the tenors slipped back and forth. The harmonies, the dissonances were breathtaking; he ignored them. To obtain what he wanted in fullest measure was his intention as well. Riches were not all, although they were enjoyable in church as elsewhere: the cloth of gold and massed cups on the altar; the curtains of pleasance; the silk brocades and the fringes that trembled over the statues of the Blessed Virgin and of St Margaret – but riches were not always enough.

So the foundress had discovered perhaps: Mary of Guelders, in her magnificent tomb in the centre of the sacristy. She had outlived her young husband by only two years, leaving to this brood of unruly children a heritage of high expectations and uncertain skills. Of course, they had been brought up by Betha Sinclair, by Whitelaw, by all the loyal, good nursemaids like Mariota; brought up in comfort. They would hardly miss their mother the Queen. Sometimes, when he found them too simple, Nicholas wished that their parents had survived, and that he had been enabled to try his wits against a grown King and his consort.

At other times he recognised the dangers of over-confidence. Whitelaw and Argyll were subtle and experienced men; so were Sinclair and Hamilton. He had pitched himself against a team as strong as any he would find in Burgundy or in Venice. Only Louis of France could give him a more dangerous match. Louis and the fat man, Jordan de Ribérac, who had sent Wodman to spy, but had not come himself, perhaps to discourage Simon from coming. Jordan despised his son, but preserved him from his own follies. Jordan didn't want hot-tempered Simon in Scotland. Of course, one day Simon would come, if only to vent his spite against Gelis. *Gaude mater miserorum.* One could look forward to that.

The singing was running, dividing, weaving and leaping like the interleaved arches that lined the aisle in which he sat. The building was so high that the voices floated, unimpeded by finial or crocket, or echoing them in their own florid patterns and knots. Bishop Kennedy must have shared some of the planning: the masons from St Salvator's were everywhere. The architect was a cousin of Jamie Liddell's, and had even Cochrane's approval.

It was as well Kennedy was out of the way, now the Bishop his nephew was making so many ludicrous blunders. The unfortunate man would be in Rome by now, with poor Jan Adorne. There was no shortage of dispatches from Rome: Julius appeared to be mortared into the bricks until Christmas, although Gregorio was returning to Venice, having dispatched all he could discover about the rich and worthy Anna von Hanseyck. The idea of Julius in love was something which, regrettably, sent all his friends into paroxysms. Tobie would have been amused, had he been here. Godscalc would have worried. Well, Godscalc didn't need to worry about anything or anyone any more.

The noise was making it harder to think. Leaning back, staring at the immense sweep of the vaulting overhead, studded with bosses, Nicholas was increasingly bothered by the strands of sound soaring over his head. He tried to envisage the text and the pictures. Christ disputing among doctors. A doubtful pleasure, to those who remembered the same Dr Tobias, or knew Dr Andreas or Master Scheves. But of course, that evaded the issue. The equivalent doctors were not of that sort, they were the thinkers of Paris and Orléans and Bologna and Louvain. Of al-Azhar and the Sankore Mosque. Humbly, he had disputed with them. Joy was what he had found. And had lost.

Gaude virgo mater pura, certa manens et secura. The last verse. Translated: secure, this mother had lost nothing by dying. He stared at her image. Behind it, jewelled baguettes, the apse windows had dulled; the light now came from the vast windows and the clerestory behind and above him. The silvered organ pipes glittered and the voice of the organ intervened. You could hear the organ in St Donatien from Colard Mansion's room. In Venice, it was the clangour of bells which made the head ache, especially in Carnival-time. *Non cessabunt,* sang the voices. *Non cessabunt, nec descrescent sed durabunt et florescent per aeterna saecula* . . . Will not cease nor diminish, but will last and flourish through all eternity.

One word more.

The echoes of the final chord settled about him. He did not immediately move: he was calculating something. When Anselm Adorne got up and walked over, Nicholas stood. He saw that Moriz and the organist had walked in the opposite direction, and were enclosed within the group of singers, as if mourning in silence. He turned his gaze back to Adorne, standing before him.

Adorne said, 'You must have been as moved as I was. I have never heard anything finer. The only version I know is from England. We had it sung at the Dry Tree. I know you are musical. When you come back to Bruges, you must let me enrol you there.' He paused. The knot of singers was still closely entwined. He said, 'Margriet came to see you.'

The Dry Tree, however vaguely religious, was really a club for aristocrats and their friends. Tommaso Portinari was a member. They had helped with the music for the Duke of Burgundy's marriage. Nicholas said, 'Thank you. Yes. I am sorry she is unwell. Tell her that I think the lady Mary will decide of her own will to stay.'

'I see,' said Adorne. He stirred. 'Here is Master Roger coming to hear our opinion. Perhaps you don't know but, preparing this work, he and his singers have had almost no sleep for a week. It was for you. He wished you to perceive a work of perfection.'

'I feared as much,' Nicholas said.

Adorne looked at him. 'It is not perhaps the impertinence it appears. It is a pity to wear out one's life solely in resistance to others, and never to pause to create something worthwhile of one's own. Especially someone as gifted as yourself. Roger has offered you music. Give him what he asks in return.'

He sounded earnest. Then he smiled and turned aside to stop and embrace Will Roger as he arrived. Nicholas heard their voices without listening to them. The door had opened behind him, letting in the mid-afternoon light. The singers had put out the lamp and, leaving the lectern, were beginning to drift forward. Adorne made a final remark and, gripping Roger briefly by the shoulder, smiled again at Nicholas and quietly withdrew.

Will Roger turned to Nicholas and gazed at him. He said, 'Your eyes are dry.' His own were sunken and very bright.

Nicholas said, 'It was passable. Why should I tell you it was magnificent? You know you can do anything, now you've done that.'

Roger showed no sign of having heard him. He said again, 'Your eyes are dry.'

It made Nicholas angry, having no answer. He gave the only answer he had. 'I didn't ask for it. You told me it wouldn't touch me.'

Roger continued to stare at him. His face, from being tired, had become heavy. 'You couldn't,' he said. 'Could you?'

Some of his prebendaries, speeding towards them, heard the change of tone and slowed down. Exhausted, ecstatic, the others were transported still.

Nicholas said nothing. Will Roger suddenly said, 'You bastard! You blocked it. Did you? You blocked it with something.'

He had blocked it. He might as well admit it. 'I had a lot to think about. It wasn't my idea,' Nicholas said. Now the others were slowly gathering round. On their faces the elation of the performance was starting to ebb, leaving starkness behind.

Roger said, 'You didn't hear *anything*? Not even the end?'

Gaude virgo mater pura . . .

Nicholas said, 'The sound came through. I didn't listen. I'm sorry.'

Whistle Willie said, 'If the sound came through, your mind heard it. Sing it.' All the singers were close. There was a rustle. Roger said in an angry aside, 'You don't know,' and turned back to Nicholas. 'Sing it. Any part.'

It was ludicrous. He was poised to make some joking remark; to convey soothing excuses; to leave.

He couldn't do it. He couldn't deny, for his own peace of mind, what he had just been given. He let Whistle Willie's fierce gaze remain locked in his own, and unwillingly opened the evil, infallible bank of his memory.

It was a tenor part that came to the surface, from the later verses, when the weight of the music had first begun to break through. That he could recall it, with all its fluid turns and rapid ornaments, signified nothing; his musical memory was like that. He could hear the other four parts in his mind as he began to reproduce, sotto voce, the one he had chosen. It required concentration. He sang as if he and Willie Roger were face to face and alone, since that was how he felt. It was some moments before he realised that the other parts were not in his head, but were being taken up, one by one, by the other singers. Taghaza, Taghaza. The texture floated, complete: a ghostly furnishing below the high vaults.

When the verse ended, they were all gathered close and Roger, who had never moved his gaze from his face, lifted his choir-master's hand. 'Do you remember the rest?'

He did remember. This time he summoned his voice, properly

placed on the reservoirs of its air; and the others did likewise. The interweaving now was not faint but firm and rushing and brilliant: glass and paint and silver and stone. It swirled through the spaces and quickened. The fierce *Amen*, when it came, struck the roof and dissolved in a curtain of echoes. The organ pealed and pealed and pealed, and the singers stood, flushed.

Unobserved in the shadows, Father Moriz stole to the door and addressed the man who, arrested, had stopped there to listen.

'Master Roger will get his Play now. Perfect as that was perfect, whatever it costs.' He mopped his face, which was moist. 'I am disturbed. I may have been wrong.'

'No,' said Anselm Adorne. 'No. Your instincts were right. There is the proof.' His lashes were wet; he made no effort to dry them.

The priest said, 'There is also the root of my concern. To divert a brook is one thing; to divert a river is quite another. You will still compete against Nicholas?'

'I must,' Adorne said. 'And with my whole heart. My house depends on me.'

'Good,' said the priest. 'And for his sake, I might hope that you'd win, were I not paid by the Bank, and bound to try to outguess you, as he will. I should leave the church now, and so should you. It will permit them to float to some inn and get drunk. The Most High, I feel sure, will absolve them.'

Chapter 15

GREGORIO OF ASTI left Rome in October in order to await the birth of Margot's first child in Venice. He was aware that Julius, daily expecting to welcome his Gräfin, was disappointed by his departure; but his wife, his darling, vivid and firm as a nut in the hedgerow, naturally came first.

Her pregnancy had been untroubled from the start. They were not foolish enough to view this as an omen. Margot's bloodline bred aberrations. Because of it, she and her first husband had had no children, and after he died, she and Gregorio had lived without marriage or children because of it. The turning point had been Gelis's son. Aghast for Nicholas, revolted by Gelis's tale of betrayal, Gregorio had given no thought to the coming child of that betrayal. It had been Margot, no less upset, who had steeled herself to go to Gelis and offer to share her self-imposed exile and stay to look after the child when it was born. Later, sickened by what Nicholas had been made to endure, Margot had changed her allegiance, and helped to bring together father and son.

It had been, for her, a series of long and difficult trials. She had learned that a bond with a child will overcome anything. She had learned from the steadfastness of Nicholas, who had shown no doubts about accepting his son, however malformed. She had realised with horror that Nicholas, knowing her history, had assumed that the care of his invisible child had required her special acquaintance with deformity. And that Gelis had allowed him to think it, even when the child had been born without fault.

Margot had found it hard to forgive Gelis van Borselen, but now she was ready for children, Gregorio's children. And if they were less than perfect, they would be born into a love which would compensate. Gregorio felt as she did. He had already sent for old Tasse.

In Rome, alight with Pope fever, the thick insect-ridden heat of the summer moved hardly observed into autumn as the stately delegations followed their harbingers into the city and every bank struggled over its ledgers to keep afloat in the torrents of ducats, the snowfalls of bills of exchange that arrived with their masters.

Handsomely quartered in the Canale del Ponte close to Hadrian's Bridge, the financial sector of Rome was inhabited by astute men of many nations who knew each other well. Success in a new papal era depended on a supernatural adroitness in identifying new trends; in finding a path through the smokescreen of hints and rumours and misinformation that swirled daily through the community; and above all in plucking what information could be had from the incoming embassies, from the highest officials to the lowest page-boy or groom.

Lazzarino of the Casa Niccolò had been selected as factor in Rome because of his skill in this respect. The most inoffensive and obliging of men, he took his listening ears to all occasions of note and said nothing; his reports told what he had learned. His wife, more naturally opinionative, had the sense to appear gentle also. Their aptitudes fitted in well enough with the more flamboyant personality of Julius, who was happy to leave the dull work to the agent and buff up the Bank's social relationships in his own style.

By the time Gregorio left, the English embassy was already over: a constipated group under Goldwell, dispatched to bring the obedience from a King newly back on his throne, who desired the fact to be noticed. Florence followed: not on the prodigious scale of Milan, but rich enough to make the eyes water. It was led by Lorenzo de' Medici, and included a column of wains requiring thirty-five horses to pull them, and loaded with, among other things, four hundred pounds' weight of table silver.

For lodging they had the hospitality of Lorenzo de' Medici's two uncles who ran the Rome Bank and, more grandly, the extravagant palace of Cardinal Orsini, whose eighteen-year-old niece was the wife of Lorenzo. With the party rode five other envoys, the orator Donato Acciajuoli and a Martelli among them, and an assortment of Levantine exiles including a girlish young half-Greek called Nerio. There came also a crippled kinsman of Acciajuoli's whose presence would have turned Nicholas cold, had his thoughts not been directed elsewhere.

Julius had no qualms when this particular gentleman stalked into his house, the wooden leg perfectly managed underneath the long skirts of plum velvet. Gazing at the smooth bearded face and dark eyes, Julius noted the silvery hairs, the sharper bones, but conceded that the man had worn well since the day that Claes had snapped his leg off by accident. By what passed for an accident, in those light-hearted years when men perceived only Claes, and not Nicholas.

Acciajuoli hadn't borne him a grudge; had indeed passed him a few business tips well worth having, even if there had been a sting, now and then, in the tail. Nicholas seemed to find the fellow lowering, which was natural. Acciajuoli was a man who had seen Nicholas, his back buttered, in jail. Nicholas hadn't been anyone's padrone then.

Julius thought the Florentine sly – his Greek blood – but would hardly call him malignant. They said he had approached Gelis in Florence two years ago. No one knew whether he had offered her anything, or asked her to do something, or had been merely obeying a whim. He was an inquisitive man. At this very moment, goblet in hand, he was enquiring about the arrival of Anna. It was a dull, clammy day, and they were sitting in the loggia in the garden, not far from where Ludovico da Bologna had once placed himself.

'The Gräfin?' Julius said. 'Many of our clients, as you might expect, are coming to Rome. I believe she is one of them.'

'Of course,' said the Florentine soothingly. 'I forgot. She is a shareholder in the Bank's newest ship. I am told your splendid merchantman is sadly delayed? Some dispute in the boat-yard at Danzig?'

'One expects it,' said Julius. 'There are others.'

'Skiffs and doggers and balingers, in little boat-yards in Scotland, so rumour says. Not very palatable news for your Hanse friends in Cologne. Unless, that is, you mean to recover your fleet from the Doge? The old *Ciaretti*, the pirated *Ghost*, the battered *San Niccolò*? Venice would have a right to complain. But who could blame Nicholas, retired to his love nest in Scotland, if he lost interest in fighting the Turk on the Euxine, or in Persia, or the Khanates?' He smiled, and laid down his cup. 'I hear his wife is pregnant again.'

Despite himself, Julius could not resist it. 'Not unless miracles have happened. The best news we have received is that he has refrained from breaking her other arm. He is where he is, on the affairs of the company. After that, he is committed to Burgundy. He will come back to the Somme when the spring land campaigns open. He couldn't sail for the East if he wanted to.'

'Even for gold?' the Florentine said. 'Or perhaps he thinks he will divine all the gold he requires in little Scotland, as he thinks he has identified all the alum in the Tyrol? I have to tell you that the Vatachino think he has allowed personal matters to stifle his genius. The gold in Scotland is trifling. The sale of other alum will be prohibited so long as the papal mines have the monopoly.'

Julius admired his own beautiful hose. They were of knitted silk, with three pearls down each side. He said, 'Run by the Medici.'

The Florentine tilted his head. He, too, was admiring the pearls.

He said, 'Operated by the Bank of the Medici. Also the newly opened magnificent mines in Volterra, a commune under the influence of Florence.'

'Another source of rightful pride to Messer Lorenzo,' Julius said. 'One has only to hope that the rumours of unrest in Volterra are baseless. Also the tales of useless stockpiles of alum, over-produced and offered at too high a price. After all, the profits are to finance the Crusade you mentioned. The spring sailing to Persia. The peregrinations of Father Ludovico, the Patriarch of Antioch. The marriage of Zoe. I believe Messer Prosper de Camulio has been seen in the city. One might imagine that even the Genoese think that papal alum may not, sadly, achieve all that it might.'

There was a silence during which Julius, smiling, studied the toe of his slipper. Whatever one might think of him, sometimes Nicholas got it just right. Then the Florentine said, 'I have a message for your Master Niccolò. The Medici have lost none of their power. And this is a different Pope, with different policies. You may have fewer friends now, and those you have, may be dispersed very soon. The Vatachino must watch out for themselves.' He paused. 'In this new world, it pays to be Greek.'

Nicholas had said that as well. Nicholas, in the closely written pages ciphered for Julius alone, had suggested paying particular attention to the quandary of Zoe, tender unmarried heiress to the brilliant lost throne of Byzantium. Failing her brothers, who were too young to lead armies, the husband of Zoe would have the right and the duty to drive the Turk from his Empire. Once, with the blessing of Cardinal Bessarion, it had seemed that Zacco of Cyprus would make Zoe his bride, and Cyprus an outpost of Byzantium. It had not suited Venice. Cyprus was to be a Venetian arsenal, a floating war-machine against the Grand Turk. Zacco, discontentedly rattling his chains, had instead married Catherine Corner, half Venetian, wholly the daughter of a princess of the lesser Greek Empire of Trebizond.

Catherine's uncle was in Persia now, urging her great-uncle Uzum Hasan to lead his armies against the Sublime Porte. It would embarrass the Turk to have the White Sheep attack from the south. It would embarrass them more to be attacked at the same time from Moscow. As would occur, one might hope, if Zoe, daughter of Caesars, gave her hand to the Grand Duke of Muscovy. The widower Ivan the Third, the lord of White Russia; and the fated successor, perhaps, to Constantine Palaeologus, the last lord of Byzantium.

Julius said, 'How right you are. Greece! Fount of all civilisation. Although, in my days serving Cardinal Bessarion, I never found him less than complimentary to us Latins. I take it that you are attending his ritual welcome to the Florentine embassy? If anything has gone amiss with your invitation, I should be happy to write you another. I have the Cardinal's confidence.'

'I should have expected no less,' said Acciajuoli. 'He reposes the same confidence in the Latin Patriarch, your much-travelled Father Ludovico. The Cardinal has even found, in his wisdom, a willing partner to finance his new printing schemes. The Vatachino have his confidence too.'

'Really? A little more wine?' Julius said. 'So Anselm Adorne made some investments in Rome?'

'As to that,' said the Florentine, 'you must ask his son Jan. I believe he is hourly expected at the Flaminian Gate – that is, the Porta del Popolo. The Scots bishop called Graham is with him. But why speak of business? I prefer to give myself completely to pleasure. Indeed, I look forward to the Cardinal of Nicaea's reception to which – I believe – I have been invited. Nerio will know.' He laid down his cup with a smile. 'No, I thank you. It is a fine vintage, but I must leave.'

'Nerio?' Julius repeated. Seeing the other man rise, he remained standing. He put down the flask with a certain care.

'The young lad who was exiled from Trebizond. Duke Charles made him welcome at Bruges; Alighieri knows him, of course, as does the Cardinal. Perhaps you remember; you met him in Venice.'

Julius remembered. He said, 'Is he here?'

'Outside. He hesitated to intrude.'

'But bring him in!' Julius exclaimed. He knew he had flushed. He saw it reflected in the boy's face as Nerio entered; in the lustrous dark eyes fixed on his, above the delicate chin, the curling lips, the exquisite nose. In Venice, Nerio of Trebizond had caused a great deal of mischief by ceasing to dress like a man. Now, the long lashes flickered once; then, smiling, Nerio touched the one-legged man on the shoulder, his white fingers smoothing the velvet.

'Sit, sir,' he said. 'I am sure Master Julius does not expect you to stand.' And turning: 'Monsignore, I am happy to see you.'

'And I, you,' Julius said. 'You are with the embassy? Are you enjoying it?'

'He is with me,' said the Florentine calmly. 'I thought it was obvious.' And, indeed, as the bearded man resumed his seat smoothly, the youth sank to a stool at his knee. After a moment, the man's hand touched his neck, and then rested there. Feeling it, the boy smiled; but the dark eyes were still fixed on Julius.

Julius poured a full cup. 'You will drink with me, Nerio, I hope.' Carrying over the wine, he brought to mind something about Tilde

in Bruges. Tilde complaining of Catherine her sister, and how she
filled the Charetty–Niccolò house with her ardent young followers.
And the rumour he had heard more than once: that they were not
there from love of Catherine, these charming young men. Of whom
Nerio had been one. And Diniz, Tilde's husband, another.

He gave Nerio the cup, and said, 'I am glad to have caught you. I
expect you will be on your travels quite soon.' Their fingers touched,
by no volition of his.

The older man spoke, with no trace of jealousy, but rather a hint of
well-bred amusement. 'We shall be here for a week or two yet. There
is plenty of time.'

Trotting back and forth to the Apostolic Palace, prayerfully prodding
its solitary mule, the complement of the Scots lodging in Rome
heard the same news of impending arrival, and expressed its excited
alarm.

'Expected hourly!' said the Abbot of Cambuskenneth, wringing out
the hem of his robe and sitting down in the communal parlour. He
lifted both little feet and watched his man draw off his boots: they
came off so easily that the man nearly sat in the fire. Henry Arnot
grinned, and then gave a great howl. 'Patrick Graham coming here! I
cannot believe it! Arches will crumble, temples fall, catacombs fill
with absconding prelates and cattle. Why here?'

'Because he can't afford anywhere else,' said the brother of the
Abbot of Melrose. 'At least he'll help you win your campaign for
Coldingham. He's still Bishop of St Andrews, or was when I was last
at my desk. All your musical friends will be pleased. And you like
Anselm Adorne.'

'I don't like his son,' said Henry Arnot. 'No. That is uncharitable.
I would wish no further ill on a young man who has had to travel
from Bruges with the Bishop of St Andrews. Such a catastrophe,
when you remember his uncle. But a family tree is a salad of many
herbs.'

'Henbane,' said John Blackadder.

'Not the first day,' said the Abbot. 'Later, perhaps.'

Even before leaving Bruges, Jan Adorne had thought of henbane. By
the time he had crossed the Alps and accompanied the Bishop of St
Andrews through Pavia, Bologna, and Viterbo, the eldest son of
Anselm Adorne was contemplating something more sudden with
blood in it. It was not so much that Patrick Graham was short-
tempered and greedy, had acquired too many illegal offices and was
failing to pay for them. It was because he complained all the time.

Last year, on his long, painful pilgrimage, Jan had fallen out with his father, the autocratic, demanding, exigent Baron Cortachy. But his father had been a model of self-control compared with this man of the Church, obsessed by his own royal blood. His father, grieved though he'd been over Jan's silly behaviour in Venice, had forgiven him in the end, and had said nothing of it back there at Calais, although he had not allowed him to come with him to Scotland. If Jan had been given a punishment it was this, to come back to Italy, the place where he had made a fool of himself. But he might have made a fool of himself anyway, if he'd stayed with his parents. They had no right to do it. His father and mother had no right to shame him, at their age, with their lust. To make a new child together, and to send him away.

Repressively, he made the best of it. A qualified lawyer, with years of training at Paris and Pavia, he must set to and start his career. Every offer in Bruges had fallen through. In any case, there was only one path to the heights, and that was through office in Rome, and the kind of situation the last Pope had offered. That Pope was dead, but his nephew was still in Rome, still a Cardinal. And Cardinal's secretaries had been known to become Popes themselves, in the fullness of time.

Not that Jan's ambitions stretched quite so far, or were quite so weighty. He knew he lacked concentration, and would have to curb a taste for student frivolities; but provided he were in the right company, it should be easy. He hoped to meet no one who had seen him in Venice, and had been thankful, in passing through Pavia, to find de Fleury's physician no longer there. Dr Tobias had gone to the Count of Urbino, either to cure his marsh-fever or to attend his wife through her ninth pregnancy. She had already given day to eight daughters, but such was the mystical reputation of the Banco di Niccolò that a son was no doubt considered assured. Jan hoped with all his might it would be a ninth daughter. He hated Nicholas de Fleury and his whole heartless, mercenary crew. Henbane would be too good for him, too.

It was raining in Rome. Once, he had found the city exciting. Slowly, after the return of the Popes from Avignon, the new houses and mansions, inns and villas, fountains and stalls had begun to cluster again round the bridges, and the two principal roads to Ostia and the north. Some of the converted palaces stayed the same, but churches were acquiring new faces, and costly and elegant buildings were rising now for the Roman nobles, the Cardinals, the Conservators and the municipal authorities, with fine gardens and salons and halls where precious things could be displayed. Only a few months

ago, Jan and his father had been shown the Pope's own collection in
the Palazzo San Marco: the gems and medals and bronzes and
cameos; the twenty-five charming altars with their mosaics; the jewelled vestments and ivories; the hundred gold coins, the thousand
silver; the modern arras from Flanders; and the golden vases commissioned from Florence. It was said that he had offered to build a new
bridge for Toulouse in exchange for a cameo.

All that had been the Pope's. When, only this January, Jan had
received the news, kneeling, that a post would be his with the
Cardinal of San Marco, his future had seemed brilliantly assured. He
would live in the Palazzo. The ceremonies of the Vatican, glittering
and ornate, confirmed the promise of a career that – provided he now
kept his head – might astonish and humble his father. The whole city
seemed ready to blossom. St Peter's itself had acquired a flight of
new marble steps, magnificent statues. There was no end to what
might be going to happen.

Then the Pope died. Life continued. Building continued. But now
Jan remembered more clearly the other aspect of Rome which had
been forced on him by his antiquarian father, who had dragged him
remorselessly from Colosseum to Forum, from arch to pillar, from
towering baths to underground tombs. Looked at thus, Rome was no
more than a stackyard: a hilly wilderness of rough grass and cracked
stone within a circle of walls far too big for it. Most of the ruins had
been quarried, the shapes of theatre or temple half lost and the bricks
exposed, thin and reddish under the marble. Incinerated marble
offered a rich profit in lime: they had discovered as much in
Alexandria.

From the heights, its towers foreshortened, its gardens concealed,
the Eternal City looked neglected and pagan; a place of marshes
and mounds choked with sanctified offerings, its surface pitted and
pustuled with domes, circles and crescents; home to robbers and
beggars, where packs of dogs strayed and animals rooted even as far
as the old Ponte Rotto, and dead men were found every day. That
was the country inside the walls, where rich men might wall off a
vineyard or a well-protected villa near to the jetty for Ostia. For
business, one had to stay in the crowded part, even though two riders
could scarcely find room to pass in some of the unpaved, crooked
lanes.

Strangers entering Rome, however, would see only what was impressive. Here, the wider roads, although only surfaced with dirt, led
between tall houses whose porticos admitted glimpses of green, handsome courtyards. From time to time they would open into wide
flowered spaces round a church or a monastery, or a piazza where the

Cardinals' houses were hung with paintings and tapestry, and the streets were laid with fine carpets on feast days. Once, it had seemed very fine. Now, he was afraid to think anything.

He delivered Patrick Graham and his servants to the Scots house and fled, as he had explained that he must, to the hospice of the French nation. It was untrue that he had arranged to live there: he had to pay extra before they would take him. His father had expected him to stay with the Bishop. He couldn't stand any more. He wanted to speak the French they all spoke at home, a reminder of Paris, the happiest time of his life.

It was bitter, then, to find there no one that he knew; no one who had travelled as he had. The young men were moved to remark on his beard, the sacred mark of the pilgrim; two years in growing, and carefully kept to impress the late Pope's nephew, the Cardinal Barbo. They asked, open-eyed, if sheeps' eyes could be chewed, or gave you a fright the next day in the chamber pot. They enquired whether Arab wives kept their veils on before and during the act, and who shaved them. They wished to know how his cousin pissed, dressed as a boy. They put something into his ale, and after he had been sick, slapped his back and told him he was one of them now, and tried to take him off for a night in a bawdy house.

Sallow and shaky, he took his letters at first light to the wonderful Palazzo San Marco, and left them with the Cardinal's chamberlain. He had hoped to be invited inside: his father had written already, and the Cardinal might have expected him. But His Eminence, said the chamberlain, was much occupied, and it might take some time to arrange an appointment. He trusted that Signor Adorno was in no haste to leave Rome.

It was dispiriting. He wandered about in the rain, avoiding the houses his father knew. When he had braced himself to return to the hostel, striding in and slamming the door like a magistrate, it was to find the parlour empty but for a well-built middle-aged man in fine clothes whose slanting eyes and classical cheek-bones he remembered at once. Jan Adorne froze.

'I startled you,' said the Banco di Niccolò's notary Julius. 'Look, don't hold it against me. I've forgotten everything that happened in Venice; and anyway I'm here to give you a hand. You're here to see Cardinal Barbo.'

'How did you know I was here?' Adorne said.

'I called at the Scots lodging. My God, I remember the Bishop from Linlithgow. I don't know how you got here alive. I would have killed him, and then cut my own throat. You know that Nicholas is in Scotland with his family?'

'My parents will be there by now,' Adorne said. The wave of nausea was receding. He straightened his back.

'I shouldn't worry,' said Julius. 'They'll enjoy sparring with one another, Nicholas and M. le baron your father. I only mentioned it to show that no harm came of all that nonsense at Venice. Nicholas took proper care of the child, and he and his wife are together again. And Simon de St Pol is shown up for the cur that he is. Wait till Nicholas gets him.'

'He could be dangerous,' said Jan Adorne. 'His father more so. Afterwards, I thought his father was behind it. Jordan de Ribérac.' He paused. 'My father had nothing to do with it.'

'We know that,' Julius said. He lifted an eyebrow. He said, 'I wonder. If you're not going to eat me, M. Jean, could I beg a little refreshment? I've been waiting a long time.'

He said it in French. Jan realised he had been speaking French – Savoyard French – from the beginning. He said, 'Yes, of course. I'll call for something,' and went off to find servants. When he came back, he was already half composed, and by the end of the meal more at ease than he would have thought possible. They had talked of a great many things: he could not remember how many. And Julius – he was to call him simply Julius – had offered to obtain him an invitation to Cardinal Bessarion's great reception for the Florentine embassy in the Palazzo Colonna. At which, he guaranteed, Jan would come face to face with Cardinal Barbo.

By the time he saw Julius to the door and the others came back, Jan felt perfectly able to deal with them, answering their gambits like a tolerant uncle, and even able to laugh at some of the adventures with which they attempted to shock him. They also told him something of Julius, who had made an impression, it seemed, during his stay in the city. Apparently he was in love with some countess, and was expecting her to come to Rome before Christmas. Her name, as he understood it, was German. They said he had bribed the watch at the Flaminia to tell him the moment she appeared.

Jan was amused. Julius had said nothing of it, which made him appear both more human and a good deal less Olympian. He had confided to Jan that sometimes he found Nicholas too brutish for comfort; and his wife was a witch. Julius thought it a mistake for any man to father a child except in the first flush of youth. It was unfair to the child.

Jan agreed.

Chapter 16

STATELY, WHITE-BEARDED and chaste, the Cardinal Bessarion thought a great deal about banks. It was one of the reasons why, today, he was holding a reception for the envoys of the Republic of Florence in his home, the splendid Palazzo Colonna. Splendid, but not extravagant. Not at all. This was not a household noisy with hunting-dogs, flute-players, jesters. To build the Palazzo San Marco, the late Pontiff had required that a whole quarter of Rome be torn down. But in all this vast complex of houses and courts, the many lodgings which adjoined the Church of the Holy Apostles, there were only twenty servants to see to the needs of the Cardinal, his household, his scribes and his pensioners. Yet no one could deny that his house was well run, his table generous. To bankers, especially.

Sadly, this afternoon Lorenzo de' Medici himself was not present, having been summoned from Rome by the increasing unrest in Volterra. The Holy Father had voiced his regrets, but made sure that Lorenzo received a gift of two classical busts and his pick of the late Pope's collection of gems at a very reasonable price. The other envoys remained (including the inestimable Donato Acciajuoli), for there was no doubt, of course, that the Florentine Bank would continue to manage the finances of the Papal See, and to export its alum. The Medici Bank, and not the Pazzi, or the Banco di Niccolò.

The Cardinal Bessarion – moving hospitably from one group to another; speaking to his scholarly house-guests, his fellow exiles from Trebizond, the orators of Florence – had not forgotten the Banco di Niccolò, ruled by this young Burgundian who did not know what he was or what he was doing. In all the years he had known Nicholas de Fleury, either through their infrequent meetings or indirectly through that zealot the Patriarch of Antioch, the Cardinal had never given up hope that the man would eventually bring himself and his Bank to the aid of the Church in the East.

The Cardinal had not given up hope because, although his interest in de Fleury was purely political, as was the Patriarch's, his experience of human nature was wide, and he had observed some contradictions to which da Bologna had not given note.

According to his former clerk Julius, as well as his own observation, the man Nicholas had heard at least some of the teaching at Louvain, could read, and knew languages. According to the merchant Michael Alighieri, now knight and chamberlain to Duke Charles of Burgundy, the young Nicholas had been a silent observer during the Emperor's famous gatherings of scholars at Trebizond, and during his wanderings after, had drifted through several studios on both sides of the Alps. According to the seamaster and merchant Benedetto Dei, who traded in Africa, the man Nicholas had attended the schools of the Sankhore University for many months, placing himself in the hands of the finest Arab teachers of the day.

Yet nothing of it was visible. Questioned, the Burgundian evaded the subject. He entered no discussions, took part in no debates. Here, last Christmas, he had broken bread with Callistos, Laskaris and the Cardinal's own dear Perotto. He had listened to Regiomontanus, who had tried to draw from him his experiences in Timbuktu and beyond, but with no success. Once, perhaps, the reticence had been rooted in shyness, but that was true no longer; the man was disarming in converse, conveying all he wished to convey, with some wit.

Perhaps the habit of self-distrust in personal matters was hard to break, once ingrained. Perhaps he feared, as often happened, that in saying something, he might not be able to prevent himself saying too much. Or perhaps, since he came from humble beginnings, he had discovered early the secret of a kind of contentment, and preferred to float through life on this familiar raft, rather than plumb below, and risk finding turmoil and pain, or a mission which his mind or his soul could not abandon.

Such a man would act like this and, seeking justification, would make himself a false purpose, creating an earthquake out of a sneeze, and a burning wound from the scratch of a fingernail. He had seen it happen, in women as often as men, and it never ceased to exasperate him with its waste. He had never found a solution.

And now Nicholas de Fleury was in Scotland, they said, and perhaps there would be no other chance to convert him, for Cardinal Bessarion himself did not expect to remain long in Rome. Sixtus had come to the throne of St Peter from humble beginnings. As Francesco della Rovere, he had studied here in Cardinal Bessarion's house; had been encouraged to teach on Duns Scotus. Now he was Pope, and the relationship would be too hard to sustain. Bessarion would be found some distant post, as the other foreigners, the other friends of Pope Paul would be scattered. He would be gone, very likely, before Nicholas de Fleury had cause to come back.

But that was next year. Meanwhile, the Cardinal could make sure of the marriage of Zoe. He did not speak of it now, moving among his eminent guests, but the question of Zoe was another which rarely left his mind.

A slender Greek princess of twelve, misty-eyed, her cloudy hair veiled to her hips, Zoe had come to Rome with the two youths her brothers after her father the Despot had died. That was six years ago. The precious family, orphaned, bereft, had understood no Italian; the Cardinal had gathered them round him and spoken in Greek. They must do all that was asked of them. They must talk, sing, pray in the Latin rite as they would be taught, for if they deviated by one inch, the Pope their host would discard them. One day they, the grandchildren of the Emperor Manuel, would go forth and, God willing, teach the two churches of Christendom, the Latin and Greek, to unite. But first they must learn the ways of the Franks. They must survive.

The child's marriage had concerned him for years. She was without financial resources. However exquisite the girl, Italian princes demanded a dowry. The man who would make Zoe his bride must value her not for her wealth, but for the one priceless asset she had: her claim to the blood of Byzantium.

Once, it had seemed to the Cardinal that the wild young King Zacco of Cyprus would take her, securing his throne, for Zoe was second cousin to Carlotta his rival. But Venice had seen a more direct advantage in forcing upon him – there was no other phrase – the daughter of Marco Corner and Fiorenza of Naxos. The Cardinal knew more than might be expected of Fiorenza and Violante her sister, wayward beauties with unfaithful husbands.

Nevertheless, in the war against the usurping Turk, the Venetian–Cypriot match could be useful; and so could the disposal of Zoe. Zacco's small paper bride, sulkily pure, represented a physical link with Uzum Hasan and his Turcoman armies. Young Zoe's husband, if she married the ruler of Muscovy, would embody the impetuous might of White Russia. Both princes hated the Turk.

There was a third power, as yet unmentioned, which the unsavoury skills of the Patriarch might yet tempt into the arena against Mehmet the Conqueror – had indeed been expected to do so, before Nicholas de Fleury had forgotten his promise and turned his back on the East. But no one openly mentioned that. No one spoke of the Golden Horde as the allies of Rome.

*

Jan Adorne arrived late, having spent half the day in the Leonine City as co-opted *giovane di lingua*, attempting in languages other than Latin to disentangle the Bishop of St Andrews's sins of commission from his sins of omission. The trouble with Patrick Graham was that he had been spoiled all his life: given a prebend, aged fourteen, by Pope Nicholas; elected Bishop of Brechin by Pope Pius before he was thirty. By the time Bishop Kennedy died, his nephew's transfer to become Bishop of St Andrews was already negotiated, at a price of 3,300 gold florins. After that, every fresh appointment had brought its own problems.

Descendant of kings, the Bishop was, of course, loftily sure of his worth and his rights. But the favouring Popes were all dead; his uncle was dead; and there was a limit to what the Adorne family, however willing, could do. Yet Graham seemed to be foolishly persuaded that, having fallen out with half Scotland, he could expect the new Pope to befriend him. He was so grotesquely certain, indeed, that you would think he knew something Jan didn't.

But at last the lawyers rose from the table, and Jan was able to rush, deafened, between the armourers' shops on the bridge and through the mud to the portico of the Banco di Niccolò, where he found that Julius had already left for the Bessarion reception. 'Dragging his feet,' said the porter, with a grin. 'We've just had news that a client is coming, and Master Julius was keen to stay here to greet her. You may see her yourself. The Cardinal has agreed to receive her at the Palazzo if she cares to attend.'

Jan searched his memory. A countess. A German countess with whom the lawyer was flirting. He wasn't interested. Except that, if she came, it would keep Julius occupied while Jan found the late Pope's nephew Cardinal Barbo, and reminded him that, among all his new-acquired treasures, he might count on Master Jan Adorne of Paris, Pavia and Bruges as his most sparkling, his most willing amanuensis.

The rain pattered on the orderly bushes and trees in the courtyards of the Holy Apostles, the only uncooperative element so far in the dignified reception taking place in the Palazzo Colonna. Receiving Jan Adorne, not the last of his guests, Cardinal Bessarion was gracious, for the sake of Anselm Adorne his father, and because of the pilgrim's beard the lad kept, soft and yellow and light as the aigrette of a dandelion. Putting his own interpretation on the boy's wandering gaze, he directed him towards Julius, who had caused him to be invited.

The Cardinal recalled that a lady was also to be expected. He was

resigned. There were others present: it would not be disruptive. He
was accustomed to managing diverse assemblies such as this: so soon
after the papal election, there were bruised sensibilities everywhere;
he was in practice. Alighieri, the Florentine merchant from Trebizond, had promised to bring the envoy of Uzum Hasan, the adroit
Turcoman called Hadji Mehmet who had formed part, long ago, of
one of Ludovico da Bologna's fund-raising tours of the West, and
was so employed once again.

Julius would know him. Hadji Mehmet had been in Venice in
February, when de Fleury had somewhat cynically vanished from
view, having committed his Bank to the West. Jan Adorne would
presumably know Mehmet as well. The Genoese had a stake in the
Levant. He must introduce young Adorne to Bishop Bonumbre.

'I don't see him,' said Jan.

'Who?' said Julius. He tore his eyes from the doors.

'Cardinal Barbo. You said –'

'Did I?' said Julius. 'Oh well, there are still some people to come.
Make yourself at home. Find a girl. You'll never taste better wine:
the best in Candia. Wasted on Greeks.' Someone addressed him in
Greek, and he responded, bright-eyed and fluent with a ready reply.
Jan wandered off. Painted ceilings. Fine doorways. Elegant windows.
All that the looters had left after Pope Martin's death, with what the
present incumbent had added, which was modest in scale. But, as
Julius said, the wine was good.

Alighieri had not yet come with the envoy from Persia, an irritation
which the Cardinal quelled, although he had wished Acciajuoli to
spend some time with them both. He was pleased therefore when his
major domo came to his side, and a moment later the solemn Turcoman stepped through the doors, followed by the Florentine agent.
The Cardinal had walked forward, smiling, and was greeting them
both when he saw that the newcomers were not alone: behind them
stood two other men, the elder of whom was the Franciscan Patriarch,
Ludovico da Bologna, of that particular Order of Observants of
which Bessarion himself was Cardinal-Protector.

With no obvious haste, the Cardinal led Alighieri and his envoy
across to the Florentine group, introduced them, and returned. Provi-
dentially, help was at hand.

'Ah, Master Julius,' said the Cardinal. 'You know, of course,
Father Ludovico, whom we are delighted to welcome. Perhaps you
also know ...' He hesitated, recalling only that the child, far too
pretty for comfort, was a protégé of Acciajuoli's one-legged kinsman.

He perceived, with mixed sentiments, that this time the boy was unescorted.

'Nerio, isn't it?' said the notary. 'And of course, we entertained the Patriarch at the Casa in August. How are you?'

'How do I look?' said the Patriarch. 'No nearer to Constantinople. No nearer to hanging the Turk from the top of Sant' Angelo. Libido, cupidity, voluptuousness and delectation stand in the way. I hope you are enjoying your wine. Is Jan Adorne here?'

Under the Cardinal's surprised gaze, the two younger men, Nerio and Julius, looked at one another, and then suddenly broke into smiles. The smiles made Bessarion feel weary. The Patriarch, unde-terred, continued. 'I have a letter for him. Is he the idiot he seems to be? I pity his father.'

'He wants to work in Rome,' Julius said. 'Perhaps that answers your question. He's over there. I'll take you to him. Nerio can join us in a while, if he wants to.'

'Wait,' said the Cardinal. '*Hospites tamquam Christus suscipiantur* – Master Adorno is your guest and mine, and I will not have him distressed. What is your business, Patriarch?'

The priest looked surprised, his curling black hair at all angles. 'He was expecting to see Marco Barbo. The Cardinal gave me a note for him.'

It seemed innocuous enough. Bessarion nodded and turned to the sprightly young man, but Nerio was already locked in gay talk with three Greek theologians, two of whom Bessarion had never seen smiling before.

Jan Adorne saw Julius coming. The burly man at his side was a priest, although the mighty crucifix on his chest had something oriental about it, and he was coarse-skinned and black-haired as an ape, with a kind of grim simian mockery, too, in the thrust of his lip. Planted before Jan, he spoke.

'Ludovico da Bologna, my boy; Patriarch of the Latins in the East. You walked in my footprints on Mount Sinai last year, when that whisker you have was no more than a coating of mould on a cheese. I met your father in Bruges.'

'He is in Scotland at present. I know you, of course, by reputation, Father,' said Jan. He kept his face straight. He remembered even his cousin Katelijne having to keep her face straight, when listening to his father on the subject of Ludovico da Bologna.

'Then you'll not be surprised,' said the Patriarch, 'if I tell you that Moses or not, every man that climbs Mount Sinai seems to return, in my experience, either a saint or a goat. Nicholas de Fleury comes down a virgin, and the pilgrim Adorne staggers home and gets your mother with child.'

'They are husband and wife,' said Jan. His face burned with anger and shock.

'You're happy for them. I'm glad. So what did the Adorne family expect the Holy Father to jump up and do for them? Install you in the Palazzo San Marco to count the cameos and oil the ivories and wax the bosoms and buttocks of the Nereides? Everything changes when a Pope dies.'

'There was nothing for me in Bruges,' Jan said. He hardly knew what he was saying. He was watching someone approaching.

'The Bastard Anthony wouldn't have you, I heard,' said the Patriarch. 'But God alone in His wisdom knows why your father sent you back to Rome. The meek, joyful pursuit in nakedness of the naked Christ it might be, but a troubadour of God you are not. So what are you looking at?'

Jan continued to look.

'My dear,' said Nerio. 'How delightful to see you again. Are you recovered?'

Cold nausea filled Jan Adorne. Through the mists of carnival Venice he had pursued the wraith of an exquisite girl, masked, alluring. It had ended in public, in shame, with Jan vomiting drunk, and his love revealed as a cruel, pretty boy: Nerio from Trebizond. Julius had been there. Julius, standing beside him, was smiling. Julius had known that Nerio was coming today.

Jan swallowed. He said, 'Do we know each other? Forgive me. The Patriarch and I have some business together.'

The dark-lashed eyes laughed into his face. 'So fickle? Pray continue. I can wait. Antioch! Now I know why Syrians call it *le pissoir*!'

'You should go there,' said Ludovico da Bologna. 'Provided you can find out which *pissoir* you are made for. Meanwhile, stand there and be quiet. Master Julius?'

'Yes?' said the notary. His voice had lost some of its amusement. Jan Adorne stared at the floor.

'Nothing seems to surprise you,' said the Patriarch. His voice, momentarily, appeared almost agreeable. 'Every event bears the pricks of the drawing-compass. You can probably guess, for example, the contents of the paper I am about to hand Master Adorne.'

'An indulgence?' said Julius. His voice was amused again. 'Or no. Master Adorne here could hardly afford it. He has spent it all on libido, cupidity –'

'Who better should recognise it?' said the Patriarch. He turned the hedge of his brows upon Jan. 'Have you no sense? Perhaps the bishops in Scotland may deny their jewels to their see, but the wealth of St Peter by the Election Capitulation cannot be alienated. All that Paul owned passed to Sixtus. Sixtus has charge of the fifty-four silver shells filled with pearls, and the single diamond worth seven thousand ducats. A million ducats' worth in jewels alone, many of them sold to the Medici already. What dream of wealth did you have?'

'None,' said Jan. 'I wished to serve the Cardinal of San Marco.'

'And who is the Cardinal of San Marco? The nephew of the late Pope. Is it likely that this dogged Sixtus will bare his gums to welcome a Barbo, or the Cardinal Borgia his friend, or even the lord Cardinal-Protector our host? Bessarion and Borgia and Caraffa are foreign barbarians, the only three in the whole Italian Electorate. These are four Cardinals who will be found suitable tasks far from Rome.'

'I have heard nothing of it,' said Jan.

'You will, in a matter of weeks. Three of them are to be sent abroad to seek help against the Grand Turk. Caraffa will lead the papal fleet in the spring. Ask my lord Bessarion, if you doubt me. He is going to France.'

'And Cardinal Barbo?' said Jan. He was merely thankful that, minute by minute, he was achieving answers, and controlling the heave of his guts.

'Cardinal Barbo leaves for Germany, Hungary and Poland with the smallest of retinues. He has sent you a letter, to explain and express his regrets. Had his uncle survived, no doubt he would have found you a post. He is a good man: you would have benefited from it.'

'He will be away a long time?' said Jan.

'How long will it take to stir the Emperor Frederick to war?' said the Patriarch. 'An aeon, do you think? And Barbo will get no quick answer from Poland, nor much of a welcome from the King Casimir's friend Buonaccorsi, whose conspiracies threatened his late uncle's life. Although, to be sure, Zacco sheltered the miscreant, and Sixtus might give him an amnesty. But no. There will be no quick return for Marco Barbo. You must look for employment elsewhere.'

'I have no other prospects,' said Jan.

'You have the Bishop of St Andrews,' Julius said. His voice was a mixture of reproof and surprise. 'A Scot, a friend of your family, pledged to a long sojourn in Rome. Surely it is ideal? You cannot wish to go home, to watch your father grow poor, losing ground to the Banco di Niccolò; to find your mother inattentive, and busy with napkins and milk.'

'Indeed, you must not fly from Rome.' It was the voice of Nerio, sweetly appealing. 'Now all your friends have discovered you. The great Nicholas himself must surely come one of these days.'

'I hope he does,' Jan said loudly. Suddenly, all his squeamishness was replaced by anger. He turned and looked at them: the winsome face of the Greek with its glittering eyes; the slanting eyes and curled lip of Julius, whom he had begun to think of as an ally. And lastly, at the brooding, powerful person of the Franciscan, watching him narrowly. It was to the Franciscan he spoke.

'Is this how you treat a man who has walked through the desert; who has given his time and his strength to visit the Holy Places, only for the reverence of God? Is this how you treat a man coming to serve Christ in His City, however poor, however inept he may be?'

He turned on Julius. 'You pretend that Nicholas is a match for my father. I know what is happening. I know what my father is doing. We are laughing at you, the Vatachino as well. You were relying on your new ship from Danzig? You will never get it. Who do you think has delayed it?'

He turned back to the Patriarch. 'Why do you waste time on Nicholas and his henchmen and their catamites? I went to the Holy Land for my faith. He went for gold and for commerce, and broke every promise he made about lending his help to the East. Such a man can never succeed. Already we have usurped his printers. Caxton in Cologne is undoing all that he planned with the Hanse. My father has kinsmen, colleagues, contacts all through the Levant; the Knights of Rhodes know what they owe us. My father can call on all such help, and the loyalty of his own town of Bruges, and the high regard and respect of the Duke. What is the Banco di Niccolò?'

'Catamite?' Nerio said. 'Does Nicholas have a catamite?'

'He is talking rubbish,' Julius said. 'He is angry with his father – I can understand it – and with himself for having to defend him. Anyway, Jan himself prefers girls. Nerio should know.'

'It must seem a strange taste,' said Jan. He was still speaking loudly. The Cardinal, glancing over, could be seen speaking in a low voice to some servant. Jan said, 'Your own runs to older rich women. I thought we were going to meet Anna von Hanseyck with her dubious offspring? Or has she heard what we all know, that you are a bastard yourself? That you stole from Bessarion when you were his clerk and will steal from any master, or mistress no doubt. Or are you really besotted, and mooning after a woman who laughs about you with her friends? I should like to meet her. I could tell her something.'

'You may have the opportunity,' said the Patriarch calmly. 'If I am not mistaken, the lady is about to arrive.'

Jan Adorne heard it, breathing hard, and felt himself turning white. In the heat of the moment, he had meant all he said. He had not expected the Gräfin herself to appear. He drew himself up, and was surprised when Julius, too, took a quick step forward and fell silent. The boy Nerio, after looking from the one to the other, had turned his smile on the great double doors of the hall which stood open. Beyond them, several people were waiting. One, the Cardinal's major domo, stood with head bowed. One, a very young girl plainly gowned, appeared to stand in attendance. Two men stood beside her, presumably from the Cardinal's household. To the right of the doorpost a second lady was waiting, of whom nothing could be seen but elegant rings, and the fall of exquisite silk from one sleeve.

The major domo, a Cypriot, straightened. The girl curtseyed. The major domo entered the room and his guest took her place at his back, the two men falling in behind with the girl. The Countess, it was apparent, was diminutive, but wholly composed. Although her person might be obscured by the bulk of the Cypriot, her robe swept the tiles, it could be seen, without trembling; the set of her arms, it was plain, was relaxed.

The procession halted. Julius took another pace forward. The major domo raised his wand and with deliberation, stepped to one side. There was a collective sound; not quite a gasp.

'So there is your whore!' cried Jan Adorne; and burst into laughter.

The servants behind must have been waiting: as he uttered the words, they grasped his arms and pulled him backwards, and through a discreet door. He made no resistance. He had shamed Julius, as Julius and Nerio had shamed him. And yet, he still could not believe what he had seen.

Indeed, the Gräfin Anna von Hanseyck had turned out to be small; short would be the better description. Indeed, she was splendidly dressed in a gown of heavy silk in deep blue, whose volume and cost could only be guessed at. Its oversleeves, embroidered and gemmed, were of velvet, and jewels were bound into her hair and appeared to encircle her throat. Appeared, since her neck was so fat that its corbels concealed all that might lie in their creases. The same amplitude invested her clothes: the rounded bastion of the lower torso and the twin parapets of the bodice, with between them a nook-shaft fit for a putlog and hoarding. The oversleeves, falling back at the elbow, exposed silk-covered arms stout as balusters and wrists whose brace-lets seemed pressed into place with a chinsing-iron. The face was round, the expression benign, the thick-painted eyes little short of magnificent. But nothing softened the terrible truth. The creature was vast. The sweetheart of Julius was the fattest person Jan had ever encountered.

He let himself be taken off and sent home, still hiccoughing weakly. So he did not hear the major domo make his announcement, in Latin followed by Greek. *My lords, ladies and gentlemen, pray honour the Despoina Zoe Palaeologina, niece of Constantine, lately Imperator Constantinopolitanus; honour the prince Andrew Palaeologus, Despot of the Morea; and honour the prince Manuel Palaeologus, his brother.*

'Jan thought she was your lover. Do you have a lover?' said Nerio to Julius.

'None of your business,' said Julius, choking. There were tears in his eyes. The lady had begun, in a stately way, to make a circuit of the far end of the room. He said, 'She's just been painted for Muscovy. Do you think the panel was big enough?'

'All princesses are beautiful,' murmured Michael Alighieri, joining them. 'All paintings proclaim it. All envoys call them so, for fear some turn of the political wheel may make it necessary to believe it. All speak of Catherine Corner as an angel of pulchritude: you have probably seen her. And before you call it hypocrisy, Patriarch, recall how you fumed long ago over that *stinking Greek turncoat*, Zoe's father. But now she is a valuable pawn, is she not, in your game?'

'Poor Ivan. Poor Zacco,' said Julius. He began to laugh again, very quietly.

'Holy Church,' said Father Ludovico, 'does not have recourse to pawns. Here is the Cardinal. He will tell you. The lady is the Pope's beloved daughter in Christ. On the day she marries Duke Ivan of Muscovy, she will draw the worth of her dowry and more from the returns of the Tolfa alum mines. So the papal alum will pay for the downfall of the infidel. And should the Golden –'

'Enough,' said Cardinal Bessarion. 'This lady lives under my roof, and will be respected. Master Julius, you have leave.'

Julius flushed. He said, 'Monsignore. I have to apologise for Adorne. He is young.'

'He is not helped,' the Cardinal said, 'by his friends. I should like you to retire. This reception in any case is nearly over except for my private guests. I shall send for you presently, when I have a communication about banking matters. Patriarch, a word.'

The two men paced off. Julius, still scarlet, smoothed his doublet and began to move to the door. Nerio walked with him. 'But it was worth it!' said Nerio. 'Poor boy, it was worth it! I suppose there is nothing for him but the Bishop of St Andrews? He looked very glum.'

'There never was anything for him but the Bishop of St Andrews,' Julius said. 'He'll have to make the best of it, like everyone else. That's my cloak. It's still raining.'

'So it is. Which way do you go?' Nerio said.

'Not in your direction,' said Julius.

There were fifteen taverns in the centre of Rome. Jan began with the Sun, which was just off the Campo de' Fiori, and worked his way through the rest until he began to distrust his legs. Then he returned to the hospice and, taking a razor, bloodily hacked off his beard.

Julius walked in the rain until he was sure Nerio was quite out of sight; then he held his sword down and ran to the Casa Niccolò. He took the shortest way, which meant the most crowded, looking all the time from side to side without seeing anyone he knew. He passed within sight of the Palazzo San Marco and a number of taverns, but Jan Adorne had long since gone from his mind. His cloak was soaked and his boots and fine hose were stinking with mud. As he came near the Canale, the rain stopped, and a watery sun touched the overlapping red roofs and the white loggias of the international money market of Rome: the foreign banks with their strange food and odd tongues and busy, busy counting-houses.

Outside the pale portico with its vines, he saw a magpie flash of the Niccolò colours: Lazzarino had set someone to look for him. Julius increased his pace. By the time he arrived, Lazzarino himself had come out. He looked composed, but called across with a little more emphasis than was customary. 'Our client has arrived. She did not wish to trouble the Cardinal, and preferred to wait for you. I have placed her in the garden chamber to rest.'

Julius nodded. Shedding his cloak, he saw a manservant he knew in the room with his porter, and smiled at him as he passed. There was no sign of anyone else. Julius walked through the house.

The garden chamber was small, and during winter was closed off from the loggia, although the garden could still be admired through glass. The light from the sun, weak and low, touched the windows to gold, and rimmed the hair of the woman who rose at once as he entered. Her face was lost in the dimness, but he smelled her scent, and heard, in the stillness, the sound of her faint, exact breathing.

Then he whispered, '*Anna!*' and crossed; and threw himself at her feet.

Chapter 17

NEWS FROM ROME travelled badly in winter: it would be two months before Nicholas, in Scotland, learned all that Julius and Lazzarino in their separate ways would send to tell him of these events, and at least as long before he would hear from Gregorio. The Bank had to put up with these delays, as had its competitors. Dispatches, although out of date, arrived in Edinburgh that autumn in the usual steady stream: in repressive mood from Achille in Alexandria; from an agitated agent in Damascus; from Paris and Orléans and Lyons; from Lisbon and Valencia and, nearer at hand and much more recent, from Diniz in Bruges and certain unspecified persons in Antwerp, London and Newcastle, as well as from Tom Yare in Berwick and from Eric Mowat, moved discreetly from Copenhagen to Bergen.

Nicholas read them at night, when his work on the Nativity Play had temporarily ceased, for the business of the Bank had to go on. When the wax-wrapped duplicate ledgers arrived in their regular satchel, he rarely let a day dawn by without opening and studying them – and for their style, as well as their contents. Things changed quickly. Men changed quickly. A new wife, a new mistress, a bereavement, a quarrel; men were human, and nature enforced its priorities. And hence the reports upon which his business depended – the situation, problems, intentions of powerful men – might be incomplete, or unintentionally biased. Or intentionally so. There was that to beware of, as well.

In between the dispatches came other communications: sometimes testy personal scrawls; sometimes carefully penned lines with many abbreviations, displaying the grand seals of abbeys and duchies. These were borne as a rule by persons who had come to Scotland by licence to work until Yule: difficult men and cantankerous persons for the most part; artistic, flamboyant persons such as Nicholas had loved ever since he was Claes, and whom Gelis detested.

Laying his careless, extravagant plans for a careless and extravagant Mystery, Nicholas had always envisaged bringing artists from overseas, although equally he intended to sequester all the talent – or even the non-talent – he could discover in Scotland, and spend time on giving it classes.

Now he had been proffered a challenge. A small affirmation of the immortal status of man had taken place: a work of music created which represented the supreme endeavours of one gifted idiot and his friends. Nicholas was morally bound to do no less for them. A Pasche Play was out of the question – he would not be here for Easter. Therefore the royal Nativity Play must be his test piece, his offering.

Instead of ten months to prepare it, less than four, including the work he had already half done. Instead of a week-long performance with half-trained actors, and amateur craftsmen, a performance of one afternoon, to which would be brought painters, sculptors, carpenters from Bruges and Lille and Brussels and Tournai; scribes who could copy sixty pages a day; tailors who were accustomed to dressing an Entry at speed; men who trained men to walk like young women; men who made wigs for God. That did not take account of the materials which had already come and which continued to come in the holds of hired ships.

Only he did not need an engineer or a Master of Secrets, for he had John and himself. And he did not need a master craftsman, for Cochrane was that. And he did not need musicians, for he had the core of the new Chapel Royal with Whistle Willie at its heart and its head.

For all the people around Nicholas – those who feared him, or loved him, or were anxious for him – that autumn in Edinburgh was a strange one. In the Castle the King, having commissioned the Play, watched his own dearest plans take second place to a spectacle. Silent, obedient, barren, the Queen saw it as well. Without M. de Fleury's financial reserves and sympathetic encouragement, James was not likely to leave her this spring to become a second Alexander. His brother Mar sulked, and jeered at the painter who came to take a likeness of the King for a placard. The King, annoyed at the jeering, had dismissed the artist after a sitting of no more than ten minutes but, being ingenious, the fellow found another rough sketch at the moneyers'.

In the Casa Niccolò in the Canongate it was the same. Govaerts, as ever, controlled the business, but admitted to himself it was less stressful when Nicholas was abroad than when he was physically present but almost wholly engaged in other concerns.

Nor was it better when John le Grant and Father Moriz arrived, angered at the interruption in their difficult programme. All that was left in full swing was the boatbuilding, which de Fleury wasn't crazed enough so far to compromise. John however had to abandon his guns and replace them with quite different mechanisms and finicky castings: hours of concentrated fine work for the benefit of a Christmas playlet. Being John, he presently took fire and would have refused to do anything else. Moriz, suspended between the true God and one made of hide-covered clay, took longer to become reconciled, being disturbed by both his own conscience and suspicions of Nicholas. Meanwhile the business did without both of them. Only the goldsmith, who always worked directly to Nicholas, appeared wholly happy.

Archibald, Abbot of Holyrood, was happy because he was an able, energetic man who didn't mind his entire yard being dug up and remade to hold a long rectangular platform with a stand of seats on two sides, and an end which was fixed to the porch of the Abbey. Beneath the yard was positioned a network of rooms, pits and tunnels, some of them filled with machinery. Above it were workshops. Sometimes Abbot Crawford would make his way there after matins just to smell and look at the pigments: sinople and cinders of azure, verjus and brown of Auxerre. There were two pounds of vermilion, at seven shillings the pound. And all the scenery was painted on vellum, not paper; so that nothing could buckle or flake. His highly numerate intelligence kept track of some of the costs.

He was content that the money was being spent in his yard (with the promise of permanent compensatory improvements). The more money the King lavished on this, the less there would be for any nonsense such as leading armies to France. Duke Charles had just made a pact against France with his new allies England and Aragon. It was not a bad thing that de Fleury was here, and Adorne, the other Burgundian. God forbid that Charles of Burgundy should surround himself with clever men.

When the actors were chosen and the rehearsals began, advertised by the clang of the bell, the Abbot lingered to watch the men hurrying to and fro, their rolls under their arms. The rolls so carefully copied in his own cloisters, each man's part on a strip. Sometimes de Fleury came himself, brandishing the traditional baton of the Protocolle, the man who carries the book of the play and directs it. The Abbot armed himself nowadays for his exchanges with the Burgundian. De Fleury, said Bishop Tulloch – and he agreed – was both a fathomless danger and an ally worth having. It made for stimulating encounters. The virtues of bourgeois *cortesia*.

The musicians practised where they had begun, in the collegiate church of the Trinity, learning the music as it was written. The singers had been joined by a child of fragile beauty called John, the son of one of the actors who, like his father, appeared on the recommendation of the Abbot of Holyrood. Roger, who suspected everyone's musical taste but his own, heard the child once, and that night changed three pieces to accommodate him. His sister, equally angelic, was too young to sing but was given a role as a cherub. As for Will Roger himself, his condition varied through all this time between a state of violent happiness and violent anxiety. He forgot to eat, until the nuns noticed and began sending down baskets.

In the High Street of Edinburgh, one of the few mansions unaffected by theatrical madness was that of Anselm Adorne. There, in his office, Adorne quietly conducted his business with the men who slipped in, sometimes after dark, to talk to him or bring him dispatches. Martin of the Vatachino saw him there, or, with discretion, in Martin's own house in the Cowgate. However occupied he might seem to be, Anselm Adorne did not now underestimate Nicholas de Fleury of the Banco di Niccolò. And neither did his nephew, Sersanders.

His niece Katelijne he preferred not to involve. She was busy enough in all conscience, running to the Prioress's house and her duties over the street, or to de Fleury's house to interfere with the Play, or here to sit with Margriet, with or without the two Sinclair cousins, Betha and Phemie. He himself did not impose his presence on that part of the house which was women's business. All Margriet's women friends came to see her; the Queen sent small gifts; and the lady Mary, Countess of Arran, sometimes seemed to live in Adorne's house as much as her own.

There was a more settled look now to the Countess – something of resignation, perhaps; and she had made her peace to some degree with her brother. After the first weeks as guest of de Fleury, she had been allowed to move to the monastery of the Greyfriars, not far away. The children visited one another, and she seemed to prize the company of both Nicholas and his wife. She had also recovered her affection for Margriet. If she had blamed the Adorne family once, she did so no longer.

To her husband, Margriet seemed better. Adorne spent time with her, when the others had gone, and sat hand in hand, and read to her, which she always liked. She had never been interested in music, so he set his own lute aside, and devoted himself to what would please her best. He had brought Dr Andreas to live in the house, just to be sure. She did not speak of Nicholas any more, which was as well.

The house of Nicholas, across the street, was – by his own decree – the centre of the whole enterprise of the Nativity. To it, in the early days, came the groups of powerful merchants, the craft-masters, magistrates, lawyers: the men of title and office whose support, guidance, licences, local knowledge, and participation he was going to need. Later, it was the technicians who came to confer, when the rooms the lady Mary had now vacated became a drawing-office, and the stone-lined chamber whose purpose had never become clear suddenly turned into a storehouse of volatile powders and precious metals beaten into strange shapes.

Gelis had been consulted. It made sense, she supposed, that the Ca' Niccolò in the Canongate should be left undisturbed, to continue trading in privacy. She herself was an excellent organiser. In a project like this, which was something like planning a war, she could become its quartermaster, handling the accommodation and feeding of the multi-national brood which wandered arguing uphill and down between her house and Holyrood, and even assisting the Abbey to provision the performance itself, when engineers and performers, guards and musicians and the spectators themselves required to have access to food.

What she could not yet guess was why Nicholas was doing it in this way. His own capacity for planning was unquestioned, but so was his instinct for good business. It was clearly useful to dazzle the King and to make a killing from all the Bank was procuring. The rest, however, didn't make sense: the wholesale dedication to this one little project of the Bank's senior technicians, and – more wasteful by far – the personal undivided attention of Nicholas the padrone himself.

He had never fully explained it, even at the beginning when, seated uninvited in her room with Jodi self-attached to his knee, he had asked whether she would like to help plan it. All she gathered then was that he had offered to furnish a play, and was now expected to produce one for Christmas. He had sounded, if anything, resigned.

She had resisted involvement at first: it was not any plan of hers to assist him. She changed her mind, in the end, for several reasons. For one thing, the prospect of an early departure of the Boyd family had seemed wonderfully appealing. It also appealed, she observed, to Mistress Clémence.

Later, she heard rumours of a wager to do with Willie Roger, but she doubted if that was the whole story, or his approach to her that day would have been different. She remembered, for what it was worth, that he had been firmer than usual with Jodi. Except when carried, Jordan de Fleury was not encouraged to put his arms around Nicholas. It was a confiding habit he had, of showing open affection to everybody, and Mistress Clémence did not usually check him, unless she thought him too forward. She did not check him that day, nor intervene, of course, when Nicholas did.

In the weeks that led up to Christmas, Gelis was present at most of the gatherings held in her house. During those meetings she sat, largely silent, watching Nicholas manipulating people: so inoffensively sure; so good-natured; so deeply autocratic. Away from the conference table she watched him handling the staff of her house; and the boy Robin and Archie his father, who dropped in most days; and Jodi's nurses; and Jodi. The weeks went by and Jodi, whistle in pouch and wearing the large knitted hat from which he would not be parted, wandered talking in English and French from house to garden to workshop, breathing heavily as he drew crosses and windows on two inches of paper with Tom Cochrane's graphite; standing thumb in mouth watching John le Grant fashion two little wheels in order to make a number of others revolve. He stopped holding his arms to be lifted, and spent less time with his parrot, except for four days when Nicholas was away.

They said Nicholas was divining, and indeed reports confirmed that he had been in the west to fulfil some commission connected with minerals. He took Alonse, but not Robin. Everyone, returning, was very secretive, and she caught the end of a peppery clash between Nicholas and the priest, Father Moriz, who was generally stationed at Holyrood. In divining, obviously, Nicholas was open to rebuke by the Church. It did not seem to disturb him: he looked cheerful, as if glad to have the interruption behind him, and turned the unflagging energy once again upon his labouring colleagues. He spent a little time, as was usual, with Jodi, but made no excuses and gave no appearance of making amends for his absence; after a short, sulking interval, the relationship was as it had been before. Nicholas was an expert with people of any age, and planned for the long term.

It was then, moving up to the date of performance, that he engineered a moment alone in a room with his wife. She came to it bearing a list. In conference, they had been discussing a mountain of details: chains and straw for the streets of approach; turf to mask the trap-tops; ale for the erectors of awnings; and a request on behalf of the pulleys for a supply of pork fat from the butcher. Someone reported the theft of their piss-flasks and tournesol, which deprived them of blood. Blood was discontinued.

'Grass,' Gelis continued, proceeding down her column of *dubia*, 'for the donkey called Abraham. When am I going to see all these performers?' No one had been allowed near the rehearsals.

'Not until the day, and by paying full price. Guild rules,' Nicholas said, shutting the door. They were alone.

'No special family rates?' Gelis said. Her heart beat like a drum at a hanging. She had always admitted the force of his physical presence, but had found methods, in public at least, to resist it. She had been less prepared for the strain of being coupled, however briefly, however selectively, with his mind. On shipboard, his companionability had been a veneer; here, it was genuine. For the space of this project, she, too, had become part of his team, and had been treated to the same magical mixture of mischief and concentration. For nearly two months, she had fought against the enchantment. It was temporary, temporary, *temporary*. When the Play was done, it would stop. She would stop it.

But now, she thoughtlessly followed his mood. She said, 'Family rates and good seats. Or I'll ask Willie Roger to smuggle me into the Trinity. I could begin singing the tunes so that people don't want to hear them again.'

'That for certain,' said Nicholas. Then, perhaps regretting the insult, or the joke: 'You'll hear enough of them afterwards to deafen you. Joy plays the organ and Memory works the bellows and the Suffering Servant hangs himself from the bell-rope. I wanted to ask you something about Jordan.'

'Young or old?' Gelis said. She stayed calm.

'Both are continually in my thoughts, but in this case the younger.'

'He calls you Doc-Doc,' Gelis remarked. 'It began while you were away.'

He smiled immediately, forgetfully using both dimples. 'Origin, Pasque, I should guess. A local nickname. Not obscene, to my knowledge.'

'Doctor?' she guessed. She was curious.

'More like Odysseus polymetis, the sort of knave who makes deals under carts. I am flattered, I think. Gelis, I should like to take Jodi somewhere when all this is finished. Bel of Cuthilgurdy is here. Here in Edinburgh.'

She looked at him. Since they had resumed their notional life as a family, he had always asked permission, like this, to take Jordan away. It was part of the unspoken pact. If he did so, so must she. But this time, she had to consider his motives. Bel, neighbour and friend to de Ribérac's family, had been close to Nicholas and to Gelis in Africa, but had since lost her trust in them both. An affectionate visit from Nicholas might well re-attach Bel to himself, while underlining the transgressions of Gelis. Odysseus polymetis, indeed. Gelis said, 'Where is Bel staying?'

'In de Ribérac's house. I noticed smoke, and asked who was there.'

'Fearing, of course, it might be Fat Father Jordan or Simon. My dear! What a bad moment it must have been!' Gelis said. 'A nasty bite for the ass called Brunellus. I have no objection to your taking Jordan to Bel's. She will mother you both.'

He said, 'I want Bel to see him, that's all. He needs godparents.'

'Godparents?' she echoed. A pain ran through her and vanished. She said, 'You are thinking of a sort of insurance policy, as with a ship? If we sink, Bel of Cuthilgurdy will rescue your offspring? A regular contract, I suppose, with negotiated increments annually. Or is that risky? She might dispose of us both and lift the money.'

'Would you consider Bel as a guardian for Jordan?' he said.

She said, 'You are serious.'

Nicholas said, 'You raised the subject yourself, after Hesdin. I know Bel is close to the St Pols, but I trust her. And Mistress Clémence would go with her, if you agree. She is very good.'

'She is very good,' Gelis repeated. Then she said, 'What is this? A tragic revelation? You perceive yourself as a vessel of death? I shouldn't expect to need Bel even if you were to perish tonight, to the ruin of four hundred men and a donkey. Wolfaert and his wife would rear Jordan with their own children. A van Borselen upbringing, away from anything Simon could do.'

'Simon might frequent Bruges,' Nicholas said. 'Henry might be sent to train in some ducal household.'

'They are back from Portugal?'

'Not so far. But they won't stay for ever. Shall we agree on a compromise? If you outlive me but pine from remorse, Jordan will go to Wolfaert in Veere on your death. If I survive, then I may ask Bel to take him.'

Since it began, she had been growing more puzzled. She had plans for after the Play. She thought she knew his. There were always risks in his life, but none that quite explained this sudden ordering of his affairs. She said, 'Nicholas? What are you expecting?'

'A genteel argument,' he said. 'Otherwise nothing of note, even though I am in your room, and we are married. *Virginité voluntaire*, like Mary and Joseph. How timely.'

'What are you afraid of?' She refused to be deflected.

'Or might there be a delicious, remote possibility of *union charnelle* if I suggested it? Does it move you when I soak a bed, or shut the door firmly and sit down like this? Would it move you if –'

'It would not move me, except to make me depressed, if I had to bear your whole weight here and now on my bed.' She snapped, in response to that insulting, deliberate voice. By no remote chance did he mean what he said. The end would not be permitted to happen that way, and he knew it. She said, 'How can I discuss Jordan's

future unless you tell me what threatens it, and how soon?' She
paused. 'You want me to think you are going away after Yule.'

He laughed. 'I want you to think I want you to think I am going
away after Yule.' He was smiling directly at her, without the dimples.

'But you are going to take Jordan to see Bel.'

'After the Play. Yes. Otherwise you might think you know what I
am going to do. And you don't, Gelis,' he said. 'But if you want to
play on, then so be it.'

'Of course I want to play on. I am practising Comedy,' Gelis
retorted.

He smiled a little and rose, collecting his satchel. It was so smooth.
Suddenly, it was all much too smooth for her temper. She said,
'What a callous fool you are, Nicholas. Have you ever given this a
thought until now? What would your Jordan have done if I had
listened to you on Mount Sinai? What if you and I still die together?
What then?'

'Bel could go and live in Veere. Wolfaert would love it,' he said.

It still sounded smooth, but it was not: he had gone rather white. It
might mean little. It might mean that he had nothing like the
defences that she had imagined. And, unexpectedly, he didn't stop,
but went on, as if under compulsion.

'I thought of Jordan as much as you did that day. I made the same
choices that you did, over and over. If you forget that: if you forget
why we are together at all, then we should have walked over.'

She rose slowly, her gaze locked in his. Her view of him shimmered.
She heard him take a single short breath; and then he turned and
walked to the door.

She stood, watching him leave. He was on his way, she knew, to a
score of different places, ending at Holyrood. In the doorway he met
and spoke to someone, clearing his throat. The other voice was that of
the Sersanders girl, Kathi. By the time the exchange ended, Gelis
was ready for her, but for the tremor that could not be stilled in her
hands.

From pique or from tact, Katelijne Sersanders had gradually stopped
coming to the house in the High Street as the enterprise matured,
and with it Gelis's involvement. She had also abandoned Willie
Roger. Nicholas, wholly immersed, had not particularly noticed her
abstinence: just now, as Gelis had heard, he had paused chiefly to ask
after her aunt, who was within six weeks of her delivery. Almost
immediately, he went on his way, and Kathi knocked and came in.

'Chess?' Gelis said brightly. 'I was eavesdropping.'

The girl shook back her hood. Her hair was short, like Gelis's own,

though caught up and pinned to look longer. It was easy to forget
that this large-eyed child had travelled as she had through the Egyptian wilderness, and was just eighteen, and interfering, and
marriageable.

Katelijne Sersanders said, 'I didn't mean to disturb you, but
Archie of Berecrofts wants you to come to supper tomorrow, and his
housekeeper has sent a bundle for Robin, and there's a treat for the
parrot, but he has to sing for it first. The chess is just a sort of joke.'

'You are going to tell me that Nicholas plays,' Gelis said. Speaking
his name was an effort.

'I expect he does,' Katelijne said. Her voice remained, as ever,
perfectly sensible. It occurred to Gelis what a good nun she would
make. She listened to Kathi explaining the joke about chess. It
concerned an English translation of a book by Jacobus de Cessoles, in
which everyone from the Duchess Margaret in Ghent down seemed
to be taking a hand.

'The French is so difficult? What is it called?' Gelis said. She
relieved the girl of her bundles and brought across a platter of
sweetmeats. The plate shook and she lost one.

'*The Game and Playe of the Chesse*. No, the translator's forgotten
his English. He's in Cologne, hence the appeal to the Banco di
Niccolò. Master Julius tried to help by sending a verse or two to M.
de Fleury, and M. de Fleury just made it worse. That is, you couldn't
print it. You couldn't even repeat it.'

'You couldn't?' said Gelis teasingly. She had almost recovered. She
realised suddenly that Kathi knew it.

'Oh well,' the girl said, and gravely began to recite.

It was Nicholas at the top of his bent: scurrilous, witty, engaging.
She could hear every shade of his voice in the words. Gelis said, 'You
should tell that to your uncle. It would cheer him. What do you think
of the Nativity Play? Are you going to watch it?'

Katelijne Sersanders hadn't seen it; no one had, but as far as she
knew, the whole of Edinburgh and Lothian was going to watch it.
People were coming from everywhere. Her aunt couldn't attend, but
Katelijne and her brother would describe it all to her later. 'It would
be nice,' Kathi said, 'if her child came at Christmas. It might be born
hearing some of the singing. A gift of music from Magus Will Roger.'

'And a gift of poetry from a somewhat inebriated German *fatiste*, I
gather,' said Gelis. She paused. 'You are not going to shame and
astonish me with the news that Nicholas has translated the text?
While playing chess with one hand and beating a drum with the
other?'

'I don't know whether he writes,' the girl said. 'Phemie does, and my uncle. I think a lot of people have helped. But we shan't know till next week. Won't it be dull when it's over? What are you going to do?'

In her head, in her heart, Gelis stifled an inclination to desperate laughter. 'I don't know,' she said. 'That rather depends upon Nicholas.'

Chapter 18

ITHERTO, WHEN SET in the highest gear with every wheel spinning, Nicholas had been taking his share in a war, or contributing to a scene of international negotiation, or at the very least deploying whip and reins to preserve the multiple concerns of his Bank during some heinous crisis.

Now he was exerting the same extreme concentration of skills for the sake of one brief event: an ephemeral work which, once over, would leave nothing behind it except, of course, bills. It was his belief and intention that, subjected to such an overwhelming concentration of effort, something unique might be born. Something not only unique but superb. Something not only superb but close to a vision he had, but had never put into words: something soaringly wonderful. From this area of his thinking, all cynicism, for once, was debarred.

He knew by now his own gifts. As the weeks went by and the hour of completion approached, he saw every task duly executed; the ocean tamed; the advancing waves drilled into order. In the days before the performance the lists shrank, ticked off one by one, and the shouting began to die down, and the yard of the Abbey of Holyroodhouse, veiled by its awning, emptied of arguing men in cloth tunics, became a silken pavilion, a mysterious cavern where the spoken word lingered like incense, and trumpet peals mixed with the tassels, and a voice sang, inward and solitary, from a tunnel of cloud.

It was too soon to slacken, and too soon to hope, and too soon to wonder. Nicholas worked, smiling, even-tempered, a never-failing source of solutions and calm. During that last week he did not go near his business, but slept in snatches on a truckle bed in the Abbey, and ate what people put in his hand.

The Secrets had come. Many of the experiments were his own, devices to play on the senses. The lighting was put into place, misty, magical in the grey air; and the smoke in its dusky colours; and the palette of incense and spices. Below the covering turf, John's gleaming wheels turned without sound. Screened off, alone, Nicholas watched the Angel of the Annunciation spread his swan-wings and float, his yellow head bent, while his son's childish voice swayed at his side, a silvery air-thread in water. Nicholas stood, considering sound and its trajectories, and Will Roger walked about with him, and the players.

The costumes arrived. The actors, word-perfect, were permitted to leave their chambers of study and be shown to their places. Nicholas had sat by their desks many times. Now he used all his knowledge of them to help carry them through this last stage. The prompts and signals began to receive their rehearsal: he had not allowed the intrusion of placards. He had not permitted anything which would destroy the fragile illusion: the awe, the pity, the beauty, the triumph of the birth of a child.

He did not think of his son, his mother, the women he loved and had loved. But soothing the boy who played Mary, his fingertips on his shoulder, he was conscious that shadows were present; that far off in Venice a woman in travail with her first child was also here in his thoughts. And somehow the intensity of his conviction seemed to transfer itself to the boy, and the blood returned to his face.

Battle pitch can be sustained for only so long. In every campaign, success depends on the skill of its timing.

The day before the performance, Nicholas worked without respite from long before first light, as did all his henchmen. Even Sandy, pale, with glittering eyes, was no longer the King's brother, but a willing part in something close now to mystical. That night, Nicholas sent everyone home but the guards, and walked up the hill to his house in the High Street.

Gelis was awake, and opened her door. The house was silent. He stopped.

She said, 'Take my bed. I shall wake you.'

'Will you?' he said; and came in, as if he were a friend; as if all distrust had been neutralised. He stumbled once, reaching her bed, and meant perhaps to rest there and untie his doublet and shirt, but in the event he simply sank back and slept as he was.

The brazier whispered. Its dull red and blue light touched the cushioned settle to which she retreated, her eyes on the low curtained bed. A single candle stood by his pillow, illumining the dense, springing hair, the ends of his lashes, the bridge of his nose. His hand, smudged with dried paint, lay open as if appealing for something. His face was closed in the absolute peace of dreamless sleep; she could not hear him breathe. All the vigour, all the intelligence, all the cruelty were in abeyance, till he should wake.

She had watched him like this once before, during the long agony of their duel in Venice. His sleep had been unnatural then, and full of torment. And she, watching him, had been tormented as well; consumed with anguish and bitterness, for fear he would wrest back his child.

He had taken Jordan. Then he had sent for her.

I made the same choices that you did, over and over. She knew that he had. She knew why he had.

In time, the candle guttered, and she rose stiffly and went to extinguish it. She paused at his side.

His face was invisible, but he was still deeply asleep. He had turned once, half constrained by the close-fastened doublet. It would be the task of a moment to free him, leaning circumspectly, unloosing the buttons. When she last eased the clothes that he slept in, it had been long ago, and she had been unmarried in Bruges. Then he had lain warm and resistless like this, closer than this, and smitten by sleep for a sweeter reason than this, or the pains of divining. She could do it again. He would not waken, but he would know, when he rose, what she had been thinking of.

She snuffed the candle, and left without touching him.

He slept for four hours, rousing of his own accord an hour before dawn and presenting himself, freshly dressed and new-shaven, to apologise and thank her as any normal man might. Leaving, he turned to ask her if she meant to come to the play and bring Jordan, and smiled when she said yes. She would not see him again until the performance was over.

She felt tired but content, even triumphant. His day had come, and hers with it. She had been put to the test. And there was nothing, today, she could not do.

In Edinburgh that day, the house of Anselm Adorne was one of the very few still to be occupied. From end to end of the town, the crooked streets were all empty; their inhabitants tumbled down to the foot of the Canongate and flushed up the mountain behind, as if the ridge were indeed the chute that Nicholas once had called it. The buildings lining the ridge were hung with banners, to honour the guests of the King.

It had come to James some weeks before that, instead of grudging the cost, he should be exploiting what promised to be the finest single work of prestige he could show, outside Mons Martha the cannon. One did not invite crowned heads to such an event. Those who came, however, represented their lords, and themselves were powerful noblemen, who would take back to their shires, their duchies, their kingdoms the reports of what Scotland could do. And when a funeral loomed, God forfend, or a marital feast, or a coronation, James would be pleased to consider the loan of his musicians, costumes and experts to those princes who lacked them.

The procession down from the Castle was a triumphant one therefore, despite a shower of rain; and the comfort of the royal stand, when they reached it, drew exclamations from the eminent visitors. They gazed at the face of the Abbey before them, hung with arras and garlands. They studied the silks of the awnings, the veiled and silent box of the stage in the centre below them. They were offered mulled wine and talked, while the benches were filled, and lamps and braziers glimmered, warming the air. From the well of the Abbey arena there arose the buzz of a beehive: the expectant murmur of two thousand curious souls. Then a fanfare of trumpets rang out, and the curtains raced back from the four walls of the stage, light as smoke. Behind them was Paradise, furled in sweet-scented clouds, beyond which glinted the slow-moving wheel of God's angels and the celestial throne, bright as the sun, with, kneeling beside it, a mighty-winged Gabriel. Then, from a core of dizzying radiance, the voice of God rolled, sending his herald to earth.

It had begun.

Many who were not present would later describe all that happened thereafter, for the report of it, borne on the wind, carried far. A man digging peats was petrified where he stood by the sudden silence as the curtains were drawn, and then by the gasp, and then the snatches of a single voice speaking, so terrifying and rolling and deep that he crossed himself. The voice stopped. Then the breeze slammed forth the peal of an organ, followed by a susurration like a wheatfield under rain, that swelled and swelled until it burgeoned into the voice of a full choir in song. The man leaned on his turf-spade and listened.

Dr Andreas cried, 'But you must be glad! Shout for joy! One glorious effort, and all your labours will be at an end! See, give the woman your hand. Praise God and shout!'

A play could take all day or a few hours. Your Nativities, with six or seven scenes, were sometimes over by noon, but not this one. It was the music. Not just the 'Ave Maria' and the 'Angelus ad Virginem' for the Annunciation, and a bit of something for the Salutation of Elizabeth, but a lot of singing no one had ever heard of before. And then when it came to the Shepherds . . .! Everyone afterwards said it must have been during the Play of the Shepherds that the dance music came in, and between it the gusts of laughter, which you wouldn't expect.

Later, it came out that the shepherds were speaking in Scots, and making jokes that you wouldn't believe. Not that all the rest was in Latin, they said. A right mix-up of tongues, as if the story of Mary and Joseph belonged to everyone, as you could say that it did. The fun of the shepherds, they said, was what broke your heart when it came to the Manger, and the holy music was mixed with the lullaby. *Lully lullay, hail my bairn, hail my King, hail my darling.* You could hear that as well, from the hills.

Noon came and went. It rained a little, and ceased, and rained again. The peat-cutter worked slowly, cutting in rhythm. Across the marshes and plains, others listened. At the Abbey of Holyroodhouse, the scenes unfolded one by one. The Star burned. Glittering Herod sent out his messengers and ripped the leaves from the books of his lawyers, the fires of hell licking his throne. Kaspar, Melchior, Balthasar spread their jewelled robes and knelt, and myrrh and frankincense scented the wind. Over Paradise, palace and stable the cloud banks lingered and passed, tinged with sound; flushed with close-woven plainsong; opulent with polyphony; pierced by trumpets and clarions, dulcions and clarsachs, schawms and viols: *Ne timeas, Maria*, Gabriel sang.

Instead of seedlings and moisture the wind distributed words, and sighs following words – *Ave Gloriosa!* Swirling about the small hills: Craiglockhart and Blackford and Braids, music fell like ash on their slopes; and the voices of children – *pleni sunt caeli gloria tua* – were borne by the stout vanes of seabirds winging from Cramond to Bass. Watching them, men saw that the underclouds carried thumbprints of light, and sudden colours, and once a spray of crackling sparks, as if someone had grated down a half-pound of thunder and lightning, and tossed it for joy.

Dr Andreas said, 'Of course you are tired, but your baby is not! He is angry; he is straining to meet you; you must give him your strength. Brace yourself. Push!'

Towards the end, there was nothing but music: noble; expansive. The light blazed, and the Star, and the poetry ceased, giving way to the voices, at first transparent and low. The music thickened, beginning its climb. The secret trumpets suddenly burst into sound from the roof-tops, and the four organs began their low thunder.

Dr Andreas said quietly, 'Take your time. Rest. The boy will wait. The Bride of God suffered as you are suffering, and also had joy.'
  Anselm Adorne said, 'I do not want this child. Save her.'

On the stage, in the stands, nothing moved except a veil touched by the wind, or the threads of a child's hair, or the sudden spark of a jewel. The sound reached its apogee, vibrating through earth, flesh and bone, physical and spiritual at once; plangent, tender, triumphant. *Emmanuel!*

The paean stopped. The silence clamoured and raged, beating about in distraction like a soul torn from its casing and lost. Then it deadened and the people stirred, and moved, and made their opinion known.

In the house of Anselm Adorne, a woman was screaming.

Jordan screamed. At first, Nicholas did not hear him, such was the uproar about him. His fingertips ached. He saw that the Queen was weeping, her face concealed in her kerchief; that all the men and women he could see had tears on their cheeks. On the stage, everyone was looking at him, and he tried to break from his stiffness and smile, but it was difficult. He felt Willie Roger's hand at his neck. The composer's face, contorted, produced no words at all. Nicholas smiled at him too. Then he heard Jodi crying, and looked for him.

Gelis was there, attempting to comfort her struggling son. She was white. The child pulled himself free and stood apart, his eyes clenched, his mouth open, shrieking. She said, 'He won't say what is wrong.'

'Jodi?' Nicholas said.

The child opened his eyes, his chest heaving. Nicholas knelt and, stretching out his cramped hands, closed them fast about the boy's doubled fists.

'Scream,' he said. 'Scream for me, too.'

Gelis exclaimed. Clémence of Coulanges touched her, and spoke with a smile. 'It is nothing. When you are a child, you think that something wonderful will go on for ever. And that was something wonderful, was it not?'

No one had left. Like Jordan, they remained in their hundreds, close to the stage, as if by adhering to it, the experience would somehow continue. Jodi's screaming had died, replaced by ordinary sobbing. Nicholas looked round, and Mistress Clémence drew out a kerchief and knelt. Presently, with a glance for permission, she lifted the boy into her arms, and did not chide when he laid his cheek to her neck and cuddled close. Nicholas watched, and then turned the same smile to Gelis, who did not smile back. Then the royal party arrived.

He was used to it. Even at this extraordinary moment, he found the right tone, the right expression, the right words to deal with the chaotic mixture of raw sensibilities and royal formality. It was the same, after that, with everyone else who surged round him, securing him as in a clamp to the place where it had happened, although it was over. He became aware in due course that, although he had not escaped, at least he was mobile: that a phalanx of companions composed of his actors, engineers and musicians was moving him steadily away from the scene, and uphill. Just short of his Canongate house they formed a barrier and drew him through it, and forbade others to follow until he was indoors, in the Casa Niccolò, in his own house.

Will Roger was there, and Tom Cochrane, and John and Moriz and half the polyglot crew who had helped him to do what he had done. And Gelis. And Katelijne Sersanders.

Will Roger said, 'Come, my bastard Flemish apprentice. Come, you amazing man. Come and get drunk.'

If he couldn't scream like a child – and he couldn't – it was what he wanted most at this moment on earth. Except that he had seen the face of Adorne's little niece. Nicholas said to her, 'What?'

She shook her head. Her eyes spoke, and the tears on her cheeks. He said to her, 'Come to my room,' and threw a word over his shoulder to Roger. Belatedly, on his way through the house, he saw that Gelis had followed. She was right; he had no wish to stop her. In the privacy of his own chamber, Gelis drew the girl down to a seat while he closed the door and dropped kneeling before her. 'Kathi?'

She said, 'I've just been told. My aunt was brought to bed of a son during the Play.' She stopped, looking at Nicholas.

He wondered if she thought the significance had escaped him. He said, 'Tell me.'

She said, 'They saved my aunt. The boy was born strangled. He died.'

Nicholas rose to his feet. 'No,' he said. 'There was a knife.'

Gelis dropped her arm. Kathi looked up, her lashes stark as boar-bristles. 'They cut the cord with a knife. The cord strangled him.'

His head swam. He said ridiculously, 'How do you choose?'

Kathi frowned. She said, 'My uncle chose to let the child die, to the risk of his soul. Men make decisions.'

'Pawns cannot make choices,' said Nicholas. 'Doctors can. The cyrurgyens ought also to be debonayr, amyable and to have pytye of their pacyents. Was Dr Andreas there?' He did not know what made him think of William Caxton. For no reason he pictured Anselm Adorne's condemned son as an angel of beauty; a golden child like the one in the play. He began to feel even more strange.

'Dr Andreas was there,' Katelijne said. She added quickly, 'It wasn't your fault. Nothing was. I must go. I wanted to tell you.' She was looking at Gelis.

Gelis said, 'I am so very sorry. Can we do anything?'

'No,' the girl said. 'I must go.'

She was halfway to the door before he realised he had said nothing more. He said, 'Kathi. Shall I come with you?'

'No,' she said. 'Rest. It was glorious. It was the crown of your life.'

The door closed. He sat, rather suddenly, conscious through the cloudiness in his mind that he had been wholly inadequate. His skin was clammy. Shreds of old emotions, old tragedies wrapped themselves round his thoughts, mixed with the sadness of Adorne's loss and other deaths, other burdens he could not understand, which seemed to lie on his shoulders. He felt ill, and adrift, and afraid.

Gelis said, 'Are you going to be sick? Even Jodi wasn't as over-excited as that.'

He had forgotten Gelis was there. He had even forgotten the Play. Of course, that explained how he felt. He said, with a certain effort, 'Not unless you pay me for the performance. Did you enjoy it?'

'Enjoy what?' she said. Now that he looked at her, she was sitting upright in her splendid court gown and veils, her hands clasped in her lap. They were glistening white. She looked as if she meant to be there a long time.

He said, 'I had better go back to the others.'

'I have something to tell you,' she said. 'Something you wanted to know.'

He got up. 'Later,' he said. 'Later, please, Gelis.'

'No,' she said. 'We have been interrupted so often, that I think it must be now or not at all. It won't take long. Sit down. Mourn the Adorne child a little before you plunge into all your well-earned festivities. After all, its death *was* your fault.'

He remained standing. He said, 'You needn't go on. Kathi knows all that you do.'

'And thought you required reassuring. Why? Because she knows, as you and I do, that for the sake of your precious Boyds, Margriet was compelled to travel to Scotland. But for the Boyds and the threat of your Bank, Adorne might never have undertaken his Levantine journey. But for the long separation, Adorne might not have been careless: Margriet might not have had to suffer this child.'

He said, 'I really shouldn't say that to Kathi. She would find it, as I do, unforgivable. The rest, even for you, is special pleading. It could all have happened perfectly well without me. Is that all?'

'You don't care?'

He said, 'Of course I care. A child is dead.'

'But you don't accept any blame. You never do. My sister Katelina, for example.'

Then he sat down. He said, 'Go on, then.' However he felt, this was something that had to be faced, that he would not try to escape. Katelina her sister was dead, but Gelis had never forgotten that he had been her lover when young, and was the father of Henry her son.

It was not the only sin she held against him. He was about, now, to hear more. Unless he did, he would never fully be able to assess the depth of her anger, and the strength of her resolution. And with an enemy, one should always do that.

Gelis said, 'A child is dead, and you care. I am glad. You cared for Katelina as well, or so you tell me. You cared for her on her death-bed in Cyprus, when she was innocently caught in the siege of Famagusta. So young. So lovely. A tragedy.'

'We all know that,' he said.

She said, 'Only Katelina wasn't accidentally trapped in Famagusta, Nicholas; she deliberately went there. She went there to die. She went there in the hope – in the certainty – of being killed, because she was pregnant.'

Her eyes were shining. She knew what she was saying. If Katelina had been pregnant, it was not by her husband. Simon had not been with her for months. But Nicholas had. He waited, and then said, 'So, go on.'

Gelis said, 'Have you no comment to make? Katelina had to arrange her own death because she was carrying a second child planted by you, and she couldn't hope to cheat Simon again. So she arranged to die, and take your unborn child with her. The Dry Tree. The Immaculate Conception. I thought you should know. You would want to mourn that little child, too.'

He had no comment to make, because his thoughts had become tangled again, child for child, death for death; even to a sense of children unborn, still folded aside in their hampers, awaiting their part on the stage. Katelina, Adorne. The death of a child, decreed by its parent, so that another should live. Both Katelina and Adorne in a way had been guilty of that, but their sons had not breathed, smiled, cried, trusted. *Say good night to the dark.* He had killed his own son.

The words had no sense. In a distorted way, they made perfect sense. He wondered if it would have been a son Katelina was carrying. He wondered many things, but dared not let himself think of them, because Gelis was waiting, and this was a stage in a very long war. He found his unseeing gaze had fixed on Gelis's fair, bright-eyed face. It was full of mockery, beneath which lay a curious attentiveness.

He said, 'I don't know whether or not I believe you. I should need a little more proof. I can only take this for what it is, a sign that I am succeeding a little too well.'

He stood up and smiled. 'Was it so good, then, the Play? Was it so very good that you couldn't bear it? Then, of all praise I have had today, yours has to rank as the highest tribute of all. Thank you, Gelis.'

The clutter had left his mind, along with everything she had told him; set apart for the future behind the mental wall he knew so well how to raise. He watched her straighten, frowning, and deepened his smile. She could see that, superficially at least, she had failed. That in every other way she had succeeded, she could only surmise.

In the distance, footsteps made themselves heard. Gelis drew breath, then thought better of it and turned to the door. There, she looked at him again. 'You have nothing to add?'

'Mistakes happen,' he said. It was true. Planning could only take you so far. She could take that however she pleased.

She didn't please. Her face changed, filling with something more violent than scorn. Then she walked out, the door swinging behind her.

The rolling step of Roger approached, by now unmistakable. There were others behind him. The time for celebration had come.

Chapter 19

FROM THAT TIME on (people said), the sun and the moon shone out of the backside of Nicol de Fleury, and he could do what he liked. The King loved him. The people loved him. Only the Lord Treasurer cursed him on the quiet.

It was not quite as rumour had it, of course, but it had increased the renown of the Bank. Even Govaerts was prepared to concede that. The real celebrations had taken place the following day, when the same Nicol had thanked his colleagues in generous Burgundian style, and they drank together all day and all night, with no water, by God, disgracing anyone's cup.

After all that, it was not surprising, either, that the patron of a bank, having for so long neglected his business, had to move his bed and office back from the High Street to the Canongate. It pleased the King, amid the Yule feasts that followed, to have instant call once again on the Burgundian's services, more especially since Adorne, of course, was understandably absent.

As to that, it pleased the King even more to see how kindly his little Queen treated the poor sick lady of Cortachy, showering her with delicacies as she recovered from her confinement. Since the afternoon of the Nativity it seemed to James that there had been some change in Margaret his spouse. She had asked Willie Roger, his musician, to repeat for her several of the verses that had caught her fancy that day, and to rewrite some of them to suit her voice and her lute. It was, however, usually Nicol de Fleury whom she invited to sing for her. The lady Mary was sometimes allowed to come too.

The visitors left, and the yards in the High Street and in the Abbey of Holyroodhouse returned to their previous state, to the disappointment of Jodi and the delight of the Abbot, who immediately set about his rebuilding, all of it distinguished by his personal monogram. The collegiate church of the Trinity, which had filled its coffers by renting itself out as a music-room, made known its loyal desire to commission a triptych depicting the monarch, his Queen, and Edward Bonkle, the Provost of Trinity. The initial response, such as it was, indicated that a donation in cash might be preferable.

The Palace's caution was justified. The bills for the Play were coming in, together with those for the Court's dress and entertainment for Christmas. All of it confirmed what was already apparent: James was not likely to lead an army next year into Brittany without a package of gifts, loans, bribes, requisitions, dowries and taxes on a scale hitherto unknown. Taxes depended on Parliament. He had no son yet to farm out in marriage. And the King's loans from the Banco di Niccolò were of such a dimension by now that John Laing the Treasurer laughed when the King proposed an extension.

The Franco-Scottish courtiers, through all this, said nothing. Andro Wodman and William Monypenny kept to themselves whatever they knew or suspected of the dual interests of Nicholas de Fleury. A Scottish army was, after all, only one of his promised objectives.

Twelfth Night passed. Michael Crackbene returned, arriving by night at the house in the Canongate and slipping prudently through Govaerts's room before announcing himself to vander Poele. To M. de Fleury. The session with vander Poele – M. de Fleury – was as effing difficult and as effing fascinating as it usually was, and he deserved the flask they shared afterwards. Mick Crackbene knew how successful he'd been. It was ninety in the hundred certain that everything would be in place, and on time. He said, 'It's lucky for us that Adorne isn't going. Sersanders hasn't the experience.'

'It wasn't so lucky for Adorne,' de Fleury said.

Crackbene looked at him, surprised, and remembered something. He said, 'It's a pity Ada never learned to decipher. She says there are a lot of old papers in Coldingham, just piled on the monks' shelves.'

He waited for, and got, de Fleury's real bastard's stare. He knew who Ada was, and how long Mick had been bedding her. De Fleury said, 'I thought she could count, at the very least. How many have you got between you by now? Three?'

'Two,' said Crackbene shortly. It was true, for the moment. He had had no idea he was watched.

'Two and eight-ninths, I am told,' de Fleury said. 'It's your affair. I have no objections. But hear this. No one steals anything or searches for anything at Coldingham without my instructions. That is an absolute embargo. Do you understand?'

Crackbene understood. He didn't trust vander Poele either. M. effing de Fleury.

It fretted Martin of the Vatachino, as well, that Anselm Adorne refused to leave his wife's side, or break the period of mourning for his infant. The nephew, who thought a lot of himself, was not helpful. 'You have the plan all made. The master is coming, isn't he?'

'He'll be here and in place by next month. You are going yourself?'

'Of course,' said Anselm Sersanders. 'Someone has to protect my uncle's business. You have a full crew?'

'Near enough,' Martin said. 'I need a purser, that's all. It should pierce that Olympian complacency just a little. You know we've cornered the paper?'

'For Colard?'

'And others. It has a unicorn on it. Very appropriate.'

'So he can't print,' Sersanders said.

'He can, but it would cost him. And he doesn't have the reserves. He can't have. Not with all he's loaned the King, and spent on the play – how does he expect to recoup that? And he's vowed to redeem all his gold from the Knights: that'll involve some outlay. And Beltrees. The sums they've spent on that castle!'

'I heard that was the fault of his factor,' Sersanders said. 'With Bel of Cuthilgurdy to encourage him. Does she belong to the Vatachino as well?'

Martin had laughed. His teeth were bad: in the red-head's pale skin they looked like the gravel grin of a snowman. 'I wouldn't know. David and I only work with Egidius, and our sub-agents are with other firms. I don't see why we shouldn't have women, though: it would certainly brighten things up. Your sister Katelijne for instance. There's a sport.'

Sersanders was silent. He was trying very hard, and so was his uncle, to keep Kathi ignorant of what they were doing. Business was a cut-throat affair, best left to those who comprehended it. And anyway, her constitution was weak.

Into the trembling kaleidoscope dropped the news from outside, nudging, shaping. Late in January, the dispatches from Rome: telling of Jan Adorne and the Bishop of St Andrews; of the presence of Nerio and the Patriarch; of the departure of the Legates, including Bessarion and Barbo; of the coming union of Zoe and Ivan of Muscovy; of the plans for the joint spring attack on the Turk. The report to the Casa Niccolò was signed by Lazzarino; Julius had already departed for Venice. The reports to Anselm Adorne, and thence his niece and his nephew, were from Jan Adorne himself. He expressed the hope, at the end of the volley, that his mother did well, and his sister or brother, whichever had come.

Late in February, a dispatch came for Nicholas alone from Gregorio. He read it in his room, before he unpacked the rest of the satchel, ready to read and annotate and discuss it with Govaerts. It was in the lawyer's usual black ink and forceful penmanship, but this time different from any he had received from him before.

Nicholas, I have a son. I have a son born in' December. The birth was easy. It was like seeing a flower reach for the air, and then open. I was there. Margot and I held him in our arms, weeping for joy.

His name is Jaçon. He is perfect.

Nicholas rose, paper in hand. Soon, he would take it down to the counting-house, and they would celebrate. He would tell all the others who knew and remembered Gregorio, and they would write letters, and mobilise gifts, and send such a parcel over the Alps as would break the backs of the mules.

Only later did he sit down again to read through the rest, and found what he had not seen before.

The only sad note is the news I have of dear Tasse. She was to come, as you know, to help Margot. She was well when she came, sprightly as ever; but her footing was not what it had been. She drowned, Nicholas: stumbled into the canal when out buying linen to sew for the child. By the time she was found, she was dead.

She would so have loved Jaçon. We gave her a fine burial, as you would have wanted. It is a loss for us all.

It is a loss for us all. Tasse, the little servant, herself beaten, who helped – as others had done – to make his boyhood bearable after his mother had died. Who, once Nicholas was out of his apprenticeship and married, had come from Geneva to serve Marian de Charetty, his wife. And who, after Marian's death, had lived in genteel retirement, to be brought out again to what should have been her last happy years with Gregorio, blessed with a child.

Presently, as he had intended. Nicholas folded the letter and, taking the satchel, went to break the news to Govaerts and the rest. Presently also, as was his custom, he left the Casa Niccolò and walked up the hill – hailed by casual company; frequently halted – to spend the night in his pretty house in the High Street with his wife and his child.

Immediately after the King's Nativity Play, he had had to make several decisions. Business invariably stopped during Yule, but he had lost a great deal of time, and had expected to return to his plans unimpeded. Instead, there had come the changed circumstances of Adorne, and the effect on himself and his schemes of the faultlessly timed intervention by Gelis. The specifications to which he had been

working had altered, and hence the machinery had to be tested again;
reassembled; its components altered if necessary. The other *machiniste*
had altered his programme. He himself had to devise his response.

He had given himself three days' delay before he dealt with it. To
begin with, he had the excuse of the celebration that followed the
performance, and then the further excuse of its consequences, which
were drastic enough. During that period, he concluded without too
much trouble that he must return to what passed for normal life in
the same house as Gelis. There were several reasons, one of which
was the continued wellbeing of Jordan. The rest had to do with Gelis,
and himself, and her sister.

In the three days of his grace, he had opened the barriers of his
mind – as he must – and lived again through all that had happened in
Rhodes and in Cyprus eight years ago, and compared it with what
Gelis had said. He heard again what Katelina had told him, and the
words of her Arab physician. *To a mind delighting in tactics and
devices, grief is not a familiar factor . . . In the simplest of games, one
person at least knows the pain of doubt, or defeat . . . Success seldom
teaches what is worth knowing.* The wisdom of a great man. But
nothing had been said of a child.

He knew that Gelis believed what she had said. It was not necessarily true. He must, then, pursue it with her; settle it once and for all.
If she were wrong, something might even come of it.

So he had prepared to go to the house in the High Street, and also
to make the difficult visit to Bel. He wished, with black and desperate
humour, that the egregious Willie Roger were going instead, or the
superior Adorne, or the disapproving Father Moriz, or any one of the
meddling homespun philosophers who had so recently, so piously
attempted to break his life in half. But for Gelis, it might even have
worked. He might be carrying back to his marriage all his newly
discovered ideals; his dedication to dedication; his resolve not to
squander his genius. He ought to sell seats for both meetings and get
Roger to play in the interludes. He should never have touched the
Nativity.

He was calm enough nevertheless when, on the third day after the
performance, he entered Gelis's house and walked into her room,
causing her to drop what she was holding. He said, 'Why so surprised?
I told you I was coming to take Jordan visiting.'

She was alone in the parlour, dressed softly as often happened
these days, with her fair hair unbound. She said, 'I see that you
believed me. Or is it the wine?' She picked up the object, a wooden
gun, and, carrying it to the door, spoke to someone and came back
without it. She studied him again. 'Jordan will be ready whenever

you like. Did you want to ask me something? About Katelina?' She took a chair, waving him to another.

'I wanted to tell you something,' he said. He remained standing.

'You preferred her, on reflection, to me? How in particular did she excel? Tell me. Show me.' And, as he glanced at the door: 'No one will come in,' Gelis said. 'You may be quite explicit.'

Then he walked to the window and turned. He said, 'I wanted to tell you what I knew of her death. I left her in Rhodes. I heard that she was about to sail home to Portugal when she learned that Diniz, her husband's nephew, was in Famagusta in Cyprus, and elected to join him instead. She didn't kill herself. She was mortally wounded during the siege of the town. I know that was true. I was a prisoner in Famagusta myself. I was there with Diniz in the last days of her life, and worked with the Arab who nursed her. He didn't mention a child. Nor did she.'

'Of course not,' Gelis said. 'Wouldn't you claim that she adored you? Wouldn't she want to spare you the pain and the guilt? Wouldn't she swear others to secrecy? After all, the coming child must have been yours. Simon was in Portugal. Or was she promiscuous?'

'I don't know,' Nicholas said. He felt tired. 'She was your sister.'

'Alone and pregnant,' Gelis said. 'Frightened; caught in a war. Knowing that she had already borne you one child, and managed to pass it off as her husband's. But another? She couldn't explain that to Simon. He would kill her, and your bastard Henry, and you. So her solution was to go where her pregnancy would never be discovered, because she would be sure to die first. As she did.'

'I am sorry,' he said. 'That is no more than guesswork. Would she lie when she was dying? I think not.'

Katelina had not, in the end, been afraid. She had been concerned about sin, the sin they had committed together, and he had comforted her. Simon would never know; and if they had betrayed Simon once, he had betrayed Katelina his wife many times. He had told her that if atonement were required, he, Nicholas would willingly pay for it.

As he was doing.

He said, 'So, you see, there is no proof of the pregnancy, and everything points to it being untrue. What astonishes me is not that you believe it, but how and when you decided to tell me. That, from your point of view, was a mastercard – the last, it might be. So why play it? Why throw it away?'

'I spoiled your Play for you,' she said.

'A moment's gratification, for that price?'

'I don't know.' She affected to ponder. 'I deserve some amusement, don't you think? And I did have a reason. I should prefer your whole attention, Nicholas. The quest for beatification is all very well, but first of all you have to clear me from your way.'

'I am quite content to have you where you are,' Nicholas said. 'In my house, with our excellent child. If you impede me, I shall tell you.'

She gazed at him. She said, 'You really think, don't you, that you are omnipotent? There is no proof, you say. Did you ask me? No, you assumed it. So why not ask me now?'

His throat had dried. He took his time, and said, 'I am asking you.'

She smiled. Her hair, wheat-coloured, strayed over her cheek and her skin was polished like ivory. She said, 'Then here is my gift to you. You spoke of Abul the physician. He nursed my sister, with Diniz to help him. He could not keep the complications of her condition from Diniz, young as he was. Diniz knew she was bearing your child. He was forbidden to tell you.'

'But he told you?' Nicholas said. The boy Diniz, now a grown man. The hesitations, the compassionate gaze, the unexpected tenderness now and then.

It was true. And Diniz had known.

She was hesitating. 'Ask Diniz,' she said at last.

He said, 'Perhaps I can guess, without asking. Diniz told you what he didn't tell anyone else – not me, not Tilde, not even Tobie or Godscalc. He told you that Katelina was pregnant, but that she insisted I should never be told. And if that is not a lie, at least it confirms that she wanted to spare me; that there was nothing but affection between us. She died smiling, Gelis. She chose to come to me; she chose later to do what she did. I would have stopped her from going to Cyprus. But she didn't give me the chance.'

He could see her breathing, long and slow, with a shudder. She spoke abruptly. 'So you were the love of her life, and she died for you. Is this, then, how you take the news, with your damned reasoned arguments? *She died for you!* Isn't she worth a pang, a single sign that you cared? Why show nothing for her, when you can make thousands weep over a play-show with tinsel and dummies?'

'Because you are here,' Nicholas said.

'Without which you would be rocked by contrition?'

'Without which I might have the memory that she meant me to have. Of an idyll. Of an idyll now spoiled, as you spoiled the Play of the Nativity.'

'*Was* it an idyll?' she said.

'Under a waterfall. You remember. I talked in my fever, and you memorised every word. Katelina was frightened of butterflies. And one of my other friends – one of my wives, at the time – had upset

her. It was the least I could do, to console her. Really,' said Nicholas,
'the butterfly episode was truly quite charming. She was wearing –'
  'No,' Gelis said.
  'That is, she was fully clothed when I saw her first. Then –'
  'No,' Gelis repeated.
  'But you wanted to know,' Nicholas said. 'When I came in, you
begged me to tell you. Exactly how did she excel? Be explicit, you
said. Why not show me?'
  'You never stop,' she said. 'You never know when to stop. Some-
times you fill me with horror.'
  'Good,' he said.
  Outside the room a child shouted, and the voice of Mistress
Clémence could be heard, and the cackle of Pasque. Someone knocked
on the door.
  Nicholas rose. After a moment, Gelis stood also. She said, 'You are
taking Jordan to Bel. With Clémence? Or not?'
  'With, I think,' Nicholas said. 'I shan't keep him too long. I am
glad we talked.'
  'Are you?' she said. 'We must do it again. And meantime, which
house are you planning to live in?'
  He showed his surprise. 'Where else but here? Unless you don't
want me?'
  'Never that,' Gelis said.

The house of Jordan de Ribérac was quite close: between the top of
the High Street and the Castle itself. To reach it, Nicholas had to
traverse the busiest width of the road, including the graveyard and
King's park of the church of St Giles, and the houses of well-doing
burgesses, all of whom knew Nicol de Fleury, and most of whom
were inclined to fall into step with him as he passed. Mistress
Clémence held the boy by the hand, and saw that he responded
politely to all the introductions, without which he would have paid a
great deal more attention to the dogs and the pigs and the gulls.
  Nicholas conversed smiling with everyone, one hand to his hat, his
heavy cloak swirled by the wind. Once before he had come to meet
Bel of Cuthilgurdy at this house, his thoughts chaotic as now. Then,
he had known he was going to meet his wife's lover, and to see for the
first time his unacknowledged son Henry, the handsome, spoiled
child of Simon's wife Katelina. Now, a greater irony, he was deliberately presenting to Bel his undoubted son by Gelis, Katelina's young
sister.
  There was no danger that Henry would be here; the two children,
half-brothers and cousins at once, would never meet, if he could help

it. And even if they did, they would appear less alike than most cousins were: Henry tall and blue-eyed and fair at eleven; Jordan brown-haired and chubby at three, with two remarkable dimples to Henry's one.

Two sons. Now he knew there might have been three. But what he had just learned he had to obliterate from his mind, together with all emotion. He remembered talking of bastards to Gelis. *You may have made a better start than you know*, she had remarked. She had nearly told him after the ball-game, but had waited. Despite what he had said, Gelis played her cards well.

He conducted Mistress Clémence to the door. He had informed her about the vicomte de Ribérac who owned a castle in Scotland and enjoyed an estate and high office in France. He had explained that the vicomte's Kilmirren was not far from his own place of Beltrees. He had further explained that Mistress Bel, the widowed lady within, had been a friend of de Ribérac's family, and had travelled to Africa with M. de Fleury himself and his wife. Nicholas said, 'She would have made a better man of young Henry than his father and grand-father have done. She is a good person to turn to in trouble, even though her tongue can be sharp.'

'I shall remember,' said Mistress Clémence, whose linen headgear nothing ever dared disarrange. She glanced at the child. 'I dare say she knows all about parrots, as well.'

'There is very little about parrots she does not know,' said Nicholas seriously, and knocked.

He had sent young Robin to say he was coming. Belatedly he had reviewed his choice of that particular messenger, and cursed himself quietly. There was a stage between obsession and idiocy. As an antidote, he had chosen to bring Mistress Clémence along with the child. An upper servant from Kilmirren opened the door, and they were shown into Bel's chamber.

She looked the same at just over fifty as she had when they had quarrelled more than two years before at Kilmirren. He had bought Lucia's land, and Bel had professed to think that she, too, was homeless. She had kept her house. It had been a way of warning him, he thought, that he could not necessarily count on her. She needn't have troubled. He saw, amused, the two women exchange stares as he introduced them: Mistress Clémence upright, composed; and Bel blunt-featured and squat, with her grey hair bundled up in a napkin. Next, Bel lifted her eyes and ran them over Nicholas, much as his armourer did. Then she looked at the child. 'Eh,' she said. 'Eh, the wee man.'

Nicholas said, 'He understands a little Scots.' Mistress Clémence said nothing at all but, drawing off Jordan's great hat, flicked his hair and crossed her wrists, the hat dangling.

'Never tell me!' said Bel of Cuthilgurdy, laying a hand to her lips. She took it away. 'And French as well? They tell me the bairn can speak French?'

Mistress Clémence looked surprised and then brushed the child's ear with one finger. '*Madame demande . . .*'

The child interrupted, smiling with confidence at the old lady. '*Oui, madame,*' he said. 'Aye, mistress. God strake him, he's near chowed aff ma prick.'

His eyes sparkled with triumph. Bel flung back her head with a shriek. She was laughing. Mistress Clémence said, 'Forgive him. I am afraid . . .'

'I speak Scots,' Jordan said.

'And you have a parrot,' said Bel. She spoke in French.

'*Un méchant, oui. 'Suis alloui,*' continued the linguist, with the same unalloyed confidence.

'Jordan!' said Mistress Clémence.

'Oh, never heed, never heed!' said their hostess, switching tongues. 'Weans and wames are near the same word, with guid reason. And if ye canna understand that, the lad's father will tell ye. Is he allowed a piece of marchpane?'

'Me?' said Nicholas.

'You? It would turn black on your tongue. I was about to ask Mistress Clémence if she would like to take the wee man to the parlour. There's something there for him to see.'

'*Quoi? Quoi donc?*' said Jordan. His hair curled like a terrier's round his neck, and his cheeks had turned crimson with pleasure.

'*Tiens! Tiens! Comme c'est gars bachique! Va-t-en, tu l' verras,*' said Bel. The child ran off with his nurse, and she watched him. The door closed. She said, 'I've fair amazed ye. How d'you think I kept an eye on young Henry there, travelling to Ribérac? What tongue d'ye think I spoke, living in Lagos? What tongue do you ken that I dinna ken?' She turned back. Her eyes were still brilliant.

'You can't swear in Greek,' Nicholas said.

'I can so,' she said. 'From the same source. And if I had the beak, I'd take a lesson or two in emasculation forbye. D'ye want this child?'

'I took a lot of trouble to get him,' Nicholas said. He sat down.

'I heard,' she said. 'Show me your hand.'

It puzzled him for a moment; then he remembered Dr Andreas. He held out his right hand, thumb and forefinger uppermost, his eyebrows raised. There was nothing to see. He had watched Gelis glance at it also. 'They told me you were divining,' Bel said.

'It was easy this time,' he said. And keeping his eyes on her face: 'Of course I want him. I want him to live with his parents. I brought Gelis back.'

'Henry lived with his parents,' Bel said. 'And none could be prouder than Simon. So what spoiled Henry, and how will Jordan be different?'

He could display, when he liked, a masterly lack of involvement. 'Jordan *is* different. Ask Gelis.'

Bel folded her arms, not an easy convolution and therefore all the more positive. She said, 'Well, well. Was that what ye wanted to know? I havena spoken to Gelis since ye brought her to Scotland. I didna see her in Bruges: she'd left for the Holy Land with Anselm Adorne. I wasna in Venice. I spent time with her here, when she served the lady Mary afore you and she married. And I remember the pair of ye before that: never a kind word between ye in Africa, and never a sheet between you – or time for speech – when ye came back.' She paused. 'They say that lust burns itself out.'

'You remember a lot,' Nicholas said. 'Do you remember that she slept with Simon, and tried to pass off Jordan as his?'

'But you've forgiven her,' the old woman said. 'As you told me, you went and brought the lass back. Jordan is to grow up different from Henry, oh aye. Gelis has changed, oh aye aye. So have you, wha could deny it? That's why wee Robin was sent me: *Here's a nice, fresh little lad who admires the new Nicol de Fleury.* The de'il kens what harm you'll dae him. And now Mistress Clémence de Coulanges is brought: *Here's an upstanding, principled woman who would only work for an upstanding, principled man.* For shame! Ye'd mak God himself gnap on his thumbnail.'

'What do you want?' Nicholas said.

'I thought I had it,' she said. 'I saw your Play.'

He did not immediately answer. 'But?' he said eventually.

She never avoided his eyes. Hers were round and clear; insignificant in colour; set on either side of a turnip of nose, in a shapeless face blanketed by a creamy, powdery skin with no lustre. From the paleness of her brows, she had once been fair.

She said, 'I have no need to tell you. I hoped you'd leave Scotland.'

'So that the vicomte and Simon may come back without risk?'

'Without risk to whom? They willna keep off for ever,' she said. 'Take Gelis with you. Take Jordan.'

'And abandon Beltrees?' he said. 'After all the gold you have squandered there on my behalf? I forgot to thank you for that.'

She didn't answer. He said, 'You know, I take it, who brought Jordan to me in Venice. Katelijne knows too.'

'You were meant to stay clear of Scotland,' she said. Her voice, which could grate, was low and curt.

'I don't always do what others want,' Nicholas said. 'It must be my upbringing. How sad. At least I shall spend the summers away. I have to be in Artois by June. But I am afraid I shall be back. And Gelis. And Jordan. Do you think they will approve of my Beltrees? Or your Beltrees, ought I to say?'

She thought, turning over his answer. Then she said, 'You havena taken them there?'

'I haven't had time. But Oliver Semple has to go back in February. He could take them. And if you were at home, you could explain all its extravagant pleasures.'

'You're speiring at me to spend time with Gelis? Why?'

'With Gelis and Jordan,' he said.

'Why?' she repeated.

'For Godscalc,' he said.

She unfolded her arms. After a moment she got to her feet with deliberation and set the door open, after which she came back. He had risen. She said, 'Gin ye were a wean, I wad strike ye for that. Nicholas, Nicholas . . . what path are ye set on? What would Godscalc feel but heartsick if he saw you? Is this all his agonising was worth? Or your own?'

He returned her gaze. His face, he knew, contained no trace of apology, or appeal, or indecision. In the distance, the child's voice could be heard approaching. This time he did not trouble to smile. 'Entertain her at Beltrees,' he said. 'Or you might regret it one day.'

As Nicholas de Fleury remained so brilliantly visible that festive Yule and the weeks that immediately followed it, so by contrast the house of Anselm Adorne remained quiet, though not lacking in visitors. The Baron tried not to deviate from his plan, but continued painstakingly to interweave the complicated threads of his embassy and his personal business, always looking to the future, and taking account of the new land he possessed and his increased duties in Scotland and Bruges. He continued to confer in private with Martin. He perused, too, but did not discuss with his womenfolk, the letters which came to him from Genoa and Danzig, Rome and Cologne, and his own agents and partners in Bruges. And, of course, from his daughter in England.

He now knew, from Jan, that the plan had succeeded: that de Fleury's new ship would not be here by the spring, whereas his own vessel was on its way with its cargo, in immaculate order, in exemplary time. He knew that Diniz, de Fleury's Bruges manager, was uneasy over the outlay in Scotland, and over the padrone's winter isolation from Venice and Rome and the Low Countries, as the French–Burgundian truce showed signs of wearing thin. He also knew, but could not explain how he knew, that the effort to divert, to reshape, to tame Nicholas de Fleury had failed.

Adorne had never spoken of this to Kathi, and at present she was wholly devoted to the care of Margriet, like the other kind women and Andreas. The German priest had, he thought, recognised a little of what was being attempted, but had called to leave his condolences, not to chatter. The same applied to the three generations of the Berecrofts family. They said the young one, the boy Robin, was going to Nicholas to train as a squire. Kathi maintained it would do him no harm. Kathi was too young to remember Felix de Charetty, who had also had dreams.

There remained the musician, Will Roger, who had begun it all with his motet. Long ago, even without Phemie Dunbar to instruct him, the Baron Cortachy had recognised that the Englishman's truculent moods, his battery of invective and blandishments were no more than weapons: the siege machinery of his ferocious commitment to his art.

Adorne had not attended the Play. He had not been there when de Fleury, fulfilling his promise, gave Roger the creation he had asked for; but he had spoken to those who were present, and had learned from their silence as much as from their speech. Will Roger, exchanging words after the funeral, had simply said, 'God preserved you from watching it. It would have been wrong.'

'Everyone tells of your music,' Adorne had said.

'Oh yes,' Roger had said. 'I made music. But this man who wastes time as a merchant – this man put together shape and texture and light and matched the music to movement. Or mismatched it, out of sheer screaming arrogance. He got van der Goes – he got the best artists in Europe to copy the paintings by Lippi and van Eyck and Petrus Christus. He did the Strozzi–Fabriano Magi in its gold frame, and replaced the painted figures with live ones – can you imagine that? The dove was *real* – it fluttered down the nine golden rays to Mary's cloak and nestled there. You couldn't see the mechanism or hear it: the angels floated, the demons from Hell swirled and flew. The shepherd's bob of cherries was real, and so were Gabriel's garlands and the stem of white lilies. And he prodded the spoken word into it all, never forgetting that the most fearsome sound a man hears –' He stopped.

'What?' said Adorne.

'– is no sound at all.'

Adorne did not speak. At length he said, 'And it was done as he wanted?'

'As in war,' Roger said. 'For the space of one day, they would have followed him into Gehenna. He could have razed Rome or retaken Jerusalem.'

'Now he knows what he can do,' Adorne said. He waited. 'What is it? You cannot think you have lit the wrong fire?'

'I think I have stamped it out,' Roger said.

Adorne straightened. 'Surely not. You wanted him, and so did I, to recognise what talents he has and put them to use. Now the world knows he can do it.'

'They will forget,' Roger said. 'A play, a piece of music are soon wafted away. They will not hold him to it, and he will not listen to me again, or to you. I wanted him to do something well, but I forgot, idiot that I am, what theatre teaches. It teaches power.'

'Is that bad?' Adorne said.

Will Roger looked at him. He said, 'When I train my musicians, my choir, I have absolute power for a short time. For me, that's enough. In military life, a man learns as he rises, from humble lanceknight to captain, from captain to Constable. But in business? The patron of a company exerts power, but not over a clamouring crowd: his men are scattered, he reaches them scribe to scribe, person to person.'

'You are saying that the experience of mass command was a shock? Was too much? Was something he would be afraid of applying to other parts of his life?'

'I don't know,' the musician said. 'If I were God, I'd kiss that man and offer him pardon, provided he produced plays such as that through eternity. As it is, he has gone back to his worm-cast. He has returned to his petty affairs as if it never happened.'

He spoke as if it were a matter of personal grievance, but there was another emotion beneath. Adorne said, 'It is lonely, the life of a leader. The herd offers companionship.'

Will Roger looked up. 'What herd will he fit into now? Whatever he does, he is isolated by his own gifts. If he doesn't put them to use, he's in limbo.'

There was a silence. Adorne wondered, in a detached way, if Roger thought he was drawing an analogy: if he conceived that Adorne's own career – ducal adviser, burgomaster, royal envoy – in any way resembled that of a dyeyard apprentice. Then he realised he was being ridiculous, and smiled. He said, 'You think he has failed to take the chance that you offered him – that we all offered him. But he can never be quite the same. And because of you, a great thing has been done.'

'It has been done by a cripple,' said Roger.

Last of all, just before Gelis left for the west, she learned from Archie of Berecrofts that Nicholas had come to visit him.

Since they possessed adjoining houses, this was not unusual. It seemed, however, that Nicholas had had no particular purpose, except that of commending young Robin, and of obtaining Archie's consent to remove the boy for a little from Edinburgh. When asked where he was going, Nicholas had referred vaguely to Moriz, who had established some promising ventures on the Fife and Lothian coasts.

It had always been Gelis's plan to survey her husband's new castle of Beltrees; especially since Nicholas had so markedly omitted to take her there. She waited. Through her work on the Play, she had become well acquainted with their Renfrewshire factor. As soon as Nicholas proved indeed to have left for the east, Gelis arranged to ride in the opposite direction with Master Oliver Semple. Prudently, she took Jordan with her, and Mistress Clémence and Pasque to attend him. It was cold, but her thoughts and her plans were most cheering, and Jodi liked horses. In any case it would not be very long, she suspected, before his father rejoined them.

She forgot, because it seemed to have no present relevance, the conversation Nicholas had once begun about Jordan's future. She enjoyed good health herself, and Nicholas displayed all his usual energy. His final visit to Jordan had been if anything over-exuberant, although against custom he had brought the child something to play with, and had extracted a promise to do with a lengthy poem he wished to hear on returning. The poem would take some weeks to memorise, which he might or might not have guessed. Mistress Clémence at least would take the hint; and the child seemed undisturbed by the imminent parting. His father had vanished on business before, and come back. Equally, since Nicholas had chosen to leave, Gelis saw no need to inform him that she and Jordan were not staying in Edinburgh. He would learn soon enough.

Just before Gelis left, she learned with pleasure that Crackbene had come ashore in a hurry. She wondered if Nicholas had noticed that Martin had vanished. She did not know, and no one told her, that John le Grant had gone from his lodgings as well. She saw no cause at that point to regret having told Nicholas the truth about Katelina.

Part III

Spring, 1472

THE CRAPAULT OF HELL

Part II

Chapter 20

TO MANY PEOPLE in Edinburgh, it was perfectly obvious why the younger Burgundian had left town. The theories did not always coincide, except in so far as all agreed that a massive money-making adventure, of advantage to them all, was about to be advanced to a brilliant conclusion. After which, as was known, Nicol de Fleury would leave to join his army abroad until the summer campaigning was over.

The project was, of course, to do with the production of salt, for which de Fleury had the lease of the Hamilton rights on both sides of the Forth. Alternatively, it had to do with the mining of coal, extensively used in the pans, and also profiting by the Bank's remarkable success in the field of sophisticated hydraulic engineering. Or if it were neither of these, then it was concerned with the casting of cannon, now brought to such an improved level that before you knew it (men said with a wink) Scotland would be exporting to Mons.

Money changed hands.

There was a rumour about precious metals, but the knowledgeable declared it ill-founded: the man had ridden eastwards, not west.

There was some talk about fishing.

Asked to opine on the subject, Archie of Berecrofts said less than most, although in fact he knew something. The world might think that Nicol de Fleury had dropped by to talk about Robin, but that was the tale they agreed on. What Nicol de Fleury had wanted was not a few weeks of Robin, but the company of Archie his father.

It had been hard to refuse. The old man had refused for him. 'My Archie's a merchant. He's nae mair tae say tae a line o' dried fish than a line o' raisins wad flush up a fishmonger.'

'You sell herring,' said Nicholas.

'Oh aye,' said old William of Berecrofts. 'And I'll tak' a share in your trade. But a piece of Archie you'll not can get, my fine lad. Berecrofts needs him.'

'I can go,' Robin had said.

The eyes of William and Nicholas had met. Nicholas said, 'I think Berecrofts needs you as well.'

'Berecrofts will get me,' Robin had said. 'When I'm trained. You promised to train me.' He added, 'Or I'll complain to the King.'

Nicholas winced. Old William said nothing. The father, biting his lip, looked at the boy. The grandfather, breaking his silence said, 'Take the lad. 'Tis time for his blooding.'

Of the three men paid to spy upon the Burgundian, it was the bearded man who followed him when he left. De Fleury's cavalcade was quite small, and not overburdened with luggage, so that its pace was quite brisk. Nevertheless it was easy to follow, depositing its belongings in Leith, and passing on to the outcrops and saltflats further east, where Moriz the German priest joined them. Then, just as they prepared to move on, a messenger came with some news and the whole party turned back to the house in North Leith in a temper. You could hear the shouting clean through their windows. Then a servant emerged, and spurred off back up the road to the Canongate.

The bearded man went to report. The man who had arrived in such haste was Michael Crackbene, the company shipmaster. And the news he had brought could be guessed at.

The second spy, discreetly placed in the warmth of the stables, was able to see the bustle of servants, and was quite ready to follow when de Fleury emerged from the house followed by Crackbene. They made for the strand where the doggers were building. Directing the work was the Bank's red-headed gunner. There was an acrimonious passage between them, then de Fleury returned to the house.

The second spy sent a message to Edinburgh:

De Fleury's new ship failed to come. They are taking one of the doggers, and ordering another to follow. The herring have nothing to fear; nor has his lordship.

Robin said, 'I think someone is watching us.' Standing at the window of the Leith house, he peered through the horn and was careful to keep his voice firm. If the rest could hide their dismay, so could he.

'He is welcome,' said Father Moriz, the German. 'We shall still sail tomorrow. Are you afraid of small boats?'

'It is twenty tons, for God's sake,' said the engineer, John le Grant. 'All you need to know is which side to be sick over.'

Robin kept quiet. He had been to Aalborg once with his father, and he hadn't been sick. He was used to small boats. He had just looked forward to something magnificent. And although no one had told him very much, he could make guesses.

Later, when supper was over and the fireside flask had gone round, he spoke his thought to M. de Fleury. 'Now we shall have to fish.'

The dimple he hated appeared. 'It is what one usually does, in a fishing-boat.'

He was obstinate. 'In one as big as the ship that isn't coming from Danzig?'

'How much you know,' said his master. 'That is the ocean there outside the firth. What else would a ship do but fish?'

'Rob other ships,' the boy said. 'Baltic ships trading in herring.'

The dimple deepened. 'An interesting theory. Have you shared it with anyone else?'

He was honest. 'My grandfather wondered. He says Master Crackbene is known.'

'Mick?' M. de Fleury addressed the broad-shouldered seamaster. 'Are you known?'

'I hope so,' said Crackbene. 'Or I have been wasting my time.' And everyone laughed.

Then they were at sea.

At first, he believed they were going to fish, for they struck out as you would expect, into the ocean. He was accordingly mystified when they changed tack to bear persistently shorewards. Questioned, the crewmen ignored him. There were only eight, and none of them Leithers, although he thought he recognised one: a man who sometimes plied between Dysart and Eskmouth. Finally, he asked the German chaplain where they were going.

Father Moriz's eyebrows vibrated, and his streaming eyes stared accusingly over the scarf wrapped about his nose and his mouth. He pinched it down and answered, if curtly. 'There is a harbour. I understand we have people to meet.'

'Back in Scotland?' yelled Robin.

'Can you not tell west from east? Yes, back in Scotland. A respite at least from the wind. Are you not glad?'

'And then what?'

'And then, if you insist, you will be told everything,' said Father Moriz.

It was a tidal river they entered, full of sandbars and crowded with fishing-boats. Behind the jostling masts there stretched sheeted water and marshes; what else the masts hid was not apparent until they had dropped anchor in the deepening dusk and were promptly hailed from a skiff at their lee. The men who came aboard from her were not only strangers, but only one of them spoke a language he knew. They were greeted by Master Crackbene, who in turn presented them to his employer.

Presented was not the right word. They spoke to M. de Fleury as free men; as Master Crackbene did when he was forgetful or angered. And M. de Fleury, broaching the ale-keg himself, answered the strangers in kind. When Robin scrambled to help, M. de Fleury said, 'No. We're leaving in half an hour. Pack.'

Father Moriz was busily strapping his coffer, and the engineer's modest bundle was ready, as was that of the sailing-master himself. Like the others, M. de Fleury had brought almost nothing: it would not take long to pack. Robin himself had more garments than anyone. He had been told what to bring. He found, heaving bags into the skiff, that he kept catching his breath with excitement. Then he was in the lighter himself, and the strangers had joined him, with M. de Fleury and the three Company men, and the dogger was already weighing anchor, ready to sail off without them.

He sat and watched it diminish until its lamp splintered and shrank among the rigging and masts of the fishing-boats. Then something heavy and dark took its place. A dam gate. A mill-house. A castle. A ship without lights, with water chuckling around its curved sides, and three towering masts stroking the stars. A caravel of two hundred tons, hidden here. A glimmer showed him the name. It was a strange one: the *Svipa*.

Someone spoke; someone answered. A ladder came down in the dark and Master Crackbene climbed up it, followed by all the Company men. He was last. He looked over his shoulder and saw that all the strangers were coming aboard too, with their luggage. He stepped into the waist of the ship, and Father Moriz took his arm and steered him aft to where the poop castle should be, and the cabins. A curtain moved, and he was pushed forward into a chamber whose swinging lamp dazzled him.

Shaking hands with M. de Fleury inside was a man with a cynical face and a bundle of frizzled black pelt on his crown which turned out to be hair. 'Eric Mowat,' said M. de Fleury, introducing him. 'Our agent in Denmark and Bergen. All went well?'

'Never better,' said the black-haired man, greeting each of them. 'Not a wheesht has got out. Ye'll be first at the hallost, never doubt it. Aye, the laddie. Ye'll need some guid sturdy claidin' for this one.'

Robin saw he was being addressed. He gave an agreeable smile and cast a hopeful glance at M. de Fleury, who sighed.

'I promised to tell you.'

'Can I guess?' Robin said. 'The Danzig ship arrived after all, and you hid it.' Everyone smiled, which was what you risked when you made guesses.

M. de Fleury said, 'She would have been seen passing through from the Baltic. Besides, this ship isn't new.'

Now Robin looked about, that was obvious. He said, 'But she's beautiful.'

'She should be,' said M. de Fleury. 'A two-year-old two-hundred-ton ship with a caravel hull, built from the finest imported wood and hemp cordage for a Bristol consortium of merchants. Since they were trading mainly in other folks' goods, no one objected when Crackbene restrained them. He freed the seamen, returned the cargo to its proper owners and ransomed the merchants, retaining the ship for our trouble. Crackbene brought it to Montrose before Christmas.'

It was piracy. It was double piracy. It was wonderful. Robin said buoyantly, 'To sweep the herring grounds before the Hanse boats trouble to get there!' He had to shout, against the sound of running feet and calls and clanking outside. The ship trembled.

M. de Fleury said, 'I'm glad it seems like that. Someone will tell you the rest. John, outside if you will. Moriz, Master Mowat will show where our gear is. Robin, stay out of the way. I want to get out on this tide.'

'Get out where? To fish?' Robin said. 'To stay ahead of the ships from the Baltic?' He followed him out of the cabin and gazed. Where all had been darkness, now the estuary was filled with small lights, bobbing as the fishing-boats opened their ranks. The moon laddered the sea where they'd been.

M. de Fleury had gone. It was the red-haired engineer who glanced over his shoulder. The engineer said, 'He'd no business bringing you.'

Robin stopped. The chaplain said, 'His father allowed it.'

'To fish for herring,' said Master le Grant. 'Can you see Nicholas fishing for herring?'

'Then *what*?' Robin yelped, forgetting his manners.

Father Moriz took him back to the cabin. Mowat went out. The chaplain sat, and drew Robin down with him. The chaplain said, 'You are bright, but that is a man of exceptional cunning. Don't think shame you can't match him. It is true that the Baltic ships don't know we are here. Neither does Anselm Adorne.'

'*Anselm Adorne!* But he's going home to Bruges.'

'He couldn't stay because of his wife. But he has a ship. His nephew Sersanders is going to be with it. And so is Martin their partner, the agent of the Vatachino our rivals. Their vessel is hidden as we are, to keep out of sight of the Hanse.'

Robin was silent. Then he said, 'Sersanders doesn't know we are here.'

'No.' The priest waited; then said, 'It was Anselm Adorne who arranged to delay the Bank's new ship in Danzig. Nicholas would have done the same. There is a rivalry between the two men.'

'I wouldn't have told anyone,' Robin said. Then he said, 'Are we going to fight the other ship?'

Father Moriz patted his shoulder and leaned back. 'Not if all goes according to plan. We are making for the same markets, that's all. And he is off the west coast, and better positioned to reach them than we are. But he has no idea he should leave quite so soon.'

The same markets for what? Frowning at the jolting black hide of the curtain, Robin tried to recall what he had glimpsed in the hold. He had seen sleeping animals penned, and stout boxes, and signs of considerable provisions. He had seen barrels of salt, and bales with coquet seals on them. He had seen casks of water and boxes of fish-hooks – boxes with hundreds of fish-hooks. And he had observed, in swathes and coils and bundles, more fishing-lines than he had ever seen at one time in his life.

He said slowly, 'But we aren't going for herring.'

'No,' said Father Moriz. 'We aim higher than that. We aim to serve Christendom – which has, you may have noticed, one hundred and sixty-six fast days per year, forty of them in Lent – with a fish that is greater than herring; that will endure without salting; that will transport to every clime, while exacting the highest of prices. We are going to fetch stockfish.'

'I am sorry,' said Robin. He was sorry for the priest, who had spoken so bitterly; he did not understand why.

'It is not your fault,' said Father Moriz, recovering. 'I cannot say I approve, but I would rather be here to influence what occurs if I can. You understand this is a field of great competition, where rights are already pre-empted and disputes are not taken to court, but settled at sea. We shall be away for some time.'

Robin thought of the great northern sea, washing Denmark and Norway her vassal; embracing England and Scotland, truculent neighbours; surrounding the islands of Orkney and Shetland, so recently Danish. He said, 'Stockfish are cod. Stockfish are cod, caught and dried by the sun and the wind.'

'So I believe,' the priest said. 'And so, with a warehouse in Leith, a boy will know what an old man from Augsburg had to be told: that the cod is a creature of habit, and will come at a certain time every year – at this time, as the year turns to March – to the place where it best likes to fatten and breed. And there, well before the spawn can begin, and during the weeks of rich feeding, when they are at their ripest and heaviest, men will gather and catch them. And you will perhaps know that of all the known world, there is one favoured spot where they come, and where all those hunting them will come also.'

'The Westmann Islands,' said Robin. He thought the priest was teaching him some lesson. Then he saw he was not.

'We are going to the Westmann Isles,' said Father Moriz. 'We are going to tamper with Nature, defy law and cheat pirates. We are going to multiply fish for the Lord. We are going to sail the stiffening ocean to Iceland.'

As he spoke the anchor-chain rattled. The squeak of the windlass had ceased; the tow ropes took up the strain. The *Svipa* slowly came into motion, swaying through the long sandy channel that would take her to sea. The priest rose and went out. Robin stood at the door, silent with shock. The Mouth of Hell was in Iceland. He had heard mariners talk. You could see the column of smoke from the mountain when you could see nothing else. Smoke and fire rising straight from the sea.

He thought of the deep shell of the ship, packed already with clothing and provender; the food and water and ale, the livestock and the well-equipped cook-room; the fish-hooks, baskets and lines that were to feed them on their long stormy journey, and then make them rich, if they lived. He thought of the other shapes he had seen, which were cannon.

In the last week of February, when his father had been at sea for a day, Jordan de Fleury left his house and his toys in the High Street and travelled with his nurses and mother to Dean, a little south of the new hall of Beltrees.

He bore the journey quite well, despite the cold and the wind, since Oliver Semple, who led them, had lodged his party sensibly between simple stages, and since the boy had his mother's especial attention. No mother, naturally, was perfect, but the lady Gelis paid strict attention to her child's care, and spent time in his company. She spent less time, as was natural, when her husband was at hand to distract her, and now might seem to be repairing the omission. Or she might be reassuring herself of the child's affection. Parents could become jealous, at times, of each other. They could become jealous of the child's nurse.

Mistress Clémence, alive to such dangers, had averted them. The present threat was not to her authority but to her job. Although Dean Castle was no longer hers but the Queen's, the Princess Mary was lodged there with her children. With her fractious Boyd children, who had responded so well to Jordan's nurses. Mistress Clémence wondered whether, if it came to a tussle, the royal household would accept Pasque as a servant for Jamie and Margaret. She feared not.

Gelis herself took profound pleasure in the ride. Brought up to the dunes and slades and wide skies of Zeeland, she preferred the bracing shores of the east, but the softer valleys and moors she now entered had been home to her when she had served the young Mary, and she was pleased to be back, even so close to Kilmirren. She shut her mind much more easily now to the recollection of what she had done there. Her sister Katelina had seduced her future husband for a purpose, and so had she. She despised Simon.

No, she could dismiss that charmless small episode. It was over, and it had led to success. In all but a few minor instances, Nicholas had acted as she had expected and planned. She knew him. However skilful you were, if you had no real objective in life, you would lose. She was filled, as she rode, with exultation dimmed by an ache she did not want to identify; but which made her think, unexpectedly, of her father. In any case, Nicholas would be back soon enough; and would find her at Beltrees.

North of Dean, and close to the house of Kilmirren, which was empty, Bel of Cuthilgurdy heard of Jordan's arrival at the Castle. Indeed, Oliver Semple was the first to ride over and tell her of it. He added, 'The woman says she's going to Beltrees. I can't stop her.'

'Why should you?' said Bel. She had made a point of cultivating the de Fleury factor, and had acted as his confidante and friend when awkward decisions fell to be made about furnishing Beltrees. When he had raised the question of expense, for example, she had always invited him airily to place the blame for this bed or that plate on her shoulders. A family man, and well connected to others of substance, Oliver Semple had said plainly enough that he had never seen silver-gilt of such weight in a laird's house: was she trying to ruin the fellow? He knew she had strong views about Master Nicholas de Fleury, Knight of the Unicorn. She did not tell him that, on matters other than furnishing, she might occasionally choose to do what Nicholas de Fleury asked of her.

So now she said, 'If you're worried, why not let me take the blame of her visit? The lady can come and stay here. If she wants an expedition to Beltrees, she can have it.'

'She wants to lodge there,' Oliver said. 'It's not seemly. Unless of course you'd fancy keeping her company. We'd need a day to redd it and warm it and get childer to cook and to serve.'

'You do that,' said Bel. 'I'll invite her.'

After he had gone, she sat and stared at the fire for a long time; then she heaved herself up and went to hold a council of war in the kitchen. The house was accustomed to visitors. But this time she liked to think there might be a wee knave and his nurses to care for. A wee laddie with dimples called Jordan whose sorry motherless sibling was far away now.

When Nicholas failed to arrive at Dean Castle, Gelis set out to move, as she had intended, to Beltrees. She also decided to accept Mistress Bel's proffered company. It might, if nothing else, even the balance. After all, Nicholas had taken the chance to put his side of the case. Gelis ought to be surprised that Bel even wanted to see her.

Arrived at the old lady's house, Gelis refused to feel guilt at Bel's manifest disappointment that the boy was not with her. The child was none of her business. Nicholas was not a widower yet. Instead of chattering about the progress of Jordan, Gelis described for her the present horrors of Dean. The Castle, with three children in it since Saturday, was a place of unrestrained uproar. The Princess, her moods vacillating between apathy, acceptance and anger, wanted the children with her at all times. Further, in a misplaced effort to help, the King had dispatched his other young sister to stay, with Katelijne Sersanders in attendance.

'Then you're lucky,' had been Mistress Bel's comment, as they sat on either side of a board, eating dinner. 'There's a hard-working lass with a touch for young children. But you'll ken her better than me. From Bruges like yourself, and she stravaiged all over Egypt, as ye stravaiged all over Africa with your man. She did what she thought right for the child, not for him. She doesna take sides.'

Gelis did not contradict her, for what she said was quite true. For what it was worth, Katelijne Sersanders made her own decisions. Gelis said, 'She's young; she likes to be in the midst of this drama or that. But she has her own troubles at present. Her aunt is still very unwell. In fact, her uncle was glad of the chance to send Katelijne away for her own sake.'

Bel looked up. 'She gets over-tired.'

'It may have been that. But I'm told that Dame Margriet is to go back to Bruges as soon as the weather allows. Dr Andreas and her husband will take her, while the girl is away. They felt Katelijne had done more than enough, and shouldn't be asked to abandon her life here. They are probably right.'

'You ken that but she doesna?' said Bel.

'The Princess was asked to help keep her busy at Dean. By the time the girl leaves, her aunt and uncle will have gone.'

'That seems cruel,' said Bel. 'Where is her brother?'

'He has been found some task to keep him away for the moment. I think it is cruel,' Gelis said. 'But it may have been what Margriet wanted. She hoped that Katelijne would marry in Scotland. The girl was young to nurse a woman in childbed.'

'From what I have seen of Katelijne Sersanders,' said Bel, 'she will marry whoever commonsense tells her to, and will have as many children as she knows will be reasonable, while conducting a perfectly satisfactory life that has nothing to do with either. In Kathi, the fire burns in a different place.'

She spoke in earnest. Gelis was almost tempted to respond in the same vein. 'You talk as if I could be jealous,' she said.

'Do I?' said Bel. 'Well, that would be foolish. It would presuppose love, or at least ownership. And even if that were to be the case, it is not the girls in his life that you should fear. Or not unless they are as clever as you are.'

Gelis pushed her plate away smoothly. 'He is not a lover of men.'

'Heaven forgive me,' said Bel. 'Could you have known Umar in Africa, and think of nothing but physical love? There are two kinds. There are two hundred kinds, come to that. And if you are going to be jealous, you had better be jealous of them all, for one of them will take Nicholas from you.'

Her gaze was direct and uncompromising. Gelis met it in the same way. She said, 'This is not a subject I want to discuss,' and Bel, shrugging, desisted. They rode to Beltrees next day, a Wednesday, in the rain, with Oliver Semple and two grooms to guide them.

She had expected something grandiose and found it, inside. But the buildings themselves, when they had ridden the length of the gentle grey loch and over the brow of the hill, were simple in line, although the architect had been given, or taken free rein to embellish the gutters and windows. The principal edifice was a tall restored keep, to which a new range of buildings had been added. A company of horse could have found quarters within and outside the walls of its courtyard, and the guest-chambers were equally spacious. There were signs of an elaborate garden. It had been built, Gelis guessed, both as a challenge to Kilmirren and to match it. Certainly, it would be an adequate station for defence or attack. It was not, however, the flamboyant base for a barony.

She said as much to Bel, walking through the principal room of the tower and opening one of the windows. Bel licked her finger and, joining her, removed a spot on one of the painted panes. She rubbed it squeakily dry before answering. 'You think he wants a title for Jordan.'

'I'm sure he does,' Gelis said. 'And, of course, for himself.' Bel was looking at her. She waited to see what the old lady had to say.

Bel said, 'I wouldna quarrel with that. I've changed my mind these last days. I'd like fine to see Nicholas de Fleury settled here. And yourself. And the bairn.'

'Would you?' said Gelis.

'Why so surprised?' the old woman said. She turned aside and shifted a basin, rearranging the flask at its side. Both were of silver.

Gelis said, 'I slept with Simon.'

'Everybody has,' said the old woman. 'You'll not do it again. Nobody does.'

'I kept the baby from Nicholas,' Gelis said. 'You were against that.'

'I wasna against your wedding,' the old lady said. 'And he's got his child now.'

'You blamed him for Lucia's death,' Gelis said. 'He's killed others. He nearly killed Simon, and Adorne. He nearly killed me.'

'Did he?' said Bel. 'I thought the fall was an accident.'

'I wasn't talking of Hesdin,' said Gelis. 'He tried to get me to –' She stopped.

'What?' said Bel of Cuthilgurdy. 'What, Gelis?' The cold light on her face made her look older even than fifty-two. Then slowly her expression changed and, stretching one hand, she shut and fastened the window while she drew Gelis away with the other. Her fists were puffy and small; her touch so light Gelis could hardly feel it. Bel said, 'Come to the brazier. We're not going to talk if you don't want to. You're saying, if I understand you, that Nicholas is not to be trusted, and I won't say you're wrong. But ye came back.'

'For Jordan,' said Gelis. There was a painting with a watered silk hanging, and a walnut firescreen, and an inlaid desk with a beautiful hourglass standing on it. The cushions were of tooled leather with tassels.

'And you are staying for Jordan?' the old lady said. 'If Nicholas makes Beltrees his home, you would stay here? Or if he goes, will you let him?'

'*Let him?*' said Gelis.

'Oh, yes,' said Bel. 'You are holding each other. That much is obvious, even to me.'

They stood facing one another. Gelis turned and touched the basin that Bel had aligned. She said, 'So what were you trying to do? Beggar him?'

Bel smiled. It was a tired smile, but with a good deal of mischief still lurking there. She said, 'Just say I was trying to save him from spending it on something much dafter. But I'd help him win to a title. For Jordan's sake.'

Gelis said, 'Which Jordan? If Nicholas wants to establish a dynasty here, don't you think he'll get rid of both Jordan de Ribérac and Simon? Unless they get rid of him first.'

'They arena here,' said Bel of Cuthilgurdy. 'And he is. Come. Master Oliver will expect us downstairs.'

They did not talk of Nicholas directly again, Bel being, as Gelis knew, an (astute) respecter of boundaries. In the days that followed they gradually fell into something extraordinarily like their old easy companionship, riding, walking and talking on the boundless variety of subjects on which Bel had an opinion, usually provocative. It was a respite. But, as the days went by and Nicholas failed to appear, an end had to be made. Bel made no objection when Gelis announced her departure to Dean, and they rode back to Bel's house and parted. She had been away for six days.

Returned to Dean, Gelis found that nothing had changed save for the departure of Katelijne in the wake of a summons, it seemed, from her brother. The reason was not crystal clear, except that it had to do with her ailing aunt Margriet. Wiping compassion from her freckled young face, the lady Margaret proposed that Dame Gelis could be her attendant instead. Dame Gelis, in a single smooth diplomatic operation, made her peace with the Countess, persuaded Margaret that the Countess's attendants would be far weaker card-players than she was, and extracted herself from Dean with her nurses and Jordan. In any case, Jordan wanted to go back to Edinburgh and say his long poem for papa.

It was a disappointment for everyone when the High Street house, when they reached it, proved to have no word of papa. Depositing Jordan, Gelis rode down to the counting-house in the Canongate and fared no better with Govaerts. M. de Fleury had left for the coast and had not yet come back. Applied to, Archie of Berecrofts took off her cloak, gave her warm drinks, and explained apologetically that her crazy husband had been for over two weeks at sea.

'At sea!' Gelis exclaimed. 'I thought –' She broke off.

Archie grinned. 'He's a secretive bastard. Wanted me to go with him. He had this idea of arriving before anyone else at the herring grounds, but his big ship from Danzig wasn't ready. So he took the new doggers from Leith. Two of them.'

'They won't get very far,' Gelis said.

'They don't have to. The grounds aren't all that many miles off. But a dogger can't stand up to a Hanse ship. I thought they'd be back before now, glad of whatever fish they had managed to catch.'

'Has it been stormy?' she said.

'Nothing out of the way,' Archie said. 'Nothing that Nicol and Robin, for God's sake, couldn't handle.'

He smiled, so that she shouldn't guess how erratic the weather had been, and that his anxiety was far keener than hers. Nor did he say, because he assumed that she knew, that Anselm Adorne and his wife had departed for Bruges in her absence. It was only when, leaving, Gelis asked after Katelijne and her aunt that Berecrofts realised that the girl was no longer at Dean; and Gelis learned that Katelijne had not come back to Edinburgh.

Gelis said, 'I am sure there is no cause for alarm. She will be with Sersanders her brother.'

As was often the case with the van Borselen, Gelis was not just inadvertently right, but catastrophically so. Having seen off his uncle and aunt, Anselm Sersanders followed his predestined plan and crossed to the west coast of Scotland. After a sojourn of two days at Ayr, he was able to greet and board the great ship of his uncle. On the same day, the fourth of March, Sersanders wrote and dispatched a farewell note to his sister at Dean.

In this he told her, in the kindest way possible, why their uncle and aunt had gone home without her. In his pride and delight he went further, and informed her where he, Anselm, was going, and why. It did not occur to him that his ship might wish to stop overnight for fresh stores, or that a courier from Ayr to Dean Castle might arrive, in hope of reward, the same day.

Kathi read her brother's letter alone and sore-hearted. Love had prompted her uncle to spare her; he had not known that she did not want to be spared. The sprawling writing continued, uneven in its excitement. *Guess what, Kathi!* Uncle Adorne had a ship freighted and hiding all winter in Donegal. It was coming to pick up her brother at Ayr. He was to command it in place of his uncle, and Martin of the Vatachino was coming to help him. And they were going to return from the north with a fortune.

So far as she knew, her brother had never commanded a ship in his life. He was similarly ill-equipped to deal with feminine logic, believing that, dazzled by the bravura, she couldn't work out with ease what a herd of puerile merchants was blundering into. Exasperated, she put her mind to a little hard reasoning.

The ship was fully freighted, deliberately positioned in Ireland, and hiding. Ships had been known to do that before fairs, to scoop a valuable market. They hid from rivals, and also from pirates. But there were no fairs in the north worth this trouble; her uncle would hardly circumnavigate Scotland to end up in Bergen op Zoom.

But the fortune was to come from the north. Was the ship concealed because the trip was illicit? Martin of the Vatachino would have no qualms, she was sure. But Uncle Adorne, magistrate and Burgundian councillor, engaged in illegal trade?

It was possible. Driven by unusual provocation, it was possible. So what illegal profit could tempt a man to sail north at the tail end of winter?

There was one. Thinking of it, Katelijne remembered what the lady Gelis had said about the whereabouts of M. de Fleury. Still thinking, she went to make arrangements to pack, while searching her memory for someone else who had talked of the north, but not recently: someone who had stayed with her uncle in Bruges. Then she remembered who it was.

She went and found the lady Mary and lied. She said her brother had summoned her.

The Countess was in one of her moods. 'You want to *leave*?'

'I must. Today, my lady,' Kathi said. 'But Dame Gelis will be back very soon, and Jordan is happy here. I was telling him today how you bought his father's lovely parrot three years ago. And then you found a new house, with little birds with great red beaks all round it.'

'Poffins,' said the King's sister. To Kathi's distress, her eyes filled with tears. 'Our little house on Nólsoy that summer. We were safe. He taught me –' She broke off. A tear rolled down her cheek and Kathi took her hand in both hers.

'The Earl your husband taught you to fish. In the Faroe Islands.'

'Only on Nólsoy. I told you, we were hiding. All through the summer, ships came into Tórshavn from Iceland, for stores and shelter and pilots. We had to stay hidden.'

'Iceland,' said Kathi.

'From the cod-fishing in Iceland. Sometimes they came in with dead men, or wounded. Everyone fights over stockfish: a single ship's load is worth seven hundred pounds, did you know? They fished all that summer we spent there. Then the Earl and I left to come south. Our baby was born at your uncle's in Bruges. Jamie, my darling. I shall never see Nólsoy again. I shall never see Tom again,' the Countess exclaimed, and cried harder.

Later, she tried to recover her calm. 'M. de Fleury said I must be patient, or I could endanger Tom's life. I must think of Tom, not myself.'

Kathi gritted her teeth. She said, 'It was M. de Fleury who helped you escape.'

The Countess gave a watery smile. 'And his shipmaster, Crackbene. Crackbene had friends in the Faroes who helped us. But yes: without M. de Fleury, Tom and I would never have been together in Nólsoy, with the poffins.'

'Dear M. de Fleury,' said Katelijne.

'Why?' said Betha Sinclair, coming in with a brisk curtsey. 'What has he done?'

'Nothing,' said the lady Mary, drying her eyes. 'We were just talking of Nólsoy.'

'Were you?' said Betha Sinclair. 'And persuading Kathi, I hope, not to leave.'

Kathi could not tell them the truth. She could only repeat that her brother had called her to Edinburgh. She found herself moved and distressed by their determination to keep her at Dean. She rode off wretchedly in the end, with Betha standing foursquare and cross in the doorway, and Jodi waving happily from the arms of his nurse. Margaret, pleased to have one keeper the fewer, was already tormenting poor Pasque.

Katelijne travelled quite a respectable distance before she ordered her escort to turn about and spur to a gallop. They were surprised, but they did what she asked. Ayr was not far away.

Chapter 21

HALFWAY TO THE islands of Orkney, with the *Svipa* pitching and rolling and the sea crashing green into her waist, it occurred to Nicholas, as it still occasionally did, that he was happy. Since this could have nothing to do with the weather, which had been consistently fearsome, it must have evolved from his memories: home-made rafts on the lake at Geneva; his first tuition from John on the voyage to Trebizond; his first command of his own ship at Lagos. And despite all that later had happened, the tranquillity of the Nile and the Joliba; the sail with John, full of hope, to Alexandria; the cloudless small passage from Gaza. The voyages, high in expectation, here to Scotland. The healing sweetness last spring, with his son.

But of course, past contentment was not the sole cause of his pleasure. He liked the physical challenge, and the camaraderie, and the isolation from the rest of the world. Isolation from all responsibility save that owed to the ship and its men.

This ship named the *Svipa*, the *Whip*.

He spoke to the helmsman who was lashed, as he was. Lutkyn Mere was a pirate, of Danish birth, and spoke several languages. Most of the crew did; although at present he had to converse in broken Danish with Yuri and Dmitri, the Muscovite father and son. There was an Orcadian related to Mowat who spoke all the Scandinavian tongues, and two from the Baltic, fluent in German. Between them, they could navigate from Finland to Greenland and back. The rest of the seamen had spent the last years crewing and fighting with Crackbene. He had known them all by name before twenty-four hours were out. He would trust few of them on land and all of them at sea.

John and Moriz had reached, he supposed, the same conclusion. John the mathematician, whose calculations Crackbene respected. The dwarfish chaplain from Augsburg who, through resolution or prayer, had found his sea legs at last, and his appetite. And Robin, whom he had not meant to bring at all.

When Berecrofts the Younger wouldn't come, Nicholas had had to make up his mind quickly. He had made this decision before: to allow a boy to prove out his manhood. Felix de Charetty his step-son had died. This voyage, central to all that he planned, was unusually dangerous. He had not pretended otherwise to Archie of Berecrofts – but he had not said, either, what their real destination was. Had he known, Berecrofts might not have allowed Robin to go. It had therefore been the decision of Nicholas, not of Archie. He knew what Moriz thought of it, and of him. Then he looked at Robin's ecstatic face, and listened to his shouts as he raced up the rigging with Dmitri, and thought that he had been right. Dmitri was only a year older than Robin, and Yuri had brought him. It didn't strike him that Robin was happy because *he* was happy.

Lutkyn shouted something, and he answered. It had to do with the herring fleet. The Moray Firth had been covered with boats, and the caravel had gone far out to sea to avoid them. He was already resigned to doubling the length of this part of the voyage; the weather couldn't be helped. They would meet other vessels no doubt, and would claim to be bound for Deerness. It was early: they might be believed. But even at the wintry beginning of March, there was traffic at sea.

The stop in the Orkneys was vital; but then so were all the components of this expedition. Adorne had accused him, with Roger, of achieving nothing complete; of attempting nothing with a whole heart. John and Crackbene could have enlightened them. It was true, he could not compare what he had done in December with this. That had been wholly within his control, and enacted in a single long day. This was a scheme quite as intricate, prepared over a very long time and necessarily unrehearsed and full of imponderables.

He had found it a relief. He had drawn upon all his strengths for Willie's Play, and had been rewarded. Yet in the end, empty of emotion after the white-hot intensity of the experience, he had come to question that sense of transcendental fulfilment. The ecstasy of creation had been there. But there also, he saw, had been ecstasy of quite another kind: the man-eating pleasure, for a space, of absolute personal power. An airless, passionate place where, for a time, he could foster those he wished to bind to each other, and to him. *A hatchery of chicks is ready and will be emptied this day.*

It was as well, perhaps, that Gelis had destroyed the blazing moment so deftly.

Before Godscalc's death, he had discussed this other project with

Crackbene, and Crackbene had dismissed it as crazy. 'They'd slaughter you. Everyone would.'

Nicholas had been irritated by Mick's lack of vision. 'They'd try
to. They needn't. Look. The Hanse – the Baltic ports – got a
monopoly of the cod-fishing in Iceland, provided they paid dues to
Iceland's masters at Bergen. That didn't last. Now, the only Hanse
ships left paying at Bergen are the annual big vessels from Lübeck
and Rostock and Stralsund, and all the others are sneaking to Iceland
direct, and battling among themselves for the illegal catch. So not
only fish are getting killed, I grant you, off the Westmann Islands;
but there are fortunes being made. Why not by us?'

'We haven't a ship,' Crackbene had said.

'Then get one.'

'Once we get one, it will be known what we're doing.'

'Will it?' had said Nicholas.

A pause. 'You'd have to get to the fishing-ground first. Even then,
you'd find the *Pruss Maiden* likely creeping up on you. And then
forty others.'

'We have a master gunner,' said Nicholas. 'And yes, we'd need to
get there very early, before the convoys arrive.'

'In March. In the Arctic Circle in February and March.'

'The Westmanns are south of the Circle. You've done it before.
We've just talked of it.'

'And even if the foreign ships aren't there, the Icelanders will be.
Their Governor's Danish. They're an island colony ruled by Denmark like the Faroes. They have a contract with the official Hanse
ships, and that's all. They don't like it; they hate it, but they're
helpless. As I said, they'll slaughter you to save their own taxes and
skins. Or if they don't, there will be an inter-state row and they'll
hang you.'

'You've forgotten,' said Nicholas. 'The King of Scotland is being
contracted to Margaret of Denmark.'

'Are you simple?' had said Crackbene, who occasionally forgot he
owed Nicholas anything. 'How in hell can the King of Denmark
afford to fall out with the Hanse? And King James, so far as I've
noticed, doesn't have any uncles or aunties in England. What do you
do when a fleet of bullies from Hull sets about boarding you?'

'I'll think of something,' Nicholas had said. The scheme was
possible. He had seen at once it was possible. Mind you, he hadn't
guessed at the time that Anselm Adorne would find out what he was
building in Danzig and decide to compete. But it created interesting
odds. The Banco di Niccolò against the Hanse, the English, the
Icelanders, the Vatachino and the sea. He would have laid a good

wager with Roger except that if he didn't win, he wouldn't be in a position to pay him.

In the event, they didn't sink between there and Orkney, although they lost a sail before they got into Scapa, and even there the ship needed four anchors. Mowat went ashore first, and came back with good news and an invitation. The yoles were built and delivered, and no one had spotted them. Bishop Tulloch was not on the island. And they were welcome to rest as many nights as they liked at his second cousin's.

'Where are we going?' asked Robin who, in his new element, was becoming forgetful of form like Mick Crackbene.

'To spend the night ashore and take on provisions. Make the most of it,' Nicholas said.

Robin scrambled down to the ship's boat beside him. 'Yoles are boats.'

'That is correct.'

'Fishing-boats, clinker-built, with one mast and three pairs of oars.'

'A team can build one in three or four days,' Nicholas said. 'In any small corner. Provided they are given the wood.'

'The Earl of Orkney –' began Robin in a great burst of realisation.

'There is no Earl of Orkney,' Nicholas said. 'Only a Bishop. And he is away. The omens, in fact, are quite good.'

They were storm-stayed for three days on Orkney but kept away from the other bu farms and the castle. Some of them had been here before; none seemed surprised by the rolling moors, the looming menhirs, the sheer red cliffs from which waterfalls spouted upwards. English ships had also touched there. Robin, the climber, brought back battered hooks found embedded in fish-bones. Crackbene recognised them.

'But last season's,' he said. 'And don't concern yourself. Going north, the English ships prefer passing by Shetland.' He paused. 'But all the same, we ought to get on.'

'How near are we?' said Robin.

Crackbene stretched and looked down, hands on hips. Like all of them, his face showed a rough salty stubble, and the deep indents at his nostrils looked grim. M. de Fleury was the only person who joked with him. He said, 'We'll be halfway in two days.'

'Halfway!' Robin said.

'The Faroe Islands are halfway, near enough. We lost a day here, and we had a slow start with the dogger. We're going to an island only two hundred miles east of Greenland.'

'I know,' Robin said.

They boarded next day, the fifth of March, at Deer Sound, having left Eric Mowat behind. Robin was sorry. Parting, he had tried to say something about Orkney. 'It isn't really like anywhere else, although you think it's going to be.'

Mowat had grunted. 'Picts and Irish and Vikings. You won't find that mixture anywhere else, although Caithness comes closest. The history of Orkney was written in Iceland. The great earls lie here. They say you can hear the voice of Thorfinn in the wind.'

'Who was Thorfinn?' Robin said.

'A better sailor than any of us,' said Eric Mowat. 'And the greatest earl of them all. His son Paul had a granddaughter who carried the earldom of Orkney to the Scots Earl of Atholl. A daughter a few generations on brought it to the Earl of Strathearn. And a girl descended from them gave the earldom with her hand to a Sinclair, and one of *them* was to sail further west than most men live to describe. Picts, Irish and Vikings. You can push the blood from one line to another, but it remains aye a powerful ichor.'

'Dysart,' Robin said suddenly. He thought of the crewman he had noticed, in the boat that had brought him to Montrose. He said, his voice hollow, 'Lord Sinclair's land is between Roslin and Dysart.'

Mowat grinned at him. 'Aye, a great place for the herring, the Forth. A few well-built doggers can earn their price there.' He contemplated Robin more seriously, and feinted a blow to his chin. 'Come away! It's the mark of your master's fine native cunning, not sorcery. You wait and see what happens in Iceland.'

'The Mouth of Hell is going to open, they say. Dmitri says it will open this year.'

'Then let's hope you get your trading done first,' Mowat said. 'Then Hell can do what it likes with the Lübeckers and the Vatachino and the rest.' He paused. 'It's only a mountain, you know.'

'I know,' Robin said.

They reached the Faroes a day later than planned, on the Sunday. They were sure, that is, that it was Sunday. They had Crackbene's word, supported by Lutkyn and Yuri, that the crags and drengs that passed, inch by inch in the fog, belonged to the Danish archipelago of the Faroes. They were meant to be seeking the shelter of Tórshavn. They could not even see the sea. Between the regular nerve-fraying blares of their own trumpet, they could hear the regular plop of the lead-line, and beyond that, a subdued piping of seabirds, and far, far distant from that, a lowing of elf-horns, or of trolls, or of small, invisible boats also mournfully announcing their presence. Eventually they dropped anchor and lay unpleasantly rocked by invisible rollers, while a skiff was prepared to take the patron and Crackbene ashore. Father Moriz and John declined the privilege.

Nicholas said, 'You're sure you don't want to come?' Suspended in fog, his gilt-bearded face looked capable of biting off hands, like a leonine post-box.

'We don't mind,' said the German priest blandly. 'Ask where we are, and if they reply in Chinese, come and tell us.' Then he went back to the cabin, where he was beating John le Grant at a stiff game of cards.

The boat returned full of stores, and proceeded to ply back and forth. The ship lurched as its holds were replenished and then became preternaturally quiet, except for the groans and bangs and creaks of its timbers and rigging. All the crew were on shore, except for the card-players and a couple of watchmen.

'It *was* Tórshavn,' said Moriz. 'And the right harbour. Isn't it unwise, allowing the seamen on shore?'

'No,' said John, picking up cards. 'They need the change, they need the girls, and there's nothing to get sick or drunk with. Why did you come on this voyage?'

'To prove that I'm unshockable. Godscalc asked me my opinion of Nicholas.'

'Godscalc's dead.'

'I still hope to give him my opinion one day. Why is Nicholas here? A cargo from Alexandria or Crete would fetch thirty times what this will profit.'

John had looked up. He said, 'Ask Nicholas, and tell me if he answers. Officially, the returns will be rich. Unofficially, he's hoping to tempt out and damage his rivals. Secretly, if you want my opinion, he's running away from himself. Do you hear something?'

'*Sir!*' It was one of the watch, in a whisper.

John said, 'We are coming.'

On deck, the muffled voice of the incoming horn was unmistakable, its direction uncertain. Slowly it grew more distinct. It was not until the vessel came close, slipping into the principal harbour, that they saw the ghostly line of its lamps, and its dimensions.

Nicholas was in a tavern with Robin at the time, concluding a deal with Crackbene and a Faroese pilot called Torolf Mohr, while fog curled through the turf roof and round the edge of the door. The contract was not for themselves. Torolf, a self-assured man with one eye, had already stuffed the ducats into his purse. 'Any friend of Crackbene's,' he was repeating with casual joviality. 'I am minding that couple you sent up to summer in Nólsoy: how the man fretted and fumed! Three times a week he rowed over in secret to Tórshavn: the little wife never knew. But the next batch of Føroyar young, I can tell you, had a fine cross-bred kinship among them. Would that be the ship we were talking of?'

Robin jumped. Nicholas flung open the door, having crossed the matted dirt in two strides. It was a ship's horn. He refrained from swearing. 'It can't be. You say they all use the main harbour?'

'They all do. You're safe where you are. But you'd better get your men aboard and get out. You can't bribe the whole of Tórshavn. Whoever it is, they'll learn that you've been.'

'It can't be helped,' Nicholas said. Crackbene had already left. It was good news in one sense: the men would still be sober enough to rouse out. In another sense it was startlingly bad. Either his competitors knew to be early, or they were faster by far than he bargained for.

It could be dealt with. Only one vessel had come. By the time it could land a shore party, the *Svipa* could be preparing to con its way out. All the time he was helping Crackbene to scour through the huts and herd his seaman back to the ship, Nicholas was working out where the incomer could have come from.

He was answered just as he embarked on the final trip from the shore to his ship. The Faroese pilot called Torolf stood above and spoke from the wharf. The fog curled behind him. '*Ey, Svipa!*'

'So?' said Nicholas.

The man's one eye beamed in the light of his lantern. 'The ship that came in. It is the one we were speaking of.'

Damn. 'The ship from Ireland?' said Nicholas.

'From Killybegs, yes. You were right. You will need me.'

'She's big?'

'*O, jà!*' The Faroese grinned. Stretching one arm, he described an immense, waving line with the lantern. 'Four hundred tons, twice your size. Its name is *Unicorn*.'

Then Nicholas swore, so that the Faroese laughed out aloud. The Faroese said, 'It is your title, *nei?*'

'Others hold it as well,' Nicholas said. 'But I don't think they should have a ship to go with it. Do you?'

'We shall see,' said Torolf Mohr. 'But make haste. Put to sea. Let the lad off at the skerry. *Bless', bless'.*'

Nicholas had borrowed a boy to lead them out through the channel. He signalled his oarsmen to pull, and called thanks. '*Takk! Takk fyri!*' But Torolf had already gone.

Aboard, he found the orderly chaos of departure, and had to resist the impulse to shout. The other ship would know of his presence by now, but Martin and Sersanders still had to revictual and take on a pilot. In this fog, they were unlikely to catch him, and probably knew it.

Even so, the *Svipa*'s progress seemed painfully slow, swaying along the fjords between shadowy cliff-faces and fingers and pinnacles, banded with mist. And when at last the wind started to come, dispersing the mist, it pranked from every side, funnelled this way and that between cliffs, so that the ship shook with the tug of her gear. Although they knew these soundings so well, the Føroyar were oarsmen, not sailors. The wind was no friend in these parts.

As arranged, they landed the boy at the end of the channel, by a grassy shelter picked out by the moon. Then they moved away, and broke out their sails, one by one.

Nicholas stood on the foredeck with John. The sea opened, a glimmer of crests in the dark. Above, the sky was broken with stars. The ship leaned and dipped to the deepening waves; its speed quickened; its uneven voice began to ease towards melody. He could feel the mood on board altering too, as resentment faded, usurped by the first tingling spark of excitement. Soon he would order up ale for all, and some food. Robin said, 'Sir?'

Ready-witted, ever-present, ever-helpful, Robin of Berecrofts had already proved himself his father's son; and Nicholas had rewarded him with fair, but not undue attention. Robin had his own people and, trained, would serve them in the end, not a stranger.

Nevertheless the boy had worked hard at Tórshavn and was due some return. Nicholas said, 'What? You wanted to stay in the Faroes? The Boyds enjoyed it. Well, one of them did.'

'No,' said Robin. 'That is, I know. I didn't mind having to leave. I thought there was something you ought to be told. Martin didn't hire your man Torolf for the *Unicorn*.'

Beside them, John had spun round. The boy's face, dripping with spray, was rather pale. Nicholas said, 'Explain, please.'

The ship lurched. The boy staggered and recovered at once, his hands stiff at his sides like a soldier's. He said, 'Torolf offered, and Martin refused him. They've taken a pilot called Mogens Björnsen. He knows Iceland well.'

Nicholas stared at the boy, who met his eyes. He always did. So when he spoke to the lad, it was with more restraint than he felt. 'Robin, how do you know this?'

'I told him,' said someone defiantly. '*Ey.*'

He thought at first it was Dmitri, stepping out from the dark of the hatch. Then he realised that the unbroken voice was not his. Finally, he recognised whose it was.

He said to John, 'Tell the helm. We turn back.'

John, with an effort, turned his gaze from the speaker to Nicholas. 'You'll jeopardise the whole ship.'

'Not if she's rowed to the hut,' Nicholas said. 'She can wait with the lad until morning.'

'No, she can't,' Robin said. 'She's risking her life as it is. Let her speak.'

'Well, Katelijne?' said Nicholas.

Chapter 22

FOR MANY REASONS, not least to do with his boyhood, Nicholas Fleury was on the surface an equable man. Of recent years he had begun, as a matter of strategy, to allow himself some show of temper; and more recently still, there had been occasions, some regrettable, where his exasperation had outstripped his control.

The debt he owed Katelijne Sersanders was a profound one. At the moment, it didn't exist. She was here, on his ship, in jacket, tunic and hose, a woollen cap on the hair cropped from Egypt: a well-born unmarried girl of eighteen, niece to Anselm Adorne, sister to Anselm Sersanders of the powerful *Unicorn*. When Nicholas said, '*Well, Katelijne?*' he made no effort to hide what he felt.

He saw her swallow. Then she said, 'I am your hostage.'

The lid of the hatch was no place to pursue that. He said shortly, 'To my cabin,' and holding the curtain aside for the girl, closed it in the faces of Robin and John. If he knew him, Father Moriz would appear soon enough. The ship continued on its course; the girl stood facing him, her hand on the bulwark. He said, 'Sit.'

She sat. She folded her hands where her lap should have been. She said, 'I warned Sersanders not to hire the first man you sent him. I'm sorry. But now I'm here, they can't attack you or your ship.'

'Jesus Christ,' Nicholas said. He took a breath. 'Does your brother know that you're here?'

'He will now. I left him a message.'

'He knows I have the *Svipa*?'

'We heard as soon as we landed. I slipped away then, and came here.'

'After making sure that Torolf was rejected. You think I would bribe a pilot to mislead his employer?'

'I knew you would,' the girl said. 'As soon as I learned what my brother was doing. As soon as I heard you had dashed out of Edinburgh.'

'How? You were at Dean Castle,' he said.

'Your wife joined us after you'd gone. My brother wrote me from Ayr. The lady Mary talked of your link with the Faroes. She hid in Nólsoy when Tom Boyd and she first fled from Scotland. Her son was conceived there. She speaks with tenderness of the idyll you made possible for her. Her summer alone with her husband.'

'I note the vinegar,' Nicholas said. 'But you didn't have to come and rebuke me in person. You had only to mention all that to your brother.'

'But then he would have attacked you,' she said. 'Now he can't.'

'No. But I can attack him,' Nicholas said. 'Nothing personal, of course. But the Bank has a stake in this trade, and I plan to put another through Martin.'

She said, 'Their ship is bigger than yours.' She paused. 'Don't blame Anselm. I forced him to let me sail with him.'

'Of course I blame him,' Nicholas said. 'And you. I should take you back to him.'

'Then you would lose your ship and your men. M. le Grant was right. And after all this trouble, I wouldn't reach Iceland. They were going to leave me till summer in Nólsoy. Nólsoy!'

'And look what happens there,' Nicholas said. He spoke absently. He said, 'Kathi?'

'*Jà*,' said Katelijne. She never blinked.

'Mother of God, don't *do* that,' Nicholas said. 'Are you doing all this just because you want to go to Iceland?'

'Of course,' Kathi said.

Her eyes shone. She loved adventure. She loved any kind of adventure, as he ought to have remembered. Father Moriz, hauling open the door to the cabin, stopped and looked at them both. He said, 'What are you doing? What is she doing here?'

'We are all,' said Nicholas, 'going to Hell. Come and join us.'

They got there in three remarkably satisfactory days. Among the crew, it was recognised almost at once that the girl was not the padrone's young piece, as assumed. This was made exceptionally clear by the priest, who had given his cabin to the young person. Thanks to Kathi (they used her name freely), the *Unicorn* wouldn't harm them, and the master wouldn't force an attack. Why the girl was doing it all was a mystery. She wasn't sweet on either Mick or de Fleury, far less the two older men and the 'prentice. She seemed more like a boy than a maid. Christ, did you see her run up those ropes like a squirrel?

Nicholas had her ordered down twice, before he found she was as sure-footed as he was. She was more competitive in all things than Robin. Like Gelis, she could sense the mood of a ship, and work to keep the crew's loyalty. But Gelis never wasted her time, as Kathi did, with ceaseless activity. Kathi did things because they occurred to her, and not with any permanent object. She was like a storekeeper filling his shelves with delicacies that instantly perished. In time, he let her race where she wanted, and sometimes competed against her. He did not always win.

He had, of course, lectured her about her foolhardiness. She was aboard, among men, with only the priest for a chaperon. The voyage was dangerous. Her reasons, however altruistic, might never be recognised or believed: she could be labelled a traitor, a spy or a hostage.

'I know,' she had said. 'But you can't put me back on the *Unicorn* now. It would be suicide. And anyway the damage is done. And further anyway, if we all survive, I can get myself back home with Sersanders, and no one will know I ever left him.'

'You are absolutely right,' Nicholas said. 'I can even suggest what you might do with the two shiploads of men you are going to have to bribe to keep quiet till you're dead. Kathi, I shall try to look after your brother, but I can't promise the same for your uncle's ship. Do you understand?'

The clear eyes didn't change. He was left to review his own words, and regret them. He saw her follow his thoughts with a half-smile. She said, 'My uncle has other things on his mind. Yes, of course I understand. Tell me your plans if you like. It won't hurt me. Sersanders will be doing the same.'

Then, for the first time, he gave all his mind to what she had done. He said, 'I thought you would have gone back to Bruges with your uncle and aunt.'

'They didn't tell me they were going,' she said. 'They left while I was at Dean Castle. They want me to stay in Scotland, and do well, and marry. It is right that I should do what they want. They have been a father and mother to me.'

'But you would rather have gone.'

'Oh yes,' she said. 'But Dr Andreas is there to take care of her. He will be better than anyone.'

'So that is really why you are rushing to Iceland. I'm sorry,' he said.

She looked up and smiled. 'I had other reasons. No, they are right. I should marry soon.'

'I hear there are suitors,' he said. 'Someone, for example, not too far from Berecrofts?'

Her smile remained, full of friendship and mischief. 'Perhaps. My uncle has several favourites, all kind men, and good. He says the choice may be mine.'

He thought of Gelis's sister, forced into a loathsome Scottish betrothal and repudiating it with such violence in Bruges. The suitor was dead, and so were the parents who picked him. 'Do you like them?' he said. 'Your uncle's candidates?'

'I'm in no hurry,' she said. 'But yes, I could share a house and a family with one of them. I should like to have sons like your Jordan. He enjoyed the ponies at Dean, and the country.'

'Of course. You said Gelis came.'

'Not for long: Bel of Cuthilgurdy took her off to see Beltrees. I hear it is a beautiful place. You would make a good lord of the manor.'

'You have been reading my mind,' Nicholas said. 'A coat of arms, do you think, with a fish in it?'

'And a tree, and a ring? It's been done. I'm going to bait hooks. What about you?' said Katelijne.

'The very same thing,' Nicholas said. She thought he meant it; until she saw him with John le Grant, supervising the emplacement of cannon. The *Unicorn* had no artillery. She would have to decide whether to say so.

She remembered le Grant in Egypt. She liked his unsentimentality, and his fervour for the things that he created, such as the machines for the Nativity Play. Since she came on board, she had encouraged him to talk about it and he had done so, in bursts of impassioned exposition, his fingers stabbing, his chalk slashing out diagrams. The sliding of the scenery thus. The smoke, the vapours, the lights orchestrated thus. The ghosts of the Prophets – how did she imagine that had been done? The unbearable light for the Deity? The paintings that moved?

She asked intelligent questions, and he went on to relate to her, chuckling, the fearsome tally of near-disasters that they had overcome, all of them, that terrible, that miraculous day. He spoke like a man starved, recalling a banquet. She realised that, since the immediate intoxicated aftermath of the Play, he had never been allowed to digest what had happened, or even refer to it. M. de Fleury had made it impossible.

It worried her. She learned quickly that Father Moriz was baffled as well. She had heard a good deal about the chaplain from Germany. It was he and Will Roger, they said, who had involved M. de Fleury in the Play: for the sake of his voice or his character, or perhaps both. It didn't seem to have worked. The Play, in all its purgative glory, was past; and M. de Fleury had sailed off to Hell unredeemed, and was about to start a small war over fish.

Tackled in private, Father Moriz admitted that he shared her regrets. 'But,' he said, 'I see we are two people who do not easily give up on the gentleman. You are here, then, hoping to turn him back from this unsavoury venture?'

'Of course not,' she said. 'But I had nothing better to do, and he does need a sharp word now and then. I couldn't leave it to Robin.'

'To Robin. Of course. Although I doubt if I have ever seen M. de Fleury receive a sharp word from Robin.'

'I goad him. Robin looks after him. Until someone else comes who can do it.'

The priest studied her thoughtfully. He had a large, unkempt head and a short neck. He said, 'You are risking a great deal to do so. So is Robin. I am not sure if his father appreciated as much.'

'Robin would have come anyway,' Kathi said.

'Indeed? His father would be relieved, nevertheless, to know you are here,' the priest suggested.

'I suppose so,' said Kathi. 'He likes M. de Fleury as well.'

In Edinburgh, Archie escaped from his father and strode with his news to the house in the High Street. Gelis received him, but didn't ask Mistress Clémence to leave. She had bound her hair up again. Archie smiled at the nurse and young Jordan, but spoke to Gelis at once.

'I've just heard where they are. Has Govaerts told you?'

'They?' she said.

'Robin and Nicholas.' The child, who was playing with wool, looked up at his mother. So did the nurse.

Gelis said, 'Govaerts told me this morning. They have gone to Ultima Thule, that desert that lies in the ocean.'

'He told me he was fishing for herring.'

'He told me the same. Place thy trust in cod,' Gelis said, 'rather than in *aleci rubei*, or red herrings. What else have you heard?'

'That the Vatachino have a ship there as well,' Archie said. 'Sersanders, Adorne's nephew is on it. And his sister Katelijne.'

'What?' said Gelis. Of course, she liked Kathi too.

'She joined her brother at Ayr and sailed north.'

'Why?' She spoke as if he might know. He could only guess.

'On an impulse, it seems. The ladies at Dean didn't know until later.'

'But why?' said Gelis again.

'I don't know,' Archie said at last. 'Upset over her uncle and aunt. Worried about her brother and Nicholas. Maybe even she wanted to go. You know Kathi. A one-person tornado. Thank God Robin is there.'

The nurse was looking at him. He added, 'He's a helpful boy.'

Unexpectedly the nurse spoke. 'It is spring. Young people embark on adventures. They are in capable hands.'

'You are right,' Archie said. He knelt and took some of the wool. 'Your papa has gone to the top of the world. What will he bring you?'

A slow dismay spread across the boy's face. The nurse picked him up and sat down. 'He will bring his two ears,' she said. 'And some ice. He will bring some ice from Iceland to keep fresh that long, long difficult poem, so that when papa asks, there it will be, all the verses like new. And papa will be so proud.'

Soon after that, Archie left. He had come to soothe and be soothed, but remained troubled. Nicholas had deceived Gelis; he had deceived Archie himself, and taken Robin his son into danger. But you couldn't hold a boy – or a girl – from adventuring. And the nurse had been right. It was spring. The boughs in his orchard were sturdy with thickening twigs, and the sun was warm through the glass in his windows. The sea was blue in the spring, and there was a harvest in it for everyone.

The sea was blue, the colour of cobalt. The sky and the sea were both blue, and both vacant. The sun illuminated the sails, and the bright knitted hats on the heads of Katelijne and Robin in the mast-basket of the Banco di Niccolò's *Svipa*. 'The mainland of Iceland,' Kathi said, 'is a fifth bigger than Ireland, three-quarters empty, and you could put the entire populace twice into Venice.'

'Including the trolls,' Robin said.

'Including the trolls. The Danish Governor lives in the south-west. The Danish Bishop lives a day's ride from that to the east. The Burning Mountain is further east about the same distance.'

'The Mouth of Hell,' Robin said.

'The Mouth of Hell. They call it Hekla. It opens once a year and swallows the damned. Henne is painting it. There are other hot mountains as well. You can tell them by the white clouds above them.'

'Unless they're exploding.'

'Unless they're exploding. Then you tell them by the black smoke and fire.'

'And the boiling hot fountains,' said Robin. 'You can tell those by the steam. What do you think we'll see first?'

'I see it,' said Kathi. Her voice faded, and then gained a resolute strength. 'M. de Fleury, *black smoke*!'

'The children are frightening one another,' said Father Moriz. He turned an inquisitive eye upon Nicholas.

'You underestimate them,' Nicholas said. The call from the mast-head had reached him. He tilted his head and made a soothing remark. It was something about voting for Beelzebub. Then he turned back. His voice was still soothing. 'The mountains smoke a great deal of the time, Lutkyn says; it doesn't mean anything. Except that we are about halfway there, and the *Unicorn* hasn't caught up.'

The priest said, 'I hate to say it, but it looks as if you were right.'

Nicholas grinned. So far he had been gloriously, happily right in all his guesses. The *Unicorn*'s problem was the same as his own: how to obtain a full load of fish and get away before the Hanseatic ships came to blow them out of the water.

The *Svipa* had a head start. Instead of trying to race them, Martin would surely consider alternatives. Every inlet on the south coast of Iceland was known to have its store of dried cod: stockfish already in store and ready to sell to incomers. By visiting the best of these now, the *Unicorn* could expect to arrive in the Westmanns with its holds already well filled, and would require no more than a little brisk fishing to leave well ahead of the opposition, including the *Svipa*.

Moriz said, 'He's running into a noose of your making.'

'What noose?' Nicholas said. 'Poetic ropes, like poetic justice, are invisible, especially on mythical animals. The beards of women, the roots of stones, the sinews of bears, the breath of fish, the spittle of birds and the noise of the footfall of a cat made the cords that they used to bind Fenrir. Absolutely no residual evidence: they threw the poor brute's case out of court and he didn't even get compensation, although he did make a strong point with Odin. Never mind. Come and dice with Old Nick. First prize, Valhalla; second prize, you get cuckolding Vulcan. Moriz, you *are* Vulcan, I never noticed till now. John? Mick? A wager?'

His delight, his childish delight, the delight of childish anticipation ran through the ship like phosphorescence and carried them across the cobalt-blue sea until, between the sea and the sky, a white surf line appeared. A surf line that thickened and shone and took to itself glinting small shapes in a landscape of long gleaming whalebacks. On the sea just in front was a handful of rocks set in dust.

The dazzle of white came from the glaciers of Iceland. The rocks were the Westmann archipelago. The dust was the fishing flotilla of Iceland, busy there. It was spring in the orchards of Edinburgh, but Iceland in March floated pure as the hot-mountain clouds, white as mist, white as steam, white as snow, save for the fingers of smoke from the pyres of the damned.

Under the hand of Mick Crackbene, the *Svipa* sailed innocuously towards the storm of shrieking gulls and plummeting gannets and dropped anchor well short of the fishing. Then Crackbene went and stood in the prow while the sails were stowed softly as eggs, the awnings rigged, and the ship set to rights after her voyage.

The *Svipa* swung. Forward, the cook had set up his fire and his oven: smoke rose and was snatched by the wind, and a tapping told of a keg being broached. The gulls at their masthead had left to join those over the Icelanders, for the fishing there had continued, even if every man turned now and then to glance over his shoulder and stare. The faces, hatted and hooded, were generally bearded and seemed curiously pale. It could be seen, between waves, that most of the boats had only two oars or four, and some of them were made of pieces of driftwood.

The moments went by. Oddly, the flotilla had thickened. A swirl was created within it, caused, it was apparent, by incomers from beyond; in particular a much larger boat approaching the bank from the shore, having set off, it was clear, as soon as the masts of the *Svipa* were seen. The flotilla embraced it and then, moving apart, allowed the new boat to row through and pass it. Now it could be seen that this was many times the size of the others: a dogger, recently built of good wood, and obeying a firm sweep of multiple oars. A man stood in the prow, and the men behind him were chanting. They were coming straight for the ship.

Then Michael Crackbene leaped up to the peak of the prow and cupped his hands round his mouth.

'He's going to say "*Ey*",' said Katelijne.

'*Ey!*' said Crackbene. And in the boat now surging up to their flank the blue eyes, the myriad blue, icy eyes opened and shone.

'*Svipa, ey!*' bawled the man from the boat. And the cry was taken up, from boat to boat under the gulls until all the faces were turned to Mick Crackbene, and smiling.

Peace, not war. They were in Thule and, thank God, they were welcome.

Only Katelijne, watching the dogger arrive, was disturbed. She said, 'The fishermen know Master Crackbene. They're coming aboard. Where would they get a new boat of that size?'

Robin wouldn't have told her just yet. It was John le Grant, on his way to the steps, who seized the chance to explain. 'Could you not guess? We built the doggers in Leith, exchanged them in Orkney for yoles, and presented the yoles to the Icelanders, together with one twenty-ton dogger that can fish as far out to sea as the Hanse ships.'

'In return for what?' Katelijne said. But she knew almost before she was told. In return for all the existing stores of dried cod, and the fill of M. de Fleury's holds, if he liked, in fresh landings. She should have guessed. She should have managed to forewarn her brother. Betha Sinclair, so anxious to keep her at Dean, had known of her father's Orkney involvement. Only Kathi had been blind.

The dogger, arriving, made fast to *Svipa*'s side and the oarsmen slowly clambered aboard, heavily creaking.

'Don't laugh,' Robin said. 'They're wearing sheepskin made supple with fish-oil. It's waterproof.'

'I'm not laughing,' Kathi said, and departed. Robin looked after her.

'She'll be all right,' said the chaplain. 'Divided loyalty is an upsetting thing, with or without halibut-oil. Give her time.'

Robin said nothing.

Father Moriz surveyed him. 'Some of that was new to you also? I share your doubts, but lives may be saved. The *Svipa* can be freighted and leave in two weeks, before anyone sees or can stop her.'

'Except the *Unicorn*,' Robin said. He wasn't stupid, and he didn't want to be soothed. He was anxious about Kathi's brother.

The priest removed his handkerchief from his nose, and replaced it quickly. 'The Vatachino have no more right to be here than we have. With no stockfish to buy, they're going to be far too busy catching wet fish to complain. And even then, they'll have to leave if the Hanse come.'

Robin said, 'Won't the Icelanders be punished for selling to us?' Below, the dogger's master was calling to M. de Fleury.

The German smiled. His eyebrows, fluttering, made him wink. He said, 'I doubt it. They are tough. Royal officials have been killed in the past. We are more in danger than they are.'

'If a Hanse ship were to catch us,' Robin said. M. de Fleury had made a remark, and the dogger man was waving his arms.

'We must hope that it doesn't,' said the priest.

'It has,' Robin said. 'Father, you've got your hat too far over your ears. That's what the man from the dogger is saying.'

The priest dropped his handkerchief. 'What?'

'Ever since we came in, there's been a Hanse ship hidden there in the harbour. The *Pruss Maiden*, they say. Her men watched us come in. And now she wants her full due of stockfish, or she'll sink us.'

Apart from a carrying voice, the man who brought the bad news, by name Glímu-Sveinn, possessed the shape of a dicker of hides and a jaw as long as his beard, above which bulged two ferocious eyes in a ring of white lashes. Nicholas absorbed what he said and pondered all through Lutkyn's translation, having already picked up the gist. He hoped the others were doing the same.

It was, of course, catastrophic. A mature man would have wept. Arrived at Ultima Thule, faced with six well-oiled aliens and a thundering threat from a Hanse ship, Nicholas experienced a jolt of pure juvenile pleasure. He said, 'Lutkyn, Yuri and Mick: let's have the ale up, and a brazier, and as much as there is of the beef. And then, my friends – then, my friends, let us see how we can help one another.'

It took an hour, but he got the help that he wanted. He had known that he would. It was the end of the winter. They had been living on dried saithe and blubber and poffin, and their beer had run out after Yule. They owed him for the boats. And after the *Svipa* had gone, they could fish for themselves and the *Maiden*.

He had to sober them up in the end, and they left thanking him and stuffing gifts into their jackets. They had to be reminded to appear on deck quarrelling, and to row away shaking their fists. Their faces were grinning, and Glímu-Sveinn, gesturing from the prow, revealed an astonishing pinch of pink silk between buttons. Fortunately the watchful Hanse boat was behind him. Then Nicholas ordered his own skiff to be launched, and stamped down into it with a great show of annoyance. He felt remarkably cheerful.

During all this time, in the cabin, John le Grant was obeying orders and enlightening his fellows, among whom he included the girl. 'There's only one harbour in the whole of the Westmanns, and the *Pruss Maiden* of Lübeck is in it. It came early from Bergen to trade. It's licensed by Denmark. It came primed to buy the whole season's dried stockfish. Now it hears the stockfish's been sold and it's sitting there brooding, because it's sure no other ship beat it from Bergen.'

'Will it know who we are?' asked Father Moriz.

'Its master's acquainted with Crackbene,' said John. 'He kens the *Svipa*'s a pirate, but not that it's bought all his stockfish. For a start, he's sent his skiff to the cod banks to watch us. It's the wee boat painted blue over there. If it sees fish coming aboard, it'll turn tail and report to the *Maiden*.'

'We have the guns,' Robin ventured.

There was a silence. Then the engineer said, 'Aye, son, we have the guns. But the *Maiden* has more. It's a merchant ship, as big as the *Unicorn*, but packed with goods to sell rather than salt. It isna equipped for fresh fish. So it'll make a real murdering hunt for the stockfish.'

'Which is where?' Moriz said.

'On the Westmanns, in caves. They'll not find it. But if we try to bring it on board, they'll see us.'

'Sink the blue boat,' said the boy Dmitri.

'Then the *Maiden* itself would come out and attack us. The Iceland-ers couldna help. They can risk unleefu trade: they canna fight against cannon.'

'So?' said Dmitri.

'So put yourself in the other man's place,' said their female hostage, who was a very good mimic. 'What do you know of the *Pruss Maiden*'s master?'

'Too much,' said John le Grant. 'Kathi, I dinna think you want to hear this.'

'I think I'd better,' she said. 'Who is it? Someone who doesn't like the Vatachino?'

'Someone who doesna like Cologners, anyway,' le Grant said. 'Moriz, the master's Paúel Benecke of Danzig. They've hired the de'il to bring the *Maiden* to Iceland. And so long as we're here, he'll suspect us of trying to corner his stockfish.'

'Until the *Unicorn* arrives,' Kathi said. 'You're going to save yourselves at the expense of the *Unicorn*.'

'Maybe not,' the engineer said. 'First off, we have to convince the *Maiden* that we don't have the stockfish, and we dinna ken where it is. Nicholas is doing that now. Come and see.'

By the time they stood at the rail, the shouting had stopped and the big dogger was already far off, pulling hard. Nearer at hand, the *Svipa*'s skiff was also departing, but in a different direction. M. de Fleury stood in the prow in a threatening attitude.

'He's going to the blue boat,' said Kathi, in a voice of discovery. 'He's going across to the *Maiden*'s blue boat, and he's going to accuse them of stealing his stockfish.'

'That's the idea,' said John. 'He'll claim he's just been told there's none left, and doesna ken who to blame first. They can even board us and check that we're empty. Then they can start to wonder where else to look.' His voice faded.

'Not for long,' Kathi said. 'Do I have to keep mentioning the *Unicorn*?'

'I think,' said John, looking at Moriz, 'that Nicholas might have a plan for all that. Why don't I go down and find out?'

He and Moriz left the deck. Kathi returned to the rail. The *Svipa*'s cockboat was now further away. Robin said, 'The blue skiff could keep him as hostage.'

'M. de Fleury? He's within bowshot. The archers are covering him. No one's worried. Look at Dmitri. He's giggling.'

'I know,' Robin said. 'I know it's a very good trick. But what will happen when the *Unicorn* comes? What will the *Pruss Maiden* do?'

'Ask yourself,' Kathi said. 'You know M. de Fleury, or you ought
to. He won't kill my brother. Enjoy it.'

It was the way she sometimes addressed her young cousins. She
shut her lips, and Robin looked at her in surprise. Then he said, 'Of
course it's going to be all right,' and settled his young arms on the rail
close to hers.

Chapter 23

THE *UNICORN* TOOK three days to arrive, the delay being purely strategic.

On its very first landfall, near the island of Papey, the man Mogens got news of the Lübecker. The *Pruss Maiden* had left Bergen early, and was already inside the Westmann Isles' harbour. An unknown ship had since passed the same way. As to stockfish, Mogens added, there was hardly any to be had in this fjord, but he was arranging to barter for what there was. A pair of shoes for three fish; fifteen fish for a firkin of honey. They bought, and moved on.

The second ship must be de Fleury's. Having suffered the tantrums of Sersanders all the way from the Faroes, Martin would willingly have kept the news from him; as it was, it precipitated another outburst of temper which made Martin twitch. He wished the young lord and his sister to perdition.

The Vatachino, in his view, had had no need to resort to a syndicate. His invisible chiefs had insisted. The ship was Adorne's, and so was that part of the risk. His sea captain Svartecop was good. It made sense to include Cologne merchants, since that prince-bishopric had renounced its Hanse partners. He understood all of that. But Adorne had been unable to come, and Martin was saddled with this young Flemish aristocrat who couldn't keep his own sister in check. And de Fleury had found a new ship and, enticing the girl, had attempted to handicap Martin.

Well, de Fleury could try. But now the head of the Banco di Niccolò faced a far greater threat in the *Pruss Maiden*. The Lübecker was a big ship: at least as big as the *Unicorn*. And it had the right to sink the *Unicorn* and the *Svipa* whenever it pleased.

It seemed to Martin that there was no immediate call to arrive at the Westmanns. He would have to go there eventually, and put his boats down, and his cod-lines, and fish. Half his cargo was salt. It would be shameful not to utilise that, or his barrels. He would, of course, invite the wrath of the virtuous *Maiden*; but bribes might work, and a certain low cunning. Also, the more Martin delayed, the greater the chance that the *Maiden* would clash with the *Svipa*. The smaller vessel could never prevail, but de Fleury might damage the other. A crippled *Maiden* might not relish more fighting. And de Fleury wrecked, sunk or captive would be a truly acceptable bonus.

The *Unicorn* lingered, therefore, off the uncomfortable surf of the coast. It didn't suit Adorne's nephew, of course. But as Martin did not fail to point out, it was Anselm's fault that the girl had come anyway, and if the *Svipa* fell to the *Maiden*, she would be treated well as a valuable hostage. Whereas with three ships in battle, who could control where the missiles would fall?

Privately, he was amazed at Sersanders's naïveté. The child was known as a pert little madam. If de Fleury hadn't got to her first, presumably all the crew had, from the mariners downwards. A round of shot would be the kindest solution.

They got even less stockfish at Horn, and plunged along the black and grey shores to Dyrhólaey, a nightmarish outcrop of rock with two holes in it. The boat going ashore half capsized in the thundering surf, and all they got was a Gothic halibut, a bundle of saithe and some feathers. He paid them in cloth, and was glad to explain that he had no packets of iron, or timber, or flour. Even so, had the sea been less rough, he had a notion that the Icelanders would have rowed out and boarded him. Rowing back, they had to tow out the halibut, and it fell twice from the hook of the pulley.

That afternoon, the sun dimmed, the sky darkened, and they had their first fall of snow, reducing the horizon to the point where Mogens refused to sail further. It might have been worse. The *Unicorn* was a commodious ship, with plenty of fuel for her cook-fires and braziers, and they had grown inured to the pitching and rolling. Only, when the snow finally ceased, Mogens decreed that they could not reach the Westmanns by dark, and must therefore remain one further night where they were.

It meant that he had to give up the advantage of surprise: his masts would be seen by the Lübecker, and alert what remained of the *Svipa*. They had expected, all through the night, to hear gunfire, but nothing penetrated the shriek and bluster of wind and the incessant thunder and boom from the surf.

He hoped that bastard Crackbene was dead. He was in two minds about de Fleury himself. It had been dinned into him often enough. The Vatachino wanted him spectacularly ruined before anything else. Martin had an idea that, back in Cairo, his friend David had deviated from company orders, but de Fleury had somehow survived. Martin didn't mind. He didn't refuse easy prizes. But he also enjoyed the occasional personal campaign against a man he truly disliked. He had disliked Nicholas de Fleury ever since he, Martin, had been made to tumble down a Venetian staircase. Naturally, he discussed none of this with Sersanders. Girl or no girl, he didn't need permission to ram and scuttle the remains of the *Svipa*. The Lübeckers would get all the blame.

If Martin had prayed, you could say he was partially answered. The weather next day was fair enough to set sail before dawn at slack water, and presently cleared to reveal in the distance the scattered grey and white rocks of the Westmanns, with a haze of gulls finer than gnats, and a dissolving speckle of minuscule fishing-boats, rising and sliding over the crests. He glimpsed the needle-tops of three masts, too far off to identify. One ship. One victorious ship, no longer lurking in harbour, but fishing at ease off the cod banks. One ship which, having dispatched its first prey, might be persuaded to share the grounds with a generous rival. With a ship that happened to be much its own size.

Then, the answer to the rest of his prayer, the weather closed in.

They made their way from that point without sails, even then pushed by the wind faster than Mogens wanted to go. The snow turned to slush on the decks, but slid from the leather and wool of the crewmen plying the lead, and peering chilled from the baskets, and craning down on each side of the prow.

Eventually, Mogens had them lower the boat, and took it himself, with a boy and two oars, digging against the receding tide. Sersanders went with them. Martin stayed behind with the Cologne agent Reinholdt, and Svartecop took the helm. The tide had turned an hour after midday. They were to arrive on the west-going stream with the wind at their backs, Svartecop said; and with ample time to deal with the *Maiden* by nightfall.

It was like the entry into Tórshavn in fog, except that this time they were forewarned and ready. They crept on through the haze. They were emerging with care from between the ghostly five-hundred-foot walls of two islands when Martin's prayer failed, and the snow-curtains started to thin.

The first objects to darken the sky were the massive cliffs, white with foam, of Ystiklettur. Beneath them lay the mouth of the dangerous creek, the passage that led to the Westmanns' sole harbour. They had reached the right spot. The mother holm of the group lay before them. Martin stood beside Svartecop and gazed.

No ships speckled the base of the cliff, or made themselves known through the roar of the surf. The outer passage was empty; the inner harbour was hidden from view by an upheaval of unnatural heights. To the south, the horizon was bounded by the curve of the island's steep shoulder, jutting into the thundering sea. Within its embrace, and at no very great distance, floated a packed mass with the appearance of birds: perhaps a raft of incoming poffins, preparing to return for the spring to their slopes.

They were boats. These were the fishing-boats Martin had glimpsed only that morning; perhaps two hundred makeshift small craft tilting and dipping at anchor, their lines streaming drowned in the sea. Beyond them, alone, was the three-masted ship. It looked small.

The lookout saw it, and let out a shout. The word passed from side to side and down to the boat, where Mogens stopped rowing and started to turn. Then the lookout bellowed again, causing Martin to hammer his fist in delight on the rail. The ship they were looking at was not the *Pruss Maiden*, it was de Fleury's. The *Pruss Maiden* had gone, perhaps without ever sighting the other. De Fleury's ship was intact, or so it would seem from the way it was riding. Its men would be fresh. But the *Svipa* was half his own size. There were no laws and no codes among pirates. The Banco di Niccolò's vessel was his. Together, of course, with all the fish it had caught in the meantime.

Everyone knew they had a prize in the offing. The Cologner smiled. Svartecop looked over for orders; already the excitement had spread through the ship. Mogens, from below in the sea, was calling in Faroese, and the master, handing over the helm, began to bellow instructions. He stopped. The fellow Sersanders, standing up in the skiff, had raised his voice and was contradicting him loudly. The bowmen, who had started to hurry, stood still.

Martin sighed. He caught Mogens's eye. For a moment, he contemplated the merits of deafness. Given the simplest of signs, Mogens would be happy, he knew, to render Sersanders senseless. On the other hand, Sersanders's uncle was one of the syndicate, and his niece was on de Fleury's ship.

Martin hoped, if there was a Hell, and if it were near, that it was preparing to accept two strongly tipped candidates. He nodded and turned, and to a stupefied audience issued new orders. The ship was to stand down its armed men from the foredeck, prepare a defence, and await his command. It was safe. They were not yet within bowshot range of the *Svipa*. Martin didn't care if the girl died, or Sersanders, but the Baron Cortachy would. And at the moment, he had no one to blame.

Mogens and the boy came on board. Martin was thinking out what to do next when the voice of Sersanders reached him again. He was still in the skiff, calling Martin. Martin said, 'What?'

Although he might seem a youth, in fact Anselm Sersanders was his uncle's agent in Scotland. One had also to bear in mind that, although short, he was an excellent jouster, and a man well enough respected in Bruges. Standing in the well of the boat shouting up, he looked cold and determined and angry. The oarsmen were huddled behind him. He said, 'I'm going to row over and fetch back my sister. Drop anchor and wait. Then you can do what you like with the *Svipa*.'

Svartecop looked at Martin and away. 'Why,' said Martin. 'What an excellent notion. Of course, they may try to keep you as hostage.'

'He won't trouble,' Sersanders said. 'And if he does, at least I'll be with her.'

'Of course, there is the boat,' Martin said. 'If you don't come back, we shall have lost a good boat.'

'Buy another. Go and do what we planned, and go home. So long as you don't provoke Nicholas, he's not going to want to make trouble. I'm sure there's enough fish for all.'

'Except stockfish,' said Martin thoughtfully. 'I rather wondered about the shortage of stockfish. Does it look to you as if the *Svipa* is laden? Of course, the fish may have been bought by the *Maiden*. Ask him, Master Sersanders. If you get the chance, ask M. de Fleury.'

From the deck, Martin watched the skiff leave, threading its way into the distance. None of the creaking small boats tried to stop it. He watched until it prepared to round the far side of the *Svipa*. The young man's eyes were fixed on the ship, which showed no particular sign of awareness. Indeed, the only sounds to be heard were those of a number of lethargic voices combined in some sort of ale-sodden ditty. Those in the skiff might have noted that one of the singers was female.

'Holà, *Svipa*!' called Anselm Sersanders.

Walking into sight by the rail, Katelijne refrained from answering '*Ey!*', and not merely because M. de Fleury, possibly short of patience, was not far behind her. Instead she said quickly, 'Anselm. Come up.'

The face in the boat, ruddy within its light beard, wore its familiar expression of harassed obstinacy. Sersanders said, 'I've come for you. It's all right. Come down.'

'I can't. Come up. Leave the boat and come up.'

'You can't stay, Kathi. Come. He can't stop you.'

'No,' his sister said. Her eyes shifted sideways and back. She said, 'Quickly, then,' and opening the rail very fast, stepped out and trod on the ladder. Sersanders set his foot on a rung and stretched up. His sister seized hold of his hand, and instead of stepping daintily down,

hauled him up with a disjointing yank. He clung to the walloping
rope and exclaimed. He saw someone else was behind her: the large
person of Nicholas de Fleury. De Fleury smiled. His powerful hand
released the girl's grip and firmly shoved her back upwards on board.
His equally punctilious foot, following through, courteously punted
Sersanders face down in the boat. Sersanders sat up in the skiff, his
nose bleeding.

'Sorry,' said Nicholas cheerfully. 'She said no.' He had stepped
back and pulled up the ladder.

'I said I couldn't come down!' said Kathi furiously. 'Look what
you've done! I asked him up! Let him up! Anselm, you don't know
what's –' She stopped, being deprived of the means of continuing.

Nicholas kept his hand over her face. 'Anselm?' he said. 'She is
well. She is protected. So far as all at home know, she has never been
out of your sight. She is staying here as my special insurance, and you
are staying with Martin as his. You are being thrown off this ship.
There is no way you can board it. Turn, and sit up, and tell your men
to row you as far back to your ship as they can. And if anything
happens, lie down.'

'What do you mean?' Sersanders said.

'What I say,' said Nicholas de Fleury; and removed his hand from
the face of the girl.

'Katelijne?' her brother said.

And very shakily, his sister answered. 'I think you should leave.'

There was nothing more he could do. The ladder had gone. The
rail was lined with men even bigger, it seemed, than their patron.
Sersanders picked himself up, and sat down, and gave orders in a low
voice to the oarsmen. They grasped the shafts of their blades, and the
boat slowly rounded the stern and began to pull away from the *Svipa*.
He sat this time in the prow, so that his accusing gaze rested all the
time on the face of his sister. She was pale, and staring too; but not at
him.

No one was looking at him. They were all looking past him, and
up. He turned to see why. He was confounded by a sudden frenzied
hauling of lines in the cod-boats. He perceived the *Unicorn* where he
had left it, but now its decks were a curious antheap of jostling men.
And he saw, emerging from the back of Bjarn Island, a dragon. No,
not a mythical beast; but the vast high-decked bulk of the licensed
Hanse ship the *Pruss Maiden*, preceded by a gentle puff of white
smoke from its bows.

The *Svipa* had not been alone. Nicholas de Fleury had saved his
own cod by agreeing to be the Lübeckers' mussel.

*

Martin had no chance at all. The first shot, a warning one, fell into the water and sank by the *Unicorn*. The other cannon were trained on its deck. And by then the Lübecker was so close that the best its victim could manage was a defensive burst of stray bullets and arrows.

Martin was wearing his cuirass. He had already drawn his short sword when Svartecop laid a hand on his arm. 'It isn't worth it. I know Paúel. He wants the loaded ship, and its merchants to ransom. Let him have them.'

It sounded suspicious. 'But you and the men?' Martin said.

Svartecop grinned. 'Lutkyn, Paúel, Colombo, Ochoa de Marchena, Mick Crackbene, myself – we belong to the same brotherhood of *classionarii*, sometimes on one side, sometimes another. Paúel knows what gold I have, and will take it. Next time I will take his. Our crew are select; he will probably keep and employ them; Mogens too. He is telling you to throw down your arms and let him board. Only don't tell him who Reinholdt is. He despises Cologners.'

Martin took the advice. He had no one else to consult: Reinholdt had small wish to fight, and Sersanders had not returned from the *Svipa*: presumably he was now fast in irons. De Fleury must be scared, or mad, to trust the *Pruss Maiden* to keep to its bargain. This might be the end of the *Unicorn*; but very soon, according to Svartecop, the *Svipa* would find itself the next prey of Paúel Benecke. Martin of the Vatachino went forward bitterly to speak to his captors, but beneath the undeniable rage was some satisfaction. If he was to suffer, then so was de Fleury.

Outwardly placid, the *Svipa*, swaying at anchor, was corporately quite aware of the anomalies in the situation. It heartened Kathi to observe that M. de Fleury at least appeared inwardly placid as well; and sufficiently easy of conscience to take his stance on the deck with her, watching. The rest of the ship appeared plunged into activity.

Half the fishing-boats had now dispersed towards the south coast of Iceland, two hours away, and the *Unicorn* and the *Pruss Maiden* were linked together by grappling irons and cable. She couldn't see the skiff that had carried her brother.

M. de Fleury said, 'It's all right. They stopped rowing when the trouble began, and Sersanders is being taken ashore by the fishermen. They'll see he has shelter and food till it's over.'

'How did you know he would come to try and fetch me?' Kathi said.

'Because he's touched, like his sister. But if he'd stayed on the *Unicorn*, he would just have been ransomed with everyone else.

Benecke wants an intact vessel, and cargo and money. There wasn't much danger.'

'So you rather hoped he would stay,' Kathi said.

'Well, of course. Your uncle has plenty of money, and Sersanders would quite enjoy Lübeck. The beer is stupendous, they say.'

'Lucky Martin,' said Kathi, gazing to sea.

'Yes. Well – I do have plans for him.'

'Amazing,' said Kathi. 'And for me, I am sure. What did you tell the *Maiden*'s blue boat? That if the whole season's stockfish had gone, then Martin must have it?'

'More or less,' M. de Fleury said.

'And now that they see the *Unicorn* doesn't have it, Benecke will know that you have?'

'I have?' said M. de Fleury.

'Yes,' Kathi said. 'That *was* what you were taking on board every night you were waiting for Martin?'

'You didn't drink your drugged claret,' said M. de Fleury.

'I would have drunk it rather than the syrup Mick serves. So what are you going to do when the *Maiden* comes to make you her prisoner? You don't think she's going to leave you alone?'

'No,' said M. de Fleury. 'But they'll take an hour or two to fix up the *Unicorn*. Put their prize crew on board. Transfer the best of her cargo. Blacken Martin's eyes if he's cheeky.'

'Lucky Martin,' said Kathi again. 'You can't fly. Benecke would outsail you. You can't sail in the dark: it's too dangerous. And what's going to happen to Anselm?'

'You're going to join him,' said M. de Fleury. 'Don't tell me you didn't guess that.'

'On the south shore of Iceland. In Hell.'

'Naturally.'

'When?'

'When it snows. Yuri says it's going to snow in an hour. Blinding snow; the kind that will stop them moving themselves or the *Unicorn*. It usually lasts for two hours.'

'How does he know?'

'Ask him some time. Either the *Unicorn* will pick you up, or I will. In the *Naglfar* if I must.'

Then she stared at him. 'I'm not going. Anyway, how in Heaven's name could the *Unicorn* . . .'

'You can't *guess*?' said M. de Fleury. 'You deserve to be stranded. Kathi, get ready to go. Robin will help you with clothes for your brother. The *Maiden* has cannon. And if the oratory palls, there might be a scuffle on board. Heigh-ho, you know how it is with rough boys.'

She knew how it was. Of course, he wanted her out of the way. He even wanted her safe, and her brother. But transcending everything else was his anticipation of the excitement ahead, from which she was excluded. The dizzy, glorious contest, with cannon, against a man he had never met, but who was said to be the best of his kind. He might be speaking to her, but M. de Fleury was thinking, all this while, of Paúel Benecke.

She said, 'I think you are right. Yes, I'll go.'

She would have preferred him to look mildly pleased; but supposed that his lack of surprise was a compliment.

The snow came in an hour, and as soon as it closed white around them, the yole arrived, and Nicholas sent Kathi off with a man he could trust and could spare. Then he joined Crackbene and John and Lutkyn and Yuri and Moriz, and all the fun started.

It was unlike the Play. Everything was based on guesswork. It had been guesswork that Martin would linger, hoping that the *Maiden* would finish Nicholas off, and in fact allowing him leisure to load up his stockfish. It had been a guess that the *Unicorn* would come when it did, using the first of the tide, and allowing itself plenty of daylight. It was pure luck that the snow had come, too; and that Glímu-Sveinn had proved to have a sense of Ultima Thulery fun, and to be so very pleased with his dogger.

He wondered how humourless the Danziger Benecke was. Crackbene and Lutkyn called him a brilliant mariner; a man who became bored with the routine of the Hanse and now worked as a mercenary. A man so lucky and rich that crews begged to join him. A man who, within the last year, had captured and held to ransom both John of Salisbury and the Lord Mayor of London.

Now Paúel was working for Lübeck and, while fishing himself, was entitled to stop other nations from fishing or trading off Iceland. He might have noticed the yoles and dogger and drawn some conclusions. The Icelanders would not, Nicholas thought, mention stockfish, but Paúel might guess. All in all, it seemed he was unlikely to honour his promise, and let the *Svipa* slip scatheless away, keeping its reward of three days' hurried fishing. The fact was that the *Svipa* was nothing. The capital prize was himself, patron of the Banco di Niccolò – a capture to make the Bank rock, if the concern for a baby had shaken it. And, of course, Benecke could expect gold for the Sersanders youngsters. For though they were no longer here, Martin thought they were.

He had said as much earlier to Moriz, who had stared at him with disbelief. 'Martin's ship belongs to Adorne! How could he wish to harm the young people!'

And he remembered his answer. 'Martin won't fire a gun against Adorne's niece or his nephew. That's Benecke's privilege.'

Benecke had several options, when one gave it some thought. He could challenge the *Svipa* to surrender and use his own guns to beat down and board it. Or if unwilling to damage his ship, he might man and send in the *Unicorn*. Or he might land the crew from the *Unicorn* and attack the *Svipa* from both ships at once. Nicholas wished he knew more about Benecke.

Then had come Yuri's prediction of snow. Ravens and Yuri knew when snow was coming. So did other men, advising the *Maiden*. 'So think of Benecke,' Nicholas had said. 'We all know snow is coming, then darkness. Benecke doesn't know me, but he knows Michael Crackbene. Mick, what does he know? That you wouldn't give up. That you came up to Iceland last year and probably delivered that boat against stockfish. Would you go home without collecting the fish?'

'You might,' Mick Crackbene had said. 'He doesn't know you. Neither really does Martin. They might think you would reconsider the risk to your Bank and cut your losses.'

There had been a silence, indicating that a number of others thought the same. John had been grinning.

'On the other hand,' Crackbene added, 'he used to know Ochoa de Marchena.'

Ochoa de Marchena, now invisible, had once been entrusted with a cargo of African gold belonging to Nicholas. Ten minutes alone with Ochoa would tell Paúel exactly what Nicholas was capable of. When that snow fell, Paúel would know the *Svipa* wasn't going to flee, or abandon its fishing, or give up its feud with the *Unicorn*. The column of black smoke, thin against the grey sky and white snow of the land, caught his eye at that point. He had said, 'I don't suppose any other useful augurs have appeared that might be convenient? An opening of the Crapault d'Enfer?'

'You never know,' Crackbene had said. 'But the reverse of hellfire seems to be likelier. Frozen pack ice all the way over to Greenland; foxes and bears coming ashore; snow in March. They say the hot springs have increased, which means something is boiling up somewhere, but I don't think the sea will divide. Plan for snow. Benecke will. Benecke will stay till it lifts, confident that you're not going to run. Then he'll come for you.'

It had been good advice. That was when he had sent out to find Glímu-Sveinn.

Chapter 24

T HE SNOW FELL for two hours, as any Muscovite could have predicted. And, in the icy seas off the Westmann Islands of Thule, three well-found vessels each sought to make use of it.

On the *Svipa*, the work was already done: the weapons and cannon and armour prepared; the grappling irons laid out; the instructions given. When Nicholas gave the order to stand down and eat, he made sure that the food was the best they had left, and that there was enough ale to lift the heart without drowning it. Robin, torn between worry and ecstasy, obeyed his commands in a dream, and excitement sparkled like lightning in summer.

On the *Pruss Maiden*, men ate as they worked, but bore no grudge, because the Danziger had made them rich men, and they were going to be richer. The *Unicorn*, empty, would have recouped all the cost of the voyage. But it had proved to yield much more than that: an international broker to ransom, and a man who, on courteous questioning, had proved to come, would you believe it, from Cologne. But better even than that was the cargo, the surprising high-quality cargo lodged among all the barrel staves and the salt, and now being deftly transferred to the *Maiden*.

The *Unicorn* had been proposing to trade. The absence of stockfish must fairly have sickened them. The men chattered and laughed as they worked, and swore that Paúel Benecke was the best man off dry land.

Paúel Benecke, a jug of beer to his hand, sat apart in his room with his lodesman and studied the drawings before him. Stanislas, an old colleague, dared to speak. 'You say he will stay, like a child, to confront you. With what? He is half your size. He did not take the *Unicorn*. We did.'

Benecke spoke without looking up. 'He has cannon.'

'There is no sign of them.'

'Of course he has cannon. He would have left three days ago if he hadn't. And a bigger crew than we think. He is equipped, as we are, for taking prizes.'

'He didn't know we should be here.'

'No. He came intending to fight with the broker. You heard the man Martin. I think de Fleury still wants to capture the *Unicorn*. That is the other reason he stayed.'

'And to find the stockfish,' Stanislas said.

Paúel Benecke let the map close. 'Great Christ, the man has the stockfish already. Did you not hear the Icelanders talking? They call him Nikolás-riddari, the Knight Nicholas, as if he were a talisman of some sort. That is why, before it is night, we must take him.'

'If the snow stops,' the pilot observed, and was quiet. He knew the shipmaster Paúel of old. A brutal, dedicated privateer while at sea, and a dilettante owning farms, castles, women at home. Many mercenaries – the Count of Urbino for one – behaved so, despising their underlings. Stanislas admired his employer, and didn't give much for the chances of Nikolás-riddari.

On the *Unicorn*, even the prisoners were asleep.

There was no need to be vigilant. Just before the snow fell, the last of the boxes and bales had been hoisted across to the *Maiden*, and the skeleton crew had come on board, after which the grappling irons had gone, and the two ships had anchored apart. Enclosed in its circle of snow, the captive ship might have been quite alone; none, it was sure, could interfere with it; and its new crew, leaving a watch, were thankful to huddle under whitening awnings close by the fokkedeck, while her master and mates were lodged in the broad poop.

Lying trussed below in the hold, Martin of the Vatachino listened to his fellows complaining, and wished he could watch what Benecke was going to do when the snow ceased. Indeed, he would like to have helped him. The ship swayed to the west-going current. The wind, gusting along her high sides, caused her gear to rattle and knock, and the slap of the waves vibrated through the rubbish-strewn void below decks. Their voices boomed. It pleased Martin to think that if he survived, de Fleury would soon be in equal discomfort – perhaps on the *Maiden*, perhaps in this same windowless prison. It would be dark in three or four hours. Benecke would want to storm and take the *Svipa* before then.

Although a far-travelled man, Martin had little interest in maritime matters: the crew worked for the merchant, not the other way round. When the water-sounds from the keel became louder, he thought at first that the tide must have turned. Then he remembered that this could not be so: the ebb was not due to begin until darkness. It was some moments later that he, and all those with him, realised that their vessel was actually in motion. Mogens Björnsen the Faroese began to shout something, while Martin lay and attempted to think.

They were not going to sea. That would have been preceded by the stamping of feet overhead, the chant of the marines and the squeal and creak of the winches. They were not going to sea; they were simply changing their present anchorage. The snow must have stopped, and Benecke was moving forward to confront the *Svipa*. And to help with his capture, the damned Danziger was taking the *Unicorn* with him.

Mogens the Faroese was still shouting. Martin gritted his teeth and shouted back. 'They must be bringing us into the fighting.' The noise of turbulent sea was increasing: he could hear a distinct chuckle and flow, as if the water were under his elbow.

His elbow was wet. His padded tunic was wet. He was reclining in a vigorous small stream of liquid. Martin sat up. Crashing and rolling, the bound form of his pilot thumped against him. 'I said,' said Mogens loudly, 'we're running in front of the wind. We've broken loose from our anchors. Shout! Shout!'

'We're leaking!' Martin said. Around him, men had started to bellow.

'We'll leak a lot more when we land on the rocks. Rouse the bastards! Hey! Hey!' Mogens shrieked.

Martin's heart started to thud. 'Don't they see?'

'It's still snowing, for sure. We'll crash, and they won't even notice. Bang your heels! Yell!'

'How long have we?' Martin said.

'With a north-east gale at our backs, and in the height of a west-going current? Minutes,' said Mogens Björnsen. 'Yell!'

The snow started to wane. Nicholas said, 'Stations, everybody. Get ready. It's happening.'

The crew on the *Maiden*, avarice lending them speed, had finished their stowing, eaten, and were proceeding to arm for assault when the message came from the after-deck: to go to positions, and wait. The snow-veil was lifting. Animadverting upon the distant, cowering form of the *Svipa*, no one immediately thought to check on their first prize, the *Unicorn*. It was left to Benecke to discern, through the swirl of the flakes, that there appeared to be nothing but sea between himself and the clifftops of Bjarnarey. For a moment he thought the damned ship had gone.

It couldn't have; he knew that. The prisoners could not have burst free. No one could have sailed in the snow. And, staring breathlessly from the height of the mast, he saw that of course he was right. The captive crew of the *Unicorn* hadn't sailed his prize anywhere. It was the ship itself that was loose, and was now running, lurching and yawing towards the jagged rocks of the holm. His eye told him that it had not dragged its anchors: it was moving too fast and too wildly for that. The bloody ship had no anchors at all.

He dropped to the deck, shouting orders, his eyes on the runaway vessel. Its decks were full now of men. Someone threw out a kedge, then another. The steps came down, and the skiff came alongside: they had only one boat, he remembered. If they were wise, they would tumble into it all the men and the weights they could spare and tow it behind as a drogue. All around him, his own men were running, manning the helm and the capstan, preparing to break out a sail. At his ship's side, the two pinnaces were drawn in and bouncing, awaiting their crew and himself. The *Maiden* couldn't move fast enough to do any good, but the skiffs might get there in time, or at least would help to save what could be redeemed. He raced to the steps.

He didn't go down, for there was nothing to go to. The waves, the cold green waves were buttoned with the dark heads of men, and the boats were two shivering nests of loose planking which disintegrated, as he watched, into single crescents of timber, undulating out of his sight.

Paúel Benecke said, 'Pick up these men. Navigator, a course as close to the ship as you can. If they fend off a strike, we may save her. If not, we take back our own men and the broker. Are they towing the boat?' The skies, leaden with wind, were losing all light. It was half an hour to full darkness; forty minutes before the ebb started to run, with all the harm that might do to the *Unicorn*. He saw that no one had answered his question because it had answered itself. As the *Unicorn* sped to destruction, it dragged no laden pinnace to brake it; only a starfish of dismantled timber spreading out on the sea at its side, and scoured by the disorganised flap of its rudder. As he watched, the *Unicorn* struck.

You would think the crash of it jarred through the *Maiden*, the way that silence fell, if you could have silence in a fast-sailing ship with a big working crew in full action. Then they all looked at him.

Nails.

Paúel Benecke knew what had happened, as if he had been watching it all. As if he had been able to pierce the ill-timed, monstrous screen of the snowstorm and set eyes on the nodding hoods, the claw hammers, the shears; the small busy cod-boats like corks, mobbing the flanks of the *Unicorn* and withdrawing what held it together. He knew that somewhere on shore, carefully pouched, every nail from these three boats was sitting. The anchor-cables hung shorn; the anchors were marked, no doubt, for easy retrieval. Everything of iron had gone, even to the hinges on the *Unicorn*'s rudder.

And at last he realised why it had happened, and why he should have heeded the boasts of Ochoa. The crash of the *Unicorn*, still in his ears, had coincided with another crash from behind. At his side, catching his eye, a cascade in the sea was descending. He spun round then, as did they all, and looked into the confident guns of the *Svipa*.

Nikolás-riddari. Amid the rattle of orders, standing firm, as he spoke, to be armed, Paúel Benecke found himself moved to a grudging delight.

Nicholas said, 'Well, John. The mainmast, if you please, and then the mizzen. Boatmen ready. Hackbutters ready. Grappling hooks ready. Mick, you have the helm. Father Moriz?'

'It is unethical,' said the voice of Father Moriz from halfway up the mast.

'It will save lives,' Nicholas said. 'You're the only one who can do it. Do it.' Beside him on the crowded foredeck the fuses burned and the cans stood ranked with their powder. It appeared a little less orderly on the *Maiden* where someone stood, fully armed on the after-deck. A thin man, of about his own height. Paúel Benecke, for sure. Paúel Benecke, one hoped, in a towering temper.

Nicholas smiled, and put back his helm, and lifted the speaking-trumpet.

Temper was an indulgence of fools: Paúel Benecke had never been known to lose his. When the *Svipa* failed to fire off its guns, he put it down to mishap or mismanagement, and ordered a cannonade of his own. It should have been simple. Both ships were still sailing west by south-west, the space between them too small for comfort; the space between himself and the cliffs even smaller. A shot from each of his guns should resolve it. And so it might, had each gun not worked loose from its swivel plate. Because, they found, its nails had all vanished.

It was then, from the other ship, that the hail came.

De Fleury, if it was he, was a big man, and fluent in the German the Hanse merchants spoke. With moderate politeness, he was inviting Benecke to take the way off his ship and surrender.

'You must excuse me, Nikolás-riddari,' Benecke said, cupping his hands. Then, gesturing, he sent for a trumpet. Every moment's delay was of use. The cliffs were ahead. In a very short time, he must either turn or tack to the south, presenting his beam to the guns of the *Svipa*. He needed time to set guns amidships. Those in the poop were already half restored to their moorings, and his hackbutters and bowmen in place. There were more of them than *Svipa* carried. The trumpet came, and Benecke spoke through it. 'I have no quarrel with you. You must excuse me. A ship has run upon reefs. Men are dying.'

'We shall gladly offer our chaplain,' said the hollow voice helpfully. 'Meanwhile, we are too close for our guns to miss. I suggest that . . .'

'Fire,' said Paúel Benecke in a murmur. He did not speak through the trumpet, but directed it at the gunner beside the one culverin primed and ready. The gunner lifted his taper and stretched. The roar that followed came not from his gun but the *Svipa's*. With intolerable prescience, de Fleury had fired before he did.

It was a direct hit. The mainmast broke with an echoing bark; the noise shot about within the deeper reverberations of the cannon, and the ship jarred as if rammed. He would have been thrown off his feet but for his grasp of the rail. He knew from the screaming behind that some of the men in the stays had been hurled to the ground; he could see others clinging. Arrows were flying aboard. He lifted his mailed arm to his bowmen, to command them to answer the fire. There was a hiss as they shot. He found, to his amazement, that his arm would not drop to his side.

He assumed at first, with annoyance, that he had been wounded. Then he saw that a thick piece of cordage had settled across his gorget and cuirass, and was tightening fast. He drew out his sword, but already his feet were leaving the deck. He dangled, half-choked. Men were picking themselves up and running towards him, staggering as timber and blocks rained about them. The cans had spilled, and there was powder all over the deck; he saw his gunners, returned to their posts, looking up at him with blankest astonishment. Then, with a stupendous jerk to his ribs, he was taken sailing over the gunwales and across the patch of rough sea that separated his ship from the *Svipa*. He saw there was a ship's boat below.

He gave the whole matter a moment's consideration: they had rigged a cargo hoist from a spar, and someone had hurled over a noose. They did such things, he had heard, in the Tyrol. He gave further consideration to the benefits of travelling light. He was sufficiently stirred to decide to make his own gesture. As he swung over the boat, he lifted his sword and slashed through the rope by which he was suspended. He rather hoped, as he landed in a welter of splintering timber, that he had killed somebody.

*

'He's broken his arm,' Robin said. 'Father Moriz says he's black and blue everywhere. He's got a cut on the face from his helm, and a stave got through the joint in his greaves and he's still got a headache from being knocked out by the fall. Otherwise he's just fine.'

It had been his first engagement, and there had been eight injured and no dead, and they had taken Paúel Benecke hostage, and the enemy's ship had surrendered, to save the life of their famous commander. For the moment, Robin had forgotten that the enemy was the man who had the right to be here, and that M. de Fleury was the pirate.

Father Moriz said, 'Get that boy out of here. I am ashamed. I collaborated in a piece of chicanery while men on Adorne's ship were drowning.'

'The *Pruss Maiden*'s physician has gone to them,' Robin said. 'In our boat, with a crew from the *Maiden*. There's no one of Ser Adorne's on the *Unicorn* now, just the Vatachino and their friends. And they're on rocks: they can't drown, and it's dark now. We'll put it all right in the morning.' He lingered, reluctant to leave M. de Fleury. It was as if the magic would stay if he stayed. He longed to tell Kathi.

M. de Fleury said to the priest, 'There. Do you hear? God and St Barbara will forgive you. Do you think our Flying Danziger may be visited?'

'I suppose it is safe. John and Crackbene have returned from his sickbed with their lives. I dare say so will you, provided his teeth are removed.' Father Moriz sounded sour. Robin was sorry. He bobbed up hopefully when M. de Fleury rose and made for the door, but was told firmly to go off to bed.

Laid in the dimly lit quarters usually occupied by Crackbene and his companions, Paúel Benecke wore, inadvertently, the livery of his captors, being picked out by the white of his bandages and the black of his bright eyes and his lank hair and his beard. His feet, projecting over the end of Yuri's mattress, were long and bony and thin, and he had the frame which in a sick man seems gaunt, and in an active, lithe one is simply due to a misarticulation of the limbs. He looked, for a man covered in bruises, quite at ease. 'The Nikolás-riddari,' he said. 'I am told you kept a knife at my throat until my deputy agreed to surrender.'

'The Bergenfahrer,' Nicholas returned with equal politeness. 'By that you may know how highly you are esteemed in the Artushof. Being practical men, my crew would have bargained and sailed off.' He sat. 'Apart from your freedom, is there anything I may offer you?'

'Your master gunner,' said Benecke. 'He is good. Engrained powder, not riddled. One of sulphur to seven parts of saltpetre and two of charcoal, unlike most. And I'll swear my man went to fire before he did.'

'He is John le Grant,' Nicholas said. 'I hope you made him an offer.'

'He prevaricated. Trained in Germany, I hear. Your chaplain also is German.'

'My counter-masters are Danish and Scottish and Muscovite. Crackbene was born in mid-ocean. I have no one from Poland as yet.'

It was not an observation he would have made, for example, to an Ochoa. He risked it because of something he glimpsed in the man's face. Nothing of appeal, nothing of complaisance, nothing of softening but something. A gleam, perhaps.

The man said, 'Perhaps we are good at prevaricating as well.' He let a pause develop before adding, 'I hear you have friends in Murano.'

Nicholas lifted his brows. 'And little good have they done me when it comes to getting ships built. But I always say it's good to have friends on an island.'

'I would not deny it,' said the other man. 'You are familiar with Venice, of course. I hear their custom is to whip a nail-thief round the Arsenal, with his nails hung in ropes round his neck.'

'Indeed?' said Nicholas. 'Ropes round the neck. A barbarity. Why did you cut yourself free? If you had hit the sea, we couldn't have saved you.'

'I contemplated it,' the man said. 'But it seemed a trifle flamboyant. The Hanse don't pay me that much. No. I cut the rope to remind myself not to be so stupid next time.'

'You didn't think I would sail up behind you?'

'I assumed that, having arranged the diversion, you would fly. I apologise.'

'Apology accepted,' Nicholas said. 'Although, of course, there was no question of leaving. Why should I? After all, I helped you to capture the *Unicorn*, and in return, you sanctioned two weeks of authorised fishing. I have to thank you.'

There was a silence. At length, the thin man said, 'You are staying to fish?'

'There is still room in the hold,' Nicholas said. 'And all that salt in the *Unicorn*, if it hasn't dissolved. And while we fish, I trust the *Maiden* will wait in the harbour. Minus her remaining masts and her sails and, of course, without yourself until you are better. But we shall be sure to reunite you all with one another about the time that we leave.'

The man stared thoughtfully at him, saying nothing.

'That is,' Nicholas went on, expatiating. 'You are a Hanse ship
from Bergen, and licensed. I shouldn't want to interfere with your
fishing. Only to do all mine first.'

'And the *Unicorn?*' asked Paúel Benecke gently.

'A wreck. The prize of the first person to reach it. I have sent your
scaffmaster to watch her tonight, and we shall see what needs doing
tomorrow.'

'I seem to remember,' said the other, 'that I was the first person to
reach her?'

Nicholas pondered. 'I have it,' he said. 'You take the man Martin
to ransom, and I shall take the equivalent worth from her cargo.'

The other man thought. 'That seems fair,' he remarked.

'Good,' said Nicholas. 'Where I come from, we seal a pact with
some wine. That was what was wrong with the last deal we made.
There was no wine. You remember.'

'I am not sure that I do,' said Paúel Benecke. 'But I am willing to
celebrate this one. Nevertheless I have to warn you: I have a very
hard head, as you see.'

'Would you like to make a wager?' said Nicholas.

Two hours after midnight, a semaphoring lantern in the cold windy
dark announced the return of the boat which had gone to the wreck of
the *Unicorn*. It was full of exhausted men on their way to the *Maiden*;
their physician, grim of face, insisted on boarding the *Svipa* to report.
Father Moriz, roused, met him and listened. Then he said, 'Follow
me. The patron will have to hear this.'

Had he been less disgusted with Nicholas, he would have left the
man outside the cabin. As it was, the priest flung open the door and
ushered him in. 'Go and tell him yourself.'

'Which one?' said the physician distastefully.

Father Moriz moved forward. The bodies of Crackbene and Lutkyn
Mere, both snoring heavily, first caught the eye, an overturned
tankard between them. A third recumbent form, languidly stirring,
turned out to be that of Paúel Benecke, his bandages scarlet.

'Dear God!' said the physician, starting forward. 'Dear God, is that
blood!'

The Danziger slowly looked down. 'Dear God,' he repeated. 'Oh,
dear heaven, thank heaven, it is. Is there any more of the wine?'

'Behind you. You lost the wager,' said Nicholas. 'Check. Yuri, you
bastard, it's check.'

'It isn't,' said the voice of the Muscovite. The box upon which the
chess was laid out could hardly be seen, so fragmentary was the
candle beside it. Both the players sat preternaturally upright.

Father Moriz said, 'You're both drunk. I thought you were waiting for news of the *Unicorn*.'

'Are we?' said Nicholas.

'No,' said Yuri.

'Yes we are,' said Paúel Benecke from the floor. He had lain down again.

'But not till the candle goes out,' Yuri said. 'We have a wager.'

'You are not concerned about fifty men's lives?' Moriz asked.

The Muscovite sketchily crossed himself. 'When the candle goes out,' he said. 'Mate.'

The candle went out. 'Hell,' said Nicholas.

'Not here,' said Paúel Benecke drowsily. 'You do not invoke Hell on this island. Who won?'

'He did,' said Nicholas. His voice, in the darkness was placid. 'Martin is going to Moscow.'

'What?' said the physician.

'Martin of the Vat – Martin is going to Moscow,' said Paúel. 'Yuri has won him from Nikolás.'

Father Moriz, groping, found the lamp and laid hands on the tinder. 'Martin is not going to Moscow,' he said. 'Nor is anyone else on the *Unicorn*. The doctor is waiting to tell you his news.' The lamp flared, lighting his inimical, troglodyte's face.

On the floor, Crackbene turned over and mumbled. Lutkyn snored. The bandaged Danziger opened one eye and then closed it. 'Tell us,' he said.

Yuri was clearing the chess from the box. The pieces clicked into their bag, or on the floor, or slid from the folds of his clothing. 'Tell us,' Nicholas echoed. He made no effort to help.

'The *Unicorn* has gone,' said the doctor.

'You missed one,' said the Danziger. Stretching his unbandaged arm, he picked up a crudely hewn queen.

'You missed them all,' said Father Moriz.

'They've sunk?' Nicholas said. His beard gilded the rims of two dimples.

The German priest leaned over the table and slapped his face hard with one palm. With the other he swept the cups, the bag, the table, the pieces to the floor. Then he sat down beside Nicholas, who was staring at him in a slow, aggrieved way.

'The *Unicorn* has gone,' repeated Father Moriz. 'Not sunk. Not wrecked. Not floating upside down on the tide. But sailed away with Svartecop and Mogens and Martin, after they patched up the damage – superficial – and bribed someone to find enough nails, and planted all the *Maiden*'s prize crew on the rocks and abandoned them. The

Maiden's men were very cold. The doctor here had to revive some of them. We brought the worst cases back, and will fetch all the rest in relays.' He broke off. His chest heaved like a portative organ. He said, 'You had better play another game, for a different prize.'

'Oh,' said Nicholas. He was looking at Benecke.

'Ah,' said the mercenary, returning the look. Between the knobs of his throat, something quacked. Nicholas coughed. The cough turned into a splutter. Then he laid his head on the table and laughed. On the floor, the bloodstained master of the *Pruss Maiden* brought his knees up and began laughing too. Yuri looked cross and, still looking cross, slid under the table.

Crackbene opened his eyes. 'What is it?' he said.

Nicholas rested his chin on his hands. Happy tears had run into his beard. 'We've lost the Vatachino,' he said. 'They've sailed off with their ship and the salt and all the bits of the cargo that Danziger Diavolo here didn't transfer from its hold and its arse and its fokke-deck. You could say,' added Nicholas wildly, 'that the *Unicorn* has fokkedecked the *Maiden*.'

'I didn't hear that,' said Father Moriz. 'Nor did the doctor.'

To his surprise and gratification, Nicholas sat up and gazed at him, clearly half sobered.

'Bloody hell,' Nicholas said. 'Now I'll have to sail over and bring back the Adornlings.'

Chapter 25

To ANSELM SERSANDERS, aged twenty-eight, factor, business-man, representative on this expedition of his eminent uncle the Baron Cortachy, the resignation in de Fleury's voice, had he heard it, would have been the last straw in a bale of such offered over the previous twelve hours, and all of them short.

His ruined sister had refused to leave de Fleury and join him. De Fleury had kicked him off the ship and virtually into the prison hold of the *Pruss Maiden*, except that the Icelanders had got to him first. And now the Icelanders had dumped him on the south shore of Iceland and taken his boat, leaving him in a hut hanging with fish and choking with smoke composed in equal parts of seaweed and sheep's trittles and cow-pats. When he ran out again shouting, they only waved as they rowed off without him. The shore was thick with fish-guts and cod's heads and whale blubber which sagged and squeaked under his feet.

After a while, he sat down and waited. It was possible that the Hanse ship would be outgunned by the *Unicorn*. Martin, whom he didn't particularly like, was nevertheless one of the toughest men he had met, and would not quickly give in. If they won, they would come for him. He was coldly furious with Nicholas de Fleury, who had sold them all to the *Maiden*. He would have sold Kathi too, he supposed, if he had thought it worth while.

The cold reached through his jacket, and he got up to walk. He didn't intend to go back into the reeking hut, or any of the other humped grassy mounds, which were also cabins, built of rocks stuffed with grass and roofed with turf. Round about them were the fish-cleaning trestles, the vats of unspeakable offal, and the wind-huts where the grey fish hung drying. The people working all about, their knives flashing and sucking, were women. As they worked they chanted and chattered and looked at him, calling and giggling. He ignored them, although he observed without conscious volition the wet, powerful ankles and feet; the rounded bosoms and bellies like fish-floats; the golden hair plaited round the strong necks. He didn't know what language they spoke, having only German and no Scandinavian tongues.

He knew what language they spoke.

When the snow began, and he was forced to return to the hut, he found two of them there, lifting a mighty cauldron on top of the fire, while a hooded figure with reptilian finger-bones hooked live mussels on lines coiled in a basket. The younger girl stared, all the time she stirred the mess in the pot with a ladle. At first he could see only a heavy white scum, as of sheep grease. Presently, as it warmed, it suggested other themes, partly blocked by his pink swollen nose. It was the only recent service that Nicholas, damn him, had done him.

Then he heard, through the snow, the voices of men; and among them, incredibly, the animated, cheerful voice of his sister Katelijne. Anselm Sersanders rose and ducked through the door, to stand lowering. The girls came out behind him, and the woman. All the nearby huts emptied. They all stood in the slush smiling at Kathi, as a fisherman carried her up from the boat on his back.

She looked pretty. That was the first thing he saw as they set her down. She looked clear-eyed and red-cheeked and happy, with none of the anxiety she had shown when he was trying to persuade her to part from the *Svipa*. He exclaimed, with relief, 'You got away!'

The men round her were grinning. 'Well, not exactly,' said his sister. 'I was invited to leave. *Her se Gud. Hvad heittir thú?* May I come into your house?'

She was not speaking to him, but to the women. He had to guess what she said. When the women replied, Kathi laughed.

'What?' said Sersanders. 'Can they take us back to the *Unicorn*? Can we leave?'

'No. They ask how many babies we have,' Kathi said.

'Who?'

'You and I.'

'Tell them we are brother and sister!'

'I have,' Kathi said. She was bidding goodbye to the oarsmen, each of whom kissed her on the mouth. She kissed them all back and returned. 'We can't leave. The Hanse ship has taken the *Unicorn*. If we go back, they'll hold us to ransom. If we wait, it may work out all right.'

'How?' said Anselm Sersanders.

She looked at him thoughtfully. 'M. de Fleury has a plan.'

'I'm sure,' said her brother. 'To leave.'

'No. To do with the *Unicorn*. He said if you and I stayed, we'd be picked up.'

'Who by, do you suppose?' enquired her brother. 'You say the *Unicorn* can't, and the Hanse ship doesn't know we are here. They'll all leave, Nicholas too, and we're stranded. That's why he put us off, isn't it?'

'I guessed he was getting sated with me,' Kathi said, 'that last moonlit night up the mast-basket. Anselm, don't be an idiot. He put us off because he's got a plan to deal with the *Maiden*, and he doesn't want us about if there's fighting. If it works, he will come, or the *Unicorn*. If it doesn't work, I fancy he'll tell Benecke where we are, and we'll be taken prisoner as we should have been in the first place. Aren't you getting cold?'

'No. He's tricked you. I'm going to do something.'

'What?' Kathi said. 'We're in the midst of a snowstorm. It'll be dark in two hours. Whatever happens, the fishing-boats will find out and we'll hear. If it's bad news, you can think what to do in the morning. Is this the house you were in? Something's cooking.'

He followed her in, arguing still. The old woman stood up, the fish-forest parting above her, and Kathi, smiling, went over to speak. They talked for a long time. The cauldron reeked of mutton and sheep grease and fish. Kathi, returning, took up the ladle and dipped it. She said, 'It is Tryggvi-Sigurdsson's house. He is doing something for Nikolás-riddari, but will be back when it is dark. She apologises for the fishing-hut; their farmhouse inland is much bigger, and Glímu-Sveinn's farm is the biggest of all. She says it's the custom to lodge foreigners in the church, but there isn't one handy.'

'There is a cathedral,' Sersanders said. 'At Skálholt. Ask where Skálholt is.'

'Why? We're not going there,' Kathi said. 'Oh Anselm, look.' Her ladle, dipping and stirring, had brought up a fish. Its eyes had withered. The next attempt produced a long slackened form, its neck drooping. 'A cormorant,' Kathi said. 'Or a shag? And oh, *look*.'

She paused. Sersanders said, 'Oh Christ, I can't bear it. *Kathi!*'

'I know,' she said sadly. 'A poffin. The poor little bird with the enormous red beak and the feet. They made love beside them on Nólsoy.'

'Who made love? Kathi, don't cry. Kathi, sit down, it's all been too much, I've been thoughtless. Kathi, they won't make you eat it.'

'I know. I don't mind. It isn't that,' Kathi said. 'But what will they do if he dies?'

'Who?' said Sersanders.

'The parrot,' said Kathi. 'It made me think of the parrot. Come and help her bait hooks while we wait.'

'No, thank you,' said Sersanders.

The news came, brought by Tryggvi-Sigurdsson after dark. The *Ein-hyringr*, the *Unicorn*, had dragged her anchor and run on the reefs of Bót Bay, with what loss no one so far had discovered. The *Pruss Maiden*, forging out to recapture her, had been set upon by de Fleury and crippled, her mainmast gone and her master held hostage.

'Paúel Benecke's ship has been captured by *Nicholas*?' Sersanders did not want to believe it.

'So it seems,' Kathi said. She had had some of the broth, and was eating a pudding made of moss cooked with milk. 'M. de Fleury means to lodge the *Maiden* inside the harbour in daylight, and then fish the cod banks until his holds are quite full.'

'And the *Unicorn*? Martin, Mogens and Svartecop?' Sersanders said.

'The *Svipa* is sending boats through the night to try and help the prize crew and our people,' Kathi explained. 'There's a doctor, it seems, and Father Moriz will make them do what is right. That is, if M. de Fleury claims the *Unicorn* and its cargo, I don't suppose Father Moriz can stop him.'

'But I can,' Anselm said.

'I'm sure. And Uncle Adorne and his lawyers. But nothing can be done until daylight, and even then, Tryggvi says, the *Svipa* will have to see the *Maiden* is settled in harbour before M. de Fleury can think about coming in to the mainland for us. So we might as well lie down and sleep.'

'I shan't sleep,' Sersanders said. 'I don't propose to wait to be picked up and ransomed by Nicholas de Fleury.'

'But you can't do anything now,' Kathi said. 'Tryggvi's mother has made you a bed in the corner. I'm just outside in a hut with the girls. I'll see you at first light.'

She looked perfectly cheerful. The apprehension or despair of a short time ago seemed to have passed. It was characteristic of Kathi: one minute living at ten times the pace of anyone else, and the next moment exhausted. She left. He stumbled, led by the grandmother, to his bed, which was a slab of basalt covered with sand and a mattress. On top was a thick, faded eiderdown, smelling of fish. The old wife patted him down and went back to the fire, where the two girls were serving their father.

Sersanders took off his boots. After an interval he lay back on the mattress, his rolled jacket under his head. Someone pulled the feather-filled cotton over his body, patting it gently. He closed his eyes, and was surprised, opening them, to find that the lamps had gone out, the bog-cotton wicks having expired in a warm stench of fulmar. Someone was still pleasantly patting the quilt. He realised that the patting hands were not only on top of the quilt, but smoothing restfully under it, and that one by one his points were being drawn undone and apart. In the glimmer of the low fire he saw a dark yellow plait swinging loose, then a pale one. Presently the girl on one side of him lifted the quilt and slid in, to be joined by the girl on the other.

Affrighted, he lifted his head. He discerned the snoring form of his host, bedded on the far side of the hut. He saw the old woman still sat and toiled at the hand-lines, her lidless eyes fixed on his face. He made a sudden involuntary movement, and one of the girls laughed aloud. The grandmother smiled like a leaf, plucking, plucking the molluscs and ramming them ceaselessly down on the hooks.

At dawn they had to shake him awake, snug and reeking of fish, and with a fair attempt at sang-froid he managed to assume his clothing under the quilt and venture into the half-light outside. He found Kathi up, fed and being taught how to slit and gut cod. Beside her was a bucket of fish-heads and a vat full of livers and bladders and oil. She put the knife down and waved. 'I can give you some news of God's chosen victim, the *Unicorn*. Guess?'

Her eyes were sparkling. 'They saved it?' he said.

'Better than that. It rescued itself before anyone reached it. It got itself off the rocks, and managed to sail out to sea and escape. It's free! Uncle Adorne's ship is safe, and the Cologner and Martin and everyone!'

He realised that his lips were drawn back like a gargoyle's. He said, 'Now pretend you haven't been fooled, Master Nikolás-riddari. Where did the *Unicorn* go?'

'South. Home, of course. They'll be home before us; they don't even know that we're here. It doesn't matter. M. de Fleury said he would come if they didn't. Anselm, isn't it splendid?'

'You don't know anything,' said Sersanders indulgently. 'And they haven't gone home, I would bet on it. And I don't intend to wait for Nicholas de Fleury to condescend to pick us up, if he ever would, which I doubt. No. Clean your hands. Get your bag. I'm going to find us a boat and some horses.'

'Turn round,' she said.

He looked at her, puzzled, and turned.

It was an odd time, he thought, to admire scenery. Certainly, the landscape had been obscured before, and he had had other things on his mind. He still had. To please her, he studied the view: the plain of the delta, and the snow-covered lava beyond. They were pink. He said, 'Very nice.'

'Very nice,' Kathi repeated. She gazed at her brother. Then she turned back to the sight which she hadn't even wanted him to observe: the distant place where the sky was still dim, and an ethereal city swam in the air – a marble confection of mosques and towers and tombs which hung sugar-pink in the dawn. It lasted one moment more; and then the light changed, and showed the massifs and the peaks to be lifeless.

Spiralling into the paling blue sky were two thin columns of smoke. Two, not one.

She said, 'Look. I'm not going anywhere. I'm waiting for M. de Fleury.'

Her brother faced her. She had a feeling that she was still misunderstood. He said, 'Kathi, I know what it's like. I can't boast. I'm no prude. But Nicholas de Fleury doesn't want you. You would never be more than his mistress.'

'Heaven preserve us!' said Kathi. She rolled up her eyes. '*Anselm? Listen!* The reason I didn't go back to Bruges is because Uncle thinks I should find someone in Scotland to marry. Poffins in soup. I don't mind. But having decided to stay, do you think I'd waste my maidenly charms on a much-married husband and father?'

He said, 'So come to Skálholt with me.'

'Why?' she said. 'Anselm, why? If it's over, we ought to wait and go home.'

'It isn't over,' he said. 'And we can get ourselves home without the help of the Banco di Niccolò. It's going to be Nicholas's second surprise. If you're frightened, I'll go on my own.'

'And desert me?' said Kathi. 'Abandon me at the portals of Hell? Relinquish me to the clutches of –'

'You've just said the opposite,' said Anselm unkindly. 'You don't want him, he doesn't want you, and you are on kissing terms with the entire population of Iceland, so far as I can see. You don't need me.'

And that was true, Kathi conceded; but silently. She gazed at him with wistful affection tempered with admiration. He looked remarkably fresh. She wished, for the hundredth time, that he would marry.

'I'll come with you,' she said. She hoped she hadn't given in too abruptly. She was dying to know what he was up to. She had made up her mind, long before, that she was going to make the most of her journey to Iceland. She just found Anselm a boring companion, that was all.

Nicholas came to land that afternoon, arriving in someone's flat-bottomed boat not much larger than a Thames shout, Robin with him.

It was later than he had planned. The *Pruss Maiden* had taken time to disable; now it was lodged with the *Svipa* in the sheltered north bay of the harbour. The fish-cleaning stations were in place on the shore by the ships, along with the trading-booths and the tents they'd brought with them. It was the usual practice, when southern fleets fished at the Westmanns. If any Icelanders had been rash enough to set up summer house, they were thrown off and their hovels re-occupied. Only the Hanse ships could operate here. Or, of course, anyone crazy enough to have captured one.

As a place of residence, the mother holm of the Westmanns had few attractions to offer. Like the parent Iceland itself, the island was uneven and wild, its surface contorted with misshapen mountains, its sea cliffs defended by ferocious rock-teeth and reefs. Against the white of the snow the bright tasselled pavilions, diced with colour, might have blown from a tourney in Florence until you saw how they shook in the wind, the snow sliding glazed down their sides. There was one spring of water, half frozen.

The scream of the birds never ceased, nor the howl of the wind, nor the surf-roar. It was not a haven of quiet.

When he left, the fishing had already begun, and the yoles were coming back to his men with their catch. One of his ship's boats was in use, and the other, damaged by Paúel, would soon be out of the carpenter's hands. The rest of the fishing was being done for him by the Icelanders. He reckoned that three days or four would complete it. He had some salt, but not much: most of the barrels were now filled by the pre-empted stockfish. He remained ineffably pleased about that. No one liked to handle green fish: the cold, aching toil of the gutting; the blood and the offal. But it would all fetch its price in the market. He would even fill and tow the *Unicorn*'s boat, which had carried Sersanders to the *Svipa*. The Icelanders had returned it.

He used a borrowed boat now, on his way to collect the Sersanders siblings. When at the last moment Benecke asked to go with him, Nicholas agreed on a moment's reflection. He should be back before nightfall. And all his best men were on board behind him: Crackbene and John, Lutkyn and Yuri and, of course, Moriz. Their guns were trained on the *Maiden*, and there were watches on each of the hills. It was not impossible that another ship would arrive, but unlikely. And if it did, it would be well advised not to make trouble.

Nevertheless, to have the *Maiden*'s master at his side was not a bad precaution. Added to which, he liked the man as much as he mistrusted him.

Today, the blizzard might never have been. The sand of the strange double coastline with its dangerous surf was quite black, and even the Markarfljót strand, when he reached it, was glistening grey and not white. Only through the haze of the smoke could you see banks of brilliant purity which might be clouds, or uplands, or mountains. There were, he noted, two columns of smoke in the sky. Robin's head turned towards them, and away.

He walked on through the settlement, with Paúel and Robin. Women and children clamoured about them. The stench of fish was appalling. There was no sign of Sersanders, or Kathi. Then he heard what the women were saying. Robin, who was also a pupil of Lutkyn, halted beside him. He said, 'She was longing to visit the mainland.' He sounded apologetic.

Benecke said, 'Something is wrong?' Beneath the leather cap over his bandage he wore a permanent, black-bearded leer. He knew the girl had fled from her brother's care to de Fleury. He was unlikely to believe she had come to his ship as a peace-maker.

Nicholas said, 'They're not here. They've gone inland, it seems. You'd better go back to the ship. It'll be dark pretty soon. I'm coming anyway, to get some provisions. Then I'll sleep here and collect the pair of them tomorrow.'

'Where?' said Benecke. 'They are surely not coming back here?' He was not smiling now. He suspected.

'Probably not,' Nicholas said, after a pause.

'Then let them go,' Benecke said. 'Unless the girl matters a great deal, why trouble?'

His eye glinted. It pleased Nicholas to notice his injured arm, tucked into his jacket. At the same time, he cursed Katelijne Sersanders. She should have stayed. Then they could all have gone back on board, and he would have paid someone to find and bring back her brother. And if they didn't find him, he could damned well hide here till some ship came. For choice, a greedy big Hanse ship from Lübeck.

Nicholas turned from the Danziger's black, cynical eye to the clear supplication of Robin's. Nicholas sighed. He said to Benecke, 'What did you hear?'

Paúel Benecke smiled. He said, 'I heard the word *Einhyringr*.'

'All right,' Nicholas said. He had made a criminal slip over that vessel. There was no way he could keep it from Benecke. He turned his back on the crowd and made the best of it. He said, 'The *Unicorn* hasn't gone home.'

'It hasn't come here,' Benecke said. 'We should have seen it, or heard.'

'No,' Nicholas said. 'It hasn't come here. But they all know where it's gone. So did Sersanders. He's taken his sister and set off by sea to the mouth of the Thjórsá. From there, they'll ride to the Bishop at Skálholt. Then, with his help, they'll cross to the Danish Governor's house near Hafnarfjördur and either join the *Unicorn* there, or ride down to the south coast at Grindavik. As I said, the *Unicorn* didn't go south. It circled the Westmanns, and came straight back to the south-west of Iceland.'

He kept his voice even. He didn't feel like keeping it even, because he knew he had been fatally stupid, and his only comfort was that Benecke hadn't guessed either. Nicholas said, 'Didn't you wonder about the *Unicorn*'s cargo? All that salt . . . Yes, of course Martin was going to fish. But all those small, compact high-value bales in addi-tion? We thought it was barter for stockfish.'

'By the Virgin!' said Benecke. His teeth showed neat as pebbles within the black beard. 'Your cannoneer might have told you. He knows, if anyone knows, what the ingredients of gunpowder are. My poor Nikolás, Martin has gone to buy sulphur at Hafnarfjördur! And unless you lift the guard from my ship, you cannot stop him!'

It was difficult, after that, to maintain any ascendancy. They did return to the ship, where Nicholas acquired certain equipment, and left behind certain explicit orders for which he would one day be thankful. It was all he did leave behind: Benecke insisted on coming back to Markarfljót with him, and in the end he gave in and took Robin too. If they were going to wander about, he would need an intermediary posted at Markarfljót. That would be Robin's job. Robin, who had hoped to wander about with him, agreed in a way half jubilant, half subdued. Then they all three left the ship, and returned to the shore they had just left.

They passed the night as Sersanders had done, in Tryggvi's ill-smelling hut. Tryggvi was not there: he had put to sea with Sersanders and Kathi, with a son to help with the rowing and to handle the ponies they would hire when they landed. On winter-weak beasts, it would be a day's ride to Skálholt, or more.

It sounded a laborious journey, but it was safer than most. In theory, you could make the whole trip directly on horseback, but that was to ignore all the rivers: those fast, swollen Icelandic rivers that dragged men and horse into crevasses and overturned ferries in spate. Nicholas was thankful that Kathi had not chosen that way. And for the journey from Skálholt, she would have the help and advice of the Bishop.

From the beginning, Benecke set out to irk him. 'Let the fools go,' was his refrain. He said it again, as they sat in the hut before bed-time, drinking an anonymous soup provided by a crone and two giggling girls. 'The *Unicorn* may have loaded and gone before they get there.'

'Will it?' said Nicholas. Robin was nodding: sleep would mend the hurt of his banishment. Nicholas felt no remorse.

Paúel Benecke replied with an amiable sarcasm. 'You think the Danish deputes should impound the *Unicorn*, since it is not a tax-paying ship from the Hanse? They should. But your friend is astute. Your friend Martin has guessed that a small gift to the Governor and the Bishop may not go amiss. There is no such thing, you see, as an absolute monopoly.'

'You surprise me,' said Nicholas.

'Do I?' said Paúel Benecke. 'So, how far will you put yourself out for this girl? For that is all it amounts to. There is no other reason for following.' He paused. 'Of course, were you to release me and my ship, we could waylay the *Unicorn* for you, and expose those improper practices.'

'I should not dream,' Nicholas said, 'of putting you to any such trouble. As for our strays, I put them on shore, and promised to lift them. If we find them at Skálholt, I hope you will support me with the authorities.'

'I wonder,' Paúel Benecke said. 'I might denounce you as an unlicensed pirate, and return to do as I please with my ship.'

'The first half would be easy,' Nicholas said. 'But I am afraid that if you returned to the harbour without me, my master gunner would be seized with alarm. Do you want to come then, or not? Robin could take you back now if you wish. You have the use of only one arm.'

'But I do not keep my brains in my arm. No, I shall come with you, Nikolás,' said Paúel Benecke. 'And disport myself in this fishy Paradise guarding the smouldering portals of Hell. I hear there have been horse carcasses found, and cattle-sheds fallen in splinters. I hope you have weapons, or spells.'

'Of course,' Nicholas said. He had weapons. He had no intention of arming Benecke. He saw no reason, indeed, to believe him.

That night, they slept in the cabin Sersanders had used. When, half awake, Nicholas heard the girls creep giggling in, he told them to go, without consulting Paúel. Robin appeared to be sleeping.

He used the remains of the night hours to think, as once he had used calculation to neutralise music. The aridity of one part of his life was not something he normally dwelled on. When not in the same house as Gelis, he found it possible to repress that particular hunger reasonably well, as he could train himself to drink water. There had been times when the need had disappeared, and others when he had been able, in his own interests, to harness it. This night on shore, although unplanned, had called for no particular effort; but the frank availability of the girls, and a sudden sense that there had been commerce here, stirred a current kept carefully stagnant.

He was forced to recognise it next day, when the soaking, stormy boat-trip was behind them and the hooves of their low, shaggy horses were tripping through uneven snow on the way north to Skálholt. The first climb up from the shore had been toilsome, with the Danziger and the horse-minder behind, and the menhir of Glímu-Sveinn himself in the lead, the spare ponies plodding between them. Then they left the roar of the river and entered silence and sunlight, with no sound but the jingle of harness, and the snuffling white breath of their mounts, and the occasional deep-chested bark of the dog Glímu-Sveinn had brought with him.

Strung over the snow, the piebald ponies glowed in the oil-yellow afternoon light, their manes erect, their shadows prancing beside them. They kept their even, hobby-horse gait over an invisible track which ran from one man-made cairn to the next; for under the snow on each side was a lava-field, and on top, sticky sepia and white, lay the boulders and blocks which had not been created or tossed there by man. And beyond that were the heights.

It was upon these that Nicholas rested his eyes as he rode: upon the swooning battlements and immaculate cones of a landscape moulded by chance, random as primaeval shapes under sand; rounded; melting; softly enamelled with snow.

The snow was not white. The snow was the yellow of cream, and the shadows on it were blue. The snow shone in the sun, and the breeze of their passing was fresh on their cheeks, but so light in itself that it hardly stirred heavy cloaks, or parted the pale, heavy fur of the dog. And so transparently clear was the air that the eastern glaciers lay, rank upon rank, as if iced on the blue of the sky for a feast, or a wedding.

In Edinburgh, there had been gales. In the lands that he knew, there was no terrain like this, nor such light. Nor such golden, golden light.

Behind Nicholas, the Icelander did not speak. Gradually Paúel Benecke also fell silent, and Glímu-Sveinn rode alone by the dog which looked up at him from time to time, its feathered tail waving. Once, a flock of ptarmigan rose, white on blue in the sparkling air, and once an eagle passed with its shadow, to a frisson of bird-cries below. 'Take heed of any falcon you see,' Glímu-Sveinn said. 'Emperors have given a coffer of pearls for our falcons.'

His eyes on the eagle, Nicholas made no response. Into his mind had come something grave, to do with his child. Part of his consciousness told him that, whatever it was, it was not fatal. Part of his mind attempted to turn his thoughts back to the present: to the beauty and silence through which he was riding. He wished he could soar alone, like the eagle. Or that one person was with him, to whom he could say: *Match this beauty, this white and gold beauty, with yours.*

It would soon be time to camp. As the sun declined, so, like dancers unveiled, the far-off slopes and ridges and gulleys revealed themselves to the altering light. Curves and lines in the snow gleamed like script; harness dazzled, and where the horses had stepped, a crusted sparkle of gold rimmed the prints.

By the sixth hour all had dimmed, and their tents were put up by the seventh near a farm, at the onset of darkness. His pavilion, for himself and Benecke, had come from the ship and was ungainly and tall. The Icelanders made a home from three poles, two of them upright, with a cross-pole of eight feet between them. The cover was wadmol, its white folds pegged and weighted with baggage. For mattresses, they employed slabs of turf from under the hook-saddles, and the farmer gave them some dung for their fire, and a wooden pail of warm milk, and some curds. There were no girls in the house, it would seem.

Viewed from the blue dusk of their shelter, the distant tableland glared like their fire, and was quenched. They talked as they ate. After a while, when all the news had been exchanged, and the pointed – the surprisingly pointed – cross-questions had ceased, Nicholas contrived to lead Glímu-Sveinn to speak of his island as once it had been.

The first to come had been the Culdees: Irish monks, Robin had told him, who worshipped Christ on St Serf's island in Fife as well as here, on the islets of Iceland, and who knew the pink-footed geese in both lands.

Then had come the Norwegian settlers, worshipping Odin and Thor, whose hammer-symbols and giants and trolls still haunted the fiery hills and the caves and the fissures, even though Christ had ousted Odin, and there were devils with new names in Hell. Glímu-Sveinn was familiar with all the stories because, since his ancestors came, they had been related over and over through the dark nights, and written down, and made into poetry, and sung. Everyone in Iceland knew who his ancestors were. Every farm, every hill, every rock had its name and its story. The plague had come twice this last century. The Black Death had killed half the populace. But still the vellum rolls were kept in their coffers, and for those who could not read, the farmer would tell over the tales in the evenings, or give room to the travelling bard, who paid his way with his stories. 'Who were your ancestors,' asked Glímu-Sveinn, 'ten generations ago?'

And Nicholas laughed a little and said, 'I do not even know who my father might be.' It sounded friendly. It didn't need to be true.

By then Benecke had fallen asleep on his bed, and soon Nicholas joined him. After that, he wakened and slept, and occasionally attended to the health of the fire. Once he saw Glímu-Svein silently rise and move out, a lighted spar in one hand and his knife in the other. The dog had been uneasy and jumped up and went out with his master. Then they both returned and the Icelander went back to his tent, saying nothing.

Nicholas lay and considered. He had put aside the matter of Kathi. She and her brother had passed; the farmer confirmed it. They would have reached Skálholt this morning, and might already be embarked on the last of their journey. He would catch up with them. He would reach Skálholt tomorrow. What happened then might be amusing.

Now he should sleep, but could not. He wondered if Glímu-Sveinn had daughters. He wondered how Sersanders had fared, and was faring, and if his sister had learned of the hospitable customs of the country. She would greet the discovery, he knew, with genuine laughter.

It was not how he felt. He didn't know why, tonight of all nights, he should remember the scents of an African night, the pillowed dunes of a much smaller island; the arms in which he had lain – on which he had lain – over and over. The sense of loss, of foreboding stayed with him till dawn, and caused him to reply curtly when his prisoner rallied him. He regretted it, and shook off the mood. It was not Benecke who had turned out to be humourless. He busied himself, packing up, and noticed that nothing had changed about the two fitful emissions of smoke on the horizon. The demons which stoked them were absent. The demons, damn them, had been busy elsewhere.

Chapter 26

IN EDINBURGH – the ancient epicentrum towards which, in counter-flow, there had streamed for six months all the molten concerns of the Banco di Niccolò – in Edinburgh, no word came from the north. In the house in the Canongate, Govaerts prosecuted his business tight-lipped with his hard-working staff of the counting-house, and maintained and developed all that the padrone had instituted with the great officers of the Court, and the Court itself.

He did not find it especially easy, for although some – the Lords Sinclair and Hamilton – were prepared to be remarkably patient, his grace the King and his brother were not. And although his master's lady herself did not trouble him, he had to suffer the daily importunities of Berecrofts the Younger. A father's feeling: it was natural enough. There were times when Govaerts wished, none the less, that Nicholas had left the boy Robin behind. He was only thankful that news of the whole escapade had yet to strike Venice.

It had of course travelled to Bruges, and from there to the Burgundian camp. He could imagine Astorre's spit of disgust. It meant little. Whatever his boy chose to play at, Astorre was confident that he would return to his real task unimpaired. Astorre was looking forward to fighting this year.

Sometimes, his thoughts straying, Govaerts allowed himself to wonder what Zacco of Cyprus would think of his Nikko de Fleury, if he thought of him at all, while he had David, the dark-eyed David of the Vatachino, at his side. In uncharitable mood, Govaerts occasionally hoped that somewhere in the far north, Nicholas was slicing up David's friend Martin and feeding him to strange foreign ducks. He also wondered about the Gräfin von Hanseyck, who would have had a share in this venture, had the Danzig ship been finished in time.

Gelis did not keep to the house. The Play had made her more friends than she had possessed in her years with the Princess, and other doors opened, of course, to the wife of her spouse. It was not her intention – not yet – to disillusion all these decent, tedious people: to say to them, Do you never ask yourself what kind of man performs best on a stage? What person is this with the calculating efficiency of a quartermaster; who can command and drive people as a general does, or seduce them with cunning? There are men of genius, and there are tyrants, and there are men who might be either or both.

She did not go back to Beltrees.

Mistress Clémence concerned herself, as was correct, with nothing at all but the child. When the fever first attacked, in the early days of their return to the High Street, she did not trouble the mother, but embarked, with Pasque's help, on all the usual remedies, for children are sick for many reasons, not least because their playmates are absent. When, however, the pustules appeared, she sent at once for Conrad, the physician who served the royal children in Dr Andreas's absence, and went to break the news to the lady of Fleury.

If there had been any doubt of her love for the child, her distress would have seemed to dismiss it. All her actions were bold and immediate. The sickroom was shut off. Commands were sent to William Scheves and the Prioress. Berecrofts the Younger, swiftly obeying her summons, arranged to vacate his family house by the Avon so that the child could be tended apart. Mistress Clémence remained in isolation by the bedside, aware that in particular a messenger had been sent to the King, and to his sister at the Castle of Dean. Several ailments struck thus. Some were innocent. One was the disease that men ranked with the plague.

Dr Conrad, of course, was aware of it. As the illness developed, he frequently came and sat with the child, speaking sensibly to his nurses and discussing methods of easement. He did not answer Pasque's aggressive questions, and Clémence asked none. It was too soon. Time would tell. Then one day he had returned from his supper below to come to the bedside again, and had removed his hand from the whimpering child to exchange smiles with the nurse and with Pasque.

'The sickness of the water-pox, not the other. It is plain. A bath in warm water in which starch has been dissolved. Prevent him from scratching. Keep him away from other children until the blisters have healed. In three weeks he will be well. I shall go and inform Mistress Gelis, and convey the news to the Castle.'

Jodi, who did not know he did not have smallpox, burst into tears, and was prodigally comforted. Later, alone with Clémence in their room, Pasque spoke her mind. 'That lady,' she said. 'Does she care for the garçonnet, do you think? Or was she afraid, if he died, to have to confess to the father?'

'Surely she cared,' said Clémence de Coulanges. 'And it is as well, for Master Jordan is fond of her.'

'Accustomed to her,' said Pasque. 'As he is accustomed to everyone. I expect that woman will come.'

'Which woman?' asked Mistress Clémence. It was surprising what Pasque understood.

'That widow who lives in the west, Mistress Bel. The master took Jodi to see her in Edinburgh. You went.'

'I remember,' said Mistress Clémence. 'Yes. I suppose she might come, when she hears. And, of course, the father is expected back soon, with young Robin.'

'No!' said Anselm Sersanders for the third time to his sister. They sat in her room in the guest-quarters of the Bishop's Cathedral at Skálholt, which was a collection of snow-plastered buildings surrounding a handsome small church made of wood. The roofs were of much-nibbled grass covered with footmarks, and blackened and singed from the smoke from the kitchen. There was no fire in Kathi's room, which contained a standing bed and a chest and a basin, and bore signs of an abrupt evacuation. Three women's shoes of differing sizes lay under the bed, and the curtain over a corner proved to have a thick sheepskin garment hanging behind it. It was a man's. It looked dirty, but comfortable.

Kathi herself was dressed like a very small man, in boots and leggings and a belted tunic down to her knees, peasant-fashion. She sat on her bed swinging her legs while Sersanders thumped himself down on the box in a pet. Old eider feathers swam from the cushion: he sneezed. He said, 'I am not going back to the *Svipa*.'

It was hard luck, Kathi knew. Sersanders never forgave Fate for its blunders. Victory over M. de Fleury had been so deliciously close. Here they were, the strenuous journey from the Markarfljót behind them, and a mere day's ride between them and the *Unicorn*. First, they had been prevented from leaving because of a dearth, so it seemed, of fresh horses. And now here was the Bishop's bailiff, just back from a visit to Hafnarfjördur, to tell them that there was no point in going at all. While they were stranded at Skálholt, the *Unicorn* had loaded and gone.

It was smart, even for Martin. But of course, he wanted to protect all that sulphur for their uncle. He wanted to get home really fast, avoiding anyone else, such as a vindictive Paúel Benecke and the *Svipa*. And of course (as she said to Sersanders) Martin could have had no idea they were hoping to join him. He appeared to believe her.

She had continued. 'It's good news really, when you think. The ship will get home. Uncle will recoup all he lost from the cargo, and it will pay nearly as well as the fish. And we can go back on the *Svipa*.'

That was when he said, 'No!' for the first time. He did not mean to go back with the man who had exposed Uncle Adorne's cog to the *Maiden*. He intended to wait for the Bishop, and then return south in his Buss.

'The Bishop's out of the country,' said Kathi with involuntary fondness. Her eyes watered.

'And very likely the *Svipa*'s out of the country,' said her brother. 'If the *Unicorn* thought it wise to get out, I don't suppose the *Svipa* is going to linger. Nicholas will complete all his fishing and go. He'll be gone before we could get back.'

'No, he won't,' Kathi said. 'M. de Fleury said that he'd come for us. What's so shameful about letting him do it? He kept us safe, whatever he did to the *Unicorn*. It's just normal good manners to him.'

'Then he'll land, find we've gone, and go away.'

'Do you think so?' said Kathi. 'All right. Let's go back to the delta with Tryggvi, and if the *Svipa* has gone, we'll ask if the *Maiden* can take us.'

'Kathi,' said her brother with unnatural gentleness. 'If Nicholas captured the *Maiden*, the *Maiden* will either be towed home by Nicholas, or he'll steal her cargo and sink her on leaving. I rather hope that he does; the Hanse will hang him.'

'Oh,' said Kathi. She frowned. 'Is that why you don't want to join him? You'd rather like him to outrage the Lübeckers?'

'No! Don't be silly. Of course not. If he's decided to do something mad, he won't stop just because I arrive. I just don't want you involved in the fighting.'

'You don't,' Kathi said.

'I don't. So we're going home by the Buss. Settle down. We'll have horses, they say, by tomorrow. You,' said Anselm, 'can do what you like. But I thought that I'd get up early and try for some falcons.'

'Oh,' said Kathi. She had stopped swinging her legs. 'I shouldn't mind that. Where do you find them?'

He opened his mouth. 'You're not coming.'

'Yes, I am,' Kathi said.

'No!' said Anselm Sersanders for the third time.

Nicholas, considering later that magnificent morning scamper to Skálholt, also considered the pure impatience Glímu-Sveinn must have felt, burdened with two irresponsible men, mad as berserkers, and one of them maimed in one arm. The exhilaration of the light and the snow was their only excuse, added perhaps to some childish denial of the awe that had smitten them. Also it had to be admitted that Glímu-Sveinn himself was preternaturally dour, so that the competitions between Nicholas and his fellow privateer became progressively wilder. It was as well, in fact, that they arrived at the smoking enclave of Skálholt when they did.

And even then their buoyancy was not impaired, for although the news at first appeared bad – the young man and the *junfrú* had arrived the previous day and had left early that morning – a further explanation by the steward who ran out to meet them had caused Nicholas to break into laughter, and Paúel Benecke to parade a picturesque glower. The *Unicorn* had arrived at her harbour, purchased her fill of Krísuvík sulphur and left.

Wearing his elegant doublet and pourpoint as a banker, Nicholas ought to have regretted the news, which represented a prestigious success for the Vatachino. It had been a piece of fine opportunism, which had taken some application and guts to achieve. He didn't wish Martin well, but he could respect him.

Wearing quilted cotton and leather and sealskin, with a yellow beard and a round sheepskin hat on his head, Nicholas didn't give a horsehair button for Martin, but experienced a juvenile pleasure in finding that he had sailed off without Sersanders and Kathi. That was when he learned that they had gone, but only out to hunt birds for amusement. They were both staying at Skálholt, with the bailiff.

The bailiff, a hearty, flushed man with a paunch, appeared a little confused by Benecke's presence and, once he had recovered, extraordinarily anxious to explain. He spoke a form of tongue Benecke recognised, and at length, the Danzig captain broke in. 'Herra Oddur, I know the Governor has many cares, and the Bishop's door must be open to wayfarers. Had my ship been in Hafnarfjördur yesterday, perhaps the *Unicorn* would not have departed so easily. But it was not, and I don't blame the Governor or the Bishop. Which way did the young people go?'

'You would like to follow them?' the bailiff said. He looked from one visitor to the other, and then glanced to one side at Glímu-Sveinn.

'They have gone to seek falcons,' said Glímu-Sveinn. 'Or so your men tell us. Perhaps we should wait.'

'It is a fine sport,' said the bailiff. 'There are horses. We had some trouble bringing them in, but they are here now. You could eat, and ride out to your prisoners. You will take them to Bergen, for avoiding taxes and trading unlicensed?'

There was a pause. The black-bearded visage of Paúel was grave. The Icelander shuffled. Now, Nicholas thought, one of them will mention that the Hanse captain Paúel is my captive, and the bailiff will have to decide what to do. He waited, his face as solemn as Paúel's.

Glímu-Sveinn didn't speak. Paúel Benecke said, 'When I catch him, Martin will answer in Bergen. The brother and sister are not worth the trouble; we shall take them back to their homes on our ships. As for Síra Nikolás here, I owe him much, which I intend to repay.'

'I guessed as much,' Nicholas said.

'I am sure of it,' said Paúel Benecke. 'Meanwhile, Herra Oddur, we should certainly enjoy a hunt for these birds.'

'I shall send a man with you,' said the bailiff.

'I shall go,' said Glímu-Sveinn. 'Where were the gyrfalcons last seen? There is no better fellow than Tryggvi to find them.'

'My own man is as good,' said the bailiff. 'Tryggvi and his son had to go home. I have sent Sigfús Helgason with the young man and his sister.'

'He is a thorough man,' the Icelander said. He was a man of few words, Glímu-Sveinn.

'What do you think?' Benecke said when, leaving Skálholt behind, they set out over the snow on fresh horses. It was an hour before midday.

'That you're a lying bastard,' Nicholas said, 'and so is he.' He switched to Icelandic. 'Glímu-Sveinn? Is Sigfús Helgason good?'

'He is good for some things,' said the man. 'His thirst is best of all.'

Nicholas glanced at him. Loading the ponies at Skálholt, the Icelander had said very little. They had been given all they could carry in the way of food and drink and provender. Fetching it, with the eager help of the boys of the house, Nicholas had noticed the barrels of ale in the barns, the kegs standing stuffed full of moss, the piles of sacks bulging with meal. Some Icelanders, they said, had never tasted a loaf in their lives. The Bishop was rich.

They loaded, too, as was customary, what they must have for survival as well as for sport: tents and staves, rope and fuel, and the inevitable bags with the horse-shoes. There were only nine ponies, and Glímu-Sveinn had elected to send the horse-handler home.

He had kept the dog. In the yard, the dog had behaved as if tied to its master, standing with its eyes on his face, or trotting briefly away, and returning. Nicholas had called out to one of the boys. 'What do you think? Can dogs foretell a change in the weather?'

The boy had laughed. 'They won't go out if there is a storm

coming, that's for sure! They know the signs. Our house ravens as well. And the buntings sense when to come in and lie snug. We had a covey this morning: see there.'

Thinking of it, Nicholas now studied the sky as they rode. It was clear. They traversed the same butter-gold dreamland as before, the Icelander riding in front, and the voluble Paúel at his side. The dog kept the horses in line, swerving and scampering about, now on top, now shoulder-deep in the snow. The way the bailiff had indicated was east. 'Towards Hruni. That is where Sigfús was proposing to take them. The white gyrfalcons follow the ptarmigan.'

Glímu-Sveinn had grunted. When questioned he had shrugged his wide shoulders. Like most of his race, he was thick-set and long in the trunk, bred from generations of riders and rowers. Ten generations or more. After a while he had observed, 'There are rivers to cross. But for falcons, it is worth taking trouble.'

Far to the east, the sun gleamed on the glaciers. To the north, across the snows of the vale, lay a range of gnarled and sheared cliffs streaked and speckled with white, and garnished with mountainous boulders. To the south-east, a white mountain smoked and far beyond it, almost too far to be sure, there rose smoke from another.

'Hekla and Katla, I am informed. Are you frozen with horror?' said Paúel. 'Because if so, look there and blench. We have come to the river.'

It was an unpleasant river: broad, and plated with grey and white at the edges. The running currents were not at once apparent; in places the surface was turgid, or mixed with the chopped and scurrying pools of the frustrated flow. There was a ferry, Glímu-Sveinn said, on the other side, which would come to their horn. The horses would swim.

'The horses will float,' Paúel Benecke said. 'Mine is lighter than water, save for his spine, which is halving me like an Icelander's saw or a cheese wire. They tell me they drowned a bishop nearby not so long ago.'

'He didn't understand the local customs,' said Nicholas. 'There are several methods of dropping a hint.'

The ferry was labouring over. It looked highly unsafe. It came closer. Nicholas said, 'For example ... What did you say about saws?'

Benecke looked at him. Glímu-Sveinn had already dismounted, and was leaping down to the river-bank, shouting. The ferry bumped and splashed its way into the shoals. There was one middle-aged man at the oars. The rest of the old boat was empty. But all he could see from above was blotched and stained and clotted with blood.

Paúel Benecke swore. Below, the Icelanders exchanged hasty words. At length Glímu-Sveinn came back. His face above the long beard was veined, and his shallow eyes bulged. He said, 'Is the Frenchman a fool?'

'He's a Fleming. Sometimes. What has happened?' Nicholas said. His chest eased.

'The farmers had to butcher a horse and take it over. They found it disembowelled on the bank. I will help the boatman sluice out the ferry, but we ought to cross over at once.'

'But what killed it?' said Paúel. 'Demons? Trolls? Those black dwarves who live underground and drag men to their red smoking caverns? And why is Sersanders a fool?'

'Bear,' said Glímu-Sveinn. 'Every year the white bears arrive on the ice-floes from Greenland. They are spent with walking and hunger; many die. But if they are skilled and hunt well, they gain strength. Sigfús knows, if this Sersanders does not.'

'What has he done?' Nicholas asked.

'Nothing yet,' said the Icelander Glímu-Sveinn. 'He is three hours ahead, to the north-east, with Sigfús and the maiden. The ferryman took them over. He told them of the tracks of the bear, and the tracks that showed that the bear had a cub. White bear-cubs are worth more than falcons. In some kingdoms, white bear-cubs command as much as a ship full of grain. They have gone to follow and take it.'

'Do they have weapons?' said Nicholas.

'Bows, and nets and spears, I am told. And Sigfús never parts from his axe. It is still not enough.'

'For a cub?' Benecke said.

'The cub is bad enough,' said Glímu-Sveinn. 'But if they take the cub, the she-bear will come for them. The ferryman says there have been white foxes about for a week. The white fox follows the bear as a scavenger. The bailiff should have heard the reports.'

He broke off. He said, 'If they give Sigfús ale, he will do anything. If Sigfús dies because of the Flemings, I will kill them.'

Nicholas looked at him. He thought of their night together before Skálholt. He remembered how the man had risen at night, with his dog, to check that all was well. He had thought his concern was for the weather.

But he had not known that bears were in these parts. The bailiff had known that.

'The bailiff must think *we* are fools,' Nicholas said, 'never mind Sersanders and his sister. I will not tell you what I think of him. But we are three grown men, one of us native. I will not ask either of you to risk your life for these people, but if you will help me track where they have gone, I will look after it.'

It was surprising how much Icelandic Benecke could understand now. He said, 'A thousand-pound bear? My dear Nikolás, you do not need us for that. Thanks to you, I have lost the use of one arm. I am going to rest it.'

The Icelander stared at him. The dog, gazing up at his master, was growling. In a moment, Nicholas felt, the Icelander would start growling as well. He felt unalloyed gratitude to them both, even if they didn't understand one another at all. He said to Glímu-Sveinn, 'He doesn't mean it. He's coming,' and after a further glare, the Icelander turned and went down to the boat.

Paúel Benecke said, 'Don't you understand a categorical refusal?'

'No. And you can't even spell it,' Nicholas said. He led the way down, pulling horses behind him.

Benecke came with his own. He said, 'This is really exceedingly dangerous.' He sounded petulant.

'Blame Herra Oddur, or the Bishop,' Nicholas said. 'They wanted you killed. Anyway, you can't afford to run away now. Men would laugh at you.'

'No, they wouldn't,' Benecke said. 'There would be nobody left to tell them what happened.'

'Not even you,' Nicholas said. 'If you go back without me, John will kill you. It's white bears or nothing.'

They argued all the way over the river, while the horses wheezed and snorted at angles behind them, their eyes rimmed with white, their broad heads shoved into the current. In the boat, the dog shivered and whined. Nicholas was thinking about Glímu-Sveinn, all the time he was talking. Until now, he hadn't been sure how far to trust him. Paúel represented authority, and by bartering fish for the dogger, Glímu-Sveinn had committed a crime. He owed something to Nicholas, but need not put himself out to preserve Benecke's life any more than had the bailiff.

But it was more complex than that, as the outburst just now had revealed. *If Sigfús dies because of the Flemings, I will kill them.* Glímu-Sveinn despised Sigfús. He had no relationship, good or bad, with Sersanders. He was giving form to a sense of unease that now appeared to have a reason behind it. Benecke played no part in the equation at all.

Nicholas understood that, because he too had been aware of unfocused foreboding. He had experienced this manifestation of it often enough in the past: from Julius, complaining of some trouble Nicholas had got Felix into; from Tasse in Geneva, when he had lured another boy into mischief in an obstinate rebuttal of misery; from his mother, when he had dragged off her baby half-sister into some wild children's

game. They had all exploded like that, until he had learned to do
things on his own.

He had not felt like this when his mother died. He had had no
foreboding at all. It was only in recent years that he had found
himself beset by strange fears and premonitions; punishment for
crossing some mystical threshold. He had felt the sense of danger
again, ever since setting foot on the banks of Markarfljót.
Now, like Glímu-Sveinn, he supposed that he had discovered the
cause.

He put his gloved hand to his throat, and saw Benecke watching
him, but in fact he felt better. Sersanders was sturdy and well trained
and armed, and the guide was not surely a cipher. As for Kathi, she
was probably match for any three bears. Despite himself, the excitement rose in his blood. Kathi had not wanted to miss this experience,
and neither did he. It was the threat of the intangible which had
shaken him. But of course he could not predict. He had not been able
to predict the death of his mother.

Now there were practical things to be done, and they did them.
The ferryman would not come with them, but helped them catch the
ponies as they landed downriver and took the three men into his
cabin for soup. It was wise, although they wanted to hurry. And the
ponies had to be reloaded with the necessary gear ready to hand.
Nicholas uncased two crossbows and, keeping one, gave the other
with its forked bolts to Benecke. The Icelander already carried a
spear and a knife and an axe: it would do.

When they left, the dog was put on a lead. It ran back and forth
barking and no one attempted to silence it. At intervals, Glímu-
Sveinn set his lips to his horn. The wind, which had risen a little, was
blowing against them, but Sersanders might hear. There were no
prints, or none yet, where they were riding, but Glímu-Sveinn
seemed to know where to go. Between the bogs and the streams and
the lava, there was probably not so much choice.

After they had been riding for some little while, they were surprised
by a brief fall of snow; a shower so fine that it sparkled like dust in
the sunshine. When it ceased, the distant landscape vanished, white
as a veil, and then returned bit by bit, in coins of picturesque detail.
In places, the sky was pewter and purple, flat as a plate, with the
cones and glaciers dazzling below it. The wind strengthened. Presently Glímu-Sveinn stopped.

'What?' said Benecke.

'They have doubled back to the north. They have gone to look for
a ferry to recross the Hvíta.'

'Oh?' said Benecke. 'Where are their prints?'

'After the snow?' the Icelander said. 'But if you look, there is the mark of a horse-shoe, in the lee of that boulder.'

Nicholas said, 'It could be last week's. Are you sure about this? We have seen no sign of bear. Even the dog has stopped barking.'

'He was excited,' the Icelander said.

'He was excited every time we diverged to the south. I think the bear and the bear-cub are there.' Nicholas spoke harshly, with reason. Every time he looked to the south, his nape pricked like the ruff of the dog, and he wanted to cringe. He repeated, 'The bear is in the south.'

'You know this land?' said Glímu-Sveinn. 'No? Then listen. There are no fish south of here, and no ptarmigan. If this bear has a cub, then I know where she is going. So will Sigfús. So do the foxes: I have seen the prints. Perhaps the foreigners will abandon the hunt; we cannot tell. The only sure way is to track down the white bear and kill it, so that we may all go back safely to Skálholt. I am going north.'

'The danger is in the south,' Nicholas said.

'Then it is another danger,' said Glímu-Sveinn.

'Listen,' said Paúel Benecke.

The sound came from the north and the east, fragmented by the increasing interference of the wind. Not a scream or a roar, but the high nasal yapping of falcons, mingled with another call, powerful and barking.

'I hear it,' said Glímu-Sveinn. 'You wished to see more of our fine eagles, *nei*? There they are.'

Nicholas and Benecke stared at them: a cluster of specks to the north, circling and swooping. Benecke said, 'That is a sad sight. I am sorry, my good man. We should change horses, and hurry.'

They hardly spoke after that, but followed Glímu-Sveinn's hammering heels as he thrust his little beast forward, never ceasing except over the bogs and the lava, where he let the animal pick its own way. Once, when the footing was good and the pace swift, Benecke said, 'Tell me about the girl.'

'She is Adorne's niece,' Nicholas said.

'And therefore intelligent, I should suppose? She wanted you to follow?'

'She knows me well enough to expect it. She enjoys novelty: so do I. She is not,' Nicholas said, 'playing at maidens and dragons.'

'You reassure me,' said Benecke. 'I always preferred the dragon to that simpleton George. You are lovers? Or she wants you to be?'

'For the last time —' began Nicholas.

'— you are like brother and sister.'

'Not even that. We are, if anything, brothers,' said Nicholas. He stopped, surprised to think how true it was. He added, 'She is like a young brother.'

'Indeed?' said Benecke. 'And you think that is reassuring?'

Then they got to the river. They dismounted. This stretch of the Hvita was wide, with snow powdering the slush at the edges, and whitening the wide banks of sand which divided the fast, thrusting currents. There was no snow on the outcrops of rock which also stood in the path of the flow, with spume dashing man-high, and shards of ice sliding round them like salmon. The water was white and heavy with discoloured debris, but there was no pumice that he could see. He had been told (by Robin, in tutor/grandfather mode) that pumice was the froth of the lava, and sometimes covered the sea so that ships couldn't sail. This water was merely opaque and angry and noisy.

The noise was indescribable; so great that Benecke had to hammer his shoulder to make him look where Glímu-Sveinn was pointing. First he indicated upstream, where you could see the birds of prey now – more of them, and nearer. And then the Icelander turned his wrist down, pointing to the idling edge of the river, where the slush was coloured pink, and the thick milky water was marbled with blood.

Nicholas turned to his horse, took out his crossbow, and settled the quiver with its barbed bolts at his side. He saw Benecke was doing the same. Then they set off to lead their horses along the bank towards the birds. The packhorses were already tied tail to harness and, but for the dog, would not have followed. Nicholas realised that the dog was barking and snarling, and had been for some time. After a bit Glímu-Sveinn stopped, lifting his arm once again. He wore woollen gloves, with a second thumb sticking out from his little finger. The hand of a troll.

The bank had become steep, the noise hollow. He was pointing away from the water, to a confusion of hoofprints, and then the clear footprints of people. Two of them had worn fine leather boots. The third wore the soft sealskin shoes of the Icelander, drawn together and sewn in one piece, teasing the snow with the fur on their soles. Sersanders, Kathi and Sigfús.

'This is where they saw the bear,' Glímu-Sveinn said, 'and dismounted. They would arm, as we are doing. Whatever it was happened there, just beyond the next bend of the river.'

There was no blood on the snow, only footprints. They followed the tracks round the bend and, sickeningly, half the river below them ran red. The red came from an island in the centre: a bank of gritty black sand like the others but not, like the others, whitened with snow. The surface was covered, in this case, by the immense yellow-white corpse of a bear. Its two large cushioned hind feet, pronged with black, lay pigeon-toed under its rump, and birds hovered over its flank and its head, scolding the little delicate fox, white as down, already busy there. You could see the dead beast was a female, in milk. Everything, including the fox, was blood-splattered.

'*Hà!*' cried Glímu-Sveinn. '*Hà!* Sigfús is sober!'

'Are you sure?' the Danziger said. 'If so, where is he?'

He was speaking in the wrong language; and in any case, Nicholas had already arrived, jumping and sliding, at the bottom of the bank. The birds rose and hovered, complaining. The fox had turned and continued to gnaw, his eyes fixed on the horses and men. He was a good distance away, and there was a deal of fierce white water between them. Benecke arrived, and set his hand to his bow. Nicholas stopped him. Benecke swore.

Nicholas said, 'Look. Three sets of prints. They shot her, and came down, but she swam to the island and died there. They tried to wade in and came back – see the prints. Then the sealskin shoes went back downriver alone.'

'Why?' Benecke said.

'To fetch help. To get a boat. To bring back ropes, if they didn't have any. The bearskin was valuable. But no one was hurt – there is no blood above the edge of the water. And if someone had drowned, the other would have gone with Sigfús. By the way, he *was* drunk. He was staggering.'

'Unless they were both swept away,' Benecke said.

It had been what Nicholas was afraid of at first. Then he had found the other footmarks, booted, impatient, walking up and down and then turning to reclimb the bank. Nicholas walked over to where Glímu-Sveinn had joined them. 'What has happened?' he said.

The Icelander lifted his shoulders. '*Putt!* The fools! The carcass is ruined! They were unable to cross; Sigfús has gone to get help. There is a farm five miles to the south. We passed near it. But they have filled him full of ale, and he has lost his way, or fallen asleep; who can tell? So after waiting a while, they have grown impatient. The fools!'

'You saw the footprints above? They've ridden after him?'

'How would they know where to go? No. They have continued upriver, to the north. Why, I cannot tell.'

'Then we must follow,' Nicholas said. 'Or I must follow. You should try and find Sigfús Helgason, should you not? With your dog?'

Dogs could find human beings under nine ells of snow, Robin had said. You wouldn't find nine ells of snow anywhere here, unless in a fissure, or a hole in a lava-bed, or unless the snow started again. The water still sparkled in sunlight; the snow that clouded its banks was nothing but eddies scooped up by the wind.

Glímu-Sveinn said, 'I cannot leave you.'

'But there is a ferry,' Nicholas said. 'A ferry, you said, to the north? We shall take six of the horses and follow the prints of the young people. Then the ferryman surely will help us. Leave the bear. It isn't worth salving. Find Sigfús and join us once he is safe.'

'You didn't ask me,' said Paúel Benecke ten minutes later. They stood, mounted once more, looking after the vanishing Icelander.

'You've no say. You're my prisoner,' said Nicholas. 'Why? Have I done something to frighten you?'

'No,' Benecke said. 'We have abandoned our guide and his dog. We are two men in a strange land in charge of a handful of horses with, I fear, more snow on the way, and a track to follow which may soon be obliterated. I have never felt happier. Where is the bear-cub, do you suppose?'

'Pursuing Sigfús, very likely,' said Nicholas. 'And if he isn't, he's smaller than you are. Do you know what I think?' He had started to ride. Benecke followed.

'You don't think,' Benecke said. 'They were right. They said you were a furious maniac.' His eyes were gleaming.

Nicholas said, 'I think our Flemish couple have gone to the springs. Kathi wanted to see them. They're over the river.'

'What springs?' Benecke said.

'Hot springs,' Nicholas answered. 'Great big enormous boiling hot gushers, leaping a hundred feet high. Bubbling mud. Steaming pools. Seething rivers. They're all over Iceland. People cook their food in them, and dry and wash out their clothes, and bathe themselves every *Thváttdagr*, Saturday. They changed *Fryádagr* to *Föstudagr*, Fast Day, but of course they eat fish every day, so they could call it Sinful Blood Pudding Day for all that it matters. Anyway, they got tired of Freya, according to Glímu-Sveinn:

> *'I will not serve an idle log*
> *For one, I care not which;*
> *But either Odin is a dog*
> *Or Freya is a bitch.'*

Paúel Benecke moaned. 'You *are* a maniac! You meant to go to the springs all along!'

'No. Kathi did. But I must say,' Nicholas said, 'that now I have leave of Besse, I shall enjoy it.'

He frowned at Benecke's uplifted brows. 'The great white bear.

The Muscovites, I am told, call him Mishka, and the Mongolians refer to him as Ese, grandfather. Once, long ago, a young priest called Isleifr from Iceland carried one as a gift to the Emperor, and lived to become Bishop of Skálholt. Nowadays, when one does something without leave in Iceland, one does it by permission of Besse.'

'The tale of your life, I suspect,' said Paúel Benecke. 'And of mine, I have to admit. So yes. Let us go. Let us go and visit your devilish cauldrons. I have no desire to meet this Sersanders, but I am much looking forward to the acquaintance of your young brother Kathi.'

Chapter 27

'I TOLD YOU,' said Katelijne Sersanders. 'I told you he'd come. Tie it tight. Tighter. I knew he'd come. You'd better be ready with a merry quip about the *Unicorn* and the sulphur. Now throw it in.'

With a jerk of pure exasperation, her brother did as she asked. He said, 'Nicholas doesn't know about the *Unicorn* and the sulphur. He's probably sunk the *Maiden*, killed its captain, and thinks that it wouldn't do any harm to ingratiate himself with the Icelanders and me. God knows the Bishop and the Governor are not fond of the Hanse.'

'I'd be surprised if they were,' Kathi said, 'considering how much money they make behind the Hanse's back. I'm going to call again. Stop your ears.' She had tried to teach Sersanders falsetto, but he had never been in the Tyrol and couldn't split his voice into three. She warbled for a long time, with some pride; and was gratified, once again, when someone warbled back promptly. It was nearer.

Sersanders said, 'You know, if the wind gets up again, he'll walk straight across and step into every hot cauldron and boil.'

'Broth again,' said Kathi automatically. It was true. When the wind rose, or it snowed, you couldn't distinguish the haze from the vapour. She said, 'He'll stop till it clears, or his guide will. And he'll follow the staves. How many should we cook for, do you think?'

'Two,' said Sersanders, gazing into the distance. 'That's all I can see. Six ponies, Nicholas and his guide. I suppose it's his guide. He's wearing a hat and a boat-cloak. *Tell me* before you make that sound again.'

'Sorry,' said Katelijne, uncupping her mouth. It had been less a cry of welcome than a crow of shared pleasure for M. de Fleury. He had rounded the hill as she had, lured by the white drifting steam from beyond it. And now he was standing gazing at what lay before him: the whole vast sloping terrain, white and grey, grey and black, of the fuming crust of the earth, below which seethed and bubbled the deep scalding vents from which rose the steam, the sulphur, the mud, the jets of sizzling water and the rivulets which boiled their way through the snow.

As the cry echoed over the waste, Kathi felt the pressure change under her feet. She looked down. Something spoke: a dark sound below the splutter and hiss of the field. There was a trembling pause. With a roar, the basin behind her gave birth to a fierce jet of steam, followed by a mounting volley of water. It rose and spread in the sunshine and dropped, while the steam blew and rolled in the wind, obliterating the distant figures of ponies and men. By the time it cleared, the beasts had been hobbled, and the men had started to move, and were making use of her marker-staves. There were not very many: they came from Sigfús's spare tents. She wondered how Sigfús was. She wondered what guide M. de Fleury had got, because he wasn't walking in front, as a guide should.

She said to her brother, 'You jumped. You thought it was ours.' The geysirs exploded at different intervals. She had chosen the big one to prime. She hoped it would wait until M. de Fleury was here. She had timed it. She had packed it with turf. Sometimes it came when you didn't expect it. The first time, their tent was too close, and Anselm had been rather angry. Now she thought he was enjoying it almost as much as she was. She wished M. de Fleury would hurry, and then cautioned herself. Shag in soup. She stood, beaming.

M. de Fleury, when he came up, looked as he had on board ship, blithe as frost on a window. She said with satisfaction, 'You came.'

'Well, I had to,' said M. de Fleury. 'After all those distress signals from Anselm. Now I'm bloody going away. He hasn't got long golden hair. I'm not going to marry him.' He was speaking in old-fashioned German, which was quite close to the Norraena tongues.

'He was going to marry me,' said the man with M. de Fleury, in the same language. He had a black beard, and an arm in a sling tucked into his jacket under the cloak and a bandage under his hat. He was not an Icelander. 'But now I have seen his sister, I am not sure of my constancy. In any case, you, Nikolás, cannot even arrive in time to kill bears, never mind dragons. Introduce me.'

'Your future bride, Anselm Sersanders, and his sister,' said M. de Fleury obediently. 'Anselm, embrace Master Paúel Benecke, Danish representative of the Hanse, whose sulphuric wish is to make you his prisoner, were it not for the fact that he is my prisoner already. You may kiss. What is that?'

'Dinner,' said Kathi. 'Step back.'

'What?' said Paúel Benecke.

'Oh my God,' said M. de Fleury.

The ground, which had begun to throb, growled. This time, the vibration came from below, not behind. This time her geysir was coming. She said, her eyes on M. de Fleury's face, 'You had really better stand back.'

He said, 'All right. Take me,' and allowed himself to be pulled back by her gloved hand. He said with surprise, 'You have only five fingers.'

'Christ,' said Paúel Benecke. 'Be quiet, you fool.'

She had seen it three times. She had never seen it like this. To begin with, the subterranean explosions were much stronger this time: eight of them, and growing in violence, so that the ground shuddered under their feet as if it were about to rise up, or buckle, or split. With the eighth came the first gush of scalding water, a mighty column hurled into the air with a thunderous hiss, and dissolving into clouds of white steam. It was followed in quick succession by others. Lumps of turf spurted up. Boulders flew, rocketing into the sky and bursting high over the billowing clouds. The columns rose higher and higher with a shocking roar. The main eruption, driving upwards in a single terrible explosion, ripped off the side of its base and shot a hundred feet in the air where it whistled, a boiling, unbroken pillar of water.

This time the spout had brought something with it that was not a stone or a turf, and by playing under the thing, sustained it high in the glittering air, pagan with rainbows. Staring upwards, Benecke broke his dumbounded silence and swore. Kathi clutched at her brother. M de Fleury tilted his head back and gazed.

Jerking to and fro in the sky, rising and falling, danced the torso of a white-shirted man, arms outstretched. Its legs and its head were horribly missing.

The jet dropped. The thing tumbled into the basin and lay in the steam, rocked by the receding water. There was a throaty gurgle and silence, but for the mutter and hiss of the great evil field.

'Plates?' said M de Fleury. 'Napkins? Knives? Or are we supposed to tear it apart with our fingers?'

Paúel Benecke pulled off his felt hat and let the wind play about his dank hair. 'What is it?' he asked. His voice shook.

Upon the good-looking face of Sersanders there appeared an exuberant grin. 'It's my spare shirt,' he said. 'A ptarmigan in either sleeve, and a breast of lamb packed in the body. Kathi's idea. We buried a pan loaf as well, but I don't think it's risen. Not so high, anyway. Nicholas? Come on. We did all the work. You go and retrieve it.'

*

They held their feast in the tent; and although the birds fell apart in a welter of feathers, the mutton was done to a turn and went down well with some ale of the Bishop's. 'We shouldn't have let Sigfús have any,' said Kathi, 'if we'd known he'd been drinking already.'

'He has that reputation,' Nicholas said. Since the geysir blew, Paúel Benecke had never removed his eyes from Kathi, even when the geysir blew again.

'Oh,' said Kathi.

'I wish someone had told us,' said Sersanders. 'He was drunk as an auk. He would have scalded to death in the hot springs.'

'So might you,' the Danziger said. Kathi looked at him.

'Well, we were sensible,' Sersanders said. 'We sent the man back with the bear. He said he knew of a farm. I'm afraid it's too late for a pelt from the she-bear; the foxes will have stripped her by now. I expect you saw her. Didn't you have a guide?'

'Glímu-Sveinn. We sent him back with his dog to find Sigfús. You said Sigfús *went back with the bear?*'

'He knew of a farm with a sledge and some ropes. If he ever got there.'

'He means the bear-cub,' said Kathi modestly. 'We caught it.'

Paúel Benecke removed his black stare to Nicholas. 'Your young brother,' he said. 'So what now?'

'Glímu-Sveinn will find the farm, the bear and Sigfús, and they will all duly arrive back at Skalholt, demanding a price for their services, which they will receive.'

'Or if we perish, they sell off the bear.'

Kathi said, 'They didn't make us come here.'

'No, you were coming here anyway,' said Sersanders sourly.

'So was M. de Fleury,' said Kathi. 'And aren't you glad?'

'I'm glad,' said Paúel Benecke cheerfully. His beard was covered with grease. 'I'll stay as long as you like, but I have to say this. I think Herra Oddur is going to be a very surprised man when he sees us.'

'When he sees Kathi and me,' Sersanders said slowly. He generally reached the right conclusions eventually. 'But you're from the Hanse. Or was he suspicious of Nicholas?'

'I think,' Nicholas said, 'that he thought we were all cheating Bergen together. He couldn't make out Paúel's intentions, but felt a lot safer without him.'

There was a pause. Sersanders said, 'And what are Paúel's intentions?'

'Ask your friend Nikolás his intentions,' Benecke said. 'It is my ship which is dismasted and lying under his guns.'

'I was relying on the bear,' Nicholas said. 'We began with Paúel's head and his arm, as you see. A trifling effort would finish him off. How about if we tied him into his shirt like the sheep? He'd go high. Anything over two hundred feet'd be a record.'

'You're going to hold Paúel Benecke to ransom?' Sersanders said. He sounded irritable.

'Well, that would be stupid,' said Kathi. 'M. de Fleury would have to stay a pirate for the rest of his life. Mind you –'

'It *is* rather attractive,' said Nicholas. 'I have access to a Greek-speaking parrot and some unclaimed treasure and the crew have learned to chant "Hale and Howe Rumbylowe" and all the right ditties. I even know a one-legged man.'

'What has that to do with pirates?' Kathi said.

'He *is* one. I suppose,' Nicholas said, 'the world is full of natural pirates and those who are trained by their nurses. Ask René of Anjou. Ask the Emperor Frederick. Ruthless.' He paused, feeling slightly distrait. Outside, the small geysir rumbled and then began to spout in vehement gusts. It was disturbing. Sersanders got up and went out.

'So who goes to prison?' said Kathi.

'We haven't decided,' said Paúel. 'You wouldn't like to come to prison with me? We have some delectable tortures in Bergen.'

'Nobody is going to prison,' Nicholas said. 'But don't tell Sersanders, he'd be so disappointed. Kathi. I want to spring the springs. Are you coming?'

Kathi jumped to her feet. To the pleasure of Nicholas, so did the Danziger. Even Sersanders, although muttering something about returning to Skálholt, joined them outside in the glittering, shifting, rumbling playground of giants and dwarves and accompanied the three of them on their tour. They were moved to imitate the puttering mud, warmed their hands in the streams, blew alcoholic fumes into the profound, steaming basins. They collected stones and fed the gurgling orifices and counted in unison until the geysirs burst forth. They put Sersanders's hat into one, and a glove which emerged like an insect.

They made up rhymes and spells and orders which they timed contrapuntally to several geysirs at once, after they had found how to set the explosions. Sersanders, relaxed with judicious applications of wine, joined in boisterously. Benecke played his supporting role without stint, but without giving voice. It was his dry remark which at last made them all stop and listen. 'Snow is coming. You should strike your tent and move, while you can see.'

It was, of course, sensible. Sersanders agreed. Nicholas, deeply involved with Kathi in a monstrous experiment with the largest geysir, felt like being obstinate, and was. After a sharpish argument, he gave in, largely because of a short fall of snow which, while it lasted, reduced visibility to nothing and made the risks of leaving the hot springs quite apparent. It happened again before, laden, they managed to walk half of the way to the horses. By common accord they sat down where they were until it ended. The ground was warm. The next random step might have plunged any of them into a simmering basin. The snow, fine as powder, danced about them in clouds and so did the steam mingling with it.

'Unlike Hesdin,' Nicholas said, 'everything works.' The remark had no point, except to himself, but Kathi took him up anyway.

'I knew you would enjoy it,' she said. 'Lucifer, Master of Secrets. Did you notice the rainbow? A *regnbogi Nikuds*, they call it. Nikudr is the old name for Odin. Old Nick.'

'Robin told me,' he said. 'It is also the name of a water-goblin with inverted hooves. You can't tell whether I'm coming or going, so help me Freya and Thor and the Omnipotent God. Do you know the expression *concupiscientia oculorum?*'

'Visual curiosity, leading to sensory and imaginative excitement. It's a sin,' Kathi said. 'And you've got it much worse than I have. Why did you leave Robin back at the Markarfljót?'

'I wanted a holiday. Robin believes it his duty to keep me advised about my duty. St Cuthbert's sandals. I got paralysis of the feet.'

'You made him your page,' Kathi said.

'I also prefer to take him back alive to his father,' Nicholas said. 'Was that thunder?'

'No. You should have taken the trouble to bring him. Don't you see how he has changed in five months?'

'You mean he's getting younger?' Nicholas said. 'That would be a distinct help. Look, I like him. He was disappointed. He'll get over it.'

'You sound,' Kathi said, 'as if you think you're doing more for him than he's doing for you. And you're right in thinking he's more mature than you are. Dr Andreas believes you're fourteen.'

Nicholas turned and stared at her. Her knitted hat lidded her eyes. Behind him, Sersanders had jumped up and was standing impatiently. He had an idea that, also behind him, the Danziger had heard every word. Nicholas said, 'I wager he said you were fourteen as well. Anyway, what's wrong with being fourteen? Holy Jesus, that *was* thunder. Wasn't it?'

'That was thunder!' said Sersanders, bending down.

'Wrong!' said Kathi. 'As declared St –'

'– as declared St Augustine's congregation at Hippo when he

misquoted the Bible. Your brother isn't St Augustine. He's right. Thunder.'

Unusually, she insisted. 'It was the geysirs. Several at once. I felt them. My Sole cleaveth to the Pavement. Didn't you?'

He felt them too, as she spoke: several extraordinary thumps underneath him, followed by a long shiver. Behind him, Paúel scrambled to his feet. He said, 'If the wind would drop, we could hear.' A moment later he said, 'Someone is calling.'

'The Destroying Angel,' Nicholas said. 'Thor the Thunderer, Father of Slaughter and Desolation. Troops of infernal spirits passing by, bearing the doomed. It's calling Herra.'

It was the voice of Glímu-Sveinn. Talking, Nicholas had begun to heap their belongings together, his eyes meeting those of the other two men, who at once came to help him. The snow was thinning, and the voice repeated its call. Nicholas said, 'Answer back, Kathi,' and as she launched into her high, clear warble, added his own remarkably powerful voice.

This time they all felt the shaking, followed by a long rolling boom underground. At the same moment, there was a short, loud report from directly over their heads, followed at once by another.

'Thundering applause. We are *all* correct,' Nicholas said. 'St Augustine *and* the Hippos: I'm going to start walking forward. If you see the poles, take them to walk with. If I fall in, I'll bubble.'

'I shall walk beside you,' Benecke said. 'Stretch your arm. Sersanders, walk behind touching your sister. If one falls into trouble, the other can help.'

The snow was thinning. The wind was so fierce at their backs that they had to brace themselves, deafened, but already they could see a short distance. Then the wind rose higher yet, flinging the soft powdered snow into the air while they felt their way forward, half blinded. They set their feet where the snow lay intact on the lava; sometimes ankle deep, sometimes up to the knee. Once they stepped across the black steaming line of a stream; once Paúel's foot slipped on the snow-covered ice of a basin, and his cry warned them all. Behind the wind, they heard several times more the shouts of Glímu-Sveinn, guiding them over the patched and dangerous waste.

Behind them, as they crossed it, they also seemed to hear, raised in concert, all the myriad cavernous tongues of the springs; the glottal, gurgling voices of trolls, the subterranean chortle of demons. The wind rose until they could hear nothing else; and then ceased. The haze parted. The landscape lay, steaming, distinct, at their feet. And beyond the springs, beside the shifting shapes of their horses, sat the mounted figure of Glímu-Sveinn, his arm raised.

Nicholas shouted and, raising his own arm, increased his speed to a circumspect run. Benecke, now apart, ran beside him. Kathi said, 'Listen. Stop.'

Nicholas stopped and looked round. So did Benecke. Sersanders said, 'Don't be silly. Come on, while it's clear.'

Kathi said, 'Listen.' Her face, losing its liveliness, had become intent. She said, 'There is nothing to hear.'

Nicholas returned to her side. For a moment he stood. Then without saying anything he walked back over the snow to first one dark, steaming vent, then a second. Beyond that was the icy-rimmed basin upon which Paúel had slipped. He stood there for what seemed a long time, and then saw that Paúel was standing beside him. Neither spoke.

The fifty-foot basin was dry, which was normal. The water which had recently filled it had spilled from the edge and was still making its way, steaming, tricking over the snowfield. The central pipe still emitted steam, which blew about in the abated breeze. The geysir was one they had timed. The water retreated sixty feet down the pipe, boiled, ascended, and finally exploded once more in the air. Nicholas stepped into the basin and looked down. He heard Kathi call out in warning, but Paúel beside him made no effort to hold him back.

There was no danger, because there was no sound of simmering water. There was no sound, because there was no water and, as he looked, the upper surface of the pipe became dry. The geysir was dead. And so, inert in uncanny silence, lay every spring in the field. The steam, as he watched, began to thin and to fade. Dry and silent, the crust of Hell lay around them, the voices withdrawn.

They stood, looking about, while in front of them, Glímu-Sveinn called again, pointing. They turned to the south-east. Against a deep charcoal sky, a white mountain glowed in the distance. From it trailed a plume of pale russet smoke.

'Hekla,' Benecke said.

Behind Hekla, to the east, lowered the mighty Vatna glacier with its burden of ice three thousand feet deep. To the south floated the great southern glaciers of Myrdals and Eyjafjalla, over five thousand feet high: a pack of icy-blue whalebacks against the dark sky from which arose, feather-white, another column of vapour. Nicholas studied it, one hand at his throat. He said nothing.

A flock of crows fled overhead in an abrupt storm of noise. A moment later, like a darn in the silence, could be heard the faint scratchy sound – *reu, reu, reu* – of hastening ptarmigan. Then the silence returned. Benecke said, 'I think we should hurry.'

Watchfully then, all four of them started to run. Around them, the tormented arena lay cooling and dumb, its violence throttled, its trickling waters and mud-beds congealing. Now and then, something pattered or cracked. Once, Sersanders attempted to speak, but Nicholas shook his head. Glímu-Sveinn had the answers.

Glímu-Sveinn, his beard in his chest, sat and watched them approach. He had roped the horses together; they stood in a huddle, their great heads poking over each other's backs, their eyeballs glittering. The Icelander's wide otter-eyes were veined red. He said, 'Mount, and throw down anything you do not need. You felt the tremors?'

'The springs are dry,' Nicholas said.

'All this last week the ice-caps have shrunk, and for two days the ewes have held back their milk. I should have known. I will take you west with my family, and from Skálholt you will go to the Governor's house at Bessastadir. When it is over, he will find you some ship.'

'We have ships,' said Benecke sharply. They were already mounting.

The reddened eyes turned and glared into his. 'You cannot reach them. The valley of the Markarfljót will be impassable. Even the Hvíta has changed since you crossed it.'

'Why?' said Anselm Sersanders. Beneath his tight hand, his pony was wild-eyed and fidgetting. The spare horses were trampling and snorting. Sersanders himself appeared alert and determined, the way he did in his armour when fighting. Kathi wore the same expression. For once, they looked like brother and sister.

The Icelander turned and spoke to them all. 'There have been earthquake tremors all afternoon. Among the geysirs, you would not distinguish them. There will be more. They are dangerous in themselves, but also, they affect the rivers, the glaciers. They can cause a *skidáfall*, a landslide, a snow-slip. The thunder, too, can bring very bad lift-fire.'

'Lightning,' said Kathi.

'It can kill men, and horses. And at the very worst, with all this motion, the fire-pipes in the mountains may crack. Hekla may explode.'

'When?' said Benecke. 'How soon might it happen? How will we know when it starts?'

'You will hear it. The smoke will darken. There will be a smell of sulphur perhaps. It can happen quickly, or it can delay for some days. But long before the explosion, you will be travelling west. All those who live in the plains are preparing to round up their beasts and do the same. My family too. I have just come from there. We can be

with them in an hour, if we hurry; and travel together to Skálholt by
dark. Come. Come.'

'And Sigfús?' said Kathi. 'Did you find him?'

Glímu-Sveinn looked at her. He said, 'He is dead. I followed his
tracks to the farm, but the farm was no longer 'there. The shaking had
brought down the snow, and a landslide of boulders beneath it. The
wreckage was strewn all down the hill, and there was nothing of the
farmer and Sigfús but a bloodstained shoe and some rags. I left them.
I had to find my own home.'

If Sigfús dies because of the Flemings, I will kill them. Glímu-Sveinn
had meant it. But Fate had buried Sigfús in the end and, faced with
the danger to his own house and his duty – to his credit – to his
travellers, Glímu-Sveinn had not wasted time on a search. Whoever
lived at his home – elderly parents, sisters, infants – needed him
more.

Nicholas said, 'We are grateful that you came back, and for your
offer to help us. I have only one thing to ask, very quickly. Does one
mountain unsettle another? Are you afraid only of Hekla?'

'Hekla is nearest.' The Icelander paused. 'It has been known.
Hvallavellir disturbed can rouse Hekla.'

'And Katla?' Nicholas said.

'It is not impossible. But it is a nightmare I for one will not
contemplate.'

'No. Take us to your house,' Nicholas said. 'And on the way, if you
can, take us past the place where Sigfús was killed. We should speak
of it to his widow, if we meet her.'

Sersanders's expression changed, and he opened his mouth. Before
he could mention the cub, Nicholas said, 'But of course we must
hurry. Lead on.'

During the journey, they spoke very little, each of them braced for
what might be going to happen. The soft ground beyond the geysirs
was difficult, and the ponies jibbed at the ropes which held them
together instead of the dog, left behind to herd Glímu-Sveinn's
animals. The ferryman's hut, when they reached it, was empty, and
the river itself seemed to have tilted, with shallows where there had
been none before, and deeper currents racing like horses. The water
was saddle-deep in such places, and the ponies paddled like crabs,
before scrambling up the steep opposite bank. Even the roar of the
upper creek and the falls seemed thinner and lighter.

After that, oddly, the wind came once again, whistling and whining
from a different direction and erratic in force. It stripped the snow
from the ground and hurled it into their faces in long stinging

swathes, stopping their breath. Before them, the layers of lava displayed arching streamers of snow, coldly bridal. Despite the chill and the buffeting it restored, for a while, a sense of healthy normality; even the clamour of it was welcome. Then the wind dropped as abruptly as it had risen, and the veils cleared to show them the glaciers again, and the rough whitened ground, and Hekla, with a brown column of smoke puffing into the sunless air. Near at hand lay a vast black escarpment, its lower slopes burdened with snow.

Glímu-Sveinn said, 'There was the farm.'

Kathi made to ride forward, but the Icelander stopped her. 'The snow is soft. We do not know how deep it is. It is best not to go near.'

'Let me try,' Nicholas said, and dismounted. Immediately, Sersanders slid off his horse.

Benecke said, 'We should hurry.' In his voice was more than impatience.

Kathi said, 'Yes, Anselm. Come.'

'I must just –' Sersanders said. He began walking forward. He hadn't even taken a pole. Nicholas watched him, his hand at his throat.

'Well stop him!' said Kathi, with exasperation.

Glímu-Sveinn had begun to urge his pony forward. Nicholas said, 'No. Give me a pole and some rope.'

'Why?' said Benecke.

'*I've found it!*' shrieked Sersanders suddenly. They could see him up to his knees in soft snow, attempting to dig something out with his hands. As he spoke, he half sank out of sight and hauled himself out again. Then he started tugging again.

Nicholas began walking towards him very slowly. Behind him, Benecke was using his one useful arm to detain Kathi. Benecke said, projecting his voice, 'If you pull anything out, you could dislodge all the snow piled above you.'

'What?' said Sersanders. His face, red in the whiteness, was beaming. 'It's the bear! Unblemished pelt! Come and help me!'

His voice echoed. Nicholas listened, and swore. Once this had happened to him, in the Alps. Correction: he had made it happen. This time, the hapless Sersanders yelled, and a rumble answered him from over his head. Nicholas uncoiled his rope and hurled one end as far as he could towards Sersanders who, staring up, noticed and caught it. He had wrapped it once round his wrist when the avalanche fell.

It pulled Nicholas with it. He felt the drag on his arm as Sersanders was tossed down the slope far ahead of him, and then himself lost control of the rope under a shower of angular rubble. He lay, mildly concussed and empty-handed until the movement and noise died away, and then threw off the snow on his shoulders and lifted himself cautiously up to look round. Behind, Benecke was still holding Kathi but the Icelander, gripping rope, was on all fours and crawling forward. He was carrying two planks of wood.

Nicholas said, 'Throw them. I'll find him.' He didn't have to speak very loudly.

Glímu-Sveinn said, 'What is that?'

The knot was sodden: Nicholas had to drag off one glove, and pull the thing over his head. Then he let the stone hang, without answering. The vast, heavy silence had fallen again. It made it easier to concentrate, and also more difficult. The pendulum started to swing. Nicholas said, 'He is over there. Give me a board. Follow me if you like.' Behind him, he heard Kathi's low voice, talking to Benecke. He followed the pendulum. His hand was so numb that he felt none of the cord's violent friction. He was confident of success. The avalanche had been brief, and Sersanders had been braked by the rope and couldn't be deeply buried. They had to find him quickly, that was all.

Skilled at moving over the snow, Glímu-Sveinn led, and Nicholas followed, articulating directions. The pendulum had no doubts about where it was going. At the place where its swing was most violent, Glímu-Sveinn carefully pushed down his pole, and met resistance. Together he and Nicholas dug, and Adorne's nephew was there, half stifled and shocked, and with an ankle-bone snapped, but alive.

Returned to his horse, wrapped in wadmol, he sat with chattering teeth while Nicholas faced Glímu-Sveinn. 'What was that?' said the Icelander. The man from Danzig, mounted again, was gazing thoughtfully at them both, while Kathi bent over her brother, padding and binding his ankle. Nicholas could not see her expression.

Nicholas said, 'It was a pendulum. It's often used overseas to find water. Sometimes it can find people too.'

'Anyone can do it?' the Icelander asked.

'If they have the knack. Glímu-Sveinn, there is someone else under the snow.'

Kathi looked up. 'Bodies,' the Icelander said.

'No. Someone living. It could be the farmer, or Sigfús. But it would take longer to find him.'

'Why?' said Benecke.

'I knew Sersanders,' Nicholas said. He turned to Glímu-Sveinn. 'How near is your home? Could you take the others there, and come back for me?'

The pale blue eyes stared at his. 'There is nothing there. This young man needs attention. We must go.'

'There is something there,' Nicholas said. 'Someone. A man.'

Kathi said, 'It is not the bear, Glímu-Sveinn. Nikolás-riddari has a gift. He can find people.'

'And nails?' said Paúel Benecke. 'Is that how you did the trick with the nails? A magician, forsooth.'

Nicholas could think of nothing to say. There was blood in his hair and his face stung, but he hardly felt it. His head felt swimmingly empty and his chest, by contrast, unpleasantly tight. He said, 'If we leave it, it will be too late.' He spoke directly to Glímu-Sveinn, with a sort of irritated anger which increased as he found the man was looking away. Then he saw, to the right, a mounted figure approaching them: a white-bearded man who was hailing them in Icelandic. Glímu-Sveinn called back, and turned.

'My father's brother, come to tell me to hurry. This is what you will do. You and he will look for this person. I will take the rest to my house and return. If you have not found him, you leave. Hekla is smoking.'

'It isn't Hekla,' Nicholas said. He felt he had said it before, and was annoyed at having to repeat it.

Benecke made a remark. 'You said the danger was in the south, as we were coming here. Isn't that Hekla?'

'No,' said Nicholas. 'Further south. I think it is Katla.'

'I hope not,' Benecke said, after a pause. 'One would have to think of our ships.'

'I am thinking of them,' Nicholas said. 'I am not going with you. After we get out this man, I go south.'

'Without a guide?' Benecke said.

'I shall find one. You see,' Nicholas said, 'they are expecting the explosion from Hekla. They will have to be warned.'

'And if you are wrong?'

'Then that will be best of all,' Nicholas said.

They must have gone, after that, for he found himself alone in the snow with Glímu-Sveinn's uncle, who immediately launched into angry abuse. Then the old man crawled about hawking and spitting, and complaining at everything Nicholas did. But like his nephew, he was a master of locomotion over treacherous ground, and accepted directions, although he cackled with temper when the directions proved wrong, as they often did. Then suddenly the sense of Sigfús came flooding in, as had never happened before with someone he didn't know, and the pendulum span higher and higher, and Nicholas pointed and spoke.

The old man got there before him, but even when both of them dug, there was nothing to see, and he had to keep urging the old man to continue. Then his numbed fingers stubbed against something that could have been a rock or a board or a box, but proved to be a sleeping man's head, with a half-melted cavity around it. From the drinker's nose, Nicholas would have guessed it was Sigfús, even without the old man's surprised croak. They pummelled him like a piece of blue steak all the time they were digging him out, and wrapped him in everything they could find, and started a fire with a door and a section of table. And all the time the old man was perfectly silent, although he still spat now and then.

When they heard the hooves coming back, there was only one hour left of the day, and the brown smoke of Hekla had merged into the violet-blue of the night. Nicholas had expected Glímu-Sveinn. With him were Kathi and Benecke.

Glímu-Sveinn said, 'You found him.'

The uncle, roused, launched into a mucilaginous monologue. Nicholas let him rant. He felt physically beaten, as might be expected after his recent experience. He felt the sickening lethargy that came with the pendulum. It had almost felled him in Venice, when he had used this power to hunt down his son. This jealous power.

He knew, beyond doubt, that he had been right about Katla. And his ship was there, a few miles off shore, unaware and waiting for him. A pony tossed its head with a chime of its bridle and he received the image, at once, of a bowl, and a carob seed tapping and tapping. Nostradamus had also been right.

Glímu-Sveinn was speaking. Glímu-Sveinn was saying, 'The *junfrú* has said this has happened before. You are a sorcerer.'

Nicholas got to his feet. It was an effort. He said, 'My magic is white. My ship carries a priest.'

There was a silence. Then Glímu-Sveinn said, 'Your spirit tells you that the furnace of Katla is about to burst through her ice? You know how terrible this will be?'

'Help me to warn them,' Nicholas said.

Glímu-Sveinn said, 'The Markarfljót valley will flood with torrents of ice. Scalding water will rush through the rivers, molten rock through the fields. All that lives in the *sandur* will be swept out to sea, and the parboiled bodies of fish and of men will toss through the arks of their houses. Any ships within reach will be swamped.'

'Help me get there in time,' Nicholas said, 'and my ship can save people.'

'And mine,' Benecke said. 'I am coming. So is Katelijne. Sersanders would be with us, but for his injury. He will be taken care of by Glímu-Sveinn's people; they and Sigfús will see that no harm comes to him now. Are you not proud of us, selfless as we are?'

'Yes. We need a guide,' Nicholas said.

'I will come,' said Glímu-Sveinn. 'My uncle will see to the household.' He looked defiant and uneasy at once. The rest of his family were fishing from Markarfljót. Because a buried man had been found, he was placing his trust in another man's instincts.

It hurt to smile. Nicholas smiled and said, 'Let us guide each other. *Ave Maria, gratia plena, Dominus tecum.* Lead me to your bliss.'

Chapter 28

DURING THE DAYS of his absence, the caravel of Nicholas de Fleury rocked in the harbour of the Westmann Islands and received, with its fish, those ounces of information which contrived, despite everything, to travel from Hafnarfjördur and Skálholt. As first one day passed, then a second, Father Moriz prevailed upon Crackbene to invite on board Stanislas the lodesman of the *Pruss Maiden*, and share the news with him.

From Nicholas and Paúel themselves, they knew of the *Unicorn*'s insolent expedition, and of Sersanders's intention to rejoin his own ship with his sister at Hafnarfjördur. They knew Nicholas and Paúel had set out to pursue them.

By the second day after their departure, they were receiving further snippets. Faster than anyone expected, the *Unicorn* had picked up its sulphur and gone, allowing barely enough time for Adorne's nephew and niece to have joined it.

Later, one of the yoles arrived and delivered a message. Tryggvi and his son had returned, those Icelanders who had escorted Sersanders. Because of a shortage of horses, Sersanders and his sister had been unable to ride on from Skálholt and had thus missed their ship. So far as Tryggvi knew, the pair were at Skálholt still.

'In the custody of Nicholas and Benecke, by now,' le Grant said. 'I'd like to have seen Sersanders's face when they arrived.'

'It cannot be easy for his sister,' said Father Moriz. 'How strange that Tryggvi was dismissed. And that there should have been no suitable horses.'

'And that Martin should turn round so quickly. Still,' said Crackbene. 'Now de Fleury will bring the young people back. They will start a choir on the way, I shouldn't wonder.'

John le Grant grunted. He said, 'You've just about got all your fish?'

'Yes,' said Crackbene. 'Stanislas is pleased. We are full, and the

Maiden is starting to load. If de Fleury comes back by nightfall tomorrow, we could sail the next day, the quicker the better. There's word of an incoming ship.'

'Nicholas could come back faster than he went out,' said John. 'I don't know why he went round by sea, when he only had to cut across a few rivers. He might be coming down the Markarfljót by now, if he's feeling less timid. He might be arriving today.'

They heard the horn from the hill an hour later; followed at once by the watch with the news. 'A three-masted ship, Master Crackbene. Some distance off, but the fishermen know it. Sir, it's the English privateer called the *Charity*. And it's under Jonathan Babbe, with his own special crew of Hull men.'

'Is it, by God,' said John le Grant. His freckled skin had turned red.

'They say he drives every other ship off the grounds. They say he came into this harbour last season, and killed every man who didn't make way fast enough. They say he landed boats wherever he could, and seized the fish and slaughtered anyone who resisted. They say –'

'We know,' Crackbene said. They had discussed this: he had orders to deal with it. Peaceful incoming ships were to be left unmolested. Ships displaying aggression were to be engaged by both the *Pruss Maiden* and the *Svipa*, which would share any booty or prisoners. Crackbene's eyes were bright with anticipation.

John said, 'I'll go and see to the guns. Stanislas will need help with his masts.'

'I've signalled him over,' said Crackbene. 'He can pick up his bows and his gunpowder now, and when you're ready, you can check over his cannon.'

'You are arming the *Pruss Maiden*?' said Moriz.

'We're no match for the *Charity* on our own. So long as de Fleury holds Paúel Benecke hostage, the *Pruss Maiden* will do as she's told. If Benecke's dead, we hope no one will find out till later. Meanwhile, let's climb a hill. I want to look at this fellow Jo Babbe.'

They climbed the hill. The air was searingly cold, but the wind hardly fluttered their cloaks. Over the thick, lazy swell of the sea, the fishing-boats were curvetting towards home. The gulls and seals had all gone. In the silence the surf sighed, and lingered, and whispered. Moriz said quietly, 'John?'

'I see it,' the engineer said. 'It's big, but we could take it, the two of us, if we have to. He's becalmed, I would say. He may not even get here before nightfall. We'll be in position outside before then.'

'John,' said Moriz again. 'Look at Hekla.'

*

Robin of Berecrofts stood on an opposite height, also looking.

He climbed this cliff every day, frequently soaked by the waterfall which flowed over it. The cliff was part of the long range of mountains which formed the base of the Eyjafjalla glacier, and the waterfall was the meter by which the fishermen of the Markarfljót measured the wind. If the waterfall climbed into the air, they didn't go out.

From the cliff, he could see across to the Westmanns, and mark the yoles and the dogger as they plied in and out with their catch. He couldn't see the *Svipa* or the *Pruss Maiden*, but he knew they were there. All the messages Crackbene had received had come from him. It had eased the hurt to his pride to realise how essential was his role by the shore, a link between M. de Fleury and the boats. Only since the smoke from Hekla had thickened, he wished M. de Fleury would hurry.

Wiser now than the men on the ships, he didn't expect M. de Fleury to lead the way down the vale of the Markarfljót. Every year, in the dark and the snow, the farmers walked two hundred miles to the coast to greet the incoming cod, swarming to fatten and feed before spawning. And bad as that was, the subsequent easing of winter softened the bogs, and brought heavier spates from the glaciers. The safest way, of all the difficult passages, was the one M. de Fleury had already taken, following Kathi and her brother. Mixed with Robin's anxiety about his employer was a not dissimilar foreboding about Katelijne Sersanders. Even given the easiest route, you couldn't depend on either of them to keep out of trouble; and neither knew when to stop.

Robin had taken precautions. He had made sure that a boat was set apart to bring them back from the Thjórsá. All the fishermen knew to look out for them. Every traveller who rode in or forded the river was questioned. And just in case something went wrong, he paid a man at Hlídarendi, up the river, to watch out for news from the north. But M. de Fleury would only try to come down by the Markarfljót in an emergency, and the emergency was not likely to be created by Hekla. If there were any danger from Hekla, M. de Fleury would lead them all west, and hope to come back by boat as before. If Hekla exploded, its gas and ashes and lava would destroy anyone on his way south from Skálholt.

In the end, the tales that came from Hlídarendi were not about a band of rash travellers, but about the weather. There had been thunderstorms in the north, and rumours of earth-shocks. Also, as could be seen, the smoke from Hekla had changed. It seemed less than ever likely that M. de Fleury would try to come south the direct way. Time passed, and uneasiness lay over the settlement. Then, when the fleet came in at dusk, the men splashed ashore shouting news. A privateer had been sighted: the notorious *Charity*, with a reputation for stealing fish and attacking its rivals. Now they had man as well as nature to contend with.

It did not take them long to decide what to do. The fishermen of Markarfljót proceeded to pack up their stocks and abandon the station.

Part of the work was completed that evening, while the Englishmen were too far away to do harm. Robin helped. Already the sheer bulk of the catch was overwhelming; by the end of the season, every man could have his tail-mark on six hundred cod, to pay for all he must buy for a year. To have it seized was to lose life itself. So the fish were packed first, to be rowed up the coast and stowed underground inland, in safety. By the time darkness fell, many of the boats had already gone to the west and some of the huts were half empty. The *Svipa* knew what was happening. It was aware that its lifeline with Robin was lost. If it wanted his news, it would have to send its own skiffs to collect it.

That night, Robin was too tired to sleep. Like the others before him, he had been given a place in the cabin of Tryggvi, and had succeeded in lying alone without offending his daughters – an exercise in tact which his father had taught him some time ago. His father was always gentle with women; even unreasonable women like Kathi.

Thinking of Sersanders and Kathi, he remembered something Tryggvi had happened to say about the Icelanders' dislike of their foreign tithe-levying bishops. He had heard the same grumbling in Orkney, which led him to wonder whether the Bishop of Skálholt and Bishop Tulloch might not have much in common. It would explain how Sersanders had felt sure of a welcome in Iceland – a welcome spoiled by the Hanse-owned *Pruss Maiden*. Had the *Maiden* not arrived before time, the *Unicorn* might have expected to fish unmolested, and unmolested escape with her sulphur. Martin of the Vatachino was sharp.

He remembered other things Tryggvi had told him about Herra Oddur, the bailiff. Sersanders had wanted to go hunting gyrfalcon. He should have been stopped, Tryggvi had said. It was dangerous. There were bears about. One couldn't blame Tryggvi for obeying the bailiff and not staying at Skálholt. Fortunately, Robin himself had no conflict of duty to worry him. He would be of little use in a sea fight with the *Charity*. And if – when – M. de Fleury arrived, he would certainly expect his page to be waiting.

Forty miles to the north, in a basalt chapel the size of a hen-coop, the awaited party lay stricken with sleep, having launched on a journey none of the four would have chosen, however wild some of them were.

Left alone in the last hours of daylight, they had been forced to hurry through rivers and snow, to escape a night in soaked clothes in the open. They had also been forced to hurry by Nicholas who, abetted by Kathi, had transformed his fatigue into an antic simulation of energy which had astonished Glímu-Sveinn and induced the disgusted Danziger to compete, loudly complaining.

Even when tumbling, numbed, into the chapel, they had been given no rest, but had been set to finding writing materials. None was to be had. On their travels over the mainland, they had passed other churches like this, with the bowls of curds set on the altar and the stockfish stacked at the walls, together with the priest-farmer's boxes of tackle. Sometimes the pastor's own empty coffin would lie on the steps, prudently completed when wood could be had. Other mortals, with worse luck or less foresight, might be found at the back of the church, neatly stitched into wadmol and patiently awaiting the next season's timber.

There were no corpses here, which was as well, considering the building was eight feet in width, and only a small man could stand head unbowed. There was no paper either, and the only Gospel the altar produced was a heavy old block made of wood, on which oaths had been sworn long ago, Glímu-Sveinn said, when the real book had been stolen or rotted. In the end, apologetic in their necessity, they added the *Helga Bok* to the fire at which they were drying their clothing, and Nicholas knelt on the floor and scratched a map on the hide of his jacket, reaching from where they now were to the coast, and containing all the detail that Glímu-Sveinn could give him.

If nothing happened, Glímu-Sveinn said, it was possible – it was just possible – that they would reach Hlídarendi by the following evening. There was the Rangar river to cross, and its tributaries. There was rotten ground under the snow; unseen bogs; and new crevasses sprung by the shocks. There might be more shocks, and more thunder. And there was Hekla to pass, and then the *jökull*, the glacier which overlaid Katla.

'The Rangar,' Kathi said. 'It means the wrong-running river, because its bed has been distorted by lava.'

'I know,' Benecke said. Glímu-Sveinn had gone out to the horses. De Fleury had risen and walked to the back of the church, swinging the jacket. Benecke said, 'I had the happy idea that if all the rivers dried up, we could cross them. Our friend says that we could, except that the burning lava tends to flow down the river-beds. Is he a magician, or does he just think he is?'

'M. de Fleury?' said the girl. 'He found Sigfús.'

'So what is he doing now?' Benecke said. His arm was still sore, but he had got rid of his bandage, which he felt made him look slightly ridiculous. He was remarkably tired.

'I'm sorry,' said the girl. 'It seems to use up his strength. He either had to overdo it, or not get here at all. Tomorrow might be as bad. But we have to hurry.'

'So he's divining?' Benecke said. He began to get up.

The girl pushed him down firmly, on his sore arm. She said, 'If he's getting any good advice, I don't think we should interrupt him.'

'Advice?' said Paúel Benecke. Embroiled with lunatics, he was torn between impatience and curiosity. He said, 'He can get messages *from the ships?*'

'In their own argonaut,' the girl said. 'Very salty, some of the language.' She then relented, saying, 'You'll get more out of him, really, if you pay no attention. He doesn't like doing it.'

'What a pity,' said Paúel Benecke, his face bland. 'What else can he reluctantly divine underground? Alum? Silver mines? Diamonds?'

The girl laughed. Her skin was blotched with cold and folded into lines of exhaustion, but her eyes were bright as a monkey's. Nicholas de Fleury, also smiling, had come to stand beside Benecke. He said, 'Don't think of it. My fees are too high, and you haven't a chance of coercing me. But you may be glad to know that everyone, at the moment, is as you left him.'

The girl looked up. 'Robin is still on the shore?'

'Yes,' said de Fleury. 'So let's sleep. We have a race with the demons tomorrow.'

Benecke was sound asleep when, at the hour the Icelanders called *ótta*, Nicholas de Fleury silently rose and made his way out of the church. A long time elapsed. Kathi, accustomed to the courtesies of travelling, made no effort to follow until, lying there, she realised at last why he had gone. Silently she wrapped herself in her bed-fleece and went out.

First she saw the sky, covered by the stars the Icelanders used to count time. Among them was Sirius, which they called *Loki-brenna*, Loki's fire. Below the stars was the dim white of snow, and black against that, the stolid forms of the ponies. The Burgundian was standing beside them, his face turned to the south. She walked to his side and, pausing, looked at the same view: of the *jöklar* like clouds in the sky, ridge upon ridge, and above the furthest of them a sparkle, as if the fires of Loki were playing about it. The air was so still that the faintest grumble of thunder could be heard, even from such a distance. Katla, not Hekla. And from Katla or Hekla, the thing she had sensed, that had brought her out here in the first place. The faintest odour of sulphur.

She said nothing, but looked up at the singular, well-liked man standing beside her, and after a moment he returned the look with one of his own which bordered on helplessness, but in which rueful-ness also played some part, and regret, and awe, and – contradicting them all – a suffusion, bright as Loki's fire, of contentment.

Nothing was said. In such a silence, even a whisper would annihilate sleep. In any case, there was nothing to say. The danger was there and increasing – the sulphur betrayed it – but as yet no glimmer of fire beaded the sky; no fissures gaped; the only voice was a low one and distant: that of thunder. They had talked with mock solemnity of the Twilight of the Gods, of the fires of the damned; but if you had knelt at the altar at Sinai, and had stood where Moses stood, and had experienced, in a cold northern town, an exaltation of the spirit which, all unbidden, had carried with it the soul of a child, then you believed in one God and in submission to him. You also believed – contradictory as that air of contentment – that it was right to submit only when you had fought to the uttermost of your powers.

She had meant to say commonplace things: *If anything happens, I shall try to do my best for the child, and for Gelis.*

Then: *As you choose to do this, so Robin has chosen his way, and neither of you must regret what may happen.*

If I do not survive, make my uncle your friend.

And, of least importance of all: *Of course, Paúel Benecke is waiting to kill you. But he will want to do it in style, and you will probably stop him, one way or another.*

After a while it became cold, and she pressed his arm and went in. By dawn, they were all up and travelling.

To the leaderless Hanse ship and the *Svipa*, it was apparent under the same paling sky that the English vessel had approached through the night. The wind, now from the east, rose and died but provided some help, and their oarsmen had been working. Their course would take them to the north of the fishing grounds, which did not bring them close to the Hanse ship or the *Svipa*, but was still within range of their guns. They had sent no signals, although Crackbene had brought both his ships early from harbour and lay at anchor, ready for anything.

The *Pruss Maiden* was now armed. Lacking their master, the crew were far from anxious to fight, but they had been reminded often enough that Paúel Benecke's life depended on how well they acquitted themselves. And to see off the English ship, after all, was their duty. To make sure they understood this, John le Grant had gone over, with a handful of men, to work as sailing-master with Stanislas. He spoke fluent German, and was known by reputation to them all. Father Moriz stayed with the *Svipa* and Crackbene, and watched the sky to the north and north-east.

They had all seen the changes, even before the last of the Icelanders came to warn them that they were leaving the settlement. The young Herra Robin, they added, had refused to come with them.

Father Moriz was angry with everyone, and especially with Crackbene and John. The *Charity* had been here before: they would see the smoke, recognise the danger and leave. The *Svipa* should send a crew to the settlement to stay with Robin and rescue both Robin and Nicholas, if Nicholas came back by land.

'It is impossible to come by land,' Crackbene had said. 'Also, the Icelanders say the *Charity* has never seen an eruption and will attribute the fishermen's flight to their cowardice. They will be disappointed and angry. They will either storm the settlement, hoping for fish, or will try to attack and sink the Hanse ship in particular, taking her catch and destroying her witness. We can't afford to spare the men for a boat. And if Katla erupts, the boat would be commandeered.'

Then Moriz had asked: 'You say Hekla would kill. How would Katla erupting be worse?'

After Crackbene had answered, the priest sat silent for a few moments. Then he said, 'To avoid a death such as that, we should have to stand fifteen miles out to sea?'

'Or more,' Crackbene said. 'The decision is mine. There can only be one master on any ship.'

On the Markarfljót, the day began long before dawn, when the lamps were lit and the work of loading and disembarkation started again. It continued all morning under a thunderous sky, while the ether crackled like cannonfire, and the lightning played blue on the crests of the Eyjafjalla Jökull. Every now and then their breath caught with the smell of it. It smelled like gunpowder.

Every boat-load Robin helped to shove off tried to get him to come, and described what would happen if he stayed. He refused them politely, as M. de Fleury would have done. He considered, all the time, what M. de Fleury would do, and what a sensible man ought to do, and tried to follow the mean. Kathi, he knew, would concede, if with reluctance, that he was right. M. de Fleury was not a sensible man.

*

Commonsense tracks the way across deserts; faith and laughter sustain those who cross them.

Glímu-Sveinn had faith, and had prayed aloud at the altar before leaving the chapel.

> *'Almattigr Gud, allra stetta*
> *Yferbiodandinn, engla og thioda,*
> *Ei thurfandi stadi ne standir . . .'*

'It is from an old poem,' M. de Fleury had said, when Kathi asked. 'All-powerful God, Who presideth over all orders of beings, both angels and mortals; Who, independent of place and time, continuest undisturbed in Thy sovereign power . . . I ask of Thee, that in Thy great mercy, Thou wouldst grant me what I implore with a submissive soul –'

'A dish of beef collops with ale,' Paúel Benecke had interrupted. 'Since you're asking. Shouldn't we go?'

'When we've settled this wager,' had said M. de Fleury, staring at him.

For three of them, a dedicated levity was their chosen shield against what was to come. The fourth, being an Icelander, had his own form of strength, and was to show it on that first killing stretch which was to take them south to the farmhouse of Selsund, a halfway station where they could take time to rest. They each had three lean-bellied animals, economically laden; and must ride them hard over the snow-covered lava, for after Selsund was passed, the basalt ridges and the bogs and the Markarfljót would hinder all progress.

That was the plan. The rest was outside their control. The Hades within Hekla might explode, and send its flames down the mountain behind them. Ahead, the Plutonic cauldron within Katla might rise, and give its glowing carpet of ash to the wind. After Hlídarendi, the danger would be nearer and worse.

At the outset, M. de Fleury had claimed that the thunder was a stroke of good luck, since it would alert the fisherfolk to the danger of Katla. He said if they could smell anything, apart from each other, the stink of sulphur would be noticed as well. He said that if they had any sense, they would all get out to the west, including Robin. It annoyed her, since she knew he didn't believe it. She was arguing when the Danziger had interrupted.

'Excuse me, but are you proposing to call this man *M. de Fleury* throughout this entire journey? You realise he could fall into a crevasse while you are still pronouncing his name?'

She had, with annoyance, felt herself colouring. Then M. de Fleury had said, 'I think she thinks it's a charm against evil. She can call me what she likes.'

'Then for God's sake, tell her to call you the same as everyone else.'

'That wouldn't be very polite,' said M. de Fleury. 'I don't know why she doesn't call me Nicholas.' He addressed her mildly. 'Do you want to call me Nicholas?'

He had looked reasonably patient, and probably serious. Under the circumstances, it clearly made sense. 'All right,' said Kathi. 'It's shorter.' Then they were off. When she had breath at all, she tried to get used to it, while reviewing her precise situation.

They carried some hay, and had fed the horses from a small store they had found in a cave. They had kept the makings of one single tent and their survival supplies, including some oddments of dried fish and blubber, a lump of tallow and a flask of sour whey. Glímu-Sveinn led, followed by the head of the Bank of Niccolò, followed by herself, and with Benecke in the rear. His mount had a bell on its harness, the way they had in the Tyrol. M. de, now Nicholas, had lifted it from the church. He probably wished, Kathi thought, that he had crampons and snowshoes and servants with baskets of food and warm coaches on runners to meet him. Well, it had been his idea to come fishing for cod.

Paúel Benecke said, 'What are you grinning at?'

'Something Tryggvi-Sigurdsson taught me,' she said. 'Do you know the Icelanders make up lampoons they call *nídvísur*? *Rude* lampoons?'

'Oh my God,' said M. de Nicholas. 'All right. You begin.'

At the end, Glímu-Sveinn unexpectedly broke into a guffaw of appreciation and without prompting, launched into another. She didn't understand all the words, but she could tell M. de Fuf-Nicholas did. Halfway through, the skies emitted two loud reports, then a third, even louder. These were immediately followed by a flicker of horizontal blue light. Her pony laid back its ears and the one behind overtook her in a cloud of flying snow, stumbled, fell, and threw Paúel Benecke hard to the ground, thereafter tumbling itself and breaking a leg. Glímu-Sveinn got down and killed it, she didn't see how. Then he hauled the shaken Danziger to his feet, and with M. de dammit began to redistribute the baggage. It was done very quickly.

'Come on,' said M. de Fleury. 'The thunder's moving north and we're going south on our reversible hooves. It will be like Paradise in Hlídarendi.'

They remounted. Glímu-Sveinn placed the Danziger's new pony behind him and *Nicholas* rode behind her with the bell, which he had announced was an E. There ensued a profound discussion on the Icelandic Scriptures, which held (*Nicholas* said) that all boys were born tuned to A, while baby girls emerged squealing in E. Twins, he added, required resolution. He went on to mention that the inventor of harmony was Nibal, brother of the smith Tubal-Cain.

'Horse-shoes,' said Benecke, out of consideration, no doubt, for his feminine company.

'Nails,' said *Nicholas* dreamily. 'Five thousand, as I remember. No, I'm wrong. That was Tubal the Paralytic. Also Isachor, Architriclin and Eve. Eve, served straight from the rib with a fig-leaf. Glímu-Sveinn, I'm sorry.'

He shouted the last bit. He was sorry, it was all too clear, because he had allowed his pony to set feet on an ice slope. By the time his voice started to rise he had already failed to slew it round out of its slide, and it was slithering helplessly downwards. He fought for a few moments more, and then jumped for a pillow of snow, the reins still grasped tight in his hands. He held them as long as he could, then released them with a curse. It reached Kathi in an incomprehensible hiss like *No mattresses.*

Glímu-Sveinn, dismounting, ran forward. Kathi did the same and then stopped on the brink of what she found was the lip of a crevasse. The pony had slid to a halt on a ledge, and was peering upwards, its two forelegs scrabbling. Every now and then it licked at the rock as if hungry. Benecke said, 'Is it worth it?' Glímu-Sveinn, leaning down, had wrestled M. de Fleury to safety. Both their faces were blue.

'I think so. It shouldn't be hard,' the rescued man said, and trudged off to unfasten the rope.

He was mistaken: it *was* hard, and all of them were breathing painfully before the pony was finally back above, shaking, and *Nicholas* had mounted another. He had been right: they had lost one horse already, and their lives might depend on these creatures. To her narrow gaze, M. de never mind seemed to have suffered no disabling injury; or none worse than his captive, who was grinning again. She wished to God she didn't have to think what to call him.

They set off at a dangerous jog. The thunder delivered a sudden cannonade, and the lightning danced with reptilian flickers. She could hear it crackling. Above them, Hekla was releasing spurts of saffron and dusky brown smoke and, to a person of credulous disposition, appeared to be rhythmically changing its shape. Her head, but not her ears, received the impression of a cavernous sound: her throat was coated with sulphur. She turned her head to the Banco di Niccolò. 'So you cried in E.'

'That was the bell,' the Bank said. 'The As, the divine and *Almáttri Æss*, were all mine. The horse was a G.' The ground suddenly staggered, and his horse slipped and recovered, rolling its eyes.

Kathi's mount jibbed and she controlled it. Her back ached, and her thighs were chafed raw. Glímu-Sveinn said, 'I do not think we should waste time at Skard. I think we should make straight for Selsund.' He had a harsh voice.

Selsund, when they reached it, was deserted. Stiff with cold, aching from the difficult ride; filled with apprehension and unpleasant vapours, they dismounted with resolute badinage, built a fire, and found a pot in which to simmer a snow-broth. Kathi's eyelids started to droop. Then the cauldron gave a loud rattle and she jerked awake once again, until the shaking petered out. Paúel Benecke said, 'We are halfway to Hlídarendi. We could probably outride an eruption by now.'

'And if Katla also breaks open?' Kathi said.

'People survive. They speak of wooden churches swimming whole out to sea. You will rejoin one of our ships. Come to Poland.'

'I didn't know you were necessarily returning to Poland?' Kathi said.

'You know of someone who could stop me? Your brothers are children.'

'Brothers?' said Kathi.

'Your merchant friend thinks of you as his brother. Didn't you know?'

She was so pleased that she felt herself flushing. Then she caught the Danziger's expression and laughed aloud. 'Sergios on horseback. It's only an allusion.'

His annoyance visibly deepened. He said, 'Then I have no rival? All the simpler. Come to Poland.'

'You have no rival,' she said, and showed him a smile of genuine and unaffected goodwill. 'Paúel, you are not in the race.'

Chapter 29

IT WAS AN EFFORT, when they had eaten, to leave the shelter of Selsund and, laying sodden gloves on freezing harness, to face the white, ice-bounded wastes of the south.

The wind had dropped. The dark smoke behind and the white that rose far ahead now climbed straight into the air before spreading. Before they left, *Nicholas* had peeled off and slung down his jacket, and made Glímu-Sveinn point to the route he expected to follow. It was no more than a guess. On the gouged and rock-scoured area they were entering, there would be water everywhere. At the end, Kathi had said, 'Where is Robin?'

Benecke, fastening his coat, had glanced at her sardonically, and she was sorry she had asked. But after only a moment, M. de Nicholas said, 'He is still on the shore.'

'And the ships?' Benecke said. 'Surely you can tell us what has become of the ships?'

M. de Fleury looked at him. 'Only that the people I left are still there,' he said.

'And Hekla and Katla?' the Danziger persisted. 'If you can find water underground, can't you tell what is rising?'

'Maybe,' said M. de Fleury. 'But what good would it do if I did?'

He had turned then and mounted. It was a precise answer, whatever Benecke thought. He and the Banco di Niccolò were committed to the men on their ships, trapped there awaiting them. And it was too late for the Icelander and Kathi to break away on their own. The pendulum had been consulted, and had spoken, and she knew what it had said.

This time, by request of the Icelander, she rode in the front by his side, instead of behind. She forced herself to speak, gathering together her scraps of the language. '*Glímu* means wrestler, doesn't it?'

He didn't look at her, only at his pony, and the ground ahead.

'*Já*,' he said. And after a while: 'It is a good sport. It is what we do on the strand, when the weather is too bad for fishing. We wrestle, and race. There is plenty of daylight in the summer.'

'And in the winter?' Kathi said.

'Ah,' he said. 'Then there is none at all, or very little. That is how the storytelling began. When darkness falls, we sit on our mattresses in the bed-hall and work and tell stories. I work my loom, and Hristin my wife riddles the straw from the eider feathers, and my sons cut up ox-hides for ropes, and my daughters sew.'

'You read and write,' Kathi said. 'Great writings have come out of Iceland.'

'Once,' Glímu-Sveinn said. 'Once, when farmers were rich, they travelled often to Norway and Denmark, and their sons were educated there, and others were taught by the priests. Now it is only the foreign officials who can afford to be educated, and some of the priests cannot write. We teach ourselves, when we have oil for the lamps. Fortunately, all men have memories.' He paused. 'I would ask you something, Junfrú Katti.'

'Of course. Ask,' she said. He had turned. His face was withered with cold, his shallow eyes icy blue.

He said, 'Is it good magic, that your friend has? He says that it is. Do you believe this?'

It was the question occupying them all. There is a grammatical right, a geometrical right and a theological right. And there is the enigma of Nicholas de Fleury. She looked Glímu-Sveinn in the eye and said, 'I will answer you when you tell me what you were doing outside the farmhouse at Selsund.'

Their ponies slithered and trudged. Hers pecked, and his hand came out to steady it. A veil had dimmed the horizon, as if the thunderstorm had overdrawn the day's light. Glímu-Sveinn said, 'We are a Christian country, but there are spirits older than Christ. Some places are known for them. If I have a little extra whey, or some tallow, I leave it.'

'His magic is good,' Kathi said. 'It found Sigfús. It has found others. It is good because Nikolás-riddari did not seek it, and does not want it, and uses it only out of necessity. His chaplain permits it.' She didn't mention divining for metals. She hoped he would remember the effort it had taken to find Sersanders and Sigfús.

'I see,' said Glímu-Sveinn. 'I thought perhaps he was like Sorcerer-Hedin, who was *skoll-víss*, deceitful, and could be hired to cause death; but perhaps he is more like Gunnar Hamundarson. You have heard some of our stories?'

'Who was Gunnar Hamundarson?' Kathi said. She glanced round briefly. Behind her, an approving Bank jerked up one of its borrowed four thumbs.

'A fine man. His home was in Hlídarendi, where we are going. They say he sits there today, chanting inside his burial mound.'

'How did he die?' Kathi said.

'They winched off the roof of his farmhouse and killed him. He was the dearest friend of Burnt Njall. You know Njall's story, *nei*?'

'Tell me,' Kathi said. There were five hours of daylight still left. Or less, of course, if either one of the mountains gave way. Enough to get to Hlídarendi, and hear Gunnar singing inside his grave-mound, but not enough to get to the shore, and Robin, and safety. They had to live through the night to have a chance of that.

Glímu-Sveinn told his story, his voice jerking and hoarse in the absolute silence. She strove to follow it. Behind her, the two men were silent. She supposed Glímu-Sveinn had taken on himself, for the present, the role of entertainer to give them a respite – and also, Kathi thought, to bring back to mind those firelit winter days with his family, with the busy hands of his sons and his daughters about him. She glanced at him now and then, but he was always looking ahead.

That was the good part. Very soon after that, there was no room for tales, for the obstacles in their way were increasing. At first, they tried to circumvent the abrupt gullies, the fierce narrow streams and the bluffs, returning when they could to their route. Then a sigh and a whine brought a gust of frolicking wind and a haze of snow fine as dust, which forced Glímu-Sveinn to dismount, for both landmarks and track were now masked, and there was no chain of immaculate cairns in this tumbled and changeable territory, where even magnets were useless.

For a while the Icelander walked, probing ahead with his stave. Time went on, and the snow-haze persisted. Finally, he halted and pushed back his hood. There was snow on his cheeks as well as his beard, and his pursed lips were blue. He said, 'We can go on, or we can dig in until it clears.'

'Will it clear?' Benecke said. 'In time to reach Hlídarendi before dark?'

'It would have to clear at once, and even then one could not be sure,' said Glímu-Sveinn.

'Then surely it is better to go on?' Benecke said. 'You are a man of this country. Even blind, a man can tell where he is by the wind, by the light, by the slope of the land. Nikolás-riddari?'

He was not at once answered, and when the other man spoke, he seemed to be thinking. He said, '*How lovely the slopes are.* But here they alter, and so does the wind. In the desert, a blind man uses his nose. We can be guided by the smell of the sulphur.'

'And by your magic,' said Glímu-Sveinn. 'If it reads true. Can you
not tell where to go?' The wind wailed.

'That isn't fair,' Kathi said. 'We are all tired.' It disturbed her to
have him called a magician.

He was already answering Glímu-Sveinn, his voice even. 'I don't
know Hlídarendi. I can take you, without deviation, to the person
waiting at the mouth of the Markarfljót.' He paused and then repeated, '*Without deviation.*'

Glímu-Sveinn put his hand on the saddle. He said, 'Not even an
animal could travel blind from here to the delta. Ravines and rivers,
ridges and crevasses stand in the way.'

'But an animal, even blind, could pass from here to Hlídarendi,'
Benecke said. 'The terrain is easier, is it not? And Hlídarendi is on
our direct route to the mouth of the delta. If Nikolás uses this
instinct, he could guide us as far as Hlídarendi by nightfall. And then
tomorrow, when we can see, we can cover the worst twenty miles to
the coast.' He looked round. 'We have nothing to lose. I propose that
we start, with Nikolás in the lead.'

'No!' said Kathi. She knew the concentration it needed. His senses
fixed on the distance, he couldn't look out for himself.

'*Nei,*' agreed Glímu-Sveinn. 'He and I will set off together, linked,
and leading our horses. The spare horses follow. The *junfrú* rides
after, and then Herra Paúel with the bell.'

'You need a bell for the leader,' said Kathi.

'We don't,' said the Banco di Niccolò. 'The leaders will proceed on
their own, singing versicles. Or *nídvísur*, if you prefer it. Let us
begin.'

'Wait,' said Kathi. She dropped from the saddle and stepped
through the snow to Glímu-Sveinn. He had pulled forward his hood.
She took his two thick arms in her grasp and kissed him. '*Benedicte,*'
she said. The snow from his beard brushed her face; he kissed her in
return, the courteous Icelandic salute, his hands on her shoulders.
Then she turned and went back to her horse.

'Now me!' called Paúel Benecke from behind, but she didn't look
round, although she raised a glove in cursory acknowledgement.
They had been joking, and would continue to joke, however little she
trusted him. But whether you believed a diviner to be god, or man, or
to possess the worst features of both, the person bound to him was
staking his life, his one ordinary life, by that deed.

At first, it seemed as if they had made the right choice. After a slow
and anxious beginning, the wind dropped and visibility returned, and
with it their landmarks. It was evident, too, that the violence within

the two mountains was still contained: the smoke was no worse, and the underground movement had ceased, as had the thunder. For a while, the earth seemed to have recovered its voice: the ponies snuffled and blew, their shoes thudding in snow and rapping upon the bare rocks; at one point they heard the croaking of ravens.

Twenty-four hours had passed since the field of the hot springs had become silent. She had thought, as anyone would, that the danger would steadily escalate, but Glímu-Sveinn said that sometimes the shades below could not make up their minds as to which fires to stoke, or decided to tease, by alternately fanning and choking them. He said, however, that once such a force had begun, it could not subdue itself for very long, and that the outcome would be all the more violent. They must not be deceived into stopping.

He had hardly spoken the words when the wind rose, this time from the east and the south, and bringing sulphur mixed with fresh snow. Behind her, Kathi heard Benecke swear, but Glímu-Sveinn simply dismounted again and paced forward, shafting the snow, his head bent to catch the level, spaced observations of the diviner. There were three hours of daylight still left.

It happened twice more, the second time as they were fording a wide, shallow river. A short while before that, two of the ponies had fallen and been unable to rise, and of the nine they still had, none had strength for more than a short spell of riding, and all were weak-footed and worn. All of them baulked at the water and had to be beaten down the steep rocky bank to commit themselves to the stream. M. de Fleury said, 'They have to be whipped, for their lives and ours. We have an hour to do it in, Kathi. Glímu-Sveinn says we are near.' Then she helped him.

The snow came just as they entered the water. The two banks disappeared, and all that could be seen was the dark water racing, with the white snowflakes dancing above it. She had early been taught not to look at fast water, but there was nothing else to fix her eyes upon here, and the bottom was full of ruts and loose stones, threatening to turn her ankle as she felt her way over. The current coursed up to her knees and her thighs: she was already soaked to the waist, if not numbed. Glacial water would have been a really bad joke; the Bank said: 'God be praised, *not* a jökulár river.' She had expected the Hanse to respond, and he hadn't. Now she called, 'Where is Paúel?'

They were almost in midstream; Glímu-Sveinn, wading ahead, had his arms through the reins of two ponies and was roaring at three more who were plunging and scrabbling at his side. She had her own; behind, the Banco di Niccolò was dragging two more. Of Benecke, his horse and his bell there was no sign.

Glímu-Sveinn turned round, with difficulty. He bellowed, 'Shout! He is probably over the river.'

'I didn't see him,' said M. de Fleury.

'Then leave him,' said the Icelander. 'You think this is bad? Wait until there is snow and no light.'

'All right. Take the *junfrú* ahead and I'll follow.'

'We need you,' said Kathi.

'Not now. Hlídarendi is not far away. Even blind, Glímu-Sveinn can make his way from the river, he tells me. Anyway, I'll be back before you get all the ponies to land. Take my two; let them swim. And if you find Benecke on the other side, shout.'

'No!' said Kathi sharply. Ahead, she could hear the Icelander cursing. Suddenly, there were two horses threshing about at her side and she could see nothing but a receding back, the snow closing about it. The Banco di Niccolò, ridiculously going back to trace and rescue the Hanse because, despite everything, he rather liked him.

Ahead, Glímu-Sveinn had discovered a shoal and was standing in it, the water up to his ankles. Five of the ponies were scrambling up, shaking, beside him. As she prepared to address him, she observed the water actually recede from his island, so that the Icelander was standing dry-shod, looking astonished. He looked astonished for a brief moment more; then with a roar he dived fully clad into the water. The horses jostled and scattered into the shallows.

Where they had been, with a rumbling crash a jet of steam rose in the air, almost as white as the snow-clouds. She was still looking at it when Glímu-Sveinn seized her ankles and, bringing her down under the water, pushed her with him, half under, half out of the river back to the bank they had left. There, taking her full weight in his arms, he wrestled her to the top of the slope where, choking and retching, she turned to look back.

Thick as the trunk of a tree, the cascade stood in the heart of the river. The steam, transformed into blistering rain, fell scalding back to the cold rushing water. She heard the screams of the ponies and the hissing splash as they plunged off downriver. Breathing harshly, Glímu-Sveinn was half sitting beside her. She looked up at him, gasping, and saw him staring over her head.

A single pony stood further along the same bank, its reins dangling, its drooping head turned from the snow. Below it, someone seemed to be sleeping. She saw it was M. de Fleury, his soaking coat already patched with red slush. She struggled to her feet and went over. He was not sleeping or dead, but had been knocked momentarily unconscious. As she watched, he started to stir. His knuckles were reddened.

A man shouted, in German. 'Are we not lucky, dear maiden? Another moment, and we all might have boiled. As it is, you have come back to succour us.'

Paúel Benecke, who hadn't crossed over. Paúel Benecke, seated not far away on the snow, his eyes bright, his bandages red with fresh blood.

She plodded up to him, dripping. 'Do you think so? What happened?' she said.

He raised his voice. 'To poor M. de Fleury? It seems that my pony thought he must be a water-horse, and gave him a kicking. I expect he will live.'

She said, 'The pony kicked you as well?'

'We all became excited,' he said. He had to shout over the roar of the water. He was yellow above the black beard, and for some reason, she perceived with satisfaction, he seemed unwilling to walk. She thought she knew what had happened. She also knew which patient most deserved her attention. She turned, ignoring Benecke's plaintive mock protest, and expecting to see Glímu-Sveinn already helping M. de Fleury to sit.

Instead it was the reverse. The Icelander remained crouched where she had left him; motionless, his fixed gaze on the ground. And it was the injured man who was holding him, murmuring.

She could not hear what he said. The ground drummed under her feet; the air shook with the roar of the river, and the boom and hiss of the rocketing spout. Kathi stumbled down and knelt by the farmer. He looked the way a man looks when his heart has failed. She cried, 'He carried me over.'

'You couldn't have stopped him,' M. de Fleury said. His face was pale, and there was blood in his hair, but his voice was quite clear. 'Glímu-Sveinn, what do you feel? Does it hurt?'

The beard lifted. It might have been a nod. His eyes turned up, and he made a sudden, lumbering movement that threatened to tear him out of their grasp, but M. de Fleury held firm, and together they laid him back on the ground. Kathi said, 'Let me look.'

He was unconscious. She rested her hand at his neck and his wrist as he lay. She said, 'His heart is beating. A flutter.' She had seen enough doctors at work. She did what she had seen others do, and M. de Fleury sat back in silence and let her. She wondered, as she worked, whether they had done this for the poor throttled baby, Margriet's baby. She was reminded, not for the first time, of the bear-cub under the snow and banished the thought, as before, to the recess where it properly ranked. M. de Fleury rose and limped across to the Danziger. Because of the noise, she could not hear what he said. In a while he came back and dropped down with caution beside her, touching the cheek of the fallen man, and then his pulse. The beat was stronger.

He said, against the noise, 'What do you think?' There was no need to say more. They had a stricken man on their hands, perhaps a dying one.

She had begun to think, as he had. They had both hardened their voices, to carry. She said, 'There's one horse. You take it. I shall stay with him.'

'No, you won't,' said M. de Fleury. 'There is a cavern back there, in a boulder. I'm packing the bastard into that, with some comforts he doesn't deserve. Then you and I get on our way.'

She scowled at him. 'And Paúel Benecke? What happens to him?'

He stared at her in his turn. 'Who in hell do you think I am talking about? Benecke, the bastard that just tried to kill me. He can't walk – I can't think why. He can wait in the cave till he's rescued. The new geysir makes a fine landmark, and if another breaks out underneath him, they can boil him and serve him with garnishing. You're riding the horse, and I'm going to strap this fellow on it behind you. All I wanted to know was if he was dying.'

'And then you would have taken Benecke in his place?'

'Are you joking?' said M. de Fleury.

The snow had stopped. Duty sent her to visit Herra Paúel Benecke in his cave before she departed. To her prejudiced eye, he appeared to have many more comforts than he deserved, including a mattress and a garment of M. de Fleury's own, but not the hide coat. He wore, in addition, an insolent grin.

Kathi said, 'Whatever happened to you, you deserved it.'

'It was worth trying,' he said. 'You couldn't persuade him to put the old man in here, and take me?'

'No,' she said.

'But you won't forget to send someone back?'

'If there is anyone left to send,' Kathi said.

She said it jokingly. Furious though she was, she left without destroying his hopes with the truth. They had no guide from now on, only a senseless man strapped to her saddle. Now they had to rely on themselves to follow that primitive scratched map on the jacket; to distinguish the mountains of Thríhyrningur and Thórólfsfell and look out for the canyon of Bleiksárgljúfur; to make the appalling journey alone in failing light that would take them at least to Hlídarendi. Nor did she tell him the worst news of all. Robin of Berecrofts, said the pendulum, was no longer at the mouth of the delta.

It meant, at best, that the ships were standing off out of danger, and had taken him with them. It meant, at worst, that when they reached the coast, there would be nothing there.

They crossed the river lower down where, her companion said, the water promised to be pleasantly warm without skinning them. He guided the pony while she walked with the Icelander's stave; and she helped haul the beast up the opposite bank. She was not sure when she had ever been so tired in her life, but there was no point in saying so.

There was no sign of the ponies. Steam drifted down from the spout, and the gulley carried its roar: they still had to speak with raised voices. Apart from one joke, neither mentioned the cascade again. If it could happen once, it could happen again under their feet. When they had at length reached the height of the bank, she did look across to the three peaks of Hekla. The smoke was still brown. It seemed to her that there was a glow at the base, but she might have been mistaken. Then they had to climb.

She knew then how tired he was, too. Glímu-Sveinn had brought them over the terrain, but it was the remorseless concentration of the diviner which had guided them through the fogs of blown snow, and kept them moving always surely south. She had already realised that, without Robin to act as his magnet, M. de Fleury would in future be powerless. But meantime the landmarks were there to be read, and they must do what they could.

She had never before embarked upon a sustained and dangerous trial in partnership with one person. Illness had taught her endurance, and her travels in Sinai had tested that same endurance in different ways. In the four years of her intermittent acquaintance with Nicholas de Fleury, she had observed and enjoyed his preferred methods of relieving boredom, or reassuring the insecure, or exposing to ridicule any obstacle unfortunate enough to stand in his way. It had not occurred to her that he would not work with a partner as he worked with a group, some of whom he wished to keep at a distance. She had competed with him in sport several times, and at games and in song. She had touched, mostly by accident, upon moments of both violence and tragedy in his life, including the death and presumed death of two women, and the recovery of his son. As a result (she had been told), he thought of her as a young brother.

In fact, he did not treat her as either young, or a brother. He talked as to a partner, and entirely about what they were doing. She saw that he had made a practical compound of their assets: her lightness and speed; his strength, so long as it lasted, and his experience from his months in the Tyrol and from the mountains of Asia and Italy. She let herself fall into his way of discussion, light, economical, and to the point, which provided its own stimulation without any painstaking banter. Problems arose, and were solved.

She was able to ride very little. Burdened with the unconscious man, the pony had to be coaxed down the icy sides of a gorge, and up through the opposite ledges. It could step from rock to rock with precision, but would not jump over a chasm. At times, she protected the Icelander with her arms as the pony scrambled about, and wondered if he would not have been better off in the dark and peace of the cavern. But Paúel Benecke was not a man to waste time over a farmer and, given the chance, would see to his own safety first. She had little compunction over Paúel who, if he were found, could wield all the authority of the Hanse. And if Hekla burned, he would be as safe as they were.

They lost a great deal of time circumventing a bottomless creek which, alone, either of them could have bridged or leaped over. There were two streams to cross, neither as wide as a river, but fiercer. Early on, they had achieved a physical congruity not unlike, she thought, that of a small team of acrobats, from which the horse was not excluded. Their limbs, their shoulders, their combined motive power were all part of the machine they had assembled to take them alive through this journey.

Agile and slight as a marmoset, she explored for him, using him as a ladder, climbing over his shoulders to test some high crumbling spur. In his turn, when the leap was too great or the water too violent, he carried her in whatever unorthodox way allowed him to manage the pony. Their hands in their soaked gloves gripped and grasped one another and they smiled, even though it was painful to breathe. She was too tired to remember what she was to call him, and so called him nothing at all. She kept watching what his beard revealed of his face, but his eyes remained clear and intent, although their setting was chipped out of lava. He was extraordinarily even-tempered. As darkness began to come on, and over and over again they were baulked by some hazard, he simply evolved different plans, and she abetted him.

Soon it was apparent that they were not going to reach Hlídarendi. Also, as the snow around them grew dim, she saw something else. Beneath the seething smoke-clouds of Hekla, a smouldering glow had appeared in the vacant dark sky filled with silence. Very soon after that, like a monster disturbed, the ground beneath their feet grumbled and stirred, and was quiet. With one accord, then, they stopped.

He said, 'So the secondary plan. We have ten minutes of light. We gamble on reaching Hlídarendi, or we use the time to dig in where we can.'

He didn't have to expound. If an eruption took place, they would be as well or badly off here as at Hlídarendi. In any case, the farmhouse at Hlídarendi, though providing comfort, would be deserted. By now, everyone within reach of both mountains would have left. Robin had gone, and at least the ships had received some sort of warning, if not the one they had striven to bring them. Now they had no one to think of but themselves.

She said, 'The pony is failing.'

He said, 'Then we look for some shelter.' On his own, he would have taken the gamble, she knew. So would she. But to lose was to find themselves caught in the cold and the dark with a sick man who could not survive it.

They found a place just in time: a flaw in the lava, half tunnel, half cavern, and dry beyond the drift of blown snow. As they were lifting the Icelander down from the pony, the animal dropped. She knelt beside it a moment, then unstrapped and brought over the saddle to where the sick man was lying. His eyes were closed, but he was breathing. When she came back with the saddle-turf, her partner had made the leather into a pillow, and laid his jacket over the man. She said, 'We can burn the turf now.'

'Ah,' he said. 'Poor little pony. Well, now he has a life after death. He will make a warm bed, for a while. He will give blood to mix with our whey; we need the warmth and the nourishment. And if the lava entombs us, we can skin him and eat him before we start on each other.'

He had begun to move Glímu-Sveinn to lie in the curve of the horse's round belly; she helped him. He said, 'I'll unpack and get stones. We'll light the fire and block up the entrance, once the light goes.'

His coat had been stained with Paúel Benecke's blood. His rough tunic beneath was also stained. She said, as they worked, 'What did Benecke do?'

'He thought I'd come back for him alone. He had a few stones, a bit bigger than this. It was to look like a drowning.'

'He liked you,' she said.

'But he didn't believe that I'd free him. He's proud of his reputation.'

'*Vanitas*,' Kathi said. 'So what did you do?'

'I had a few stones as well. Now he is alone, and we are not, and that is all the difference, really, between us.'

His voice receded. He had walked to the mouth of the cavern, now a deep purple-blue against the black of the walls. She sat where she was, on a bit of turf, because her legs didn't want to walk any longer. She saw him in silhouette, leaning against the dark rock. She said, 'Is he all right?'

His head turned, a change in the outline. 'Who?'

'Jordan,' she said.

'Oh. Yes,' he said. 'And Gelis.'

She said, 'What is it like? When you concentrate?'

'Exhausting,' he said, with a half-smile she could hear. Then he said, 'No. Warmth. I can feel him.'

She said nothing. He added, still with the half-smile, 'With Gelis, it is just exhaustion. But that is because her thoughts are concentrated on me. Hard to circumvent.'

'But she can't tell where you are? Shouldn't you teach her?'

'Goodness, no. It's my strongest weapon,' he said.

She waited. If he wanted to speak, then he would. Later, he might come to be sorry. In the end he said nothing, but presently turned and made his way back to the invalid's side. He lowered himself down beside him and took up the tinder. It was so dark they could barely see one another. He said, 'There are things better unsaid. You never speak of your parents. May I ask?'

'How we came to be with Uncle Adorne? It's no secret. My mother fell ill when we were young. Not a family illness: the kind that comes with great pain, and destroys all the power to reason. She was like my uncle before that, fair and graceful and kind. My father couldn't bear the change, or us, reminding him of her. It was best we leave Ghent.'

He said, 'I don't remember you. I remember Sersanders in Bruges.'

'I wasn't born when you first came to Bruges. I don't remember you either. A name. Claes. It annoyed Sersanders, that you always seemed happy.'

'I'm glad I annoyed him,' he said.

After a while, she said, 'What was your mother like?'

It sounded callow: the remark of a child. It was, she had long known, the most important question anyone could ask of Nicholas de Fleury. And she had earned the right to ask it.

Apparently he recognised that as well. He waited, but in the end he replied. 'Loving. Terrified. Sad.'

'*Terrified?*' she said. She could hear her own horror.

He said, 'You know Jordan de Ribérac.'

She couldn't ask any more. She knew Jordan de Ribérac, after whom his own son had been named. He did not speak again.

She closed her eyes. When she opened them, it was upon the ruddy light of a fire: sparkling buck-bean turf stuffed between a glowing heap of small stones. There was a folded cloth between the dirt floor and her head, and her own coat, dry now, was tucked in around her. The light flickered on the shape of the horse, and the form of Glímu-Sveinn lying against it. She could hear his uneven breathing.

Closer than that was a hand, slowly stilling something bright on a cord. She said, 'Don't stop. If you must.'

He lifted his head. She wondered if he had slept, and thought not. She wondered whose minds and hearts he had been visiting. Did they know? Did Gelis ever feel her husband's thoughts touching hers, day and night? He had said hers were on him, which made his task in some way more tiring. She wondered if he had ever had cause to trace herself, or Sersanders, or her uncle, and found the idea both unflattering and hurtful. She gave him credit for realising this.

He said, 'I have something to tell you.'

She knew before he spoke, because she had heard it. 'Katla?' she said.

'Yes. You can see the white of the steam, even from here. But something else.'

Glímu-Sveinn was alive. She said, 'What?'

He lifted his hands. There was blood on one finger. He said, 'I remembered to ask the right questions. Kathi, Robin is near.'

His face, his voice said it all, good and bad. The boy was alive. By coming to find them, the boy had thrown away his own chance of survival. She said, 'How near?'

'Quite close. Kathi, he can't find us. I can find him.'

'In the dark?'

'It isn't dark now,' he said; and rose, wincing a little, to his feet. 'Come and see.'

She went out. She faced west, and saw above her the ink-blue of night. She faced north, and a lantern hung in the sky; or it might have been the basket balefire of a castle, or a burning thicket of thorns that threw off a continuous low sparkle of red, but yet was not consumed. Above Hekla floated crimson-lined clouds. Below floated the shoulders and spires of snowy eminences, all frosted like sweet-meats with pink.

The south was different. In the south, a field of dazzling white champignons ripened and burst in the dark. Beneath them was a point of red light.

She said, 'It has begun. How long before they erupt?'

'I don't know. I'd rather leave now. And I'll be quicker alone.'

She said, 'Well, at least you don't have to bother with food. Take the stave. Take your jacket. Glímu-Sveinn will be warm enough now.'

He was going on foot. His special sense wouldn't show him the route, it would simply take him direct as a bird to the boy. There were no birds to be heard now, unless the iron-beaked ravens were there, attentive and hovering. And although there was light, it was little enough to show the way to a man who could not fly. A man whose feet were torn with lava, like hers, and who was almost too tired to walk.

She prepared and gave him a stirrup-cup, with plenty of blood in it: the first genuine *hesta-skál*, he remarked, that he had ever been offered. Then he smiled at her and, bending, gave her the courteous Icelandic kiss on the lips. '*Guds frida veri med ydr*,' he said. The peace of God be upon you. 'I will be back.' And he left.

Glímu-Sveinn snored. The fire burned for a while, and she used it to attend to his comfort and her own, and to warm some of the drink for herself. When the last flame flickered and died, she gave in at length to her anxieties and, wrapping well, slipped from the cave.

Outside was a wonder of light. One by one, the seams of Hekla's dark garment were bursting apart to expose the living core. The flames, higher now, were both yellow and red, pushed about by the curdling smoke, and their light flickered and streamed over the ghostly beds of the snow. Now the air shook with the sound of muffled explosions; now there resounded a group of ringing reports, upon which the golden spray rocketed. *Colpito*, a hit.

If the north was crimson and gold, the south was a shimmering miasma of white, drifting steam shaken by sudden explosions, and stained with darker effusions shot with red. The distant concussion from both labouring mountains was almost continuous, as from a battery of John le Grant's guns, or the noise of a crowd watching Florentine football, or of an audience roused by a play. There was thunder pealing in the steam above Katla, shot with blue light.

Thunder-makers need not be gods, other people could do it as well. Copper sheets; carbon powder. Vif argent for silver; pigments and resin and gouache for colour and glitter. White lead and red ochre; sheets of glass; gilded tin; turf to pack round the traps, or the geysirs. Two little bellows for Hell. Eleven innocent dolls for the Massacre.

She had read the bills of lading. They did not actually reproduce, in any play she had read, the scalding torrents that would presently flow; the rumbling ocean of fire that would appear on the ridges above her and crawl thickly down; the clouds of brilliant dust that would darken the stars, setting light to her clothes and her hair. But men could create them, of course, if they tried: Negroponte; Constantinople. A diadem for God, and wine for the actors.

She thought of the man who had left her, taking his own life in his hands to turn a boy back to safety. She was aware that he would not think in those terms: that before the spectacle of the night, he would be no more capable of reasoned thought than she was; but would be riveted, despite all the horror, by the greatest performance in which he would ever take part, with the gods themselves as Masters of Secrets. She guessed he wished there had been music.

She knew he would try to come back. She thought of the Icelandic:

> *All ills shall cease;*
> *Baldur shall come . . .*

So they said of the White God, Baldur the beautiful, destroyed by Loki and waiting through all eternity for the call that would summon him back. They didn't say it of a clever enigma whose chief achievement was to have founded a Venetian bank. The word of his death would travel quickly: to Venice, to Rome and to Bruges, to Brussels and Brixen and Bourges. To Cyprus, where he had almost tamed a young king. To Timbuktu, and a tomb. To Edinburgh, where he had a son. The Banco di Niccolò is dead, and shall not come again.

She was standing there still, unaware of the cold, when above the grandeur of unearthly percussion, she heard the rattle of harness, and turned.

Dark on the snow, jogging across the ridges below her, were ponies. A dozen, twenty; their riders cracking their whips, their torches streaming innocent light, Baldur-light.

One rider led. One rider, familiar with the route, came racing over the snow and drew his mount to a quick halt on seeing her.

Her reason told her it would be Robin. Then she saw that Robin was there, far behind, his face lit as bright as the torches. But the person who was standing here in the snow was her friend.

She ran towards him then, surprising herself and probably him; impelled by a surge of heart-felt fervour which moved her to fling her arms round him and cling, her cheek deep in his stained sheepskin coat. She clasped him, and he in turn closed his own arms about her, her head under his chin. Swept together, they sank comfortably into one another, and she felt him for the first time profoundly relax, as a warm and loving friend might.

There was nothing to put into words. His embrace said it all: his safe, indestructible grasp, his secure hands. When in the stillness she began to draw breath, it was not to overwhelm him with speech; only to utter his name – so difficult, recently, to remember.

'Oh, *Banco*,' she said.

She was so close, she felt the spasm that developed into a hiccough of laughter. His clasp broadened. Then he set her away from him, his palms on her shoulders. She laid her hands fast over his.

Somewhere in the sky to the north, there was a crackling roar, and their faces were lit by the flame-gush that followed. He released her softly and said, 'We must hurry. Glímu-Sveinn? We have a litter, and men to take him.'

She said, 'He's still there. I'm so glad. What about Pauel?'

Robin had come. He said, 'One of his own men is here. And two Icelanders, who have been offered a boat if they find him.'

'A boat?' Kathi said. 'I thought all the yoles and doggers were spoken for.' Her eyes were on her friend, her halting friend, who was pulling over a horse.

'An *English* boat,' Robin said. 'Wait till we tell you.'

Katelijne Sersanders carried only a half-memory of the torchlit ride to the coast beneath the greatest display of pyrotechnics she was ever to see in her life. She was surrounded by familiar faces. When she could no longer bear to touch the ground or the saddle, they wrapped her in fleece and handed her from man to man through the night like – like a bear-cub. For seamen, they were uncommonly tender, but the grasp was never the one that she sought. When she asked, Robin said, 'M. de Fleury is here. He is safe. He is quite tired as well.' It made her sick, to think she could be so thoughtless. She didn't ask for him again, although she looked about when they arrived at the shore and waded out to the skiffs that awaited them. One of the skiffs did not leave, because it was waiting for Pauel.

The Mouth of Hell opened when they were a long way out to sea, and the glacier over Katla lifted its city of ice into the sky. Rowing, they watched, and Kathi watched with them.

Now, you could no longer diminish what was happening by translating it into human dimensions. This was not a play. This was the hurling into the sky of thousand-ton blocks of ice, glinting and roseate in the thundering night. This was the discharge of millions of gallons of boiling water, plunging down from the mountain in a wild dashing glitter, outrunning the billows of its own pink-flushed steam. This was a spectacle of red and gold flames, of spinning fire-balls, of swathes and columns of sparkling ashes and sand. This was the crack of thunder and the roar of explosions and the massive, evil susurration of the deluge, continuous as the hiss of the sea. This was the Twilight of the Gods.

Nicholas watched it begin from the strand, where he had forced them to lay him until the last boat should leave. Kathi and Robin had gone. Glímu-Sveinn was safe, on his way by boat to where his family sheltered. He had wakened once, from the turf bed they had made for him, and had peered about, frowning and mumbling.

'Well, old man,' Nicholas said. 'Odin heard you, or some other god. And there is a purse in your shirt, to show that foreigners can even be grateful. Get well. Ask your wife to forgive us.'

He did not know if he was understood, but he thought so. When his time came to go, the Icelander looked at him, moving his hand, and Nicholas stretched over, smiling, and took it in his own lava-flayed palm.

After that he lay still, drifting out of consciousness; awaking to the grinding cramps of his over-strained body, the burning pain of raw flesh in his hands, his limbs, the soles of his feet. Iceland and Egypt. His eyes were open when they brought Paúel Benecke down to the beach, the excited voices loud with relief in the reddening light. They carried him across in a cloak; he was yellow with pain but grinning crookedly still below the black beard. 'Nikolás! I hoped never to see you again. Are you dying?'

'Ask me tomorrow,' Nicholas said. 'If you can.' The earth wavered and shook; he could hear the rumble of another explosion beginning.

Benecke turned his head. 'I mustn't keep you. You know, I didn't expect you to save me? Why did you?'

'I don't know. I wanted a favour,' Nicholas said. He watched them place Benecke in the skiff; then they came back for himself. As they left, the glacier rose into the sky, filling the air and the sea with its light, and the numbing roar followed.

There was a long way to row, for the *Svipa* had anchored many miles from the shore, the Hanse ship alongside. Benecke had fallen silent. Nicholas drifted into some form of awareness, his half-open eyes resting on the spreading glory before him.

In the presence of that, everything he had ever done appeared futile – even the music, the Play, the one private creation into which he had poured all that he had, for its own sake alone. Or so he had thought, until Gelis had shown him that it was only a refuge, that was all. And a tempting one, for someone brought up as he had been. An easy way to learn to love power. And so he had fled, seizing upon this venture in Iceland; this chance to return to the anonymity of the machine. He had destroyed all John's pleasure, and Roger's, by acting as if the Play had never been.

Iceland should have been simple: some hard work, some hard play, a little trickery, and he would have returned with his load, having executed his personal plan, and bested a rival or two. But Katelijne had come, and he had had to place her and her brother in safety, and then go to recover them. Otherwise he would never have been on the mainland of Iceland at all, or here when this happened. Otherwise he wouldn't have burned his fingers, yet again, on an instrument that was not meant for him; that was tuned too high, and too low, and demanded more than any human being could give. The music he wanted to live by was the safe, mediocre span in the middle, where nothing would tear him to pieces; neither a black country, nor a white. And even if he didn't think so; even if he decided to burn and be damned, it was useless. Nothing, nothing in all the world could match the wonder of this.

There was no one to whom he could say that. Or no, perhaps one person: Katelijne Sersanders. He still would not say it. He smiled, as the journey ended and the ships loomed ahead. He knew what her first words would be, speaking in awe of tonight. There should have been music.

Part IV

Summer, 1472

THE MULTIPLICATION OF PAINS

Chapter 30

AMONG THE RICHER class of dealers and traders, the disappearance of the principal of a bank in search of profit is not a matter of immediate concern. His non-return, as weeks go by, creates anxiety. The owners of banks obviate this, where they can, by the dispatch of consoling reports to their agents. From Nicholas de Fleury came nothing for four wintry weeks. And the message that did come, in the end, was carried by no agent of man, but arrived as dust on the wind.

Nicholas had taken certain precautions, but it had not been his intention, setting out, to unsettle the market by dying, or by occasioning rumours of death. By the end of the first week in March, his own counting-house in Bruges knew where he had gone, and the news spread to the financial arms of the French and Burgundian and Angevin courts, and thence to their princes. Captain Astorre heard, and was impressed. Anselm Adorne learned of it as he stepped from his vessel at Sluys, but did not even reply to the man who hurried to tell him, however unexpected the threat to the *Unicorn*. He had other things on his mind.

The relatives of Gelis van Borselen wondered if she were about to become a rich widow, and whether they would be expected to find her a husband. The vicomte Jordan de Ribérac sent a message by one of his ships to Madeira. It said:

I think you may now come home. Your late wife's good-brother would appear to be either lifeless or greatly subdued, and I should value your presence in Kilmirren.

These reactions were however highly subjective, and the business of the Bank was not, in such a short time, disturbed. Indeed, the news had no time to reach Venice and activate the orders Nicholas had so judiciously sent there before he left Edinburgh. That is, Gregorio would have hesitated about carrying them out. Julius would have obeyed them regardless.

In Edinburgh, closer to events, the merchant class evinced a
guarded interest in reports of the venture; interest which blossomed
into a worldly-wise pessimism when members of the Berecrofts family
were not within sight. The magnates, pursuing their own affairs and
the affairs of the country, said little, although individuals tended,
with the passage of time, to find themselves closeted in contentious
dialogue with their King. Mistress Clémence de Coulanges, in the
High Street, watched the lady Gelis respond to the waiting, while
ushering the lady's son, with a firm hand, through the character-
threatening perils of convalescence.

Pasque, who had made herself reprehensibly absent during all the
first stages of illness, recovered her nerve as soon as the spots began
to disappear, and was to be found several times a day hopping,
juggling or playing tunes on the comb for the edification of young
Master Jodi as a kind of atonement. The offer to send her to Dean,
where the Countess of Arran's two children were equally smitten,
had also had some effect. For a while, Mistress Clémence had expected to see Bel of Cuthilgurdy, the elderly lady who had a kindness
for the sick boy. Instead, it turned out that the lady had generously
offered her assistance to the Countess at Dean, where Mistress Sinclair, they said, was overworked and short-tempered these days.

Mistress Clémence listened to everything, and permitted the
younger gentleman of Berecrofts to visit the sickroom when he came
to call on the Lady. Jordan reminded him, she thought, of his son.
Master Roger also came once, with a very small kettledrum. He was
not invited again.

Then the *Unicorn* sailed into Leith, and Master Martin of the
Vatachino rode into Edinburgh looking, they said, as if he had swum
all the way from the North Pole himself, but openly triumphant. The
Cologne merchant Reinholdt was with him. Naturally, they went to
Adorne's house to begin with, for Martin still had to make his report,
even though Adorne was in Bruges, and his nephew Sersanders, it
seemed, had elected to remain temporarily in Iceland.

After that, word of what had happened in Iceland did not take long
to spread. First, that the Vatachino had achieved a brilliant if oppor-
tunist success, not only bringing back their great vessel against the
most vicious odds, but having as cargo the finest quality of Icelandic
sulphur, to be sold off in Bruges as soon as the ship was in a fit state
to take it. The partners in the *Unicorn* venture were rich.

The rest of the story, picked up by Pasque and conveyed to
Clémence, was one that merchants avoided when speaking to Gelis
van Borselen, although the news would reach her eventually. Many
people had seen Master Martin marching down to the Canongate to

burst into the Banco di Niccolò where, it was said, he had stormed at de Fleury's man for an hour.

By nightfall, everyone knew what Nicholas de Fleury had been up to in Iceland: preserving his own illicit cargo, in return for exposing his fellow-Burgundian's ship to the Hanse. Further, he had caused the *Unicorn* to run on the rocks, from which it had only saved itself by a miracle. The last seen of the same Nicholas de Fleury, Martin was happy to say, was gun to gun with the Hanse ship the *Maiden*, whose captain Paúel Benecke had a sharp way with a person who didn't deliver.

'And the little maiden? Katelijne Sersanders?' had asked Mistress Clémence, hearing it all from the voluble Pasque.

'Ah!' said Pasque. When she said Ah! in that fashion, Mistress Clémence always wished she had not asked.

'Ah, the poor silly child,' said the woman. 'They have attempted to hide it, you know. They would like you to think that she stayed with her brother. But the girl ran away on her own, and was with M. de Fleury for six days, before her brother went to persuade her to leave. He never returned. They are at the bottom of the sea with M. de Fleury. Will our terms of employment remain the same?' Pasque said. 'The Lady might even want to increase them.'

That was on Tuesday, the twenty-fourth day of March. For two days the lady Gelis stayed at home, save for one visit to the Bank at the Canongate, and one to the house of Adorne, where she heard the account, in person, of Master Martin. During that time, she behaved as she usually did, although her complexion was pale, her eyes darkened, and she could not disguise her disinclination for food. The household were proud of her stoicism and served her in whispers, even though it was not absolutely sure that M. de Fleury was dead.

On the third day, in a fashion no one had contemplated, the doubt was resolved. An English privateer, foundering off Dunbar, had been seized as a prize and brought into harbour, where it was discovered that this ship also was returning from Iceland. If the state of the *Unicorn* was bad, it was a wonder that the *Charity* had stayed afloat at all, with her strakes splintered with balls, her sails patched and both her boats missing.

Half her crew was missing as well. According to Jo Babbe, her master, she had sent two boats to make a peaceable landing on Iceland, when she had been set upon by the crews of two skiffs from the *Svipa*, the vessel of Nicholas de Fleury. After some severe fighting, the Englishmen had been tied up and handed to Icelanders, the two boats confiscated, and a message sent to the Hull ship advising her to get off at once, reinforced by some shots from a cannon. Without a proper crew, they had been unable to respond and without boats they could hardly go fishing. They had turned and sailed off, intending to demand compensation from the Banco di Niccolò.

'They'll be lucky,' had said Govaerts, arriving from the Bank to report to the lady Gelis. The words sounded more defiant than flippant. He was nervous. Mistress Clémence, who had been asked to remain in the room, saw her employer observe it and brace herself. The child was not present.

Then the lady Gelis said, 'You did not come to tell me only that.'

'No,' Govaerts said. 'I have more news. I should not have believed it, except that I went and saw for myself. The ship, the *Charity*, is covered with ash.'

'It happens,' Gelis said. 'They use Greek fire in fighting.'

'*Covered* with ash,' Govaerts said. 'Not consumed. It began to fall as they sailed south, so heavily that the sky was black as night, and they could not see one another twelve inches apart. Before it fell, they saw the mountains of Iceland explode. The flames rose so high, Babbe says, that they saw them two hundred miles off. They fled because of that, not only because of the *Svipa*.'

'And the *Svipa*?' Gelis asked.

'Remained behind with the Hanse ship, the *Pruss Maiden*. They were waiting, it seemed, for word from on shore.'

'Both of them?' Gelis said.

'Babbe didn't want to confess it, but apparently both the *Svipa* and the Hanse ship had sent to attack him on shore. Both ships were still in good order. If they had fought one another, the fight had been stopped, or resolved.'

There was only one question to ask, and for a long time, she did not ask it. Then she said, 'For whom were they waiting?'

By then, Mistress Clémence knew that the reply was one that Govaerts was unwilling to give. She did not realise, until she heard it, how bad it was going to be.

Robin of Berecrofts had taken part in the fighting on shore and when it was done, had ridden inland with men from both ships. For M. de Fleury had not been on the *Svipa*, nor had the girl and her brother. All of them were in the interior of the mainland with the Hanseatic master Paúel Benecke. And they were still there when the mountains exploded.

'I am sorry,' Govaerts said. 'But there has to be hope. The ships would not leave until M. de Fleury and the others were found.'

'But the ships themselves may have burned,' Gelis said. Then she said, 'When will we know?'

Govaerts said, 'Eric Mowat is on Orkney. As soon as he is sure.'

'How will Orkney know something is wrong?' Gelis said, and then stopped. 'Ah. The ash.'

'Swift as the wind,' Govaerts said. 'I have to ask you. Would you like to come to the Canongate house, and wait there for news? Your rooms are there. The Berecrofts family are waiting as well.'

Clémence sewed, jabbing and jabbing. Then the Lady said, 'I think that would be best, of course. Thank you. Jordan can stay here with Mistress Clémence and Pasque. Do you not think so?'

She was asking Clémence her views, and Clémence agreed, her voice quiet. The child was her charge, not its mother. And she thought, once the word travelled west, that she might have company in any case very soon.

Because Govaerts was steward and manager both, the house and bureau of the Banco di Niccolò in the Canongate was as impeccable when Gelis came there that Friday as it had been five weeks before, on the February day when Nicholas and young Robin had left. Before she went to her rooms, she walked with Govaerts through all the offices, showing Nicholas's household and clerks that she was not distraught, but was waiting with patience for news, as they were. Showing them, in case they feared for the future, that she was not merely a cipher.

She had thought, of course, of what would happen if Nicholas was killed before their mutual game came to an end. She had achieved some of the objectives she had set herself that wedding night, awaiting his step on the stairs, although they hardly mattered if he were not alive. There were some hurdles, some traps she had prepared and fiercely wished him to face. Now he might not. She could not complain. She had taken a gamble that the game could be played, rounded off, and completed; if it did not do that, she had lost everything. But then, so had he.

She thought of the girl Katelijne, and the rumours. The priest was there, and could scotch them, but she was sorry, for the girl's sake. She was sorry, for several reasons, that the girl had gone to Iceland at all. But she was certain beyond possible doubt that Nicholas would neither have touched her, nor allowed her to be touched. It shook her sometimes to see proved, over and over, that in this, the one glorious indulgence he had always permitted himself, Nicholas could will himself to abstain.

There had been only one exception she knew of, and that had been Simon's wife, her own sister. But Kathi was not Katelina. Kathi was bright. She liked to parade her independence, but she would never – could never arouse him. Gelis was indifferent to Kathi. Her anger sprang from the knowledge that twelve years ago Nicholas would have abstained, had the young Katelina not possessed the looks and the art to seduce him. Katelina, however, could not have kept him.

She did not sleep. She heard the cavalcade as it swept under her window from Leith Wynd, and even heard the crash of Berecrofts's door as it was flung open. Then it was upon her own door that someone was hammering.

Archie of Berecrofts stood outside, with Govaerts half dressed beside him. Archie said, 'There is a ship in the road. They think it may be the *Svipa*. Dress. I'll take you.'

She dressed, and had to stop to retch even though there was no food in her stomach. She had thought she did not care. She was wrong.

The ship was still in the road by mid-morning, when she reached Leith along with Archie and Govaerts and all those who could be spared from the Banco di Niccolò. It was raining, with heavy gusts from the west – one of the reasons why the vessel was sheltering in the midst of the estuary. A boat waited to take them all out there to join it, so this time she did not have to play her part for the crowds on the jetty. Even if royalty came, she would see Nicholas first.

The crossing was rough. Govaerts was sallow. Berecrofts said, 'I'm sorry. Will the motion disturb you?'

He, too, looked sick, but with the pallor of strain, emphasised by his natural fairness. She thought of Simon, and of Simon's heir Henry, and compared that spoiled brat with the thoughtful boy that Robin had become; and the sickly wooer in Flanders with this kind and courteous young merchant, no older than Nicholas, but free of that furious dedication to excess.

She reassured him, and smiled as best she could while she kept her eyes on the ship. A three-masted caravel, heavily down in the water, with two ships' boats also sluggish behind her. Men in the rigging. Men lining the poop, the forecastle, the waist, but too far away to be recognised. Then beside her, Archie suddenly moved. He said, 'It is the *Svipa*.'

A moment later he said, 'He is there. Robin is there.'

She was not looking at Robin. Her eyelids fluttered. Her eyes, blurred with rain, peered at each glimpse of the ship, with its beading of blockish forms and pale faces. Her gaze, but not her mind, registered the red hair of le Grant, the short priest, the big Scandinavian Crackbene, the beardless young face, yes, of Robin, the flying hair of a girl. They had pulled off their caps and were waving them.

Her mind and eyes together saw Nicholas, standing at the furthest end of the poop. He had not uncovered his hair but she recognised him, as she had recognised him under the archway at Hesdin. And she knew, distant from each other as they were, that his eyes were on her boat, and that his gaze was only for her.

She pressed her hand on Archie's shoulder, and stood. On the ship Nicholas hauled off and semaphored with his hat to no one in particular. Then he made a single extravagant gesture which seemed to include all his people, the ship, and the cockboats.

The gesture said, *Success, riches, victory.* His face, and the faces of all they could see, now coming fast into focus said, *We are tired to death, and we have seen things we do not yet wish to speak of. But we are here.*

She sent Archie first up the ladder. Moving past the boy, entwined with his father, she stood before Nicholas, and, as once before, found herself without words. This time, returning her gaze, he did not taunt her. Instead, placing his hands on her shoulders, he bent his lips to her mouth, then removed them. He had not kissed her on the lips for four years. He had embraced her only once since their marriage. '*Ey*', he said, with one dimple.

Behind him she saw the girl Katelijne, her eyes twinkling. There was no malice in her face, or in that of Nicholas. His lips had been chilled; the contact had been of the slightest. Some sort of token, a gesture, a wry joke. Except for the look in his eyes.

They crowded together for the sail into Leith. The ship ploughed into the waves, and everyone shouted. Listening, Gelis learned something at least of what had happened in the north. The role of the *Unicorn* was not entirely made clear, nor did the sardonic references to the *Maiden*'s Paúel Benecke in any way agree with what Martin had told her. It seemed that Benecke had also been rescued, and the two ships had sailed for some time in consort. According to Robin, they had played competitive havoc when storm-stayed in Orkney. She stopped listening after a while, the better to scrutinise Nicholas.

He had not been desperately ill, and he was not seriously damaged, it was clear. But eight days before, she did not need the priest to inform her, he had not been capable of sailing this ship. And the girl Sersanders, despite her animation, was visibly weak.

Her brother, it seemed, was still with the Icelanders. 'He is safe. They will send him back with some ship. You didn't bring Jordan?' Nicholas asked.

They were temporarily alone; the ship was preparing to anchor. She was herself again, too. She said in a low voice, 'You don't know what has happened?'

He was watching Crackbene, Eric Mowat. He transferred his attention. 'Don't trouble,' he said. 'I know Jordan has been ill, but not
gravely so.'

Unchastened, she returned to her usual voice. 'It was the water-
pox. He's better, but house-bound. Will you come to the High
Street?'

'Later. Would you wait for me there? There are some things I
must do.'

She understood. His cargo was fish for the Low Countries, and the
faster the delivery, the higher the price it would fetch. Victualling and
repairs would have to start straight away, so that the *Svipa* could set
off tomorrow. She said, 'The *Svipa*. A suitably menacing appellation.'

'I know. Childish,' he said. 'I decided to change it last week to the
Merrybuttocks. We held a ceremony of re-dedication off Nólsoy.'

'Oh,' Gelis said. 'It doesn't seem much of a change. Will it
translate, do you suppose, into Venetian?'

'It won't have to,' Nicholas said. 'It's staying in Scotland. The
King has promised to buy it after this shipment. He's always wanted
a fleet. He'll probably call it *The Lion*.'

'You don't *want* it?' she exclaimed.

'I don't need it,' he said very reasonably. 'I should have the Danzig
ship soon, Merrybuttocks Two or Four, and they're building me
more in the Arsenal.'

His gaze had shifted to the shore, where she saw a flag had
appeared. As once before, Alexander Albany had rushed down to
meet him. She saw Crackbene was grinning.

Enlightenment dawned. She said, 'You're not coming to Edinburgh
at all. You're going to celebrate your arrival all night at the King's
Wark, or Lamb's.'

He half pulled a face, but his eyes were still elsewhere: on flaming-
haired John, on the Russian oddity and his son, on the infamous
Dane. 'We have something to celebrate,' he said.

'And spend the rest of the night in a bawdy house?'

Now he was paying more heed. He said, 'Leith does have the best.
And really, I *am* thinking of you, as you noticed. I hope to return to
my patriarchal commitments shaved, clean, freshly attired, and professionally reduced to that state which will least discommode you. Do
you mind?'

'I am glad to hear it,' she said. 'Will one night be enough?'

Father Moriz returned with her to Edinburgh, carrying Katelijne
Sersanders on the saddle before him. Behind her rode Archie of
Berecrofts, his voice lifted, as if in protest, to Robin, his son. He said,
'I am proud of you!'

'I couldn't stop them,' said Robin.

The *Svipa*, now the *Merrybuttocks* (Nicholas having spoken the actual truth), sailed with Crackbene the following day, leaving behind it a number of persons in precarious health. Among them was the musician Will Roger, who had added himself to the festivities at nightfall; and who now took Nicholas under his charge.

'When is your first meeting?'

It was then an hour after noon. 'Now,' Nicholas said.

'Who with?'

'With the King.'

'Sandy will tell him. When he sees Sandy, he'll know not to expect you. Do you know he's written to the Pope about suppressing Coldingham Priory? I'll get my choir. You'll get my choir. Never mind. Do you want to go home, or to your bureau? Do you want Govaerts to report to you first?'

'He has,' Nicholas said. 'He brought me clothes, too. Willie, would you just say nothing and get me up to the Castle? I want to change in your rooms, and drink all your beer, if you have any.'

'Beer?' said Willie.

'I got used to beer,' Nicholas said shortly. 'The sophistications of travel.'

His protector's silence lasted all of ten minutes.

'Do you want to stop?'

'No,' said Nicholas.

Seven minutes.

'Talking of beer. Was it true you became friends with Paúel Benecke?'

'Yes,' said Nicholas. 'Apart from the fact that we each had a good try at killing the other.'

'Oh,' said Will Roger. 'Maybe you won't get your Danzig ship, then.'

'Maybe I will,' Nicholas said. 'If he knows what's good for him.'

'Oh,' said Will Roger.

Five minutes.

'Was that true what you did to the Hull ship? What did you call them? The Chinchins?'

'I didn't fight the Hull ship. John and Moriz.'

'Whoever. They took away their cocks and their fokkes and handed the crews to an Icelandic harridan who'd already captured and kept English prisoners?'

'As John said. Willie, I don't want to talk about it.'

'You wouldn't let me play my drums either. What's wrong with telling the story? You've had a great victory. You'll have to talk about it up at the Castle.'

'You didn't see it,' Nicholas said.

'John described it. You all did. You saw off the Hanse; you saw off the English; you nearly saw off the Vatachino. And you come back with a treasure in stockfish. Why not bang your own drum and mine?'

'Because God's drums were better,' Nicholas said.

There was a silence. Surprisingly, Roger had understood. He said, 'You mean when the mountains exploded? But they all got away. They had warning. It wouldn't harm anyone. A few fish.'

'They fled where they could,' Nicholas said. 'Our ships carried them, too. But the old and the sick and the young wouldn't all get away. No one knows where the lava is going to burst out, or which way the rivers will flow, or how the scalding water will fall from the glacier, and where it will pour out to sea. When the ash comes, it sets light to everything. The sheep burst into flames. Women run about with buckets over their heads, trying to herd in the beasts. But even the families that we saved couldn't take their livestock with them. And when the water enters the sea, the fish will die too.'

'Nicholas?' Roger said.

Once he couldn't start. Now he couldn't stop. 'They say, after the last time, that the rivers and sea were full of boiled bodies, fish and human, jostled together. So there will be no fishing this season, and no moss and no hay and no grazing, therefore no sheep and no cattle for milk and for meat, and no horses to load up or ride on. And they can't expect any help from King Christian of Denmark, who has had to pawn away Orkney and Shetland already, and who can't even protect them from Jo Babbe.'

Roger said, 'Would he sell Iceland to Scotland? Is that what you are going to suggest to King James?'

His voice had become very quiet, for which Nicholas was thankful. He let time pass, and not only because he was feeling unwell. Eventually he said, 'Scotland couldn't afford it.'

Then Willie Roger looked round and said, 'Well, you'd better get down, if that's what beer does to you, and get rid of it.' He waited and said, 'What's wrong? It wasn't your fault. There is nothing you can do for them.'

'No,' said Nicholas angrily. The anger was not against Willie Roger but himself, because when he made a plan, he liked to stick to it.

In honour of a few of his other plans, he sent a message, before he presented himself at Court, to Mistress Clémence at the house in the High Street. At the Castle, he was taken immediately to the monarch's private apartments in David's Tower. He was received in the room with the canopied chair and grandiose fireplace, generally used to impress personal heralds and foreign magnates of the medium rank.

Beside the King was his brother Sandy, suitably sobered and changed into jewel-buttoned velvet, as was Nicholas. Seated elsewhere in the room were my lord of Caithness, once Earl of Orkney, Lord Hamilton, and his own landlord, Semple of Elliotstoun. Among the King's chamber men standing behind was Andro Wodman, Scottish Archer. The Queen was not present, nor was the King's brother John, Earl of Mar. Nicholas made his required bows and waited, while the King examined him from the chair.

James, Third of the Name, would be twenty quite soon, and the months were firming his face and lining the over-dry skin, though he still sat on his cushion like a youth who preferred tilting or hunting to dealing with papers and numbers. Since the Play, his way of speaking to Nicholas had changed, but it was five weeks and more since they had met.

He said, 'Master Nicholas of the Unicorn, we warn you to have regard for our nails. Every nail in this room has been counted.' He then burst into laughter, politely echoed by the elders in the room, although Sandy, origin of the anecdote, merely grinned.

Nicholas said, 'Sire, your nails are the Nails of Divinity, sacrosanct as those pinning Thor's shrine. I bring you a gift, which I have left in the hands of your steward; and also news of a good venture.'

'A gift?' said the King, and waved to have it brought in. It was a pretty sight: white fox furs and swan feathers. It was of course designed to pass from the King to the Queen. Then that was over, and they let him sit down and relate the long tale of the voyage. He was good at it by now.

With James, the gift; then the story; then the business. The lords, aware of what was necessary, were patient as well. Only at the end did Nicholas describe his cargo, and William Sinclair sat up. 'Fifteen hundred pounds' worth of stockfish!'

'Thanks to you, my lord. Without the dogger and yoles, it could not have been done in the time. The fish are already dried, and fit to travel anywhere. I have unloaded what was ordered at Leith, and the rest is already on its way.'

'And you say there was no trouble?' said James.

'The Hanse ship was not, of course, happy with the situation, but I was able to arrange, I think, that there will be no complaint. It has returned to Bergen with a full cargo.'

'And the other ships?'

'The Baron Cortachy's ship, the *Unicorn*, was somewhat resented by the Hanse and also by the Icelanders, but managed to escape, as you know, with a load of sulphur. I rather think,' Nicholas said, 'that an accommodation had been reached with the local officials, and in particular with the Bishop. I did not pursue it. One would not wish to offend the Church. I am not sure, however, if they would be welcome again.'

'And the English were pirates and cannot complain. While you, of course, had our personal sanction in our capacity as a son of Denmark. That may now be ratified.'

'My lord,' agreed Nicholas humbly.

'And the share of fish we agreed on be apportioned.'

'My lord, it has been arranged already. Also, the ship will be yours as soon as she has delivered her cargo. I am honoured to think that she comes to you bearing a victory.'

'Ah,' said the King. He looked about. No one spoke. He said, 'You are a Burgundian, but your Bank's clients belong to no single country. You lease your army to Duke Charles, but it has done little that I have heard of. A whisper has reached me that you have been received at the French Court, and have even discussed a possible contract.'

'I rarely listen to rumours, my lord King,' Nicholas said. 'But it is true that I try not to discriminate. You are speaking, perhaps, about Brittany?'

'You have heard of our own glorious plans,' said the King. He was flushed. 'We have always hoped, as you know, to lead an army this summer to France to aid King Louis in taking back his Dukedom of Brittany. Now Parliament has voted the money, and the Lord Monypenny has come to assure us that in return for our help, a portion of Brittany will be ours. Your ship, therefore, is of great value to us.'

'I am honoured,' Nicholas said.

'But equally,' said the King, 'there are new financial commitments which I had hardly contemplated when we spoke of this last. Briefly, I have no money with which to pay you.'

Nicholas manufactured an expression of pain. It was not very hard. He added some meekness, and a good deal of perplexity. He said, 'Then, my lord, I do not know what to propose.' He didn't suggest waiving the price. The King knew what he owed him already, and so did he.

There was a silence. Then Semple said, 'My lord King. If I might make a suggestion?'

There was no such thing as walking alone down the High Street to his house. Apart from the escort which had already attached itself to him, he had accumulated a scurrying crowd by the time he came to his front door, and had to waste time answering questions and throwing remarks to them all. Then he managed to enter. The porter knew him these days. He did not try to see Gelis, but went at once to the rooms where Jordan was.

The boy was there and awake; the nurse had got his message. The boy rose very slowly from his play and stood looking, unsmiling. It was the first time Nicholas had seen his eyes full of anger. He thought that they had probably succeeded, if the child felt sufficiently safe to show what he felt. He felt the gaze of the nurse on his face.

The child's skin was sprinkled with blotches. Nicholas said nothing of them, but kept his own face open and pleasant, dropping comfortably on his hunkers. He said, 'Maman kept telling and telling me to come back. I should do what I am told.'

'I do what I'm told,' Jordan said. After a while he said, 'What were you doing?'

'I was buying fish for the King,' Nicholas said. 'I saw a white bear and some falcons. If I didn't have to come home, I could have caught one for you.'

'I could catch a falcon,' said Jordan.

'Could you? Then perhaps you should come with me next time. All I could get you was this. I had a horse. This was my whip. See, the handle is carved from the bone of a beast called a whale. Hold it.'

Jordan held it. The horsehair, dangling, lay on the floor. He moved it up and down, hissing. Mistress Clémence said, 'Master Jordan rode with the family at Dean Castle. He had to borrow a whip.'

The wooden horse he had painted was quite near. Nicholas perched on its back and said, 'Come. Show me how the whip works.'

Soon after that, the child settled quite naturally on his knee, and began to ask the first questions, and then to chatter. Mistress Clémence moved back and forth, fetching milk for them both, and poking the brazier, and finally sending Pasque for the tub and undressing the boy for his bath while the conversation went on. Then at last, sitting wrapped in a towel on his father's knee, Jordan said, 'Poem.'

Nicholas said, 'I like hearing poems.'

'Poem,' said Jordan. And struggling down, he stood, breathing heavily, and recited.

It was a long poem, and although he hesitated once, he remembered it all.

Nicholas stared at him with vast and clown-like astonishment. 'Now that,' he said, 'is the longest, finest, best-spoken poem I have ever heard. Are you really Jordan de Fleury?'

'Yes!' said the child. He jumped up and down, making noises.

'Yes, you must be. And here is Mistress Clémence so proud, and I am proud, and so will maman be, when I tell her. And now I suppose I will have to take you sailing with me on my new ship? Do I have to?'

'Yes!' shouted the boy.

'With me and maman and Mistress Clémence and Pasque?'

'Yes! Yes!' screamed the boy.

'And what do you think the ship should be named? What is my name? What is your name? Should the ship be called the *Fleury*?'

'He will never sleep,' the nurse said, over the squeals.

'Yes, he will,' Nicholas said. 'For we are not going sailing just yet, and I am going to bed too, and in the morning I shall still be here, and I shall come and see him. *If* he has gone to sleep.'

He saw the boy placed in his bed, and the nurse followed him out of the room. She said, 'He is very young to take on rough seas.'

He smiled. 'I'm not proposing to go back to Iceland, Mistress Clémence. I hope you have no objection to a summer in the Low Countries, while I look after some business. My wife will be with us, and my step-daughters will be near, among others. He can have a pony, if you think he is ready for one. But there is time to plan: we shall be here for another three weeks at least.'

'He is a good boy,' she said.

'I can see that. And you have been a good friend to him. Thank you.'

She went back into the room. Limping to the head of the stairs, he thought again how skilful she was at not asking questions. He hoped she didn't really know how he was feeling. And now he had to go and see Gelis.

He took out a lion, tossed it, and clapped it on the back of his hand. A sound made him look up. Mistress Clémence, bearing a lamp, had emerged from the boy's door again and was looking at him with curiosity. He said, 'Face or pellet?'

'Face,' she said at once.

It was face. 'Damn,' he said. 'I have to stay sober.'

Gelis was reading. Gelis was wearing a night-robe he had cause to recognise, and had unbound her hair, so that it fell over the silk, wheat on ivory. Her skin was flushed from the warmth of the brazier, and the lamp on its stand at her side glowed on the cushions, the carvings, her thin-fingered hand on the vellum. She wore several costly and beautiful rings. The lamp-oil was scented.

'You should try halibut-oil,' Nicholas said. 'Or fulmar. Very easy to repel people with fulmar. Were you expecting Simon or someone?'

Her eyes were *jökull* colour, and patient. 'This is how I always retire. You wouldn't know.'

'And that is true,' Nicholas said. 'I have just told Mistress Clémence that we shall be leaving for Flanders by the end of April. I have to see to the business and settle Astorre.'

'I hope you asked her if the arrangement would suit her?' Gelis said. 'She is an excellent woman.'

'I did, and she has agreed. You have no option,' said Nicholas, taking a seat uninvited. 'Apart from anything else, I hear that the good vicomte de Ribérac has set free his impetuous son. Simon could be back in Scotland by May.'

The artifical surprise covered, he thought, a real one. She said, 'I thought you didn't mind if we resumed our affair?'

The doublet irked his bruised skin: he pulled open some of the buttons and relaxed, clasping the cords of his shirt to his chest. 'I thought he wanted to kill you,' he said. 'But you may have more recent advice. In any case, I'd prefer to be present. In the same country, that is. Otherwise people would watch you too closely.'

'So he and I have to wait until winter?' she said. 'That seems a little unfair, after last night. Who was she?'

'The connection of a frequenting man. No one you know. It was all done, as I said, for your benefit. May we move on to some planning?'

'You are lying. Why?' she said.

In fact, he was not. He stared at her until he thought her colour changed. Then he said, 'Why was that so important? It doesn't trouble me when you lie. You detest Simon, and if you aren't frightened of him, you ought to be. You made him look like an idiot.'

'But you'll protect me when we come back in the autumn. Don't you know,' Gelis said, 'how hatred and love come together? It might be dangerous.'

'I know,' he said. It was a general affirmation. It amused him to see that it made her first flush, and then become very pale. Then he turned the talk to the humdrum matters of their exit from Scotland and he saw her engage her intelligence. She understood the importance of Burgundy to their future. The supreme importance, if the Duke were to obtain the sovereignty that he wished, and the Emperor were to support him. Then bankers would come into their own.

At the end he stood with an effort. 'Thank you. I must go to bed.'

'You are short of sleep.' She rose also. 'How do you know you can afford a new house in Bruges? Beltrees must have emptied your purse, and I don't see the King rushing to repay your investments in Scotland.'

'Ah. You saw Beltrees,' he said. 'I am sure Bel displayed all its advantages. How shall I pay? You forget the stockfish.'

'But,' Gelis said, 'that depends on the market at Bruges. And Bruges is nervous over the Hanse, and might even refuse a cargo of pirated fish which has deprived the Hanse and cheated the King of Denmark of his taxes.' Her voice was mild, and her eyes were *jökull* colour again.

He said, 'Bruges refuse me?'

'Bruges. Reinforced by the opinion of one of the Duke of Burgundy's principal councillors, and of the new Conservator of the Scots Privileges in Bruges. A recent appointment by James your young royal friend,' Gelis explained. She refolded the robe at her breasts and shook out her sleeves with elegant care. 'Conveying, as you know, remarkable powers and perquisites. Stephen Angus will continue at Middleberg, but the new Conservator at Bruges is Adorne.'

Cold as *jökull* ice. Hot as the inferno beneath it. He said slowly, 'I didn't know.'

'It was arranged as he left. The documents have been drawn up to ratify it. Everything you now sell between Scotland and Bruges will be subject to the Baron Cortachy's scrutiny. You have lost your Flemish market.'

'But,' he said, 'Bruges is not the only market in Flanders. May I help you with that?'

Her fingers fell away from her gown as he settled it. He smoothed her sleeves and stood back to admire them. He said, 'The van Borselens have very good taste. It was really quite a coup to marry into them . . . Did I say I was selling in Bruges? Did I say indeed that our house would be in Bruges? Perhaps you didn't know that I had a bureau in Antwerp?'

'No,' she said. She backed and sat on a cushioned chest, frowning.

'And a small staff, and a warehouse, and a bodyguard. I arranged to deliver my stockfish to Antwerp. The buyers are waiting. Ships will move them to France and to Spain, and will come back with wine and salt, some of it mine. And meantime, the *Merrybuttocks* will return, to be transformed into *The Lion*.'

He saw her seeking wildly for the flaw. She said, 'He couldn't pay for it. The King couldn't pay for it now.'

'So he has just told me,' he said.

'And so?'

Watching her, he was sorry, but not greatly sorry. She knew him well. She already understood, without knowing how, that he had eluded her. He could read her, as she could read him. He said, 'He paid me in lands and a title. Beltrees is a barony.'

There was a long silence. She said, 'From when?'

'There will be a ceremony. You will take part. So will Jordan.'

She said, 'Bel said you would do that.'

'Bel might well guess. She dissipated all my liquid assets. Isn't it lucky,' Nicholas said, 'that you didn't divorce me? Now look what has happened.'

She stood up. 'I won't stop,' she said.

'Of course you won't,' Nicholas said. 'That is why I came back.'

The safe, mediocre span in the middle, which didn't tear you to pieces. Neither of them would stop, however minor the tussle might seem on some scales. At the same time, even though it was minor, he felt the wrench, as he always did, when he left.

The ceremony he had spoken of took place before the end of the month, on the day that his new ship from Danzig sailed into Leith roads. She was the size and weight of the *Unicorn* and the *Pruss Maiden* and more modern than either. Her name, as Jordan spelled out, was the *Fleury*.

Her owner boarded her bearing a different name: Nicholas de Fleury, Lord Beltrees. The formal ceremony of investiture at the Abbey merged, later, into the informal ceremony at sea of christening and departure. John had the honour of taking her out as her first master, and Moriz sailed as her chaplain. They lost a tide, because the young royals could not be persuaded to leave.

In the end, they tumbled into the boats as the *Fleury* prepared to raise sail. Willie Roger lingered behind.

Nicholas said, 'I'm not taking you. I'll be back in the autumn. For God's sake, I'll keep telling you all I hear about your Chapel Royal money and Coldingham.'

Roger said, 'It isn't that. I've talked to Moriz and John. You're taking Robin.'

'Well?' Nicholas said. He was taking Robin, because he wouldn't inflict on Robin the mortal wound of leaving him behind. He was taking Gelis and the child and his nurses. He did not need to concern himself with Kathi, for she had already left Scotland, and before that she had been ill, and under the jealous guardianship of the Prioress. Halfway through April, word had come that Sersanders had found a ship to take him from Bessastadir straight home to Bruges. A few days later, she had got herself a passage to Flanders, and the Priory had reluctantly released her. She had only been waiting to hear from her brother.

Willie Roger said, 'You are all together. You'll all be together in Flanders. It's bad. You need to get rid of Iceland.'

'What?' Nicholas said.

'Or you'll let it blunt you, like Africa. I thought we'd write plays together,' said Willie.

'You did. Well, get in some better beer, and I might. What makes you think I don't want to?' said Nicholas. Luckily, Roger never knew when he was lying. He didn't want music. He was plagued enough by the sounds in his head. Gunnar, chanting from inside his burial mound. The voice of Thorfinn on the wind: *a better sailor than any of us*. Old loyalties, old battles, old dreams.

He pushed Willie along to the steps. 'Get off, or they'll rescind all your sinecures. I'm not going to Flanders to mourn over Iceland. I'm going to fight for Duke Charles, and tell King Louis how lucky he is, and persuade Henne Memling he's got a picture all wrong, and arrange a welcome for Julius.'

Gelis had heard him. 'Julius is coming to Bruges?'

'I hope so,' said Nicholas. 'Bringing with him the widowed Gräfin Anna von Hanseyck, part-owner of the vessel on which we now stand. Iceland is forgotten. Why should a man visit Iceland, unless to sift through the shades of the underworld, looking for his next incarnation?'

'You're drunk,' Willie said.

'I am. But not as drunk,' Nicholas said, 'as I'm going to be.'

Chapter 31

IN THE FIRST days of May, Margriet van der Banck, dame de Cortachy, loved and loving wife of Anselm Adorne, died in her home at the Hôtel Jerusalem, Bruges, in a chamber filled with her children. Her oldest son, Jan, summoned from Genoa, was by turns desolate and furious, blaming his lady mother for succumbing at all, and especially for being so thoughtless as to die before his arrival. Even the very grand funeral was already over, and the guests and kinsfolk departed, with the exception of the nuns, friends of his sisters, who were staying to look after the children and order the household; and Jan's two Sersanders cousins with whom he had never seen eye to eye.

The house was stinking with incense. On the day of his arrival, he went to pay his respects in the crypt and found himself in the company of two weeping servants and someone from the Dry Tree praying in front of the altar. He entered, with some trepidation, upon his first meeting alone with his father, who seemed worn and pale; but the initial constraint melted before the warmth of the Baron's welcome. They embraced each other, and Jan wept. Later, his father was ready to hear a little about Jan's shameful treatment at the hands of the Curia, and the preposterous position he had been placed in, *vis à vis* the Bishop of St Andrews in Rome. He noticed after a while that his father's attention was slackening and, breaking off, advised him kindly to rest.

It surprised Jan next day to find his father had left the house for the first time, it was said, for many weeks; and that he was remaining abroad, evidently with the intention of dining at the home of a friend. Dr Andreas was also elsewhere. Jan left his brothers and sisters and, changed into a rather fine gown, went to call on a few friends himself.

The town of Antwerp was flat. To Gelis van Borselen, brought up in the low lands of her name-country, it should have appeared reassuringly familiar: a relief from the spiny ridges of Edinburgh, the funnelled views, the shrill winds. Instead, she found herself established in her new home with a reluctance which became apprehension, for it was only mid-May, and Nicholas was no longer consistently present. And soon, when he rejoined his army, he would be elsewhere for weeks at a time.

She had already endured his five-week absence in Iceland, but that was a single project, now finished. For half a year before that, their daily lives had been shared. She knew where he was, and she heard what he was doing. In some things, they had even acted together: in the ceremonial visits to Court; in the social life of the merchant community; in the making of the Play, which had seemed, at first, to offer such a manifest opportunity, and then had been revealed as the greatest threat, perhaps, she had yet faced.

While he was there, she could create her planning around him; when they were apart, his unpredictability baffled her. You would think, from the tales he freely told, that he had been perfectly candid about his voyage to Iceland. Only she noticed the lacunae: the parts which none of them ever discussed or explained. The girl Kathi, sometimes helpful, could not be reached. Archie had extracted what little he could from young Robin, but the boy had been reluctant and awkward. If there had been a dark side to that visit, a romantic young page was unlikely to know.

It fretted her, this impenetrable barrier. She was reminded of the swift, merry stream they all talked of, usefully busy, until suddenly the wholesome rock splits and the scalding marrow spurts forth. She was made anxious by any untoward influences – those of Africa, of Sinai, of the Play – that threatened to move Nicholas to another dimension; that had the power to replace logic with something more powerful. She did not want an emotional crisis of that sort again. Or not until she was ready.

Visitors came to the house. It was built of red brick, one of a row in a narrow street to the west of the Cathedral and not far from the river upon which Antwerp lay. It was smaller than the great house in Spangnaerts Street, but sufficient for herself and the child and the nurses and household attendants. There had been an agent, Jooris, occupying the upper floor, who had discreetly moved out to the riverside, where the counting-house and the packhouses were.

She knew why she had been settled here, because Nicholas had told her quite frankly: to avoid repeating the experience she had already had, living as an object of curiosity in the Bruges house run by Diniz and Tilde. She had brought that upon herself by her connection with Simon, and Nicholas showed little sympathy.

The other reason she understood even better. Simon's heir Henry was now a page with her van Borselen cousins, living either in Bruges, or at their castle sixty miles north of Antwerp at Veere. And if the handsome Simon, at forty-seven, had cause to dislike her, she knew without doubt that this boy of eleven held her and her child in abhorrence. Mistress Clémence had been warned never to take Jordan to Bruges or to Veere, nor to allow him to be taken.

There was no harm, of course, in Wolfaert van Borselen and his wife calling on Gelis at Antwerp, provided Henry did not come with them. Indeed, they came sooner than she had expected to congratulate her on her new status. Nicholas, who was there at the time, received them solemnly, and the charming docility of Jordan transfixed them. Mistress Clémence, presented, described him as a sweet-natured child, and later found herself drawn into gracious conversation with the lady Charlotte de Bourbon, married for four years to Wolfaert, and now expecting her third. Pasque was presented.

Gelis, smiling continuously, found that she had caught her own husband's eye, and freed it immediately, to quash any suggestion of conjugal conspiracy. She averted her gaze after that, aware now that his amused gaze seldom left her. For a moment it felt like last summer: herself a shadow, an echo, and Nicholas her invisible watcher. When their visitors left, and when, later, he himself departed to Bruges, Gelis even experienced some relief. She wished him well, cynically, of his business, and then felt a pang, for he was also going, of course, to condole with Anselm Adorne on his loss.

Nicholas had not been in Bruges for three years; not since another death, the death of his friend Father Godscalc. After that had come his work far afield: in the Tyrol and Egypt, Cyprus and Venice, Scotland and Ultima Thule. Throughout, he had never deliberately lost touch, save for the time of his disappearance with Jordan. Now, arriving at Bruges, he had called first at the Hôtel Jerusalem and found Adorne and his eldest son absent; and next at his own house in Spangnaerts Street from where, although pleased to embrace and admire his step-daughter Tilde and her baby, he had continued almost at once, to seek Diniz and all the élite of the town at a feast of the White Bear Society.

Nicholas de Fleury, burgher of Bruges, had long since been admitted to this, its most prestigious club, whose bulk shadowed the bridge of the great merchant quarter, and whose emblem, the *het beertje van der logie*, gazed from its niche towards the opening of Spangnaerts Street. A merchant prince and a baron himself, the head of the Banco di Niccolò had no difficulty entering here. Indeed, the moment he sent in his message, young Diniz came bursting into the hall, to hug him and drag him into the banquet.

Adorne was present. It was the first thing Nicholas saw as he was welcomed into the chamber, where the songs had begun although half the food still remained on the table, and a willing place was being found as they crowded about him.

Adorne wore black and looked blanched; in his eyes was a record of a long and wretched vigil. The others fell back as he came forward. He said, 'Nicholas? I have to congratulate you and thank you. You deserve the honour, and I am glad of it. My nephew will thank you in person. But I owe you more than I can say for what you did for Anselm and Katelijne in Iceland. Come, sit with me.'

'That is generous of you,' Nicholas said. 'I came to speak to you: to say we have no words, Gelis and I, for your loss. It is mine, too. I shall never forget her.'

'Thank you,' Adorne said. 'I should not be here, but Jan must leave for Rome again very soon, and I wished to present him here first. There he is.'

There he was. Unlike those who had jumped up to greet Nicholas – the famous faces of Gruuthuse and Metteneye, de Walle and Reyphin, Vasquez and Bonkle and Cant – the eldest son of Anselm Adorne had remained firmly seated, deep in talk with someone unknown bending over him. It was not unexpected. The last time they had met was in Venice, during Jan's brutal teasing by Nerio, the young Greek beauty disguised as a girl. Unfortunately, the seat now offered Nicholas lay between Anselm Adorne and his son.

Sighing invisibly, Nicholas sat. Jan looked round. Before he could speak, the singing had started again. It was the custom, after a feast, to call on each guest to perform, and Nicholas de Fleury was known for his fiendish ability to reduce a room to wails of painful enjoyment. He was invited to entertain almost immediately and did so. He was a natural mimic, and it came easily. After that, others obliged, and he had time to eat and drink, and look round.

Tommaso Portinari was absent. There was no sign of Anselm Sersanders, and those members who were related to the Duke of Burgundy were also missing; but that was understandable. He had heard the rumours of trouble himself, meticulously forwarded by Astorre and by Diniz. He wondered what Adorne was making of it all, now one supposed he had time to turn his mind to the future. The truce between France and Burgundy was meant to last another month yet. If it broke, Scotland would immediately be involved. And Anselm Adorne was now deeply identified with Scotland.

Jan Adorne said, as if he had spoken, 'What a pity you will never be able to sell fish in Antwerp again. The King has forbidden it. All Scots merchants must sell to Bruges, and my father is Conservator of Scots Privileges in all the domains of the Duke. Do you know what that means?'

'Yes, I know. It is a great honour. Jan, I came because of your mother. I know you will miss her so much. What are your brothers and sisters going to do?' He kept his voice quiet. Under the chorusing, no one could hear them.

'It means,' Jan continued, 'that for his lifetime, my father has power to govern and direct and administer law to the Scottish subjects in the dominions of Burgundy. He is allowed to tax staple wares for his salary, and can arrest anyone who won't pay him. And all because of the way my father represented the nation of Scotland not only at the papal court and in Christian countries, but among the barbarous nations of the Saracens and the Turks. You represented nobody but yourself.'

'Did it seem so? Then the misfortune was mine, in having no son who could write about it. Your father must be proud of you.' He turned to Adorne. 'And I dare say Jan has brought you the latest information from Rome. What of the papal Crusade?' It was all he could think of to say. The song then being sung was not very papal, or welcome to a man still in mourning.

'Your reports, I am sure, are as good as mine,' said Adorne. 'The combined fleets have presumably left for the East, your own ships among them. They will do what they can. The main assault, as you know, is next year. And the fund-raising legates have gone – Cardinal Bessarion towards France, and Cardinal Barbo to the Emperor Frederick, unfortunately for Jan.'

'I heard,' Nicholas said. 'But Bishop Graham has found him a post?'

Jan Adorne opened his mouth. 'Unfortunately,' said his father, 'the Bishop, although a good man, is receiving less support than he would like from King James. Or perhaps it is fortunate, for Jan is able to render him help so long as he stays in Rome. Once the Bishop goes home, Jan will have to seek other employment.'

'Perhaps I can help,' Nicholas said. 'Or Lazzarino my agent, or Julius. Added, of course, to your own excellent circle of friends.'

'The way you helped my mother and father?' said Jan in a low voice. 'My mother might be alive today, without the burden of the Earl and Countess of Arran all those months. My father *thanked you* for what you did for my cousins. What did you do? Betray my father's ship to the Hanse, try to wreck it; have one cousin captured and take the other aboard and debauch her!'

'Jan!' said Adorne, also quietly. He had turned his back on his neighbours.

'This is not the place,' Nicholas said. 'But I must speak for your cousin Katelijne. She came aboard to prevent us from fighting. She came immediately under the care of my chaplain, and stayed so. Her brother was never in danger of being captured. As for the device to rid myself of a pirate ship and a rival, I must claim that to be quite legitimate. Martin would have done the same in my place.'

'A pirate ship!' said Jan. His voice, properly scathing, disregarded a protest from his father. 'The Hanse believe they are the only authority, but there are others more private. My father was sanctioned by the Bishop and Governor of Iceland.'

'And I by the King of Scotland,' said Nicholas dryly. 'I fancy that my next cargo might even be permitted in Antwerp, under the circumstances.'

Jan looked at his father. After the first moment of surprise, Adorne's lips produced a wry smile. He said, 'My compliments. I believed my staff-work was good, but I see yours is better. You did well.'

'But you got the sulphur. Martin is a very shrewd man,' Nicholas said. 'Although careless. He really should have checked what had become of Anselm and Katelijne. Where is Anselm?'

'I hoped you would ask,' Adorne said. He turned in his seat, opening the conversation again to the table. He called across. 'Jehan: Nicholas is impatient to talk to my nephew.'

The solid cheeks of Jehan Metteneye quivered. 'Patience! Patience! He will be here!'

There was a ripple of laughter. Nicholas put on a complaining face. 'There is a secret. I am excluded.' All the eminent faces were smiling but one. Louis de Gruuthuse, conveying an unspoken message. Nicholas acknowledged it equally silently.

Jan said, 'He's willing to speak to you, now you have forgiven your lady wife. You were talking of Julius, your lawyer.'

'Yes?' said Nicholas. Some of the diners had risen and were crowding round the inner door at the end of the room. He added, 'He is coming to Bruges. You might see him.'

'I hope,' said Jan, 'that he is bringing his new lady with him. A gräfin. Perhaps you have met her?'

'He is bringing a lady,' said Nicholas. 'But no, I have not met her. You have?' The doors at the end of the room were slowly opening.

'Oh yes,' Jan Adorne said. 'A vision of beauty. A little lacking in height, but the horizontal aspects more than make up for it. In fact, I have seldom seen a comparable girth outside a cheese-house. I should think he had to roll her over the Alps like a barrel, even to the danger of scratching her paint.'

'Jan, that is ungallant,' said Adorne sharply. 'Nicholas, I am sorry. No gentleman speaks thus of a –'

He stopped because his voice was drowned out by cheers. The doors stood open. The crowd before them fell back. Nicholas stood, and so did Jan and his father. Then Nicholas started to laugh.

Entering the room, limping slightly, was Anselm Sersanders. His face was smiling; his dress, after the travel-worn quilting of Iceland, was stylish and rich. And by his side, two porters were trundling an object.

It looked at first like a crate on four wheels. Then, as it stopped at the end of the table, Anselm leaned over and drew back the covering cloth. Nicholas saw that it was not a crate but a cage. A stout cage with thick iron bars, within which sat something enormous and furry and white. Sersanders put his hand through the bars and scratched the object under the chin, and the object sniffed him.

It was a white Greenland bear. Nicholas said, '*Há!* The cub? Anselm, this is the *cub*? You went back for it?'

'Of course,' said Anselm Sersanders. 'Meet the *het beertje* Besse, gift from the White Bear Society of Bruges to the great and powerful Charles, Duke of Burgundy, Count of Flanders and everything else. Uncle, come and shake hands.'

'I don't think so,' said Anselm Adorne, with amusement. But he walked over, Nicholas with him, and stood in front of the cage. Nicholas said again, 'That's a *cub*?'

'Well, they're born in winter,' said Sersanders with mild irritation. Can't cross the ice till their second year. Bears are big.'

'Katelijne caught *that*?' Nicholas said.

'I helped her. I brought it back on my own. Well, with the Icelanders. So. Better than stockfish, do you think?'

'It depends what you feed it on,' Nicholas said. 'Anselm, I do think that is enterprising. Where do you keep it?'

He waited until the noise and laughter increased and the talk became general, and then made his way to where Gruuthuse stood a little apart. As Anselm Adorne was a loyal officer to the Duke, so the Gruuthuse family were one of the bastions of Burgundy. In their palace in Bruges had lived the exiled English King and his brother, before their triumphant return the previous year. In the same house, Gelis van Borselen had lain with her future husband for the first time since she seduced him in Africa. Nicholas said, 'Something has happened?'

Gruuthuse said, 'You have spent a long time in Scotland.'

'The winter. My army is still on the Somme, and I am here with my gunner as promised.'

The other man's face had always been lined, now it was more so. He said, 'I told Duke Charles, but you should go to Arras to speak to him yourself. The King of France's brother has died, poisoned, they say, by his order. The Duke of Brittany is preparing to march. It seems very likely that our Duke will then take the field.'

'Breaking the truce?' Nicholas said.

'An oath made to a murderer is no oath. Your lady is with you?'

'Gelis is well,' Nicholas said. 'She is in Antwerp. I shall return there tomorrow, and then report to the Duke. Are the English likely to send troops?'

'They have sent them already. A thousand archers to Brittany under Earl Rivers. We may tempt them to invade France with us yet,' Gruuthuse said. 'There is enough land in France to please everybody.'

Soon after that, the party broke up. Nicholas, setting off to walk down the short slope with Diniz, was stopped by Anselm Sersanders, expansive in drink. 'You haven't seen Kathi.'

Adorne and his son had gone home. He didn't want to see Jan again. The moon was up, and it was a long way to the Jerusalemkirk. Nicholas said, 'Anselm, I love you and her and the bear, but not tonight. And I'm going to Antwerp tomorrow.'

'Then come tomorrow, before you set out.' Sersanders paused. 'I heard how you found me and Sigfús. I heard how you set out to find Robin. I don't agree with the Church.'

'They have to be careful,' said Nicholas. 'It's all right, I'm not going to beat up Jan Adorne, although I'll wring Nerio's neck if I ever meet him. Tell Kathi I'll come early tomorrow, and you both ought to be proud of your bear.'

It was easy to say. When the moment came to leave for the Hôtel Jerusalem the following morning, he stood in the stables doing nothing, until stirred by the mock-annoyance of Diniz.

Guds frida veri med ydr: the peace of God be upon you. He had not been alone with the girl since those words were spoken, in the thundering dark, with the doom-fire of the gods in the clouds. Until last night, he had pushed aside all he knew of that tongue, as he had buried the language of Umar.

This girl was not Umar. The situation was not at all of that kind, except in so far as it was a relationship, disembodied as that of the mistletoe, which found its nourishment in strange, diverse places: in the excitement of danger; in the marriage of music and words; in understanding allied with compassion. Until now, he had not fully realised how privileged he had been, knowing Katelijne Sersanders.

Since Iceland, her illness had kept them apart. At Leith, she had been swept off by Father Moriz and Archie of Berecrofts, and after that the nuns had not allowed her visitors, not even when, grudgingly, they had allowed her to sail off to Bruges.

There were nuns, too, at the Hôtel Jerusalem, but when Katelijne spoke to them mildly, they left him alone with her in Adorne's parlour. He had been there many times in the past: sometimes with Marian; sometimes as a boy about to be condemned to a night in the Steen, or a thrashing. Adorne had been lenient, on the whole, for a magistrate.

His niece was brown-haired, not fair, and smaller than you would expect of the family. Her slightness made her almost invisible, as did her dark high-revered gown, and the black veil that covered her cap. He thought of Sersanders's portly white shirt in the geysir. She said, 'Do we shake hands? I am sad, but not dying. *Ey*, Nicholas.'

'I liked Banco,' he said. 'I'm so sorry about Mistress Margriet. I'm sorrier than you know. I heard you got back in time, and I'm glad.'

'So was I. She liked you,' she said. 'Anyway, you had nothing to do with her death. She knew the risk. She wanted that child. They sang Willie's Nativity music at her funeral.' She stopped and said, 'You don't need to talk about that. Won't you sit?'

He found a seat, since she did. He said, 'I mustn't stay long.'

'You are going to Antwerp with Diniz. Sersanders told me. What do you think of the bear?'

'He went back for it. He is an idiot. So are you.'

'He wanted Uncle to have it, in case the sulphur didn't arrive. He knows you saved his life. He is truly grateful.'

'It's all right,' Nicholas said. 'I've already told him. I won't lambast Jan, or not while he's in Bruges.'

'Oh dear,' Kathi said. 'Do you know the Bishop of St Andrews?'

'Not well enough to re-educate him,' Nicholas said. 'What is the main trouble? Money?'

'A bit. He holds too many benefices and can't pay for them. And there's Coldingham, too. I know,' said Kathi, looking cross, 'that Willie Roger *aches* for his Chapel Royal choir, but it would be a great boon to Jan and the Bishop if the King would change his mind and not suppress the Priory and give Willie quite so many tenors and altos. It's been a very fine religious establishment. Dr Andreas says their school was so good that foreign colleges took their orphans for nothing.'

'How does Dr Andreas know?' Nicholas said.

Kathi grinned. 'He looks after Ada's children when they need it. The Crackbene–Crabbe tribe are old friends, didn't you know? Also, he fancies Ada, I think. Much chance of that, of course, while Mick is about.'

'You are opening my eyes,' Nicholas said, 'to Dr Andreas.'

'Really? Have you never noticed?' Kathi said. 'Necromancers, astrologers and ordinary prophets: women fall at their feet. Diviners as well. You want to watch. Well, it's too late now, I suppose.'

'Much too late. Does he draw up horoscopes?'

'It would be odd if he didn't. He's a by-blow of the astrologer John of Vesalia, the town doctor of Brussels. John of Vesalia was rector of Louvain when Bishop Kennedy was there, blazon three weasels. You know all that. He made those awful predictions in January when the fiery star flew across. Dr Andreas says you ought to be careful.'

'Of women?' Nicholas said.

'Of divining. He says the future can open when you don't want it to. He thinks you should lead an ordinary family life, and keep away from the occult.'

'He does? Or you do?' Nicholas said.

Her colour had risen. She said, 'I do, as well. I wouldn't tell you, if you weren't a friend. I know what it's like when everyone tells you what to do.'

It was enough to shift his thoughts from himself. He said, 'Who are telling you what to do? The *nuns*? Because –'

She gave a genuine laugh. 'Don't worry. Father Moriz has almost excommunicated himself, putting my case. But there is a strong feeling I should enter a nunnery. The Patriarch of Antioch suggested it first.'

Nicholas said, 'What in God's name would you do in a nunnery?'

'Then what should I do?' Kathi said.

It was a plain question, asked without coquetry. Asked by a friend, and not by a young sexless person to be protected. He said, 'What is your illness?'

For a while she was silent. He saw that, unusually, she was not surrounded by work, the traces of a dozen fleeting occupations that might be currently filling her day. She said, 'I don't know. I have no warning of tiredness, as most people have. I do too much. I make extravagant use of my energy and call on all my reserves until I collapse. Bad for me, bad for my heart.'

He said, 'So they want to limit what you do.'

'That is what they say, Dr Andreas and Dr Tobias.'

'But that is not how you want to live.'

She looked at him. 'That is not what life is for.'

'But there will be no life,' Nicholas said. 'You will burn yourself out. The nunnery would be another sort of death, in your case. You need a regulator; someone who will let you do what you want, but stop you from excess. Is there no one?'

She did not answer. She said, 'Does Gelis stop you?'

'Me?' he said.

'Yes,' she said. 'I told you what Dr Andreas said. Are you not driven as well? To waste no time, to take every chance, to try everything?'

He began to say, 'But I am never –' and halted.

'Never harmed by it? Tell that to your doctors. Tell your doctors that you never have waking dreams, that nothing ever confuses you. If I know, Gelis knows; but while you are competing against one another, she won't help you. So I say what you have just said to me, but I'll go further. You need protection. You need Gelis. Make peace with her.'

Her gaze, level on his, was clear as peat water. Good advice. Sensible, unbiased advice. He said, 'She won't stop until it is resolved.'

'Until what is resolved?' Kathi said. 'Until she has proved herself cleverer than you are? She may be. If she will only be happy when she thinks she is, then give her that happiness now. Once she has proved herself, then the race will be over.'

'Will it?' Nicholas said. 'And what if she discovers she has been permitted to win? Also ... it isn't merely a race. I am receiving a punishment.'

'Which you think you deserve,' Kathi said.

'Which I know I deserve.'

'And you are throwing away happiness, both of you, because of that?'

'Happiness?' It stunned him, to be talking to anyone about this.

The girl looked at him, astonished. 'Nicholas, you love her. You must know it. She must know that you do. Why on earth would you have wasted these years if you didn't? Bring yourself to think of her. You nearly didn't come back from Iceland. You'll be in the field with your army this summer. If you don't stop it all now, you will be dead before the race is ever finished.'

'I do think of her,' he said. He spoke to himself.

After a while she said, 'I have said too much. Will you forgive me?'

'I expect so,' he said.

She was standing. She said, 'And if I need your help, may I come to you?'

It brought him to his feet. He said, 'Kathi, of course. I am sorry. It was like Hekla and Katla at once.'

'Someone had to say it,' she said. 'Before you go, I have something to show you. Did you know that Jordan was riding at Dean?'

It was hard to concentrate. He said, 'Yes. I thought of buying him . . . Kathi?'

'I guessed you might. I have a pony,' she said. 'In the stables. If you like him, I'll sell him to you. He seemed just right for Jordan. But from you, not from me.'

He said, 'Jordan won't bring us together. He is the barrier.'

'No. You are wrong,' she said. 'You are wrong. When she is free to love you, she will love Jordan.'

Later, he rode into Antwerp with Diniz, the pony trotting beside them; and took the child out, and visited the warehouses, and had supper with Gelis and Diniz. Afterwards, he broke the news to her that he could stay for only a day, and then must leave for a visit to Arras. He tried to speak as he normally did, and thought he succeeded. He had attempted to set aside all that had been said that morning, for otherwise he could not continue with what had to be done. He would have to think of it some time. He supposed he would have to think of it some time. But he didn't see how he could expunge the plan of four years on a whim. He didn't see, as of now, how he could bring himself to discard it for any reason, for he was afraid he would discard himself with it.

He did not tax her then with her other visitors, although he knew she had had them; and further knew who they were.

Chapter 32

MISTRESS CLÉMENCE SAW the visitors, but it was not her place to remark on them; nor on the arrival of the extremely valuable pony, of which on the whole she approved.

Pasque had no such inhibitions. 'At last, he treats the boy as he should! Remind him what a baron's son is due! There are those – you know them – who would have silver harness by now. A miniature helmet.'

'A page?' suggested Mistress Clémence. 'And therefore no further need of his nurses? Pasque, the bath has to be emptied.' There was no point in explaining. This was a father who did not give bribes. The pony, therefore, represented something else: an apology for a long absence past, and another to come. Perhaps a very long absence.

The day of his arrival from Bruges, there had been something about their employer's appearance which she did not like, taken in conjunction with Lord Beltrees's apparent inability to avoid life-endangering activity. He had displayed a little too much attention to Jordan, shaking Jordan's sense of security. His wife had not noticed, which was rare for her. Mistress Clémence sometimes wished, watching the Lady watching her husband, or keeping vigil during his absence, that Gelis van Borselen would have some care for his health. Some gentlemen, unevenly matured, went all their lives in need of a little nursery discipline.

Nicholas took John le Grant with him to Arras, but left Moriz and Robin at Bruges. If there was to be war, there was a lot of planning to do.

And there was to be war. The first sight of the tumult in Artois confirmed it. At Arras, only forty miles north of Amiens and thirty-four east of Hesdin, the Duke received him at St Vaast in a room jostling with captains and messengers, and crashed his fist on the table.

'What is this man doing here?' His long, full face, glaring at Nicholas, was crimson. 'You took my gold, and turned Scottish whore for a barony! You said they would never raise an army against us, and they are sending six thousand soldiers to France!'

'My lord,' Nicholas said. 'When the army comes, kill me.'

The Duke paused. 'It is not coming.'

'They cannot afford it,' said Nicholas.

'My lord of Cortachy believes otherwise,' the Duke said. 'Anselm Adorne brought us sulphur. What do you bring?'

'The man who will use it,' Nicholas said. 'Master John le Grant, who might otherwise be fighting the Turk. We place our souls as well as our hearts at your service.'

Later, alone in the rooms they'd been given, John said, 'The man's crazy. Does Scotland really owe you that much? I thought they'd raised the gold for the army.'

'They have,' Nicholas said. 'But James wants to lead it, and they won't allow that while he's childless. Dreams of Alexander and Hercules. Rubbish.'

'Dear, dear,' said John le Grant. 'What it is to be young and romantic and have well-travelled friends. The Duke is childless. That is, he's only got the one girl from his previous marriage. Whoever marries her is going to do well, and make a few changes. Perhaps in the long run we'd be better backing France.'

'That's all right,' Nicholas said. 'We're doing that, too.' The Duke was crazy: rich and impatient, and greedy for honours and land and a name that would match that of his warrior forefathers. A triple invasion of France was one of his dreams for the future. His more immediate desire was to retrieve the two border towns he had lost the previous year to the King of France. He had published two manifestos accusing Louis of France of killing his own younger brother by *poison, sorcellerie et machinations diaboliques*, and had some new banners made inscribed *VENGEANCE!*

To Nicholas, the future looked mildly promising. He rode into Arras. The following morning, racing ahead of his cohorts, Captain Astorre burst into his patron's rooms like a ready-spurred cock from its basket.

'Claes! My boy!'

'Nicholas de Fleury, Lord Beltrees, to you,' said John le Grant acidly. 'Have you got any decent gunners there yet? One who can strike a spark from a flint?'

Everything flowed off Astorre when there was a battle in prospect. He embarked on a ten-minute lecture on strategy. Louis was currently five hundred miles away with his army. When he came north to attack, he'd choose Brittany. 'Scare them into surrender, he'll think, and then turn back to us, before we've had time to do all that much damage.'

'Have we time to do all that much damage?' Nicholas said. Astorre had let his beard revert to black streaked with white. The girls were either departed or dropping like plums.

Astorre said, 'Depends what kind of damage you mean. You and I could launch a nice little series of sorties, tip out a few garrisons, and begin to hold a good solid line threatening Paris. That'd change Louis's mind and bring him scurrying up to the conference table.'

'But?'

'But you know mercenaries.'

'We're mercenaries,' Nicholas said. He liked annoying Astorre, who turned puce.

'Are we?' said Astorre. 'Are we? I've yet to see any body of men under me behaving like Hagenbach's bloody Alsatians.'

'All right,' Nicholas said. 'You're saying that the ducal army won't consolidate without better discipline, and that's a point I shall make with the others. Now let's talk about guns.' He could see John's hair growing ruddier. John enjoyed sailing, but his heart was really in proper guns, with masons and platforms and carriages, and barrels and barrels of gunpowder.

Much later, when platters were empty and the wine nearly done, Astorre said, 'The barber-surgeon went off. I'll get somebody. Unless you've someone permanent in mind.'

Nicholas said, 'Get someone temporary,' and met Astorre's one gleaming eye. He did have someone permanent in mind: the same man as Astorre. Jan had spread the news, as he had spread the news about so much else happening in Rome. Dr Tobias, former physician to the Charetty company, was surprisingly about to return to the field. Having successfully brought to delivery the Count of Urbino's ninth child and first son, he was leaving to follow the Count into action.

Jan had wondered why, with the Count's thanks in his pocket, he'd bothered. Nicholas supposed there was some discernible reason. Urbino had always been a hero to Tobie. He had been in battle with him before. And from the very beginning, Tobie had been involved in the Charetty interest in alum. Now the alum mine in the Florentine subject-town of Volterra had occasioned a power struggle between the Medici and those who disagreed with them. Lorenzo de' Medici, infuriated by the revolt, was calling for troops from Milan and the Pope and the Count of Urbino to help put it down. And where Urbino went, Tobie would go.

Tobias Beventini, physician, had left Nicholas before, unable to tolerate what the others had learned to ignore, because he understood it better. This last year, it had seemed that he had vanished for good. But if he had, it was odd that he should want to return to an army again. And when and if Urbino completed his task, Tobie would have to consider where next to go. Nicholas remembered something Kathi had said. He was a good doctor.

Astorre was speaking. 'And the boy. You were supposed to be bringing the boy to be trained?'

Nicholas looked at him. 'Aged three and a half? Trained for what?'

Astorre looked impatient. 'What do you mean? The boy. The other boy. The son of the merchant. Your page.'

His head cleared. 'Ah, Robin. I will bring him. He's worth teaching. Will you do it? Stretch him. I don't want him coddled, but I'd rather not have him killed.'

'Killed?' said Astorre. 'Men don't get killed in these wars, except over wagers while they're sitting down waiting. These aren't proper wars.'

They spent next day between the camp and the commanders. The following afternoon, leaving John, Nicholas prepared to make his one visit home before the start of the campaign. By home, he supposed he meant Antwerp. It seemed a long way away. From there, he would go to Diniz in Bruges, for he had a business to order as well as an army. He was leaving Moriz to help. And Julius might have arrived, with his chubby Gräfin.

All the women Nicholas knew had speculated about Julius and his new conquest – Julius, who had seemed so devotedly self-centred and single. They didn't seem to consider, as Julius undoubtedly had, that at a certain stage in a man's life he would be seen to require an establishment, and a hostess to run it. A rich hostess, for preference. Looks would hardly matter. All the time his friends had known him, Julius had had a very mild interest – almost no interest at all – in what Nicholas had always regarded as the best and cheapest pleasure in life. Perhaps he was about to be converted.

It was then the beginning of June, and the country was bowered in green. Going home, Nicholas travelled by Ghent, the shortest route back, since he had recently spent a great deal of time in the saddle. When he left Ghent on the fourth day of the month, he had something under forty miles still to cover to Antwerp. Nothing warned him to go to Bruges first, for although the thought of Gelis seldom left him – he had told Kathi the truth – he had refrained from divining.

Alone among the inhabitants of the matroneum at Antwerp, the elderly handmaiden Pasque was both carefree and happy. As she had absorbed Edinburgh, so she absorbed the quays and the ramparts and the markets of her new home; loftily inquisitive, she was acquainted with every washerwoman in the town in two weeks. Pasque preferred Antwerp to Scotland. In Antwerp they spoke God's own tongue, if you could imagine God with a cleft palate.

Certainly, when the baby's father departed for Arras, she tried to convince Mistress Clémence that a little visit to Coulanges and Dijon would also do the child good, but the undoubted distance between Artois and the Loire was against it. However, she was not truly cast down, even when the boy Robin arrived one day from Bruges with a message that took Mistress Clémence away (the Adorne children were ill), thus leaving poor Pasque to shoulder the labours of two. In fact, when she pointed this out, the lady Gelis hired another to help her, a devout, hardworking woman called Bita who went to her devotions at the same time as Pasque, and whose son was a baker.

Shortly after that, the lady Gelis herself was called to Bruges to meet a banker from Venice, and Pasque's happiness was complete. Despite the young man Robin's mild protests, she allowed the child that day to do whatever he liked; and even though he was a little sick after supper, she jigged and sang until he was laughing again, and put his dress into the tub, and promised him that next day he would wear his very best clothes. And the lad Robin, even though he pulled a long face, burst into laughter as well at her jokes. He was a pretty fellow, and was going to break a few hearts.

The next day, since she had not had time to get him quite into her ways, he objected, though politely, to some of the things she proposed, but at length agreed to go with her and the boy to the Grand Market, provided one of the house men-at-arms went along with them. The fair was on, so they had a very good time, and were given cakes by the son of her friend, and a drink of free ale by the other son of her friend, whom she hadn't mentioned. Then, while the child had his sleep, the lad Robin went off to his lessons with the master-at-arms who had been found for him near the fort, and who was going to make him into a chevalier. Pasque had just closed her eyes too (Bita was cleaning the child's little boots) when she was wakened by an argument in the street and the trampling of horses, very loud between the two rows of houses. She got up and opened the shutters.

Below, at her door, was the Duchess of Burgundy. Even as Pasque let out a scream, she saw it was not the Duchess of Burgundy, and that the splendid horses and harness, the liveried grooms and the upturned face of the opulent lady belonged to someone she knew: to Charlotte de Bourbon, dame de Borselen, whose husband was the lady Gelis's very grand cousin.

The Lady, gazing upwards, was smiling. 'Why, we know one another! Is it not little Jordan's kind nurse? Do you think we might rest for a moment, even though your master and mistress are away? You will understand, being a woman. Pregnancy makes one a little tired.'

She had so much brocade in her gown that you couldn't see how far gone she might be, and her headdress was sparkling with gems. She was thirty, near enough. She was no chicken. Pasque knew, without being told, that this was a lady who would dress her little boys in fine silver armour, and have two under-maids for each nurse. Without a moment's delay Pasque tripped down the stairs and let the party into the house. There were only three of them, apart from the grooms: the lady Charlotte and her step-son, named Paul, and a bright-faced young girl with brown hair, who introduced herself as Catherine de Charetty.

Pasque had heard the name. She knew that monseigneur's first wife had two daughters, of whom this must be one. The girl was unmarried, and the young man, Paul van Borselen, was clearly her suitor. Delighted, Pasque scampered about, scolding the steward and shouting into the kitchen and sending Bita to wake up the child.

It was the child they had travelled to see. The young man was indifferent, and the lady Charlotte of course had already met him, but the girl Catherine could hardly contain her impatience while the cakes and the wine were brought in. Then the door opened and Jordan stood there, not quite as starchily neat as some liked, for his best clothes had suffered that morning, but a proper boy for all that, with his ruffled brown hair and grey eyes and cheeks scarlet from sleep. Then he smiled, for he liked meeting people, and the Charetty girl started to weep.

The lady Charlotte patted her hand. 'Come,' she said to the child. 'Come and meet your step-sister Catherine, and hear what a treat I have decided to give you. You are going to come and stay with us all. While your mother and father are busy, you will come and sail in our ships, and play with my little children, and Pasque, of course, will come with you too. Would you like that?'

He would like that, said Jordan, getting some Scots words into the greeting by mistake. Pasque, seized with ecstasy, saw that even this was a blessing, the van Borselen household being familiar with Scots. The child was in the arms of his new sister Catherine. Pasque left him there and, skipping, went off to pack.

The leader of the household bodyguard, a busybody, had sent to fetch little Berecrofts who came running, all sweaty from fighting, and looking as if the Turks had come to the door. He knew the Lady perfectly well – he had been there when the family visited – but you would have thought he was Mistress Clémence herself, the fuss he made about the child leaving home. It wasn't until the dame de Borselen asked him sarcastically if he thought the boy would be safer with him than he would be with his own blood relations, that the youngster mended his manners.

Even then, he wanted to come and bring all his bodyguard, until the lady Charlotte, with the same chilly patience, pointed out that the household retinue of the van Borselen was perhaps adequate for most occasions. She did agree, however, that Lord Beltrees's page might go with her, finding his anxiety – if misplaced – highly commendable. By the time they left, she had recovered all her gracious good humour.

'Now,' said the Lady. 'Now at last we may do what best pleases us, and show this little Jordan the pleasures of Veere.'

Racked with anxiety, Robin of Berecrofts remained obstinately attached to the side of the child as they embarked on their journey of pleasure.

Awaiting his master in Antwerp, he had been given no office to perform, other than that of being useful, and pursuing his training. He knew that the son of a banker should always be guarded from kidnappers. He further knew that Nicholas de Fleury had enemies, and would have preserved Jordan from Simon de St Pol, for example, with his life. Unlike Mistress Clémence, he had been given no specific instructions about excluding Jordan from Bruges or from Veere, simply because he would have asked questions, and Mistress Clémence did not. Also, no one had dreamed that the child's mother and nurse could be absent at once.

Leaving Antwerp, Robin had considered, frantically, whom he should warn. It was the third day of June, and Nicholas de Fleury had been away for nine days and was momentarily expected to return. Meanwhile, the lady Gelis and Clémence were both in Bruges: Clémence at the Jerusalemkirk, and the Lady at the Casa Charetty–Niccolò with the lawyer Julius from Venice and a rich German lady investor. Even if Robin sent a courier now, neither could come within three or four days. Also, the van Borselen were Jordan's own relatives: it ought not to seem as if Robin, on monseigneur's behalf, did not trust them.

Robin scrawled a note to be given to his master, and left another for Jooris, the agent. The next rider to Bruges was to tell the lady of Beltrees that her son was in the house of her cousin at Veere.

*

Gelis and Katelina van Borselen had been members of a very great family; Gelis still was. Their territory was Zeeland, and their home was on Walcheren, the stranded island north-east of Bruges whose southern shore was the mouth of the Scheldt, leading to Antwerp, and whose opposite shore lined the Veergat, the waters of which served the trading port of Bergen op Zoom. Placed between Bruges and the Baltic, Zeeland's wealth lay in trade and in shipping. Her lords intermarried with the Counts of Flanders and the Dukes of Burgundy and the royal house of Scotland, and were showered with formidable honours.

The late Henry van Borselen, lord of Veere, had carried Mary of Guelders to Edinburgh to become the Queen of James II; and twenty years later had borne Edward of England to his throne. Henry's son Wolfaert, now over forty, had brought up young Sandy, the Scots Duke of Albany, and had possessed, briefly, the Scottish earldom of Buchan; his first wife had been sister to James II. Charlotte, second wife to the same Wolfaert, was of royal French as well as ducal Burgundian blood. Louis de Gruuthuse, married to a van Borselen, had become lieutenant-general for the Duke in these lands and had housed the English King during his exile. The family van Borselen were skilful survivors.

They also possessed a magnificent home. The approach to Camp-veere – the old ferry to Campen – was both by road and by water, and made to enchant a small boy of three and soothe the fears of a man of fifteen. The seigneurial boat, with its strong oarsmen and magnificent awnings, pranced over the sparkling waves, and Jordan's new sister fed him sugar almonds. Embraced by the competent arms of her sweetheart, Jordan rode through groves and beside streams and pools full of herons, and screamed at peewits and at the black-headed birds he had fed at the Nor' Loch in Edinburgh, which his sister called *mouettes rieuses*. In Walcheren everything laughed, even the gulls.

Occasionally Catherine cried, Robin observed, from pure happiness. He had heard – everyone had – of the great scandal of her silly girlhood, from which she had been rescued by her mother's young second husband. Robin realised that she loved Nicholas de Fleury, and hence his son; and the last of his fears was assuaged.

The castle of Zandenburg, once a fortress, was now a hunting seat for the van Borselen, and also a place of business, as were their other houses in Flushing, in Bruges, in Champagne. The black and silver family arms were painted over the great gothic entrance gate, and in their chapel within the vast church of Our Lady, and flew from flags at the port: the small harbour whose jetties, though simple, could accommodate ships of any size. The anchorage outside was calm. And from Veere to the sea represented a voyage of less than two hours, free of rocks or of shoals. The Veergat almost never had ice.

So, more and more often, a little fleet from Scotland or England or Denmark was to be found unloading at Veere. And, while Bruges and Calais might at present hold the monopoly, Veere was there, with its humble advantages, and when one town or another fell out, Veere ran seductively into the gap. Veere was no virgin.

If the lord Wolfaert, his mind on these matters, was vexed by the incoming cavalcade, he was courteous enough to show no sign of it. When little Lodewijk, two, and his baby sister, screaming, made their appearance, Robin realised at last why no pains would be spared to make this visit agreeable. He found himself thankful that Pasque was the immediate quarry, substituting for her absent superior. He didn't think Mistress Clémence would have liked Veere.

While the children were carried off to eat and to sleep, Robin found himself included, awkwardly, in the family dinner. He was accustomed enough to a table of state: his father and grandfather were not solely merchants, and round their Lanarkshire board would feed chaplain and tutor and secretary, factor and steward, just like this. As a page, his position was low, although in deference to his master he was placed at the same table. Next to him, already seated, was a boy of eleven.

Robin collected his French. 'We haven't met. My name is Robin of Berecrofts. May I join you?'

The boy looked up and smiled. The smile was breathtaking; his voice, low and sweet, answered in Scots. He said, 'I know what your name is. Fuck off.'

No one from the family had noticed. There was no other seat he could take. The boy, having spoken, lowered his stupendous lashes over his glorious blue eyes; a beam of sunlight turned his hair to pure gold. Wolfaert van Borselen, from the end of the room said, 'Ah, Robin. Is it Robin? Quite; yes. Robin, meet my young kinsman, your mistress's nephew. Henry. Henry de St Pol of Kilmirren, a welcome addition to our little brood.'

Robin, rigid, gave a bow and sat down. The boy, lifting his head, gave him a smile as sweet as the first, and transferred it modestly to Wolfaert van Borselen. 'My dear surrogate father,' he said and, still smiling, hacked Robin under the table. Robin, gasping, didn't even think to kick back.

This was the boy born to Gelis van Borselen's sister, now dead. This boy's father was Simon, monseigneur's worst enemy.

The meal passed in a blur. The boy, for most of the time, turned his back on him. Robin spoke, as well as he could, to the others beside and across from him; his attempts were regularly nullified by the boy who, turning round, would engage him, always charmingly, in horrifying murmurs.

'Don't you agree the lady Charlotte is gross? On the other hand, you can couple with her for three months and more without penalty. I'll show you how to unlock her chamber. Was your mother a whore?'

'What? No!' said Robin.

'Paul's was. Paul is my lord Wolfaert's bastard,' said Henry, waving to Paul at the other end of the table. 'He has others, of course, but he usually pays seamen to claim them. He once had four girls in a night. I once had two, end to end. What about you?'

'I don't believe you,' said Robin; but the boy had turned away, and the man next to him was staring, so that he began talking to him rather wildly about Scotland. It came to him, sickeningly, that this boy was Nicholas de Fleury's nephew by marriage, and the first cousin of Jodi.

The next time the dulcet voice spoke into his ear, it was to mention monseigneur. 'But who,' Henry said, 'can claim these days to be conceived in lawful bed? I can, of course. Your master does not even know who his father might be – his mother, poor bawd, was open to all passing traffic. And it is hardly to be expected that Catherine over there didn't pick up the trick – wave! See, she is smiling! – with lusty young Claes in the same house. Then he abandoned her – you do know? – for the boys in a Trebizond bath-house, leaving her to earn her keep in the bed of a murderer. Catherine and Paul, the bawd and the bastard! A marriage, wouldn't you say, made in heaven?'

'I beg your pardon,' Robin said. 'You are wrong. And even if you were not, Lord Beltrees is your own uncle.'

The change in the seraphic blue eyes turned him cold. Then, after an interval, the boy spoke, less guardedly than before. 'Claes,' he said. 'The ape is called Claes, or maybe Lord Billygoat. His wife might enjoy thuggish handling, but Claes vander Poele shares none of my blood, and his son is the son of an animal.'

'Henry?' said the lord Wolfaert's voice. It was impatient, not shocked. He had heard the tone, not the sense of the outburst.

Henry turned his bright head, his face pale. 'My lord, forgive me,' he said. 'But I cannot bear to hear light words of my mother, even though she is dead, and I know my lord of Beltrees is happily married. If you will excuse me, I shall go to my room.' A tear had caught in his lashes.

'Of course,' said the seigneur of Veere slowly. He watched the boy leave, and then returned his heavy gaze upon Robin. The table was silent.

Robin got to his feet. He said, 'I am sorry, my lord. The young man was mistaken. But if you will excuse me, it might be better if I go to my room also.'

'You are excused,' Wolfaert said; and turned to his neighbour.

Robin did not go to his room. Instead, he followed the noise to the nursery, and dragged Pasque out of the room. 'We must go home.'

It was like holding a chicken. 'What? What? Are you crazy? We have hardly arrived!'

He tried to explain. But even if he had known her vernacular, her desire to remain would have thrown back a legion of Goths. 'So you and some spoiled child have quarrelled! You are the guest! Go to the lord, and apologise, and make your peace! Or if you cannot admit you are wrong, then go home. We do not need you,' said Pasque.

'You do!' said Robin. 'Pasque, he could hurt us.'

'Hurt old Pasque? A silly boy of eleven? Go along,' said the woman. 'Find the boy. Make it up. I am busy.'

He saw, soon enough, that it was hopeless to argue, and that he was unlikely to make an ally of Pasque, or the bodyguard. He had no case to make, other than an account of a conversation, which the boy would deny, and a feeling of extreme foreboding. The boy was only eleven, and parroting the language of elders – but even so, what had happened was not accidental. Robin had been placed in disfavour, and it would take little more to persuade the lord of Veere to send him home. Robin did not know why Henry should want that, but he proposed to make sure it didn't happen.

Chapter 33

ROBIN OF BERECROFTS had little vanity – his father and grandfather had seen to that. But he had a sense of pride and of fairness, and he had to sacrifice both in order to stay at his post beside Jordan that day. There was no appeal. Even if the lord of Veere were not wholly deceived, the boy Henry was well born and his kinsman, and Robin was the page of a man who could have no love for Henry's father.

His plan had been to stay with the child while it slept. Instead, curt words and raised eyebrows forced him out to the butts to help retrieve arrows, and to hold the pennants for the pony-racing that followed. The lords and their friends worked Robin hard, but the June sun was high in the sky, the pleasure-grounds were green and tree-shadowed and pleasant, and he would have borne them no grudge, had he not been aware of a growing unfriendliness, so that no matter how fast he pelted about, the shouts from the players became brusque and impatient. And as it developed, he watched Henry's smile.

He learned to admire Henry. Young as he was, the boy must have trained long and hard with a master to attain such proficiency. He was also inherently gifted. He managed his horse, big for his years, with the grace and strength of someone much older, and his eye was razor-sharp.

Robin knew. The arrow that slightly missed its route pierced his skin by so fine a margin that, although he bled, he deserved no attention other than an irritated order to watch where he ran. It was Henry's horse, alarmed by his presence, which reared and came down, shouldering him to the ground. And it was Henry who, almost winning a cast, had his aim put out by Robin's sudden appearance and throwing, grazed Robin's thigh with his lance before being dislodged by his horse from the saddle.

Ladies ran to the fallen boy's aid, but Henry leaped to his feet and gallantly absolved Robin from all blame, while agreeing, limping over the grass, to take his ease for a while. The lady of Veere had emerged, with the children. Jordan, walking sedately with Pasque, saw his new sister and ran to her lap, where he sat, being courted with sweetmeats. Robin could hear his high voice, and see the ladies round him exclaiming and laughing. Henry smiled, showing one dimple.

Robin went to sit beside Jordan, but the lady of Veere wished to speak to him. Listening, he was advised that, being a boy among coarse-living men, he had not yet learned to conduct himself as gentlemen did, but should try and learn from example. He heard that it was positively atrocious that a youth of his years should attempt to strike a valuable animal and injure its rider, and moreover spread malicious tales of his host and his hostess and their guests. She wished him to know this, and to understand that she would take no severe action, provided the misconduct halted at once.

Robin bled, inside and out. Robin said, 'My lady, anything I have done, I have done unknowingly, and out of ignorance. Please forgive my lack of skill. I would not harm you or yours, not for the world.'

The lady of Veere looked surprised, and her face softened a little. But when the meal was over, he found himself chivvied into the sports field again.

His lesions ached, but at least he knew now what to expect (or so he thought), and whatever Henry might do, he managed somehow to avoid him. The child Jordan played among the women and babies. It was only when the call came for golf that Robin felt the first breath of danger. Any game with a ball would attract Jodi.

The clubs came, and the heavy balls fashioned of wood. Robin took one, and gave it to Jodi. Henry strolled up and took it away. 'Did you want a ball, Robin?' he said. 'I shall ask the lord of Veere to spare you one later. But really, we need them all now.' He went off, and Jordan looked up, his lip trembling. Catherine kissed him. 'Come and play with me instead.' Then someone shouted for Robin, and he went.

They played rovers at first, hitting the ball from place to place: into trees and over walls and into pools, from which Robin retrieved it. Twice it made its way back near the children, and twice Jordan scrambled up and, trotting, attempted to capture it. Each time Robin got there before him and, picking him up, carried him back to the others. Jordan squealed at him with frustration, and Robin had no way of explaining.

Miraculously, the third time was spared him since the lady of Veere, standing up, ordered her lord to take his party elsewhere, for the sake of the little ones. Robin looked at her in a fervour of gratitude, and then dashed off to serve as he might.

He was not needed for long. Already the golf seemed to be palling. They listened to Henry when, boyishly shy, he asked if they might not ride to the dunes and shoot rabbits. He added, thoughtfully, that he was sure Robin too would enjoy it, despite not, of course, having a weapon.

Robin agreed. He hoped that Henry was as accurate with a crossbow as he was with the other kind. He proposed to do his very best to keep behind Henry. He didn't know whether to be glad or not when he saw that monseigneur's step-daughter Catherine had left the child in order to ride to the beach with her sweetheart. He felt alone, and not alone. He was a person, as he had been in Iceland, riding up between Katla and Hekla. He was monseigneur's representative.

Soon after that, he saw that Henry was missing. He wheeled his horse and, ignoring a peremptory shout, spurred back the way he had come. He did not realise, then, that the girl Catherine had turned to come after him, or that it was Paul van Borselen who had shouted.

Later, he pieced together what had occurred at the castle. Later, he could imagine how Henry, arriving back, had abandoned his horse and, making for the discarded kolfs and the balls, had lured Jodi into following, tap tap tapping the wood, making it bounce out of sight through the garden. Through the garden, the park and the fields until the castle was well out of sight. Then he invented a game. Jodi trotted, and his cousin bounced the ball after him.

The laughing gulls must have had the best view: the three-year-old chuckling and stopping; the ball thudding up to his feet; Jodi bending to seize it and then, reminded, staggering on, frothing with laughter. And stopping. And watching the ball bounce again, while lissom Henry, big cousin Henry, pretended to be unable to catch him. While behind the child, nearer and nearer, was the ditch, the deep drainage ditch of the flatlands.

By the time Robin saw them, far in the distance, the ball was no longer trickling to the child's feet but bumping against him; gently at first, with a little rebound, and then harder, so that Jordan cried out and turned, tears of surprise in his eyes. And then big cousin Henry, instead of comforting him, took out another ball from his sleeve and, dropping it, drew back his club. Jordan watched him perplexed, without moving. Then some hint of what was happening must have reached him, for as Henry bore down on the ball, the child turned and staggeringly ran.

Robin heard the crack of the ball and Jordan's scream. He saw the ball chop in the air, a speck in the distance, and the white, fixed stare of Henry behind it. He heard the rap as the ball fell, then the crack as the club again caught it. The double sound, repeated over and over, reached through the quiet like the cluck of a bird, or a man alone, tapping a hammer. Only, ragged and faint as the wail of a leveret, there came too the cries of the child whom the ball was pursuing.

A single hard shot would have felled Jordan and killed him at once. That was not Henry's aim. Henry was deliberately whipping him on to fall and drown in the gutter behind him.

Then Robin shouted. Behind him, unexpectedly, he heard other cries, and the thud of other horses from his own hunting-party overhauling him. A deep voice roared: that of Wolfaert van Borselen.

Henry's face lifted, white as a shell. Briefly, he hesitated. Then he drew a great breath and, racing forward, stopped at the ball, and raised his club as a hunting-cat would stretch out its forearm. For like the hunting-cat, he was smiting to kill.

There was no chance they could stop him. There was no chance that anyone could stop him, even the rider who burst through the trees from the castle and scored through the grassland like fire, crying aloud as he came.

Henry heard him. Henry glanced round, once, with no real surprise on his face. Then his head lifted, to weigh up his target. He positioned his club without haste, and without haste swept it down to connect, clean and hard, with the ball. There was a click and a whisper as the solid boxwood shot through the air. There was no doubt that it would strike the child's head. Henry had all the skills of his father.

While it happened, the horseman behind was riding flat out. Robin saw that he leaned to one side, the reins in one hand and a kolf in the other. Memory, uncontrolled, showed himself as a boy, also eleven, standing on the flat sands of Leith and watching a cold, distant man, the same man, dispatching a tzukanion ball far out to sea. He saw that there was a ball now in the grass ahead of the rider, one dropped by Henry, and that Nicholas de Fleury was riding towards it.

He saw Henry swing up his club and glance round as the other man shouted. He saw Henry prepare for his stroke, his eyes on the staggering child. He saw Nicholas de Fleury lift his club in turn for the stroke that would kill Henry as Henry killed. Just before the moment of impact the man's face, so unlike, was blank, uncannily blank like the boy's. The sieur de Fleury called, one final explosive cry, and then closed his grip and aimed.

Far ahead, through his panic, Jodi heard his father's voice, the familiar, trusted voice, calling his name. Oblivious of the ball whistling towards him, he tried to turn but could not. Soaked and frightened and sobbing, he lost his balance and fell, just as the boxwood hurtled up, and sped over his head to skid glistening into the turf.

Behind, all the clamour broke off. The sieur de Fleury's club dragged and bounced over the ground, aborting its shot. The horse cantered on. The rider hurled the kolf from him. It sped hissing and whining to dig, splintering, into the ground. Then its wielder was level with Henry de St Pol who stood motionless, scornful, waiting for the great blow that reached him, and felled him.

No one moved. The boy lay on the ground. Then Nicholas de Fleury walked past him, and threw himself down by the small, mewing child in the grass.

Robin was first to rush up, his throat choked. The girl Catherine dismounted beside him, saying nothing. Her stepfather Nicholas did not look round. The only sound was his voice, conducting a long peaceful monologue as he sheltered the child with his shoulder, and blew its nose, and wiped the mud from its cheeks. It sobbed intermittently, and his fingers caressed it. When he addressed them, it was in the same conversational tone.

'Berecrofts, you will take Jordan back to the castle, collect the slut who helped you bring this about, and return to Antwerp at once with them both. Van Borselen will give you a guard and a wagon. There you will remain until Mistress Clémence will join you. You will not go out, or take the child out for any reason whatever, and you will stay until you receive further orders. Are you capable of understanding all that?'

The child, clinging, claimed his attention, and his fingers, circling, gentled its head. Catherine de Charetty said, 'Robin is injured from trying to protect him. Henry did all he could short of murder to get Robin thrown out.'

'And you stopped it, I see.'

She flushed and paled, her face lined with anxiety. 'None of us realised at the time. We were stupid. Let me take Jordan. Let me go with Jordan to Antwerp, with Paul.'

Her stepfather looked at her, as to a stranger. 'Why not?' he said, and got up, lifting the child in his arms. 'See,' he said. 'Catherine has almonds, and Robin will let you ride on his horse.'

'And maman?' said Jordan. His heart pumped like a bird's.

'Maman is in Bruges,' said his father. 'You will see her soon. *And so shall I.*'

They left, and Wolfaert van Borselen, dismounted, stood in their place. He said, 'What can I say?' He sounded hoarse.

'There is your pupil,' Nicholas said. 'He speaks for you.'

The boy Henry had got to his feet. Expertly delivered, the blow should have broken his neck. At the last moment, the man had held back. As it was, the boy swayed. The whole side of his face was discoloured, and his pupils were so distended that his eyes appeared black, and not blue.

'He is scum,' Wolfaert said. 'I should never have taken him.'

'He is the son of your cousin. This is a house expected to breed and train leaders. You were sent a savage and have done nothing to curb him.'

Wolfaert said, 'He caused no trouble before.'

'Are you excusing him?'

'No. But the fault isn't all mine. You and your feud with his father –'

'And the conduct, you would say, of your other cousin, who slept with his father?'

'You said it, not I,' Wolfaert said.

'Just to remind you. You knew. So that any fool but you, my lord, would have been on the lookout for trouble.'

'I beg your pardon!' Wolfaert was flushed.

'I am not ready to give it. This boy is afraid that mine has a claim on his father. He wants him dead. Am I right?'

He turned on the boy who returned his stare from under drawn brows. 'Of course,' Henry said. 'A bitch litters. The product is dung. You and him.'

Wolfaert lifted his arm, and then dropped it.

'What a pity,' Nicholas said, 'that I wasn't wearing a ring. My lord? I need transport.'

'Anything. Anything. Food, a wagon, an escort. And for this knave, a prison cell in the castle.'

'I am a van Borselen,' said the boy. His face blazed.

'You are a St Pol, nothing else,' said the seigneur of Veere. 'I have disowned you. Beg your life from this lord.'

'What lord? This cuckold?' said Henry.

'Did you speak? Don't speak,' Nicholas said.

'How will you stop me?' said the boy.

'With a gag. Will your men remove him, my lord?'

'Where?' said Wolfaert.

'Oh, to prison,' Nicholas said. 'But not for long. An hour, maybe. I have to send off some messages. Then I am taking him with me to Bruges.'

'Tonight?' Wolfaert said. A man of conscience, he tried to dissuade him, but was clearly quite thankful to fail. He knew Nicholas had already ridden from Antwerp. In fact, he had set out that morning from Ghent. Nicholas hardly remembered it, through the pure, high, white fury that burned, Loki's star, in his mind and his senses.

*

It was a fast journey, fast as he wanted. He slept, he thought, in the van Borselen boat which took them from Flusa over the Scheldt, but no one mentioned it; the small armed escort provided by Wolfaert were silent throughout. Henry's eyes followed him in the half-dark but Henry said nothing: Nicholas had sealed his mouth, as he had promised, some time ago. He took a room for a few hours at Sluys, which they reached after midnight, and changed Wolfaert's horses for some of his own, which were kept there at stable. At three in the morning there was an outcry from the place where the men-at-arms were sleeping with Henry: the boy had been ungagged on his orders, and on some excuse his escort had untied his hands, and he had nearly escaped, wounding the innkeeper. Nicholas dealt with it as Astorre would have done; the men-at-arms muttered behind him. By dawn they were riding into Bruges with the first of the packhorses and wagons, and Nicholas was at his own door.

The night porter was sleepy, and unknown to him. Nicholas kicked the door from his grasp and, when men came running half armed, made known his opinion in a few suitable words, and had his escort made welcome and led to the kitchens. He gave the leader his purse, entire, as a gesture to Wolfaert, but the man's eyes, as he thanked him, were aloof. Henry stood, his face grotesquely bloated, and shivered while everyone stared. His hands were tied and his lips bound again. Nicholas hooked him by the shirt-collar and pulled him indoors and upstairs, passing familiar faces but not looking at them. No one spoke. Since he did not know which door was Gelis's, he hammered on them all. A baby started to cry.

Father Moriz said, 'What are you doing?' He stood by the stairs, fully gowned, and smelling of candles.

Nicholas said, 'Where is Gelis?' Behind the gag, the boy was sobbing quietly.

The gnarled, truculent face surveyed them both. Moriz said, 'I will fetch her. Go to the parlour. Who is this?'

Nicholas said, 'Gelis knows.'

'Go, then,' said Moriz.

In the parlour, which was unlit as yet by the dawn and quite empty, Henry ceased sobbing at once. His eyes sneered.

'Your moment is coming,' Nicholas said. He found tinder and lit all the candles, so that the boy's misshapen face glimmered and gleamed. Then he untied the gag.

'Your wife is a cow,' Henry said. 'I have seen both her dugs down her dress.'

The door opened abruptly. Henry stopped speaking. 'Nice attempt,' Nicholas said.

It was Diniz, looking heavily worried. 'Come in,' Nicholas said. 'Who sent Catherine to Veere?'

Like the good man he was, Diniz swallowed his questions. He said, 'Paul invited her. She is friendly with Paul van Borselen. I hope – I hope nothing has happened to her.' His eyes were on Henry.

The door opened again. It was Tilde, Catherine's sister, in her bedgown. Diniz said, 'Nicholas is asking about Catherine.'

'Why?' said Tilde. 'She's at Veere. Is something wrong?' Her eyes fell on the boy, and she gasped.

'This,' Nicholas said, 'is Henry, son of Simon de St Pol. Diniz may remember him as a child in Madeira, where he expected to enjoy my execution. Did Diniz not tell you this?'

Someone made a sound, and suppressed it: Henry, his hair aureoled by the light. He spoke in a whisper. 'I was four years old when it happened. I asked you to forgive me.' His eyes were full of tears.

'. . . And has since,' Nicholas continued, 'escaped a charge of attacking a princeling and attempting to blind him in Scotland. You didn't know this? You didn't know about his father and Gelis?'

Diniz said nothing. Tilde looked uncomfortably at her husband. 'We had heard. But –'

'You had heard. You knew that Henry de St Pol had been sent to the household at Veere. You knew that my son was at Antwerp. You knew that I was absent. And you did nothing about it, so that your sister not only went to Veere, she allowed Wolfaert's wife to bring my son there. Yesterday. Friday. Yesterday, without mother, father or nurse, Jordan and Henry were together at Veere.'

'Robin was with him,' said Gelis. 'Robin and Pasque.' Moriz had brought her. She stood in the doorway, her hair rough on her robe, her face ghastly. There were others behind her, one of them Julius. She said, 'Nicholas?' Then her gaze fell on the boy.

'So if Tilde and Diniz helped it to happen,' Nicholas said, 'what about Jordan's mother? Pasque, you say. Do I remember appointing Pasque as senior nurse to my son? She cleans the floors well, it is true, but cannot really be expected to prevent the lady of Veere from walking all over them. Mistress Clémence is the senior nurse. Where is she?'

'*What has happened?*' said Gelis.

'. . . Or do I know? Looking after the motherless infants of Anselm Adorne. I sympathise. But Anselm Adorne has many children, and you and I had only one. Still, perhaps you were right. One should be magnanimous. Jordan's mother, unlike theirs, was alive and could care for him. Except – how extraordinary! – Jordan's mother left Antwerp as well.'

'Tell me. *Tell me*,' said Gelis. '*Where is Jordan?*'

'You have to ask me?' Nicholas said. 'I have been in Arras: how should I know? You mentioned Robin; but Robin is fifteen and quite as overawed as Pasque when a great lady breaks all the rules.'

'Robin didn't know,' said Gelis flatly. 'Robin didn't know of the danger. I did. It is my fault. It is all my fault, whatever has happened. Nicholas, have pity. Is he dead?'

Father Moriz said, 'Let him answer that question alone. None of us has a right to hear it. Come. Let us go.'

'No!' The scream of the boy stopped them all. 'No! Don't go! He will kill me!'

The eyes of Jordan's parents had locked. Nicholas said, 'He will never forget what has happened. He is alive.'

She stared at him, her eyes blank. The boy, throwing himself at her feet, clung to her gown. 'Help me. Help me. He will tell you terrible things.'

Slowly, Gelis looked down. 'Did you harm Jordan?'

Exposed to the light was the profile of a white and gold angel. Then it turned, showing the closed eye, the thickened lips, the gross swelling, black, red and blue. Henry whispered, 'I couldn't do it, what Robin does. I couldn't. I couldn't. And when he makes me, I bleed.'

Gelis pulled her skirts away. The boy subsided, his face running with tears. Nicholas said, 'Is that what you told the men-at-arms? Henry, why did I strike you?'

The boy sobbed. He said, 'Because I wouldn't – wouldn't stay in your bed.'

'But, Henry, you and I had our quarrel in public,' Nicholas said. 'A dozen people were there, including the lord Wolfaert of Veere. They would say that your tale was a lie. They would say you were punished because you had secretly attempted to murder your cousin, forcing him to run to his death.'

'It isn't true!' Henry said. 'He was running from you. I didn't want him to bleed. I was saving him.'

Someone made an odd noise: probably Julius. Father Moriz wore a look of disgust, and Diniz had put his arm around Tilde, his grip convulsively tight, his face wretched. Gelis, pallid as a Venetian mask, looked first at the boy, then at Nicholas. Then she bent, and took the boy by the ear and pulled him up. He stopped crying.

She said, 'My dear Henry, that is one accusation that will never stick. Truth apart, the lord of Veere will see that it doesn't. Which is the side of your face that doesn't hurt yet? Because if you wait, I, too, am going to present you with a mark of my feelings for you.'

She had actually lifted her hand when the boy tore free and made for the door. There, someone caught and removed him. Nicholas concentrated on Gelis. He said, 'Thank you. I always hoped to be credited with my preferred vices, at least. So why did you decide to leave Jodi? He asked for you, by the way, between screams.'

The group at the door had dissolved. Now Father Moriz, stretching his hand, drew Tilde and Diniz out of the room and, shutting the door, stood inside. He said, 'Stop, Nicholas. You are not yourself. Go to your child, both of you. So long as he is safe, nothing else matters. You have, I am afraid, found the miscreant.'

'Where is Jodi? Is he downstairs?' Gelis asked.

Nicholas slammed his palms on the back of a chair. 'My God, do you think I would bring him here? He is in Antwerp, and will stay there. As soon as Mistress Clémence returns, Pasque will receive her wages and go. Robin will be sent back to Scotland. The guard has already been doubled. What sort of mother are you?'

'You left him alone?' Gelis said. 'After all that, you left him alone in order to come here with Henry?'

The priest said, 'Catherine de Charetty is also with him, and Paul. The men downstairs told me.'

There was a porcelain vase on the table. It was Indian, and had been in the old house as well. Nicholas detached a hand and, lifting it, hurled it with a crash on the floor. 'I asked you a question.'

She looked up, her eyes wide with shock. 'You didn't care about Henry. You left Jordan because you wanted to do this to me. What sort of father are you?'

'To do what to you?' Nicholas said. 'Ask you questions you are ashamed to answer?' He lifted a glass flask and balanced it.

'I'm not ashamed. I was asked to meet Julius and his client. You were away. She owns half the *Fleury*.'

'The monumental Gräfin,' Nicholas said. He lifted the glass vase and smashed it straight down. The fragments flew everywhere. 'You were avid to meet her. Didn't you know that Charlotte, that stupid woman, wanted your nurses? She didn't care what happened to Jodi. Jodi thought Henry was chasing for fun. Henry pushed him like a ball, striking him further and further. The last shot of all was aimed to kill, at his head. But he fell.' He moved about, touching one thing after another. He saw a casket of Marian's.

Gelis said, 'You were away. You could have given Jodi these two weeks at least. I'm sorry, but Father Moriz is right. We'll talk when you are sober.'

'It is your fault,' Nicholas said. He held the casket, and thought of Marian, and opened his hands in spite of it all. It fell, and Gelis cried out.

He said, 'It is your fault that Henry thinks that your son is Simon's. That is why he is trying to kill him.'

'And what about you?' Gelis said. 'Why did you come here with Henry, instead of staying with Jordan who needed you? Why have you dashed to abuse me, except to hide from yourself what has really happened? What you can't bear. What you want to punish me for. But it isn't my fault, is it, what has happened to Henry? It isn't my fault that –'

'Stop,' said Nicholas. He found he had stepped across and was holding her hard, one hand over her mouth. Glass crunched under his feet. Her eyes, Nordic-blue, stared into his, exploring them, puzzled.

Father Moriz shouldered between them, breathing hard. He said, 'Gelis, get out.'

She pulled her head free, and Nicholas let his hand drop. 'We haven't finished,' she said.

'You have,' said the priest grimly. 'Stand back.'

Nicholas stood back. The fury, evaporating, left a white haze. The door opened as Father Moriz walked to it, holding Gelis. Mistress Clémence stood there, with another woman. Mistress Clémence curt-seyed to Gelis and the priest and looked across to where Nicholas stood. She said, 'I am free to go whenever you want me, my lady.' She paused and said, 'I have to tell you that Master de St Pol is asleep and well guarded, and has been seen by a doctor. Also that . . .' She hesitated, glancing behind.

The other woman said, 'Also that his tale of abuse was untrue. He is untouched and whole, apart from some well-deserved bruises.' She appeared to smile at the priest. She said, 'Clémence will see to the lady Gelis.'

Gelis went out, with Mistress Clémence and Moriz. The sun silvered the glass on the floor, making rainbows. *Regnbogi Nikudr.* The same woman's voice said, 'When did you last eat?'

He tried to focus. A youngish woman, with the dark hair and bright complexion of the Irish, such as you found sometimes in Iceland, or Spain, or the Western Isles. Her eyes were like violets. He smelled her scent, and heard the sound of her faint, exact breathing.

She said, 'I have had a tray put in your room, and a bed made up. Come. I will show you.'

She left him at the door.

When he woke, he had slept the day through, and it was evening. His head was heavy from the long sleep, but he felt better, and competent. When he appeared, no one expressed surprise. They treated him, he thought, as if he had been ill. He said, 'Where is Mistress Clémence?'

Gelis said, 'I thought you would want her to go back to Antwerp. She is on her way now. The boy Henry is still asleep.'

'I see,' Nicholas said. The priest sat, saying nothing. Diniz gave him some wine, which he didn't want, and pressed his shoulder lightly in passing. Diniz, he remembered, knew a great deal too much. Someone had cleared up the glass.

Tilde, who had not brought in her baby, was preparing to say something. Nicholas forestalled her. 'I'm glad Clémence is going, but of course Catherine will have been a great help. I'm sorry, Tilde. I'm sure, but for her, it would have been worse.'

'And but for Robin,' the priest remarked. 'It is your affair, of course. But Robin was ignorant, too, of the dangers. Have you even heard his side of the story? Whatever it was, he has already proved his loyalty and his courage ten times over this year, and you are a fool to forget it.'

Nicholas remembered, with difficulty, having made some arbitrary decisions about the future of Robin and Pasque. He recalled very clearly some of the things Gelis had said. She had regained her tranquillity this evening, and her hair had been dressed with meticulous care. He said, 'I think I should probably cancel everything I said this morning and start over again. In any case, I have to ask your forbearance, all of you. I can't give any more time to the business or to my family. I have to go straight back to the Duke.'

'War?' Julius said. His voice lilted. Nicholas saw, clear-eyed now, the changes of the last year: the sleekness that Rome and Cologne had wrought in him. Or, of course, other things.

'Yes,' Nicholas said. 'You don't want to come?'

'I'd cede my place,' Moriz said. 'I have had my fill of John and his guns for a while. Do you have to go?'

'I have a contract,' Nicholas said. 'The business depends on good faith. It will be over in four months or five, and then we can arrange for the winter in Scotland.'

'The barony?' Julius said, with friendly insolence. 'You can manage your business from there?'

'I don't expect to indefinitely,' Nicholas said. 'And meantime, I have you and Diniz and Moriz and Gregorio, not to mention those who do the actual work. I can get to Bruges in two weeks, and Venice in six if you make a mess of it. We'll talk after supper.'

'You have something else to talk of,' said Moriz. 'The boy.'

'That foul-mouthed little blackguard?' said Julius. 'Lock him in the Steen and get rid of the key. Or he really will kill someone one day.'

'Will that help?' Moriz said. 'His father might be even more dangerous.'

'Send him to Simon,' said Diniz.

Gelis glanced at him. The others showed no surprise at his curtness. Diniz and Simon de St Pol were related; but not even kinship could make Diniz excuse the boy Henry.

Gelis said, 'Simon has left Madeira, it seems. If you free Henry, they might both go to Scotland.'

Julius had walked to the door, apparently hearing a step. He said, 'If they do, I think the kindest thing you could do, Nicholas, is to find some baronial reason for hanging them. My lady?' Opening the door, he was ushering somebody in. He said, 'Nicholas? Have you met the Gräfin Anna von Hanseyck?'

No monumental countess appeared; merely the violet-eyed apparition of the morning, with her dusky hair bound up in voile. She smiled. She said, 'You don't remember. You were asleep on your feet. How do you do?'

'Better than I did this morning, thanks to you,' Nicholas said with extreme smoothness. He wondered how on earth Jan had made such a mistake. He wondered how on earth Julius had met her. He knew Gelis was watching.

Julius said, 'We were talking about what to do with the monster. What do you think?'

She walked across and sat beside Gelis. Her gown of fine taffeta was cut plain as a child's. Gelis had met her, of course, in Cologne. Gelis could have corrected Jan's mistake, if she had heard it. The Gräfin Anna said, 'What do I think? That we should none of us waste our time guessing. Lord Beltrees has decided already.'

'Nicholas,' Julius corrected her, smiling.

'We do not know each other well enough,' the Gräfin said; and Nicholas did not contradict her, for he disliked the free use of his name. Her French, though inflected, was well managed.

He said, 'Yes, I have decided what to do about Henry. There is nothing you need to arrange. I shall be taking him with me tomorrow.'

His eyes were on Gelis. She said, 'Where?'

'To my camp,' Nicholas said. 'He has been taught the arrogance of a knight. Now he ought to practise the knock-about life of a soldier.'

Moriz got to his feet. 'Are you serious? A boy of eleven, made to live with a mercenary company at war! Is this your punishment?'

'Yes, it is,' Nicholas said.

'Well, I must say,' said Julius in astonishment, 'I'd rather like to see that. My God, he would get his deserts. From the other men, if not from the enemy. Mind you, if he survives –'

'If he survives, he will turn into a professional thug,' Gelis said.

'And whether he survives or not, Simon will come for you. What are you thinking of?'

'Jordan,' Nicholas said. It silenced her, for the moment.

'But also the boy?' said the Gräfin beside her. 'Forgive me: my child is a daughter, but spirited. She may become wilful one day, but will always follow a noble example. This boy has been unwisely reared. He may find a new inspiration.'

'It is too late,' Gelis said. 'The bond is too strong. Simon depends on him. It will not make Jordan safer.'

'Then, failing the army, Henry must be dealt with by the law,' Nicholas said. 'Perhaps you are right. Simon can pick a fight with the magistrates, not with me. Will you take him to the Steen, or shall I?' He did not look at Diniz, who had been silent since his single remark.

She gave in, as he expected: the army was preferable to disgrace. They all agreed, with reluctance. It was just as well, since Nicholas had already visited Henry and, locking the door, had told him where he was going.

Alone through the day, the boy had had time to review, perhaps, what he had done; and to worry about what might now happen to him. A grown man would have done so, and a grown man might have lounged before him like this, insolence on his damaged face, concealing his fears. Nicholas saw that Henry's supreme confidence was not assumed. Whoever had dared to touch him would soon answer for it to his family The fact that the van Borselen side of his family had rejected him seemed to count not at all. Henry had never thought much of a mother who had died when he was three.

So when Nicholas, perched by the door, twirled the key and told him what was to happen, the smile left the boy's face. For a moment his lips opened, then he stood.

'Oh no,' Henry said. 'Oh no, you stupid animal, you can't get away with that. I demand to see a magistrate.'

'They're all busy,' Nicholas said.

'You won't? Then I'll shout,' Henry said. He walked to the window and opened it. He said, 'You really shouldn't have locked the door before you walked in to rape me. I want to be kept safe until my father comes.'

'I said you'd say that,' Nicholas said. 'Actually, they're all waiting down in the yard hoping you'll favour them with some technical language. Really, away from the wharfs, I've seldom met anyone so obsessed with the business of reproduction. One wonders what your home life is like. In any case, as you surely must know, a doctor has already reported you to be in a state of infantile purity.'

'Some liar paid by you,' Henry said.

'I couldn't afford him. Dr Andreas is, among other things, a household physician to King James of Scotland. No one,' Nicholas said, 'is going to tolerate any more of this conduct. You attempted to kill a young child. You should hang for it. Be thankful that today I am feeling more lenient.'

'It's an excuse,' Henry said. 'You could never touch me if my father were here. You're a coward. You're a traitor as well. You're going to force me to fight against Scotland's allies, and whatever happens to me, you'll say it wasn't your fault.'

'You'd rather hang?' Nicholas said. 'I can arrange it.'

'You can't!'

'Would you like to place a small wager?'

The boy stared at him. Nicholas gazed back, holding in his mind the sound of the ball and the club, and the screaming. He said, 'In any case, I didn't say I was sending you. I am going with you. You will enjoy that.'

He watched the boy's eyes, and the gleam that came into them. The boy said, 'I might.'

'On the other hand, I might make sure that you don't. That depends on you. We leave in the morning.' He rose and paused. 'Don't you think it a pity that this had to happen?'

'Yes. I should have killed him,' said the boy.

Nicholas de Fleury rode off to Arras next morning, Julius beside him, and did not have to bind the boy Henry's mouth, for it remained set and closed. He said goodbye to the others in public, and to Gelis in private so that his household might retain their illusions. He thought he had secured, with her, the protection of Jordan. He was removing the worst of the danger. And if Simon set foot in Bruges or in Brabant, he would know, for he had returned to his divining, understanding as he now did that it was to be his master for life. He did not kiss his wife because, this time, no one was watching.

The Gräfin Anna came to see Julius leave, and he bent and saluted her hand from the saddle. His face was flushed. She touched his knee, and then walked over to Nicholas. 'You are well?'

'Yes,' he said. He smiled as he usually did.

'Good. I didn't wish to trouble you this time with business, but that is why I am here,' said the Gräfin. 'I do not like to see the brilliant guardian of my investments risking his life for no reason, so I shall express the hope, if Gelis allows, that you return safe, and return often. I admire what you are trying to do for the boy.'

'Don't,' said Nicholas. 'He won't thank me.' Moving off, he didn't look round, but felt, he thought, the remarkable eyes following

Julius, or himself, or both, all the way up the street to the White Bear. At the junction he turned, but the only eyes following him were those of his wife.

Chapter 34

ON THURSDAY THE fourth of June, the day of the fracas at Veere, the Duke of Burgundy launched his army into the field under the black and purple legend VENGEANCE! VENGEANCE! By the time Nicholas de Fleury reached Arras on the ninth day of June, the Duke had advanced thirty miles to the castle he still possessed at Péronne, situated on the river Somme between the French-manned towns of Amiens and St Quentin. From that highly provocative spot he crossed the swampy frontier of the river into enemy land and marched south, burning hamlets and crops as he went. On Thursday the eleventh, when Nicholas reached him, the Duke had taken up quarters on his way to the well-garrisoned French town of Roye, and was awaiting news of a foray by his van.

His main army was still camped around him. Before reporting, Nicholas went and found Captain Astorre, who was playing dice outside his tent. Astorre said, '*Merde*, you took your time. Master Julius!'

'I wanted to know what you were spending all that money on,' Julius said. 'Now I see. Can you put up with me for a week or two?'

'If you say so. I'm short of a notary. Well, boy! But I have to tell you that you won't find many banquets or princesses here. Nor much fighting maybe, not in this war. And who's this? That's not the son of the merchant?'

'No,' Nicholas said. 'That's the pig-sticker in the poke. This is a somewhat saddle-sore Henry, come with reluctance to serve under you and me and anyone, really, who wants something tedious done for them. He may be apt to wander off, so I want him looked after by two willing men who, for a consideration, will not let themselves be bribed, stabbed, shot, seduced or led to believe that on any excuse whatever, this boy may leave camp.'

'Annoyed you, has he? Can he ride? You couldn't ride,' Astorre said. 'You couldn't shoot, either.' The faces round the dice-board were grinning. Astorre could get his own back sometimes.

'I was only pretending,' said Nicholas agreeably. 'You're lucky this time, he can do both. But that's all he can do. He thinks rough work beneath him.'

'Oho!' said Astorre.

'It *is* beneath me,' said Henry.

There was a chorus of good-humoured groans; the boy's eyes flashed. They were sapphire-blue, and his hair was like corn. The face beneath it was rather less swollen than heretofore. Nicholas said, 'And that had better be the only thing that's beneath him, or on top. Do you hear me?'

'He's yours?' said Astorre with perfect understanding.

Nicholas laughed. It took an effort to avoid the boy's eye, but he caught the edge of Julius's amusement. He said, 'Yes, he's mine.'

Later, coming back from the Duke's room, he walked round the camp greeting everyone, and then held a company council of war in Astorre's tent, with John le Grant and Julius and Astorre's deputy Thomas. He deferred, as always, to Astorre and noted that, in his turn, Astorre deferred to the master gunner. He had already confirmed that his hundred lances were trimly provided for, and in excellent heart. As for the rest, Astorre was the leader, the executive. Nicholas was not here to captain a company, but to join the band of policy-makers, the councillors of the Duke.

Astorre's view of what was happening was accurate. The Duke had put into the field about five thousand men: enough, if all went well, to frighten Louis into surrendering the Somme towns; enough to fight with if necessary. With the help of Brittany and a vast English army, it might even have been enough to topple Louis from the French throne; but Edward of England was not sufficiently sure of his good-brother of Burgundy to send his soldiers to help him just yet. A little injection of archers to Brittany was about the right response. Aunty's wool.

So far, the Duke's strategy appeared reasonable. The leaders were keeping the main body of troops well together, to guard their heels against harrying parties from St Quentin and Amiens. They had sent a small squadron nine miles to the east, to invite the little town of Nesle to surrender. It held no mighty force, only a company of five hundred franc-archers from the Isle de France, come to do their tour, tax deductible. There had been no need for John's guns and, so far, no proper fighting.

'I told you,' said Astorre. 'And they won't find much resistance in Nesle. Le Petit Picard will go by the book. We'll have more fun at

Roye. Fifteen hundred middling archers but some men-at-arms who might know their business.'

'Listen to him,' John said. 'He still wishes he were fighting the Germans or the Swiss or the Lorrainers.'

'The French aren't bad,' Astorre said. 'But their crack troops are all going to the Brittany border. We might never get near them.'

John staged a yawn. A captain's reputation grew with the quality of his enemies. It was one reason why Nicholas had never tried to tempt him to Scotland. To suit Astorre, a place had to be a notorious cockpit as well as a wealthy state or duchy or kingdom. Astorre had been happy in Cyprus.

Nicholas allowed Astorre the five minutes he deserved for his prejudices, and then proceeded to do what he had come for, which was to receive the reports of his officers and confirm that the company continued to be well run, well provisioned and in a fit state to perform, when called upon, the duties for which Burgundy was lavishly paying them. He also heard such complaints as there were – far fewer, now that the fighting season had opened. He also noticed, as always, the sharpening caused by John's presence. The company was proud of its artillery, but wanted no one to forget the soldier's traditional skills with the sword and the bow.

He thought, walking round afterwards, that Astorre's men were pleased to welcome their owner, and to show others that, by coming with them, he valued their campaign. Most of them he could put names to at once: some from their weeks together outside Hesdin, some from long acquaintance dating back to the Italian wars, and Rhodes and Cyprus and Trebizond; even to when he had just been an apprentice called Claes. He showed that he remembered, without singling them out in particular, and they treated him with the mixture of camaraderie and respect which had long been the norm. Then he left them and went with Astorre to visit the other commanders. He was there when they were all summoned, without explanation, to the Duke.

When he returned to Astorre, the rumours were already spreading, and Julius and John and Thomas were all there awaiting him, while the soldiers sat round their cooking-pots in the dusk, watching their faces. Nicholas said, 'Come into the tent. Then you can go out and tell them.'

It was news, you might say, of a victory. There were other over-tones, as reported back from the vanguard at Nesle, but the gist of it was that Nesle would give no further trouble, and the squadron would shortly rejoin the main body, prepared to march forward.

It became clear, in an indistinct sort of way, that the garrison at Nesle would give no further trouble because they had all been murdered or hanged or had been permitted to leave provided their hands were chopped off. The fault, it finally emerged, was that of the townspeople, who had killed the herald sent to bid them surrender, and then had unchivalrously dispatched two more of the besiegers during an equally sacrosanct truce. The Duke of Burgundy's vanguard, retrieving their dead, had announced that Madame de Nesle might leave if she pleased, with her servants and moveables, after which the garrison would be put to the sword. She had left, and it was.

'No need for that,' Astorre said. 'My God, were they bloody Albanians?'

'They broke the truce twice,' Julius said. 'War is war.'

'Astorre means,' Nicholas said, 'that you should make friends as well as make war, so that when you eventually take over the land, the natives are nice to you. They are not going to be nice to us.'

'Or Duke Charles,' said Astorre gloomily. 'So wait till the news gets to Roye. They'll fight to the death, mark my words.'

'Or surrender,' Nicholas said, 'to keep their hand in, as it were. Towns may fall flat from now on.'

'Will you wager?' said Astorre.

'No. Well, small towns, perhaps. The Duke is in a state of entrancement, and planning to curvet into Nesle over the bodies tomorrow. But I don't think the Duke will encourage anyone to do it again. Not if he can stop them, that is.'

Three days later, they set off for Roye. Before they left, Astorre took his employer into a corner. 'That young fellow Henry.'

'Yes?'

'Oh yes. Don't take that tone with me. That limb of Satan is the son of your friend Simon de St Pol of Kilmirren. You didn't tell me.'

'You didn't ask.'

The single eye glittered, manfully keeping its temper. 'Julius tells me that boy tried to kill your young Jordan. Julius tells me he stabbed you in Scotland. Julius suggests this is a boy who would benefit from first-class battle experience in the forefront of all our best actions. I thought I'd mention it.'

'Julius is mistaken,' Nicholas said. 'And when I want you to do something, I shall tell you myself. I brought Henry here to be taught, but not in battle. You trained me. I still have the marks of it, damn you. Train him.'

Astorre grinned. 'Doesn't do to play favourites. I let you take what was coming, and you managed. But you were one of the lads, and when they finished kicking you about, they accepted you. This one thinks he's a lord.'

'So it may not work. But it's worth trying,' Nicholas said.

'Is it?' Astorre said. 'If he can't change, he'll go back the same murderous brat. Worse than before, to blot out the failure. I've seen his face, looking at you and the rest of us. You want to watch your back with that one.'

'That's why he's got his two handlers. Let them provide themselves with a good barkable dog, and lie at night with their sheep. They do the watching.'

'I've told them. I've told them, too, to look out for the father. Sure as death, Simon will come when he hears.'

'Perhaps,' said Nicholas diplomatically. In his view, Simon would not be allowed to come when he heard. Nicholas knew who would come.

Determined as an irascible wasp, Louis of France completed the ordering of his dead brother's fief and, riding north, proceeded to conduct two wars at once single-handed. Before he had even left for the Loire, he had ordered guns and men to be sent off to Angers. From Selles, he castigated the Clerk of the Treasury of War for failing to supply pay for the army in Picardy; from Montreuil-Bellay he sent the missives that dispatched the Grand Master of the Household to join the Constable against the Burgundians. When the news reached him of the massacre at Nesle, he was roused to a state of high fury, only surpassed the following day, when he heard that Roye had surrendered, and the Burgundians were advancing on Montdidier. In the King's opinion, the Constable should be making no effort to hold minor forts such as these, but instead should be allowing the Burgundians to take and wastefully man them.

By the sixteenth of June, Roye had surrendered; by the twenty-fifth, the Duke of Burgundy was entrenched outside Montdidier which, far from resisting, very properly flung its gates open and was duly garrisoned by the Duke's soldiers. Louis, learning of it, was highly gratified.

The next news was far more important. The Duke, apparently about to turn north into Normandy, had allowed one of his rasher captains to make an attempt on Beauvais which, half succeeding, had caused the Duke to bring his whole force across to support him. As from Saturday the twenty-seventh of June, the town had been invested by the Burgundians.

'Well?' had said Louis, pacing back and forth on his horseman's legs. Beauvais was not Nesle or Montdidier. Beauvais, only forty-eight miles from Paris, meeting-point between Paris, Flanders and Normandy, was important. 'Is this our bad luck, or the chance that we have been waiting for? Can it hold out? Can we increase the garrison sufficiently to persuade the Burgundian army to entertain us to a long siege?'

'Sire,' said the messenger. 'Provided the walls withstand the initial attack, there are reinforcements on the way such as will cause the Duke more damage than he ever thought possible.'

His commanders, when summoned, agreed. The Noyon garrison was already detailed to strengthen the city until the Grand Master should arrive with his army; this force would be followed immediately by M. Gaston du Lyon and two other lords with their troops, and another body of two hundred lances. The Provost of Paris had undertaken to send his commanders, and wagon-trains of food and munitions would be readied in Paris and Rouen. Beauvais would resist its besiegers.

'If the walls stand,' the King said. 'You say that the Duke has brought up his full battery of artillery.'

'Sire,' said his adviser. 'The walls are thick, and the spirit of the people is high.'

'I am sure it is,' said the King. 'But the Duke's cannon are famous, and he has a master of ordnance better even than d'Orson, I hear. So should one not take such steps as one can?'

'Undoubtedly, monseigneur,' said the adviser.

'Undoubtedly. You will send therefore,' said Louis, 'and bring me the vicomte de Ribérac.'

In Italy that same June, the Count of Urbino's siege of the town of Volterra came to an end with a reasonable capitulation. By its terms, the Medici protected their local interest in alum, and the Volterrans (or most of them) gave up to Florence their semi-autonomy, on the promise that their possessions and property would be safeguarded.

There was a little delay, during which those Volterrans who still had misgivings gave voice to them. During this space the mercenaries within Volterra's own walls, growing impatient, threw over their contracts and set out on a methodical if drunken looting of the city which paid them. Not to be outdone, the unpaid mercenaries of the Milanese army outside entered the town and made sure of their share. Very soon after, the rest of the Florentine army, defying its leaders, rushed into the town and completed its sacking.

On the eighteenth of June, the third day after the surrender, Federigo da Montefeltro, Count of Urbino, one of the great commanders of his age, finally reduced his unruly army to order. But for Volterra, it was too late.

Tobias Beventini, the doctor who had accompanied the Count through so many of his campaigns, did not take part, with the Count, in the three days of festivities in Florence, during which lands, houses and vases of bullion were presented to the conqueror, together with a silver helmet studded with jewels and bearing the crest of Hercules trampling on a griffin, the device of Volterra. He waited until it was over and then went to the Count and, with sorrow, resigned his commission. Then he packed, and took horse for Venice, and those friends who would welcome him.

Arriving at the Banco di Niccolò, he found – as he had expected to find – a thriving business, a group of old friends, and a new one – the child, now seven months old, born to Gregorio and Margot his wife. Tobias Beventini was just over forty, unmarried (although not necessarily celibate), pink, bald, and short-tempered, but he liked children. The boy, whom he took at once on his knee, had inherited the scythe nose of his father but also much of his mother's good looks, and for a long time they spoke of nothing else. Gregorio knew about Volterra and, decent man that he was, had made sure that it need not be talked of, until Tobie was ready.

He was not ready yet. There were plenty of other questions to discuss. In the sixteen months since he left – since Nicholas vanished from Venice, that dark Carnival night – an astonishing amount seemed to have happened. Supping at the crowded company table he received a barrage of information and gossip of the spicy kind he had missed more than he knew. He heard about Julius.

'A *gräfin*?' Tobie exclaimed. 'What does she see in him?'

'A handsome man,' had said Margot, laughing.

'And someone who, without charge, will help her increase and manage her money.' Gregorio's view was more prosaic.

'But they are not considering marriage?' Tobie enquired.

Margot looked at her husband and smiled. 'Julius would marry tomorrow. But the Gräfin, after all, could choose whom she pleases, with her fortune and her rank and her looks. Nevertheless, perhaps love will prevail.'

Then it was late at night, and Tobie and Gregorio and Margot were sitting alone, and Tobie gazed into his cup and said, 'Tell me about him.' He didn't have to say whom he meant.

Gregorio looked at his wife. He said, 'Nicholas writes; but everything we know is second-hand. We were wrong in our fears. He lives with his wife and his child, and has gone out of his way to have her accepted. His work in Scotland has been prodigious, and she has partnered him. The torrential energy is the same: he knows all that the Bank is doing, and since he came back has never stopped organising, except during the few weeks he was in Iceland and for a little while after. They all needed time to recover.'

To diagnose, one listens and watches. Tobie repeated, 'All? Who?'

Margot didn't look up. Gregorio said, 'John was with him, and Moriz. And Robin, the son of a Scots merchant, who went as his page. And Katelijne Sersanders.'

'*Kathi!*' he said. His nose tickled. He sneezed.

'With her brother. She had some crazy idea of protecting them both. Nicholas should never have let her come: they always end up in escapades of some sort. This time she could have killed herself, and Nicholas came back in a fairly bad state. Moriz says he had been divining.'

'What happened?' Tobie said.

Margot answered. 'Afterwards? Kathi had to come back to Bruges for her aunt, and Nicholas and Gelis went to Antwerp.' She smiled. 'Nicholas bought a house in Antwerp four years ago, but didn't tell anyone. Gregorio was furious.'

'Why?' Tobie said. He wished he were less tired, or less drunk. None of this was what he had expected.

'Why Antwerp? Secrecy, we suppose. He hadn't decided yet what to do. And now it removes Gelis from the gossip of Bruges. People still talk about Simon. And he thought it would keep Jordan safe.'

'Jordan?' The gross man, Simon's father came to mind.

Margot said, 'What are we doing, keeping you sleepless on your first night? The rest can wait till tomorrow. Come. Gregorio will take you to your room.'

He remembered who Jordan must be. 'The child?' he said. 'Keep him safe from what?'

Then he read the letter from Moriz in Bruges that she showed him.

After a while, he looked up. Margot had gone, and Gregorio was sitting quietly, nursing his cup. Tobie said, 'Henry tried to kill the little boy?' The boy Robin had been there; the new page who had been taken to Iceland. He wondered who Robin's father might be.

'He tried to kill Nicholas too, a while ago. I remember Henry from Madeira. The little brute should have been hanged. As you see, Nicholas has decided to chastise him himself. I shan't mourn him.'

'It may be the other way round,' Tobie said. 'Dear Christ . . . What did Gelis do?'

'Moriz doesn't say. Henry is her nephew. Presumably she would think the army less humiliating than prison. And when Simon de St Pol does descend on them all, it will be Nicholas he will single out, not his wife.'

There was a long silence. Then Tobie said, 'You said we were wrong in our fears. You haven't said that we were wrong to have fears. Nicholas and Gelis are not together from love. Why are they together?'

'I don't know who could tell you. Kathi, perhaps,' said Gregorio. 'They are waging a war, Moriz thinks. An impersonal war, it seems to me, of skill and attrition, rather than something sprung from contempt, or hatred or loathing. For her, the child is of importance because it is important to Nicholas. For him, the child has a right of its own.' It might have been Gregorio's own deduction. More likely, it was the conclusion – the informed conclusion – of Margot.

'What is he like, the child?' Tobie said. 'Hounded from person to person, how has he grown?'

Gregorio looked at him, smiling. 'Are you afraid of another monster in embryo? Veere gave him a fright, I am sure, but there has been a continuity of upbringing, Moriz says, which has not spoiled the child or warped it so far. And even its nurses have no complaint against Nicholas as a father. He has impressed them, I am told.'

'And he has taken Henry with him?' Tobie said. 'Perhaps he means to train him as well.'

'No,' Gregorio said. 'The consensus is that Simon's son is not worth redeeming.' He paused. 'You know Nicholas would welcome you back.'

'Would he?' said Tobie. It emerged more sharply than he meant, and he was sorry.

'Well, we should,' said Gregorio.

In Antwerp, as the freshness of June merged into the heat of July, Mistress Clémence of Coulanges was pleased to find that the child Jordan de Fleury, responding to firm, kindly treatment, was virtually himself once again, although a little inclined to cling, and to ask for his father. His extreme distress at the mention of Veere had caused Mistress Clémence to advise against repeating the visit, despite the lady of Veere's many kind invitations. Happily, Jordan's mother fully agreed. Mistress Clémence was gratified.

In some ways it was a pity, for the wide skies and soft sands of Walcheren would have been pleasant in summer. But there were other meadows, other beaches; and excursions were easier than they had ever been, with the size of the bodyguard at her command, and the amenability of Pasque, who had received a great fright, and who in any case melted into complaisance, given the presence of jolly, muscular men in her kitchen. The helpful Bita, despite her even more helpful relatives, had been dismissed.

There remained the Lady. By now, it was perfectly clear, to Mistress Clémence at least, that this was not a marriage of indifference, no matter how much time the parents might spend apart. Returning from Bruges, the mother had been distant in manner for several days.

Of course, her lord had blamed her for what had happened, and Mistress Clémence herself felt some guilt. She had seen jealous children before, and spoiled children. She knew what they could do, and she knew the anger they provoked in shocked adults.

Even so, she thought the lady Gelis had been unprepared for her husband's treatment of the St Pol boy. Oddly, the good-looking woman, the German, had been more discerning, both towards the unfortunate boy and the sieur de Fleury. Mistress Clémence had admired her competence, but thought it as well that she had returned to Cologne. This marriage had enough to contend with.

Certainly, the husband had taken steps to keep in touch with both his wife and the child; the tales that came were often amusing, as one heard the Lady relating them. It could be taken for granted that she was more anxious than she showed.

Such parental attention was helpful when the boy Robin of Berecrofts came to leave, for the child had come to think of Robin in much the same possessive terms as his father; the disappearance of both to Iceland had taken some time to forgive, and Jordan did not enjoy tales of the sport that Master John or Father Moriz or especially the demoiselle Kathi had enjoyed in their company.

Robin himself would miss the child, Clémence thought, although no blow would ever be as great as the dismissal he had suffered at Veere. At first he had waited, withdrawn, for the threatened orders. Next, as the days passed, it seemed likely that the sieur de Fleury had either forgotten him, or was going to leave him neglected in Antwerp. Then one day the boy, flushed, had received a letter in his master's own hand which had redressed all that silent misery in one stroke.

It contained an apology, it would seem, although in what words the boy did not say. It also contained a request. Until the future of Henry was settled, it would be advisable, said the sieur de Fleury, that Robin and the young St Pol should not meet. Robin therefore was to place himself under Diniz at Bruges, there to continue his training in arms, and to study the methods of the Banco di Niccolò. Thus, whatever was destined to happen, he would return to his father with something of value.

Robin had left for Bruges the same day, with the regular courier. He was not going to war, but at least he was going to the heart of the Flemish business, where all his master's dispatches first arrived. Robin already knew Catherine de Charetty. Now he would meet the other step-daughter and Diniz her husband. And nearby, of course, were Katelijne and Anselm Sersanders.

Jordan's manner became petulant for a while, and Mistress Clémence dealt with it with her own brand of patient remorselessness. She was sorrier for the mother. Scotland might have been alien, but it had provided the lady with a busier, more companiable life than she now led in the isolation of Antwerp. She wondered if Dame Gelis allowed herself to remember, now and then, her castle of Beltrees and her houses in Edinburgh and the Canongate; and whether her husband would have been astonished if she did.

Chapter 35

OUTSIDE BEAUVAIS, the Duke of Burgundy's summer campaign proceeded to fulfil all its unfortunate promise. The initial impulsive assault might have succeeded, had the attackers possessed a few proper ladders, and a little more ammunition for their guns. The town should certainly have fallen when the Duke himself turned back to invest it, with John le Grant and Jacques d'Orson controlling the artillery. And even though the citizens proved to be positive Tartars, hurling fire-faggots in the faces of the attackers and repairing the breaches almost before they were made, the town would have capitulated soon enough had it not been immediately and extravagantly reinforced from behind, at the one spot Duke Charles had insisted on leaving unguarded.

The air above the Burgundian camp hung thick with agonised oaths. 'Holy Mother!' cried Captain Astorre. 'They were most of them bloody women! Did ye see the one with the hatchet!'

'I thought she was looking for you,' Nicholas remarked.

'I'm not surprised,' Julius said. 'Women getting excited. They don't want the rude soldiery tramping through their clean parlours.'

'God's toenails!' said Astorre. 'Where have you been? They're keeping the Bresle gate on fire with bits of their own houses! I tell you, the women round here are worth more than rich German countesses!'

'It's a *pucelle* tradition,' said Nicholas soothingly. All the commanders were grumbling, and the Italian captain was speechless; he began to think he might have got Astorre to Scotland after all. There was nothing more he could do. The strategic advice went to the Duke, and the Duke vetoed it. Everyone had heard the shouting from the Grand Bastard Anthony's tent, when even his powerful half-brother couldn't shake Charles's belief in his own perspicacity.

Nicholas had made some attempt at persuasion himself, but his role at this court was that of financial and political adviser; his company was part of the army. He was aware that the sense of frustration was general in the inner administration as well, extending even to the Duke's most loyal friends: Philippe de Commynes, his Master of Household; the Chancellor Hugonet, who kept day-to-day command of the affairs of the duchy, and of the ever-changing trains of envoys – from France and Milan, from England, Naples and even from Scotland.

Duke Charles had called Nicholas before him after the Scottish embassy. One of the equerries, he was almost sure, had been Andro Wodman. There had been no chance to drop a hint about the Duke's military tactics, since the tirade merely covered all the usual complaints about Scotland. Nicholas recapitulated, humbly, all that he had already offered in the direction of loans, ships, guns, and long-term Scottish planning.

'But Iceland!' the Duke had interrupted. 'What can you do for us in Iceland, except waste time and resources on a personal business adventure, and force the lord of Cortachy to do the same!'

'But he has received a great honour as a result,' Nicholas had protested. 'Anselm Adorne is now the Scottish Conservator in Bruges, and trusted by the King, as I am.'

'And now the King has gold!' the Duke had said, switching complaints. 'What will he use it for? To send an army to help France?'

'As my lord has already heard, I am sure, the Scottish Parliament has forbidden the King to lead such an army, and it will not leave without him. What this has achieved,' Nicholas said, 'is to provide the Scottish King with the money he craves to improve his own estate, so that he has no need of a French pension.'

'Such as you have,' the Duke said. 'Depleting the French treasury, the argument ran. You want to go and see him this summer, you said.'

'There is a difference,' Nicholas said. 'If I am killed, my successor will not fight for France. Kings die young in Scotland and a pension, once arranged, is easily continued.'

The Duke had grunted, and soon he was dismissed. The Chancellor Hugonet had been present throughout: a friend of Adorne's, but in other ways a man worth cultivating. Some time after that, Nicholas went and sat on the grass beside his legal partner, stretching his legs. 'Julius, did you know Cardinal Bessarion should be in France by next month?'

'I knew he'd been made Papal Legate. I thought he was too ill to travel. Where's he going?'

'Not here,' Nicholas said. 'He wrote to the Duke, but Charles isn't taking advice, as we've noticed, even from Sixtus. He's travelling through Lyons to the Loire. I'd like to see him.'

'So should I,' Julius said. 'Why not? It's easy. We just abandon the siege and tell the Duke we're going to go off for a few weeks to France. He won't worry.'

'No, he won't,' said Nicholas mildly. 'I've got leave already. If I'm going to keep up the fiction, I have to report to Louis some time. Then I bring back all the French secrets to Burgundy. But not until we've taken Beauvais.'

'You devious . . . Can I come?' Julius said.

'Ask me later,' said Nicholas. He waited. He knew Julius wouldn't like that.

Julius said, 'You won't be sorry to abandon the brat. You know everyone thinks he's your son?'

'I hope so,' said Nicholas. 'And don't deny it. It may keep him alive a week or two longer. I've even told Hugonet that he's called Jordan.'

'Why?' said Julius.

'I don't know. Word gets about,' Nicholas said.

In private, Nicholas gave some consideration from time to time to the matter of Henry, just as, among his other business concerns, he allotted time to his wife and son Jordan. The couriers who passed regularly between the camp and his office in Bruges connected with others from Antwerp. He knew what Gelis was doing, and Jordan heard from him every few days. They were compiling a poem together.

He was not compiling a poem with Henry, unless it were the groundwork for an epitaph. The irony of the situation was bearable only if ignored; the fact that Henry de St Pol of Kilmirren, jokingly rumoured to be his son, *was* his son. Julius, of course, had no idea of it; nor had Astorre. Diniz had guessed. Wherever he was, Tobie knew; and carried the paper that proved it. And Gelis had guessed, for her dead sister Katelina was Henry's mother who, marrying Simon, had persuaded him that Henry was his child. Which Simon, thank God, still believed. For if Simon ever learned the truth, he would kill Henry.

The problem, at the moment, was to prevent Henry from killing the man who had shamed him at Veere; whom Henry knew only as Nicholas de Fleury, a base-born apprentice with a grudge against Simon his father. Initially, Nicholas had placed the boy entirely under the rule of Astorre, and from Péronne to Nesle, had remained out of his orbit. It would be hard enough for a self-willed spoiled child without the thought that his captor was gloating.

The first reports indicated a sullen silence, as he expected. In a few days, that had changed. The boy, said Thomas (Thomas!), was amazingly quick on his feet, and he would thank everyone to give him first call on him. It emerged, as time passed, that Henry was not only fast but eager and biddable. Give him your spurs to get ready, and they were shining like mirrors. If you fancied an onion, he'd find a garden and dig till he got one. He'd groom the dirtiest horse; run the most strenuous errands; lug water; start fires; find fresh straw for the bedding. After one little jib, he'd even started to empty the night soil. And all with a smile, as sweet as you please, with that dimple.

A pretty boy. Naturally, after all that had been said, none laid a finger on him. But the women of the camp chucked him under the chin, and pulled him close on the grass for a cuddle, and he always smiled, with that high-flushed rose-leaf skin and the glowing blue eyes. A lovely boy, who only looked sad when someone mentioned the sieur de Fleury. It began to be discussed in the tents, how he had come to be beaten so badly by the padrone. If the two had been intimate in the past, there was no sign of it now. The boy would not talk, but somehow the rumour went round that he had been asked to do unspeakable things, and at length had refused. Certainly, on the few occasions when he had to report to the sieur de Fleury's own tent, the spring left the boy's step and he loitered, with despair on his face, not a smile.

The rumours reached Nicholas through Astorre. He confirmed them for himself, witnessing the boy's bright face and willing manner, and also the change that occurred if their glances happened to meet. Standing before him in his tent, Henry cut a figure both timid and brave; at times he would shiver. On his face, for Nicholas alone, there would be fixed an expression of mockery: an almost irresistible invitation to hit him. It pained Nicholas, almost, to disappoint him.

For a boy of eleven, it was clever: it was diabolically clever. But he was only eleven, and even when driven by hatred, could not deny his nature for ever. The day came when, his head turned by the rough camaraderie and the increasing show of goodwill, he volunteered shyly to share in some of their games. The fierce ones were beyond him, but his accurate eye and superb training gave him an advantage with the bow and even the crossbow that they thought at first freakish, and then greeted with good-natured praise. He should have accepted it, and returned to his tasks. Instead, day by day, he continued to vie with them, and sometimes to beat them. Then, when he sat with the women, he boasted.

At Beauvais, he received a black eye, and Astorre went to see Nicholas in his tent. 'The brat's in trouble.'

'No longer everyone's friend?' Nicholas had guessed most of it.

'He got tired of that. Now he's trying to play them off one against the other. Soon they'll realise what he's up to and do for him. He's disrupting the company.'

'At eleven?'

'I've seen one woman do it,' said Astorre. He paused. 'If you don't care what happens, do nothing.'

'It's all right,' Nicholas said. 'I'm arranging for him to go. Meantime let's give him to John to look after.' He had seen Henry up at the battery, watching the fast, heavy work and the thundering roar as each cannon spoke. His face had been avid, intent. Neither gunner would care for it much, but John had more patience than d'Orson, and would stand for no nonsense. And given something to master, the boy might forget his vendetta.

It was about then, or just before, that Nicholas chose not to contradict the rumour that had spread about Henry. It had arisen, he supposed, as a result of the tales about Jordan at Hesdin. It was known that he had brought a young son to camp. Few people would remember what he was called, or his age. And thinking Henry that son, men would – perhaps – stop short of actually killing him. It might also persuade them that his tales of abuse were unreliable. There were other potential benefits.

It worked, after a fashion, during the first weeks of their investment of Beauvais. During two weeks of continuous firing, Henry learned something of the art of gunnery, and grew to treat John with a mixture of hate and respect to which John remained exasperatingly indifferent. It ended when the Duke, casting aside all the protests of his officers, assembled his entire force before the gates of de Bresle and de Limaçon, and ordered them to take Beauvais by storm. It was dawn, on the twenty-eighth day of June.

Had it been launched in the first two days of the siege, the attack might have succeeded. As it was, six score Burgundians were killed and a thousand more injured before the Duke's men were flung back by the solid force of seasoned defenders within. During the assault, the heavy artillery was directed away from the walls and the bridges, and latterly was unable to fire, for fear of killing men in retreat. It was late that evening when, resuming his post at the gun-battery, John le Grant noticed that something was wrong.

The aftermath of any battle is a chaotic affair. The garrison of Beauvais, firing steadily from the walls, had made the withdrawal as dangerous as the assault had been, and the retrieval of the dead and the wounded went on for some hours. Nicholas, who with Julius had taken his share, and had seen his own men drop around him, stayed in the field with Astorre until all the company had been returned or were accounted for. It had been a wasted effort. Everyone knew it.

Astorre, bending over this pallet and that, spoke in tones that were heartily cheerful, but walking back to the tents he cursed under his breath and his shoulders were bowed. Nicholas felt the same weight of anger and weariness and parted from him without speech. He had almost reached his pavilion when John le Grant came running up in the half-light and, shouting, pulled him aside.

Nicholas, hitting the ground, thought at first that John had lost his mind and attacked him. Then the roar of an explosion cracked through the air, and his shadow lay black on the dust which everywhere else had turned a flickering red. He rolled over and turned. Behind stood a column of fire where his pavilion had been. The screaming came from his horses, and descending fragments of cloth were already setting light to the tents next in line. After the first shock, men had begun running with water. Julius raced calling among them. 'Oh my God. Is he dead?'

'No, I'm not dead,' Nicholas said, and stood up, his eyes fixed on John's. 'You knew.'

'He's in my tent,' le Grant said. 'I found the culverin covered with gunpowder, but managed to put out the fuse. He couldn't help bragging about what else he'd done.'

'Who?' said Julius.

'No one,' said Nicholas. 'It was an accident. Spread the news. I don't suppose anything can be saved?'

'What do you think?' Julius said. 'Both your horses have gone. No men – your servants were lucky. What else did you have?'

'Papers. Nothing,' said Nicholas.

Papers. A poem. A drawing. He did not need to ask whom John le Grant had caught and confined in his tent. In a moment, he was confronting him.

Henry was not now the shivering assassin of seven who, seized with mindless horror and joy, had stood with a bloody knife in his hand, waiting for this same man to denounce him, to drop. Now Henry knew what he was doing, and was ready to answer for what he had done. He remembered his father's face, Simon's face, smiling on him that day, caressing, praising him for killing his enemies. Sitting there, with his arms bound behind him, Henry looked Nicholas in the face with the same insolence he had managed to show ever since Veere.

He said, 'Next time, I shall time the fuse better.'

'Leave us,' said Nicholas. He heard John hesitate, and then go. He found John's campaign bed and let himself down on it. His sleeve was sodden with blood not his own.

The boy said, 'You don't want witnesses.' He was jeering again.

Nicholas said, 'You planned to blow up the battery?'

'All the guns,' Henry said. 'It would have destroyed half the camp. It would have ended the war. We should have won.'

'We?'

'Us. The Scots and the French.'

'John le Grant is Scots,' Nicholas said. 'Perhaps he beat you while he was teaching you?'

'He was fighting for the enemy,' Henry said. 'He is a traitor, like you.'

'And like you,' Nicholas said. 'You had a Burgundian mother.'

The boy reddened. He said, 'I despise the van Borselens. I renounce them.'

'Your father doesn't,' Nicholas said. 'He sent you to Veere to be educated in chivalry, and instead you attacked your own baby cousin.'

'He was a coward,' said Henry.

'I think,' Nicholas said, 'that all men are cowards at three. Your father will be ashamed of you. Instead of the mortification of seeing you imprisoned in Brabant, he will suffer the disgrace of what you have done today, and the penalty you must suffer.'

'You can't,' Henry said. 'I'm a prisoner waiting for ransom. It was an act of war. It was legal.'

'My dear Henry,' Nicholas said. 'I am your uncle, and you are here to be trained in the military arts. You chose to come, rather than suffer the Steen. You have been fed, warmed and sheltered by this company and none of them, I think, has treated you with unbearable harshness. Yet you were willing to kill or hurt them at random – not just me, not just Master John, but the boys, the pages, the servants, even the women. That by itself is something that very few men could forgive. But you say you did it for France, and that is even worse, for it makes you a spy. And the penalty for spying is the most ugly of deaths.'

'I knew you would kill me,' said Henry.

'If John or I wanted to kill you,' said Nicholas, 'we should take you now from this tent and denounce you before all those you were planning to murder. You would never survive to be hanged.'

'You wouldn't dare,' Henry said. 'I am a St Pol of Kilmirren. They wouldn't touch me.'

He was breathing hard. At moments like this you could see Katelina in him: her proud spirit so fatally combined with the insensate flamboyance of Simon. What else lay there undeveloped it was impossible to say, and there was no time to find out. To reach him would be the work of years rather than months. And Nicholas could not bring himself to use force, to break that pride and that spirit together.

The only force he could use was the ordinary kind, which would be misconstrued, but which must be applied. Nicholas said, 'You have threatened the lives of many friends of mine who have not harmed you, any more than Jordan had harmed you. To be a good soldier, you must learn to be just, and you must accept punishment when you do something wrong. I am not going to take you outside. I am going to beat you. It will be no more than you can bear, but it will be a heavy beating, because you deserve it. And if I am questioned by any man, your father included, I shall explain what you did to provoke it, and they will tell you that you are fortunate to have escaped with your life. Are you ready?'

'I expected it,' Henry said. 'My father will thrash you. He will kill you. You are a fool.'

'In that,' Nicholas said, 'you are probably right.'

He called John into the tent after it was over, and caught the flash of surprise, and the even greater surprise on the face of Julius when he learned what had happened. He wondered if they had expected him to cut the boy's throat. He had the doctor visit him, and gave orders to have him well guarded in case someone else thought they'd repair the omission. Outside he found they had cleared up the carnage and set up a tent for him nearby, furnished with bits of other people's equipment. Astorre had got him a horse, and some food, which he didn't want, and a lecture which he didn't want either. Eventually he rolled into bed, but couldn't sleep.

The boy remained in John's tent, and Nicholas returned, in the following days, to the concerns of the Duke and the siege. A good watch was kept, but nevertheless in the early hours of one morning a small number of men from the garrison, mostly mounted, made a surprise sally under cover of darkness and succeeded in crossing the ditch to the encampment. There they scattered, slashing and stabbing among the nearest tents of the besiegers, as if looking for someone. The action did not last long; the tent-ropes tripped and slowed down the horses, and as soon as the camp started to rouse, the men of Beauvais turned to go.

Nicholas was already out, fully dressed with his sword, when he heard the high voice screaming above the clash of metal and the hoof-beats and the shouting. Henry, his hair aureoled by the lamplight, had burst out of John's tent and was racing towards the French soldiers. 'There! There! Here is the master gunner d'Orson! There is the banker de Fleury!'

The finger pointed at him. The riders faltered and some of them turned. A sword flashed, and he saw d'Orson fall. Then a horn blew, and with a surge they were off, all but half a dozen who closed round the boy. A man's voice shouted a question; the boy replied, his voice shrilling with eagerness. The next moment a mailed arm came down, and the boy himself was swept up and thrown over the saddle. Nicholas saw his face, bemused, looking back at him, and lifted his sword, braced for the thundering hooves and the blade wet with Jacques d'Orson's blood.

They did not come. The last he saw of them was a tight knot of men riding back over the ditch to the portals, with a glint of fair hair bobbing among them.

'What?' said Astorre. He leaned forward, staring at Nicholas. 'What are you pulling faces about?'

'Nothing,' Nicholas said. 'I told you I was arranging for him to go.'

'The French have got him,' said Captain Astorre. 'The French have taken the brat into Beauvais.'

'I know,' Nicholas said. 'And as soon as the Duke decides to get on his way, I think I might make a little journey as well. As I mentioned to Julius, I'd rather like to visit Bessarion. You'll manage without me.'

Since this was true, Astorre didn't deny it. He said, 'You think they'll let you cross France right down to the Loire?'

'They ought to,' Nicholas said. 'The Duke doesn't mind if I go, and King Louis has provided me with an extremely elaborate safe-conduct. In fact, I feel for Henry's dilemma: we are either all traitors these days, or we are loyal to everyone.'

'Speak for yourself,' Astorre growled.

'I always do,' Nicholas said.

Shortly after, in Antwerp, direct communication with Nicholas ceased, and incoming dispatches were confined to the news from Astorre. The padrone had left, it was said, on a short trip, during which couriers would not be available to him. The sieur de Fleury had begun an entirely fresh poem, which he hoped Mistress Clémence would help to continue. He also sent a new tune for the whistle. The Lady was much on edge.

In Bruges, the doctor Tobias Beventini of Grado called to express his condolences at the home of Anselm Adorne, and found himself instead in the company of Kathi, Adorne's niece, and the youthful person of Robin, the unexpected new merchant apprentice – now page, so the tale went, to Nicholas.

Adorne was out, and Robin was visiting, and Kathi was delighted to see the physician and friend of her travels.

Of this last, there was no doubt at all: her elvish face was incandescent as she flew to embrace him. 'Dr Tobie! I heard you had come! We need you so badly!'

She was too thin, she was a sprite. Nevertheless, there was no possibility that that statement referred to herself; any more than it could be relevant to the stalwart young Robin. Tobie said, 'The lord of Cortachy? I was so sorry to hear of his lady. How is he taking it?'

Only when she coloured did he realise his mistake. He said, 'Oh dear. Our other mutual friend?'

He saw the boy look at the young woman. Kathi said, 'It must seem very strange. But Uncle Anselm has many friends, and has always led a well-ordered life. And Nicholas is alone.'

Nicholas. Tobie said, 'He has friends. And a wife. And a son.' He did not add, *And two sons*. He felt aggrieved.

Kathi said, 'I haven't even asked how you are. I'm so sorry. I'm so sorry. But we were talking of Iceland. My brother has gone, and I have to go back to Scotland next week. And Nicholas is so *stupid*.'

'That he is not,' said the boy. He was smiling.

'You are both right, of course,' Tobie said. 'He is a clever man with a defective grasp of reality. Such people sometimes cannot be helped, and do no harm except to themselves. You have your own lives to lead.'

He had forgotten her bright hazel eyes. She said, 'We are leading them. It doesn't mean that we shouldn't help someone else where we can. Would you come to Scotland? We shall all be there this winter. You would like Robin's father. And there will be no fighting at all.'

'You heard what happened,' he said.

Surprisingly, it was the boy who answered him soberly. He said, 'Yes. We heard of Volterra.'

Tobie stayed a long time. He gave them his news, then listened, in silence, to the true account of what had happened in Iceland, followed by something no one else had mentioned at all, to do with a Miracle Play. When he left, in the end, they asked for no promises and he gave none. He had not called to see Gelis or the child, and did not propose to go, without Nicholas.

He had barely returned to the Bank when the courier came, riding post-haste from Florence. He carried a letter from the Count of Urbino summoning Dr Tobias to the sickbed of his wife, mother of that ninth miraculous child and first son. Battista had been seized with illness in Gubbio, and the Count was leaving Florence to race to her side.

The message was several weeks old. It had been pursuing him since the last day in June. And before he had decided what to do, a second courier had come, exhausted, in the wake of the first, with another message. The lady Battista was dead. The Count begged his friend to return.

Dr Tobias Beventini, standing alone in his room, considered two men, and his feelings and duty towards them. The choice, in the end, was not hard to make; and was based, not illogically, on something he had been told about a Miracle Play.

Chapter 36

THE CHÂTEAU OF Saumur crowned the left bank of the Loire like a wheatsheaf in marble. In place of the mighty cylinders of Angers, its towers were slender and tall, with lacy battlements and crowded blue turrets. The golden spires with their fleurs-de-lys finials lay reflected in the sliding blue water, only disturbed by the ruffling of oars. Despite the safe conduct, the last part of the sieur de Fleury's long journey from Beauvais had been completed under compulsory escort; the King of France wished no unsupervised Burgundians travelling his realm. The presence of Julius was tolerated.

Their horses sailed with them. Presently, disembarked in the flowery heat, they were led to the tall landward port which they entered over a drawbridge. They were expected by now. The captain of the castle was pleased to greet them, and have them shown to a chamber. It was understood that they wished to interview the lord Cardinal Bessarion, at present in delicate health after his arduous travels. This would be permitted. Thereafter, they would require to await the Most Christian King's pleasure. Roi monseigneur was not at Saumur.

The castle was shady and cool, and at first even Julius succumbed to the need for repose. Afterwards, he was avid to explore his surroundings; price the furniture, the woodwork, the marble, the windows; walk through the gardens; inspect the stables; accept the captain's offer to arrange a small hunting-trip or a little falconry, or a swim in the clear sandy water. Even the ladies swam, on a hot August evening.

It was a change from Beauvais.

Sometimes Nicholas went with him; sometimes not. Since he was nineteen, Nicholas had been handling Julius. The inquisition had occupied all the earlier days of their trip, and Nicholas had dilated obediently on all the subjects Julius had raised, except those to do with personal relationships, when he became first obtuse and then mildly deaf.

The rest of the time was more enjoyable, filled with the kind of chatter and hilarity natural to a meeting of two men who had known each other in one case from childhood. It was well over twenty years since Julius had met the boy Nicholas in the bullying household in Geneva of his great-uncle Jaak de Fleury; and since then he had twice saved his life. They talked of Tasse, now dead, who had been kind to them both; and of Tilde and Catherine, whom Julius still couldn't take seriously. He asked, as only Julius could, what Gelis made of her husband's first marriage to Marian de Charetty, which was, after all, the start of his fortune and so not to be sneezed at.

'I don't know. We never speak of it. Are you going to marry your Anna?' Nicholas asked.

Julius had blushed: a remarkable sight. He said, 'If I do, it won't be for her money.'

'I've met her. I believe you,' said Nicholas. 'How did you find her? She's beautiful.'

'She found me,' Julius said. 'Through the Hanse merchants in Cologne. She had all this property from Wenzel, her husband, and wanted to realise it all and invest it. She applied to several others, but we offered the best proposition.'

'How much did that lose us?' said Nicholas amiably.

The flush had become even deeper. 'Nothing. We made a profit. You can see the books if you like. Gelis was there at the time. She'd remember.'

'Calm! Calm!' Nicholas had said. 'I've seen the books. I was joking. I shouldn't blame you if she owned all the *Fleury* instead of half of it. So are you going to ask her to marry you?'

Julius, unusually for him, had been silent. Then Nicholas had said, 'You want to, I'm sure. So why not? You're afraid she'll refuse you?'

Julius had said, 'I have nothing. I don't know who my parents were.'

'That may be, but you are far from having nothing. And beautiful as she is, she hasn't married anyone else, or even spent time with anyone else from what you tell me. Would you like me to plead for you? I can give you a fairly good character.'

He didn't think Julius would take him seriously, and he didn't. He said, 'If anything would ruin it, that would. I have to wait. I must be sure. With someone like that, you only get one chance.'

'Well, don't wait too long or I'll catch her for Jordan,' Nicholas said. And after that, he let the talk lapse in favour of more interesting things, of the kind that had earned them a reputation in Bruges when he was an apprentice and Julius was supposed to be governing him. Stupid pranks, on the knife-edge of criminality and dangerous in the extreme, which remained enjoyable even when muted, out of respect for their whereabouts and their age. Then their escort made its appearance, and they had to behave.

The summons to Cardinal Bessarion came on the third day. When Nicholas saw him, his face grey, his long beard spread over the sheets in the darkened chamber of state, it reduced him to silence.

Dying, the Greek who had laboured to bring together the Latin and Orthodox churches had been given an impossible task: to induce Louis of France to conduct the ecclesiastical affairs of his country according to the Pope's wishes; to reconcile France and Brittany and Burgundy, and induce them to turn their minds and resources to stemming the Grand Sultan's advance to the west.

Bessarion would not succeed. Whether presently frustrated or victorious in France, the Duke of Burgundy's mind was not on the East, but on freeing himself from his overlords, and on increasing his power and his lands in France and in Germany. Charles wanted nothing less than to be a king, or an emperor.

In Venice last year, Nicholas had cast his support and that of his Bank behind this ambition of Charles, and had given nothing to the present Crusade beyond a few elderly ships and some armaments. Julius, once the Cardinal's secretary in Bologna, had abetted him. Now they received, as might be expected, the Cardinal's measured rebuke. Without wealth, without title, without ambition, Nicholas de Fleury had stood against the Muslim in Cyprus and Trebizond; he had listened to Godscalc, his saintly confessor, and aided his attempt to reach Christian Ethiopia. Why now, laden with honours, had he turned his back on his glorious destiny?

Julius mumbled. It was difficult, one perceived, to avoid mentioning that all these exploits had come about merely because Nicholas was in the way of making some money. Nicholas himself replied clearly, with deference. His duty at present was to Duke Charles and to the home he was making in Scotland. Nevertheless, he promised all the wealth of the Bank when the Duke was able at last to send his full might against Mehmet. 'Do not despair,' Nicholas said. Julius looked grave.

'Then you must let me tell you all you need to know,' Bessarion said.

Nicholas listened, although he expected little new. By now, the Christian fleet should be attacking the Ottoman coasts south of Smyrna, while inland, the Persian leader Uzum Hasan should have launched into action, prodded by Caterino Zeno, the Venetian envoy.

Nicholas wondered, while the Cardinal spoke, how the lady Violante, wife of Zeno, was sustaining her lord's extended absence. That was something that Gregorio never happened to mention. They said that Zeno had bred the occasional bastard while on his travels for Venice. The connections would have been formed out of expediency, as Violante's undoubtedly were. Former apprentices and Byzantine princesses did not usually find themselves between the same sheets. There was also her sister Fiorenza, where sheets had not been involved. His mind wandered, and he brought it back.

The Cardinal was speaking of the Patriarch Ludovico da Bologna, who had also been dispatched to Uzum Hasan's court, this time by the Pope. Once there, he would take his persuasive tongue, for sure, to wherever it would do the most good. And from work such as his, would come the real attack, the decisive attack of the Christian forces next spring.

It was something that Nicholas, too, thought to be likely. He said so. Wishing to be honest, he added that the Bank, by then, would not be free of its commitments, but that he was certain that the Venetian Republic would do all she could.

'It is my great hope,' said the Cardinal, and his lips moved in a smile. 'And I think you will find that, by the same token, their young Queen is sent this autumn to Cyprus. Whatever others may think, it is equally imperative that Venice makes sure of that island.'

Julius glanced at Nicholas, also smiling. 'Zacco may not like it,' he said.

'Perhaps not,' said the Cardinal. 'But he would be wise not to show it. I hope he has a good friend at hand to advise him.'

He had. He had David de Salmeton, of the Vatachino. The charming David whose firm had so many connections with Genoa, which also coveted Cyprus. Adorne had been in Cyprus two years ago. Nicholas said, 'I am sure he is well advised.'

His train of thought was evidently the same as the Cardinal's. 'And,' said Bessarion, 'that excellent knight Anselm Adorne? He has not returned to the East?' He listened. 'Bereaved? I am sorry to hear it. I was aware that the son had to return home. Perhaps the young man will abandon Rome, since his second choice of post may now fail him.'

'Why should that be, my lord?' Julius said. Anything to do with Jan Adorne fascinated Julius. 'The Bishop of St Andrews is ill? Or about to go home in disgrace?'

'He is not ill,' said the Cardinal, 'And he may go home, but not in disgrace, as you so uncharitably put it. Quite the reverse. As a papal bull will shortly announce, my lord of St Andrews is about to become

Scotland's first Primate. St Andrews is being erected into a metropolitan see, and its bishop becomes an archbishop.'

Julius opened his mouth. He said, 'Nicholas?'

'I believe it is true,' Nicholas said.

The slanting eyes raked him. Julius said, 'Welcomed by whom? The Scottish bishops who are going to find themselves suffragans under him? Have they agreed? Did they know? Did the *King* know?' He paused. 'Did *you* know?'

Nicholas said, 'Four noes and a yes. Now no one has to refer an abuse to the Chair of St Peter. The Archbishop will settle it locally.'

'They'll love that,' Julius said. 'Forgive me, my lord, but a Pope two months away is sometimes a better proposition than a crazy archbishop on your doorstep.'

'I think you forget yourself,' Bessarion said. 'Will age, Julius, never cure your rash tongue? The eleven cathedral churches of Scotland now lie under the metropolitan jurisdiction of Patrick Graham, by recognising which the monarch of Scotland will obtain everlasting life and the gratitude of the Pope. Your friend Nicholas not only knew, but was wise enough to help bring it about. He will explain. I do not wish to discuss it. Jan Adorne may elect to accompany the Archbishop to Scotland; if he stays in Rome, he must seek a new master. Now may we leave the subject for others more pressing?'

They listened in silence as, collecting his strength, he told them again his objectives, and exhorted them once more to lend him their help. In the end, seeing him weary, they excused themselves and with his blessing, departed. Outside the door, Nicholas found himself called back. Shrugging at Julius, he turned and re-entered, closing the door.

The sun, finding a chink in the shutter, fell across the high bed and lit the long, bearded face of the thinker named John who had taken the name of an Egyptian, the patron saint of his native Trebizond. The man patted the seat by his bed. He said, 'Julius will question you narrowly, but I wished a little time with you myself. You are patient with him.'

'Not always,' Nicholas said.

'He owes you more than he knows. He has found a gentle companion, I believe.'

'She was in Rome. He hopes to marry her,' Nicholas said. 'It worries him that he cannot bring her a distinguished past.'

'It worried him in Bologna,' the Cardinal said. 'But a good man will succeed, whether he can claim a father or not, and there is no shame to a woman in marrying him. Then he heads his own family, and is as a tree, sheltering those of his blood whom he loves.' He paused. He said, 'I speak of you, Nicholas.'

His eyes were clear. It was painful to hold them. Nicholas said, 'I wish it were true.'

'Then you must make up for your mistakes in the future,' said the man in the bed. 'Now I have no more to say that is personal. I wish to speak to you of Caffa, and of Poland, and of Fichet and what you must do with his printing. And then – Do you see that flask over there?'

Nicholas rose. 'Yes, my lord.'

'Ah, not yet. It is Candian wine. When I have given you all my thoughts, then I wish you to pour it, and to sit by me and to talk of something quite different. Do you remember your Greek?'

'Yes,' said Nicholas.

'Yes. You have listened to me, and to George and to Ficino. You have heard us speak of your namesake of Cusa. I have never heard you talk of the Dialogues.'

He ceased speaking and waited. Nicholas said, 'Christianity and Plato? I have talked of them, but in Arabic.'

The Cardinal said, 'I was told of your friend. It was not the communion of two minds that killed him. I am dying. My chosen comfort is discourse. Indulge me.'

Outside, Julius said, 'What happened? Poor old fellow. Did he want to talk of his great days, and got rambling?'

'Professors of rhetoric rarely ramble,' Nicholas said. 'Don't be jealous, or I'll give you his lecture on Aristotle. He's moving down-river soon to Ancenis. The captain says I have to wait to be summoned by Louis. He says they won't let you stay.'

'Why not?' said Julius, incensed.

'Because I'm on his payroll and you're not. I can't help it,' said Nicholas. 'They didn't mind you seeing Bessarion, but now you have to return and do some serious besieging. If I were you, I'd go back to Bruges. Teach the women to swim in the river.'

Julius opened his mouth.

Nicholas said, 'You came for his blessing, and you have it. I am glad, too, that you came. But now the risks have to be mine.'

He felt numb: a man divided in two, of which one half was routinely socialising, and the other was set among stars. He lay awake all that night, for it would never happen again. There was no one else left.

In the third week of August, Jordan de St Pol, vicomte de Ribérac, arrived for the second time in the Loire valley and was directed to await Louis his master in the upright little castle of Les Ponts-de-Cé, once a favourite retreat of King René. He arrived in mellow temper, despite the heat of the road from La Rochelle and the complicated appraisals made necessary by the untimely demise of the King's brother, the Duke of Guienne.

He knew why he had been sent for. He might not be the horseman that once he had been, but his servants were agile and efficient. The King had told him to get the child, and he had him. The boy was awaiting him now in the prisons of Les Ponts-de-Cé. By his orders the child had not been told where he was, or who had him. He had been no trouble, they said, on the journey from Beauvais. He had even tried to be helpful. It had amused them.

Jordan de Ribérac was tired. There was no hurry: the King was still at Ancenis. The vicomte retired to his chamber and slept. Then, upon rising, he refreshed himself with a change of clothes and a modest repast with some wine. Next, he commanded the governor to show him the way to the cells.

The room they unlocked had a window, lately fitted with bars, and was better provided than most, for the place was a residence more than a keep. A figure rose from a bench.

His first impression in the half-light was that the child was exceedingly fair, which was of course not necessarily impossible. The next was that it was of unusual height – indeed of a height which *was* quite impossible. The third, when it spoke, was one of disbelief. The child – the boy – the prisoner he had caused to be kidnapped gave a cry, a loud cry, of '*Grandfather!*' Then, before he had recovered from that, the boy proceeded to howl. 'I told them! They wouldn't listen! Oh, Grandfather!' The brat's cheeks were filthy with tears.

He hated tears. He despised them. He saw, with disbelief and with fury, what he had to contend with. He said, 'Henry.'

The boy began to rush forward.

Henry. Henry his grandson. Henry, who was no use to anyone. Henry, who couldn't be used to influence bankers or armies but yet was uselessly here, a source of danger. A source of ridicule.

The vicomte de Ribérac stood in the cold little room, massive, unyielding, a bastion of disappointment and anger. The boy stopped.

The vicomte said, 'What have you done? How dare you! How dare you interfere with my plans! Get out of my sight!'

Chapter 37

THEY WERE SCYTHING the wheat as Nicholas made the gentle day's ride from Saumur north-west to Les Ponts-de-Cé, parallel with the blue drift of the Loire. The wains full of sheaves rumbled beside him and, but for his escort, he would have dismounted in some deep golden field and shared his bread and meat with the straw-hatted harvesters, and heard all their gossip. But the King of France traversed this country, pursuing the concerns of his armies, and strangers rode under guard.

It was within a few days of September, and Nicholas was glad to move. Days ago, the Cardinal had received his appointment and departed, borne on the river. He would not return. Julius had also left, to go back to Bruges, and perhaps even to Cologne: Nicholas wondered whether he would find the Gräfin waiting, or whether she would have slipped off, in her cool, competent way, to oversee some other business. He had watched Julius and his Countess together; observed the grace with which she received her admirer's ceaseless attentions. But her eyes did not caress as his did, and if their fingers touched, her breath did not quicken. You could see why he feared a rebuff.

Yet she was sensual. From long experience, Nicholas was sure of it. She had had one husband, and perhaps many lovers. They said the child was her own. It was most likely, Nicholas thought, that she was teasing Julius into losing his head. Then they would marry, and she would hold the ascendancy. He did not see how he could interfere in any way that would do good.

He observed, towards the end of his journey, that the fleur-de-lys flew from the steep blue roofs of René's elegant home, and that Louis had therefore arrived. There was no hurry, however. Had the Burgundians triumphed in Picardy, he would have been sent for long before now. Louis had kept him waiting because there were no secrets that mattered. Or no Burgundian secrets.

In René's exquisite painted chamber of audience, the bees flew back and forth through the windows and were snapped at by the dogs. The room was crowded. Nicholas, waiting aside, saw men he recognised, Gaston du Lyon among them. Louis was moving about with a jingle of spurs, joining first one group then another. When he approached Nicholas at length, he was drawing behind him another who was not French at all: Philippe de Commynes, godson of Philip of Burgundy, and – until recently – the present Duke's favourite counsellor.

'See!' said King Louis. 'See, mon brave! What do we call you? The Scots have made you a baron now, have they not? See, my lord of Fleury, what other fish have leaped into our pool from the Burgundian sea! Since M. de Commynes has joined us, we know all our poor cousin's secrets: ah, what trouble they are making for themselves in the Pas de Calais! Roving hither and thither in such anger, while all the time our captains ride ahead of them, laughing! There is nothing you can tell us that we do not already know, save only what you have done for us in Scotland. So come. Let us step aside. M. de Commynes will forgive us. Tell us – how sad it seems – why after all, our dear nephew of Scotland has found it impossible to send us an army, even though you persuaded us – you emptied our pockets – on the pretext that he would?'

They were out of earshot. At a sign, all the others drew back. Louis sat, leaving Nicholas standing.

Nicholas said, 'Monseigneur knows that the Scottish Parliament forbade it.'

'As you knew they would,' Louis remarked.

'As I was afraid that they might, so long as the King remained childless. I had private word, monseigneur, just before I left Beauvais. The Queen has hopes of a child.'

It was a gamble. The word had been no more than a whisper, and might be contradicted. But for sure, Louis would not have heard it yet.

He had not. His eyes, black as ferrets, examined him. 'Are you sure?'

'It is early,' said Nicholas. 'But it means an army may come. Also marriage alliances. It is to be hoped that the King will take the best advice about that.'

'Yours?' said Louis. 'Why were you given your barony?'

'I have made myself useful,' Nicholas said. 'My lord your royal nephew was pleased to thank me for the wealth I brought him from Iceland.'

'We heard,' Louis said. 'Wealth which makes it unnecessary for him to sue us for a pension.'

'Wealth which persuaded him to invest in a ship,' Nicholas said. 'He has bought from me the great vessel *The Lion*, which will eventually bring you his army. He has nothing left. If monseigneur wishes to bind him with a pension, then I can promise the opportunity is about to arise.'

'So!' said Louis. 'How subtle we are, serving three rulers and lining our purses. But we think perhaps that now, like Paris, you must approach your final decision. You cannot surely deceive your poor Duke for very much longer. And what has the Duke to offer compared with ourselves? You have seen our young friend de Commynes, who has just acquired land, wealth and the promise of an heiress to marry. The finest officers of our late brother of Guienne have chosen to join us, and not for a pittance. And Brittany! Why do you think we are here and not with our army in Brittany? Because the lord of Lescun, the ablest man at the side of our nephew and cousin the Duke, has just joined us, for a pension of six thousand francs, half of Guienne, two seneschalships, the command of a castle in Bordeaux and two in Bayonne, twenty-four thousand crowns in ready money, and – if we remember it all – our order of St Michael, with a comté.

'You see,' said Louis, 'what we are willing to offer to those who serve us, and in the cause, naturally, of peace? The war in Brittany, for all practical purposes, has ceased.'

'Monseigneur! I am amazed!' Nicholas said.

'Indeed. So the long-awaited English will certainly not arrive, and our unfortunate cousin of Burgundy may as well load his flux-ridden army into carts and carry them back home to Artois. The war is over,' said Louis. 'There is no more work for your company to do, and you are paid – poorly paid – by a self-willed man with no more wits in his head than a goose. Bring your army and join us.'

'In what capacity?' Nicholas said.

'Ah,' said the King. There was a table, with a small stool beyond it. He waved Nicholas to the seat and made a sign over the room. A servant, surrounded by dogs, made his way to the table and placed on it a dish of raw meat which the King fingered with his gloved hand, before selecting a piece and throwing it down. The dogs, ears swinging, vied for it, barking. Another servant brought Nicholas wine. The table was spattered with blood.

The King said, 'What did the vicomte de Ribérac promise Burgundy, in exchange for the return of his grandson from Beauvais?'

'What did he tell you?' Nicholas said.

'What you might expect. That he gave orders to kidnap your child, and his men seized the wrong boy.'

'My son is in Antwerp,' Nicholas said. 'The vicomte's grandson was with the Burgundian army, under threat of arraignment for attempted murder. Certainly, he would have an imperative need to extract him.'

'And the price?' Louis said.

'Perhaps M. de Commynes can tell you,' Nicholas said. 'The bargain was not made with me. Or perhaps it is enough to say that the vicomte has sent his son back to Scotland after keeping him for almost four years in exile. Perhaps the vicomte himself means to follow. It could harm monseigneur's prospects in that kingdom.'

'He plans to go there. He has told us,' said Louis.

'Monseigneur could forbid it,' said Nicholas. 'And ask him to bring back Simon his son.'

'Or we might let him go, and send you to counter him,' Louis said. 'We have spoken of the vicomte's position at Court, and we know you are willing to fill it. You have seen the rewards we can offer, which would include your own vicomté of Fleury. We have said that we should welcome your army. All this will happen next year, when you openly leave your Burgundian master. But this winter, we wish you to serve us in Scotland. If our suspicions are confirmed, de Ribérac's position in France will be yours.'

'And the future of the vicomte de Ribérac?' said Nicholas.

'There are precedents. You yourself mentioned Jacques de Coeur,' said the King.

The audience ended soon after. They did not speak of Bessarion, but Nicholas already knew that the Cardinal's mission was over. In the long term, it had failed. In the short term, paradoxically, it had succeeded. Brittany was ceasing to fight because her most powerful counsellor had been bought. Burgundy, unsupported, badly led, was soon, surely, to fall into truce. But that was just this year. When spring came again, all the forces would realign and reassemble. When the spring fleets set out for the East, Burgundy, Brittany, and France would not be represented.

Leaving Les Ponts-de-Cé, he was offered an escort, but chose to travel insignificantly and apparently unarmed, in a worn tunic with a hat on the back of his head and a packmule of the kind a travelling craftsman might have. He hired a boy to accompany him. He was given anything that he wanted, and carried inside his shirt a pouch of jewels, two of which had a name. Louis had been generous.

He elected to journey back along the Loire valley, with the intention of striking north some way between Tours and Blois. He had been out of touch with the Bank for five weeks, but knew from de Commynes that Astorre's company at least was intact, and little in action. His pendulum told him daily what else he needed to know. He planned to travel quickly, once he had paid a visit to Chouzy.

A prince should spend a third of his revenue, someone said, on his spies. You could say much the same of a merchant. He had no reason to doubt the record of Clémence de Coulanges and of Pasque, loyal for nearly four years to Gelis and to himself, if you excepted what had happened at Veere. Even so, he commissioned agents to check it. Reports suggested that they had spoken the truth: both had been found through the Abbey of Notre Dame de La Guiche. Pasque belonged to one of the many peasant families who supplied their daily servants. Mistress Clémence had been reared there, a dependant of the seigneur Bernard de Chouzy and his wife. They still took an interest in her, it appeared. They had come, in his absence, to visit Clémence and Pasque at Dijon.

It seemed natural; he could see nothing sinister in it. Nevertheless, since he was passing, he meant to make some enquiries, and rode unescorted and unmarked in order to do so. He left the Loire five miles short of Blois and, turning up the valley of the Cisse, rode slowly past the walls of the manor of Chouzy until he reached Coulanges beyond, where he reserved a room in a primitive tavern. He stopped at the Abbey of La Guiche on the way, and they told him all he wanted to know, even showing their records. He could see nothing wrong: the only other piece of local gossip they furnished he had already half guessed. He might have regretted his own small charade except that he was enjoying it, and he was perfectly sure, from long experience, that he was not being followed. There was even a proverb. 'It's gone to Coulanges,' they said, when something had vanished.

The valley was beautiful. Sunk on the edge of the forest of Blois, it brimmed with the scent of hot grapes, hanging heavy in the groves just above, and reverberated to the rumble and splash of the flour-mills, devouring the first of the grain of the petite Beauce. This time he could dismount and talk to the hot-faced families he found working above the sparkling water. He sat with the boy, breaking bread with them, and listening to the snatches of laughter and song. Two of the Clarisses he had met at La Guiche passed, riding mules, their gleaming wimples directed towards him, and once he saw a servant cantering past, with the Chouzy blazon on his sleeve. Later, when he had eaten and slept for an hour in the tavern, he took his horse alone and found his way through hamlets and orchards back to the Loire, where the late sun lit the sandy banks and cool water. Tying his horse, he stripped to his small clothes, and swam.

Here he was alone. The river of kings carried him onwards in silence. He became aware of the broad unchanging harmony of its passage, decorated by the liquid surge of his body, and the sweet, high flourish as it surfed about distant stones. He heard birdsong, and music, and words filled his mind like the scent of the grapes. His senses woke. Behind, in another dimension, a man was speaking in Greek. Bessarion, discoursing on Plato, on Platonic love. What he felt now, loosed to the sun and the water, was not Platonic love. It was unbearable.

Just then, he saw the men on the shore, two of them, leaning against their mounts, talking. He noticed them because of the horse, a prince of a chestnut with a cream-coloured tail, loosely hobbled, its nostrils flared, patiently watching as if it were waiting for him. Then behind, half out of sight, he saw the girl.

He knew her. The blaze of emotion stopped his throat so that he had to fight to stay where he was, against the push of the current. He saw the face, pale as a Venetian mask above the light robe, but the hair about it was brown.

He exclaimed. The girl vanished. The grooms, when he looked for them, had gone as well, and all the horses. When, lifting himself out of the water, he stood where they had been, he could see nothing, not even a hoof-mark. And behind, beyond the reedy bushes that sprang by the shore, there was nothing either: no road, no trace of a building, merely the orchards heavy with fruit, and a copse of beeches, with the smoke of a hamlet rising beyond them.

Tell your doctors that you never have waking dreams. The girl had been no one he knew. The girl had been no one.

The sun was sinking. The air, losing its heat, made him shiver. He had turned to step back into the water when the nearest hedge trembled, and he faced about, thinking he was wrong; it had been real; the grooms had come back. Instead, three different men stepped out and began walking towards him.

These were neither grooms nor casual footpads. The sun burned like fire on their helms, and the light on their chain mail and cuirasses danced sudden and bright as a spout of dazzling hot water. They all carried clubs.

He could do nothing against them but run. He flung round to do so, and met the first blow from the three others behind him.

It was not much of a fight. He nearly succeeded in dragging them into the water, and indeed had the satisfaction of seeing one of them fall with a splash. He didn't have time to discover whether he drowned, because the blows were coming too fast: on his head and face, on his belly and shoulders and back. They weren't going to kill him with swords, evidence that armed men had attacked him. They were going to beat him to death. It went on, rather nastily, until at length he lay on the ground, unable to raise his arms any longer, and

one of them knelt and raising his truncheon, brought it down deliberately across both of his shins. He heard the bone crack as he cried
out. Then they stood up, breathing heavily, and looked down at him.
One of them spat.

When they had said anything, they had spoken in French. Floating
in and out of nothingness, dizzy with pain, Nicholas made a civilised
effort. 'At least tell me. Who was so very timid that he dared not face
and kill me himself?'

Someone answered, but he could not make out what he said. A
helmetful of water brought his hearing back, and some of his sight.
The man repeated. 'We were to tell you. Monseigneur feared that if
he set eyes on your carcass, his natural reflex would dispatch you too
soon. We had orders to deliver a complaint on behalf of his grandson.
Monseigneur looks forward to completing the sentence in Scotland.'

Monseigneur. Scotland. Grandson . . .

Jordan de Ribérac.

Fat Father Jordan, who had not needed to follow him, for he had
guessed where he would go. Fat Father Jordan, who had ordered a
beating just short of death for the knave who had so inconvenienced
him. For the apprentice who, this time, had inconvenienced the
vicomte de Ribérac very seriously indeed.

Nicholas let his eyes close. When he opened them, intending to
speak, he saw the trampled strand, the broken bushes, the blood that
lay in cakes all about him, but the men-at-arms were no longer there.
He lay and watched the unvarying river, until darkness fell.

After all, he had gone to Coulanges.

In Antwerp, Gelis had reached a decision. The idea had struck her some
weeks before, just about the time the news arrived about this short trip
that Nicholas was taking. He had Julius with him, and it was not known
when he would return, or to where. He had gone, it seemed, to the Loire.

It was then the end of July. It meant at best, he could hardly be
back by September. It meant, very likely, that he might not be back
for some time.

She said nothing, but began to make her arrangements. When they
were complete, she called in both nurses and told them her plans. She
was closing the house. They were sailing immediately for Scotland.

She knew she had given them almost no time. She saw the wrinkles
of distress and perplexity begin to line Pasque's face – Pasque, with
her happy dreams of the Loire finally dashed. Her compatriot's
expression gave nothing away; Mistress Clémence stood obediently
throughout, showing no hint of distress or of pleasure. Merely she
said, 'Without his lordship, madame?'

'I have decided,' said Gelis, 'that it is unseemly for Jodi to be brought up in a fortress. Apparently my lord is to be away for some time, in which case it will deprive us of nothing to live somewhere else. He will follow us.'

Pasque muttered under her breath. Mistress Clémence bowed her head, but somewhere in the thin-boned face Gelis thought she saw a flicker of interest. Mistress Clémence said, 'The sieur de Fleury knows we are leaving?'

'He will find out,' Gelis said. 'It is only a small change of plan. As you know, we are all to spend the winter in Scotland.'

They accepted it. There was no reason why they should not. They were merely returning earlier than the master had expected; and returning without him.

She wondered how he would like that, when his pendulum told him. She knew that he, of all people, would appreciate her yearning for freedom after the anxieties and dangers of Antwerp. She knew that he of all people knew that the dangers of Antwerp were as nothing to the dangers of Scotland, where Simon de St Pol had taken up residence. She had told Mistress Clémence that Nicholas would be sure to follow. Which of course was the truth.

She did not know, making her plans, that by the time she set forth, Nicholas would be riding to Chouzy, and the pendulum upon which she was relying was about to be stilled.

Whenever Nicholas had marsh-fever, the face of Tobie was the first he saw floating above him, with its fluffy bald head and round nostrils and disapproving small mouth. It appeared always after some time: a week perhaps, or occasionally even longer. When, therefore, it materialised on this occasion, Nicholas said, 'What day is it?'

The acerbic expression did not change. Tobie said, 'You have been here for two weeks.'

'Where?' said Nicholas with vague interest. It could be almost anywhere. Cyprus, for instance. He wouldn't mind being ill with Tobie in Cyprus. When Tobie didn't answer he said, mildly insisting, 'Come on, where?' His chest, curiously, didn't like supplying his voice with much volume. Thinking about it, he realised he was quite badly hurt, as well as weak from the fever. Further thinking about it, he remembered what had caused the injuries. He remembered, too, the horses, the men and the girl who had vanished. He mentally cancelled the question and remarked disagreeably, closing his eyes, 'O God, our crucified Redeemer.'

'What's wrong?' said Tobie with anger.

It *was* Tobie.

Nicholas opened his eyes, as far as he could manage. Tobie, sitting beside him with his short lips and shining pink scalp and assortment of comical worry lines, said, 'You're in the manor of Chouzy. They found out who you were from your lad, and sent a man to the Pays de Caux to Astorre. They volunteered me to come. The Berecrofts boy's with me. Your lad has been paid off.'

'Thundering Poison,' Nicholas remarked. 'You didn't consult me.' He felt like Death chained at the feet of Fame, but perceived that some sign of *esprit* was required. As the pain penetrated, he remembered more of what had caused it. He was not yet capable of pursuing the problem of why Tobie had been with Astorre, or what Robin was doing here. He found Tobie was supporting him in order to give him something to drink.

Tobie said, 'Here. They found you by the river. You'd had a bad beating. Your ribs are damaged. One leg is snapped and the other cracked. They'll mend; they're only stiff because I've bound them. And then you got yourself some marsh-fever, which is why you're addled, as usual. Now you'll sleep, and when you wake I'll bring in the people whose house you're in. You owe them a lot.'

He heard the words through a somnolent fog. Tobie always did that: sent you to sleep just as you were about to grasp the key of heaven and hell. When he woke, his hostess was sitting at his bedside, or so he assumed her to be: a fair young woman, expensively dressed, with a three-year-old child asleep in her arms. She smiled. 'Eh bien, your doctor was called away, and I offered to sit until he came back. I am the dame de Chouzy. You feel better, my lord? I am glad.'

Nicholas said, 'I am told that I owe my rescue to you.'

'Ah! Others would have helped,' the girl said. 'But how could I let suffer the employer of my husband's own kinswoman? Clémence works for you, does she not?'

'For me and my wife,' Nicholas said. 'Our debt to her is almost as great. She has been . . .' His voice died. Although his eyes continued to rest on her, he had forgotten what he was saying. She rose, still carrying the child, and the door opened. His eyes followed her. His mind was elsewhere. She said something.

'He is not fully awake,' said Tobie's voice. 'It is nothing to worry about. But I shall watch him now. Thank you.'

The door closed, and Tobie sat down. Nicholas said, 'Why are you here?' He paused and then said, collecting his breath, 'I am awake. Why are you here?'

'Volterra,' said Tobie. 'The canonical irregularity of blood-shedding. You have it here as well. *Par saint Georges, mes enfants, vous avez fait une belle boucherie!* Thus the Duke riding into Nesle, I am told.'

'Louis is extremely sickening as well,' Nicholas said. 'So you are looking for a desirable private practice, like Andreas's?'

'What are you looking for?' Tobie said. 'They say de Commynes has left the Duke for the King.'

'I'm still with both,' Nicholas said.

'Hence the beating?'

'Not at all. The beating was a private commission. Six former Archers of the King's guard, if I am not mistaken, in the employment of the vicomte de Ribérac.'

'*Jordan!*' said Tobie. He added, after a moment too long, 'Because of what you did to Henry?'

Nicholas was unable to smile, but the idea amused him. He supposed he must look exactly like Henry. He said, 'Partly. Also, I played a trick on the fat man which he didn't like. He has threatened to finish the chastisement in Scotland. We'll see.'

'Where is Henry?' said Tobie.

'In Ribérac.'

'The vicomte told you?'

'I haven't seen him. I guessed.'

'You didn't ask?' Tobie said. 'You thrashed that boy, and saw him captured by strangers, and you didn't *ask*?'

'I didn't need to,' said Nicholas. 'Where is Jordan? My Jordan?'

'Henry is your Henry,' Tobie said. His face shone with temper. He said, 'Why do you make me do this? You need rest. This is not the time to discuss all of this.'

'It is. You made a promise to Godscalc. Henry is the heir-male of my body, and I, too, swore to protect him. He is safe. He was captured by his grandfather's orders and his grandfather sent him to Ribérac. Perhaps he will even take him to Scotland. If you give me my pendulum, I can tell you where both my sons are.'

Tobie said, 'They are both safe. I am sure you are right. Go to sleep. It is too early to talk.'

He heard himself murmur a protest, but his strength had waned, and he could feel his mind losing its grip. He said, 'I put Robin in Bruges,' and, frowning, sank into sleep.

When Tobie came next, he was awake, half sitting back on the pillows, breathing deeply. Darkness had fallen, and moths rapped on the ceiling and whirred round the blazing wax lights by his bed. The perspiration ran down his skin. Tobie said, 'What have you done? You shouldn't move.'

Every inch of his body told him that. He said, 'Send Robin in.'

Tobie said, 'He is busy.'

Then Nicholas lifted his hand from the sheet and showed the cord, and the pellet, and the map. Tobie looked at them; and went out of the room.

Nicholas lay back on the pillows. Although the shutters were open, the night seemed to have swallowed the air: his throat ached. His limbs would mend, he had been told, but he could neither walk nor ride till they did. If he over-extended his strength, the fever would attack him again. Tobie had known all of that.

Robin of Berecrofts came in. Nicholas had not seen him since that senseless dismissal at Bruges; he had tried to make amends. The boy looked pallidly resolute, like a trader caught with counterfeit stock. Nicholas said, 'Thank you for coming. You don't need to hide anything now. I know my wife and son have left Antwerp. I suspect they are travelling to Scotland, and you decided, rightly, that I ought to be told?'

'Ser Diniz agreed,' Robin said. 'I didn't know where you were. I'd reached Captain Astorre when the message came that you were here. Dr Tobie said I should come with him.' He paused. 'I can go back. I wasn't trying to disobey orders.'

'Henry has gone,' Nicholas said. 'You can stay if you wish. Do you want to fight?'

The boy's eyes gazed at him, considering. The boy said, 'It depends, my lord. The Duke has taken Eu and St Valéry-sur-Somme, but not very securely. The troops have gorged themselves in the orchards, and there is a good deal of sickness and not very much food. Captain Astorre says the rumours about secret truce talks are probably true, and he is sticking to the job of guarding Master John's guns in the rear, since M. d'Orson has – has died of his wounds. We were to tell you that his men are properly fed and in reasonable health, but he doesn't expect to see anything much more done this season. That's the situation, my lord.'

'In other words, "No",' Nicholas said.

'It is for you to say, my lord,' the boy said. Tobie, who had followed him in, had not spoken.

Nicholas said, 'I think you had better come with me to Scotland. See me later.'

He watched the boy glance at the doctor, and then bow slightly and leave. He was a good lad. Archie ought to be proud. Nicholas withdrew his eyes and turned to Tobie.

'When did they go, Gelis and Jordan?'

'Three weeks ago,' Tobie said.

'So now we can guess why this happened.'

'To stop you from going to Scotland? Nonsense. De Ribérac couldn't have known. He had plenty of other good reasons for crippling you.'

'No. He knew,' Nicholas said. 'She will be in Scotland by now.'

'You meant to take her back there in any case,' Tobie said. 'You must have been sure you could protect them. She will be in Edinburgh. Simon will be in Kilmirren. Gelis will take proper precautions. She will do all you would have done.'

'I know,' Nicholas said.

'So what is it?' said Tobie. 'That she went? Is that it? That she thinks she can force you to follow? Well, she's wrong, isn't she? Fate took a hand there, and you can't.'

'But then Fate brought you here, and I can.'

Tobie's eyes, when he faced opposition, had always seemed to become rounder and paler, while their pupils concentrated, sharp as two pins. Nicholas looked into them now, and despite his own desperation, surprised in himself a wave of relief. It came from physical weakness, and would not last. He was alone. Everyone was.

Tobie said, 'No, you can't,' as he expected.

Nicholas said, 'Then I'll get Robin to take me. You can come later. Do you want to come later? You probably don't.'

'I don't. Why did Godscalc forbid you to go back to Scotland?'

'For two years, that was all. I stayed away for two years,' Nicholas said. He had forgotten that Tobie knew that.

'And he would want you to go back now? Other things being equal?'

'Other things aren't equal,' Nicholas said. 'Simon and his father are a threat to Gelis and Jordan.'

'And to you.'

'That is their belief. Let them hold it while they can.'

Tobie said, 'That is really why you are going back? To destroy the St Pols, because of what they did, are still doing to you? And then what?'

'Who knows?' Nicholas said. 'Come to Scotland if you want to find out. I shall be there for the winter. I don't expect to be there ever again. I aspire to an Imperial destiny.'

Tobie went. Nicholas lay, subduing his anger and fear and, in growing calm, was able to assemble and contemplate, once again, the finely geared instrument he had spent so long designing, now running its course.

Soon, the portion dealing with France would find itself losing momentum and would begin to wind down and cease, once the vicomte had succumbed.

The Tyrol had completed its initial part in the plan, and was about to contribute more. One could not be sorry for Sigismond, and his Duchess had played throughout with her eyes open. He was supposed to take account of what she had done for him in the past, and he would.

He had bought indemnity from the Signoria and would not take part in the Venetian Crusade; he meant to crush the Vatachino in Europe, and if the price was the loss of his gold, he was willing to pay it. He had promised Bessarion nothing.

Adorne could look after himself. So could Cyprus. Godscalc Protector of Bridges was dead; Bessarion dying. He could not be every man's conscience.

He could not foresee the future, or not so far as he knew.. But his guess, his informed guess was that the supreme power in Europe would fall to Burgundy and its new empire, of which the Bank would be part. Fleury would be Burgundian. And next year, the business of Scotland would be over, and he would take Gelis aside and say, 'This is what lies ahead. Now, have we not come to the end?'

In that mood, he could forget the dawn over Sinai; Jordan screaming at Veere; the white death in Iceland; the miscalculation – the naïve miscalculation which had led to what had happened by the Loire, coupled with the headstrong flight of Gelis, with all its possible consequences.

Tobie had been right. He had been angry because she had forced him to follow. She would be in the same country as Simon, and without her husband. That was the real challenge she had sent him, defiantly, cynically, using against him the art she so hated. Because he could divine where she was, she would count on him to follow immediately.

And that was all right. Responsibility belongs to the person who chooses. God is without blame.

Chapter 38

PLANNING IT, Gelis van Borselen gave Nicholas three days to get to the coast and find a vessel in which to pursue her. If he were deeply embroiled elsewhere, he might take a day or two longer. Or, if he were more disciplined than she expected, he might stay where he was, until Diniz sent word of her destination. She had made sure that Bruges knew where she was going. He would be a week behind her at most, and very angry.

The voyage to Scotland was unremarkable. At Leith, she remained on board ship until Govaerts responded to her call for an armed escort into town. She made no effort to visit the High Street, but installed herself and the child and his nurses in the domestic wing of the Casa Niccolò in the Canongate. To Govaerts, she said that the private quarrel with the St Pol family had now become grave, and that her husband had ordered that until he arrived, the house should be discreetly protected, with a permanent guard for herself and the child.

Govaerts was able to tell her that Simon de St Pol had been for some weeks at Kilmirren, although his father the vicomte was still abroad. She expected Simon to move east almost immediately, and during the two days that followed, made all the outside calls that she must, before retiring to the confines of the house along with Jodi, who was pleased with his welcome, but resentful of the absence of his father and Robin.

She had no need to repeat her warnings to Mistress Clémence and Pasque, who already knew what had happened between Nicholas and Simon's son Henry. They also knew – everyone did – of her misconduct with Simon four years ago, and his rage at being used in her war with her husband. Until now, his father had kept him away.

The harassment began on the fourth day, a sign of unusual efficiency. At first it affected only the house in the High Street, which was kept in her absence by two sisters who slept in the kitchen, but came daily to serve the big house in the Canongate. It began with minor annoyances: a baxter persistently claiming a non-existent debt; the accidental breaking of shutters; the destructive robbing of the finest trees in the orchard. When Govaerts sent two men to stay in the house, they found the water barrels were tainted. It culminated in a fight in the street, after a drunk man had insisted on entering, claiming to think the place was a brothel.

In the Casa Niccolò, all the food and water was tested, and there was a guard night and day. No official complaint had been made: nothing was traceable to Simon, who had settled into his house near the top of the High Street and was peaceably dividing his time between the affairs of his estates and occasional serious consultations at the royal kennels and stables where the King, unused to incipient fatherhood, had come to value his advice on matters of venery. Simon was to all intents pure. One could not complain without regenerating the scandal.

While all the rest of the town pretended ignorance, the Berecrofts family was predictably sensible. Calling to invite her to visit, Archie had conveyed, mildly flushed, his father's considered opinion. 'I'm to say that one lassie's mistake should be noways prejudicial to a fine lady like Gelis van Borselen, and that if either Robin or your husband took a fist to that useless brat Henry, it was because he deserved it.' After a while he had added, 'In any case, what can the loon Simon do? Anything serious, and the law would clap him in prison.'

She had been touched and sickened at once – sickened as she always was at any mention of Simon. She reminded herself, yet again, why she was doing this. She also remembered that Archie of Berecrofts and his father had been threatened by Simon, once, for sheltering Nicholas. Or so Kathi had told her.

The Sersanders sister and brother were in Edinburgh: she had received greetings from both, among the other messages of welcome that had come to the Casa. Anselm Sersanders and his clerks were lodged in the house his uncle held in the High Street. Another of the Iceland adventurers had returned to his rooms in the Cowgate: Martin, the red-headed agent of the Vatachino who had outsmarted Nicholas, and brought home Adorne's sulphur from Iceland.

Gelis gathered that Sersanders had disapproved of some of Martin's performance in Iceland, and the two now rarely spoke. The sister, Kathi, was back in Haddington at her post with the young Princess Margaret, and the Princess's sister had joined them. In her present state of marital suspension, it was not surprising that poor Mary had been lodged in a convent. They said England was finding Tom Boyd inconvenient, and he might be reduced to the life of a mercenary.

Nicholas, had he been here, would no doubt be reminding the Countess that, whatever she craved, it was her duty to stay with her children. But Nicholas wasn't here.

The next person to suffer was Mistress Clémence who, disapproving of her charge's isolation, had elected to bring him a reward from the booths outside St Giles. Stalking uphill through the mud, she paid no attention at first to the jostling on the crown of the road until hands on one side dragged and tore at her thick hooded cloak, and on the other tugged and emptied her basket. She caught the lad who did that and fetched him a slap on the jaw before the rest turned her round and shoved her over the highway and down the steep wynd on the other side.

There, losing her footing, she slipped, and they kicked her between them, rolling her over and over as she gasped and flailed and tried to grip their legs and their shoes. Then they scattered and fled, as helpers poured down the hill, a girl ahead of them all who stopped her fall by flinging herself bodily below her, exclaiming. 'Mistress Clémence! Are you hurt? Lie still. Lie still, help is coming.'

It was the young girl, Katelijne Sersanders, and behind her was their own neighbour, Archie of Berecrofts.

'If you will allow me to sit up . . .' said Mistress Clémence, doing so. She pulled down her skirts, eased her shoulders and made a brief appraisal of her limbs. She said, 'I am bruised, but not otherwise injured. Perhaps you would help me to rise. Thank you. It is kind of you. I suppose the rogues have all vanished?'

They had. The crowd was too interested to do so, and she was glad to accept the demoiselle's invitation to enter the town house of the Priory of Haddington. Master Archie came with them. The nuns, fussing, took off her wet cloak and went to fetch wine. She straightened her cap. Master Archie said, 'You are a brave lady, Mistress Clémence. But you mustna walk out on your lane.'

'Are we to be prisoners?' said Mistress Clémence crossly. She had refused an escort. And Pasque was too scared to go out.

The girl Kathi said, 'What do you mean?' and the young man looked at her.

'The lady of Beltrees and the bairn. They're being secretly hounded by yon fool St Pol of Kilmirren. His fushionless brat ran into trouble in Zeeland, and Nicholas tanned him – Robin wrote me – instead of making it known to the law. And now Simon thinks he can make his wife and wean pay for it.'

'Where is Lord Beltrees?' said Kathi.

Mistress Clémence looked at her with approval. 'He is coming. The Lady expected him here before now.'

'The Lady doesna allow for evil and contrary winds,' said the man. 'It might be a good week or more before he comes. And until then, mistress, you should walk tentily.'

'Archie,' said the girl. He looked at her. They seemed to know each other very well. She said, 'Don't you think it will be a lot worse after Nicholas comes? If Simon wants to punish Gelis, he'll want her husband to see it. I think men-at-arms aren't enough. I think they need the best kind of protection. Don't you have some of the Holyrood clergy living beside you?'

'That's so. All our land belongs to the Abbey.'

'So they could put Gelis's business discreetly before the lord Abbot?'

'Archibald Crawford? Of course.'

'All of it?'

'He likely kens,' Berecrofts said.

'And he's worldly-wise. And he owes us all something for the Nativity Play. Couldn't he make it clear that, whatever Gelis has done, the Church has exonerated her? And couldn't he suggest to the Countess of Arran and the King that she resumes her old post with the Princess Mary? She'd be safe, surely, at Haddington,' the girl said. 'They all would. Anyone who touched them after that would be really in trouble.'

Mistress Clémence's admiration increased. She said, 'May I say I think it an excellent idea. So long as one bears in mind that the behaviour of the family de St Pol cannot always be regarded as rational.'

The clear eyes regarded her, and then beamed. 'So it ought to be quite interesting when the sieur de Fleury gets back,' Kathi said.

They escorted her back when she had recovered. They found the household in an uproar: the garden had been discovered to be full of black rats and Jordan had barely been pulled indoors in time.

Within two days, they were all installed in the Cistercian Priory of Haddington.

It amused Simon de St Pol when he heard, returning home rather drunk from what had begun as a royal hunting-party. The whore was scared: good. Perhaps she didn't know he had land in Dunbar.

He was about to send for his own private agent when Martin of the Vatachino was announced. But for the note he sent in, Simon wouldn't have seen him. He had lost too many business deals through the sharp practices of the Vatachino, and so had the vicomte his father. They were unpleasant rivals. That they were equally vicious opponents of the Banco di Niccolò was the only point in their favour. It was the name of de Fleury which had leaped at him out of that note.

He did not propose to treat the fellow, however, as other than *popolo minuto*. He left him standing and asked him his business. When the man took off his cap, the straight red hair was extraordinarily thick and coarse; his face, despite his colouring, had a southern fleshiness, and his build was squat. He spoke French with a hint of Catalan in it.

The man said, 'They tell me you are doing well, my lord. I came to congratulate you, and suggest how you might do even better.'

'You are resigning from business?' said Simon.

'I could,' said the other. 'I have wealth enough. But the firm I represent has made a suggestion. The St Pol and the Vatachino and the Banco di Niccolò comprise three well-established companies, each with a modest share of the market. Would it not be even better if there were only two?'

'I am listening,' said Simon.

'You are gracious. I am not – we are not sufficiently simple to imagine you would concede us the field. You will develop, you will flourish. Were you our only rivals, we should not object. As it is –'

'I have an appointment,' said Simon.

'Forgive me. Of course. I shall be brief. As it is, we should be disposed to embark on a rather more unfriendly policy than heretofore, had an alternative not presented itself. You dislike Nicholas de Fleury.'

'Who does not?' Simon said.

'But especially, you have embarked on a personal campaign against him and his wife and his son?'

'Indeed?' Simon said. 'One wonders how such gossip becomes general.'

'In which case,' said the man, 'would it offend you if I suggested that the Vatachino would be interested in joining you in this project? In lending you all our specialised assistance? Indeed, in performing whatever final acts you may have had in mind?'

'Perhaps,' said Simon, 'you would care to sit down?'

The second week passed, and the third, and Nicholas did not come, while the storms stopped all news from the south. October began.

Reared in a convent, Mistress Clémence had no objection to the Cistercian life of the cloister. The Prioress was a lady of some authority, although the Rule was in many ways lax, as tended to occur in poor countries, where the nearest well-founded buildings had to serve not only as convents but as mints and meeting-halls and national guest-houses, and as nurseries and retirement homes for the great. A well-run abbey or priory was little less than a city, with the swell and surge of the liturgical calendar married to the seasonal management of a great agricultural domain, its products, and its inhabitants.

There were sometimes more men than women in Haddington Priory, and the chambers resounded to secular music and laughter as often as they echoed with Lauds. It was, however, a good place for the young, at least below the onset of puberty. After that, it was an equally good place for concealing the results.

The child liked it almost too well; it required some application to maintain the standards of rearing to which Clémence subscribed. In many ways it was comparable to the conditions at Dean Castle the previous year. The Countess's children were indulged, but Mistress Betha had sense, and Mistress Phemie was as gentle as ever, although a little withdrawn, and seemed to have relinquished her music. The young Sersanders girl, Katelijne, was often to be heard trying to tempt her to accompany her in some piece or other, but she only succeeded when Master Roger came to teach singing, when the whole Priory seemed to glitter into the air, like a birthing of fireflies. Even Jodi, thumb in mouth, had found his way to some of these sessions and Master Roger had allowed him to stay, sometimes setting him on his knee while he played and letting him tug at the strings.

But mostly, Jodi was directly cared for by herself, for the lady Gelis had to see to the needs of the Countess, helping with her correspondence and interviewing her tradesmen, and attending her, well escorted, when she went out. And as at Dean, the girl Kathi seldom visited Jordan, although Mistress Clémence saw her watching the child now and then. But then, Katelijne herself had other occupations. With the death of her aunt, the necessity of arranging a marriage seemed at last to have been officially enjoined on the Prioress.

Katelijne was eighteen years of age, lively, and possessed of good prospects, and it should not take long. The young men all seemed reasonably pleasant, the older ones even more so. It had been a mystery to Mistress Clémence that a niece of Anselm Adorne should have been so neglected. It led to misjudgements or worse, like the unfortunate voyage to Iceland. The girl was patently innocent, but it was time that such freedom was stopped.

The autumn weather was kind. The children played around the broom-park, the homesteads, the grange; ran to follow the fowler; pretended to assist with the cutting of peats; helped to count the Abbot of Melrose's wedders; visited the swine; were shown how to beat the kirns in the dairy and peered wide-eyed into the eel-tank.

They were chased out of the brew-house and wished, but were not allowed, to carry ash and dung to the midden.

They were guarded night and day: nothing happened. It seemed either that the foolish man Simon had been outwitted, or that he was waiting for his real target, his audience. It made Mistress Clémence privately uneasy to notice the growing preoccupation of the lady Gelis, and of the girl Katelijne in particular, as October wore through, and still there was no word from the child's father.

He had been going to the Loire. By now, Mistress Clémence knew him a little, although she did not trust him: she trusted few men. She knew at least enough to be sure that his care for the child Jodi was not superficial. He would go to Coulanges.

There he would find nothing that he was not already aware of, except perhaps the comeliness of the Cisse. There were fat cattle, too, by the Loire; the grain would be sheaved; the vines would be weeping with sweetness. Perhaps, like his son, he had been seduced by the joy of the season, and not by the occult.

She had heard it whispered that he possessed powers of divining, and had used them in the Tyrol and Scotland, but she had seen no such dark side in all the weeks he had spent on shipboard in that strange idyll with Jodi, and the mysteries of Hesdin had been mechanical. Master Nostradamus had left the Loire, she had heard, and Dr Andreas was here. Yet the lady Gelis, departing so suddenly, had seemed confident that her lord would somehow know and follow immediately. And then he had not come.

The news broke through, finally, at the end of October, but not to Haddington. It came to Simon in Edinburgh because his man, riding hard from Dunbar, pre-empted the arrival of a battered vessel struggling against wind and tide to reach Leith. And although he longed to proclaim what he knew, Simon had sense enough to keep quiet. The Priory was still uninformed the next day, when Willie Roger, tired of incense and discordant noises, led his class of young adults and children out into the sun for their music, and stayed to join in their games.

Jodi was there, and the Countess's infants, although the Countess herself was at Court with her sister. There were also some of the choristers from the church of the Trinity, including a handsome man referred to by Roger as the Angel of the Annunciation, who also brought his two children. They had been given carriage from Edinburgh in the wagon-train of a merchant. The merchant had gone, but one of his wagons stood at the top of the field, full of the seed corn to be unloaded tomorrow.

The sun was bright, but the salt breeze was fresh. The little ones, wrapped in shawls, had been marshalled by Master Roger into a circle and were jumping about, shrieking words to his whistle while the older children wove a pattern around them. Every now and then they fell down. It was when the whistle broke off that Mistress Clémence first heard the squeak of the wheels, and looked up.

The wain at the top of the short slope was moving. The incline was bumpy, and at first the cart seemed to be coming quite slowly, its solid wood wheels knocking against outcrops of stone. There were more of these lower down, but the descent also got steeper, so that the heavy sacks in the wagon started to jump and to topple, and then to hurl themselves out, and bound and roll down the decline towards the children. A wheel came off and shot into the air, while the cart itself careered springing onwards towards them. The children started to scream.

Clémence seized Jodi under one arm and Mary's son under the other and ran. Roger laid hands on another two and did the same, pushing shrieking children before him. Clémence looked over her shoulder. A sack, bursting beside her, nearly knocked her off her feet and Jodi squealed in renewed anguish; the other child was rhythmically hooting, and her apron was soaked with his urine. She saw the wheel hit the ground and strike a young girl, bouncing over her. The cart crashed down where the circle had been and began to slow, its bags scattered about it. Another wheel juddered free and rolled off, and the carcass came to a halt.

There were three children lying still on the grass, and the screaming was thin and continuous, like the sound of gulls over a shoal. She let the two children down on the grass, and began to run back.

Roger was running before her. A tall man passed her, shouting. 'John! Muriella!'

She said, 'They are safe. They stayed in the garden.'

She was kneeling by the first silent heap when a man threw himself down and, thrusting her aside, began to talk to the child. She did not know all the fathers: she could sympathise, but in an emergency there was no time for niceties. She said, 'Please get back. This girl is hurt. She needs a doctor.'

'I am a doctor,' he said.

He didn't look like one. His coat was crusted with salt and his cap, knocked askew, showed a wing of insubstantial pale hair and a section of cranium. She drew breath to object, and saw what his hands were doing. He was a doctor. She got up and left.

The second child was crying, thank God, and seemed to have only bruises. She took her head on her shoulder and let her weep, her eyes following the musician as he flung himself down by the third victim.

It was not a child but a boy in his teens, one of the prebends from the church of the Trinity. He was lying perfectly quiet. Clémence spoke to the girl and, leaving her, went to join Roger. She could see, over the hill, help was coming. Among the running figures, she recognised Phemie.

Roger said, 'I think he is dead.'

'No,' said a voice. The unknown doctor, kneeling beside them. He said to Clémence, 'Go to that child. Tell them no one is to move her till I come back. The other one is all right. Do you know of a Jordan de Fleury?'

All the time, he was examining the boy on the grass. She said, 'Lord Beltrees's son? I am his nurse.'

The man looked up. His face was pink. He said, 'Then what are you doing here? It is your responsibility, I presume, to protect him? Where is he? Where is his mother? Where is Katelijne Sersanders?'

'He is there,' she said, 'and unscathed. The two ladies are in attendance at Court. It is your responsibility, I presume, to attend the injured boy under your hand, if your oath counts for anything. I will go and see to the girl.'

She saw, as she went to do what she could, that Dr Andreas was running over the grass, his box under his arm. She was relieved. One heard of all kinds of doctors.

Chapter 39

SEVENTEEN MILES AWAY, at the top of the High Street of Edinburgh, Simon de St Pol of Kilmirren took his ease with his peers at the Castle, clothed, as he had always aspired to be, in the costliest of velvet and furs and envious of nothing he saw, neither the tapestries on the wall, nor the fireplace, nor the silver and gold on the tables of the royal chamber.

Tonight, the King had arranged a small evening distraction of cards, dice and music for the pleasure of her grace his sweet lady Margaret, and in honour of the future prince or princess whom (at last) she was carrying under her girdle. It was a select company, consisting of very little more than the five royal siblings and their favourites. With the King's sister Margaret was the girl Katelijne Sersanders, about to be married off fast, Simon noticed, now that Nicholas had done with her.

With the Countess of Arran, that moonstruck cow Mary, was her lady of honour Gelis van Borselen.

It was the third time her former lover had contrived to join a company of which Gelis was part; of intent it had always been here, at the Castle, and under the most august of auspices. On the first occasion, he had seen her eyes widen; they had remained wide as he greeted her with exquisite courtesy, and continued to do so for the rest of the slight encounter. She had curtseyed shallowly in response to his bow, and had said little thereafter.

Afterwards the King had chaffed him about it, and Simon had laughed. 'She is ashamed! It became an embarrassment: I had to thrust her out of my room. In any case, her eyes are elsewhere nowadays. That doublet! My lord King has never looked more comely, in spite of the length of the trimming.'

'The fur?' had said the King, looking down. 'It is fashionable.'

'For a man of thirty. For a desk-bound merchant, weak in the loins. Praxiteles, had he but clothed his great warriors, would have

shown them wearing hose from Milan, of the kind with a spray of
gold on the uppermost thigh . . . When the Duke wears them, they
say, it is as if he were coated with honey. Command the lady Mary to
the Feast Day next week.'

That time, the lady Gelis had seemed more assured, or at least
better prepared for Simon's tactics. She greeted him as before, with
detached coolness, while as before, he showed himself sweetly solici-
tous. This time, when the feasting was over, the King invited his
sister to the dais, and bade the lady Gelis take the cushion below him,
speaking to her several times as the evening wore on, and asking to
examine her rings. His doublet that night was untrimmed.

Tonight, he greeted both his sisters almost at once, and brought
them beside him to play at the tables. Simon, too gleeful to be
apprehensive, overheard him address several remarks, in a low voice,
to the Countess's attendant. Gelis replied smiling, but glanced once
or twice at the Queen who sat at a distant table and was being plied
with attentions and wine by one of the King's chamber valets. Simon
exchanged a glance with Georgie Bell – Little Bell – who cocked an
eyebrow in reply and then turned his back on the girl Katelijne, who
was gazing at him.

Simon smiled at her too. She was no stranger, surely, to courts. A
King, at twenty at the peak of his vigour, was going to satisfy himself
somewhere. And if his Queen, a prude from her marriage at twelve,
was now looking to her condition as an excuse to refuse him, he was
going to befriend any man who could relieve his predicament. Especially if he were offered a fair adventurous foreigner, already known as
a bawd who had gone from another man's arms to her husband.

He had had no trouble convincing the King. The long separations,
the friction between the sieur de Fleury and his wayward lady were
common knowledge, as was Simon's own affair with the woman. He
had described that. He had described every detail of their conjunction;
both as it was, and as he would like it to have been. The King, when
his eye rested on the fine lady Gelis tonight, would see through her
grand damask robe to her skin, and would not suffer the itch that
possessed him much longer.

Simon proposed to make him wait for an hour or two yet. After that,
he could have what he wanted. No woman could refuse herself to a king
and expect any future position worth having. The King was seven years
younger than Gelis and eager, and personable. She would surrender. A
single night's work, properly handled, could be turned to mortify her as
she had mortified him and proclaim de Fleury a pimp or a cuckold. And
for love of the King, and his Bank, the new Lord Beltrees might even
tolerate – condone – perhaps even encourage the union. Were he here.

Simon had already seen the King's valets, and the vats of warm water were prepared. After her chatter and gaming, the Queen would be tired and retire. Then they would all retire.

It did not occur to him that his victim's mind, honed in a four-year contest of which he knew nothing, would set to work, after the first shock of perception, to assess his scheme in the light of her purpose. She saw that he wished to purvey the idea that the liaison had not been of his making, but an embarrassing affair of unquenchable lust and reluctant gallantry. He owed the van Borselen nothing now, and could risk it.

Next, he wished to prove that Nicholas, far from objecting, would share his wife with the King for whatever he might personally get out of it. The generously bewived Nicholas had done it before, after all, with Zacco of Cyprus. Zacco had accepted the courtesan Primaflora, whose arts survived death and could be studied still – sweeter than sweet, more bitter than bitter – in the arms of her husband and student.

It did not occur to Simon, the last and sorriest miscalculation of all, that Gelis might decide that what Simon had devised would perfectly suit Gelis van Borselen too. Let Nicholas wriggle out of this, if he could.

She knew of the baths. She remembered Nicholas, returning drunkly damp to her bed on the night of the Florentine football. *Should all fail, change thy country; for some cities can cure barren women.* He had protected Jodi, at least. Tonight Jodi was safely with Mistress Clémence and Willie Roger at Haddington; she had only herself to look out for. When the Queen retired, and the girl Katelijne, frowning, had followed her twelve-year-old mistress to bed, Gelis had watched, outwardly grave, while the King cajoled his older sister into coming with him to the baths, there to relax with her ladies and his gentlemen. There would be a glass of wine, a little music, some food. They would, of course, be suitably robed. It would be decorous.

They chattered, walking down the steep stairs, and she felt the King's young hand at her side. It reminded her of a masculine finger, circling a wine-glass. Simon had thought once that she would come back to him, and his son, nauseatingly, had copied his style. Henry had received his punishment now, and what Simon was planning was part of the family reprisals. Jordan's retaliation would be altogether sharper and more lethal and, she presumed, would fall principally upon Nicholas.

Her thoughts had turned that way so often that it was not surprising when, emerging from the robing rooms dressed in fine lawn like the others, she turned cold in spite of the scented steam that filled the low room. Someone had spoken her name. A courier, outside the door, was talking to Simon who, in turn, had turned back to the King. Then they all looked at her. She stood on the damp tiles and said, 'What? What, my lord? What has happened?'

The King came and took her two hands. He said, 'You must be brave.'

The Princess Mary ran up, her face worried, and placed an arm round her waist. 'What has happened?'

'A message from France,' Simon said.

'From the battlefield? Ah no!' said the Princess. 'But they have the best medical help. Tom always said so.'

They led her to a bench and sat her down. She waited. The Countess was sitting beside her and the King stood, his hand on her shoulder. He was well made. His open robe showed his white linen drawers and the haze of curling red hair at his chest. He was sweating. They all were.

Simon said, 'It was not on the battlefield. Apparently Lord Beltrees was waylaid on his way from the Loire. He had called at Saumur, and was perhaps thought to be carrying gold. At any rate, he was sprung upon when travelling unescorted, and his body lay by the river till morning. It has only lately been recognised. A vessel is bringing it home. I am so sorry.'

'There is no doubt?' said the King.

'None, sire,' Simon said. Mary was hugging her, and someone else was patting her arm. The others stood around in the steam, looking sympathetic. She fingered her hair, curling damply over her shoulders, and tried to think.

A trick. Surely a trick? But he had not come, even knowing that Jodi was in danger. He had not known. He was not coming, furious, to protect Jodi and regain face after her clever departure. He was not coming again. The game was over.

She looked at Simon and said, 'Killed by footpads, alone? I don't believe it.'

'He is dead,' Simon said. 'My man has seen him.'

'Your man?' said Gelis. She saw his eyes flicker. She said, 'Has your father done this?'

'The vicomte? No, of course not!' he said. 'The vicomte is in Ribérac, with my son.'

And then she knew it was true.

She found she was standing. Someone – Mary – was trying to lead her upstairs to her chamber, but the King considered that solitude in first grief could be cruel. He wished the lady Gelis to remain with her friends, and gave her his wine. Presently, he asked her if she thought the warm waters might even be soothing. He led her to the small tented pool, and he and Mary seated her tenderly in the warmth, and set wine before her, and fruit. Mary held her hand and talked, irritating her. She closed her eyes and leaned back, thinking of Jodi. Thinking of Hesdin. Thinking of Sinai. Thinking of the rain through an African night.

After a while Mary withdrew, leaving her maids. A little after that, it became very quiet and Gelis saw, opening her eyes, that the maids had gone, and there was only Little Bell, on a stool in the corner, drawing slow, yearning notes from the lute. Only Bell and his master who, seeing her stir, said, 'Come. The water has cooled. Here is a seat by the brazier.'

He held a great towel, and leaned a hand to help her step out. She saw his face, and remembered. She said, 'Sire, this is work for a servant.'

'It pleases us,' said the King. He set her before him and, opening the towel, wrapped it about her. He did not release her. 'It pleases us to make you warm. For we think, despite all your grief, that you have had a cold bed to lie in for some time. Is that so?'

His arms tightened. He was not very tall. She felt his fresh cheek at her neck, altering as his lips moved. His hands smoothed down the folds of the towel and then, parting it, traced the clinging lawn over her belly. His fingers began to pinch up the fine cloth.

She had lain in a cold bed for a long time. The fight was over, and self-denial was no longer a buckler, a weapon. She knew now that she had been right to regard it so, for her heart was already racing, and the tide rising, prickling her skin. Death and mating. Young as he was, James had known that one led to the other.

Lovers spoke. Lust had no need of a voice, only of signals. He loosed his hands for her turning and then set again to what he had been doing with his fingers. The towel dropped. His lashes were sandy and his lips, a little parted, were pink. The lute had stopped and Georgie Bell, carrying it, had gone to the door.

He had gone, not to depart, but to answer a scratch. Voices murmured. The King stopped and turned his head, angrily. The lutenist said, 'Lord?'

All the young man's pent-up breath exploded in anger. '*What?*'

Bell's face was red. He said, 'I am sorry, my lord. But Lord Beltrees is waiting to see you.'

Interrupted desire has a peremptory pain of its own. The young man's hands dropped, his face whitening. Gelis struggled to breathe and then, stooping, pulled up the towel and strained it about her. The King said, 'You are mistaken.'

'No, sire. It is the sieur de Fleury, just come in from Leith. He says he will wait.'

'Does he –?'

'He would also like to speak to madame. But he says he will wait until the King's grace has completed his bathing.'

He is alive. He is here. The rest meant nothing.

James turned. Looking at his flushed face, Gelis thought that, from anger and lack of control, he meant to resume. She realised that if she resisted him, he probably would. For a moment she did not know, any more than he did, what she wanted. Then she made herself passive and waited, and James, his breathing slowing, stepped back. Then she saw the whole of what Simon had intended; and further saw that Nicholas had fathomed it, and was making his indifference known. *He will wait until the King's grace has completed his bathing.*

He is alive. He is here. It has made no difference.

The King had scented deception as well. It was a common hazard, this kind of conspiracy. And it was hardly credible that Simon's man should have seen Nicholas dead, and Nicholas should be here, at such a moment, alive. The King looked at her narrowly and saw, could not fail to see, a physical distress matching his own. His face softened and, bending, he set his lips to her breast. Then he released her and went.

She dressed slowly. Her body ached, and once she caught herself in a sob. She heard the King speaking outside the door, his voice metallic and cold. He was expressing his relief at seeing Lord Beltrees in health. A false report of his death had disturbed them. The dame de Fleury had taken it badly, and was only now in a fit state to join them. No doubt he would wish to speak to the lady alone in her chamber, and tomorrow, give them his news.

She heard Nicholas answer, in the familiar, unmistakable voice. She pinned her hair into its caul and walked out of the room to the antechamber where the two stood: the King regal despite his soaking red hair and damp robe; Nicholas tall and collected, dressed in cloth more suitable for the deck of a ship than an audience. She could not look away from him. He was recounting something, it seemed. The King's face, listening, had already lost its angry suspicion. She heard Simon's name and a word of medical provenance. As she came forward, Nicholas glanced at her, and stopped. Then he said, 'Nobildonna,' and continued as if she had not been there.

'I am sorry, my lord, but I cannot stay. There has been a disturbance at Haddington. But what I have said, I will stand by. Anything of mine is my lord's, except that which might harm him.'

'She did not tell me,' said James. He was staring at her.

'She did not know,' Nicholas said. 'She was already carrying my child when she lay with the lord of Kilmirren. But she has been barren ever since. His affliction prevents procreation in himself and in all with whom he has intercourse. Any woman upon whom the King's eye falls is naturally bewitched: I cannot blame my lord of Kilmirren for what has happened, although it is true that his family bears mine a grudge. I can only express my great sorrow.'

'You did not try to interrupt,' said the King.

Her husband's lips moved in what could have been a smile. 'I thought the deed done, and would not wish to have appeared grudging.'

'It was not done,' said the King. 'Would I take advantage of a lady at the moment of her bereavement?'

'There are those who would,' Nicholas said. 'I should have trusted your grace. But the outcome is happy.'

'Except for the gentleman of Kilmirren,' said the King. Despite the freckles, he looked older than twenty.

Nicholas was looking at her this time. His voice in that last speech had sounded more normal, but his face remained blank of all expression. She said, 'I hope I am loyal to both my lord and my King. My lord, you spoke of a disturbance in Haddington?'

Again, he spoke to the King. 'I heard only just now. An accident, but none of the royal children is harmed, and our own son is untouched. There is no need, I think, to alarm the Countess tonight, but I feel my wife and I ought to ride over. If, that is, it is thought that the Countess would not object.'

'An accident? In the Priory? We shall send someone at once,' said the King.

'My lord,' Nicholas said. 'Tomorrow will do. If there is anything to be done tonight, I shall do it. I hope I have your trust.'

The King agreed, flushing.

They did not speak on the journey to Haddington, because Nicholas made it impossible to do so. Their escort galloped beside them, torches streaming. She saw they were Govaerts's men. She wondered who had sent word from Haddington, and how they had known he was back. She was ready, tonight, to credit him with frightening powers.

No ordinary human being could have activated from afar this single damning stroke against Simon: a sickening sexual conspiracy which traded on the King's naïveté, his own supposed death, and the precarious continence their duel had imposed on her. He had had her roused, she was sure, quite deliberately. He had been prepared for, had expected, consummation. Any skilled doctor could have dealt with a pregnancy. His talk of disease was untrue, but it would be believed, for it was all too verifiable that Simon was sterile. The handsome Kilmirren would now be a leper, a public procurer, a man who could be accused of attempting to end the royal line. But she would escape, as Simon's innocent dupe. She had been the King's choice. She had believed her husband was dead. But of course no one would lie with her either, ever again.

That night, arriving in Haddington, her eyes deep, her head throbbing, Gelis van Borselen found herself for the first time afraid of the future.

It was three hours from dawn. The porter admitted them. The chapel was lit, but the Priory itself lay dark and silent, as did the guest-quarters. She ran to her rooms. Outside, Mistress Clémence met her with a candle, signing for silence. 'The boy is asleep. All is well.' Her eyes moved beyond, and Gelis saw that Nicholas was standing behind her.

Gelis said, 'Lord Beltrees has just come. What happened? We were given no details.'

The woman said, 'A wagon broke free and rolled down a hillside. Three of the children were struck, only one of them seriously. Jodi received no harm at all, but sleep will help him. I shall tell him you are here in the morning.'

Nicholas said, 'You are right. We shall hear more about it tomorrow. You must be tired. And in case he wakens, here is something to put by his pillow.'

It was a large, perfect apple, still attached to its stalk, with a leaf. Mistress Clémence received it with a slight smile. 'He said you had promised one. He shall have it.' She turned and waited, her hand on the door until they left.

Nicholas said, 'Where is your room?'

Gelis said, 'There. Do you want to talk?' Her limbs ached and she shivered.

'No,' he said. 'I can't think of a subject I could bring myself to talk about. Go to bed. We shall speak, if we have to speak, in the morning.'

They had been apart for more than four months, and the last time they had met, he had broken every fine thing in the room. She had been told he was dead. She had been on the point of giving herself, out of desperation, to somebody else when she had been halted. And he knew all that, and had perhaps even arranged it.

Until now, she had never doubted that this was a war that she wanted to win. Now she was terrified. She said something, and went to her room without looking back.

*

Tied to a more juvenile mistress, Katelijne Sersanders was unable to get herself out of Edinburgh until the entire cavalcade of the King's sisters swept off to Haddington the following morning, spurred on by Mary's anxiety and held back when she collapsed into tears. The Countess would not believe the two children were well. She would not believe it until she saw them.

Her sister Margaret, whom they called Bleezie Meg in the stables, hurled herself at Phemie when they arrived at the Priory. 'Where did it happen? Are they dead? Show me!'

Phemie said to Katelijne, 'I'll show her. I think you are wanted inside.'

'Who by? Never mind,' Kathi said. Everyone in Edinburgh knew that Nicholas de Fleury had returned, and had found his wife and Simon de St Pol at the Castle. He and his lady wife had left during the night, and St Pol, they said, had gone back to Kilmirren. It was observed that Archie of Berecrofts had got his son Robin back from the war, and must be glad of it.

She was thankful about Archie and Robin. As for the rest, she refused valiantly to speculate. All she knew for a fact was that, concerned for the boy, Nicholas and Gelis had come here to Haddington. She had no trouble now in thinking of him by his first name.

Phemie's remark had been a warning. Thoughtfully, Kathi walked over the yard towards the guest-quarters. A man in a stained gown emerged and stood, his sparse hair blowing about his pink cranium, his pale eyes screwed up at the sky. Kathi cried, '*Dr Tobie!* You came!'

She was so pleased to see him that she had her arms round his neck while he was still staring. He choked, and held her off, and then hugged her, hooting himself. 'Katelijne Sersanders. You've got smaller.'

'You've got fatter,' she said. 'Oh, Dr Tobie!'

He said, 'Is this a welcome for me myself? Or do I have a feeling it isn't?'

She said, 'It is for you, if you wanted to come. Everyone likes to be needed.'

He put her down, but kept his arm round her waist. He said, 'Ah yes. But not everyone that's needed is wanted. There's the devil of a mess going on here, and I don't know what it is. I've been with him for two months and he won't talk.'

'Why didn't he come?' Kathi asked. She was leading him in towards the parlour.

'He couldn't. The vicomte de Ribérac kindly stopped him. At second-hand, with six thugs.'

She halted and looked at him. 'Simon de St Pol told the King that Nicholas had been waylaid and robbed. He said killed, at first.' Margaret, who gleaned everything, had told her. She added, 'Apparently Gelis thought he was dead. You know that Simon has been harassing her? Have you heard all that yet?'

'No. I haven't seen Gelis. I know something happened at the Castle, but Nicholas wouldn't say what.'

'Oh dear,' said Kathi. 'Well, you can't treat a dumb patient. I shall tell you all the rumours. You will repeat none of them, please, and you will kindly forget anything I say that turns out to be irrelevant. But the first thing you should know is that Simon de St Pol seems to have left in disgrace. He is not thought to be returning to Edinburgh. And if that is correct, something truly awful has happened which might stop the persecution from Simon, but which will probably bring the vicomte on the next ship. And if the sire de Ribérac hired six bullies last time, he'll likely hire sixty next, and make sure that they finish the job.' Then, calming, she talked.

Her doctor friend was very quiet at the end. She said, 'Don't say you want to go home. You haven't a home. Your home is with Nicholas.'

'He doesn't think so,' he said.

'He doesn't think so when he is tired, and hardly recovered from whatever happened to him, and when he doesn't think he wants to share secrets. Sick people don't always think clearly. You've told me that often enough.'

'I didn't think you believed me,' he said. 'At least, if St Pol is away, as you said, we may be free of some risks. I can't prove it, but I don't think that cart was an accident. Would the child not be safer in Edinburgh? Or does the termagant nurse have the last say?'

Katelijne clapped her hands. 'You have met Mistress Clémence! You are going to disagree over child-rearing, and you will end up like everyone else, by doing just what she wants. If she thinks it best to stay here, she'll stay here.'

'*That* was Mistress Clémence?' said the doctor.

'She comes from Coulanges,' said Kathi. 'Coulanges on the Cisse. So does Pasque. You have to meet Pasque.'

'Certainly, I shall have to become better acquainted with both of them,' said Dr Tobie. 'Especially since – would you believe the coincidence? – the attack on Nicholas took place near Coulanges, and he was nursed in the house of her relatives.'

'Of course I believe it,' said Kathi. 'He would have gone there to investigate Clémence, and the vicomte's men would simply have followed him. He does that. He was probably having you watched all

the time you were in Gobbio. We heard the Countess died after
having her son. I was so sorry. Tell me about it.'

She listened, for as she thought, he had been asked to go back. Dr
Tobie had been a good servant to Urbino. She wondered if he had
the detachment and constancy to make his destiny with Nicholas, and
not suffer by it. She thought that – like Diniz, like Gregorio – what
he needed most was a wife. They talked for a long time, as close as
they had ever been, and parted happy.

For Nicholas, the day was merely a continuation of a sleepless night
during which his abused body, unused to the saddle, had stiffened,
and his mood further jaundiced by the sight of Katelijne and Tobie,
united once more, talking in the yard overlooked by his casement.
His grandmothers. He wished that Tobie would go, and that the girl
would find a husband and be done with it. He dressed and, while he
still believed he could handle it, went to see Gelis.

She was always beautiful. That was the paltry aspect of this war
they were waging which, by Godscalc's decree, was already two years
longer than he had ever desired. The tragedy was that real time was
passing: years in which others would have been content to ask for less,
to take with gratitude what was there, and be reconciled for the rest
to the third-rate, or to consolation elsewhere. But even if he had been
willing, and he was not, she would never agree. Pride would forbid it,
until she was forced to cede in her chosen arena. Until she was given
pride of a different sort.

So it was terrible, as it always was, to see how lovely she was. And
being Gelis, she had scorned to dress modestly, in the peccant wife's
role, but wore loose silks which trailed from her chair, and had left
her hair straying, unbound. It was half grown again, as Kathi's was.
They had both played boys in their time, but only one of them was
playing the woman.

She said, 'I have had two separate visitors this morning. I didn't
know Tobie was here.'

'And the other?' he said. He did not want to sit down, and now
need not. He made his way to the window and leaned there.

'Katelijne. You were badly injured at Chouzy, but you were not
left for dead. Tobie says Simon must have known that.'

'Did you think it was all my plot?' Nicholas said. 'I wish it had
been. Simon merely waited until he heard I had come back, and then
timed it all accordingly. With your help.'

'I am always glad to help,' Gelis said. 'And how successful we have
been, both of us. Simon is banished from Court, and the King will be
your abashed friend for ever. So it was all inspired opportunism, the

disease story? How disappointed Simon must have been about everything.'

'I expect it was a shock,' Nicholas agreed. 'I was intended, I suppose, to stride in and skewer you both through the kidneys, while Simon skipped off and got out the wassail cakes.'

'I think he anticipated something less final but thoroughly actionable,' Gelis said. 'Treasonable protests and threats, tears, a cuckold's protest tailored to your present diminished condition, which I trust is not permanent? Or have you returned privily sealed, *Lion Sans Vilainie*, a wax lion from your wars?'

'No more nor less than Simon, I am sure,' Nicholas said. 'You colluded with him?'

Her eyes, chilly blue, closed and opened. 'Did you think it was all aimed at you? He has been attacking Jordan and me for six weeks. Ever since you elected to go to the Loire.'

He refused to digress. 'But you must have known the King's interest was being titillated, and by whom. Why did you think Simon was doing it?'

'To nauseate me and mortify you. I wasn't nauseated,' Gelis said. 'Quite the reverse. And I knew you would have no objection, since you had done the same thing yourself. Although I dare say you were not interrupted so rudely. I think I must claim a repeat engagement for that.'

'I am not sure who with?' Nicholas said.

He saw she had forgotten. Then her mind worked and she said, 'If I am thought to be infected, then so are you.'

'I don't see how,' Nicholas said. 'We haven't lain together since you descended on Simon, or vice versa. My doctors forbade it. I lied, naturally, to preserve your good name, but I'm afraid people have noticed our abstinence. If we are both ostracised, the options are certainly limited. You will have to resort to Simon for life, and I to Simon's old mistresses. Although I don't know about Ada. Crackbene would be very distressed.'

He stared at her blandly. He wasn't going to throw things this time. It went too deep for that, to a level he wasn't going to penetrate. She said, 'You seem to feel that really, it was all for the best. I'm so glad. And Simon is dealt with.'

'I'm not glad,' he said. 'Simon was supposed to be the subject of a long and brilliant campaign, culminating in a definitive foot on his throat and thirteen penitential Our Fathers in February. Now I have been compelled to excise him. I think perhaps it is worth bearing in mind. Abrupt changes can cut into a programme, and subject the players to premature hazards. All the players.'

'Nonsense,' said Gelis. 'I am inviolate. I am your game, and your life.'

Her words faded and she said nothing more, nor did he for a long time. Then he said, 'I must go and see about Jordan.'

'And that is all? You have no answer?' she said. She was sitting up.

He said, 'Gelis, I gave you my answer on Sinai.'

She remembered.

Walk over with me.

Die with me, if we cannot live without hurting each other.

Chapter 40

IN TOKEN OF his gratitude that winter, the most noble and right victorious Prince James, Third of the Name, was pleased to appoint Nicholas de Fleury, Baron Beltrees, as one of his councillors and chamberlains, and to add to his barony those lands which were necessary to round off his property. No complaint was heard from the generous donors, one of whom had already forfeited land to my lord of Monypenny, another clever man much in favour with King Louis.

James was grateful to William, first lord of Hamilton, as he was grateful no doubt to the amenable sieur de Fleury. It was popularly agreed, in an undertone, that it was not a bad thing, on the whole, to have one's lady wife surprised with the King. Especially as the candidature was now so very limited.

Following the same contrary code, the lady de Fleury was likewise allotted a cautious increase of esteem. Convinced that her friend was a victim of Simon, the King's elder sister was endlessly thoughtful. Gelis attended Court in the Countess's train, although never close to his grace; and accompanied her husband on as many formal occasions as he had time for, with all his new labours. The sabotage ceased, and in time she moved with her son back to the High Street, although very well guarded; while Lord Beltrees shared his time between that home, his Canongate house and the Castle, unless he were absent in Stirling or Perth or any of the other parts of the kingdom to which he was giving his attention.

Of Simon nothing was heard, and probably nothing would be. He had been banished to Kilmirren. One indiscretion on his part, and the banishment would become exile or worse. His self-appointed ally Martin, in the course of his travels for the Vatachino, kept Simon discreetly informed, but did not recommend action while guilt over the Burgundian was fresh. He could afford to wait. The first thing Simon had done, anyone could be sure, was to send a scream of complaint to the vicomte. And the next thing that would happen, for sure, was that the vicomte would come. As soon, of course, as King Louis would let him.

Tobie, accustomed to Nicholas's industrious guile, had never seen anything to compare with the four months that followed. Ignorant of Scotland, he spent them at the other man's side as Nicholas managed, extended, corrected all the projects originally launched with the aid of John and Moriz, Gregorio and Julius. Dr Tobias Beventini of Grado stared mesmerised at mining and draining experiments, trotted round boatbuilding yards, and met incoming ships bringing timber for the new wharves and wagons, and iron for the fine wheels and gears. He was dazzled by the splendour of the King's building plans, which lay within the competence of one Thomas Cochrane, who also provided masons for smithies and stone balls for all the new cannon. He helped check the incoming herds of draught oxen, as well as the King's special imports: the magnificent horses; the hunting dogs fine as those of King Louis, whose hounds had their feet bathed in red wine, and were set to sleep, robed in silk, in his chamber.

He helped supervise the outfitting of the King's new-bought caravel *The Lion*, and the furnishing of James's personal chambers and chapels. He rode round the acres of land where experimental crops were being planted. He saw vines. He saw hemp. Occasionally, when tired of Nicholas's more cavalier answers, he took his amazement to Govaerts.

'At least he isn't doing another Nativity Play,' Tobie said. 'I heard about that.' He saw, to his astonishment, a gleam enter the manager's eye.

'It's what finally made all the difference,' Govaerts said. 'That, and what he did for them in Iceland. The Vatachino may do well enough, and so may Sersanders, through his uncle's new post. But of the three foreign merchants in Scotland, the Banco di Niccolò is held in greatest esteem by the Court.'

Hence the dogs. Hence the furs. Hence the roaring silversmith's booth in the basement. Hence, infuriatingly, the commercial reason for two of the very few ventures that seemed to Tobie to offer hope of some sort of redemption.

Katelijne had shared the same view, in the talk – by no means all about Nicholas – which they had had before he left Haddington. 'There was a change, both times.'

'But it didn't last.'

'Not on the surface. It is all there below.'

'Like Africa?'

'I think so. He's afraid of it sometimes. That's when he will only drink water.'

'Perhaps he is right,' Tobie said. 'Violent extremes of emotion are dangerous. That kind of self-control is fairly rare.'

'Dangerous? Glass-breaking murderous dangerous?'

'Kathi,' he had said. 'I am a doctor. No. I know why that happened, and he will know it as well. I meant dangerous to the person he has made of himself.'

Just after that conversation he had gone to see the child Jordan, a visit previously discouraged. He was escorted by the two ladies Sinclair, and was able to make his bow on the way to the Countess of Arran, and ask how her children did. She remembered him also from Bruges. In the nursery, he was received by and passed into the domain of Mistress Clémence and an elderly nursemaid called Pasque, who curtseyed tittering. On the floor was a child with an apple. It looked up.

Tobie's nose warmed and swelled, and he sneezed. The child blessed him in French, with two dimples. Prompted by Mistress Clémence, it scrambled to its feet, bearing the apple which dropped as it made to shake hands. Tobie caught the fruit and placed it on his bald head, crossing his eyes.

'Papa did that,' said the child. 'Hear my poem.'

'Your poem?' said Mistress Clémence.

'Papa's poem,' said the child. 'But I did some of it.'

Tobie didn't stay long. He was used to children, but not necessarily devoted to them. He had seen all he needed to know about this one. And he didn't wish to tarnish the golden event of the day, which had clearly been already provided by Nicholas. On the way out, Mistress Clémence surprisingly suggested a turn in the herb-garden and, taking a cloak, led him outside to a bench. They were immediately surrounded by chaffinches, to whom she absent-mindedly sprinkled some crumbs from her apron. Through a casement he could hear Pasque squawking and the child chortling with laughter.

He said, 'He is a credit to you, Mistress Clémence. A charming, vigorous child.'

'A normal-enough child,' she said. She could have been any age. She looked older than she probably was, with her hair strained out of sight and her lean, erect figure. Her ankles were good. She had a nose that would make two of his snout. He had met a lot of nurses like her.

He said, 'I was speaking to the demoiselle Kathi about the accidents, and the attack on yourself. I hope they will cease now. I wanted to tell you that I met your kinsfolk at Chouzy.'

'The sieur de Fleury mentioned it,' said the nurse. 'I am glad they were able to send for you. Broken bones badly set can lame an active young man.'

'You have known him long?' Tobie said.

'For twenty months,' said Mistress Clémence. 'I was appointed, with Pasque, by the child's mother. Both parents appear satisfied with my services and I have no other plans at the moment. About the wagon.'

'The accident?' Tobie said.

She said, 'I have told Lord Beltrees that I agree that the descent of the wagon was deliberate. The boy Henry is spoiled, and was perhaps excessively punished. The family were moved to retaliate.'

'The boy Henry's bones were not broken,' Tobie said. 'He was not excessively punished.'

'You were there?'

'I was in the camp where it happened. He betrayed the men who had befriended him. But for your master, he would have been hanged.'

There was a silence. 'I see,' said the woman at last. 'I am glad. I had conceived the sieur de Fleury to be a moderate man, generally managing well under some stress. I had hoped I was not wrong.'

Generally. Tobie looked at her. 'You are not wrong,' he said. 'But if you ever have doubts, send for me.'

She was curious, which was fair enough. She knew of more than one lapse, and was uneasy about her small charge, which was commendable. She knew enough about Gelis and Nicholas to wonder what was going to happen. He shared the feeling, but had no intention of telling her so. He felt on the whole reassured.

The winter fled past, bringing extraordinary snippets of news, some amusing, some not. Two deaths occurred. Bessarion, Cardinal Patriarch of Constantinople departed life in December at Ravenna, ill and broken and too weak to return to his haven at Rome. He had achieved more than any one man in reconciling the two Christian Churches, but died unfulfilled.

The second death, mourned by suffering princes, was that of Giammatteo Ferrari da Grado, the famous physician and uncle of Tobie. Having wasted more time than he thought reasonable at his sickbed, Tobie declined to go to his funeral. His money was willed to other nephews, and his books were partitioned between them and the hospital of Pavia. His printing presses Tobie had already appropriated.

In November, a flotilla of ships conveyed Catherine Corner from Venice to Cyprus, there to take up her long-deferred position as Queen to James de Lusignan, known to his familiars as Zacco. Catherine was visibly delighted from the very first sight of her husband. The King, observers noted, was speechless. It was left to that accomplished courtier David de Salmeton, whose trading company had paid for the wedding, to articulate the King's indisputable rapture.

The usual truce for the winter was completed between the armies of Charles, Duke of Burgundy, and Louis, King of France, and the Duke filled in the time by sending an envoy to England to discuss a combined April attack on King Louis, together with a prize list of potential partitions of France. The envoy, Louis of Gruuthuse, who had sheltered King Edward in exile, was feasted day and night for two months in Westminster and Windsor, sleeping on cloth-of-gold beds in rooms hung with white silk, and being presented with the monarch's own charger and crossbow before finally being ceremonially invested with the earldom of Winchester, supported by two hundred pounds annually from the revenues of the port of Southampton. Anselm Adorne, Baron Cortachy, in whose house the Earl and Countess of Arran had stayed for very much longer, remained Conservator of the Scots Privileges in Bruges, from where he sent regular missives to Scotland.

Katelijne Sersanders his niece continued dutifully to be seen in the marriage market. Willie Roger was derisive. 'John Bonkle! My God! Why not his uncles, his father? I'd get the Trinity to rehearse in for free! Liddell. Napier. Muir. David Arnot and Conn Malloch – now *those* I'd approve of, if you didn't mind living in Fife or the Borders. At least you'd be able to sing duets with them.'

'That, I believe, is not the whole purpose and object of matrimony,' Kathi had said. 'What do you think of Ben Bailzie?'

'I saw him hanging about you. Do you really want to know?' Roger said. 'You'd be better off with me.'

'I know I should,' Kathi said. 'Let's run away. Where shall we run to?'

'Oh Kathi, Kathi,' said Roger. 'I wish that you meant it. But since you don't, I'll make you another proposal. You write down the names of your followers and I'll set them to music. Suitable music, with suitable lyrics.'

'Starting at once,' Kathi said. 'Willie? May I say something?'

'No,' said Roger.

'Then I will. I don't mind giving half measure to some people, but you would mind more than they do. Music is better.'

The one person who didn't call on her was Nicholas, and when they met it was by accident, when she was in her brother's house in the High Street, and Lord Beltrees was unexpectedly announced. Sersanders jumped up and welcomed him smiling: in Iceland, he had altered his opinion of Nicholas. Nicholas saw Kathi was there, and came forward.

They had met briefly when she came back to Haddington, on the day after his disastrous return. Then, she had hidden her pity, as he had concealed whatever he felt behind a routine display of good acting. Now, she thought, his behaviour appeared natural. He even seemed delighted to see her.

She said, 'I'm not going to say *Ey. Jà, ha, ho!* perhaps. And how is Wound Man?'

'Neglected,' said Nicholas. 'You've been avoiding me. I can't sit on anything green.'

'Well, there's a red cushion,' said Sersanders, who always lost some of his solemnity when Nicholas was about. 'She's been husband-hunting. We've just had another list, full of Dorias.'

'Well, I shouldn't pick a Genoese,' Nicholas said. 'Not with what's about to happen in Caffa and Chios. Is Mar bothering you?'

The King's brother was fourteen. 'He isn't bothering me to marry him,' Kathi said. 'He's fallen out with the King and wants to make a statement, in which I was to be a comma. I told him to wait until he could punctuate.'

'Kathi!' said her brother.

'Well, tell me if he gets into colons. I've got something to show you both.' It was an embroidered bag, which Nicholas laid on the table. 'Open it.'

The cloth of the satchel was wadmol, and she recognised the embroidery. Kathi opened it, and drew out one by one what she found wrapped inside. They were chessmen, so old that the whalebone had yellowed and there were cracks in the knights' shields and the queens' tunics and pigtails. There were runes cut very small in the base.

'From Constantinople,' Nicholas said. 'Handed down through the centuries to Glímu-Sveinn, who has sent them to me. He has recovered. Crackbene has just come back from Iceland, with news of them all.'

'You sent him?' said Kathi.

'There were things that they needed. And, of course, there was always the chance of picking up a little sulphur or some more fish. It isn't as bad as it might have been,' Nicholas said. 'The lava left them most of the pasture, and they got some of the herds out. There are salmon, and the fowling has been good. We took them meal. Shining armour and solid gold crown. I'm telling you this so that you won't mind the other news Crackbene has brought me. We've sunk the *Unicorn*.'

Her heart bumped, and then bumped again. All the bonhomie left Sersanders's face. 'Where?'

'Off La Rochelle, I believe, in the very shadow of Oléron. On its way back from Bordeaux with twenty-seven tuns of Gascon wine and a book on the Laws, but Crackbene's friends never could read. I'm sorry.'

Sersanders said, 'Burgundian sinking Burgundian? Duke Charles wouldn't like that.'

Nicholas said, 'Anselm, three-quarters of that ship is Vatachino. I have to protect myself. And although we are friends, or I hope we are, we are each fighting for our share of the trading in Scotland, and your uncle is my rival in that. He proved it in Danzig. Benecke is still very cross with you all. I am perhaps trying to show your uncle and you that association with the Vatachino can bring trouble.'

He was good with Sersanders. Kathi watched them both. A man of Martin's had been leaving as he arrived; she supposed Nicholas had seen him. She didn't like Martin, nor did her brother. For Sersanders, nevertheless, business was business. He said, 'We shall sue.'

'You can try,' Nicholas said. 'You won't find any connection between the pirate and Crackbene, or me. And of course, this conversation never happened. I just wanted to say that in one way I regretted the necessity. I shall never forget Iceland.'

Kathi said, 'You risked something, telling us.'

The dimples appeared. He said, 'Not a lot. I am a very good liar. Anselm, you know that Martin is concentrating on the towns? On deals for the burgesses?'

'I suppose,' Sersanders said, 'that he felt that you had the Court already in your purse. What do they owe you now?'

'Not as much as everyone owes your uncle's dear Tommaso in Bruges,' Nicholas said. 'I've decided to model myself on the Portinari. How many children does he have now? And getting his portrait *painted again*?'

Sersanders said, 'I heard you were encouraging the King to have his done. And John's rich father Bonkle would pay for it.'

'Hugo will make a very nice job of them both,' Kathi said. 'Altarpieces pay very well, and Maria's already managed two children by the age of sixteen: they'll need an extra panel if the paint takes long to dry. You've heard the joke about Henne's *Last Judgement*?' In fact, everyone had a joke about Henne's latest. It showed the Saved and the Damned, most of them identifiable drinking companions or debtors of Henne.

'I sent him a few tips about Hell,' Nicholas said. 'What's happened? Tani can't pay for it?'

Angelo Tani, formerly of the Medici in Bruges, had commissioned the painting for the Medici managers' chapel in Florence. His likeness appeared on the back. Tommaso loathed him: Tommaso had been left out of the picture. Kathi said, 'How did you guess? But it's going to be all right after all. Tommaso is underwriting the painting and sending it to Florence for free; it's going on the Burgundian galleys next spring. In return for which –'

'– Memling has painted him into the picture. Naked? All the Risen were nude as a needle when I saw the piece last,' Nicholas said, his expression distant. 'This huge triptych. I haven't seen Tommaso naked since –'

'Neither has anyone except maybe Maria. No. That is, Henne painted Tommaso's head on a piece of lead foil, and stuck the foil on someone else's nude body. There could be an industry in that,' Kathi said.

'There is already. Statues, even. Ask Tobie, if he'll condescend to mention Volterra. This triptych will be wasted on the Medici managers. You should get Jan to view it in situ, and report on Tommaso from the neck down. How is Jan? Still in Rome?'

'And that's another thing,' said Sersanders. He was still flushed from the blow over the *Unicorn*. Kathi saw that Nicholas had come perversely determined to have all his sins forgiven at once.

Her brother said, 'You bastard, what about poor Patrick Graham?'

'I thought you'd like his being made an archbishop,' Nicholas said. 'Patron of Jan, friend of the family. Papal Nuncio soon, I shouldn't wonder, licensed to collect Peter's pennies and shillings and pounds.'

'And that will make him popular, won't it?' Sersanders said. 'There are those who think that Scotland deserved an archbishop, there are those who resent it. Fair enough. But to help rush it through, to outrage the King and bring about a clash with the Pope was not – tactful.'

'You speak as if it happened overnight,' Nicholas said. 'With a Blackadder and an Arnot in Rome, not to mention an Adorne, the thing was hardly an impenetrable secret. It will settle. If your uncle wants some places and prebends, he'll get them.'

Sersanders said, 'I wasn't thinking only of Jan. I'm thinking of Coldingham; the Tyrolean alum; all the other disputes James has got himself into. It won't help your trade or mine if the Apostolic Camera gets annoyed and starts to call in its debts.'

Kathi said, 'We think Jan will be all right. Chancellor Hugonet's brother will take him. What will happen to poor Patrick Graham?'

'It depends how good he is at keeping his temper,' Nicholas said. 'If he's humble enough, James won't think him a threat.'

Sersanders snorted. Kathi said, 'Well, that disposes of his chances in a sentence.'

'Quicker than a statement,' Nicholas said. 'Anselm, I brought a peace offering below. Will you drink it with me if I get it?'

Sersanders, predictably, rose to perform the errand himself. Nicholas said, 'Willie Roger gave me a performance of your latest visiting-list. I thought I missed a few names.'

'Or perhaps I did,' said Kathi. 'Damn Willie's big whistle, that was private. Why don't we meet very much? Because of Gelis?'

'Various reasons,' he said.

'Gelis has your relationship and mine perfectly fathomed,' Kathi said. 'So has Dr Tobie. So have you. So have I. But if you avoid me, then people will talk. Call now and then. Or put all the visits together and take me out in an Eke Week.'

'Dr Tobie,' he repeated slowly.

Damn again. She said, 'Oh well, it was worth trying. Courage, my friend. Courage is different from hope and intermediate between despair and presumption. It's a finicky business being your comrade, Síra Nikolás.'

'I'm sorry,' he said. She could sense some of the things he wasn't saying.

'Don't be sorry. I'm not the *Unicorn*, I'm the maiden. Take courage and call. I'll be lenient,' she said. 'I shan't slip anything into your wine.'

He said, 'You wouldn't be the first person, if you did.' Then Sersanders came in.

She couldn't drink, watching him talk to her brother. Again, he looked quite composed. Doctored wine. A breach of trust but, somehow, not a recent one. Not even some sly potion of Dr Tobie's. Something much more important in his eyes, in his voice.

She wondered then if it had been in Africa; if it had been the beginning of all this; if it had been Gelis.

Courage. Courage, my friend.

You should have filled me with drink, and it would be over with. He drove the words from his mind, as he extinguished the whole of the interview he had just had, and walked downhill greeting his comrades, his friends, on the way to his Casa and the final phase of his programme.

You couldn't be brought up in Bruges and trained by a capable woman of business without knowing that the well-being of any town, duchy or kingdom depended on its fiscal dexterity. In Timbuktu, in Ultima Thule, profit and survival depended on barter: gold for salt; fish for slippers and cereals. In Florence, in Venice, in Bruges, it depended on gold, and paper promises. Paper promises flying over the Alps, expertly sanitising the profits of usury.

Gold and silver were scarce. No country liked to export its coins or its bullion, even to Rome. Nicholas had been inestimably fortunate in possessing raw gold of his own, brought from Africa. When that was done, which would be at any time now, he would have to think about claiming the rest of what belonged to him, currently in the possession of the Knights of St John.

From the beginning, his neighbours had wondered about the purpose of the stone room in his house. The advent of Wilhelm of Hall had explained it: soon the royal hats and shoulders were covered with examples of Wilhelm's art, and ambassadors accepted his chalices with unflattering astonishment. Wilhelm, you might almost say, had built Beltrees. After that, he made medals. And after that, an easy transition, Nicholas had offered his services to the Governor of the Mint.

The members of the Comptroller's and Treasurer's staffs were well-disposed men, unfamiliar with Italian book-keeping, whose task was to apply an inflexible system to an uncertain and corruptible income, often plundered at will by the Crown. The clerks did their best, and delivered their accounts once a year to the Exchequer audit. Once a year only; in summer; in June.

Meanwhile, the flaws in the structure were painfully obvious. Any man who could offer help in their predicament was bound to be listened to. And the solution was simple. Instead of changing the system, you altered the money.

Below, where Wilhelm of Hall ruled, the crucibles poured out their billon and copper, casting the bars which his printers and strikers would beat and cut into groats and pennies, farthings and placks stamped with crowns and mullets and thistles and the King's head, all of them debased and black money.

Later, when the coining irons were removed and the lockfast boxes taken away for the night, the furnace was ventilated again. This time, Wilhelm himself set to work with one striker he trusted; pouring out molten gold and stamping it with a pair of puncheons which no one would come to remove, because no one knew they existed: the coining irons for a louis of France.

Far from yielding a profit, this part of the business was ruinous. But of course, it was worth it.

He talked with Wilhelm for a while, and then went to bed in his office, since it was too late to return to the High Street. Before he retired, he unpacked the chessmen and laid them out one by one at his pillow.

Yule and Twelfth Night came and went, their social obligations fitted into the spinning bands of his projects. Most of his agents reached him through Gregorio or Diniz or Julius, who had gone back to Cologne. Some correspondents preferred to send word direct from as far off as Danzig. Jordan de Fleury reached the mature age of four.

Duke Charles used the winter to appropriate the Duchy of Guelders. The Pope and Sigismond of the Tyrol used it to prepare a plan to encourage Duke Charles to fight the Swiss.

In Scotland, her grace the Queen, eight months pregnant, found out at last about Simon of Kilmirren and had to have something slipped into her ptisan to quieten her. Her demands for the filthy whoremaster's head were side-stepped by the King, with the help of his doctors and ministers. After years of neglect, Kilmirren was at last being properly managed, with thriving flocks and good crops and a healthy trade through the haven of Ayr. The estate was paying its dues to the Crown. Provided St Pol stayed where he was, the King was pleased to regard this as a form of restitution.

The Queen, increasing sullenly, let the argument founder. It would lose nothing by waiting. And she was mollified by her latest acquisition: a packet of jewels, two of which had a name.

Andro Wodman departed. Messages to Nicholas from Burgundian Artois, heavily coded, suggested that unless England promised help soon, the Duke would cancel his attack on the French in the spring. Meanwhile, every nation was complaining of piracy, even France, whose own notorious freebooters were seldom chastised by their monarch. Whether in this connection or not, the vicomte de Ribérac had been sent for by Louis.

And lastly, an event took place behind closed doors in Cologne which Julius did not report, although it concerned the Bank, as it happened, as much as his own personal well-being. The Gräfin Anna von Hanseyck, whose unofficial man of affairs he had become, invited Julius to spend time at her side in the grand hunting-lodge of one of her kinsmen, in which she was currently resident.

The place was virtually a castle, and contained in its household many capable men, the Count's lawyer among them. After several days wholly given to the pleasures of eating, hunting and dancing, Julius voiced his discomfort. 'You said you had work for me, lady? Your friends are wondering why I am here.'

Bonne, her daughter, had come to join them: a solemn, flat-chested girl with brown hair, sucking a comfit from the heaped supper buffet. Anna had smiled, and made room for her to sit down. They were all warm from dancing.

She said, 'You are here to rest from your office. Why not? I benefit from the fruits of your labours; it is only right that I should wish you refreshed.'

Julius said, 'You have many friends as skilful as I am, or with secretaries who would be glad to advise.'

'Then I wonder why I am not using them?' the Gräfin said. 'Really, why should you be assailed so by doubts? Because for the first time I have allowed my hateful business to fall into oblivion for three or four days? I have forgotten it, and I expect you to forget it as well. Or if you cannot, come and take wine with me later, and we shall please everybody by computing my customs dues, or the profit from the sale of a vineyard.' He had not understood, until he arrived at her chamber, that she would be alone, and at ease in her bedrobe. He stopped.

'Julius! What are we to do with you?' she said. Rising, she crossed to shut the door at his back, and then, taking his hand, led him across to a seat, from which he gazed up at her. Her eyes in the candlelight were of that dense blue approaching to violet, and her hair fell divided over her shoulders. The black ends curled at her waist; the upper strands lay on her robe like embroidery. She said, 'You did not go with Gustav last night?' She wore the scent she always wore. He did not know what it was.

He felt himself flushing. He said, 'It was kind of him to ask. I was tired.'

The scent receded. She sat down opposite, on the feather pillows of a day bed hung with linen. She said, 'He wished you to go. It is a clean house. The girls would have done you no harm.'

He burned with embarrassment. He said, 'I'm sorry . . .'

Anna lay back. She was smiling. She said, 'I am honoured that you resisted, but you should have gone. I meant you to go. I suggested it.'

He said, 'You want me to leave.'

'No! No,' she said. 'How have I frightened you? You have paid me homage as a gentleman should. Had we lived in earlier times, you might have offered me exquisite poems. I was content. Then I wondered if you did not expect more of me than chivalrous dalliance.'

Julius swallowed. He said, 'I have never wanted more than the Gräfin wished to give.' He sat on the low velvet stool, his limbs at ease as if set on a side-saddle, his pulse sharp as the thud of a mallet.

She said, 'I know all your attributes, Julius, except for one thing, which I hoped Gustav would tell me. The Graf Wenzel was an old man. I loved him. But when I do not seek the financial advice of my friends, it is perhaps a sign that I desire something more from them.'

He began to rise. 'Anna!'

'. . . Which I should like to be sure they can give me. Are you a virgin, Julius?'

'No,' he said. He could barely speak.

'Neither am I,' said Anna von Hanseyck. 'There is nothing then, is there, to delay us?'

He had started to tremble. He said, 'You mean – '

The violet eyes smiled. She said, 'I am not asking you to marry me, Julius. I am asking you to show me whether or not I should like to be married to you.'

Her robe had parted a little; one of the long, straying locks was clinging half to her skin. He knelt before her, and she stretched a speculative finger, then two, to the sodden throat of his shirt. She said, 'You are so hot, Julius!'

He stayed all night. Long after, he remembered thinking, at the height of the experience, that he could have died at that hour, and not grudged it. When he finally woke, the sun shone through the lawn of the hangings and she lay, naked still in his arms, smiling at him. She said, 'Show me what you will do, when we are married.'

The marriage was not quickly achieved, for there were kinsmen to summon, ceremonies to be arranged, contracts to be drawn up. They were signed in the great hall of the castle, below the Hanseyck coat of arms, with his new step-daughter grave at his side. Then his wife led him into the banquet and they sat upon the great chairs together: Julius de Bologna of the Banco di Niccolò and Anna von Hanseyck, his bride.

He had written to Nicholas. The Cologne agent had sent his separate, studied account. Nicholas, receiving both, read them in silence, and then dispatched his congratulations, with a gift.

By that time, Nicholas himself had begun to prepare for his April departure. He worked with a progressive sense of achievement accompanied, characteristically, by a precarious and growing elation. He had succeeded. He was going to succeed. He began to recover, unremarked, the unwarranted soaring of spirits which had propelled him, in his volatile boyhood, into so much trouble at home.

Chapter 41

THE SNOW WAS not, in the first place, the fatal factor, nor was the sudden, peremptory freeze: Nicholas held the belief that he no longer found extremes of climate exciting. In any case, on that particular day, he was fully occupied in his house in the High Street, chatting to Mistress Clémence and Jordan; discussing with Gelis the routine appointments of family life.

The organisational talents of Gelis were inclined to rile Govaerts; Nicholas had adroitly identified a distinct sphere of power for each which left him under the jurisdiction of neither. In these sessions, he generally found something amusing to argue about; her views could be mordantly shrewd. In theory, it kept alive and continued the family relationship that now contained them. He did not find it easy.

He was not especially receptive, accordingly, when Kathi Sersanders skipped into the room, followed by a crimson-faced porter. The Nor' Loch was bearing. Might Jodi take part in the revels?

He perceived, of course, all the goodwill behind the suggestion, but thought it preposterous and said so. He was taken aback when Mistress Clémence, of all persons, disagreed.

'The child is growing up in captivity. He requires some stimulation. If he is with another family, and muffled, Lord Beltrees, I for one would expect him to be safe.'

'Archie has all these nephews and nieces,' Kathi urged. 'And it would show Robin that you trust him.'

'I'm not sure,' said Nicholas. Simon was in Kilmirren, but he had agents. So had Martin.

'Go yourself. You can skate. Take the lady Gelis. So long as you keep away from the Berecrofts and Jodi, you can watch them.'

'I have been taught to skate,' said Mistress Clémence. 'If I am seen there alone, it will convince any watcher that the boy is safe at home with the house guard and Pasque.'

'Well, perhaps,' Nicholas said. 'But you must not go alone.'

*

All the rest of the year, the Nor' Loch lay in its hollow below the steep ridge of the High Street and mirrored the Castle in its flat reedy expanse. Turned to ice, it now reflected the red of the sunset and the torches streaming downhill towards it, while braziers winked on its surface and candlelight began to glow inside booths. The ice, rubbed by skates and pitted with boot- and hoof-studs, unrolled like a half-frosted painting beneath the busy feet of the crowd, and from the Lang Gait to the Castle, the whitened banks threw back a scribble of noise: the excited screaming, the snatches of drumming and whistling, the yapping and barking of dogs, tinny in the sparkling air.

Tobie said, 'I thought only Netherlanders made sport on ice. Where did you learn?'

'In the Netherlands,' said Mistress Clémence.

Her face beneath the white cap and hood was benign, and her skirts were correctly shortened to take account of the skates. She was taller than he was. Tackled privately, he had protested at the whole idea of escorting her, until Kathi's elevated eyebrows had reminded him that the safety of Jodi was in question. He watched, out of the corner of his eye, a group of pretty girls laughing, stumbling and screaming. He had recently had cause to realise that the girls he noticed were getting younger and younger.

Mistress Clémence said, 'Were you at the Carnival in Venice, Dr Tobias? It must have been rather different two years ago.'

He thought of mist and water; of exquisite buildings and floating awnings of silk over the piazze; of the masked figures, mysterious and elegant, drifting from this or that performance of theatre or poetry, observing the artists of mime and of balance, following the delicate music of consorts over bridges and through garlanded alleys. He thought of the light-wreathed Canal, and the gilded flotilla of boats hung with tassels with the masked figures within, and the tables laden with wine and with delicacies. He thought of the agonised search for a child, and all that had followed.

'I prefer this,' Tobie said. 'So, probably, does Jodi's father. It will remind him of Bruges.'

'He was an exuberant young man, I believe,' said Mistress Clémence. A circle had formed round a tumbler, rearranging his limbs to the scrape of a fiddle. Smells of warm food drifted across from the booths. In a corner, a group of eight people were dancing to a pipe and screaming as they fell down. A man passed, hauling two sliding children. There were no princes here; none but the populace and burghers of Edinburgh. She added, 'It is an art, to enjoy life at different levels.'

There was a note in her voice that he put down to censure. He said,

'I doubt if he could return to that kind of simplicity, even for the sake of the child. Or not unless his active life were to be curtailed.'

'He requires some supervision,' she said. 'A return to the simple life, as you call it, may be a periodic remedy that should not be ruled out. Unfortunately, he does not seem to care for Dr Andreas, an excellent physician. I find the young demoiselle, Katelijne Sersanders, extremely sensible.'

'I know. She ought to have been a nurse,' said Tobie irritably. A moment later he said, 'There they are. Which is Jodi?'

The Berecrofts party seemed to include half the Canongate; he recognised the bright cheeks of Archie surrounded by a mob of small children and one or two older, including Archie's own. Robin, in the manner of boys, had subtly thickened in the six months of Tobie's acquaintance. His waving hair clung to his neck and his voice, neither broken nor shrill, had chosen a level which Whistle Willie said was light baritone. He was a good-looking boy, and there were three pretty girls tugging at him. Tobie felt elderly.

Mistress Clémence said, 'Jodi is the child in the brown hooded jacket with the red scarf. Between the two youths.' She had pulled her hood over her face.

Tobie said, 'The boy won't recognise you?'

'We shall stay at the east end of the loch. He will remain under the Castle, and will be taken home in an hour; you will not have to suffer for very long. Have you treated many children, Dr Tobias?'

He didn't want to talk about spots in the throat. He said, 'My work has been largely in army camps.'

'I understand. But that often entails childbirth and women's infections, does it not? And if undiagnosed, an infection can spread when the soldiers come home. I suppose a good doctor examines everyone in his camp before they disband?'

'Either that, or catch them on shipboard,' Tobie said, refraining from citing examples. 'You can't send them home with a diagram.'

She said, 'You must have been glad to change eventually to a civilised court. I was sorry to hear of the death of your uncle.'

Betha or Phemie had been gossiping. He said, 'We didn't get on.'

She said, 'People of similar temperament often do not. A spell in the field might have broadened his knowledge, and a spell of teaching might have enabled you to pursue your experiments to their proper end. I take it, since you have published nothing, that you have not completed them?'

'I beg your pardon?' said Tobie.

Her face, or what he could see of it, remained undisturbed. She said, 'It is as well to be reminded, now and then, of why one selected one's profession. There, I think, is Lord Beltrees at the Halkerston entrance. Should we move closer?'

Darkness was falling. The flaming brands swirled like the hairy-tailed besoms of comets, and the smoke from the torches badgered the cloudy white breath of the revellers. Nicholas wore a stained sheepskin jacket and scarf-cap and was skating slowly, looking about him, but maintaining his distance from Jodi. Tobie, watching with interest, saw a demoiselle in a large knitted hat disengage herself from a group of young men and skim like an arrow towards the indolent skater. Nicholas stepped aside with unhurried skill and let her flash past; she emitted a howl and cannoned through a circle and into the fire-eater, who inhaled when he ought to have blown. A vociferous crowd closed about the bellowing man. The voices of Nicholas and Kathi, soothing, could be heard in its midst. Tobie started to laugh, began to move, and was stopped.

'I think that gold has already anointed the hurt,' said Mistress Clémence with dryness.

Nicholas emerged from the crowd, which was now laughing, with Kathi at his side. Both appeared to be arguing, and she was carrying her hat, which was smoking, and had apparently been used as an extinguisher. Her coat, like his, was unkempt and curious, with the grey and oat-coloured burnish of sealskin falling under her wind-whipped brown hair. They moved past, still disputing, to where Tobie saw Gelis standing cloaked, where Nicholas must have left her.

Iceland, Tobie thought. The source of the garments, the raillery, the easy, intimate camaraderie. For a moment he saw again the Nicholas of the dyeworks at Bruges, employing all his voices and faces, expatiating, complaining. The girl, with the face of an affronted kitten, was replying in kind. Then, breaking off, Kathi swept up to Gelis and clutched her by the arm, expostulating, her free arm waving, while on the other side Nicholas did the same. Gelis, listening, smiled and replied, and the next moment the three had moved off, linked together in mild animation.

'As I said,' remarked Mistress Clémence. 'A sensible girl.'

Viewed from the height of the ridge, the rink – seventeen hundred feet long, four hundred broad – appeared a long gut of fire, from which arose smoke and smells, music and laughter.

Simon of Kilmirren turned from his window and said, 'Well? It was your offer, I believe. To perform whatever final acts I might require.'

The red-haired man beside him was already sitting. He said, 'But that, my lord, was before the family received the recent special attention of the King, and before you yourself had to leave Court. Also, I have to say that the incident of the cart was singularly ineptly carried out.'

'It was your idea, as I remember,' Simon said. 'As for the rest, no one knows I am in Edinburgh.'

'All the more reason, my lord, for exercising restraint. This opportunity is quite unexpected and there has been no time to plan. Much as the Vatachino would wish to see the end of de Fleury, I am not prepared to face criminal charges for work ill prepared.'

Simon said, 'You will let him betray you, wreck you, cheat you and do nothing?'

Martin pursed his lips. 'There are other theatres. It is our thinking at present that the final confrontation should take place outside Scotland. You need not be involved.'

'I want to be involved,' Simon said. 'Here.'

'Then you must do it by yourself,' Martin said.

The hour of Jodi's freedom began to draw to its close. It was possible, even from a distance, to glimpse him, a bundle of brown and red swinging and sliding between two bigger children; a jubilant parcel on the shoulders of Archie or Robin; a pair of ecstatic eyes viewing a sweetmeat being handed down from a stall. Tobie and the nurse, being less identifiable, held to that part of the ice nearer the centre; the other three kept to the east. A tall man and two comely girls were not easily hidden. Indeed, they were meant to be seen, as proof that the child was not there.

Sometimes, Gelis forgot why she had come, so strange and fearful was the whole experience. Since Nicholas had sent for her two summers ago, she had learned how readily the enemy could change into the apparently affectionate friend. It had happened during the work with the Play; it happened in public; it happened whenever Jodi was there. Skating among the rough, merry crowd, with fire and stars wheeling about her, Gelis felt herself again a child on the frozen Minnewater in Bruges, bewitched once more by the big man whose warm, steady hand now enclosed hers, as his other was given to Kathi, while his voice swooped, as light as their movements.

He was full of invention, and so was the girl. It began with word play and with chanting and then developed into a variety of games, sometimes the three of them on their own; sometimes appropriating other parties of adults and children. He bought everybody mulled wine and pastries from the great tent with the portable oven. They played dangerous leapfrog and danced. He borrowed a sledge and set off careering one-footed with Gelis. He took Kathi under the arms and spun with her. She flew, fast and neat as a whip, brown hair flying, her hands on his shoulders, her serviceable boots firmly together. By then, the young men had come clustering to lure her away. Set down, her cheeks crimson, her eyes brilliant, she threw out her hands in enquiring despair.

'Oh, go on,' Nicholas said. 'But keep Willie's verses in mind. Where is Willie?'

'In Haddington with the Princesses,' Gelis said. 'And just as well, too.' She paused and added, 'What verses?'

Kathi had gone. Nicholas grinned. 'All about her aspiring husbands. Don't ask to hear them: you wouldn't be able to look anyone in the eye for a week. Oh look, there's Tobie.'

Gelis knew that tone of voice. She looked first, and saw what he meant her to see. She said, 'With Mistress Clémence!'

'Kathi's suggestion,' he said. 'She says he'll end up doubting everything he's ever been taught, including his toilet training. He wasn't anxious to come, but he seems to be sticking it. Come on. I want to teach you something.'

Tobie said, 'That was rather remarkable.'

Mistress Clémence said, 'It is pleasant to see them so light-hearted. Dr Tobias, do you know the history of this piece of water?'

'The history?' Tobie said. He was watching Kathi speed off, a seal-coated mascot in a small group of covetous men. She had made Nicholas laugh again and again, and Gelis, too, had thrown herself into the sport. Now Nicholas appeared to be teaching something to Gelis; she kept stopping to laugh, and so did he. She looked beautiful. Tobie saw that he had brought her another cup of hot wine.

Mistress Clémence said, 'This is an artificial lake only thirty years old, created to defend the north side of the Castle. It is fed from the well-house over there, and by springs. Its height is controlled by a dam and sluice at the east end, by the Trinity College gardens, through which the sluice water runs. Skating is perfectly safe so long as the water is frozen quite solid, but care is required as the season advances.'

'Why are you kneeling?' said Tobie.

'To listen,' said Mistress Clémence, sitting up. 'I am sure there is no reason to worry, but if you will lay your ear to the ice, you will hear a murmur of fresh running water. It is not frozen solid.'

Tobie listened. She was right. She reminded him of a tutor he had once had and disliked. He said, 'None of the natives appears to be nervous. In any case, Jodi leaves soon. Will the Berecrofts escort him?'

'In great numbers,' she said. 'They will send us word. You will be able to rest. Do you take very much exercise as a rule?'

It was unfair. He had just bought her a pancake.

Jodi's scream, when it came, was not heard by his nurse or his parents, for the noise between them submerged it. Even Robin, kneeling to replace a glove, didn't at first understand why the child had pulled his hand away and exploded into terrified screeches, dragging his scarf down, drawing every eye to his scarlet face and petrified stare. Then the sound came to his ears: a sound no greater than the cluck of a bird, or of a man alone tapping a hammer. The sound of a quiet game of golf, newly begun just behind on the ice. The sound, to Jodi, of a golden-haired cousin hitting, hitting to hurt him.

All the terror of Veere had returned. There was no swift way to reassure him; there was no way at all to muffle the little boy's cries. If he had enemies, now he had been identified. Robin swept him up, vainly consoling. Robin's father said, 'We get him out, *now*. Christ, what is happening?'

The golfers, having barely started their game, had withdrawn. In their place a cavalcade had appeared: a team of four working horses, stud-shod, pulling behind like a fishing line an unreeling column of skaters, shouting, singing, brandishing tankards and torches as, each holding the person in front, they set to skim across the huge crowded pond.

The horses were properly harnessed, with a man on the back of the leader and a structured handgrip behind, which the head of the long train of skaters could grasp. It was the first reassuring thing that Archie saw, after he realised that the way from the pond was cut off. There were town musicians slithering cheerfully too, grasping fiddles and tambours and flutes, setting the rhythm, leading the familiar choruses. The horses, of the sturdy kind that dragged carts, responded gallantly, manes and tails full of cheap ribbons, and the column, always lengthening, began to pick up speed over the ice. Warned by the laughter and music, revellers moved out of the way, or joined in. The cavalcade covered a quarter of the loch.

They couldn't stay where they were, unable to leave, and with Jodi's camouflage gone. It was better to join in; and at the end of the loch, they could slip aside. Robin said, 'Look, Jodi, look. Come and slide with the horses.'

Tear-stained, hiccoughing still, Jodi was lifted and carried by Archie and, embedded in Berecroftses, found himself inserted in the long gliding column. The wind brushed his cheeks. The singing rose all about him. From ahead came the thud of the horses, the horses like his own pony at home. And the click of the kolf far behind had now gone, as if it had never happened. Someone put a sweet in his mouth, and someone told him to sing. His cheek bulging, he did so, and Archie exchanged relieved grins with his son as they held one another and slid. The pace quickened. They had skimmed over a third of the loch. The pace quickened again.

Robin said, 'Father?'

'Quite,' said Archie. 'It's getting too fast. Let's move sideways and take out the little ones. Can you draw up the people behind you?'

It wasn't easy. It would have been unfair to break the whole column. The mending of the gap required such attention that Robin was free before he realised that something had happened. The merriment continued except far ahead, where the songs had been replaced by shouting, and the rhythmic gallop had changed to a stutter. And as the pace of the horses had changed, so it seemed that the horses themselves were at odds with one another, their heads and bodies jolting apart so that all the smooth gliding column behind shared the disruption. And because they were travelling so fast, disengagement was deadly.

To those who watched, and those who had escaped, it seemed as if the skaters were played on a line, whipped from side to side, undulating and buckling and shedding hurtling figures, unable to stop. The main column itself could no longer control its direction, but brushed past stalls and through tents, throwing spectators sliding out of its way. Cauldrons tipped and braziers tumbled into the glittering grease. Flames sprang up. Screaming, once started, reached a pitch easily heard at the far end of the loch.

Nicholas heard it. He said, 'Jodi,' in a voice Gelis thought was quite calm. Then he said, 'Stay here. I will come back. I promise you.'

Her instinct was to go. She saw that she could only hinder him. In this he was quicker and stronger, and she need never doubt that he would do all he could. What had happened to Henry proved that. Then she thought that at least she could follow, without fear of distracting him. Everyone around her was moving – either rushing to help or to escape. She had begun to gain speed herself, when a man's shoulder sent her stumbling sideways, and a man's deliberate kick to her side thrust her hard to the ice. It was not an accident. She was being attacked.

She saw her assailant looming above her, black against the dark sky, and then the boot came down again, and there was nothing but darkness.

*

Tobie and his inappropriate partner had the best view of the disrupted column. They heard the singing procession approach, and saw the horses abruptly break pace to prance and to neigh and to struggle apart. Before the first traces broke, Tobie had made to rush to the west, and Mistress Clémence had stopped him.

It infuriated him that she could; that she was taller and fitter than he was. She said, 'The Berecrofts family are capable persons. They are there. They will be dealing with Jodi. Remember his parents.'

He glared at her hand on his arm. He had no wish to hurt her. He said, forgetting the niceties, 'Nicholas can look after himself and his wife.'

'Do you think so?' she said. 'I think the sieur de Fleury will go straight to his son, and his wife will have to fend for herself. Which may be what someone is counting on.'

He stared at her. 'St Pol is at home.'

'He wasn't at Haddington,' she said, 'when the cart slipped.'

Now the darkness was uneven: half the orderly torches were hurled aside or extinguished, and the braziers scattered. Racing back, swerving to avoid the wreckage of tents and fleeing people and tumbled and struggling figures, Nicholas plunged from near-blackness to sheets of shuddering light where flames rose to the sky and ran reflecting across new-melted ice. He stopped for nothing, but every now and then cupped his mouth and made the one call that would bring him an answer. After a while, Kathi replied, and he found her.

She was unhurt but covered with blood, one of a group working to lift a fallen horse from its victims. She scrambled to her feet as soon as she saw him, open relief on her face. She said quickly, 'Jodi's safe. They got him out at the beginning, and Robin and Archie and the others are taking him home.'

'Where are they?' he said. High above in the flickering darkness, lines of light began to appear and run like fire down the slopes of the Rock. Help from the Castle. Help, with any luck, from all those towering houses whose windows now glittered red.

She said, 'They've gone. He's safe. Nicholas, where is Gelis?'

The horse was dead. Its victim's blood spattered the ice. Where it had fallen a crack had appeared, below which he could hear running water. The ice was thick, and had not given way. Elsewhere, with a little help, it might be different.

For a moment, ridiculously, he could not move. Then Kathi pushed him and said, 'I'll come too. Find her. Find her.'

The numbing cold of the water roused Gelis to come to the

surface, and then notified her that further effort was not worth the trouble. She was aware that there was ice at her shoulder and that she would shortly slip under it. The thrusting boot appeared to have gone, but in any case, she felt no pain from its work; she felt nothing. Her eyes, blurring, rested on a sky which had turned into a portal of fire: a solemn circle of flames which would lead her to Heaven or Hell; into torment; out of it. It wrung pain from her then, to know that she was to be alone in this too; that he would never be with her; that, at last, she had lost him. She fancied she saw, as she sank, his face looking at her as she wanted him to look.

It was Mistress Clémence who, applying claustral calm and secular competence, discerned the strange burning tent and devised a means, helped by Dr Tobias, to thrust it over. When she saw the cracked ice and the pool, she set her lips and looked at the doctor, for you could see how the crust had been broken and sawn to make it unsafe to approach. Then they both saw something move, something sinking, and threw themselves forward.

A girl's voice said, 'No, Mistress Clémence. Go for help.' The girl Katelijne Sersanders, her hands gripping her shoulders. The girl said, 'Let him do it.'

Mistress Clémence saw that the father had come. She knelt up. Dr Tobias half turned, his face haggard. The girl said, 'Jodi is safe. Go for help. Dr Tobie will stay.' Then there was a great surge of water, chilling her feet, and she saw the man had dropped into the pool, breaking more ice as he went, and tugging at something below. She could not see his face, or hear what he was saying over and over. Mistress Clémence looked around her, took her bearings, and sped towards the lights on the shore. Then she changed direction, for someone had called her by name.

And is as a tree, sheltering those of his blood whom he loves.

As once before, Nicholas sank in chill water; as once before, he dragged himself out bearing the weight of a woman, pale hair on his arm. As before, Kathi was with him.

That time, it had been Simon's sister, and she had been dead. He did not know, now, if Gelis was still alive. Her eyes were closed, her flesh icy. His coat was sodden; he hadn't waited to strip. Kathi threw off her sealskin and rolled Gelis in it as she lay on the ice, and Tobie began labouring over her. Tobie said, 'Don't look, and get those things off. Kathi, look out for Clémence.' And almost at once, it seemed, a group of men were hurrying towards them, bearing a pallet and followed effortfully by a woman who was not Mistress Clémence at all.

Bel of Cuthilgurdy said, 'My poor childer.'

Nicholas heard her. It meant something. Last time she had said, *What have you done?*

It meant something. It meant nothing, if Gelis was dead.

Then Tobie said, 'Nicholas.'

And her eyes were open. And she was breathing.

Nicholas said, 'You can't get away from me like that.' And she closed her eyes again, but her lips had moved.

They had lifted her into the pallet before his mind started to work and he said, 'Wait!'

Tobie said, 'She could die. She has to be dry and warm quickly. You too. Let her go.'

'To Simon's house?' Nicholas exclaimed.

Bel said, 'It's empty. I sent him away. Do you think Clémence would have agreed otherwise?' And as he stared she said, 'I called her. She is there, preparing for what Dr Tobie might need. I couldn't wait.'

'For Gelis's sake?' Nicholas said. He had asked Bel to take Gelis to Beltrees. He didn't even know whether she liked her.

'Yes,' said Bel. 'And, since you don't ask, for yours.'

In the house of St Pol in the High Street Gelis slept, with Tobie nodding beside her. Kathi had gone, as had Mistress Clémence the moment Jodi's mother was safe. News had already come from the Canongate to say that her charge was in Pasque's care, and well. Nicholas had slept unintentionally as well, stripped and warmed and clothed in a bedrobe he hoped he was creasing for Simon, and fallen victim again to one of Tobie's innocent potions. Awaking, he had found his way immediately, corrosively, to where Gelis was, but once satisfied, had allowed himself to be led back by Bel. He was in her room now, floating still in a sump of opiates and emotion and aware that, at the moment, she was more than his match.

Unusually, she did not make for his throat, appearing willing to heat him some soup in near-silence. It was he who broke it at length. 'It was not an accident. The inner rims of the horse-shoes were spiked.' He had seen it on the dead horse. As soon as the beasts picked up speed, they would have kicked their own legs to shreds.

Bel said, 'I didna imagine the ice chopped itself up. And the sluice had been shut down. That let the springs well up and soop under the ice: Clémence heard them. So what's next? It's your shot. A band of pig-gelders and thieves to strake Simon? No one'd miss him.'

'Henry would,' Nicholas said. 'I'll leave the straking to Fat Father Jordan. And really, Simon and Henry deserve each other.'

'So?' the old woman said. 'You nearly lost Gelis. You nearly lost

Jordan. And it wasna Martin's blame this time. He wouldna give
Simon the crook of his pinkie: no one would. Simon's place in
Scotland is corrupted and gone.'

'Hardly,' said Nicholas. 'I hear Kilmirren has never been richer.
Flourishing lands, handsome castle, expensive shipping in Ayr. Fat
Father Jordan is preparing a bolt-hole.'

'Or maybe Simon has been onbeset by his conscience at last,' Bel
remarked. 'So what are you going to do now?'

'About Simon? Suggest some lines of enquiry to the magistrates.
They may indict him or not; I think not.'

'I wasna speaking of Simon,' she said. 'I was speaking of rank
stupidity and self-indulgence, and a bairn already old enough to ken
when something is wrong. But for the skill of that woman his nurse,
the skaith would be much greater already. End what you are doing.'

'End the marriage?' Nicholas said. 'Or my work? Or myself? What
would please you?'

She was looking at him in the way that hurt most. She said
unexpectedly, 'What did your friend Bessarion say?'

Tobie should keep his mouth shut. 'He rambled,' Nicholas said.
'In the way old people do. So give me your advice.'

Bel said, 'I didna want ye in Scotland. Then I thought that perhaps
that was the only solution. Now I say to you, go away.'

'I am going,' he said.

When Gelis woke, Tobie brought Nicholas to her, having warned
him what he would see. Even so, he felt sick. He said, 'You were
kicked.'

She turned her bandaged head towards him. One of her eyes was
swollen and darkened. Simon's revenge on them both. A traditional
ducking, in the traditional place for loose women. A less than traditional drowning, in the way that Simon's sister had drowned. Simon
had wanted Gelis obliterated. And the chance had come to remind
Nicholas savagely of the past, as well as make him a widower. As
ever, Simon had no idea what he was interfering with.

Gelis said, 'Thuggery seems to be the fashion this year. You pulled
me out, I'm told, with Katelijne. Practice from Iceland.' She hadn't
been by the river four years before, when Lucia drowned. She had
been in Flanders then, giving birth to their son.

He said, 'It was Mistress Clémence and Tobie who found you. I
want to talk to you when you feel better.'

'I feel better,' she said. Her face round the bruising was composed.
'What were you going to say? That I deserved it? That when you
humiliated Simon last year, you made quite sure this would happen?

That it is rather a pity you don't seem to be able to protect anybody, even Jodi? Where would you like us to hide next?'

'That depends,' he said, 'on our talk. We were playing a match. I thought we should set a finishing date.'

'I owe this to Bel? Peerless Bella?' she said.

'Bel has remarked, yes, that Jodi is growing. And time is passing in other ways.'

'I don't work to dates,' Gelis said. 'Just by result.' She shivered suddenly.

He said quickly, 'I still think we should talk. But not now.' He smiled, to make it less serious. 'If neither of us can achieve a result in five years, then I think we should both retire anyway.'

'You want to finish this year?' Gelis said.

There was a silence. He said, 'By the end of December, for choice. Think about it.'

She said, 'I used to be afraid of your patience. I asked you once if you would wait twenty-five years if you had to.'

'What did I say?' Nicholas said, as if he had forgotten.

Her breathing was shallow, and her eyes had the brightness of fever. 'You said you thought I knew my own mind better than that. I do. I know it very well. I do not want to be tied to a date.'

'But I do,' Nicholas said. 'I shan't press you. Think about it. Get well. But before we sail in the spring, I shall come to you again and ask the same question. If you are as good as I think you are, you should know the answer by then. Every trader has to set dates, or starve. It's nothing. It's a matter of calculating how soon you can be certain of winning.'

He looked back at the door, but she lay with her eyes closed. She looked frightened. But he had had to do it, or so he believed.

Chapter 42

NICHOLAS LEFT HIS wife alone for three weeks, securely attended in the house in the High Street. Her friends visited her when she became well enough to receive them, and Nicholas called on the household and Jodi, and was kept informed of her health by a belligerent and ubiquitous Tobie, who treated any mention of Dr Andreas as a threat.

The fever which seized her ran its course, and the bruises and stiffening faded. Gradually, she resumed some of her customary interests, as he began to lay aside his: sealing off veins; choosing that project to ripen, and this to remain suspended in ice. He had given her time to do the same, if she wished.

On Wednesday the seventeenth of March, the Queen's grace of Scotland gave birth to a fine, sturdy prince, baptised James. The processions, feasting and plays, ceremonies and contests brought the dame de Fleury recovered to Court, and the young red-headed princes and their sisters made her welcome, while complaining because their grand *fatiste* claimed to be too busy to help them. The Queen, hitherto cool, now became markedly gracious to Gelis van Borselen, and desired to be introduced to this Pavian physician whose uncle (she had heard) had treated half Christendom.

Tobie returned from Court somewhat flushed, and paraphrased the royal dilemma for Nicholas. 'She doesn't like it. She wants to know how long can she induce him to wait, and need she do it at all if he's got some infection through Simon.'

'I told you,' Nicholas said. 'What did you say?'

'Nothing she can quote against me,' Tobie said. 'Except that infertility isn't infectious, and the faster she breeds, the sooner it'll be over with. She hopes you're going to stay. She enjoyed your little conspiracy over Iceland.' He paused. 'Would you stay, if it weren't for Simon and his father?'

'No,' said Nicholas. He softened it. 'Scotland's too far away from the Bank.'

Tobie weighed it up. Tobie's thoughts were generally visible. He said, 'Venice would be safer than here.'

'Everywhere will be safe, fairly soon,' Nicholas said.

The last weeks fled. He had paced it well: all his business was settled; all his appointments were concluded one by one, many of them in the hunting-field, or over some boisterous sport (all countries were ruled half from horseback). By the end of March he had let it be known, as it had long been known to Gregorio and Diniz and Govaerts, that he was establishing his family in Venice.

'In the company of Julius and the delectable Anna!' Gelis had observed. 'Why did I not anticipate that?'

'It was Tobie's idea,' Nicholas said.

It was understood that next summer he was not coming back, and that, as had the Baron of Cortachy, he had placed all his flourishing enterprises in the care of his excellent agent. It saddened and even annoyed several merchants and magnates and their ladies that the castle of Beltrees, this promising venue of pleasure, was to benefit nobody, unless the Baron's guests and business partners were to lodge there, or the Baron himself, when compelled north.

It was agreed that its only purpose had been to supply him with an excuse for his title, although the more romantic believed that it had been built for his lady, who had rejected it. The lands around would, of course, provide him with a sizeable income, as Cortachy did for the other.

He had been prepared for all that, and also for the probability that he would be treated to some kind of feast on his departure. He had not expected to find that it was to be held in the royal presence at Holyrood, nor to discover its scale. He was a Burgundian banker, that was all.

Four years ago, in the opening moves of this time-blighted enterprise, he had appeared at an impromptu royal banquet in Linlithgow, at which he had acted as playmate and sycophant. Now the royal children of Scotland were grown, and had learned to befriend him for himself.

Most of the same people were here, in the tapestry-hung hall of the Lodging, whose windows admitted the scent of the wild flowers, instead of the death-chill of snow.

Adorne was absent, a widower now, but laden with appointments and honours. Standing for him were Katelijne and her brother, who had shared an experience they could afford to remember, but Nicholas, their companion, could not.

Julius was not here. He was married.

Patrick Graham, Archbishop of St Andrews, was not here, for his luck had changed for worse as well as for better. Patrick Graham remained skulking at Rome, while unfortunate accidents happened to his belongings, and the tide of resentment ran high.

By contrast, Nicholas was held in esteem: the Church was well represented at Holyrood. The Abbot his landlord, of course, and Tulloch, and Blackadder, and Knollys of the Knights of St John. And with these the great officers of the Household: Whitelaw and Argyll, Crawford and Sinclair, Semple and Hamilton.

Of the girls of that time, Joneta Hamilton had long left Kinneil, and the others were unknown except to him: the mistresses whom Simon could never again hope to enjoy. For of course, Simon was not here, nor his father. Martin of the Vatachino had also gone: to consult with his superiors, they said.

The doctors were present: Scheves and Andreas with their training in mysteries; Tobie who kept himself apart. The royal sisters glittered and sparkled at the table of honour: Bleezie Meg, the short, forceful maiden whom he had begun by half drowning, and who would dare any venture. And the lady Mary, come to honour him, despite the small comfort he had vouchsafed.

She had asked for his advice, these last days, and he had given it. He did not think the King her brother would relent. If she joined her husband, forced out of England, she would face perpetual exile, and see her children homeless in penury. Tom Boyd's own cause was lost. Now his name and his future lay with his children, and with her as their regal protector. She had wept. She would stay, with the children and Betha and Phemie. Both were here. But Betha would leave Haddington soon, with another royal infant to care for. The Queen, plump and smiling, was there.

And so were the merchants. Young Bonkle, now divorced from the Bank and trading with Bruges and with Veere. The veterans, the family names: Napier and Lauder. Andy Crawford and Richard his son. Thom Swift. John Lamb from Leith. Tom Cochrane who, from cutting and building, had discovered how to be everyone's expert. And Oliver Semple, factor, bailie and agent for more than the Beltrees land now.

And the Berecrofts family, whose roots had persistently threatened to tangle with his: old sharp-tongued Will, and Archibald the Younger, who had given him shelter, and become a steady companion to both Kathi and Gelis. And Robin, whom he was leaving. It was eighteen months since the crazy game on the ramparts, and all that had followed in Iceland and the Low Countries and France. He could teach Robin nothing now that would benefit him.

He knew the musicians who played for the feast, but Whistle Willie was there as a guest, with others – Arnot, Malloch – he remembered from Trinity. Established, pensioned, entrusted with the funds to create his magnificent Chapel Royal, Willie's fortunes also had changed, but the man had not. He sat glaring at Nicholas, defying him, forbidding him to leave the country he had adopted.

And lastly, the King and his brothers. Rebellious John of Mar, bored and sullen, who had once goaded Henry so cruelly. Sandy, whose dreams he had listened to, and who had turned to him in the last year, sitting late at night in the Canongate house with Jamie Liddell beside him, questioning, arguing, conjecturing. He had never spoken of these meetings to the King, for James could be jealous.

And James? They sat next to one another this time, Nicholas and James, in doublets and robes of identical richness, with identical chains crossing their shoulders, the unicorns glinting: the experienced man; the young King. Some things were different, some were not. This was not now a callow youth, but a man and a father, diligent, fretful, pinned by Fate and by pride to the long hours at the council table, in the assembly hall, or the chamber of state.

His mother had been a strong woman, conscientious, religious, who had ruled alone for three years, and had died when James was eleven. Her officers were around him still, reminding him of his duties. His rebellion, unlike that of Mars, was to throw aside work for the hunting-field, and withdraw from the problems of government to create for himself the courtly world of his aunts and his uncles, and the chivalrous world of his ancestors.

His grandfather had just died, but James had not mourned: it was a chance to renew all his claims to the duchy of Guelders. He had just made truce with England, but planned to break it if Louis would give him the money he wanted. He was secretly planning again to relieve Louis of the county of Saintonge. He had a son of less than three weeks whose marriage he was already considering.

Unlike Burgundy, James wanted more children and quickly, for all the alliances he must make. For many, many reasons he did not want Nicholas to leave. Towards Gelis, seated not quite so near, the King's manner was that of an understanding physician.

One gave a performance, under such circumstances, and Nicholas was a good actor. At the end, he was asked to step down and receive, on the King's behalf, a parting gift. It was a standing cup, made of gold set with stones, and fashioned in Paris. The King had not used the services of Wilhelm, although Wilhelm was now a royal servant, by a contract just agreed. Nicholas thanked his host on one knee, and wondered why all the noise in the chamber had stopped. Then the King said, 'We have another gift we have prepared for you.'

He should have noticed that Willie had gone, and the singers. He should have been aware of the sounds from outside, the gleams of light through the windows, the murmurs drowned by the animation indoors. He should have been prepared for what he saw, when the Queen led him out through the doors and into the courtyard; and then for what he heard.

They had not tried to assemble the clouds, or the moving lights or the Secrets. Joseph and Mary wore their own gowns, as did the Magi, and the children were barefoot in their shirts. Below the platform, Willie stood stripped to his pourpoint, with great anxious patches of sweat under the armpits. Then the music began, and nothing about it was makeshift.

The same sky received it, the same clouds, the same hills. Below, the resonating chamber was deeper, primed by time and remembrance. Remembrance of the birth of Anselm Adorne's child, loving gift of his wife; conceived to bring him at last the bright warrior son his heart craved. An infant cried once: the newborn prince in the Queen's arms. It was a small audience this time: only the people of the Court, and the Abbey, and those who were thought to be his intimate friends. No one moved.

Nicholas watched, re-created before him, the one selfless thing he had ever done. The great, solemn sweep of the work had been concentrated, salt upon salt, to a morsel of its full length. They had remembered their studies. The clear voices spoke, and the close-textured difficult harmonies lingered and surged once again, rising and falling, lovingly captured.

Such intensity of emotion, so compressed, could overpower a choir. The singers' eyes were fastened to Roger, who offered no comfort, no coaxing, but lashed the music out of their throats so that they sang without weakening, as if angry. Only at the end, when the music burgeoned, beginning its climb, and from north, south, east and west the silver trumpets suddenly spoke, and the four organs added their thunder, did his own face fill with what he felt for them. Then there came the silence, as happened before, and then the storm broke.

This time nothing stood between Nicholas and the warmth: not Kathi; not Gelis. Willie Roger appeared, punched him angrily in the stomach and then locked him in an incoherent embrace. The Queen, the child asleep in her arms, reached up her wet face and kissed them both. He went through the proper form of thanks to the King, and to Sandy and to all those he knew must have devised this; and then excused himself in order to climb the steps and speak to the singers, the actors, the musicians. Caught in rising euphoria, they wanted him to come with them now, and were mutinous when he had to return to the King. It was harder still to disengage from Willie.

Gelis had waited, Kathi beside her. Bel wasn't there, although he knew she was in town. He was glad she wasn't there. He had enough to contend with, without Bel.

Kathi said, 'So how did you like your present?' She was dry-eyed and smiling, but her kerchief was soaked.

He said, 'I saw you. You were singing.'

'But you didn't hear me,' she said flatly.

Gelis said something, and he automatically turned to her, smiling. Kathi was right: he had heard almost nothing. The effort of hearing almost nothing had given him an acute headache, but he had solved several unusual mathematical problems, devised a poem and run through many more while avoiding the pale stare of Tobie, who had never heard the performance before and was sitting as if axed on the head.

Gelis said, 'I don't remember if I congratulated you last time.'

Nicholas said, 'I'm sure you did congratulate me. Anyway, this wasn't my doing: it's Willie's night.'

'That's what I thought,' Kathi said. 'Did you see Bel?'

'No,' he said.

'She came late. She must have gone away as soon as it finished.'

'I'm sorry,' he said. 'But this isn't the last night of our lives. I'm not taking the habit. We'll all continue to meet, I hope, outside Scotland.'

'I expect we shall,' Kathi said. She hesitated and then said, 'The King is waiting. I don't want to keep you. I only wanted to speak of the music.'

They watched her go, and turned to rejoin the royal party back in the hall. He had been looking at Gelis all night because she was wearing court dress, with jewels he had never seen round her throat and latticing the wings of her white, floating headgear. The King had been watching her as well. Nicholas said, 'This shouldn't take long. The Queen will want to retire. Then we take our leave. Then we go out through the gardens and walk by the back path to the Canongate house. Then we talk.'

'Ah,' she said. 'Every trader has to set dates, or starve. I am to rejoice in the palace of my master.'

'Let us say,' Nicholas said, 'that we have enough on the board for a deal. Rejoicing would stretch it too far. So, to the Canongate?'

'My poor Nicholas,' Gelis said. 'By the back path? Through the gardens? Do you imagine for one moment that you are going to escape all those people outside?'

He had persuaded himself that he would. Such was his determination that the illusion stayed with him all through his last audience and past the moment when the Abbot, amiably conspiratorial, had them shown to a postern and he and Gelis slipped through. For one more moment, the Abbey garden seemed deserted and quiet. Then the glare of twenty lanterns struck him in the face, and his ears were ringing to the whoops, the catcalls, the bawling of ten times that number of people, and the saucy rattle of kettledrums.

They had caught him. They had caught them both. The crowd of his companions marched them up to Willie Roger's and there was no escape. None at all.

He got drunk very quickly, because he meant to. Gelis, who had never been there before, seemed to his vague surprise to conform easily to the new habitat, in the same way that she had come to terms with tough seamen off the African coast: in the mode of a cool, amused *donna di governo*. It was strange, because Gelis was here and not Kathi. Roger had never asked Kathi to enter this warm vinous world of music and gossip and badinage. It was not right for an unmarried girl. And, Nicholas guessed, he saw that it would have been unfair for a girl who must marry. The distaff should not have to compete against this bright, boisterous masculine world, or with the music. Luckily, they sang only ditties, obscene ones, so that he too could float, a wanton bladder, above the dead anchor-weight of his purpose. He did not remember going home.

He woke alone in his own room in the Ca' Niccolò and was amused, briefly, at the confidence implied by her absence. She required no advantages. He made, with the help of Alonse, a ponderous toilet, and eventually sent to ask her to see him. Then he entered her room, his lids protesting against the brilliant light, and said, 'Behold the winged lion. Your eyes are open. You were drinking as well. I saw you.'

'I paused now and then,' Gelis said.

Her voice was patient rather than tolerant. This time, however, he was not being received by the charming young girl in loose silks. She wore no elaborate jewels, but she was dressed as formally as for the previous night, and her hair was bound under stiff voile. *Noli tangere.*

She added coolly, 'Alonse put you to bed.'

He wondered if he had attempted to touch her and was immediately and painfully convinced that he had not. If anything in this world could be sure, it was that. He sat down and said, 'Well, we have something to talk about. You begin.'

'No apology?' Gelis said.

'No, Lady Better-than-Good. Let all receive thy pity, none thy hate. You begin.'

'Are we to have a discussion?' Gelis said. 'I thought you had submitted one simple question to answer.'

'That is the great disadvantage of being a woman,' Nicholas said. 'If you come to the conference table in that mood, you will lose. This is your Alnwick, your St Omer. I have proposed a date for the cessation of hostilities. That is, a time by which one side will have won or be about to win, or by which it will be apparent that neither can reasonably prevail.'

'Reasonably?' she queried.

'Without demanding a fight of such length, or so destructive, that the victory would be worthless to either. Pyrrhic. Puerile.'

'You are afraid of losing,' she said.

'Not at all. I am afraid of not recognising when I have won. In war, each should know the other's objective. We have come to the place where I need to know yours.'

'I know yours,' she said. She sat with her hands clasped before her, her expression watchful, attentive. He had seen her thus when faced with other problems of innovative complexity – when preparing the Play, for example. His hatred for Willie Roger, for all of them, welled.

She said, 'I have known your objective from the beginning. To live with me as with Katelina, except that I should bear your numberless children in wedlock.'

'How shaming for you,' he said.

'Do you deny it?'

'No,' he said. 'That will do, to begin with. So what did you really want?'

'I shall tell you,' she said, 'when I have won.'

He closed his eyes. It didn't help. He opened them. 'Tell me now. Isn't it your objective?'

'No,' she said. 'It is my reward. My objective is so to reduce you that my life will be as I wish, and whatever happens, you can never change it.'

He said, 'I might agree to all you ask now.'

'You might,' she said. 'But you see, I cannot trust you. Nicholas, you cannot even trust yourself.'

'And how shall I know when you have reduced me?' he said.

She said,'When you beg me to stop.'

'How optimistic of you,' he said. After a moment he added, facetiously, 'I might be quite happy, as on a recent occasion, to invite you to continue.'

She didn't reply. He said quickly, 'There is really no need to anguish over mistakes with *la cauza doussana*. I don't.'

He waited again. He knew she understood. *That sweet thing* which she had engaged in with Simon, had nearly shared with a King; in which Nicholas himself had been so profligate, was debased: there was no need to repine over that. That union, sweet beyond imagining, which once had been theirs was still inviolate, waiting. Thunder for God, if you please. But nothing lasted for ever.

He said, 'Do you hear what I am saying? If we deny ourselves very much longer, even that may have gone. There will be nothing worth having.'

She said, 'I was about to tell you. I agree. There are eight months between now and the end of December, and by that time, one of us will have outwitted, shamed, prevailed over the other. The loser submits: the victor should have the right to direct what is to happen thereafter. Is that what you wanted to hear?'

'You haven't asked my objective,' Nicholas said.

She exclaimed, 'You didn't deny –'

'I said it would do, to begin with. But suppose we regard it, in your words, as a reward. Then my objective must be the same as yours, mustn't it? To outwit you, until you have to submit. Unless, of course, you would like to accept my terms now? A child a year? I'm sure I could trust you.'

She said, 'You haven't talked to your wooden-legged friend.'

His mind clouded with ale, he looked at her, puzzled. She continued. 'Nicholai Giorgio de' Acciajuoli, the noble Florentine oracle. I heard he appeared with young Nerio in Rome. I thought I told you I once met him in Florence. He instructed that you were to have no more progeny. Your posterity is already secure.'

'You believed him?' he said. From the beginning, from his boyhood in Bruges, the Florentine had interfered.

'No. But you do,' she said. 'When you cut yourself loose from your beginnings you became easy prey, didn't you, to all the so-called magicians? Any strolling astrologer can frighten you. Even without me, you were going to fail.'

'The way I failed in Venice?' he said. 'I took Jodi from you. I can do it again. What if you grind me to powder, and are still left with nothing?'

She said, 'What do you think I have now? And what would you have? A son with no home and no future, like Mary Boyd's children?'

There was a silence, which Gelis eventually broke. 'So have we reached a conclusion, despite the condition of one of us? We meet at the end of December: the war ends; one of us will capitulate. Meantime, I am to take Jodi to Venice?'

He roused himself with an effort. 'You will be safer. Crackbene will escort you. I have my service to Burgundy; you can join me there in the autumn.'

She said, 'You would leave Jodi for so long?'

Nicholas said, 'He is older now. He knows us both well. I shall write.'

'And you will have me watched,' she remarked.

'As always,' he answered. 'It is you who placed us on a footing of war. You have money. You are free to have me followed, to employ whom you like. Only don't hurt Gregorio.'

'I am sorry,' she said. 'But Gregorio is the Bank. And the Bank is you.'

'I thought it was also Jodi,' he said.

He left very soon after.

In his room was a letter in Greek. It was the third such he had had; Govaerts knew by now to leave it unslit. He broke open the seal.

Come. Come. For love of me, come.

It was unsigned. It was addressed to the lord Nikko.

Part V

May, 1473
VOLERIES

Chapter 43

A MAN OF HONOUR, recently weighing the claims of two friends, Tobias Beventini had soberly set need against need, and had chosen.

Nicholas de Fleury chose at once, with his heart. Then, being Nicholas, he set about making his choice not only desirable, but mandatory.

He was aided, he was not unaware, by fortuitous happenings in Burgundy. He went there to free himself, and found himself already free. He left the Duke, left Astorre, left Diniz and Moriz in Bruges and, travelling fast with only one servant, arrived in Venice in May, only three days behind the cavalcade of his wife, his son and his doctor.

Cristoffels, staggered to see him, had to admit, in his incoherence, that none of the household was here: Master Gregorio and his guests had taken fowling-boats north to the lagoon, where the Bank owned an islet with lodges.

They were still in the boats when the *bissona* swept up in all its glittering splendour and the padrone stepped into the craft containing Margot, Gelis and the two children. Jodi screamed. Gelis whitened. The vessel dipped. The *bissona*, professionally detached, proceeded to the small island jetty and began to unload. Glasses winked, and a damask cloth floated over the sun. Nicholas said, '*Mon fils*, what were you aiming at?'

'That,' said Jodi, letting him go. He had been bending a very small bow at a water hen. At his feet was a bowl of clay balls.

Nicholas said, 'No, no. The bird would object. It is much more amusing to shoot people. See. Dr Tobias, Master Gregorio in the next boat. You might even reach –'

'My lord?' said Mistress Clémence.

'Or,' said Nicholas, 'it might be even better to throw them. You take these balls, and I shall take these. There! A hit!'

The balls were only made of light terracotta, and most of them missed, but Tobie was clipped all round the head until he dragged off his cap and pleaded for mercy. The show of alarm was for Jodi and Jaçon but his voice, when Nicholas disembarked at his side on the islet, was edged. 'Do you mind not doing that again? Why are you here?'

'It would have been worse with the bows,' Nicholas said. 'You would really have felt it with the bows. I wasn't needed at Court. The truce is being extended, the English aren't sending an army, and the Duke is deeply embroiled with making himself the next Duke of Guelders.'

Plates were arriving, and food. Trestles fronted the elegant cabins. Benches were being brought out, and armfuls of cushions. It was like Linlithgow all over again, except that it was happening in sunlight, on the reeded shore of a limitless pool, and everything within sight belonged to him, and him only.

Gregorio said, 'I thought King James was claiming Guelders because of his mother.'

'I pleaded his case,' Nicholas said. 'But the Duke is a very hard man to convince. He wanted the land to help make up a new kingdom. Now he may do even better than that. The Emperor Frederick is making signals again.'

Gregorio said, 'Keep your voice down.'

'What signals?' said Tobie.

'He wants his boy Maximilian to marry the Duke's daughter, Marie. In return – maybe – he'll make the Duke King of the Romans, halfway house to becoming next Emperor of the Germanies. And further in return – maybe – he'll abdicate one day and allow the Duke to become Emperor. You should know all that. You ought to be finding and treating a monarch with piles. Find a patient with piles, and no inside information will escape you. Although, of course, you did treat Urbino. What did he have? Marsh-fever, wasn't it?'

Gregorio said, 'So what does this mean for the Bank? Nicholas?'

'It means I don't sell so many secrets to France,' Nicholas said. 'We keep Julius in Cologne, and Crackbene's friends in Utrecht, and I cultivate all those charming officers of the Emperor whom I met in the Tyrol. Cardinal Bessarion talked to Frederick about us.'

'So did the Patriarch of Antioch,' said Gregorio. 'The Emperor will suspect we are resuming our interest in the East.'

'So we are, temporarily,' Nicholas said. It was easy.

Gelis was standing before him. 'Why are you here?'

'That's what I was about to explain. Because I'm going to Cyprus,' Nicholas said. Jodi tugged at his doublet.

Gregorio said, 'What for, in God's name? The spring attack on the Sultan is launched; the fleet has gone; the Venetian arms are on their way to Uzum Hasan and the Turcoman army.'

'Paid for by our stolen gold,' Nicholas said. The gold, pirated on its way home from Africa, was being claimed by the Knights of St John.

Gregorio said, 'Julius is on his way to plead that case now. You sent him yourself.'

'Then perhaps I should join him,' Nicholas said. 'Rhodes is only two days from Cyprus. Yes, Jodi. I have observed that you are there. You shall sit beside me, and Mistress Clémence will tell us what you may eat.'

'And what you may eat,' Jodi said.

'No doubt,' Nicholas said. 'No doubt I shall be force-fed with something before the day is much older.'

Two days later he left, taking Alonse; and accompanied Mick Crackbene and a pallid-faced Tobie in a hard, brilliant sail of twenty-six days down the Gulf of Venice, and east to the farthest end of the Middle Sea.

He had been force-fed with many reasons for not going: the only one that had given him pause was Jodi's face. Gelis had said nothing. He had promised her a resolution this year in the West, and he had reaffirmed the agreement. Only, on the eve of his departure, she had come to him as he stood on the balcony and said, 'Would you take me with you to Cyprus?'

The light from the water slipped over her skin and her hair and her breast, and made two translucent points of her eyes.

He said, 'How dare you? How dare you, after Famagusta?' He stood, breathing quickly, staring after her as she left.

He gave a different answer when Tobie put the same question later that night, in his room. Then, Nicholas lay in his own high-backed chair and contemplated the deep coffered ceiling and said, ignoring the question, 'Did you put something into my drink? Why am I tired?'

'Because you've seen the boy again, and don't want to leave him,' Tobie said. 'Zacco has called you, I think.'

He supposed it wasn't a very hard guess. He said, 'Either Zacco, or David de Salmeton.'

It was quite athletic, the way Tobie sat up. 'That little whore!'

'That extremely able agent of the Vatachino, currently occupying a position at Zacco's right hand, or even possibly at both Zacco's hands.'

Tobie digested that. He said, 'But Zacco has a queen now. I mean he's married to Catherine Corner and she's pregnant.' He stopped again and said, 'Or is all this in reality about David de Salmeton? He half drowned you in Cairo, and you propose to gratify yourself by making him pay for it?'

'You were closer the first time,' Nicholas said. 'I don't think the message was false. I think it was real. Do you want to come with me?'

'No,' said Tobie. 'But I will.'

At first glance, James de Lusignan, King of Jerusalem, Cyprus and Armenia, seemed unchanged; nine years after their first meeting, the febrile beauty, the loose waving hair and measuring eyes still stopped the heart. He wore light, expensive French dress; he might equally have chosen Arab or Neapolitan or Venetian attire, or have received Nicholas in the old way, casually naked, half killing some horse. They were the same age. Today he was seated on his throne in his palace of Nicosia, and something was wrong.

The surroundings were the same. Gold had been lavished on the royal apartments in recent years. Nicholas had noticed it three years ago on the brief visit which had seemed, then, to confirm his Bank's share in the Crusade: the promise of an alliance with Zacco and Cairo, Venice and Rhodes which would have placed him at the spearhead of this attack on the Turk.

It had not happened, because of Gelis and his son. He had assumed he had Zacco's hatred, as he had received the vituperation of Ludovico da Bologna and Rhodes. He had mollified Venice with money and with his ships. It was as well, because Venice was here now in strength. Not the little Queen, seven months pregnant and unwelcome, he guessed, to Zacco's fastidious eye. But all those Venetian noblemen whom Zacco had also married, his feline eyes open, his claws sheathed, because he had no alternative. He could fall to the Turk or to Venice. He had chosen Venice.

The King said, 'My lord of Beltrees. I am told this is your title. I am sure you have earned it. To what do I owe this great honour?'

Zacco's own language was French, or else Greek. He understood the tongue of his overlord of Egypt and Syria. He was speaking now in Venetian patois, the coarsened slur impressively accurate. Someone shifted behind him: the battle-scarred swarthy person of his Sicilian Chancellor, Rizzo di Marino. The Catalans and Sicilians of Zacco's close inner circle had a better measure of the Venetian temper than had Zacco. For Zacco, there were seldom any half-measures: life was a stallion to be ridden bareback, kill or be killed, for the ecstasy. It was one of the reasons he and Nicholas had always understood one another.

Nicholas said, 'Sire, last time I called, you were gracious enough to lend me a horse. Since I was passing, I brought another, to replace it. Also a white gyrfalcon from Iceland.'

'Since you were passing?'

Nicholas said, 'My notary has some business in Rhodes: a legal quibble which requires our attention. I merely wished to repay my debt, and congratulate your magnificence on your marriage to the lady Catherine Corner.'

'Catherine Veneta,' said the King. 'The Queen has been adopted by the Republic. She is a Daughter of St Mark. The Bishop of Turin, a contemptible fool, has quipped that he never heard that St Mark had been married.'

'A contemptible and an ignorant fool,' Nicholas said. 'Of course he was married. How could a man be a saint, who has fathered a child outside matrimony?'

'We must discuss it some time,' said the King. 'It will please us to inspect this horse and this bird in the morning. We may decide to go hunting.'

'I should be honoured, roi monseigneur,' Nicholas said.

Outside the audience chamber, seeking Tobie, he moved from group to group of men he had known: all guarded, all nervously welcoming. There were other men who did not approach him, some of them strangers. Among them was one face he could never forget: oval, cleft-chinned and delicate, with lustrous dark eyes and dark hair. The man had a page at his side, and both smelled of jasmine. Nicholas walked across.

'I hoped,' said David de Salmeton, 'that you would come to me. Zacco is so very much married these days that life has become perfectly tedious. You have left the lovely Gelis behind?'

'Are you still interested?' Nicholas said. 'I must tell her. Perhaps you should change places with Martin. But you would hardly expect her to break off with King James on your account. And Martin might not do so well here. I believe the Vatachino are positively flourishing in Cyprus and Rhodes. And, of course, Anselm Adorne.'

'It was kind of you to desert the field. I fear,' de Salmeton said, 'that it is too late to forge an opening now. They have even given me the Kouklia sugarfields.'

'And, I trust, some of the vineyards,' Nicholas said. 'And a ship to replace the *Unicorn*? All that exquisite claret. I did have some regrets about that.'

'It sank off La Rochelle,' de Salmeton said.

'But they saved me a bottle,' Nicholas said. 'I have it for you in my luggage. Too late to forge an opening, you think? Perhaps we should see.' He nodded and walked away, followed by the eyes of the boy. He wondered, as he often wondered, what he would do without Crackbene.

It had been obvious from the moment of his arrival that he was not going to be lodged in the Palace, and he had sent Alonse to make arrangements with the Venetian Bailie. It would have been correct – and he wished to be correct – for Messer Pasqualigo to invite him to stay. Instead, he found himself escorted, with Tobie, to the palatial villa next door, with which he was very familiar.

Tobie said, 'Isn't this where you went to your meeting three years ago? Isn't this where the Queen's Venetian family lives?'

It was, of course. It was the home of the Lord Auditor Andrea Corner, the uncle of Catherine and the most powerful Venetian on Cyprus. It was the home of young Marco her cousin, and of Marco's namesake and uncle her father, when called from his sugar estates in the south. It was also home, on occasion, to those three remarkable princesses, the little Queen's mother and aunts, with two of whom he had been memorably intimate.

He could feel Tobie walking bristling beside him as they were led in. He could feel Tobie's disapproval become outrage when the voice that greeted them, sweetly feminine, proved to be that of a beautiful boy. Nerio, well-born exile of Trebizond, had shamed Adorne's son in Venice and embellished the court of Duke Charles in Bruges and Brussels and had found himself a singular protector, by all accounts, in the house of Bessarion in Rome.

Nicholas said, 'How surprising. And is the lord Nicholai Giorgio de' Acciajuoli present also?'

The painted eyes fluttered. 'Should I have allowed him to come? But he is sensitive, and such tendresses, as you know, can breed jealousy. He is waiting in Modon. But I am to see to your comfort, and to apologise for the lord Andrea and his nephew, who have been called away. I hope, however, that you remember your Greek. And this is your charming doctor. I remember him well.'

'I remember you,' Tobie said.

Alone with Nicholas he said, as he had said all through the voyage, 'Achille told you. The Vatachino have all the contracts. There is nothing for you here now, or for the army. John and Astorre wasted their time defending a cesspool of plotting and decadence. Why are we here?'

'To be seduced in Greek,' Nicholas said.

'By that scented boy?'

'It wasn't his scent,' Nicholas said. 'Come to the balcony.'

Below, the trees of the garden were heavy with dust, and urns of flowers threw their black shadows on the pavement beside the rim of a fountain. By the fountain stood a man they both knew: a man in a turban, talking to a woman seated below him.

The man was Hadji Mehmet, the far-travelled envoy of Uzum Hasan, the Turcoman ruler of Persia. The woman was Violante, the golden princess of Naxos whose small, plump niece was Zacco's queen.

Tobie said, 'Don't.'

'Don't what?' Nicholas said. 'He's the pill, she's the . . . palliative. The Turk must be stopped. Uzum Hasan can stop him. In other words, if you can't help, don't hinder.'

He had been right. When, refreshed, they both descended, the lady and the envoy were waiting to greet them, and the encounter proceeded, fluently, on predictable lines. He found he rather enjoyed meeting Violante, for once, on something like his own terms. He paid her far more attention than he did Uzum's envoy.

In public, neither he nor Hadji Mehmet had ever betrayed anything but the courtesy due from merchant banker to senior ambassador. In fact, they had now met many times, and understood each other very well. Behind his slow tongue and stately manner, the Persian concealed a quick wit and a grasp of alien languages which had served his lord over many years, not least when leading his hundred-strong delegation to Venice two years ago, or at a seminal meeting in this very house some months before that.

With him then had been someone else: the Latin Patriarch of Antioch, who had so understandably wished to place Katelijne Sersanders in a convent, and whom Tobie had met in Urbino. Uzum Hasan made use of the Latin Church, as he employed any tool in a war that might lose him his country. Just as the Latin Church – in the person of the late Cardinal Bessarion, and his agent Ludovico da Bologna – had been and was using him. Nicholas thought of Ludovico da Bologna, and wondered where he was.

He saw Tobie glance at him, and realised that his own manner had become rather less weighty, and Tobie thought he knew why. Probably Violante with her silk gown and ivory skin and high-arched slippers of birdskin thought so too. And of course, he was not without some susceptibility. Any man would long to unfold her hair, discarding the jewels into some warm handy niche, to be recovered quite soon. He realised, ruefully, that most of the time Tobie's suspicions were right.

They supped in the garden, and were joined by the youth Nerio, who played his lute for them and sang, seated at the princess's knee. The songs, in the clear sexless voice, passed from language to language, at first amusingly daring, and then unashamedly erotic. Tobie had flushed. The woman, her eyes on those of the boy, was smiling a little, her breathing heightened. The Ambassador sipped the water that was in fact wine, with the peaceful expression of incomprehension that Nicholas now knew so well. And Nicholas, sighing, drank his wine which was in fact water and summoning all his own well-worn skills, blocked the words and music out of his thoughts. He hoped the boy and Violante were enjoying them.

They retired at length, without the Auditor or his nephew having made an appearance. Tomorrow, Nicholas was to hunt with the King. He and Tobie had been given separate rooms, which suited him well. The note he had half expected was slipped into the sleeve of his night-robe; he took it with him into the privy to read. He had already studied his sumptuous little room, with the great bed and the painted walls and the devotional tabernacle with its almost invisible peep-hole, high on the wall. He didn't mind. He had never minded giving a performance. He had never slept dressed, either, and wasn't going to start now.

He was in bed although not asleep when the scratch came to his door, and Violante entered, the candlelight burnishing her brow and cheekbones and breast. Her hair was already over her shoulders, and she wore one garment more than he did. He sat up, embracing his sheeted knees. 'Highness, forgive me. I would come and kiss your hand, were it seemly.'

She laid down the candle and allowed her high, pencilled brows to express amazement. 'How impolite. The man I once knew could not have refrained, seemly or not.'

'I hoped you'd say that,' he said, and came to her, lifting her fingers. She wore little rings on each one, and long earrings, which mixed with the screws of gilt hair that lay against her tinted cheeks. In Cyprus, she painted her lips, her eyes, her fingertips as if she felt close to home – to Byzantium, to the Trapezuntine empire of her grandfather which now belonged to the Turks. But she had married a Venetian nobleman, Caterino Zeno, who even now was with Uzum Hasan, and who had founded the fortunes of Nicholas and his Bank with an alum deal.

She also painted the tips of her breasts. Or so it now seemed.

Twelve years ago he had returned from Trebizond to find his wife dead, and this woman had offered herself as a vehicle for his pain, his mourning, his remorse, his self-hatred, his oblivion. He had no illusions about her, but he did not and never would forget that.

Then, aged twenty, he had known no mean between a caring love, merry or tender, and the violence which had to be its opposite. Now he had experienced a thousand variants, and could choose. He could offer no genuine love, but would not insult her by taking her lightly. He guessed that, no longer young, she could still have what or whom she desired. She would demand respect, but in her heart longed for excitement.

He made sure that she had what she wanted, and at a pace that suited the voracious girl she had been rather than what she was now. And although he never for a moment forgot the pious saint high on the wall, he acted as if it were not there. He had obtained from Tobie, without explanation, the potion that would put her to sleep, but she hardly needed it, although he lifted her at length from the floor, and laid her on the bed, her breath slowing, and helped her to drink. Then he put the candle out and waited until he heard the click of a door and soft footsteps retreating. He knew where her chamber was, and carried her there without incident, covering her in her bed. He had cut off a doublet button, a ruby, and left her fingers curled round it.

Half an hour later, dressed, he slipped out of the villa and found the door left unlocked in the garden. Very soon after, he stopped at another gate, and spoke a password, and was admitted into a building whose door closed behind him in darkness. He felt someone standing beside him. Then two arms closed round his shoulders: different arms, in a different way. They tightened, then dropped. A lamp glowed.

'Oh mon Dieu,' Zacco said. 'You reek of her. See, I am weeping. See, you whore, you turd, you Flemish cow-sucker, how I am weeping, because you did this for me. Did you finish her? She deserved it.'

He *was* weeping, his face screwed with manic laughter. An old cap bulged with his hair, and his clothes were ill-fitting and smelled. He said, 'See: Zacco, King of Jerusalem, Cyprus and Armenia. My lady mother said I could not escape from the Palace, but I did. It was she who said you would come back if I sent for you. And the Patriarch, when he was here. My mother said you would come for love of me and hatred of David de Salmeton. The Patriarch said you might come, but would only stay if we put Caterino Zeno's wife into your bed. Without, of course, allowing her to know that we wished her to go there. She thought she was fornicating for Venice. You know there is a spyhole in that room?'

'Nerio was watching,' Nicholas said. 'So I made my best efforts. *I* am supposed to be a whore and a turd?' He found he was following Zacco into a lit room containing two people. One was the black-eyed veiled person of Marietta of Patras, the King's mother. The other was the man he had just had supper with, Hadji Mehmet, the Persian envoy.

Nicholas knelt at the lady's feet and kissed her hand, meeting the considering gaze. He rose and spoke to the envoy in resigned Greek. 'What did they expect *you* to do?'

The man was smiling. 'Fortunately, I am not required to live in the villa, my entourage is too large. It was simple to leave. I left the note in your room.'

'Enough,' said Marietta of Patras. She pointed to a seat at her side, and Nicholas sat. Even in age, and a woman, she dominated the room, as she had pushed, beguiled and dominated her son through all his charmed, wilful life. She had been a King's mistress and also a beauty, until the rightful Queen bit off her nose. Now the veil hid the scar, but not the power.

'Enough. This is dangerous for the King. We must speak and then go. My lord Mehmet.'

'No. I will speak,' Zacco said. He had flung himself down. Now he pulled off his cap and jumped up, to begin prowling back and forth. He said, 'Nikko, listen. Venice is becoming too powerful. You know my dilemma. I must pay tribute to Cairo, or the Mamelukes may again overwhelm me. If Cairo and I are too weak, the Ottoman Sultan will have me. Venice offered to save me from that, and so I made this marriage. Now it is Venice, Venice, Venice and I may be worse off than before.'

'How?' said Nicholas.

Hadji Mehmet spoke in his measured voice. 'Unless he receives the promised help from the West, my lord the prince Uzum Hasan may not succeed in his plan to regain his lands of Karamania, and push the Sultan's land forces north. The Christian fleets have done nothing this year but make simple forays and quarrel. The promised arms and experts are delayed. If my prince fails from no fault of his own, we fear, and the King fears, that Venice will make a shameful peace with the Sultan for the sake of her trade. Thus the prince Uzum Hasan will be rendered helpless –'

'And so shall we,' Zacco said. 'And so too will the Knights of Rhodes, and the Sultan at Cairo. All need Venice but fear her and hate her. There was a rising here against ourselves and the Venetians last autumn.'

'It was put down,' said the King's mother. 'But then my son, my sweet lord lost his head when the Venetians tried to bring their ships and arms into Famagusta in April. What did you say, my son James, to Messer Barbaro? That if all the galleys did not leave in two hours, you would see that they were blasted out of the harbour? That if any men were found afterwards on land, you would make them so much dead meat?'

'Nikko understands,' Zacco said. He came to rest before him, his face set. 'We are the slave of the Sultan of Egypt. If Uzum Hasan fails, no Christian power is going to save us. We dared not let these galleys enter our harbour and anger the Sultan. However much Venice may object, we are compelled to send hackbutters to Cairo if the Mamelukes demand them, just as we must resist the Signoria when she tries to impress our soldiers for her galleys. And Venice must look out for herself. Cairo is tired of her, and may very well drive out her traders and replace them in Syria with Genoese.'

He didn't say *with Anselm Adorne*. He didn't have to. 'I see,' Nicholas said. 'So that you, roi monseigneur, and my lord Hadji Mehmet, troubled about the present dominance and future intentions of Venice, have been looking at other alliances? Always excluding, of course, the King's half-sister Carlotta in Rhodes.'

'The Knights are finding her tiresome,' said the King's mother. 'The Patriarch is there; he has told us. Once we feared Milan and Genoa with some cause, but now we cannot afford to close doors. Once too, I believe, you were kind enough, Ser Niccolò, to try to forward my son's marriage with a daughter of the royal house of Naples. Mischief-making perhaps, but there, too, circumstances have altered the case. Our Archbishop is in Naples now, arranging a contract of marriage between the King's natural son and our grand-daughter Charla.'

Charla was six, the oldest of Zacco's four natural children, of whom he was carelessly fond. The other Charlotte, his first and his favourite, would have been sixteen had she survived. She died, poisoned, it was said, by Andrea Corner the Queen's uncle. Venice, Venice.

Nicholas said, 'You must at least congratulate me on not having tied you to the princess Zoe, now in Muscovy.'

'Have you met my wife?' Zacco said. 'The happiest day of my life was the one when she confessed she was pregnant. I have never performed a harder month's work. I have had to ask Master Gentile to explain to her how the waxing belly may suffer from intercourse. My bed is barely my own, even now.'

Nicholas said, 'The King should have married the lady Margaret of Denmark. So what do you fear?'

There was a silence. The King's mother said, 'My son's child will be born in eight weeks. Whoever holds it, holds the future.'

She looked at him, and the veil blew with the force of her breathing. 'It is my intention to take the child when it is born, and hold it securely. And it is my wish that all who love the King gather round him on the day of his fatherhood, for I believe that his life thereafter will be in danger.'

'It is always in danger,' Zacco said. 'But it is true. We need friends.'

'You are asking me to stay until August?' Nicholas said.

'Eight weeks,' Zacco said. 'You are a merchant, of no single faction. You hear everything. So does David. Perhaps you are rivals in business, but you I trust, and David's self-interest I trust. The Vatachino reaped all the profits which you threw away: my life means money to them. He may of course try to harm you, and you may be frightened. In which case, run away.'

'Like the wild cow,' said Nicholas, and the King gave a snort.

'What of the wild cow?' the King's mother said.

'The bonasus,' said her son cheerfully. 'They say that in running away, it emits a fart that covers three acres and can set a forest on fire. Nikko means he is staying.'

'I am glad,' said the lady dryly. Nicholas expected no more; he knew Marietta of Patras from many encounters. She was not loved. She was feared; and the island called her Cropnose. But her son had come to manhood, and was ruling with vigour and courage, for all his mistakes.

Nicholas understood Zacco and his mother and the beliefs by which they ruled. One did not live by looking back with regret. Self-rebuke was a weakness: if one took a wrong turning and a man or a family died, it couldn't be mended. But here in Cyprus there was something he could do that seemed right: something he could achieve here in limbo, cut off from all the other fruits of his labours until he should go back, and find it ready for harvesting.

He took his leave, in due course. Hadji Mehmet had already left, having excused himself diplomatically from the hunt Zacco had announced for the morning. For this morning. For a time only an hour or two hence. Nicholas was to take part, since his gifts, after all, were on trial. He would not exactly be fresh. But then neither would Zacco.

The King saw him to the door and he slipped out into the darkness, as presently the King himself would depart for the Palace. Nicholas had no fear for Zacco: he was disguised, and was expert with his sword.

He did not think of himself.

Chapter 44

WHEN THE twenty-seventh day of June dawned, it was not at once obvious that Nicholas de Fleury was missing.

The King, usually quick to rise for a hunt, had decreed a later departure, with tents and horses and food sufficient for an expedition of more than one day. He proposed to cover the terrain towards Famagusta, some thirty miles to the east.

Tobie, breaking his fast in a leisurely way, wished him well of it, and Nicholas too. He was happy to be unwanted. Mick Crackbene was still at Famagusta with the ship, and all his mates from the past. He could join in if he wanted.

He assumed Nicholas had risen, dressed and gone to the Palace. It was not until the Auditor's steward came to the door that Tobie realised that his fellow traveller had not arrived there, and that his chamber was empty. Then they were joined by the lady Violante, her face frowning and pale and, it transpired, equally baffled. Alonse, questioned, could only say that he did not know at what hour his lordship had left, but that he had worn plain leather dress, fit for hunting, and that his sword and scabbard were gone. He had taken no horses.

'Ours were tired. He would expect to borrow or hire them,' said Tobie. 'The same with his hunting equipment. He has many friends in Nicosia. Perhaps the Auditor would kindly apologise to the King, and say that Lord Beltrees will follow?'

By then, Andrea Corner himself had entered the house, his eyes questioning his sister by marriage. The princess shrugged. The Auditor said, 'This seems strange. However. Pray ask his lordship to come when he can. I am afraid we must leave.'

Tobie watched him ride off. You could hear the barking of hounds in the distance, and then the clatter of a large cavalcade. Alonse said, 'Sir, I cannot understand it. He did not call me to dress, or to pay his respects to the household, or to find him a mount. Every other lord will have his man at his side.'

'I think,' Tobie said, 'that perhaps discretion is necessary. His lordship may have had an assignation, and has lost count of time. No one saw him leave the main gates?'

'There was an unlocked postern,' said Alonse. 'The lady Violante has asked me to list for her all those houses where he has friends. She has already sent servants running. She fears an accident.'

'Or she wants to know where he has friends,' Tobie said. His resentment against Nicholas grew. Cyprus was painful to him, as it ought to be to Nicholas. Trouncing the Vatachino wasn't reason enough to come back; nor was some self-deluding fantasy of reconstructing his friendship with Zacco. What had happened that morning was typical of the unpleasant stew of lust and intrigue that he remembered from other times.

It was only astonishing that wherever Nicholas was, he wasn't with Zacco. Nor with any of the Venetians, from Andrea Corner and Marco Bembo to the lesser merchants; nor with any of the principal Catalans; nor even with David de Salmeton and the beautiful Nerio. All of these were with Zacco, gone hunting. Which left Tobie alone with Violante of Naxos.

It had been his intention to walk round the town, and see if there was anyone left whom he knew. He found himself instead keeping company with the princess, who retained him in desultory conversation which ceased at each sound of a step. Studying her, he made note that this morning her movements were languid, and her skin was lax under the paint. He knew the signs: he was a doctor, and far from a eunuch. Zeno, of course, was in Persia. So, Nerio? Or . . .?

Or the owner of the rich brocade doublet which had lost, as Alonse had informed him with horror, one of its fine ruby studs overnight?

No wonder she was uneasy.

So when had Nicholas left the house? After he left her, but in darkness, since no one had seen him. And not, then, for a woman. For an assignation of a different kind, which the Venetians knew nothing about.

Close to noon, when there was still no news of Nicholas and the streets were emptying in the heat, Tobie made an excuse to retire and, making his way from the house, went to find the villa occupied by Hadji Mehmet.

The heavy Turcoman listened, his hands motionless on his robes, the black rim of his beard glistening damp in the heat. At the end he said, 'It was your lord's intention to hunt. The King also expected it.'

'So did the Auditor,' Tobie said. 'And the Bailie. And the stables had prepared horses for him, at the instance of Rizzo di Marino.' He paused. 'One knows that the King's lady mother has certain plans, from time to time, which she does not make immediately known.'

'She has no knowledge of this,' the Turcoman said. 'In fact, you will find that her own servants are making enquiries. Nicosia is a city of simple thieves as well as hired killers. A man may be robbed for his sword, and then left in a well or a sewer.'

'He was wearing a sword?' Tobie said.

'Does any wise man walk at night time without one?'

'Tell me,' said Tobie.

'I do not know where he is,' said Hadji Mehmet. 'I shall suggest to you that he was abroad some three hours before dawn, and on his way back to your villa, a walk of no more than five minutes. To remove him in that short space of time and in silence would be the work of several men.'

Tobie felt cold. He said, 'So not a robbery. An attack by hirelings of someone important. But why?'

'Why indeed?' said Hadji Mehmet. 'He is a banker, a guest, a Veneto-Fleming. All of Nicosia will be roused, is being roused to look for him. But there is no body.' He paused. 'Did your lord not lose a son in similar circumstances?'

'No,' said Tobie. 'That is, the child was simply taken by his own father, which gave rise to rumours of . . .' He stopped. 'Kidnapping? You think that may be all that this is?'

'Your lord is wealthy,' the Turcoman said. 'Such a wealth offered to our cause might have made a great difference three years ago. But I am neither explaining nor threatening nor promising. I know nothing of this.'

'But you might help?' Tobie said.

The man lifted his shoulders. 'I am an envoy of a foreign land, a foreign religion, a foreign culture. How might I help?'

'Because, as an envoy, you have studied these people over many months, many years,' Tobie said. 'More than most people, you can make guesses.'

'Perhaps,' said Hadji Mehmet. 'But it is my task to remain neutral. An envoy who interferes, even to solve his host's problems, is not welcome.'

'Yet, as you have said, my lord, the Bank's wealth and interest could be useful. Private advice, in such a talk as this, would do you no disservice.'

'It might do me no service,' said the Turcoman. 'I have been disappointed in your padrone before. In any case, there may be nothing wrong. It is early. He may have met friends, and even now have joined the King's party. If your other guess is correct, you will hear soon enough from his captors. For his sake, I hope that you do.'

'He came here to help,' Tobie said.

'He came here for Zacco,' said Hadji Mehmet. 'It is Zacco who has most to gain from enabling you to find him, if something has happened. But you do not know that it has.'

By dusk, it was known that the King's party was camping some twenty miles off, and that Nicholas so far had not joined them. By that time, Tobie had recruited every religious house in the capital to the cause of spreading the enquiry island-wide. He had already sent a message to Crackbene at Famagusta. There was a man with the King, paid to do nothing but ride for Nicosia if Nicholas appeared. The last official courier from the camp called to repeat the negative news, and pass to Dr Tobias the King's regrets that my lord of Beltrees had been unable to join him.

The tone of the message was coolly social, and contained no hint of anxiety; as if Zacco were drunk, or uninterested. Or, more likely, as if he wished to pretend unconcern, while his mother did all that was necessary. Although Tobie had only the Turcoman's word that the noseless lady was searching for Nicholas. She had not approached him.

Crackbene arrived late at night, with a pass signed by Rizzo di Marino. His eyes were enlarged from a ride of three hours in the dark, and his square Nordic face was pitted with dust. Violante, hearing, had come out of her chamber, fully dressed.

Crackbene said, 'Highness,' and paused.

Tobie said, 'We have no news. Have you?'

'No,' said Crackbene. He glanced at the princess again.

She said, 'You have something private to say. I shall wait below for you.'

'No, Despoina,' said Crackbene. He remembered his Greek. He had been on the opposite side in the Trebizond trade war. He said, 'It is nothing: a change of plan the Court has not yet announced. The King has been inconvenienced by a colic attack, and is to take a day's rest in Famagusta. The hunting is cancelled.'

Tobie grunted. It bore out his suspicions. The King was drunk, and some secretary had responded to his note about Nicholas.

'Is he in pain?' the princess asked.

'He was bellowing. But he was bellowing before. He has Master Gentile with him. I am sorry of course for his highness, but it frees the others. The Bailie is returning tomorrow, and a proper effort will be made to find my lord of Beltrees. You think he may be outside the city?'

'I think he would have been found by now,' Tobie said. Without consulting anyone, he had posted an announcement of a reward. He hoped to God no one ever had to pay it: Gregorio would kill him. And if Nicholas now appeared at that door with a whore in one hand and a pair of dice in the other, he, Tobie, would personally flay him.

Crackbene came and sat in a tub of tepid water in Tobie's room. Tobie was thankful to have him. The tub overflowed, but the pools of water made the room cool. Crackbene said, 'Can we be overheard?'

Nicholas had checked Tobie's room for him. It was secure. His own, he had let drop, was not. Tobie said, 'Yes. Why?'

'The King's attack,' Crackbene said. He spoke very softly. He got up and, dripping, closed both the windows; then he sat on the sill. He said, 'It isn't colic. It's the flux. The bloody menison.'

The two looked at one another. 'When did it start?' Tobie said.

'While they were eating in camp. They heard him yell from his tent, but that isn't uncommon. Then it got worse. It was known when I left that he was passing blood and screaming and cursing. He flung the bowl at Gentile while he was trying to sponge him.'

'A fever?' said Tobie.

'So they said.'

'And did he vomit?'

'From the pain. He was given something that stopped it. Corner told them to do anything that they could to ease the pain and keep his food down.'

Tobie felt very old. He said, 'You don't believe it.'

'I believe that part,' Crackbene said. 'So will everyone else.'

He cleared his throat. He said, 'I have something else to tell you. I know where Nicholas is. No one is going to kill him. And however disagreeable his circumstances, he is safer than he would be in Famagusta.'

'You are saying,' said Tobie, 'that the King has been poisoned. And that, being absent, Nicholas will be free of suspicion?'

'Yes.'

'Where is he?'

'I am not going to tell you,' said Crackbene. 'And in case it has entered your head, I didn't order his capture. I learned of it through a young friend. You make friends, at sea.'

As far as Tobie knew, Crackbene never made friends. He met people, and used them. He said, 'A man held under duress may suffer as much as another with . . . dysentery. Tell me where Nicholas is. I am going to him.'

'He wouldn't wish it,' Crackbene said. 'If you were to ask him, he would beg just one thing. And since you can't ask him, what you do will relieve his mind afterwards. Go to Zacco.'

'He has a doctor,' Tobie said.

'A man called Gentile, who owes a great deal to Zacco, but also to Andrea Corner and his nephew. They have locked the door to the royal apartments,' Crackbene said. 'No one is allowed in. No friends, no courtiers, no royal officers, unless they are Venetian. You are a Pavia physician, the nephew of one of the great medical men of our time. They will not refuse you.'

'You do not speak,' Tobie said, 'of the rewards I may garner for saving him.'

The solid figure in the window said nothing, and Tobie also fell silent, thinking of a young King: a lion, a leopard; violent, wilful, glorious in its courage and struck down on a whim.

Venice, Venice.

From the moment he opened his eyes, Nicholas de Fleury knew where he was; because ten years before, this place had been his.

His most profound recollections of it belonged to the spring, and were mixed with the scent of the sugar. The man who had caused him to be brought here of course knew all about that. Knew about Katelina and Fiorenza of Naxos; about Tobie's early, earnest experiments; about Primaflora. About the young, courageous Diniz, who had attempted to kill him. The little Catherine, nine years old, had been here with her parents. Now St Mark was her parent and, plain still and very much plumper, she had a King and an isle in her grasp.

And a man he knew had stood on this spot: something which for the first time, for the very first time made it a place of remembered fulfilment and not of reproach. He did not know why, but he knew the change would have angered his enemy. His enemy who had had him hidden here, bound, in his sugar plantation of Kouklia.

The south coast was two days from Nicosia. He had no recollection of the journey but thought, as hunger broke through the drowsiness, that someone had drugged him as he had drugged Violante. He wondered what Violante would do, when she found her favoured partner had fled. He thought of Tobie trying to raise the alarm, and finding that the hunt had emptied Nicosia of all its principal officers.

It had been very well planned. It was only strange, to his mind, that he had not been unbound and fed, as one would do if expecting a ransom; or tortured, as one might be pleased to do to an enemy; or killed, as might be a convenient way to deal with a rival.

As time went on, he saw that simple neglect would achieve much on its own. As a human being and a man accustomed to armies, he knew that in a crisis, cleanliness equated with vanity: if one inescapably stank, then one stank. The thirst was something again. He was surely not far from water. He was lying in a chamber of the old grinding hall, outdated now by the new one at Stavros, built to acommodate John's wonderful Syrian mill. In his day there had been a well-ordered viaduct, with troughs and channels, including one under this floor.

He could hear no water now. He wondered if the copper cauldrons were even still there, or had fallen to Zacco's great melt-down programme, a defiant attempt to repair his fortunes with copper coinage. Zacco was never passive; he always tried to do something. He bought what help he could, with land where he couldn't pay money. And the new owners looked for short-term profit, like this, but made no investments, for they knew how precarious his kingdom was.

Darkness came, and then light. It was, Nicholas thought, his second dawn here, which would make it four days since he was captured, and the last day in June. He hoped the grandson or granddaughter of St Mark hadn't got itself born in his absence. Babies of seven months were viable, Tobie said. Tobie claimed to have seen one cut alive from its mother.

A pang ran through him, indistinguishable from the pangs of cramp and of hunger. He had been trussed as extravagantly as if someone were going to weave from him: nothing he could do would shift the cords, and he had been reduced to bad-tempered movements to try and keep his muscles from deadening. He had got rid of the gag, but not the chain which manacled him to the wall. And now, his voice dried to a croak, he could not shout. He wished very badly that he could reach his pendulum, and had fingers to work it. And all the time he was sending exhortations, mingled with impatient curses, to the absent Mick Crackbene.

His visitor came that afternoon, with a footfall so soft that he almost missed it. Then he smelt the jasmine, pervading even the horse sweat.

Which?

He opened his eyes. 'Ah. Filipe,' he said.

On the fourth day of Zacco's illness, the clamour in the royal antechamber in Famagusta was such that the Venetians could no longer bar the way, and the door of the sickroom was burst open.

Five minutes later, Rizzo di Marino pushed his way out and called. 'Dr Tobias!'

The tone of his voice was enough, even had Tobie not heard the change in the chorus from within: the ragged shift from anger, jubilation, greeting, to muted distress, and then silence. He walked through the door as the circle round the bed shrank, muttering.

Gabriel Gentile said, 'I asked for no other physician.'

'No,' said Rizzo di Marino. 'But you have one.' The servant Jorgin stood at his side, his eyes running with tears.

James the Second of Lusignan, King of Cyprus, lay, his eyes closed, upon silken sheets stained with blood, in an atmosphere in which pastilles of scent strove with the smells of ordure, of blood and of vomit. On the pillow, the tangled yellow-brown hair was dark with sweat and the bronze skin was yellow and shadowed, the imperious nose jutting, the mobile lips slack. The physician Gentile, in his stained apron, was breathing quickly.

Tobie said, 'I have no wish to usurp you. Only I have had long experience of the bloody flux in the field, and there are different ways of treating it. Allow me to help you.'

It was not only the flux. He was almost sure of it. But he did not want to alienate this frightened man, who had seen the sickness from the beginning, and could tell him how it had been treated. He did not think Gentile, favoured for more than five years, would have taken part in a plot; but he could have turned a blind eye; or he could have been placed here to serve as a scapegoat. In which case he might be glad of help, even so late. Even so very late.

He thought, as he moved to the bed, that it was as well that the doors had been broached, and that men had at last seen their King as he was. No one could blame the Banco di Niccolò's doctor. No one could blame Nicholas now. By tonight, word would have reached Nicosia, and Crackbene might well act at last to retrieve Nicholas. Tobie, looking down at the withdrawn, suffering face, found himself hoping that Nicholas was safe, but a long distance away.

After that, entered wholly into his chosen profession, Tobias Beventini took no account of time passing, or of food, or of sleep as he worked for his patient. He had to commit the cruelty first of allowing the opiates to fade unrenewed, in order to see what he had, and what could be done for the poison. But it had had four days to work. And the answer came plainly enough through the night, in Zacco's feverish mumbles and uneven screeches of protest.

Through it all, Tobie let it be known, unwillingly endorsed by the Venetians, that any man of standing might enter the room, provided he sat in silence and out of his way. The courtiers of a lesser King would have been forbidden the chamber, to spare the dignity of their lord in this most degrading of afflictions. For four whole days, that had served as an excuse to isolate a man who would have been astounded at the presumption of such an idea: at the assumption that his subjects could embarrass him.

All his friends came. David de Salmeton was not among them, nor were the relatives of his wife. At times, through the night, he saw and recognised the dim faces. Between the bouts of pain, when the fever allowed, he would stop snarling abuse at his doctors to call to one or other of the stricken men on the bench, asking a question, demanding a service, indulging with malice in some barbed joke in a brilliant exhibition of pride. When the exhaustion started to show, Tobie prepared the potion that would send him to sleep, knowing that there was nothing to be gained, now, by stimulation.

A few hours before dawn, he dispatched Gentile to rest. As the King slept, one by one the observers also left until Tobie was alone in the lamplit room with his patient and the nursemaid who served him. When he saw the King stir, he sent even the woman away. He was not sure, but he thought he was wanted.

Between awakening and pain there existed sometimes a space where the mind reigned as it once did. Now the magnificent hazel eyes unclosed, and the King said, 'You are Nikko's small excrescence. A doctor.'

'Yes, roi monseigneur,' Tobie said.

'He was too nice in the stomach to come himself?'

'He would be here, if he knew the King was ill. He has been sent for.'

The eyes frowned, and closed, and opened. The King said, 'Have I been poisoned?'

A doctor's training is long and hard, and consists, in the main, of learning what answer to choose. Tobie said, 'I believe so, roi monseigneur. I believe it will never be known precisely by whom. I believe you will know what good might be done by accusations.'

'And will I survive?'

One could count on that question as well. With a man like this, there was no need to use words. Tobie kept still, and allowed his face to be read. The King studied him, saying nothing. Presently he asked, 'And how is my Queen?'

Tobie said, 'You should send for her, sire. And you should rest content. Whatever happens, the succession is secure.'

'Content!' the King said. It was a scream. The nurse outside heard, and quickly entered. Others came. They were in time to see their indomitable lord caught, blaspheming and shouting, in the fresh spasms of a new agony. Tobie worked as he did in the field, fast and accurately and in full awareness of all that he was doing, and what would result from it. He decided then that Nicholas ought to be allowed to come, for Zacco's sake, while his presence had meaning. It was then the second day of July.

*

Late that same afternoon, white and weary at the end of a feat of
dogged persistence, Nicholas de Fleury dismounted at the marble
portico of the royal palace of Famagusta, in face of the soaring
Cathedral. Behind that was the Citadel, and behind that the blue
water, full of Venetian ships.

Filipe had freed him, and found him a horse and brought him part
of the way. Now the youth was riding to Nicosia to fetch Crackbene
quickly. Nicholas understood, he supposed, why Crackbene had been
in no haste to mount a rescue operation himself, even when informed
by Filipe where to find him. It was fortunate that Filipe, unaware of
these subtleties, had made his own way to Kouklia to save him.

Filipe had little personal cause to be interested in the survival of
Nicholas, under whom he had suffered as an inadequate ship's boy
nine years before, off the African coast, on the *San Niccolò*. But he
had wished very much to please Mick, the big Scandinavian master,
who had helped to protect the little fool after the voyage; and had
since contrived him a post in Nicosia. And then, when David de
Salmeton had moved there from Cairo, the boy had been engaged as
his servant.

Nicholas hadn't known that: had been astonished to notice the
youth standing scented and curled at de Salmeton's side on his
arrival. But Master Crackbene had been told about his new position,
the boy had volunteered. They had exchanged messages now and
then.

Nicholas wondered what the messages had been. He had never
liked Filipe very much. But now he probably owed him his life, and
perhaps something else. If Zacco still lived.

They were not entirely willing to admit him. He was wasting his
momentum on anger when Tobie suddenly appeared, and took him
by the arm and led him in and sat him down in a room somewhere.
'He's very sick, but he'll last till you're fit to see him. Tell me what
happened.'

Tobie, being a grandmother. He told him, and was given something
sweet and rather invigorating to drink while in turn he listened to
Tobie. Then he said, 'When can I see him?'

'Now,' Tobie said. 'Sit with the rest. He will single you out, to
show his confidence in you. Then you will have to wait here until
he's alone.'

Nicholas said, 'He has survived for five days. I think you underrate
yourself, Tobie.'

'You want to think so,' said Tobie. Tobie, being ruthlessly honest.

*

He applied to the sickroom very soon after, and entered through the heavy carved door, and was met by a second barrier of odour, thick as a rug.

He had been entertained often enough in Zacco's personal chamber in Nicosia, but not here. The ornate Venetian bed stood on a platform laden with sickroom basins and tables and trays. The great *cortinaggio* still spread its covering wings, hung from its cords in the ceiling, but the silken bed curtains had been lifted and knotted, and the gold-embroidered pillow and sheets had given way to plain lawn. The doctors moved back and forth, and the nurses. There were several now.

He could see, just, the dusky figures seated on the banquettes against the glimmer of revetted marble, but all the light seemed absorbed by the bed and the slow-tossing figure upon it. The young lion whose place, impatient foot swinging, was customarily on the sill of his window, his sinewy shoulders turned to the moat and the gardens, his mocking voice offering friendship and treachery. Careless joy, careless abuse, careless love.

Now Zacco lay, his eyes burning, his body abandoned to the slow flicking movements of fever and pain, his flesh and tissue and blood seeping from him. He said, 'Ha! Nikko the lascivious he-goat, *fervens semper ad coitum*. Who are you ravishing now?'

'I shall save her for you, roi monseigneur,' Nicholas said. 'I wish I and my doctor had come earlier.'

'So do we,' the King said. 'We wished to play cards, before you had spent all your money. Your gyrfalcon pleased us.'

'I am glad, sire,' Nicholas said. Tobie signed. He bowed and, retreating, sat down with the rest by the wall. They looked at him, but none spoke. After a while the King's lids closed, and Nicholas rose quietly and left.

Most of the night, he sat by the window. When Tobie came he rose, his eyes on the round smooth-skinned face, all its colour faded from tiredness.

Tobie said, 'Before you go. What have you done about David de Salmeton? You know he has left Famagusta?'

'I know. I have laid a formal accusation against him: abduction with intent to murder. Filipe's deposition will support it.'

'De Salmeton will have escaped by that time,' Tobie said.

'I doubt it,' Nicholas said. 'After this, the Venetians will want someone to blame.'

After this. He added, 'Would the King see me now?'

'He has asked,' Tobie said.

The room was empty of spectators this time. Zacco lay still, his

hair combed, his arms loose on the sheets. His lashes, always ridiculous, laid shadows like leaves on his skin. Nicholas approached, and
knelt on the step.

The King said, 'I hear that you were prevented from coming. They
knew you might have saved me. Have you brought your magic with
you?'

He had forgotten Zacco might know about that. The pendulum lay
in his purse. Nicholas opened it, and laid the jewel on the bed. The
King did not move. 'Show me,' he said. 'Show me what it says.'

He knew what it said. Neverthless he lifted the thing on its cord,
and held it suspended. The King's eyes and Tobie's were on it. It
hung without movement, because he willed his mind to stay empty.
Nicholas said, 'I am sorry. There is no magic, sire. It merely finds
what is lost.'

'A soul? A country?' the King said. His voice, sapped of all timbre,
held a shadow of its old mockery.

The jewel glinted. Of its own volition it described a small circle,
and then another. The movement was soft on the skin; far from the
sharp angry flaying that tore the blood from the hand.

The King said, 'It moves. What does it say?'

Nicholas said, 'It says that birth and death are but rearrangements.
It says that nothing is born, and nothing dies. It says that there is
nothing to fear.'

'I fear nothing!' said Zacco.

'Then neither do we,' Nicholas said.

Their eyes held.

After a while, Zacco said, 'I asked you to stay. Many times. You
could have given to Cyprus all the riches, the labour you lavished on
Scotland. Did you love that King James so very well?'

From Zacco, dying, a spear in the side.

Nicholas said, 'There is only one James. There is only one Zacco,
and I am his to command.'

'Then we would have you command Death to go,' Zacco said.
'There are great things afoot; and we are too busy to leave.'

His face convulsed. Tobie said, 'Go.'

Next day the Queen came from Nicosia in a litter, accompanied by
her household and by her mother's sister, the lady Violante. Nicholas
watched Catherine approach, small, globular, pasty, progressing towards the royal apartments, evacuated to receive her. She looked
frightened. Violante, catching sight of him, turned, her eyes wide.
He saw the Queen flinch at the door of the bedchamber, and hoped
they had dimmed the lamps, or found a way to deaden the King's

sensibilities as well as his pain. He had been weaker this morning, keeping his voice and his rage for his doctors.

After the Queen there came from Nicosia a stream of officials and clerks, who were silently met and dispersed by the Constable. Among these was the royal chancellor and notary, accompanied by many strong boxes. The transfer of power had begun.

Last of all, there came to Nicholas a visitor of his own: Michael Crackbene. Nicholas greeted him tersely, for he felt angry, and Crackbene was coldly defensive and probably right. Even had he been brought back at once, Nicholas would have been too late to prevent what had happened. It wasn't Mick's fault that de Salmeton had been forced to leave his prisoner unattended. Filipe had done what he could, and was now in safe hands in Nicosia. And Crackbene had sent Tobie to Zacco.

Crackbene said abruptly, 'I'm sorry about Zacco. Was it the Venetians?'

Nicholas looked at him in surprise. Then he answered, 'I think so.'

Crackbene said, 'The King's mother is here. She came in a covered coach, with the children.'

And that was touching, as well as surprising. Famagusta was a Venetian fortress these days, guarded by Venetian ships. All the King's friends, all the disaffected lived in Nicosia, the capital. Famagusta was a dangerous place for the King's mother, as it had been for the King.

Crackbene said, 'They will ask you to stay on the island.'

'They will ask anyone to stay, who has money and arms. I want you to go to Julius at Rhodes, and bring him back here with a ship provisioned for a voyage to Venice.'

'The gold?' Crackbene said.

'Tell him to bring it, of course, if he has it; but there is little chance that he will. This is going to change everything.'

'And you are not staying?'

'Bring the ship,' Nicholas said.

The following day, in the presence of the court, the King made his will: '*Si Dieu fait sa volonté de moi, et si je meurs, je laisse ma femme, maîtresse et reine de Chypre, laquelle se trouve enceinte. Et, en outre, si elle met au monde un héritier, mon enfant aura la royaume.*' . . . 'If God hath his will of me, and if I die, I leave my wife Queen and Mistress of Cyprus: she who carries my child. And if she gives day to an heir, my child shall inherit my kingdom.'

He directed that, failing this, his heir should be chosen from his other three living children. He asked that on his death, all those imprisoned for rising against him should be released; and all his galley-slaves freed.

Those who left the chamber were weeping. There remained, now, only the nominal doctors whose task was to make his death easy, and the priests who filled the chamber with incense, and the murmurs of intercessory prayer.

Nicholas saw him once more, in a slow procession of men who entered the room and knelt to kiss the King's hand. He did not think that Zacco recognised him.

Late at night on Tuesday, the sixth of July, 1473, James of Lusignan died.

Earlier that evening, in a quiet rumble of wheels, a wagon set out, carrying three sleeping children back to Nicosia, escorted by the King's personal guards. After the death, no bells were rung. Only the lights remained burning all night in the tall windows of the King's marble palace; and in the Latin Cathedral of St Nicholas the painted glass glimmered, and the divine chant of ritual music, hoarse and low, hung on the warm scented air. In the stables, a lévrier whimpered.

Freed at last, Tobie went to the room of his partner and said, 'I have to take you somewhere.'

Marietta of Patras was not weeping. She had been making preparations to leave: servants ran to her command, struggling with painted chests and stiff leather boxes. Dismissed, they closed the door, leaving Tobie to usher in Nicholas, as she had asked.

She had come from her son's death-bed, but the kohl round her eyes was untouched. Only she had torn off her veil, so that they looked at the obscene crimson stump of her mutilation, and no illusion remained of the looks she once had.

She said, 'You will, of course, forsake us at once.'

Nicholas said, 'I am sorry, nobildonna.' Tobie didn't look at him.

The lady said, 'Quite. *Pour loïauté maintenir*. If the King failed to win you, who else could? Doubtless you will also abscond with the treasure.'

There was a pause. Nicholas said, 'Honoured lady, I know of no treasure.'

'Indeed?' said the King's mother. 'Yet my son referred to it in his will. A great treasure, gathered with pains and kept secret. But he did not say where it was.'

'I cannot help you,' Nicholas said.

She looked at him. 'You think not. Well, perhaps we shall see. Come with me. I have something to show you.'

In a locked room, his hands bound, sat a man.

David de Salmeton of the Vatachino was not now, Tobie was gratified to see, the superb miniature beauty of Cairo and Cyprus: the curling dark hair was tangled; the pure jaw bruised; the long finger-nails broken. His eyes, darker than Zacco's, were sunken.

His voice, none the less, was successfully sardonic. 'You, too! Come and join me. Now the goose is dead, all will wish to quarrel over who killed it.'

'Hold your tongue,' said Marietta of Patras. 'You yourself, in your greed, have ensured that while you hunted, M. le baron did not. They may not have thought of blaming you now, but they will very soon. Especially since you are held here, and impotent.'

'They?' said David de Salmeton calmly. But his fingers were tight.

'The Venetians. You killed the King, and tried to kill this merchant, they will say, out of jealousy.'

'So why are you here?' said the prisoner. His knuckles were torn, Tobie saw. However effeminate he liked to appear, David de Salmeton was well made, with a compact, muscular body. And yet . . .

The King's mother said, 'I am here to ask a service of this man, your rival. It is for my son, not for myself. I am going to ask Lord Beltrees to drop the charges against you, and let you leave Cyprus.'

'The papers are already lodged,' Nicholas said. 'My deposition, and that of the former page-boy Filipe.' It was the first time he had spoken since entering.

The cropnosed woman lifted her hand. In it were two folded documents. She said, 'In such confusion, it was not very difficult to have them abstracted.'

'I have copies,' Nicholas said.

'You should keep them. But I propose to destroy these.'

'Why?' said David de Salmeton. 'To have me fall into some accident as soon as I leave? Assuming Ser Nicholas were simple enough to allow me to leave?'

'That is for him to decide,' said the woman. 'If the Venetians cannot be made to pay for their crime, I am determined that at least they will lose their chief scapegoat. If you live, of course, you can never come to Cyprus again, and will forfeit everything here that is yours.'

'The sugar?' said David de Salmeton. 'You would give Kouklia to the Banco di Niccolò?'

'The Banco di Niccolò,' said the woman, 'may name its own price for any position, any property, any business it may desire on this island. But I gather that it would decline.'

The bound man laughed. 'He knew he could never rely on you.' The laugh caught.

'Ah yes,' Nicholas said. Tobie looked at him. He had spoken quite softly. His eyes, steady and sober, rested on the other man's face. He said, 'Tear up the papers, my lady.'

'Why?' It was de Salmeton's voice, sudden and shrill.

'For his sake,' Nicholas said.

Chapter 45

L ITTLE BOATS CARRYING cherries, or cheeses, or sprats bring the world its bad news, long before the dispatch of solemn embassies. So rumours spread to the marketplace. But before even that, fast-beating pigeons and riders and swift, secret galleys make sure that the world's leaders know what there is to know, even though they may conceal it.

Thus the news of James of Lusignan's fate crossed the Middle Sea many weeks before the black-robed ambassadors formally presented their tidings to Pope Sixtus and the Republic of Venice, or the Knights of Rhodes and the late King's half-sister Carlotta, or the Sultan Qayt Bey in Cairo; and long before an arrow borne by a racing dromedary reached a distant Persian battlefield and changed the fortunes of a prince.

One of the swifter ships, although not the swiftest, belonged to Nicholas de Fleury. The Banco di Niccolò conveyed its own first-hand account to the West; while behind, the body of a King was gutted, embalmed, and consigned in a funeral of little ceremony to the Cathedral of St Nicholas, Famagusta, denied even the marble sarcophagus his friends had tried to acquire. In Nicosia, the oaths of allegiance to the Daughter of Venice were taken, although the Venetian Bailie was unwilling to walk in the streets until supplied with a guard. A military parade was arranged, at which the spectators were to shout, 'Long Live Queen Catherine!' Queen Catherine herself clung to the safety of Famagusta, and refused to leave for the capital until her father, Marco Corner, winkled her out.

The journey to Venice was unlike any other Nicholas had undertaken in recent years. It had more in common with that long-ago voyage from Trebizond when all three, Nicholas, Tobie and Crackbene, had sailed home like this, repeating their news without respite; reminded everywhere that they were leaving behind a land open to darkness and violence.

Julius was not with them. Crackbene had beaten his ship into Rhodes to find that Julius had left the island three days before, embarked empty-handed for Venice and Germany. Anna his wife had gone with him.

'Germany?' Nicholas had repeated.

'Well, someone had better be there, if you want to know what Duke Charles will do next. And the lady Anna could help; she's a German.' Crackbene had been in a bad temper.

They sailed into Venice on Saturday, the seventh day of August, after a voyage in which Nicholas had been uncommunicative throughout, except when he had been required to repeat, yet again, the news of Cyprus. Sometimes Tobie did it for him, experiencing always the same disbelief and despair. Approaching Venice, he found to his dismay that they were bringing evil tidings to a Republic already in mourning: their stuttering Doge, just two years in office, had died.

For themselves, Tobie did not know what to expect. He shrank from the reunion with Gelis and the child, and with Gregorio and his little family. He remembered that the nurse, that self-opinionated termagant, would be there.

Through the heat of June and July, Jodi had made Venice his playground, while his mother waited, and worked. Then Julius had come, bronzed and smooth with contentment, and brought his black-haired Anna, wed but unchanged, with her light, pointed wit and amiable manner. She played with Jodi, and spoke to Mistress Clémence of her own daughter, left in Cologne. When it was time for Julius and Anna to leave, Gelis almost shared Margot's regret.

A little time later, a fast ship swept into the San Marco Basin by night and, dropping anchor, put ashore a man in a hurry, who went straight to the black-mantled Palace. By morning the galley had gone. On the surface, nothing had changed; but Gregorio came late from the Rialto that day and, instead of joining the family, went at once to the counting-house. Returned at length, he could only explain that the Bourse was uneasy, no one could quite say why. It was a question of waiting.

As once before, Gregorio himself was on the Rialto when the ship he was hoping for was signalled into the Basin. This one did not come under cover of darkness but anchored for all to see, flying two flags: the emblem of the Order of the Unicorn from its mizzen, and from its mainmast, the standard of the Order of the Sword, in the position of mourning.

The Bank's boat was already tied by the Bridge. Gregorio used it to sweep down the Canal and out to the anchorage while Nicholas was still on board with the officials who had come out to greet him. Tobie heard the lawyer's hail and met him at the companionway. He looked sick.

Gregorio said, 'What has happened?' He looked about for Nicholas.

'The King is dead. Long live the Queen,' said Nicholas from behind him. He looked worse than sick: he looked unfriendly. He added, 'I have to go to the Senate. Wait for me, if you like. Mick and Tobie will tell you what has happened. Is Julius here?'

'No. They've gone to Augsburg. Nicholas –'

'Yes?' said Nicholas, stopping.

'Were you there?'

'Everyone was there,' Nicholas said.

The news, passing from throat to throat, reached the Ca' Niccolò long before Gregorio returned with the travellers. Margot brought it to Gelis where she stood on the balcony overlooking the water.

'Nicholas is back, safe and well. They've just sailed in. Apparently Gregorio went down to meet them.' She saw that Jodi was there, sitting at the feet of his nurse. She said, smiling, 'Ton papa est en retour.' Mistress Clémence was looking elsewhere.

Gelis said, '*Nicholas!*'

'Sooner than he expected,' said Margot. She looked from Gelis to the nurse and back again. Mistress Clémence returned her attention to Jodi. Margot said slowly, 'They're saying that Zacco has died.'

'Oh,' said Gelis. Then she said, 'That explains the uneasy market. The news must have reached the Collegio already.'

'They say he was poisoned,' Margot said.

'But they didn't blame Nicholas,' Gelis said. She paused. 'Unless, of course, he has raced back, the Catalans screaming murderer at his heels?'

'Apparently not,' Margot said. 'I think they might even have wanted him to stay. I think we should be glad he has come back.'

'I don't know,' Gelis said. 'There are generally rich pickings to be had from a power struggle, if you don't mind the risks. But I expect he wanted to come home to us all, as you say.'

After that, everyone in the Casa seemed to know that the padrone was at last on his way, having reported to the Minor Consiglio on the tragic death of Queen Catherine's husband. The Palace itself had confirmed it. Sadly wild, as everyone knew, the young man had apparently indulged himself on a hot day while hunting, and had succumbed to an attack of the flux.

The travellers arrived. Mistress Clémence, standing in her

employer's hall, released Jodi, freshly dressed, to be crushed by his father and was pleased to observe Dr Tobias crossing to greet her. She said, 'It has been an unpleasant business for you all.'

'We shall all be the better for being at home,' the doctor said.

She followed his eyes. Instead of commenting, she said, 'You must have met with the flux often enough in the battlefield.'

'Well enough to know it,' he said.

She studied him. She said, 'So they let you treat the King? They must know your reputation.'

'Eventually,' he said. 'But it was too late.' He paused and said, 'The padrone and he knew each other well.'

'I can see that,' she said. 'The child will cheer him. I heard the Queen of Cyprus was near to her time?'

'I doubt if it will cheer her,' he said.

Nicholas was back, not in the autumn, but in August. Gelis, too, saw all that the others saw in his face, and felt the alteration at once, as he greeted her. Invariably, in the first moments of every fresh meeting, he showed his awareness of her, even if expressed by contradictory emotions like anger. Now, for the first time, he seemed indifferent.

She was given no opportunity to question him. A ceremonial supper had been arranged, attended by all the gentlemen of the factory. Afterwards, in the relative privacy of Gregorio's parlour, Tobie appeared intent on wresting Nicholas from the company. Gelis raised her voice.

'Before you go! Mistress Clémence is sure to ask me your plans. Are you leaving to rejoin Astorre?'

'No,' said Nicholas. 'The French war has stopped, for the moment. All the interesting events seem to be occurring along the Duke's frontier with Germany. I shall probably follow Julius to Augsburg, and then try to seek out Duke Charles.'

'And Mistress Clémence?' Gelis said. 'Or are children not permitted in Germany?'

He knew, of course, that this was not about Jordan. It was about whether the careful plan had been changed, and she might come to him now, rather than later.

He said, 'Margot says you have grown to like Venice. Why not stay for a further few weeks, and then join me?'

She couldn't tell whether he meant it. Gregorio sat, his arm round Margot, placidly awaiting her answer. Tobie glared. Gelis burned with frustration. She said, 'I don't mind. Jodi might: he has been practising hard on the water-hens. Must you hurry away? What exactly happened on Cyprus?'

He looked at her. His eyes were darkened, like Tobie's, and he had been drinking nothing but water. She had asked the question out of pure devilment; she was taken aback when he replied with subdued violence.

'Exactly? Zacco died, but I didn't. I was abducted, not very tenderly, and left without food or water, and chained. I not only survived, but I wasn't there when Zacco fell ill. You have no idea what good fortune that was. Princes envied me.'

Gregorio said sharply, 'You didn't tell us! Who did it? Nicholas, was Zacco poisoned? By the Venetians?'

'Probably.'

'And you were abducted to get you out of the way?'

'Oh no,' Nicholas said. 'I was abducted by someone paid by David de Salmeton, who hoped to extort a ransom for me which would disable the Bank.'

'But you escaped?' Gelis said.

'I escaped. And de Salmeton was caught and imprisoned. As a result of it all, I am not, at the moment, deeply attached to the *miraculosissime civitas Venetia*, and would rather be somewhere else. On the German frontier, for example.'

'And David de Salmeton? Are we meant to believe all this?' Gelis asked.

'Do you find it hard to think of sweet David in quite these terms? Tobie doesn't.'

'Nor do I,' Gregorio said. 'I hope he's dead.'

The owlish gaze had turned directly on Gelis. She said, 'Is he?'

'No,' Nicholas said. 'Not even in prison. I let him off. Aren't you pleased?'

'*You* let him off!' She gazed at him.

It was Tobie who answered, his voice curt. 'The King's mother asked Nicholas to let him go, and he did. Of course, de Salmeton can never return.'

'So where has he gone?' Gelis asked.

'There are several possible places,' Nicholas said, 'if my prayers have been listened to. But he may be somewhere else, and quite happy, bathed in a saintly light and enjoying intimacy with God. So, you want to come with me? With Jordan?'

She had goaded him, and he had replied. She stared at him, dizzy still. Then she said, 'It might be amusing.'

'It might be. Can you be packed by, say, tomorrow?'

'That's asking a bit much,' said Tobie.

'Is it? You don't need to come,' Nicholas said, getting up. 'Neither does Gelis. I imagine she can get herself over the Alps on her own.'

'Will you stop it, Nicol?' said Gregorio. 'Go and rest, for God's sake. But before you do, here's something I haven't told you yet.'

'There is no end to the Divine Bounty,' Nicholas said. 'So what have you found for me now, outside perpetual chastity?'

Gregorio ignored it. 'You remember Paúel Benecke?'

'Yes,' said Nicholas. He sat down again.

'He had a stroke of luck,' Gregorio said. 'Back in April. He was hanging about in the Narrow Seas in a caravel when he saw these two Florentine ships leaving Sluys for Southampton.'

'Goro?' Nicholas said. His eyes had begun to gleam.

'So he attacked and relieved one of its cargo. The other escaped. There's been a great fuss.'

Margot was smiling. Tobie was looking from one speaker to the other. Nicholas said, '*Florentine* ships?'

Gregorio said, 'Well, really, Burgundian ships. The ones that were built for the Crusade, and Duke Charles let the Medici use them.'

'*Tommaso's* ships?' Nicholas said. 'Tommaso Portinari?'

'I'm afraid so, yes. The one they plundered was the *San Matteo*. Full of alum and stuff. They'd wintered in Flusa, and were calling at Southampton on their way back to Porto Pisano. Benecke took the whole lot. The thing is, he was sailing under letters of marque, and his ship belonged to some Confrérie of the Church of Our Lady in Danzig. They'll never get it all back.'

'Alum?' Nicholas said. He looked dreamy.

'And cloth: gold and silk and velvet and satin. Furs and tapestries. Paintings, even. Poor Henne Memling.'

'Goro,' Nicholas said. He rose and, carrying his seat in his hand, relocated himself next to Gregorio. Then he put a hand on his shoulder. He said, 'Tell me very slowly. I don't want to get too pleased too soon. Henne Memling?'

'Two huge altar-pieces,' Gregorio said. He was crimson now. '*Huge*. On their way to be put up in Florence. And one of them was *The Last Judgement*.'

'Paradise,' Nicholas said. 'And Hell, of course. And all those nude ladies and gentlemen. Including Tommaso, with his head painted on foil, and someone else's bodily ticket to the Gates of St Peter. And Paúel Benecke has it: not Tommaso, not Angelo Tani, not the Medici. Oh, what shall we do? How can we celebrate?'

'Give me that,' Tobie said. He emptied the cup Nicholas had been drinking from, and thumped it back down by the wine-flask. He said, 'That's how you celebrate.'

'Oh dear,' Gelis said.

Margot touched her with a finger. 'Come with me. We can drink on our own.' She was exchanging smiles with Gregorio.

'In the terems,' Gelis said mildly. She tried not to show what she felt. Nicholas drunk had always been easier to manage than Nicholas tinkering about with the full unappetising range of his faculties. She had an advantage already.

The advantage was somewhat short-lived, in that the journey to Augsburg was sober to the point of austerity, and Nicholas spent all his spare time with his son. At night, he slept with the men of the party. Tobie had elected to come. Crackbene had stayed behind, prior to departing north on unspecified business. There were Hanseatic League talks in Utrecht.

Gelis had a grasp, now, of the purpose of this expedition to Augsburg in the vale of the Danube, where the Emperor and his princes conferred. Here, if anywhere, rumours and news could be gleaned. She would have liked to learn more, but attempts to discuss it with Nicholas failed. Eventually, roused to impatience, she professed an enquiry to which he was bound to respond. Now they had met ahead of time, had he considered advancing the end of the contest?

They had just passed through the Tyrol, and he was impatient because they had failed to meet either Duke Sigismond or the Duchess. Anything that annoyed Nicholas always gave pleasure to Gelis, whether she understood it or not. Unwisely, she showed it.

He said, 'Our resolution? I hadn't planned to advance it. Well, especially not after this terrible reverse over the Duke. Did you have a proposal?'

'No. Were you expecting one? I hear the lady Violante was in Nicosia.'

'You are speaking of an elective bid, rather than a proposal.'

'Which you accepted.' She kept indignation out of her voice.

'It would have been impolite to refuse,' Nicholas said.

'So you suffered it. *Noblesse oblige.*'

'I try to give humble satisfaction. A fervent fighter and untiring soldier of Christ. Although I have been known to charge tronage fees,' Nicholas said. 'One way or another. Here is Jodi.'

'So I see,' Gelis said. 'What a teacher your son is going to have in you one day.'

She had fired her dart, and he had replied, as in Venice. She had achieved nothing.

At Augsburg, they were met at the gates.

'God's toe-nail,' said Julius, when he had greeted Gelis and Tobie. 'It's like the Flight from Egypt. I never expected to see Nicholas de Fleury hanging with napkins and nursemaids and children.'

'You missed the cartload of whores,' Nicholas said. They went in by the Ulm gate. 'And what about you? Whoever thought to see Julius with a *wife*? How is your extremely beautiful, extremely brave lady?' He shook the hand of his agent and they all began to move through the port.

'You want me to say, sick of a morning. Well, she isn't. Time enough for all that. She's staying with friends. And my God, what good news from Cyprus! Venice with the whip hand at last! Now the Bank will get its chance!'

Nicholas said, 'You should have stayed on Rhodes and joined in the rejoicing.'

'I know, but I'd done all I could. The Patriarch, too. I have to tell you about that.'

'I heard it from Gregorio, or most of it. The Order insists it hasn't stolen our gold; the ship they attacked was a pirate; if we want to prove the gold ours we have to produce witnesses, bills of lading, hard evidence. We shall, when there's time. I didn't think you'd be here. I thought you would have left after the Emperor.'

In present company, Julius seldom bothered with tact. He said, 'I stayed to tell you what to do. You've to go to Luxembourg.'

'Really?' said Nicholas.

'Yes, really. Take your objections to the Duke, but not in that tone, I'd suggest. He's in Luxembourg. He wants you. He and the Emperor are going to meet. Charles thinks he's going to be crowned this autumn at last. Think of the festivities! Everyone will be there!'

'Where?'

'They haven't decided yet,' said Julius, happily.

It was a very long road to their lodging. Nicholas rode smiling, because they were drawing attention. He said, 'The festivities. They want us to advance them more money?'

'Oh, that too,' Julius said. 'But they also want practical help.'

'Practical help,' Nicholas repeated. His mind ran over the areas of contention in Europe, all the way from Denmark in the north, to lucky Cyprus under the Venetian whip. He said, 'What kind of practical help?'

'The Duke's heard of your Play,' Julius said. 'He wrote to Scotland, and asked if he could borrow the machines and the music and the artists for his coronation. He offered King James just about anything he wanted, except Guelders, and James has agreed. He's sending the lot.'

'*What?*' Nicholas said. After a moment he said, irrelevantly, 'He can't do it: it's mine.' In fact it was the King's, but the King hadn't paid for it yet. Disbelief filled him, followed by outrage. Oblivious, Julius was continuing.

'You'll get a fee. You'll get a double fee. You'll get a triple fee, because the Duke insists that you yourself direct the company. It's an order. He wants to hand a complete team of players to Frederick. You're his gift to the Emperor,' Julius explained. 'So that the Emperor can contribute to the festivities. I don't suppose they have entertainers in Vienna, apart from a few German clowns and a juggler. And Duke Charles can spare you. He's still got all the artists who worked under *Tête Bottée* Commynes for the Wedding.'

'Commynes has gone,' Nicholas said.

'Well, he wasn't the only one, was he? Anselm Adorne will direct this time.'

Tobie said, 'What's the matter? People are watching. Stop screaming.'

Nicholas said, 'I shall scream if I like. So will you, when you hear this.'

At the time, he didn't even pause to consider how the Duke knew so much about the Play. Certainly, he knew less than nothing about its significance. Nicholas perceived the Duke's attempt to appropriate him personally simply as a miscalculation; and not an intentional insult. It was something that could be corrected by a few words with Chancellor Hugonet. He said as much to Julius and Tobie that night, sitting alone with them in the tavern. Julius had been astonished and puzzled.

'It can lead to great things. Look what it did for you in Scotland. You'll have the Emperor's goodwill as well as that of Duke Charles.' And, when Nicholas still appeared unconvinced, Julius had become genuinely heated. 'Why not? If Adorne doesn't think it beneath him, why in God's name should you?'

'Sloth and other vanities,' Nicholas said. 'I have no ambition. I shall go to Luxembourg and tell his noble and mighty lordship myself. You can come with me. The Flight from Egypt can remain until they hear from us.'

Julius said, 'You aren't serious? Tobie, persuade him.'

'I'm staying,' said Tobie. 'If he's going to castrate himself, I'd as soon not be present. Let him go on his own.'

But of course, Julius would never do that. They left for Luxembourg the following day, two men and a bodyguard riding fast for the Imperial duchy on its river-girt pinnacle where Charles, Duke of

Burgundy, was gathering his resources for the lavish ceremonial and
hard talking that would, he hoped, make him a king.

The Duke received him in audience, but it was William Hugonet who
induced Nicholas to reconsider his decision. The meeting was private,
in the Chancellor's rooms in the towers of the Castle of Luxembourg,
with the sluggish waters crawling below in the heat.

It had already struck Nicholas that he might have been hasty. He
was being summoned to prepare court diversions, that was true. But
he was to prepare them for Frederick, from whom Duke Charles
wished a great favour. He, a Burgundian and a banker, was being
placed at the Emperor's side during a series of talks which would
determine the union by marriage of two immense powers; which
offered Duke Charles the chance to become King of Burgundy, King
of the Romans and, perhaps, eventually, Holy Roman Emperor
himself.

For days, for weeks perhaps, Nicholas would have a foot in both
mighty courts. He had begun to guess why. Now Hugonet confirmed
it. A tired, busy man with all the weight of the Duke's deficiencies on
his shoulders, the Chancellor made clear what Nicholas de Fleury
was being requested to do. He was to join the Emperor's court, when
it arrived. He was to urge the Duke's case when he could. He was to
listen. And he was to report.

And that, he could agree to.

Nothing happened at once. It was the third week of September
before the Emperor, at Mayence, sent to invite the Duke of Burgundy
to his congress of princes. It was to begin on the last day of the
month, and the place appointed was Trèves, the great and ancient
city of Augusta Treverorum, a day's ride from Luxembourg. Nicholas
could go there himself now. He could send for Gelis and Jordan and
Tobie. And Julius could send for his wife.

He had already told Julius everything. It would have become
obvious enough, and Julius could be discreet when it mattered. He
hoped that Julius would join him, with the rest of his team, in the
Emperor's lodging. With Anna, if he insisted.

He had sent, by now, for all the men and the materials that he
needed. He had summoned John le Grant and Astorre, with their
ceremonial guns and their agile squadrons of horsemen and jousters.
He had retrieved from all their comfortable positions the scribes and
musicians and painters who had helped him before. The crates from
Scotland arrived, although none of the Scottish musicians or artists:
he had countermanded the Duke's request about these. He need not
trouble busy men with a tiresome sea journey from Scotland.

Before he left, the drought had unwillingly broken, with enough rain to spoil the vintage and half fill the cisterns, but not enough to restore all the mills. By then, Luxembourg had assumed the appearance of a mighty Burgundian camp, with every house on the rock full of billeted officials, and two thousand tents crammed into every available stretch of high land or sward by the rivers. They quartered an army. They sheltered the ducal treasure and wardrobe and artillery. They housed the regalia of the ducal chapel, with its priests and players and choristers. They lodged the men of the travelling council. They accommodated the household officials and servants. And in a stone house on the mount, the great goldsmith Loyet was preparing a crown and a sceptre.

Everyone Nicholas had ever known in the Low Countries seemed to be there; there was no time to meet them all. He encountered René, new-chosen Duke of Lorraine, whom he had last seen in Provence two years before, at the start of the long journey which would lead to the court of René's grandfather in Angers, and beyond. He glimpsed Tommaso Portinari, and failed in his half-hearted attempts to evade him. Indeed, he was quite surprised at the strength of Tommaso's fingers, haling him outside the room where they happened to meet. 'Benecke!' Tommaso had said.

'What?' said Nicholas. He thought what a paintable face Tommaso had, with the high cheekbones and close-curling hair and sensitive face. He looked furious.

'Benecke,' said Tommaso again. 'You knew him in Iceland. He let you load up all that illegal stockfish. Did you tell him to steal my alum?'

'No,' said Nicholas. 'I've got my own alum. I might have wanted the painting, but I'm told it isn't really you. That is, the only part that's you isn't a part. Tommaso, who was it? Can I tell Benecke? He might send it back for a repaint.'

'So how did he know what the *San Matteo* was carrying?' Tommaso said. By adroit manoeuvring, Nicholas had got him outside his workshop. He opened the door and everyone inside looked up. The smell of fresh paint and vellum and oil flowed from the room. Julius waved.

'I don't suppose he did,' Nicholas said. 'Everyone knows you're rich and your ships are worth stealing, that's all. It was sailing under the Burgundian flag. If the Hanse won't respond, get the Duke to complain, but not yet. If Benecke walked in just now, he'd just crown him.'

Julius howled.

'Which reminds me,' Nicholas said. 'You're handling all the Duke's silks for the ceremony?'

'Yes,' said Tommaso. Julius had put a large cup in his hand.

'Well,' said Nicholas, sitting down comfortably, 'Julius and I are going to need yards and yards and yards of good silk for the Emperor's throne room and costumes and tableaux. Suppose you tell us what you have.'

Nicholas left soon after that, with Julius and John and Astorre, plunging down the Luxembourg cliff to set off north-east to the vale of the Moselle, the wagons rumbling behind him, and the long cavalcade of his craftsmen and soldiers trotting after.

It occurred to him that he had missed the arrival of Anselm Adorne and Jan his son, and of course Dr Andreas. He had not missed, but had deliberately avoided the other astrologer. And among all that vast crowd representing the flower of Burgundy there was one man, he realised, who must have been there all along, but had remained out of his sight until this moment when he waited, amiably sitting his horse by the towered portal, and who took off his hat and waved it as they passed.

Julius said, 'Wasn't that . . .?'

'Martin of the Vatachino,' Nicholas said. 'Tommaso's informant, no doubt.'

'I smelled the sulphur,' said John le Grant. 'I hope he's got David de Salmeton with him. By God, I'll . . .'

'No, you won't,' Nicholas said. 'Or not until I've finished with them both.'

Chapter 46

THE MESSAGE FROM Nicholas to his wife arrived in the other town of Augustus among an assortment of missives, some to his agent, and one to Tobias his doctor. He had also dispatched a small saddle, to which was attached a packet containing a drawing, a verse, and a note. Jodi pounced on them all.

During the four weeks they had been waiting in Augsburg, Nicholas had communicated with them quite often, and they had not been neglected. Tobie knew the city a little, and the agent was anxious to please. Twice, the former Anna von Hanseyck had travelled from the castle where she was staying to introduce them to friends; on a third occasion she had brought her host and kinsman, who had pressed Gelis to come and stay, an invitation she had refused with regret.

Tobie had been relieved by the refusal. He had been extremely taken with Anna, and had been forced to recognise the urbane, civilised company that Gelis could provide when she liked. But this was a family far more vulnerable than most, and for this space, he had been appointed its guardian.

Nicholas, leaving, had implied as much, without being explicit. He had talked of Jodi, and of the other boy who, unknown to most, was also his, and of the promise they had given to protect Henry.

'You have kept it,' Tobie had said. 'So far as you could.'

And Nicholas said, 'Not at Veere. If he had killed Jodi at Veere, I would have killed him.'

'But Henry isn't here?' Tobie had said.

'No.' After a moment, Nicholas had said, 'Tobie? Once, I gave you a paper. Do you have it?'

He had it. It was a document, drawn up and signed, which would prove, if it had to be proved, that Henry was the son of Katelina van Borselen and Nicholas vander Poele, now de Fleury.

Tobie said, 'It's with my notary. Why? Do you want it?'

'Not if you don't mind keeping it. But I wondered. Would you consider it a good idea to give a copy to Father Moriz?'

'I think it would be an excellent idea,' said Tobie slowly.

'You shouldn't have to bear all the onus. Did you know that Moriz was a native of Augsburg?' Nicholas had asked.

'I'd forgotten,' Tobie said.

'He might have friends; even kinsmen,' Nicholas said. 'I only mention it in case you come across them by accident. Both my sons, I am sure, are quite safe. But after Cyprus . . .' He let the sentence tail off. His face, for a moment, had looked younger than it was, whereas apprehension with most was an ageing emotion.

Tobie said casually, 'I was sorry to hear about Tasse. She might have helped you.'

He could see Nicholas draw breath, and then release it. Then he said, 'I was sorry, too. Jodi would have been as fond of her as I was.'

That was all. Then he had gone, and now the message had come, summoning them all to the Abbey of St Maximin outside Trèves, where the Duke of Burgundy, its protector, was taking up residence. Gelis brought it to Tobie, and with it, a note from a different quarter.

'From Anna,' she said. 'To tell us she's gone to join Julius in Trèves. He and Nicholas are attached to the Emperor.'

'She is German,' he said. 'She is almost in the position of hostess. And the message from Nicholas? He wants you to stay with the Duke, not the Emperor?'

'He seems to think it is safer,' Gelis said. She paused, and Tobie looked up. She had pale blue eyes, very clear.

She said, 'You know what our marriage is like? You know we compete?'

A war of attrition, Gregorio had said. And Gregorio was not a doctor. 'Yes, I know,' Tobie said.

'And you think us both childish. Perhaps we have both begun to think so, as well. Recently, we took a decision to end the competition this winter.'

'And end your marriage?' Tobie asked.

She noted his professional voice, and laughed. 'Will it harm Nicholas even more, you are wondering? I don't know. Whoever prevails on the day of reckoning will determine the fate of our marriage. And Nicholas, it seems, is even more anxious than you. This letter asks me to consider advancing the date.'

'Why?' Tobie said. 'Or as you suggest, is it just from impatience?'

She smiled again. 'I should like to think so, but no. He is assigned to the Emperor's household, and unsure what will happen, or where he will be asked to go next. October in Trèves is not so very far short of December in Bruges, where he expected to be. He suggests that, when the Duke receives his reward, so should he.'

'So he is certain of winning?' said Tobie.

'He is always certain of winning,' said Gelis. 'It is why he plays. And victory never brings him contentment, because he always chooses to play the wrong games.'

'I saw the Nativity Play,' Tobie said.

The smile vanished. She said, 'I am not going to lose him to that.'

'So who decides which are the wrong games?' Tobie said. 'You, if you win?'

'I am going to win,' Gelis said, and got up. The letters were crushed in her hand.

Tobie said, 'Well, I shan't try to stop you. Was that what you wanted to know?'

'You couldn't stop me,' she said, and walked out. Looking after her, he felt both exasperation and pity. He wondered how in God's name the outcome of a contest was supposed to create a bearable, never mind a lasting relationship. Unless, of course, the seeds of it were already there, and the implacable rivalry was not what it seemed.

Nearly fifteen hundred years old, the city of Trèves had once, for ten glorious years, been the capital of the Roman Empire of the West, and the home of the Emperor Constantine and his mother St Helena. Trèves had been attacked by the Franks and the Vikings, but her past could still be discerned: her two greatest churches marked the sites of Constantine's holy basilicas; the southern gate occupied the ruined Imperial Baths; and the northern port was close to the great Porta Nigra, the massive original entrance, twelve hundred years old, whose upper tiers, ninety feet high, dominated the city.

At the peak of its fame, eighty thousand people had inhabited the great marble city of Trèves: its Prince-Archbishop was one of the Empire's Electors, and Imperial Diets were held in the halls which, very soon, would be occupied by the Emperor Frederick and his train. Over the years, the throne room of Constantine, roofless now, had been transformed into a spacious central courtyard, its apse forming a tower, and its mighty walls of red brick provided with wall-walks and defences. Around the courtyard and beyond it were ranked the lodgings, the service rooms and the guest-quarters of the Archbishop's Palace. To these, Nicholas came with his men.

His reception by the Archbishop was muted: Jean de Baden knew all about Trojan horses, and so did his brother the Margrave. *Please the Electors*, Hugonet had reiterated, and Nicholas did his best, in between acquainting himself with the town, and the Archbishop's household, and those officials of the Emperor who had arrived ahead of their prince. He was not going to run about painting anything. He was merely going to supervise certain small helpful devices, decorations, performances and martial and musical diversions carried out by his own expert staff and agreed beforehand with his Archiepiscopal and Imperial colleagues.

The last person of the advance party to join them was the most decorative, and also the most unexpected: the former Gräfin von Hanseyck. Julius, his arm proudly about her, brought her into the room that they shared. 'Look! She hired a bodyguard and came straight from Augsburg. You remember Anna?'

Dark hair, violet eyes, a spine like the curl of a fern. 'Who could forget?' Nicholas said. 'She owns half the *Fleury*. No, of course I remember her for many much better reasons, not least that she has had the valour to marry you. I am going to toast your good luck all over again. Is my wife here as well?'

'Well, kiss her!' said Julius.

'I think,' said the demoiselle Anna, 'that you will find her in the abbey of St Maximin very soon, with your son and Dr Tobias. I was able to leave Augsburg a little more quickly.' Smiling, she stepped forward and offered her cheek, and as he kissed it, touched his arm and spoke softly. 'I wished to say how sorry I am about James de Lusignan. It is a long friendship severed. You must have been glad you were there.'

'Except that he might have been accused of poisoning him, if he hadn't been knocked on the head,' Julius said. 'The Vatachino! Do you know whom we saw outside Luxembourg? Martin! Martin, who . . .'

She moved back, and Nicholas went off to find wine and collect the others. Julius was happy, at least.

On Wednesday, the twenty-ninth of September, the Holy Roman Emperor arrived at the gates of Trèves, a day ahead of his guest. With him came two thousand five hundred nobles, four Electors, and Maximilian, his son of fourteen: blond and long-faced and sullen. Also the refugee half-brother, aged twenty-five, of the Ottoman Sultan. Like Tom Boyd, like the princess Zoe, like Sandy of Albany in his time, Calixtus Ottomanus was being fostered as a potential puppet. Everyone did it.

Two thousand five hundred German noblemen settled into the city of Trèves, and Nicholas was sent for to the Archbishop's Palace. At fifty-eight, the Emperor had a lined, bearded face with drooping eyes, and a bush of reddish hair to his shoulders. *Pene stupidum*, the late Pope Pius had called him. Almost stupid, but not absolutely so. This was a man who, apparently indolent, had controlled an empire of millions for thirty-three years, and kept all predators at bay, largely by limping sideways at the right moment. If his son married Marie of Burgundy, Maximilian would be the richest young man in the world.

The Emperor, it transpired, considered himself fortunate to have the services of the distinguished Nicholas de Fleury, Baron Beltrees, and congratulated him and his colleagues on the appearance of the streets. He examined, with faded curiosity, the renovated table fountain that John had produced for him, and uttered a question or two about the Bank which Nicholas answered with care. The Emperor knew all about the Banco di Niccolò. The Cardinal Bessarion had stayed at the Imperial court in his time, as had the Patriarch of Antioch and the Emperor's impecunious cousin, Duke Sigismond of the Tyrol. Sigismond, who had been so unsurprisingly unavailable recently, since behind everyone's back he was promoting a lunatic war with the Swiss.

Frederick knew precisely what force the Bank could or could not exert; and what it was worth in Imperial politics. That was what Nicholas counted on.

He returned to his work, and the master plan for the Duke of Burgundy's Entry tomorrow. Gelis had not yet arrived, but there was no cause to be anxious as yet. The journey from Augsburg could take well over a week, and she would have a heavy armed escort. The place where she was to stay, the town-like Abbey of St Maximin outside the city, was in a continuous uproar, as the officers of the Duke and the Abbot strove to prepare for the coming descent. Very early, Nicholas had used all his authority to secure rooms for his wife and her party. He would be sent for, he hoped, when they came.

There was no cause for anxiety, except that he had made a proposal. (*Were you expecting one? I hear the lady Violante was in Nicosia.*) Looking into the future, he had concluded that he dared not wait until December for their dénouement. The game should end before the board changed.

He believed she would be ready. The Duke's stay would last, surely, for most of October. He credited her with good planning; and he thought that, whatever her schemes, she should be able to advance them so far. And so the day of the Duke's victory would also be his. With all that entailed.

On bad days, he faced the reality. She might turn it down. She might insist on the original agreement. She might even now be on her way to Bruges, and he would have to wait suspended like this, until the end of the year. Suspended; bound as in Kouklia; while all the harvest, the sweetness might wither and die.

He should have stopped sooner. He could have stopped early this summer, but it would not have given her a fair chance. And there had been other things he must do.

The Duke came before she did, and the Emperor rode out from the city to meet him. His procession, rank upon rank, proceeded between cheering crowds along the main street of Trèves, sumptuously draped and beflagged by courtesy of Nicholas de Fleury and Tommaso Portinari and the Duke. The chevaliers pranced in the van in their glittering armour; after them marched the crossbowmen, followed by the trumpets, the heralds, the drums. The princes. The yellow-haired Archduke Maximilian side by side with the sallow young Ottoman princeling. The Prince Electors of Mayence and Trèves and behind them, his naked sword raised, the Marshal of the Empire, preceding the Emperor himself, astride a magnificent white stallion, and followed by the bishops and the rest of the nobles.

The Emperor was dressed like a Turk, in a golden robe embroidered with pearls, and bore what appeared to be a nesting swan on his head. Seeing him emerge from the Palace, Nicholas and Julius, ready to mount, had simply turned and silently shaken each other by the hand.

'That's my boy,' Julius said, quoting Astorre. Then they fitted themselves into the procession.

They were therefore among the first to emerge from the city and see, coming towards them, the procession of the Emperor's humble subject Charles, Duke of Burgundy. It was quite hard to discern detail at first, because the sunlight shone blindingly upon what appeared to be a river of mercury: fifteen thousand solidly helmeted men to the Emperor's lightly clad twenty-five hundred. Before them trotted an angel throng of a hundred handsome blond pages in blue and cream doublets, followed by a phalanx of silken-clad trumpeters and a body of the archers of the Duke's guard in their livery. After that came the fourteen sapphire-crowned heralds, a cavalcade of prelates, ambassadors and Knights of the Golden Fleece in cloth-of-gold robes, and finally, an escort of six thousand horse, followed by interminable lines of baggage and guns. The horse-cloths were gold, and fringes of bells on the harness were shocked into a fury of tinkling every time the trumpets gave tongue.

The Grand Duke rode in the middle, glistening in a golden cuirass and a black velvet cloak starred with jewels whose worth, at a quick calculation, amounted to a hundred thousand florins at today's rates.

The cavalcades stopped; the principals dismounted; the Duke knelt and was raised by His Imperial Majesty, who embraced him. They entered the city together, and spent half an hour in the marketplace, hats doffed, disputing gallantly over who was to escort whom to where. Eventually, the Duke left for St Maximin's.

Nicholas and Astorre, Julius and John repaired at last to their lodgings and were able to give voice to their feelings. John was the first to frame actual words.

'Man! Man! It was like two cooks selling meat on the causeway! All as sweet as you like, until the one fetches the other a blow on the haffet! His hat! His curly-toed slippers! Oh!'

'And the Duke's diamonds,' said Julius. 'Christ, Nicholas. Did no one know how to stop him?'

'With Tommaso there selling?' Nicholas said. 'And it's worse than you think. He's brought the Crown of Light, and the Golden Lily with the True Cross, and the twelve statues of the Apostles in gold, and the four angels and the ten jewelled crosses, and all the tapestries. It's got a hint of a message, of course: "Look how rich you might be when your Maximilian has married my Marie." At the same time, I do agree, it makes poor Turkish Frederick look like a Gibichung counting his toes. *Vero stupidum.*'

'That's all right,' Julius said. 'That's why you're here. All you have to do is sweet-talk Frederick and the Electors into crowning the Duke. Ha, ha.'

'I don't mind him being rich,' Astorre said, mopping up gravy. 'He's paying us.'

So began the Great Encounter, which was to dazzle the world with its jousts, its banquets, its pageantry for week after week through the whole of that strange, heated autumn.

The real events were less visible. The circumspect private meetings between the Holy Roman Emperor and the Grand Duke of the West remained private. The frequent hard-working meetings between the highest ministers of both parties were too passionate to escape notice entirely: rumour described the raised voices and the thumping of fists and the sudden departures, and occasionally reported that, listening to Hugonet, the Duke was inclined to pack his baggage and leave. But always, he relented.

Rumour also spoke of a third set of meetings, initiated by the Emperor on the command of the Pope. Nicholas knew about these, after coming face to face in an anteroom with Ludovico de Severi da Bologna, Patriarch of Antioch.

It was then the end of the first week of the conference, and Gelis had still not arrived. He had looked for her at the opening ceremony in the Abbey of St Maximin, at which the Archbishop of Mayence had exhorted the Duke to save Christendom from the maw of the pagan, while Calixtus Ottomanus sat picking his nose. The Chancellor Hugonet had replied with two hours of Latin oratory deploring the turpitude of Louis of France, who alone chained the Duke to his duchy. The Emperor, placed under a tapestry of Alexander the Great, had been clad in crimson and gold, and his son's long yellow hair rippled over a grand robe of red and green damask. The general impression was rich, but not smart.

Leaving afterwards, Nicholas had crossed the Abbey courtyard with Julius and his lady wife Anna. It was full of friends and spectators from the guest-lodgings.

Anna said, 'She isn't here yet, Lord Beltrees. I had someone ask. But I believe another friend has arrived. Anselm Adorne is a well-disposed man who, I think, would be glad if you made peace with his son.'

He had been transparent, it seemed. There was no reason, however, why he shouldn't see Jan Adorne, despite their disagreement at the White Bear Society. Since then, Nicholas had met the young man's father when passing through Bruges, and noted the changes that a year as a widower had brought. Anselm Adorne still carried the weight of that death, but his eyes were clear again, and he looked, if anything, younger. Now, coming to the door of his lodging, he smiled at Nicholas as he ushered in Julius and his wife. Jan hung back, his cheeks flushed against the severe black of his cap and his gown. Anna greeted his father, and then walked at once to the young man and spoke frankly.

'I've brought Julius to apologise about Rome. Will you forgive us? That silly boy Nerio bewitches everyone, and truly, Julius was looking for me, and not Zoe. You probably still think he deserves someone like Zoe, but I am not proposing to agree with you there. He is a very kind husband, when he stops to exercise his wits.'

Her smile, tentative, appealing, sought for a response, and received it. 'It was a long time ago,' the Cardinal's secretary said, with uncertain echoes of his father's style in his voice. 'I have forgotten it. And I cannot grudge him the charming lady wife he now has.' And when Nicholas, smiling a little, offered his hand, Jan flushed deeper, and took it.

Later, when the day and their talk had advanced, Anselm Adorne spoke, his eyes on the couple, to Nicholas. 'I cannot grudge Julius, either, this beautiful paragon, but it poses a mystery. How he find such a lady, and persuade her to marry him?'

'I don't know. She wanted half a ship,' Nicholas said. They had talked of nothing of consequence, because his mind was empty of everything of consequence. Nothing had touched him since he had sent that message to Augsburg: not the poetry; not the small, exquisite tableaux; not the music. He worked without thinking. Others drew up contingency plans; and prayed that the conference would come to its end while the weather remained mild and sunny, and the sewers were manageable, and the provision barges and wagons could travel, and the mills and the brewers had water. He could plan only from day to day.

He left his thoughts to find Adorne speaking. '. . . with her fiancé. Of course, she had to display him in Ghent, and in Bruges. But she should be joining us any day now.'

'I'm sorry?' Nicholas said.

Adorne looked amused. 'Kathi. Katelijne Sersanders. She is contracted to marry at last. And of course, you can guess to whom. But I am not going to confirm it. She wishes to tell you herself.'

Four days after that, Nicholas found his path blocked by the large, unkempt figure of the Franciscan Ludovico da Bologna, Patriarch of Antioch, carrying a dead duck on a string. He had recently shaved. He said, 'Ah. Lord Bullturd, I hear. Follow me.'

'Belchtrees,' Nicholas corrected, entering the small chamber after him. He thought, felicitously, of something Julius had told him. 'And how is Antioch, *le pissoir?*'

The Patriarch paused, clearly pursuing the phrase. At last: 'Nerio the sodomite,' he said with satisfaction, closing the door and dropping the duck on a board. 'Whose mother you resorted to with such vigour in Cyprus. Hadji Mehmet was shocked. And then you have the impudence to turn your back on Persia and Venice, who have kept that indefatigable envoy her husband so conveniently busy elsewhere?'

Nicholas walked across to the table and picked up the duck. He said, 'Are you saying what I think you are saying?'

'Or you'll ram that where I will enjoy it least? I said what you thought I said. Nerio is the son of Violante of Naxos. Watched you, did he?'

Nicholas dropped the duck on the floor and sat down. He said, 'Christ.' After a moment, he gave a half-laugh. 'Who was the father?'

'I'll tell you one day,' the Patriarch said. 'If you make it worth my while. So you don't like what Venice did, and have bolted to Burgundy?'

Nicholas said, 'I don't like what Venice did, but I didn't bolt. It was my plan all along. Burgundy and the Emperor.'

'Burgundy, the Emperor and the East. Now you can have power in them all, if you want,' the Patriarch said. 'That's what our meetings here are about. The Emperor has appointed a commission of Germans and Burgundians to study the Eastern question. I have the Pope's sanction to drum up money and armies. I'll get conscience money at least out of the Emperor and the Duke, and the troops they finance could be yours. Did Bessarion speak to you?'

'Yes,' Nicholas said.

'And you liked what he said, but won't throw your weight behind Venice. So what about other places that need help against the Grand Turk? Uzum Hasan isn't Venice, although he'll use them. Caffa on the Black Sea isn't Venice.'

'It's a Genoese colony,' Nicholas said.

'Not entirely,' said Ludovico da Bologna.

'In any case, the answer is no,' Nicholas said. 'Or not at the moment.'

'Not at the moment?' said the Patriarch in astonishment. 'How long would Lord Bullbelch wish the Grand Turk to wait? Two years? Three?'

'I have something to resolve,' Nicholas said.

'Well, resolve it,' the Patriarch said. 'She rode in today with that mountebank doctor. She'll be at the banquet tonight. Do you need someone to tell you how to wipe your own nose?' He stood up. 'I'll pick up the bird. I don't trust you.'

'Why ever not?' Nicholas said.

The banquet followed a mass at St Maximin. The Duke, not the man to solicit advice, had clothed the Abbot's halls of reception in cloth of gold embroidered with pearls, and himself in a golden robe to match, edged with scarlet and laden with jewels. The Abbey blazed with the Duke's chapel ornaments, and the banqueting chamber contained a complete suite of tapestries and his famous nine-storey credence stacked with gold plate. The guests sat at eighteen tables, and the meal lasted for four hours, during which forty-two courses were served.

'He's a bloody fool, isn't he? Look at the unicorns,' Julius said, nudging his padrone. There were three of them, cast in pure gold, and worth a middle-sized duchy.

Then he said, 'Ah. Pardon me for interrupting. You've noticed Gelis.'

At the end of the four hours, when he had got rid of the others, Nicholas made his way under the hanging lanterns to the two great inner courtyards, still full of subdued conversation as guests sought the fresh air. He had thought Wolfaert van Borselen might be with her; she had been seated beside him. But in the event, it was Tobie who peered down to see who was knocking, and Mistress Clémence who opened the door.

The nurse smiled, which was altogether unusual. 'My lord. The Lady will be happy to see you. I am afraid Master Jodi is asleep.'

'I should hope so,' he said, smiling back. 'And I shouldn't dream of disturbing him.' He had learned to be patient. It was nearly six weeks since they had met; but Jodi was nearly five now, and knew about absences. Then she went off, and Tobie came, with a curious mixture of alarm and relief on his face, and offered to take him to Gelis.

He clearly knew, or thought he knew, what was happening. Nicholas said, suddenly ruffled, 'Well, for God's sake get some wine and come with me. Introduce me. You've taken long enough to get here.'

'It's all right, Tobie. He's in a bad temper. It was a tedious supper,' Gelis said. She had come out of her chamber. She looked the way she had at the van Borselen table, with the light on the jewels in her hair. She looked like a fine drawing, whereas Julius's wife reminded him of a painting on gesso.

She said, 'Aren't you coming in? Both of you?' And when he moved forward she added, 'Ah. You haven't been drinking water.'

'I was nearly driven to it,' he said, 'once or twice. But I wanted to stay mellow for you.' He couldn't remember what day or week he had stopped drinking water. He was sober, he thought. Sitting down, he observed that she was extraordinarily at ease. But then she knew, as it were, that she had come.

Tobie handed him a cup and said, 'I've watered it. Presumably you don't want to be too mellow for the Emperor. So tell us the gossip. Everything.'

He told them a few things that he thought were especially funny, and Tobie talked about Augsburg and their journey. Gelis contributed, but mostly inspected him as if looking for rust. After a while Tobie got up to go to bed. 'When shall we see you? Are we allowed into the city?'

'Astorre will be extremely annoyed,' Nicholas said, 'if you don't come to the jousting. But normally, it's probably easier for us to come here than for you to come to the Archbishop's Palace. It depends how long it's all going to go on.'

'What is your guess?' said Gelis.

'Too long,' he said.

Then Tobie had gone, and Gelis said, 'Are you as drunk as you look?'

He realised he was standing, and sat down. He said, 'I sent you a message.'

'Is that all you can say?' Gelis said. 'No convincing arguments? Seductive persuasion?'

He said, 'I assumed you would have made up your mind. You usually have.'

'And you despair of changing it?'

'I may not need to. You are here.'

'You think I don't have the courage to refuse you to your face?'

'No,' he said. 'I have a more flattering reason. I think you are clever enough to have shortened your campaign to suit. I think you have done all you want to do, and that you are prepared for a settlement now.'

'Now?'

'When the Duke's business is done, and we are both free. Free to hold our accounting. Free to go where the winner chooses to go.'

'I meant to ask,' Gelis said. 'Who decides who has won? Should we not have an outside adjudicator? Nicholas?'

He shook his head. 'If you wish. I don't mind.'

'Good. But I shan't ask you to select one tonight. I doubt if you could. Let me send you home safely to bed.'

He found he was standing again. He said, 'You haven't answered me yet.'

'I thought you did it for me,' Gelis said. 'Of course I am ready. Come to me when the congress is over, and we shall arrange ours. Perhaps.'

He thought, afterwards, that her voice had sounded strained. He supposed his own had not been natural, either. So near, now.

The jousting, led by the Bastard Anthony, took place the following day in the marketplace before the guild church of St Gangolf. The gilt and paint on the tall houses sparkled, and their handsome mouldings and turrets and facings reflected the blare of trumpets and the rattle of drums and the roars of the banks of spectators. A battery of light guns occasionally banged. At noon all the churches added their muddled clangour: the measured beat of the Bürgerglocke, the chimes from the Church of Our Lady and the Cathedral. Astorre and his best men took part, and all the noblest seigneurs, including Anselm Adorne and the ablest Knights of the Golden Fleece, among them the Grand Bastard and Louis de Gruuthuse. Their shadows flickered back and forth along the west side of the marketplace: black on red walls; black across ranks of sunny faces, polished as apples, rapt and joyous.

The next day the princes disagreed, and were reconciled yet again. Two days later, the Emperor was entertained by the Duke, and the following day, the Duke was entertained by the Emperor. Nicholas went to see Jodi.

Gelis was absent, but Tobie was there, and Mistress Clémence. Poems were discussed, and the habits of pigeons, and the saddle was demonstrated. Tobie said, 'What's happening at the Palace?'

'Stalemate,' Nicholas said. 'The Duke wants to be King of the Romans; Frederick is hesitant; the Duke has laid down his terms. No coronation, no daughter.'

'He could get it,' Tobie said, 'if all seven Electors agreed. Couldn't he?'

'In theory,' Nicholas said. 'But even in theory, I've only got three of them bribed, and that isn't enough. But I'm working on it.'

'You're joking,' Tobie said.

'Yes,' said Nicholas.

November came. The sun shone. The beer began to run short, and the bread became black. Nicholas, who had not been entirely joking, cultivated the Prince Electors within reach, and Anna, who occasionally joined them for supper, commented on it.

'I don't think that even you, Nicholas, will manage to convert the Archbishop of Mayence. And two of the Duke's greatest opponents are not here. Brandebourg and the Count Palatine are bound to vote against him.'

Recently, by permission of Julius, they had begun to use Christian names. Nicholas said, 'You don't think Fritz le Mauvais might have a change of heart? No. But it only needs one conversion to tip the balance. And of course, if the Emperor decides he wants Charles to be King of the Romans he will be, no matter what.'

'In fact; but not for public consumption. And I don't think he will. There is too much French being spoken in Trèves.'

'Agents? Spies?' He had heard nothing.

'Gentlemen paid by King Louis. Or so I hear. The Emperor is afraid of a vassal as powerful as Duke Charles. To appoint him his deputy, his successor, is a big step. There are many persuasive arguments against it. The Emperor listens to these. He listens to astrologers. He is jealous of his inheritance. All his books bear the initials A E I O U – *Austriae est imperare orbi universo*. To Austria belongs the empire of the whole world.'

'So he is fulfilling his Imperial Vowels. The Duke's motto is *Ainsi je frappe*. I can see the difficulty. But of course, the Duke has no interest in temporal power. Rather, he sees himself as God's secular vicar on earth, bringing peace to the Imperial garden.'

'I thought you were in his employment,' said Anna, amused.

'That's what Astorre keeps reminding me,' Nicholas said. 'But then, I'm in everyone's employment at the moment.'

He saw nothing of Gelis, but a great deal of everyone else. Nothing moved; nothing budged. He forced himself to attend meals, and to watch what he drank, and to appear calm. He avoided Tobie.

The farce continued. During the first week in November, the Emperor decided to invest the Duke of Burgundy with the Duchy of Guelders and did so, enthroned on an open-air platform on the jousting-place in his crown and full regalia, surrounded by a forest of banners. The Duke, entering the city in dazzling procession, paraded three times round the marketplace, climbed the steps and, kneeling before His Imperial Majesty, inaudibly did homage for the duchy King James had once hoped to seize, and was invested with it.

Nicholas, exchanging signals of self-congratulation with his other exhausted organisers, felt no surprise. It was bound to happen. What was significant was that it had happened just now. A sop. A sop because Charles wasn't going to get very much else?

He had appropriated for himself a high window in someone's expensive merchant building from which to overlook the performance. His eye, idly roving, fell on the spectators at another similarly tapestried window. Someone waved.

He waved back, the sun in his eyes, and found that he was looking at Anselm Adorne. Beside him, he thought he saw Jan, and several people from the van Borselen household. Finally, he observed that someone else was waving even more vehemently: someone so small that the grimly ceremonial caul on her hair barely reached her uncle Cortachy's shoulder.

Kathi. Katelijne Sersanders. Everyone's friend.

And beside her, his hand raised in greeting, the diffident, smiling face of Archie of Berecrofts.

Nicholas failed to join them. Instead, he observed his usual custom, and mustered his hard-working friends at the beer barrel till bedtime. When he rose, rather late, the following morning, it was to find that he had a choral interlude and a playlet to arrange, and someone wished to consult him on the subject of fireworks. He wondered what the fireworks were for.

He learned, in time, that they were for the Duke's fortieth birthday, a week hence. He became extremely occupied with the Emperor's contribution. Just before the due date, a number of rumours began to be heard in every tavern, during the hours they were able to open.

The Duke had been refused the crown that he wanted, and had been offered another. Nicholas swore.

A French spy was discovered, and hanged. Astorre provided the drums.

Anselm Adorne sent an invitation, which Nicholas was unable to accept.

Tobie arrived and wanted to know why he wasn't visiting Jodi. The Duke was still thirty-nine, and Nicholas was feeling queasy as well as unfairly harassed. He said, 'Because I think I'm going to have to arrange a coronation. Would you like to do that, and I'll play with Jordan?'

Tobie, who was thoroughly pleased to be released from the nursery, stopped looking about him and sat back expectantly. 'So it's true? The Duke's agreed to lower the price for the marriage? No King of the Romans? No future Lord of the World?'

'It hasn't been announced,' Nicholas said.

'No, but rumour has it that he's settled for a Burgundian crown under the Empire. All his estates erected into a kingdom. *Plus* the duchies of Lorraine, Savoy and Cleves. The Grand King of the West. They say they've agreed on a date.'

They had. The coronation would take place in twelve days.

He had forgotten to respond. Tobie said, 'Which allows you and Gelis to plan. Doesn't it? You said you would end the war then. You look as if you need to end something. What is it? Last-minute qualms?'

He said something. He wished Tobie would leave, and soon he did.

The next day, he had to go to St Maximin's for the Duke's birthday. He called on Jodi. Gelis was there, her hair elaborate, her face tinted. She said, 'Do we have an appointment?'

He couldn't take it lightly. He didn't want to think about it at all. He said, 'The twenty-fifth of November. I shall prepare to be crowned.'

He was leaving, fast, when Kathi called to him over the courtyard. He slowed and turned. She was alone.

She said, 'I don't want you to avoid me.'

'I've been busy,' he said. 'The coronation. Your birthday, of course.'

'St Catherine's Day. They could hardly avoid it. The Bride of Christ. Do you think Maximilian looks like Christ?'

'Perhaps. If someone had just told him something that upset him,' said Nicholas. 'His birth-chart, for instance. Look, I'm expected. I'm sorry.'

'I know. Never mind. But would you meet me some time? Before the coronation? Before I'm twenty, and responsible for my actions?'

'Where?' he said. He thought of the crowded streets, the packed Palace, Abbey, courtyards.

She said, 'Outside. I thought of the river, downstream. It would be quiet on the banks.' She paused and said, 'Would you mind very much if I brought him with me?'

He had already agreed. He couldn't change his mind now. He saw her eyes as he left, but couldn't remember where he had noticed that look before.

Chapter 47

MANY TIMES BEFORE, as his suffering partners knew, Nicholas had delegated the work of the Bank to his managers. Until these last moments in Trèves, he had seldom abandoned one of his own personal projects. Now he did. The others could manage. He had no heart for it, or mind for it, either. The others could deal with the conclusion of the great conference which was to make Charles a king, but which still withheld, for the season, what he had yearned for. In the pending magnificent ceremony, for which he had come so well prepared, Charles would be crowned King of his own expanded duchy. And in return the sixteen-year-old Marie, his daughter, would be promised to the Emperor's son.

For John and Julius, it could have been worse. The preparations were already half made. Plans were far advanced for the Cathedral. The crown, the sceptre, the cloak and banner lay already burnished and brushed, and fit to be displayed in the Church of Our Lady. The thrones were being regilded; the cathedral hangings were in the hands of the jewellers; the erection of tribunes had begun. Banners were being painted and sewn, vestments chosen. The Archishop of Mayence sent for his exceptional jewels and began to rehearse the coronation mass and anointing. The masters and choristers of all the choirs started meeting in session. The tailors made and delivered robes and cloaks, doublets and sleeves, gowns and headdresses for the nobility of both sexes.

The week before his enthronement, the future Charles, King of Burgundy, ordained and presided over a series of extravagant entertainments designed to dumbfound his hosts, and to express his gratification at the outcome of the past seven weeks. Nicholas made a token appearance. Then he left to keep his appointment with Katelijne Sersanders, and the man, the Scotsman she had chosen to marry.

It was then the third Saturday in November, and the coronation was five days away.

*

Until now, the glorious weather had held. Watered by the light rains of September, the countryside had burst into a second flowering. Cherries ripened, trees blossomed; the vines above the Moselle, picked into October, were thick-perfumed and heavy with juice. Even yet, it was warm; although the mornings in Trèves were veiled by a softening mist which lingered until an hour or two before midday, blotting out the low hills about it, so that even the further bank of the broad river vanished.

Now it was mid-afternoon, and the sun was yellow and mild as Nicholas made his unhurried way out of the flagging city. The Imperial boats, with their banners, lay bright and clear in midstream, while the jetties were crowded with barges, and the arm of the toll-crane whined and palpitated. Upriver, the water combed through the nine massy piers of the bridge, thirteen centuries old, and flowed on past the pale city walls, winding north-east between vineyards and far-off afforested hills to where, eighty miles off, it would enter the Rhine at Coblenz.

Nicholas turned along the right bank, the gentle breeze fresh in his face. No one looked at him twice: no one heeded a man strolling at leisure, dressed in an anonymous pourpoint and cap, with a satchel over his shoulder. Soon he had left the bustle behind.

The river curved. There was no long view of either bank. On the opposite side, a low red slabby escarpment cut off the sky, with sunlit trees at its foot like gold fountains. There were trees on his side as well: some bright as embers, some laden with heraldic red and white berries, some with broad yellow flags. A baldaquin of living *gros point*, better than Hercules, or Alexander, or Jason.

There were fields beside him now, with cows, sheep. A fisherman. A hamlet, with the single piping voice of a child, talking, talking. Then silence again; the quack of a duck; the metallic chirp of a finch, and the soft hush at his side of deep water. He didn't look for her, because he knew she would watch for his coming. She had wished this for him: this solitary passage, robbed from the hubbub. Then she called, and he heard her.

She had found a vine arbour outside a small, crooked tavern. The fruiting was over: the leaves arching over the wooden table were yellow and large, half concealing sprigs of deflated black grapes. She had been seated facing him, opposite Archie, whose light hair he could glimpse. She jumped up. Like himself, she wore simple clothes: a plain cloak, with her brown hair scattered unbound over it. Not to be unbound, of course, for very much longer: protocol was strict about that. Her face, roused to colour by the fresh air, wore an expression he might have called resolute; then she ran forward saying,

'You came.' Berecrofts rose and emerged from the arbour as well.

It wasn't Berecrofts.

It was Berecrofts; but it wasn't Archie. It was Robin.

To show nothing would have been the second greatest feat, perhaps, of all his thirty-two years of play-acting. To respond with immediate cheerfulness, as he did, was the greatest.

He said, 'Kathi! I understand, of course. All those weeks on the *Svipa*. Father Moriz has issued an ultimatum. Come and be kissed.'

She came and, holding his arms, lifted her cheek. Not an Icelandic kiss, this time. He already knew, from their faces, that there was no question of an enforced marriage, or he would never have joked. He turned to Robin. Robin, who was half his own age.

He had matured, both in appearance and manner. That had already become obvious. He had the compact build and fresh skin of his father, and the steady gaze which was all his own. He was well born and landed; not only the son of a merchant. And two years ago, at the time of the Florentine ball game, Robin of Berecrofts had been placed under his own hand, to be trained as a gentleman, as a squire, as a knight. Most of Robin's skills were inherited, but the rest had been learned from Nicholas de Fleury of Beltrees. He had given Kathi her husband.

Robin said, 'You didn't come to see us. We thought you were shocked.' He was smiling, but his eyes held a shadow.

Nicholas said, 'I think only the truth will serve here. I didn't see you at that window with Kathi. I saw your father.'

'And now?' Robin said. 'I know I am young.'

'Are you young?' Nicholas said. 'You never seemed so.'

'I can look after her, you see,' said the boy.

And then, suddenly, Nicholas was swept by proper feeling; for this was true. Death had always been close to Kathi, fetterless sprite that she was. She had faced it, and was stoical. But now she had an anchor, a shield. A resolute person who was both of those things, but also high-spirited, and courageous, and quick. So, of course, was Archie his father. But Archie was his own age.

Nicholas saw that he had no right to think of himself, and Kathi in relation to himself. She was matched with Robin. The bravery she had shown in Egypt and in Iceland, had been equalled by Robin on the battlements of Edinburgh Castle; at the Markarfljót. He owed Robin his life. That moment of wordless reunion with Kathi, never spoken of since, had been vouchsafed him by Robin, whose face, triumphant, content, he could visualise now, printed against the cold snow, under the flamboyant skies of Hlídarendi. Kathi had fought to bring Nicholas his son; Robin had not only loved Jodi but, protecting him, had suffered hurts and humiliation in silence.

And for little reward. After Diniz, after Felix, Nicholas had distanced himself, of intent, from all the impressionable young who wished, eager, affectionate, to enter his life.

No longer. No longer for this one, at least. The boy waited, his eyes steady and clear as a shepherd's. Nicholas laughed with sudden pleasure and, walking over, gripped Robin by the shoulders, as he might a drinking-companion, and turned him round into his arm. He said, 'I am so glad about this.'

The boy's face melted. 'Now you have both of us,' Robin said.

Smiling, Nicholas shook him and let his arm fall, moving on. The water lapped. A leaf of gold kid eddied drunkenly down to the grass; his eyes followed it. Sunk beside it was the satchel he had brought. Nicholas lifted it with meticulous care. He said to Kathi, 'I have brought you a present.'

She recognised the pouch as soon as he placed it before her, and studied it as it lay on the table. Then she opened it slowly, and drew out Glímu-Sveinn's chessmen.

She said, 'No.' Her eyes were wet. The boy looked from her face to that of Nicholas.

Nicholas said, 'They were given to me in Iceland for a service in which we all shared. I should like her to remember.'

'Take them, Kathi,' Robin said. And she took them.

They called for wine then, and he made them talk and then laugh, while they drank it. They were to be married quite soon. The story of Paúel Benecke and Tommaso's picture was the success of the afternoon. By the time they walked back, the sun was yellow and low, warm as amber; and a barge, overtaking them, flitted upstream like a dragonfly, with a light at its muzzle and two fine silver wings on each side.

They had talked of the white bear. They had said nothing of death, or divining, or music, or the greatest spectacle in the world, which was God's own work, or the devil's. They had said nothing of Zacco. He wondered if they knew of Uzum's two great defeats. He wondered if they knew that Zacco's son had been born, six weeks after his death. He hoped they did not know – but they probably did – that he and Gelis would come to the end of their particular road on the day that Duke Charles was crowned.

There was no reason for them to be concerned with any of these things, for they had each other. He wondered how Nostradamus had known.

*

At the gates of the Archbishop's Palace he was met by the Chancellor's secretary, saying, 'Where have you been? You must come at once.'

He thought of arson, armed conflict, serious breaches of etiquette at the Duke of Burgundy's conspicuous celebration. Even when he reached his own room and found Hugonet pacing his chamber, he felt only impatience. Then Hugonet said, 'Are you not being paid well enough? I need your help. A matter is developing which must be dealt with, and before the Duke hears. I have to go to St Maximin. You must talk to the Emperor's men. You must do what you can, and I shall come back and continue tomorrow.'

'What is it?' said Nicholas. He paused. 'The Emperor wishes to change the date of the coronation?' He had ordered his life, so he thought. He had ordered part of it, at least; and was about, given time, to marshal the other. He realised he was incapable of waiting very much longer.

Hugonet said, 'He wishes to withdraw the crown. He wishes to countermand the coronation. He must not be allowed to.'

The dreadful campaign began. For two days, furious ministers met, and the secret of the potential disaster was confined to the reverberating walls of the Emperor's chambers. Outside, the Duke's gracious festival ended, and his guests thronged back, refreshed, to wrestle with the astonishing, the profligate, the ruinous preparations for his crowning. Astorre and John and Julius were among them. Nicholas, closeted with Hugonet's officers, was sworn to secrecy, and the Duke's state of divine exaltation was unimpaired.

It could not continue for long. On the third day, the Lord of the World summoned the Burgundian Chancellor and delivered his final decision. It was just before midnight. Afterwards, Hugonet called upon Nicholas. When he had gone, Nicholas sent for his partners.

They came, blinking, in bedgowns. Nicholas sat, fully dressed, drinking water. He said, 'Sit down. Prepare for a shock. The coronation is cancelled.'

They looked at him. '*Merde!*' said Astorre.

'Why?' said John.

'Someone, no doubt with a French accent, has persuaded the Emperor that a greater Burgundy would threaten the Empire. Frederick wants the matter dropped now, and brought up at a Diet next year.'

'Mother of God! Does the Duke know?' Julius said.

Nicholas glanced at the hour-glass. 'Not yet. Hugonet will break the news. Then the Emperor will send his official regrets later tomorrow. The day after that, the Duke will be called to the Palace for the final leave-taking, at which he will be shown every honour. I quote.'

'That's Thursday!' Julius said. 'He's leaving on the day he was supposed to be crowned! My God. The Cathedral. The robes. The hangings. The carpentry. The provisions . . .'

'And all we've done,' said John slowly. 'Nicholas! The choirs? Everything gone?'

'Not at all,' Nicholas said. 'Move them around. The street decorations can stay; everything else can be stuffed into the Palace for the Emperor's reception on Thursday, barring the crown and sceptre and banner, of course. At least the Duke's leave-taking should be spectacular, and the Emperor will have to foot all the bills. You can start on it tomorrow. Today. I have to go to the Abbey.'

'The Duke'll be mad,' Julius said. 'But I suppose that you feel you must go. And you'll want to arrange what to do about Gelis.'

'That was in my mind,' Nicholas said.

He had sent her a note, asking her to receive him on Wednesday. Today. Even now, he had not broken the embargo: merely stated that he had been forced to alter his plans. She would realise why, soon enough. Soon enough, the whole of the Burgundian court would explode, like Hekla, scorching everyone within reach. He didn't know what would happen after that, and he didn't want to wait to find out. He wanted to come to the end of this conflict, this mission, today.

Her note, agreeing, came just after dawn, brought by a man who had had to shoulder his way through the crowds in the streets. The news was out. He couldn't go out yet himself, although his own arrangements were well in hand: he had seen no point in going to bed. Now, he had been warned, he had to wait for an audience with the Emperor. He supposed he was about to be thanked and even paid for all he had done these two months, on secondment from Burgundy. For the sake of the Bank, he must comply.

The moment that he entered the Imperial chamber, he realised that he was wrong. The gifts were there on a table: a pair of silver-gilt goblets, a sable-lined cloak, a pouch, a paper folded with the Imperial seal. The Emperor sat in his chair of state, preparing to deliver them. But the man at his side was Ludovico da Bologna, who specialised in demands, not in thanks.

This time, it was the Emperor who, after the presentation, after the praise, sought to know the precise position of the Banco di Niccolò in the war against the Ottoman Turk.

Nicholas had replied, as he was expected to reply, that he was a servant of Burgundy, and that Burgundy was constrained by the threat from King Louis.

'It is understood,' said the Emperor. 'But does it seem to my lord of Beltrees that Burgundy's power, augmented by the might of the

Bank, will be directed against the Most Christian King of France? Or will it be required to waste its strength on small issues, from which the Bank might draw rather less credit?'

The voice of Sigismond of the Tyrol. The voice, even, of Eleanor of Scotland, his wife. Nicholas said, 'Highness, I understand the issues. I have to consider what will best serve the Bank. It had been my hope to return to the East representing both the Empire and Burgundy. That hope has gone.'

'Does it seem so?' said the Emperor. 'My friend the Patriarch appears to think differently. He thinks the Duke might be willing to allow us to retain your services for a little.'

'For the sake of the future,' said the Patriarch. His crucifix, big as a stirrup, reflected the unshaven part of his jowls, and his grin. 'You could take your wife and child with you. Consult them. Consult monseigneur your illustrious Duke. My lord Emperor merely requests that you give him your reply by tomorrow. He offers you material rewards, which will be made explicit. I offer you rewards at a throne higher than his.'

Then they had let him go, and he could leave for St Maximin. He spoke to Astorre, and gave his papers to Julius. He had already visited all his team. Anna said, 'But you are coming back?'

Nicholas said, 'I think it is likelier that you will all come to St Maximin. There may be ill feeling. One will have to choose one side or the other.'

She had smiled, shaking her head. 'I don't mean to suborn Julius. But I did hope that the two courts would become one. Will you tell Gelis that, whatever happens, I wish her all happiness?'

'I hope you can tell her yourself,' Nicholas said.

It was John who forced a bodyguard on him, and insisted on accompanying him to the Abbey. He was right. The people of Trèves, after eight weeks of idle soldiery and rocketing prices, had lost patience at last and, crowding the streets, were shouting abuse at every foreigner. Once, it must have seemed that the Great Encounter was going to bring a flood of prosperity to the Electorate and its capital. Now, having exhausted its supplies and its patience, the princes had cancelled the finest free show of them all, and left the citizens to the Burgundians' anger. There were no trumpeters on the Porta Nigra today.

If the atmosphere in the city was ugly, that in the Abbey precincts was one of boiling rage. Everywhere men stood in groups, and shouting sounded from casements, while servants and wagons crowded the courtyards, as the great households slowly began their dismantling. In all this, there was no likelihood whatever that

Nicholas would be received by the Duke. He could try to see Hugonet. He dismounted.

John said, 'Are ye worried? About the bairn and your lady?'

Nicholas said, 'I'll let you know when I've seen them myself. Why not go and find Tobie? I'll come later.'

Hugonet was asleep, but had left word to be wakened if Nicholas came. He sat, grey-faced, on the edge of his bed and listened. At the end he said, 'I spoke to the Duke. I recommended that, as the Duke's loyal servant, you should be allowed to remain at the Imperial court if invited. You are not, however, to take your men-at-arms, or promise them elsewhere without sanction.'

'The Duke has my word,' Nicholas said. 'I am grateful.'

It was done. Everything was done, but for one thing.

At his door, Pasque let him in, full of lustful delight over the morning of drama. She was alone, but for the Lady. Mistress Clémence had gone to the herb gardens, and Master Jodi was asleep in his room. Nicholas sent her back to her charge. Then he spoke Gelis's name, and her voice replied from the parlour. He had only to open the door, and walk in.

Five years. It was a long time for an estrangement. But for Godscalc, it would have been three, and he wouldn't have gained what he had gained; and lost what he had lost. He stood, and thought of Gelis on the other side of the door, waiting for it to open. Now, the moment of truth; no longer the fencing, the irony. He pressed the latch, and went in.

She stood facing him, motionless as a painted wood quintain. He thought of carnival-time in Bruges, and the fat, raucous child who had commandeered his company and perhaps averted a killing. The obsessive, competitive child from whom had grown the quick-tongued, vigorous girl, the magnificent lover, the ruthless opponent, and now this fine-boned, high-mannered woman with no flaw as yet in her beauty.

She said, 'Well, Nicholas?'

He did not want to begin. The hour had arrived: the culmination of all he had lived and worked for since their wedding day, and from now onwards, whatever happened, it would be different.

She said, 'I am told you have won the Emperor's favour.'

'And the Duke's,' Nicholas said. 'I can choose which to serve, or serve neither. That is all I had to establish.'

'I see,' she said. 'And now you find it hard to begin?' She still stood.

He said, 'Yes. I have no script today, Gelis, and no masks.'

'No music,' she said.

He made a sound. 'It is bad enough, without music. Do you want me to begin? Or shall we toss?' Reminded of something, he added, 'Mistress Clémence would have made a good arbitrator, except that she would learn rather too much. No one would be able to refuse her anything ever again.'

'I have an arbitrator,' Gelis said. 'Open the door.'

The adjacent room led to a passage, and to the back entrance to the lodging. It was small, no more than an antechamber; and a red-haired man was standing there, a powerful man with bad teeth whom he had last seen waving at him at the Luxembourg portal. Martin. Martin of the Vatachino.

Nicholas said, 'I thought we should be alone.' Then he stepped back and said, 'But, of course, we spoke of it.' The sense of loss deepened and spread, bringing with it a weariness which almost stopped him from speaking.

The man strolled forward, his knowing eye resting on Gelis. She hardly glanced at him. She said to Nicholas, 'Have we stunned you into silence? You want to talk of achievements, competitions. Martin is here from the Vatachino to remind you how often they've won, competing against you; how often they've tricked you and bested you; to tell you of victories you don't even know about yet.'

'How kind of him,' Nicholas said. 'He has come to apologise?'

She laughed: a small, excited laugh that he recognised; that once had been private between them, when no words had been necessary. She said, 'He has come to tell you that I work for the Vatachino. That most of their successes, and your failures, are because of my advice, my information, my help.' Her eyes were immense. Beside her, the man Martin smiled.

Nicholas said, 'Then he is your witness, not an adjudicator.' His voice was quite steady.

She said, 'Oh, perhaps. But he is here to supply proof.'

Alone with her, he would not have lied. Alone with her, he would have left aside the script and the mask, and told her as much of the truth as he dared. Then, beginning as they had begun, he would have moved, step by step, in the hope of an understanding. And one day, when it was all over, he would have told her, somehow, what he had done.

He abandoned that now, but neither did he take up his weapons. Instead, he chose the middle option, the course which he himself, in his right mind, had once dismissed.

He sat down. He said, 'If that is so, you are a threat to the Bank and a power, yes, which it would be my responsibility to appease. So give me your proof.'

*

The air in the herb gardens was mild, and the gardens themselves, remote from the turbulence at the Abbey, were reposeful and quiet. Freed from her heavy morning of duties, Mistress Clémence of Coulanges moved along the patterned walks, pausing now and then, her grey skirts slurring behind her. There were still some pansies in bloom, although the Church preferred more utilitarian plants. She saw some aristolochia, and thought she must tell Dr Tobias. If, of course, the exigencies of decampment allowed.

A voice said, 'Demoiselle?' There was a note of insolence in it. She turned.

A boy. A youth, as no doubt he would prefer to be called, of twelve or thirteen, of quite singular looks. She had last seen him in Bruges, his face swollen and bruised from a blow struck by young Jordan's father. Henry de St Pol, he was named. She said, 'Sir?'

'You don't remember me?' the boy said. He was well dressed, but hollow-eyed and dust-caked from long travelling. The sun glittered on his brilliant hair. He said, 'I thought Jordan would be with you. He is called Jordan, isn't he? The little bastard?'

There was an arbour nearby. She turned into it and sat, pursing her lips. 'His lady mother gave him his name. But I do not think if you have seen him, that you could call him a bastard. You are like your father. He is like his.'

'His father tried to beat me to death,' the boy said. 'He didn't succeed. My grandfather saved me.'

'To death? That is not like Lord Beltrees,' said Mistress Clémence thoughtfully. 'It is generally a matter of honour to choose an opponent at least as old and as skilled as oneself. But I am glad that your grandfather rescued you. Would you like to tell me about it? Or perhaps you are hungry? I have some cheese and milk in the house.'

'I am not hungry,' the boy said. He was lying. His cheeks were hollow.

Mistress Clémence said, 'Then come with me anyway. Master Jodi is there.'

'Jodi?' he said. He made it sound like a sneer.

'Men have little names sometimes,' she said. 'The name for Henry is Arigho, is it not? Dr Tobias?'

The boy sprang round like a young mastiff. Dr Tobias, quietly approaching from behind, stood still. He said, 'I came to fetch you. And do I need to ask who this is? The son of Simon de St Pol?' He had pulled his cap off, an untoward gesture he made, she had noticed, when disturbed.

'Who are you?' the boy said.

'No one who matters. A doctor,' said Dr Tobias. 'I heard you were thrashed. Lord Beltrees was beaten himself, shortly afterwards, although I am not sure he deserved it. But I think you have a family who protect you, and you should thank them.'

She was surprised. She noticed that, speaking, Dr Tobias avoided her eyes. She said, 'We were about to go and find some cheese and perhaps something a little better. Come with us.'

Only then did she notice how empty this part of the garden had become, and that there were men outside the arbour who were neither monks nor ducal officials. She saw the boy smile, his eyes bright in his narrow, white face. A man appeared, blocking the sunlight. A large, fat man who said, 'Mistress Clémence, I believe. Dr Tobias. We have heard your kind invitation and indeed, should like to accept it. A little cheese. A little milk. And perhaps even something more satisfying.'

She looked at Dr Tobias, who had pulled on his cap. A group of unknown men stood behind him. Dr Tobias said, 'Mistress Clémence, allow me to introduce Henry's grandfather. This is Jordan de St Pol, vicomte de Ribérac.'

'So you didn't suspect,' Gelis said. She had seated Martin beside her and was pouring him wine. She put down the flask and raised another. 'Water, Nicholas?' Her skin was flushed, her eyes bright. *Give her that happiness now*, Kathi had said. And Gelis was happy, even before the long catalogue of her scheming that he must listen to, that would prove that she was not just a sentient or a sensual being but an intelligent one. An organiser, an administrator. A person as competent as Gregorio, Julius, Govaerts. As himself.

'Let me think. No,' he said. 'I believe I might even risk wine.' And as she smiled and started to pour, he said, 'Of course. Isn't Gelis a short form of Egidia? And Egidius was the Vatachino's third agent.'

She said, 'I thought you would guess that. David was convinced that you . . . that you wouldn't.'

'Ah yes, David,' Nicholas said. She had hesitated, remembering Cyprus. He said to Martin, 'So you and David enjoyed working under my wife?' Martin missed it: Gelis ventured a glint of acknowledgement. Once, her name and David's had been linked. Even before Famagusta, Nicholas had been sure there was nothing in it.

'We worked together.' Martin was correcting him. 'I do not work under a woman.'

'Then for Adorne?' Nicholas said. 'Or for whom?' He refrained, with an effort, from emptying his cup at a gulp. He would have only one chance. And meanwhile, he might as well learn what he could. Martin said, 'None of us knows. The owner of the Vatachino prefers to remain anonymous.'

'Then it might be a woman,' Nicholas pointed out reasonably.

Martin stared at him with dislike. Then he said, 'Do you want to know what else Gelis has done?'

'Let me tell him,' Gelis said.

There were some surprises, and despite everything, he was glad of them. But in general, he was familiar, of course, with the areas where the Vatachino had bested him: in the sequestration of paper supplies, which had put a stop to his printing; in the alliance with the towns which had hindered his strategy in Scotland; in the Iceland expedition, which had been intended to tower over his supposed minor investment in herring.

He heard now again about those, but in terms of Gelis's personal involvement. All of it was clever. She had connived at Adorne's vital post as the new Conservator. She had learned of his new Danzig ship and had enabled it to be delayed. She had been deeply involved in Medici alum negotiations to his prejudice in Rome.

Some of it hurt. She had encouraged the Duke, at second hand, to send to Scotland for the materials of the Play, and to ask for him to come as director. It bastardised all he had done, and was an insult to Adorne's son who had died. Or perhaps only he felt that. And perhaps even he had no right to feel it.

The recital came to an end. She had proved the point he had asked her to make. She had damaged the Bank, especially in those early days in Cologne and in Bruges; and even before that, when she had set out for the Holy Land with Adorne. She had impeded his business to the point where he would have to ask her, or to force her to stop. And he could not use force.

She said, 'Well?' She looked like the girl of five years ago.

He remembered fragments of something Kathi once had said. *She may be cleverer than you are. If she will only be happy when she thinks she is, give her that happiness now.*

Kathi had been right. He had not thought so at the time. Paradoxically, his consideration then had been for Gelis: how she would feel, discovering one day that she had been allowed to prevail. And below that, another thought, born from his own experience. How, knowing what she had done – the brutalities of the wedding night; the poisonous revelations; the challenges; the cruel deceptions over the child – she would find a kind of absolution in what he, in return, had inflicted upon her. Beginning, of course, with his abduction of Jodi, and his consequent control of all that she did. For although he had invited her to leave with the child, he had known that she would not. She knew, as he did, the bond – the raw, speechless bond – that lay between them.

But now, it was different. Now, day by day, he was beginning, despite his elation, to glimpse that he had perpetrated something in the course of this feud which might deserve a far greater punishment than anything that Gelis had incurred. He had already been made to suffer by Gelis. Now, to throw away his advantage, to concede the battle, was the final restitution he could make for both her sake and his own. Then they could surely go forward, even though Gelis did not yet know what he was capable of. And after she had chosen her prize (for he was sure what her choice was going to be), he would tell her what he had done, and the reason.

So, he conceded. He said, 'I don't know what I could set against that. I could show you the successes of the Bank.'

'I know them,' she said. 'I can tell you precisely how much greater they would have been, but for me. Do you want me to stop working against you?'

He said, 'You are asking me to give in.'

She said, 'Only if you want me to stop. If what I am doing is of no consequence to you, then I shall continue. But this time, of course, I should work openly for the Vatachino. It might puzzle some of your friends.'

'It might puzzle Jodi,' he said. He saw she had forgotten Martin. She had forgotten everything, except that she had succeeded. She had forced him to comprehend, at last, what she could do. Now, she believed, he must ask her to stop.

As, of course, he must. He drew a breath. He saw her lean forward a little, and then bite her lip, for a door had opened quietly: the door to the antechamber behind her. Nicholas heard someone speak his name, and looked round. Tobie stood there.

Nicholas said softly, 'Tobie, go away.'

And the doctor said, 'Nicholas. No.'

Behind him was a boy, and a man, and a group of powerful soldiers. Three of them had faces Nicholas knew: he had fought them by the Loire close to Chouzy.

He fought them again now, as they moved into the room, but he knew it was useless. Tobie and the other man were unarmed, and there was Gelis to think of. In the end he relinquished his sword, and two of them held him until he recovered his breath and temper, and addressed the newcomers, as he should have done at the beginning. 'Monseigneur le vicomte de Ribérac. And Henry.'

'Monseigneur le bâtard,' returned Jordan de Ribérac. 'And madame. And – What are you doing here?' He was staring at Martin. His draped hat, his immense cloak filled the room.

Nicholas said, 'Won't you sit? Master Martin represents, as you know, the Vatachino. So, I have just learned, does my lady wife. We have been attempting, without much success, to resolve an unusual domestic embroglio. Perhaps, therefore, the lady might leave.'

'Unusual!' repeated the vicomte, with a vast and increasing surprise. His eyes gleamed, studying Gelis. 'The *Vatachino*! You have been acting for this contemptible firm against your own husband, madame? For how long?'

'For long enough,' Nicholas said. 'She has probably done you quite a bit of damage as well. You must take it up with her.'

He watched, out of the corner of his eye, the expressions cross Tobie's face: shock, anger, incomprehension. He wondered how this little company had forced its way into the Abbey, and then remembered that today, all the gates to St Maximin's stood open. He tried not to look at the handsome boy, at his son, who had fixed upon him from the beginning a blue stare of unwinking hatred. He tried not to wonder where Jodi was sleeping, or whether Mistress Clémence might not unsuspectingly enter the room. He speculated on where John might have gone, having failed to find Tobie. He wondered whether Adorne, if he were the anonymous employer of Martin and Gelis, might not come to witness the discomfiture of Nicholas, and remain to expel Jordan. He thought it unlikely. He wondered how long the vicomte had been in Trèves.

He said, in an interested way, 'Was it your man they hanged?'

'No,' the vicomte said. 'I am not now in the employment of France. That is what I came to discuss. But first, I am interested. Who betrayed the noble lady's guilty secret? You have just learned it, you say?' His gaze, roving, settled on Martin.

Martin said, 'She told Lord Beltrees herself. The sieur de Fleury and his lady have been in contest with one another, as I understand it, to decide who has the better talent for business. The lady has been making her case with my help.'

Nicholas glanced at him but Martin, disappointingly, failed to drop dead. Nicholas said, 'And since she has now done so, perhaps she might leave and wait somewhere else. I am longing to know why you are here.'

'I thought I had told you,' said Fat Father Jordan. He had taken a seat. It creaked, but could not be seen under the spread of his mantle. He said, 'So she has put her case. And have you put yours?'

Of all his enemies, this man could best detect what was raw, what was bruised, what was sensitive. Nicholas said, 'The debate is over. I have conceded.'

'Conceded!' the vicomte exclaimed. 'With all the tally of Nicholas de Fleury's extraordinary achievements to place on the scales! Do you tell me that the efforts of one young demoiselle, however talented, can outstrip his successes at the French Court, or in Scotland alone?'

'Forgive me,' Nicholas said. 'But since you were not here when the matter was weighed, you cannot pronounce on the outcome.'

Martin said, 'But the matter was not weighed. Lord Beltrees put no case at all.'

The seigneur de Ribérac stared. 'My dear man! You must not throw away a suit without debating it! I shall be your judge. I shall be your judge and your witness as well, for few know as well as I what you have been responsible for.'

'It is over,' said Nicholas.

'You ceded it. Why, Nicholas, did you cede it? A girl's skills against yours?'

'Because,' Nicholas said, 'I prefer to live, and I am tired of being attacked in the flesh as well as in the pocket. The Vatachino have tried to kill me once too often.'

'That isn't true,' Gelis said.

'You know it is true,' Nicholas said. 'Ask Martin here. Ask your precious David, when next you see him, how I came to be tortured, how I came to be left to drown in the cisterns of Cairo.'

'You weren't tortured,' Gelis said. 'As for the cisterns, the Mamelukes lied to him. But in any case, you got away easily.' Her brows were drawn. She looked, for the moment, like her sister.

Tobie said, 'I was there. He was tortured. He would have drowned, but for a miracle. David started it, and did nothing to stop it.'

'He said you knew about it,' Nicholas said. 'He had your ring.' He looked curiously at her face, and the horror on it, which she couldn't have manufactured. She hadn't known. He said, none the less, 'And in Cyprus.'

She said, 'He was to kidnap and ransom you.'

'Perhaps he meant to,' Nicholas said. 'But when Zacco fell ill, I was left to starve. And then of course, there was Martin, who almost managed to pitch me over the battlements of Edinburgh Castle, and sink me in Iceland. Even Sersanders, even Katelijne would have been killed, when my ship was sent to the bottom – I wonder if Adorne ever realised that?'

Martin was standing. The fat man's lazy regard dwelled on each speaker in turn. Then he returned it to Nicholas, as if encouraging him to continue.

Nicholas didn't mind. Nicholas said, 'And there was the pact between Martin and Simon. Did you know about that, Gelis? Of course, the Vatachino and the vicomte are rivals, but Martin did persuade Simon to join him in attacking their mutual enemy, the Banco di Niccolò. It was after that pact that the wagon rolled downhill towards Jodi. It was after that pact that the ice gave way in the Nor' Loch and the horse-shoes were spiked in an attempt against all of us, but chiefly, Gelis, against you.'

Martin said, 'I had nothing to do with it. Simon did these things himself.'

'Did he? Who is to say?' Nicholas said. 'But at least I can absolve Gelis from both, whatever earlier murders she was willing to help with. In these cases the Vatachino operated against her, as they did against me.' He turned his eyes to the fat man, brows raised. 'So you see, I do have reason for ceding the fight. The sooner she leaves the Vatachino, the better.'

'These are lies,' Gelis said. 'I attempted no murders.' But her voice was flat, and she was staring at Martin. The boy Henry laughed.

'Be quiet,' said the fat man softly. 'Madame, you may have attempted no murders, but you have been singularly blind, it seems to me, as to the characters of your associates. Do you still regard yourself as worthy of your husband's steel?'

Nicholas answered for her. 'I have told you. I have asked her to leave the Vatachino for the sake of myself and the Bank, which she was disrupting.'

'Which she was disrupting? Or which you let her disrupt?' de Ribérac said.

The shutters were closed, sealing off the lower part of the one handsome window. From behind them, and from the glazed upper half came the constant confused sound of wheels, and trampling feet, and raised voices. The vicomte said, 'If you shout, Nicholas, my men have orders whom to kill first. Concentrate instead on the discrepancy here. This lady says she has won. You agree. You have even named her a murderess to support it. But do we really believe that, all this time, she has deceived you? You!'

'You heard Master Martin,' said Nicholas.

'I heard you,' said the vicomte. 'It was most instructive, for it was not, of course, true. I refer to my friend Wodman, who has some interesting tales to tell of your two Scottish households, and how the one spied on the other. There were some ledgers which were left out to be seen, and others which were not. The same at Antwerp, he learned (it was expensive: your servants are loyal), and, later, at Bruges.'

'I am glad it was expensive,' said Nicholas, amused. 'You are describing what every merchant does, to confuse competitors and even the tax collector.'

'To confuse the Vatachino: my point,' the fat man said. 'And specifically to mislead the lady your wife. Certainly, there were some transactions which could not be hidden, where you had to limit the damage; and others, I am sure, which you allowed her as a sop. But it was your wife you were keeping your business from, not only Martin and Simon. Nothing ever leaked out, for example, about your real plans for Iceland. You must have given orders to someone not to tell her. Dr Tobias, for example?'

Tobie said, 'I learned about this for the first time tonight. We were all warned, naturally, not to tattle.'

'But especially, and repeatedly, not to tattle to the lady Gelis, I suspect. Come, Dr Tobias: admit it. She has betrayed her husband's plans to his rivals. Does it not please you to think that she received nothing from it? That he knew all along?'

Tobie said, 'I will not be drawn into this.' But his face, staring at Nicholas, was enough.

Nicholas swung the wine in his cup, round and round. Gelis said to him, 'You did know.' You could hear the pain of the wound. You could see it.

And so Fat Father Jordan had triumphed over them both. Gelis's shortcomings had been dragged into the open, and so had the superiority Nicholas had tried to conceal. And this time, the lie couldn't be covered. She would find out. Anyone, going over the transactions, would see how Nicholas had misled her, had taken measures to offset his losses. Nevertheless, of course, there had been serious losses. She was good.

He said, 'It doesn't matter. What you did, you did well. I couldn't have let it go on. I should have had to buy you off, or ask you to join me. That is where we shall take it up, next time.' He turned. 'M. le vicomte, what remains to be said is between you and me. Lock the others away.'

'You may be right,' said the fat man. 'Certainly, Master Martin should go. And the noble lady and her doctor may follow, as soon as we have established one thing. If there has been a contest, then certainly the Banco di Niccolò has won the chaplet, and the lady has forfeited. So soon as she admits it, she may go.'

'No,' said Nicholas. It chimed with the same word, spoken by Gelis.

'Then,' said Jordan de Ribérac, 'she must stay, and I shall convince her. There is no hurry.'

'Isn't there?' Nicholas said. 'You say that you are no longer in the French King's employment. If I called, would the Duke's men believe it?'

'It is academic,' de Ribérac said. 'You cannot leave this room unless I permit it. Your nurse stands outside that door with your son at her side, and the knife of my man at his throat.'

Gelis rose with a cry. Nicholas glanced at her. He said, 'I don't believe you.'

Martin, protesting, had been pummelled out of the room. The door shut. The boy Henry said, 'Grandfather? Will you make him come in? Let me show you?'

'Very well. Send the child in. But he is not to run to, or be touched by his parents. Is it understood?'

'Tell his nurse,' Nicholas said. He had had to know if it was true. And he had to have Jodi here, however terrifying it might be.

When the door opened again, it was to admit Clémence de Coulanges, pale as the napkin round her head except for two spots of red in her cheeks. Jodi trotted beside her. And behind strolled a man in a plate helm and cuirass whom Nicholas recognised at once.

It was mutual. 'Aye, my lord,' said the man. 'And how are your shin bones these days?' He was tossing a knife in one hand, and gripping the child with the other. Jodi, seeing his parents, reddened and struggled to run. Then he saw Henry, and gasped.

Henry broke into laughter. Henry hurled himself in front of the child, howling and waving his fists. '*Kill Jodi*,' shrieked Jodi's brother. '*Kill Jodi! Kill Jodi!*' And turned to his grandfather in triumph as the child broke into terrified screams.

'See?' said Henry. 'A coward!'

'What a boor you are, St Pol,' said de Ribérac languidly. 'Mistress, kindly bid the child stop, or we will stop him for you. The old woman was nearly as bad. Now, my lady. Shall we proceed?'

The child sobbed, the nurse kneeling beside him. Nicholas said, 'I could have killed your grandson; had him imprisoned and hanged.'

'I dare say,' the vicomte said. 'On the other hand, you needed Henry, did you not, to make others think he was Jordan? I believe the whole story is worth telling. For there is no doubt – there is no doubt at all, my dear lady, that your husband is a genius in his own way. You could never have matched him.'

'What has he done?' Gelis said. Bel's words, long ago.

'Let me tell you,' de Ribérac said. 'And you will agree he has won. And then I will kill him for you.'

Chapter 48

GELIS HAD NOT intended, she had never intended this meeting to end in extinction. On the contrary. Its purpose had been to shape her future: her future with Nicholas.

Born Egidia van Borselen in Bruges, unattractive young sister of a beauty, Gelis had been twenty-two when she had planned her life around the merry, mischievous man whom her sister, she well knew, had seduced. Katelina had always been able to take what she wanted. Even her marriage was false. She had tricked Simon de St Pol into her bed to give a name to her child, that was all. She had made a fool of St Pol. One could always do that, if one planned well enough. Gelis had been able to prove it. And if it so happened that one wanted that other, that merry, mischievous man, but wished to keep him, admiring, compliant for life, that was possible, too.

She had begun by attacking Nicholas, since she could no longer punish her sister. Aggression had become a defence, as she discovered the order of the attraction between them. Only fools, fools like Katelina, became enslaved. He would recognise her as his partner outside his bed before she became his pleasure within it. So she would keep him, as Katelina would never have done.

In all these five years, the only time she had truly imagined defeat was when he had kidnapped Jodi and vanished. Otherwise, outside death, she had been certain of winning. She had made him dance to her tune over Jodi, and in business she had wholly deceived him. The achievements of his greatest rivals were partly hers, as today she had come to declare. This day had brought, in the beginning, what seemed to be a different Nicholas, so that she had almost regretted the presence of Martin. But she meant to win, and had made her case therefore, and Nicholas, in this temperate guise, had accepted it.

But for Jordan de Ribérac, she would never have known he was mocking her. But for Jordan de Ribérac she would have taken the final step in good faith. And some day in the future, Nicholas would have turned to her and said, 'This time you were the fool, and I deceived you.'

Now that, at least, was not going to happen. She looked at him, and met his eyes, resting on hers. He said, 'I would have told you all this. I am sorry.' She did not believe him.

Nicholas stood, with the armed men behind. But now the rest of them had regrouped, as if attending an assize. The doctor sat, his mouth pursed, in a chair. Mistress Clémence had taken a sewing-stool, with Jodi beside her. Behind them, a man played with a knife, while the youth Henry stared without cease at the cousin who was also his brother. The fat man was speaking.

He had come, of course, to exact retribution for what his son and his grandson had suffered from Nicholas and also herself. She knew, she thought, the scale of his anger. This cynical championing of Nicholas had already slighted them both, and was only the beginning. She had not known, until now, that the old man had a new and greater reason to hate them. Because of Nicholas, he had been thrown out of France.

It had happened before. Then, he had been saved by a change of monarch. Now, she learned, that same sympathetic King Louis had turned against the vicomte de Ribérac, former Captain of Archers, former merchant prince, former fiscal adviser, and deprived him of his estate and his title, his property and his investments on the recommendation of Nicholas, the former apprentice.

Contracted to Burgundy, Nicholas had been working in secret for France. He had been assured of money, positions of honour. He had asked for, and had been promised Jordan de Ribérac's post, provided that he could prove that the vicomte was guilty of fraud.

'It was easy,' Nicholas said. His face was relaxed. His eyes, holding those of the fat man, were not.

'It was easy for a master of deception,' de Ribérac said. 'Thread by thread, rope by rope, the trap was spun, not over weeks, but over years. Cargoes selected and stolen, gold smuggled out. A well-found ship in the harbour at Ayr proves to be insured in my name, although it once belonged to a royal French squadron. And most damning of all, the louis d'or which over the years have trickled into the coffers of my stupid son who, never doubting their origin, has used them all on his wardrobe, his castle, his stables, his comfortable life at Kilmirren. Where did they come from?'

'I made them,' Nicholas said. 'Not personally, of course. It was expensive, but worth it.'

The doctor said, 'I find this hard to believe. But even if it's true, M. le vicomte, your son has been made a rich man. You may have lost your position in France, but you've gained a comfortable roost in Kilmirren.'

'Have I?' the vicomte said. 'Ask your young friend.' His gaze was locked, Gelis saw, in that of Nicholas. She could not read her husband's expression. Only, in the fading light, the mark on his face caught her attention: the filament of white which ran from the eye down to the natural dimple that was no longer there.

Tobie said, 'You are implying that there is some further trick?'

The vicomte turned aside. 'Trick? A trick is something performed by a marmoset, to make village louts laugh. This is no trick. It is a tragedy.' His eyes were resting on Gelis. He addressed her heavily.

'Madame, from pride, from vanity, from pique, you provoked a dangerous man, and issued a challenge. He has replied. He has replied, not by destroying you, or your pretensions. He has replied by destroying a nation.'

The doctor said, 'What?'

The fat man said, 'A man, a base-born ingenious man is asked to prove his ability. Business success is too easy. Even the slow destruction of his rivals seems to lack dash. But here is something he can achieve: something that no single person has ever aspired to before. Something that, when it is finished, will allow him to turn to his wife and say, "What can you do, what could you ever do that will equal that? I am your master."'

Her heart beat. She said nothing. Tobie said, 'The Tyrol. Or Cyprus.' He was looking at Nicholas, with something like appeal in his face.

'I said a nation,' de Ribérac said. 'The home of my son and myself; of the prudish race which cast out that trollop his mother. The country which, like Cyprus, has a young, silly Court, open to influence. Can you not guess?'

Against the wall, the men shifted. Jodi snuffled. Gelis lifted a hand to the pain in her throat. She said, 'Nicholas?'

Nicholas looked across. Outside, lamps had been lit in the yard and shone yellow through the shutterless panes, barring the nurse's white coif. It was nearly five hours since noon. Tomorrow the Emperor would open his doors for the Duke's ceremonial leave-taking.

None of it mattered now. Gelis said, 'Why did Godscalc forbid you to go back to Scotland?'

'For two years,' Nicholas said. 'It was inconvenient, but I managed to pass the time somehow.'

'Then you went back.'

'He went back,' said the doctor sharply, 'surely because the King was no longer a child, and Nicholas could expect a reasoned endorsement for all his new projects. Am I supposed to remind you about the experimental crops, the hydraulic machinery? The search for coal and silver and gold; the salt-pans, the boatbuilding? The fostering of all the civilised arts, from architecture to music and goldsmithwork? Is that a recipe for destruction?'

The fat man had never ceased to look at Nicholas. The vicomte said, 'The new crops? Useful, yes, had they not succumbed to the cold of the north, despite those acres of fine fertile ground they had occupied. The drainage? Once the experts had gone, was it not sad how many pits filled, how many of these costly pumps broke down and failed? The mining, ah yes. The art of divining, which so often underpinned a fine sale of land which later proved to be barren. Or led to exchanges of land which favoured Beltrees.'

'Can you prove that?' said the doctor. 'Nicholas bought his land from other men, or the crown.'

'From the crown,' de Ribérac said. 'From the King, who had to find a means of settling his debts. From other landowners such as Lord Hamilton, who was so generous with his land and his mining concessions that he seems to have asked our friend Claes for nothing at all in return. But when poor Thomas Boyd is sent to die on the Continent, what bridegroom do you think will be found for the Princess Mary, his sorrowing widow?'

'*Hamilton?*' Gelis said. Her mouth was dry. She had met James Hamilton often enough. He had married his first wife before she was born. They had tried to foist an old man on Katelina, and she had refused. But Mary, primed by Nicholas, would not refuse.

The fat man said, 'Do you think she is the only woman in Scotland who will suffer for this? The country is swimming in debt. Stirred to dreams of grandeur, the King has spent all he has on his dress, on his jewels, on the style of his Court; on his arms and artillery, his horses, his kennels for hunting. He is buying ships and building boats he can't pay for. When bullion comes into the country it doesn't go to the coiners: it is converted by a splendid German goldsmith into chains and adornments for James.'

'It made him happy,' said Nicholas. He remained standing quite still, wearing his tolerant face. He added, 'Go on about the civilised arts.'

She didn't need to listen, now, for she had begun to understand. How much had been spent on the Nativity Play – this spiritual salvation, encouraged by all his friends, to which end the artists, the experts, the materials had been gathered in Edinburgh for the performance of one single day? What of the music, the instruments bought, the players brought in from Brussels and Italy, the furnishing of a new Royal Chapel? Coldingham had been closed for that reason – or perhaps because Coldingham itself was becoming too rich, too success-ful, too much of an asset to its country. The vicomte was saying so.

'Also, of course, because the issue of Coldingham encouraged dissent between the King and the Pope,' the vicomte was continuing calmly. 'As did the rise of Patrick Graham, the amazing new Arch-bishop of St Andrews.'

'And the alum from the Tyrol,' said Tobie slowly.

'But that's all right now,' Nicholas said. 'Duke Charles is allowing the free sale of all Christian alum, and I think the Tyrol is Christian. At any rate, I owed the Duchess a favour.'

'Why?' said Gelis.

Nicholas said, kindly, 'Because she helped me get Jodi from Venice. She was the woman in the boat. Did you not guess even that?'

There was a scrape and a flare. Someone had begun lighting candles. The bald head and pasty face of the doctor emerged from the dusk, and the rippling jowls of the vicomte, and the strong features of Mistress Clémence holding Jodi, her eyes moving, back and forth, from the boy Henry to the man who employed her. The man who had done this.

Tobie said, 'You want us to believe that you have deliberately undermined and brought down a country. But even if you attempted it, you couldn't prove that you had succeeded.'

'Couldn't I?' Nicholas said. 'Ask the Treasurer. The Exchequer audit was held in June, after I left. And, of course, things will get even worse once the debased money has started to circulate.'

'Then the Bank has lost, too,' Tobie said. 'If you have bankrupted the country, what will happen to Govaerts and the Canongate bureau?'

'But the Bank is no longer in Scotland,' Nicholas said. 'Govaerts has gone. The Casa di Niccolò is shut, and so is the house in the High Street. I have nothing in Scotland but a tract of land and a somewhat overfurnished castle in Beltrees, which I shall probably strip.'

'So let me rephrase your good doctor's question,' said Jordan de Ribérac. 'What has this little exercise cost you?'

'Something, of course,' Nicholas said. 'But happily, I work under several names, like Egidia. I have been able to farm out the King's loans here and there, mainly among the various agents of the Vatachino and the Medici. Poor Tommaso, naked again.'

'And, presumably, poor Martin,' said the fat man agreeably. 'I have to thank you for that satisfaction, at least. Henry, do you understand what is happening?'

The boy had been fidgeting in the uncertain light. Now he came to his grandfather's side. 'He is a coward,' he said.

'Your cousin? We have established that,' said Jordan de Ribérac. 'But if you are to represent the future of this family, you must endeavour to recognise when it is threatened. This man beat you, and drove your father from Court. Do you understand what he has done to your country?'

The boy was only twelve. He said, 'He can't go back, he told lies. Anyway, you'll kill him, grandfather. And we still have Kilmirren.'

'Ah, but he is clever,' said the vicomte de Ribérac. 'If King Louis demands it, Kilmirren may be confiscated, and Scotland closed to us all. At best, the land will share in the country's impoverishment. We no longer have French estates to support us.'

'But you have Burgundy,' said Gelis suddenly. 'If you have told the Duke what has happened. And once he knows that Nicholas is secretly pensioned by France.'

The fat man sighed. Nicholas was smiling. The fat man said, 'The thought, of course, had crossed my mind. Unfortunately, your astute husband thought of it too. The Duke considers Nicholas to be his own secret agent with Louis. He has offered me a small sum for my counsel, on condition that I retire to my Madeira estates and do nothing that threatens his favourite. So where, madame, will you live? You have lost your home in Scotland, it seems.'

Gelis said, 'As Dr Tobias has said, there is no proof as yet.'

'I think there is,' said Jordan de Ribérac. 'I think Nicholas de Fleury has proved himself capable of something that very few men would have attempted, never mind achieved. Whatever else may not be true, it is certain that you must now admit defeat. He has won.'

'No,' she said.

Tobie said, 'For God's sake. You can still talk of a *game*?' His voice shook. She saw that, at last, he was beginning to believe what Nicholas had accomplished.

The vicomte looked at the doctor. 'You would rather talk about the destruction of Scotland? Let me say it again. For Nicholas, Scotland was part of the game. It was the master-work which was intended to prove – which has proved – his supremacy. I judge him the winner in this. I condemn him on all other grounds, as any fair-minded man must. What was his prize to have been?'

To have been. Nicholas said, 'That is between myself and the lady.'

She couldn't tell if his colour had changed. His expression had not. Despite the scuffle, he looked immaculate, as he always was in court dress. The knots and embroidery glinted, and although his head was bare, the trim, snuff-coloured hair was of the kind that clung to its place unless soaked, or made damp with exertion. He was not sporting, today, the broad golden chain and pendant of the Unicorn, identical to the one Adorne wore; identical to the one the King wore in Scotland. The other James, who had not been loved.

De Ribérac remarked, 'You are going to die. She will never know, unless you tell her.'

'I think she knows,' Nicholas said. 'As I think I know what her choice would have been. It might even have been the same thing.'

He was looking directly towards her, but she could not see through the twinkling light. The fat man said, 'My lady? You may compose yourself. You are in no danger from me. Indeed, you may come with my fee if you wish.'

Nicholas moved, and then stopped. The soldier behind him eased back. 'Your fee?' Gelis said.

'Do they not pay judges in Zeeland?' the vicomte said. 'My fee is my namesake, your son. I am taking Jordan de Fleury. You may come.'

'Where are you taking him?' Henry said. The nurse was sitting up, her hand on the child's arm. Henry said, 'Are you going to beat him? May I come?'

Jodi was whimpering. The lights burned. Her eyes cleared. Outside, the noise was as great, and the yellow panes were dappled with shadows. Gelis heard a distant, irritated voice that she knew. Nicholas, apparently deaf, was looking at Jodi. Behind their son, the knife glittered.

Gelis said, 'It is time to stop this,' and stood up.

The soldiers stirred. The fat man, watching intently, waved them back. He said, 'I agree. You have decided to come with me, and your son?'

'We will thrash him. We will kill him,' said Henry. The fair face was anxious.

'I think not,' said Gelis. The document was tucked in her sleeve. She knew, drawing it out, that now she had the sudden attention of Nicholas, and also of Tobie. Jodi began to sob wildly, and the nurse quieted him, watching over his head.

The vicomte said, 'What have you there?'

'No!' said Tobie.

Nicholas looked at him. Then he faced back to Gelis. He said, 'Put it away. You have made a mistake.'

'What is it?' said the vicomte again.

'Something I got from a priest,' Gelis said. She spoke to Nicholas. 'How can it be a mistake when you don't know what it is? And anyway, what does it matter? You are going to die anyway. I have to think of the future.'

Tobie said, 'Gelis. Who else may die?'

She said, 'Not Jordan, at least.'

The fat man said, 'Give me that paper.'

Nicholas said, 'Please.' His face was wholly without colour.

Gelis said, 'Have I won?'

'Yes, you have won,' Nicholas said. 'Name anything. Anything. Anything but this.'

'She hasn't!' said Henry shrilly. 'Grandfather? We're going to thrash the boy, aren't we?' He tugged at the vicomte.

Mistress Clémence said, with an air of total veracity, 'Your grandfather isn't going to thrash your little cousin, Master Henry. He is going to bring him up as his heir. He told me so.'

Henry seized his grandfather's arm, and received a blow which sent him staggering back. 'Madame! Give me that paper! Take it from her!' said Jordan de Ribérac.

Gelis, lifting her arm, hurled the crumpled ball to the floor.

Henry recovered his balance and, tugging his knife from its sheath, drove himself across the small room at his cousin. The soldier behind Jodi jumped out to stop him. Mistress Clémence flung Jodi bodily round and thrust him into the arms of the doctor. The vicomte, ignoring all that was happening, stooped to the paper as Nicholas pitched himself forward, followed by the soldiers behind him.

Gelis stood quite still, and watched. You could say that Nicholas had nothing to lose, but he didn't throw away any hope he might have of life. He twisted as he fell, avoiding the plunging arms of the soldiers. He even got to the document and, crumpling it into his fist, rolled aside, drawing it under his body. Gelis saw Jordan de Ribérac stand, his sword singing out of its scabbard. She saw the soldiers beginning to close. She heard Henry squealing and struggling, and the shrieks of Jodi in Tobie's arms. And she heard the crash as Mistress Clémence flung open the shutters and Tobie thrust the child out, while his sedate nurse, cap askew, screamed, and screamed, and screamed again into the night. And, lastly, she heard John le Grant's answering shout.

There were three men struggling still to contain Nicholas: one of them was the vicomte, his blade in his hand. Now he straightened and called. The man holding Henry released him. The rest began to recoil towards the door to the front of the house, all but the two who were wrestling, grunting, with Nicholas. The fat man dismissed one of these with a nod, and as the other knelt back out of range, the vicomte lifted his sword with both hands. Tobie started running, Gelis behind. The fat man spoke once, and then began to bring down the blade.

Gelis saw that Nicholas, attempting to rise, was looking upwards into de Ribérac's face, and that the fat man was returning the gaze. The next moment, Tobie crashed into Jordan de Ribérac, sending the unwieldy bulk staggering, and followed up with his fists. And immediately, the window and anteroom became thronged with determined men and bright steel.

John le Grant thrust past Gelis towards Tobie with four men at his back. His sword clashed once with the vicomte's, and then the fat man retreated, his blade flashing, his henchmen about him. The place where Nicholas had gone down was swarming with people: she couldn't see what he was doing. Mistress Clémence had disappeared: a moment later Gelis heard her voice outside, speaking to Jodi. Steel clattered. More men clambered in and buffeted past her. She wondered where John had found them. The candles guttered and streamed, and the room stank of sweat and leather and blood.

From the middle distance, the voice of Nicholas, in the irritated accent of one who is tired of repeating himself, said, 'Let them go! Let them *go*, you bloody fools! What are you going to charge them with?' The sound of fighting gradually came to a halt, and the room started to empty.

Gelis remained in the seat where she had dropped, on hearing that unmistakable voice. She crouched, gripping her arms, but the stomach pangs and the shivering continued. The room she sat in became gradually silent, as it had been when she was waiting for Nicholas. Finally, she was alone. She sat up, with an effort. She saw that the door was still open, and someone was standing there, holding it. She had no doubt who it was.

'Oh, there you are,' Nicholas said. He closed the door, and then smoothly locked it. He said, 'Don't be afraid. I don't want interruptions, that's all.'

She nodded, and then said, 'Yes,' because the room was so dark. She watched him coming towards her, picking his way among the fallen stools.

Nicholas said, 'He has gone. It seems to be over.'

She said, with an effort, 'And no one has died.'

'You sound disappointed,' he said. He had taken Jordan de Ribérac's chair. His shadowy outline reminded her of the fat man's.

Her shivering stopped. She said, 'You could have had him killed.' She thought of de Ribérac, fighting his way to the door. She thought of the single strange look that he and Nicholas had exchanged.

Nicholas said, 'He wanted me to.'

She said, 'Why?'

'I don't know. Because he hates me so much. I should have had to, if he had taken the affidavit.'

'He didn't? Why didn't he?' Gelis said.

'He couldn't, without taking me. I swallowed it,' Nicholas said.

Mask after mask. This one was smiling. She said, 'You couldn't have. It was vellum.'

'No, I couldn't have. But he thought I had. Now you are going to burn it.' He had pulled the thing from his shirt: now he threw it to her.

She said, 'You knew what it was.'

'An attestation that Henry is my son by your sister. I assume Tobie gave Godscalc a copy. I didn't know.'

'Godscalc gave it me when he was dying. It was only a copy,' Gelis said.

'But enough to tell de Ribérac that the hope of his house is my son,' Nicholas said. He paused and said, 'I thought the page would be blank. But you threw it down, so I knew that it couldn't be. Why, Gelis?'

'Why not? Why not treat Fat Father Jordan to some of the anguish he has dealt out to others? Why not pull that spoiled brat from his shelter, so that he can't threaten Jodi?'

'He would have died,' Nicholas said. 'Henry wouldn't have lived to grow up: not after that.'

'I wanted to see if you would try to stop it,' she said.

There was a little silence. He said, 'I was going to die, anyway.'

'But you didn't,' she said.

Another silence. 'Apparently not,' Nicholas said. 'So what are we going to talk about now? The fact that you have won? It is genuine, this time. No deception. I remember begging in very real earnest.'

Suddenly, she couldn't bear it any longer. She rose, and walked to the window and closing the shutters, turned and looked at him. At first glance, even yet, you would think he had been sitting at ease, drinking wine with his friends. The fine black doublet, buttoned up to the throat, had resisted all the mishandling: only the cuffs below it were torn, and there was a slash in his hose, showing the skin below spotted with blood.

She said, 'Stop acting. Stop pretending. The game is nothing, is finished, is void. You wrote a script for the destruction of Scotland and carried it out, just to show you could do it. And because I was your reason, you've forced me to share your guilt, too. You've destroyed everything else, not just Scotland. And just when . . .' She stopped, on a sob. She said, 'What demon gets into you, Nicholas? What demon from Hell?'

'It was your challenge,' he said. 'On our wedding night.'

'I know,' she said. 'I hated Katelina . . . I thought I hated Katelina and you. I was afraid of you. I am afraid of you, did you know that? So I hurt you, and you hurt me in return. But we were armed and prepared for it. We – I was playing for something of value, and I think that you thought so, too. But these people – Bel and Robin and Kathi, and Betha and Phemie, and Willie Roger and Sandy Albany and his sisters, and the little Queen and all the merchants, the singers, the people who worked with you on the Play – they weren't part of our vendetta. And they were not even strangers. They were friends. They were people who loved you. And you sacrificed them all on the – on the wheels of your satanic ingenuity.'

'I suppose so. St Vincent,' he said. 'I'd begun to notice I'd gone rather far. I did try to surrender the game. Now I have. Could you consider Scotland as something apart? Something I had to do for myself? Against Jordan de Ribérac and his family, not because of you?'

'Was it?' she said. 'Or wasn't it both? Wasn't it your trial piece, your masterpiece which had to be perfect, no matter what? And mightn't you do it again, just as blindly, somewhere else?'

'It was beautiful,' Nicholas said. 'Wheels are beautiful. I probably should. But it was against the others, against the St Pols, to begin with. You didn't harm us as they did.'

'Us?' she said. She tried in vain to study his face in the gloom, thinking of something that the vicomte had said. *That trollop, his mother.*

Nicholas said, 'I grew to hate the St Pols, not you. And you changed: you said so. Gelis, what did you want? When we were playing the game, what did you want for your reward?'

'What was your wish?' she asked. She felt weighed down with grief, like someone speaking alone at a graveside.

'Mine?' he said. 'But you know it. To spend my life with one person: with you. To respect you and have your respect; to trust you and deserve the same trust. And by night, to lie at your side, *so that I may give her my love, my dear love, ki mon cuer et mon cors a.*'

Who hath my heart and my body.

He said, 'And yours?'

She lifted her wet face from her hands. She said, 'The same, of course. But you can't do it. You can't do it, Nicholas. I thought we were matched, but we're not. Show me how I can trust you, show me how I can respect you after this.'

She stopped. She said, 'No one is innocent. I betrayed you as well. But not on this scale. I cannot live with you. I couldn't live with you now.'

The bond was broken. The bond they had each, she believed,

thought to be inviolate, no matter what happened. Inviolate even in death, as he had proposed in the wilderness. She had understood his sudden despair. It was as nothing compared with what he had brought on them now. What he had brought on himself.

There was a long space. He said, 'Will you take Jodi?'

She replied with another question. 'What will you do? Nicholas, they won't follow you now. None of them.'

'Julius might,' Nicholas said. She could see him slowly thinking aloud. 'And Astorre. Not John. Not Tobie, after Volterra. Not Gregorio. Not Diniz. Not . . . Father Moriz. Not you. Not you. Not you.'

'Not me,' she said. 'But we can share Jodi between us.'

'Do you mean it?' he said. Once, he had disclaimed any interest in a child reared by his wife. It had been part of the game. Then, he had been sure that Gelis would never leave him. As she had been sure.

After a moment he added, 'Clémence saved us all. Clémence and Tobie.'

'You should thank them,' she said. 'Will you stay here? Or not?'

He said, 'I had better go. It should be known that the marriage has ended. You will have a better chance on your own.'

'But you will tell me where you are going?' she said.

'Of course, when I know it. In any case, I shall see you tomorrow. And we have to arrange about Jodi.' He stopped, and then said, 'Did you burn the certificate?'

She said, 'Watch. I am doing it now. Nicholas, Jodi will never change into someone like Henry. That was Katelina's doing, not yours.'

'Poor Katelina,' he said.

Once, she would have been consumed with resentment. Now she watched the vellum blacken and burn, and then rose and unlocked the door, and went to find and send him their son, with Mistress Clémence.

He had closed his eyes. Jodi roused him, demanding tearfully from the doorway that his father should see him to bed, while Mistress Clémence, firm as ever, pointed out that other people also grew tired, and that instead, his father would tell him a story.

Nicholas told him his story, making room for them both in the chair, and stopping to answer the small, whispered questions. Has the boy gone? Is he coming back? Where is the fat man? But after a while, the old familiar tale exerted its power, and when the child spoke at all, it was to repeat an old joke, or an old verse in the usual places. Soon after that, his eyes lifted and fell.

Nicholas stopped, and smiled at the nurse, and said to Jodi, 'Bed. When I come back, what would you like me to bring you?'

'Where are you going?' Jodi said.

'That depends on what you want,' Nicholas said.

A little later, Mistress Clémence returned without the child, and took a seat at what could be called a deferential distance. He said, 'I wanted to thank you.'

'Dr Tobie helped. Will the vicomte return?'

'He is going to Madeira,' Nicholas said. 'But I am leaving as well. My wife and I are to part, and the boy will live with his mother, not me. I hope you will find you can stay with her. We owe you a great deal.'

'But you will visit?' she said.

'I don't think I can,' Nicholas said. He had begun to realise it.

She said, 'I will bring him, my lord.'

'I should like that,' he said, 'and my wife would be grateful. She wishes, as I do, that the boy should grow knowing us both.' He paused. 'You used to call him a bachique. That is Blésois, surely.'

'You would hear it at Chouzy,' she said.

He said, 'I heard it in Edinburgh.' *Tiens! Tiens! Comme c'est gars bachique*, the old woman had said.

She said nothing. He said, 'If you know her – if you ever meet her – tell her that I am sorry.'

'For what, my lord?' the woman asked. She had neither mentioned a name nor asked for one.

'She will know,' Nicholas said.

There was an interval, from which he emerged to find the nurse speaking. 'It is dark, and there is a disagreeable press in the courtyard. Would you like me to find you an escort?'

He had come with John le Grant. He would not be returning with John le Grant. Nicholas said, 'Have you someone in mind?'

She returned his slight smile with another. 'Anyone of the required competence,' she said. 'An astrologer might serve best of all.'

The small joke surprised him. He admired her for it, for of course she, too, must despise him.

Later that evening, when they all knew the truth, Tobie left Adorne and the rest, and went to tackle the seigneur de Fleury in Gelis's parlour. He thought of him by his title since he was in the process, for the last time, of excising this particular man from his life. He was also rather drunk (as was John), because the excision was painful.

The parlour was empty. When he went to look for Gelis, as eventually he did, that brave girl Katelijne Sersanders was with her. He took them both back to the room. It was still in fair disarray, but Jordan de Ribérac's chair was upright still. The cushion was an uneven patchwork of scarlet, and the back and one arm glistened with blood. Caught in one side was the tie of a small person's bedrobe. Gelis looked at it, and then without speaking walked out of the room. Tobie stood and looked after her.

Kathi said, 'Jodi was brought in to see him. Mistress Clémence would notice something was wrong.'

She was pale. She had been pale ever since he had told them about Nicholas. 'I didn't know,' Tobie said.

'He wouldn't expect you to. Are you going to leave him? Again?'

'I should never have come,' Tobie said. 'And you should forget him. He has destroyed your whole future. How could he? How could he do that, after Iceland?'

'He saved my brother. He cares for some things. The Play mattered,' Kathi said. Gelis had come back.

'It wasted money, that was all.'

'No,' said Kathi. 'And he returned when Zacco called him. And he didn't sell Iceland.'

'What?' said Gelis. She stood as if shackled by weariness.

Kathi turned. 'Denmark needs money. A little urging from Nicholas, and King James would have bought over Iceland, without means to feed or maintain it. He didn't.' She stopped, looking at Gelis. 'Where is he?'

Gelis said, 'Someone came to take him back to the city. He could be dead of his wound. He could make himself die. He could kill himself.'

Kathi said, 'No, he won't. He isn't like anyone else. He doesn't think he is important enough for any disaster to matter. What you have to hope for is that all this havoc teaches him something.'

She looked at Tobie with angry impatience. 'You know what he does. He invents, and then allows the invention to swallow him. What he did in Scotland is the most amazing thing he has ever achieved. He's still torn between pride, and an awful awakening. He has to reach the conclusion that he must never do it again.'

'How?' said Tobie.

'I don't know,' Kathi said. 'Perhaps walking away from him is the best thing.'

The man they were discussing was at sea. He had been there for a long time, it seemed; jolting, swaying, rocking. At other times, he was on the bank of a river, and in pain. When he struggled, a man held both his wrists and seemed to be scolding him. He had seen the man at Angers. But he wasn't at Angers.

For a time, stupidly, he thought – woe now to the chickens, woe to the blind lion – that he could not see. Then he realised that it was merely night, and he was lying in grass by the bank of his previous dream and drowsy, as if full of poppy, or drunk. A man bent and touched his wrist, but was simply feeling his pulse. His body was bandaged, and hurt. When several men crossed and started to lift him, he made no protest, for he thought he knew where they were taking him.

It was a surprise, therefore, to find himself in a barge, not a carriage. A magnificent barge, it was true. A ship. A ship fit for an Emperor. All the time he lay looking about, he expected to see Violante, princess of Naxos. Violante, Medea. A carriage, a beautiful woman.

A beautiful woman.

Not you, not you, not you.

'The Emperor bids you welcome on board,' said Ludovico da Bologna. And all the ghosts vanished, and reality stood at his shoulder.

Long after he knew where he was, Nicholas lay watching the lamps drop behind, over the glittering swirl of the water. The night was clear and very bright: he could see the network of vines on the hills, the mathematical hills of the Moselle, which produced so many exquisite solutions.

Trèves was behind in the darkness, taking its rest before the extravagant, difficult day when the Duke would ride for the last time from St Maximin to the Archbishop's Palace, there to receive not a crown, but (he thought) the Emperor's effusive farewell.

Soon, the city would stir. Soon, the smoke would rise into the air, the bakers and cook-shops would put up their shutters, the flash and nod of plate armour and plumes would begin to show themselves in the streets. The musicians would don their tabards and shake out their trumpets, and the horses would stand to their grooming. The Duke would don his heavy pearled robes. The Duke, who yesterday had smashed the stools in his room in his rage, would today have repressed every sign of offence, so that the populace should see not an insulted vassal, but a great lord in his magnificence, tolerating the puerile eccentricities of a man no longer fit for his office.

And some time about then, before the procession set off, a white-faced man would come rushing into St Maximin, and the news would flash from stone to stone, room to room until finally, and slowly, it came with leaden feet to the throne of the Duke.

Monseigneur, one must advise you not to go to the city this

morning. Monseigneur, we must humbly suggest that you disband the procession. Monseigneur, the Archbishop's Palace cannot receive you. Monseigneur, the Emperor's quarters are empty. The Emperor's officials have gone. The Emperor has disappeared, and so has his blond son Maximilian. The Emperor has fled during the night, boarded a ship, and is on his craven way back to his heartland, leaving a mountain of unsettled bills, and his uncrowned ducal guest to make his own common way home.

This was the ship. In its interior the Emperor and his son, so far as Nicholas knew, were peacefully sleeping, far from the incandescent rage of his vassal, who had expended three months, fifteen thousand men and a fortune upon nothing, unless you counted a minor duchy which he already possessed.

The Emperor had abandoned the Duke, but he had not abandoned the Duke's adviser and banker. Nicholas had expressed a willingness to serve the Imperial court: the Duke in his own interests had sanctioned it. It had not been envisaged, at the time, that the Emperor was about to make Burgundy the buffoon of Europe. But Nicholas could not be blamed. He was here, by permission of Besse.

By permission, of course, of the Patriarch of Antioch. Others had had a part in his silent abstraction: faces floated in his unreliable memory; his wound had received expert attention. He had wondered, vaguely, why he was considered to be worth the expenditure. He supposed that he knew.

Ludovico da Bologna, Patriarch of Antioch, had left Rhodes to come to the west to raise men and funds for the next Crusade, the next onslaught, the next attack on the Turks. The Pope had renewed his commission. The Duke of Burgundy, receiving Guelders, had offered gold and ten thousand men to lead a Crusade to the East, and had made the Patriarch his ducal counsellor and representative. The Emperor was now receiving his solicitations. The Emperor and Nicholas de Fleury.

Nicholas lay, watching fish. They approached, touched the glass, and swam off, scowling. The Emperor's barge always held tanks of live fish.

His injury, and how he received it, would have been of no interest to the Patriarch. The Patriarch wouldn't know, any more than the Emperor, that he had endangered his Bank for the sake of an obsession, or that he had lost the allegiance of all his chief officers. On the other hand, he had gold in the East. And Julius wouldn't mind what he had done. Nor, he supposed, would the patrician Anna.

It was not all, surely, so terrible. Roger could go back to England, Adorne's kinsfolk to Bruges. Hamilton would take care of Mary. Bel had connections abroad. Henry was safe.

He would never live with Jodi and Gelis again. He had always been sure, whatever happened, that Gelis would stay. He had been wrong.

'Well?' said the Patriarch, leaning above him. 'Well? Have you got rid of them?'

'It was rather the other way round,' Nicholas said.

'But you've thought of what I said? The Golden Horde are the key. You don't get anywhere by pinning your flag to the Genoese or the Venetians or the Muscovites, or to Naples or to Uzum or to the Knights or to the Tartars alone. You pander to everybody.'

'What makes you think I'm good at that?' Nicholas said.

'I knew you'd agree in the end,' said the Patriarch.

He wondered how the Patriarch knew, when it had been such a surprise to him. It was as curious as the way he had regained Umar recently, while in the haunted place where Umar had been, there was a child, and a girl. Jodi. Egidia.

They had been well matched as a pair, he and Gelis. Matched in a taste for intrigue, for numbers, for puzzles, for business and, to a degree, in the transmission of pain. It had not been a pretty war, but he had persevered, sure enough of the outcome – impatient, at last, for the outcome. And confident, too, that he would watch this son grow, as the other had not, at his hearth.

He had thrown all that away. Oblivious to all but his creation, he had been unprepared for the final awakening, and the revulsion which his schemes would evoke. And yet he should have been ready. It had all happened before. Intent upon his objective, he could set aside all human feeling, in the same way that he barricaded his mind against psalmody. As a result, men and women had died, and others had left him, as Gelis had. He would hear of her, of course, as they reared Jodi between them. He would hear of his other friends, as they abandoned him for new posts. The Bank itself would remain, staffed by strangers, stiff with formality. It was safer than friendship or music or deep discussion or the emotions – the untidy emotions – inspired by the majesty of the world, and creations of an order far greater than his.

So he told himself, in the well-deserved darkness where he had been left. Where he must cease to think of that small, surprising family he had been vouchsafed: Clémence and Pasque, Jodi and Egidia, Tobie, Moriz, John and the rest. And another person, already lost, already renounced: a friend; a precocious friend who, for a short time, had trusted and respected him, and placed her life in his hands. The only one who might have observed the broken thread in his design. Having been to Ultima Thule, he had not sold it.

He had, of course, sold everything else. It was what he was trained for.

It did not occur to him, because he was still in some ways inexperienced, that there are some things – the contents of a dovecote, for instance – which cannot be sold. For as the soul to the body, the birds will find their way back to their master.

A NOTE ABOUT THE AUTHOR

Dorothy Dunnett was born in Dunfermline, Scotland.
She is the author of the Francis Crawford of Lymond novels,
a historical sequence set in the sixteenth century; seven mystery novels;
King Hereafter, an epic novel about Macbeth; the text of
The Scottish Highlands, a book of photographs by
David Paterson, on which she collaborated with her husband,
Sir Alastair Dunnett; and five earlier Niccolò novels. In 1992,
Queen Elizabeth appointed her an Officer of the Order
of the British Empire. Lady Dunnett lives
with her husband in Edinburgh.

A NOTE ON THE TYPE

The text of this book was set in a digitized version of Imprint,
a Monotype face originally cut in 1913 for the periodical of the same name.
It was modeled on Caslon, but has a larger x-height and different
italics, which harmonize better with the roman.

Composed in Great Britain

Arctic Circle

ICELAND

Hafnarfjördur

Mt. Hekla

Vatna
Glacier

The
Westmann
Isles

Papey Island

Norwegian

Sea

Western Ocean
(Atlantic)

Faröe
Islands
Tórshavn
Nölsoy

Shetland
Islands

Orkney
Islands

Fair I.

Bergen

Deer Sound
Scapa

Moray Firth

0   100   200

English miles

Aberdeen

SCOTLAND

St. Andrews
Edinburgh
Berwick

German

Ocean

(North Sea)

DONEGAL
Killybegs

Ayr

Newcastle

IRELAND

WALES

ENGLAND

Kingston-
upon-Hull

Boston

DENMAR

Lynn

Bristol   London

Southampton

Bremen

The Narrow Sea

Bruges

Calais

Hesdin

Amiens

Somme

Rouen

Brussels

Maas

Rhine

Cologne

Coblenz

Luxembourg

Trèves (Trier)